Murder British Style

Murder British Style

NINETEEN CLASSIC COZY MYSTERIES

EDITED BY

Martin H. Greenberg

BARNES
&NOBLE
BOOKS
NEW YORK

This edition published by Barnes & Noble, Inc.,
by arrangement with Martin H. Greenberg.

1993 Barnes & Noble Books

Book design by Nicola Ferguson

ISBN 1-56619-924-7

Printed and bound in the United States of America

9   8   7   6   5   4   3   2   1

Acknowledgments

GRATEFUL ACKNOWLEDGMENT IS MADE TO THE FOLLOWING FOR PERMISSION TO REPRINT THEIR COPYRIGHTED MATERIAL:

The Four Suspects by Agatha Christie—Copyright © 1929 by Agatha Christie. Reprinted by permission of Harold Ober Associates Incorporated.

The Adventure of the Suffering Ruler by H. R. F. Keating—Copyright © 1993 by H. R. F. Keating. Reprinted by permission of the author.

Rats! by Dorothy J. Cannell—Copyright © 1993 by Dorothy J. Cannell. An original story, which appears by arrangement with the author.

The Convolvulus Clock by Ruth Rendell—Copyright © 1985 by Kingsmarkham Enterprises Ltd. Reprinted by permission of the author.

Fair and Square by Margaret Yorke—Copyright © 1982 by Margaret Yorke. Reprinted by permission of the author.

The Uninvited by Michael Gilbert—Copyright © 1962 by Michael Gilbert. Reprinted by permission of the author.

The Black Cliffs by Joan Aiken—Copyright © 1982 by Joan Aiken Enterprises Ltd. First appeared in ELLERY QUEEN'S MYSTERY MAGAZINE. Reprinted by permission of Brandt & Brandt Literary Agents, Inc.

The Dream is Better by Julian Symons—Copyright © 1982 by Julian Gustave Symons. First appeared in ELLERY QUEEN'S MYSTERY MAGAZINE. Reprinted by permission of the author.

Behind the Locked Door by Peter Lovesey—Copyright © 1978 by Peter Lovesey. Reprinted by permission of the author.

Lamb to the Slaughter by Roald Dahl—Copyright © 1953 by Roald Dahl. From SOMEONE LIKE YOU by Roald Dahl. Reprinted by permission of Alfred A. Knopf, Inc.

Contents

Murder British Style

❈   ❈   ❈

The Four Suspects

AGATHA CHRISTIE

The conversation hovered round undiscovered and unpunished crimes. Everyone in turn vouchsafed an opinion: Colonel Bantry, his plump amiable wife, Jane Helier, Dr. Lloyd, and even old Miss Marple. The one person who did not speak was the one best fitted in most people's opinion to do so. Sir Henry Clithering, ex-Commissioner of Scotland Yard, sat silent, twisting his moustache—or rather stroking it—and half smiling, as though at some inward thought that amused him.

"Sir Henry," said Mrs. Bantry at last, "if you don't say something, I shall scream. Are there a lot of crimes that go unpunished, or are there not?"

"You're thinking of newspaper headlines, Mrs. Bantry. SCOTLAND YARD AT FAULT AGAIN. And a list of unsolved mysteries to follow."

"Which really, I suppose, form a very small percentage of the whole?" said Dr. Lloyd.

"Yes, that is so. The hundreds of crimes that are solved and the perpetrators punished are seldom heralded and sung. But that isn't quite the point at issue, is it? When you talk of undiscovered crimes and unsolved crimes, you are talking of two different things. In the first category come all the crimes that Scotland Yard never hears about, the crimes that no one even knows have been committed."

"But I suppose there aren't very many of those?" said Mrs. Bantry.

"Aren't there?"

"Sir Henry! You don't mean there are?"

"I should think," said Miss Marple thoughtfully, "that there must be a very large number."

The charming old lady, with her old-world, unruffled air, made her statement in a tone of the utmost placidity.

"My dear Miss Marple," said Colonel Bantry.

"Of course," said Miss Marple, "a lot of people are stupid. And stupid people get found out, whatever they do. But there are quite a number of people who aren't stupid, and one shudders to think of what they might accomplish unless they had very strongly rooted principles."

"Yes," said Sir Henry, "there are a lot of people who aren't stupid. How often does some crime come to light simply by reason of a bit of unmitigated bungling, and each time one asks oneself the question: If this hadn't been bungled, would anyone ever have known?"

"But that's very serious, Clithering," said Colonel Bantry. "Very serious, indeed."

"Is it?"

"What do you mean, is it? Of course it's serious."

"You say crime goes unpunished, but does it? Unpunished by the law perhaps, but cause and effect works outside the law. To say that every crime brings its own punishment is by way of being a platitude, and yet in my opinion nothing can be truer."

"Perhaps, perhaps," said Colonel Bantry. "But that doesn't alter the seriousness—the—er—seriousness—" He paused, rather at a loss.

Sir Henry Clithering smiled.

"Ninety-nine people out of a hundred are doubtless of your way of thinking," he said. "But you know, it isn't really guilt that is important —it's innocence. That's the thing that nobody will realize."

"I don't understand," said Jane Helier.

"I do," said Miss Marple. "When Mrs. Trent found half a crown missing from her bag, the person it affected most was the daily woman, Mrs. Arthur. Of course the Trents thought it was her, but being kindly people and knowing she had a large family and a husband who drinks, well—they naturally didn't want to go to extremes. But they felt differently toward her, and they didn't leave her in charge of the house when they went away, which made a great difference to her; and other people began to get a feeling about her too. And then it suddenly came out that it was the governess. Mrs. Trent saw her through a door reflected in a mirror. The purest chance—though I prefer to call it Providence. And that, I think, is what Sir Henry means. Most people would be only interested in who took the money, and it turned out to be the most unlikely person—just like in detective stories! But the real person it was life and death to was poor Mrs. Arthur, who had done nothing. That's what you mean, isn't it, Sir Henry?"

"Yes, Miss Marple, you've hit off my meaning exactly. Your char-woman person was lucky in the instance you relate. Her innocence was shown. But some people may go through a lifetime crushed by the weight of a suspicion that is really unjustified."

"Are you thinking of some particular instance, Sir Henry?" asked Mrs. Bantry shrewdly.

"As a matter of fact, Mrs. Bantry, I am. A very curious case. A case where we believe murder to have been committed, but with no possible chance of ever proving it."

"Poison, I suppose," breathed Jane. "Something untraceable."

Dr. Lloyd moved restlessly and Sir Henry shook his head.

"No, dear lady. Not the secret arrow poison of the South American Indians! I wish it were something of that kind. We have to deal with something much more prosaic—so prosaic, in fact, that there is no hope of bringing the deed home to its perpetrator. An old gentleman who fell downstairs and broke his neck; one of those regrettable accidents which happen every day."

"But what happened really?"

"Who can say?" Sir Henry shrugged his shoulders. "A push from behind? A piece of cotton or string tied across the top of the stairs and carefully removed afterward? That we shall never know."

"But you do think that it—well, wasn't an accident? Now why?" asked the doctor.

"That's rather a long story, but—well, yes, we're pretty sure. As I said, there's no chance of being able to bring the deed home to anyone—the evidence would be too flimsy. But there's the other aspect of the case— the one I was speaking about. You see, there were four people who might have done the trick. One's guilty, but the other three are inno-cent. And unless the truth is found out, those three are going to remain under the terrible shadow of doubt."

"I think," said Mrs. Bantry, "that you'd better tell us your long story."

"I needn't make it so very long after all," said Sir Henry. "I can at any rate condense the beginning. That deals with a German secret society— the *Schwartze Hand*—something after the lines of the Camorra or what is most people's idea of the Camorra. A scheme of blackmail and terror-ization. The thing started quite suddenly after the war and spread to an amazing extent. Numberless people were victimized by it. The authorities were not successful in coping with it, for its secrets were jealously guarded, and it was almost impossible to find anyone who could be induced to betray them.

"Nothing much was ever known about it in England, but in Germany it was having a most paralyzing effect. It was finally broken up and dispersed through the efforts of one man, a Dr. Rosen, who had at one time been very prominent in Secret Service work. He became a member, penetrated its inmost circle, and was, as I say, instrumental in bringing about its downfall.

"But he was, in consequence, a marked man, and it was deemed wise that he should leave Germany—at any rate for a time. He came to England, and we had letters about him from the police in Berlin. He came and had a personal interview with me. His point of view was both dispassionate and resigned. He had no doubts of what the future held for him.

" 'They will get me, Sir Henry,' he said. 'Not a doubt of it.' He was a big man with a fine head and a very deep voice, with only a slight guttural intonation to tell of his nationality. 'That is a foregone conclusion. It does not matter, I am prepared. I faced the risk when I undertook this business. I have done what I set out to do. The organization can never be gotten together again. But there are many members of it at liberty, and they will take the only revenge they can—my life. It is simply a question of time, but I am anxious that that time should be as long as possible. You see, I am collecting and editing some very interesting material—the result of my life's work. I should like, if possible, to be able to complete my task.'

"He spoke very simply, with a certain grandeur which I could not but admire. I told him we would take all precautions, but he waved my words aside.

" 'Some day, sooner or later, they will get me,' he repeated. 'When that day comes, do not distress yourself. You will, I have no doubt, have done all that is possible.'

"He then proceeded to outline his plans, which were simple enough. He proposed to take a small cottage in the country where he could live quietly and go on with his work. In the end he selected a village in Somerset—King's Gnaton, which was seven miles from a railway station and singularly untouched by civilization. He bought a very charming cottage, had various improvements and alterations made, and settled down there most contentedly. His household consisted of his niece, Greta; a secretary; an old German servant who had served him faithfully for nearly forty years; and an outside handy man and gardener who was a native of King's Gnaton."

"The four suspects," said Dr. Lloyd softly.

"Exactly. The four suspects. There is not much more to tell. Life went on peacefully at King's Gnaton for five months and then the blow fell. Dr. Rosen fell down the stairs one morning and was found dead about half an hour later. At the time the accident must have taken place, Gertrud was in her kitchen with the door closed and heard nothing—so she says. Fräulein Greta was in the garden, planting some bulbs—again, so she says. The gardener, Dobbs, was in the small potting shed having his elevenses—so he says; and the secretary was out for a walk, and once more there is only his own word for it. No one had an alibi—no one can corroborate anyone else's story. But one thing is certain. No one from outside could have done it, for a stranger in the little village of King's Gnaton would be noticed without fail. Both the back and the front doors were locked, each member of the household having his own key. So you see it narrows down to those four. And yet each one seems to be above suspicion. Greta, his own brother's child. Gertrud, with forty years of faithful service. Dobbs, who has never been out of King's Gnaton. And Charles Templeton, the secretary—"

"Yes," said Colonel Bantry, "what about him? He seems the suspicious person to my mind. What do you know about him?"

"It is what I knew about him that put him completely out of court—at any rate, at the time," said Sir Henry gravely. "You see, Charles Templeton was one of my own men."

"Oh!" said Colonel Bantry, considerably taken aback.

"Yes. I wanted to have someone on the spot, and at the same time I didn't want to cause talk in the village. Rosen really needed a secretary. I put Templeton on the job. He's a gentleman, he speaks German fluently, and he's altogether a very able fellow."

"But, then, which do you suspect?" asked Mrs. Bantry in a bewildered tone. "They all seem so—well, impossible."

"Yes, so it appears. But you can look at the thing from another angle. Fräulein Greta was his niece and a very lovely girl, but the war has shown us time and again that brother can turn against sister, or father against son, and so on, and the loveliest and gentlest of young girls did some of the most amazing things. The same thing applies to Gertrud, and who knows what other forces might be at work in her case? A quarrel, perhaps, with her master, a growing resentment all the more lasting because of the long faithful years behind her. Elderly women of that class can be amazingly bitter sometimes. And Dobbs? Was he right outside it because he had no connection with the family? Money will do much. In some way Dobbs might have been approached and bought.

"For one thing seems certain: Some message or some order must have come from outside. Otherwise, why five months' immunity? No, the agents of the society must have been at work. Not yet sure of Rosen's perfidy, they delayed till the betrayal had been traced to him beyond any possible doubt. And then, all doubts set aside, they must have sent their message to the spy within the gates—the message that said, 'Kill.' "

"How nasty!" said Jane Helier, and shuddered.

"But how did the message come? That was the point I tried to elucidate—the one hope of solving my problem. One of those four people must have been approached or communicated with in some way. There would be no delay—I knew that; as soon as the command came, it would be carried out. That was a peculiarity of the *Schwartze Hand.*

"I went into the question, went into it in a way that will probably strike you as being ridiculously meticulous. Who had come to the cottage that morning? I eliminated nobody. Here is the list."

He took an envelope from his pocket and selected a paper from its contents.

"The butcher, bringing some neck of mutton. Investigated and found correct.

"The grocer's assistant, bringing a packet of corn flour, two pounds of sugar, a pound of butter, and a pound of coffee. Also investigated and found correct.

"The postman, bringing two circulars for Fräulein Rosen, a local letter for Gertrud, three letters for Dr. Rosen, one with a foreign stamp, and two letters for Mr. Templeton, one also with a foreign stamp."

Sir Henry paused and then took a sheaf of documents from the envelope.

"It may interest you to see these for yourself. They were handed me by the various people concerned or collected from the wastepaper basket. I need hardly say they've been tested by experts for invisible ink, et cetera. No excitement of that kind is possible."

Everyone crowded round to look. The catalogues were respectively from a nurseryman and from a prominent London fur establishment. The two bills addressed to Dr. Rosen were a local one for seeds for the garden and one from a London stationery firm. The letter addressed to him ran as follows:

My Dear Rosen—Just back from Dr. Helmuth Spath's. I saw Edgar Jackson the other day. He and Amos Perry have just come back from Tsingtau. In all Honesty I can't say I envy them the trip. Let me have news of you soon. As I said before: Beware of a certain person. You know who I mean, though you don't agree.—Yours,

Georgina.

"Mr. Templeton's mail consisted of this bill which, as you see, is an account rendered from his tailor, and a letter from a friend in Germany," went on Sir Henry. "The latter, unfortunately, he tore up while out on his walk. Finally we have the letter received by Gertrud."

Dear Mrs. Swartz—We're hoping as how you be able to come to the social on friday evening. the vicar says has he hopes you will—one and all being welcome. The resipy for the ham was very good, and I thanks you for it. Hoping as this finds you well and that we shall see you friday I remain

Yours faithfully,
Emma Greene.

Dr. Lloyd smiled a little over this and so did Mrs. Bantry.

"I think the last letter can be put out of court," said Dr. Lloyd.

"I thought the same," said Sir Henry, "but I took the precaution of verifying that there was a Mrs. Greene and a church social. One can't be too careful, you know."

"That's what our friend Miss Marple always says," said Dr. Lloyd, smiling. "You're lost in a daydream, Miss Marple. What are you thinking out?"

Miss Marple gave a start.

"So stupid of me," she said. "I was just wondering why the word Honesty in Dr. Rosen's letter was spelled with a capital H."

Mrs. Bantry picked it up.

"So it is," she said. "Oh!"

"Yes, dear," said Miss Marple. "I thought you'd notice!"

"There's a definite warning in that letter," said Colonel Bantry.

"That's the first thing caught my attention. I notice more than you'd think. Yes, a definite warning—against whom?"

"There's rather a curious point about that letter," said Sir Henry. "According to Templeton, Dr. Rosen opened the letter at breakfast and tossed it across to him, saying he didn't know who the fellow was from Adam."

"But it wasn't a fellow," said Jane Helier. "It was signed 'Georgina.' "

"It's difficult to say which it is," said Dr. Lloyd. "It might be Georgey, but it certainly looks more like Georgina. Only it strikes me that the writing is a man's."

"You know, that's interesting," said Colonel Bantry. "His tossing it across the table like that and pretending he knew nothing about it. Wanted to watch somebody's face. Whose face—the girl's? Or the man's?"

"Or even the cook's?" suggested Mrs. Bantry. "She might have been in the room bringing in the breakfast. But what I don't see is . . . it's most peculiar—"

She frowned over the letter. Miss Marple drew closer to her. Miss Marple's finger went out and touched the sheet of paper. They murmured together.

"But why did the secretary tear up the other letter?" asked Jane Helier suddenly. "It seems—oh, I don't know—it seems queer. Why should he have letters from Germany? Although, of course, if he's above suspicion, as you say—"

"But Sir Henry didn't say that," said Miss Marple quickly, looking up from her murmured conference with Mrs. Bantry. "He said four suspects. So that shows that he includes Mr. Templeton. I'm right, am I not, Sir Henry?"

"Yes, Miss Marple. I have learned one thing through bitter experience. Never say to yourself that anyone is above suspicion. I gave you reasons just now why three of these people might after all be guilty, unlikely as it seemed. I did not at that time apply the same process to Charles Templeton. But I came to it at last through pursuing the rule I have just mentioned. And I was forced to recognize this: That every army and every navy and every police force has a certain number of traitors within its ranks, much as we hate to admit the idea. And I examined dispassionately the case against Charles Templeton.

"I asked myself very much the same questions as Miss Helier has just asked. Why should he, alone of all the house, not be able to produce the letter he had received—a letter, moreover, with a German stamp on it. Why should he have letters from Germany?

"The last question was an innocent one, and I actually put it to him. His reply came simply enough. His mother's sister was married to a German. The letter had been from a German girl cousin. So I learned something I did not know before—that Charles Templeton had relations with people in Germany. And that put him definitely on the list of suspects—very much so. He is my own man—a lad I have always liked and trusted; but in common justice and fairness I must admit that he heads that list.

"But there it is—I do not know! I do not know . . . and in all probability I never shall know. It is not a question of punishing a murderer. It is a question that to me seems a hundred times more important. It is the blighting, perhaps, of an honourable man's whole career . . . because of suspicion—a suspicion that I dare not disregard."

Miss Marple coughed and said gently:

"Then, Sir Henry, if I understand you rightly, it is this young Mr. Templeton only who is so much on your mind?"

"Yes, in a sense. It should, in theory, be the same for all four, but that is not actually the case. Dobbs, for instance—suspicion may attach to him in my mind, but it will not actually affect his career. Nobody in the village has ever had any idea that old Dr. Rosen's death was anything but an accident. Gertrud is slightly more affected. It must make, for instance, a difference in Fräulein Rosen's attitude toward her. But that, possibly, is not of great importance to her.

"As for Greta Rosen—well, here we come to the crux of the matter. Greta is a very pretty girl and Charles Templeton is a good-looking young man, and for five months they were thrown together with no outer distractions. The inevitable happened. They fell in love with each other—even if they did not come to the point of admitting the fact in words.

"And then the catastrophe happens. It is three months ago now, and a day or two after I returned, Greta Rosen came to see me. She had sold the cottage and was returning to Germany, having finally settled up her uncle's affairs. She came to me personally, although she knew I had retired, because it was really about a personal matter she wanted to see me. She beat about the bush a little, but at last it all came out. What did I think? That letter with the German stamp—she had worried about it and worried about it—the one Charles had torn up. Was it all right? Surely it must be all right. Of course she believed his story, but—oh, if she only knew! If she knew—for certain.

"You see? The same feeling: the wish to trust—but the horrible lurking suspicion, thrust resolutely to the back of the mind, but persisting nevertheless. I spoke to her with absolute frankness and asked her to do the same. I asked her whether she had been on the point of caring for Charles and he for her.

" 'I think so,' she said. 'Oh yes, I know it was so. We were so happy. Every day passed so contentedly. We knew—we both knew. There was no hurry—there was all the time in the world. Some day he would tell me he loved me, and I should tell him that I, too—Ah! But you can guess! And now it is all changed. A black cloud has come between us—we are constrained, when we meet we do not know what to say. It is, perhaps, the same with him as with me. . . . We are each saying to ourselves, "If I were sure!" That is why, Sir Henry, I beg of you to say to me, "You may be sure, whoever killed your uncle, it was not Charles Templeton!" Say it to me! Oh, say it to me! I beg—I beg!"

"I couldn't say it to her. They'll drift farther and farther apart, those two—with suspicion like a ghost between them—a ghost that can't be laid."

He leaned back in his chair; his face looked tired and grey. He shook his head once or twice despondently.

"And there's nothing more can be done, unless—" He sat up straight again and a tiny whimsical smile crossed his face. "—unless Miss Marple can help us. Can't you, Miss Marple? I've a feeling that letter might be in your line, you know. The one about the church social. Doesn't it remind you of something or someone that makes everything perfectly plain? Can't you do something to help two helpless young people who want to be happy?"

Behind the whimsicality there was something earnest in his appeal. He had come to think very highly of the mental powers of this frail, old-fashioned maiden lady. He looked across at her with something very like hope in his eyes.

Miss Marple coughed and smoothed her lace.

"It does remind me a little of Annie Poultny," she admitted. "Of course the letter is perfectly plain—both to Mrs. Bantry and myself. I don't mean the church-social letter, but the other one. You living so much in London and not being a gardener, Sir Henry, would not have been likely to notice."

"Eh?" said Sir Henry. "Notice what?"

Mrs. Bantry reached out a hand and selected a catalogue. She opened it and read aloud with gusto:

" 'Dr. Helmuth Spath. Pure lilac, a wonderfully fine flower, carried on exceptionally long and stiff stem. Splendid for cutting and garden decoration. A novelty of striking beauty.

" 'Edgar Jackson. Beautifully shaped chrysanthemum-like flower of a distinct brick-red colour.

" 'Amos Perry. Brilliant red, highly decorative.

" 'Tsingtau. Brilliant orange-red, showy garden plant and lasting cut flower.

" 'Honesty—' "

"With a capital H, you remember," murmured Miss Marple.

" 'Honesty. Rose and white shades, enormous perfect-shaped flower.' "

Mrs. Bantry flung down the catalogue and said with immense explosive force:

"Dahlias!"

"And their initial letters spell 'Death,' " explained Miss Marple.

"But the letter came to Dr. Rosen himself," objected Sir Henry.

"That was the clever part of it," said Miss Marple. "That and the warning in it. What would he do, getting a letter from someone he didn't know, full of names he didn't know. Why, of course, toss it over to his secretary."

"Then, after all—"

"Oh no!" said Miss Marple. "Not the secretary. Why, that's what makes it so perfectly clear that it wasn't him. He'd never have let that letter be found if so. And equally he'd never have destroyed a letter to himself with a German stamp on it. Really, his innocence is—if you'll allow me to use the word—just shining."

"Then who—"

"Well, it seems almost certain—as certain as anything can be in this world. There was another person at the breakfast table, and she would—quite naturally under the circumstances—put out her hand for the letter and read it. And that would be that. You remember that she got a gardening catalogue by the same post—"

"Greta Rosen," said Sir Henry slowly. "Then her visit to me—"

"Gentlemen never see through these things," said Miss Marple. "And I'm afraid they often think we old women are—well, cats, to see things the way we do. But there it is. One does know a great deal about one's own sex, unfortunately. I've no doubt there was a barrier between them. The young man felt a sudden inexplicable repulsion. He suspected, purely through instinct, and couldn't hide the suspicion. And I really think that the girl's visit to you was just pure spite. She was safe enough really, but she just went out of her way to fix your suspicions definitely on poor Mr. Templeton. You weren't nearly so sure about him until after her visit."

"I'm sure it was nothing that she said—" began Sir Henry.

"Gentlemen," said Miss Marple calmly, "never see through these things."

"And that girl—" He stopped. "She commits a cold-blooded murder and gets off scot-free!"

"Oh no, Sir Henry," said Miss Marple. "Not scot-free. Neither you nor I believe that. Remember what you said not long ago. No. Greta Rosen will not escape punishment. To begin with, she must be in with a very queer set of people—blackmailers and terrorists—associates who will do her no good and will probably bring her to a miserable end. As you say, one mustn't waste thoughts on the guilty—it's the innocent who matter. Mr. Templeton, who I daresay will marry that German cousin, his tearing up her letter looks—well, it looks suspicious—using the word in quite a different sense from the one we've been using all the evening. A little as though he were afraid of the other girl noticing or asking to see it? Yes, I think there must have been some little romance there. And then there's Dobbs—though, as you say, I daresay it won't much matter to him. His elevenses are probably all he thinks about. And then there's that poor old Gertrud—the one who reminded me of Annie Poultny. Poor Annie Poultny. Fifty years' faithful service and suspected of making away with Miss Lamb's will, though nothing could be proved. Almost broke the poor creature's faithful heart. And then after she was dead it came to light in the secret drawer of the tea caddy where old Miss Lamb had put it herself for safety. But too late then for poor Annie.

"That's what worries me so about that poor old German woman. When one is old, one becomes embittered very easily. I felt much more sorry for her than for Mr. Templeton, who is young and good-looking and evidently a favourite with the ladies. You will write to her, won't you, Sir Henry, and just tell her that her innocence is established beyond doubt? Her dear old master dead, and she no doubt brooding and feeling herself suspected of . . . Oh! It won't bear thinking about!"

"I will write, Miss Marple," said Sir Henry. He looked at her curiously. "You know, I shall never quite understand you. Your outlook is always a different one from what I expect."

"My outlook, I'm afraid, is a very petty one," said Miss Marple humbly. "I hardly ever go out of St. Mary Mead."

"And yet you have solved what may be called an international mystery," said Sir Henry. "For you have solved it. I am convinced of that."

Miss Marple blushed, then bridled a little.

"I was, I think, well educated for the standard of my day. My sister and I had a German governess—a Fräulein. A very sentimental creature. She taught us the language of flowers—a forgotten study nowadays, but most charming. A yellow tulip, for instance, means 'Hopeless Love,' while a China aster means 'I Die of Jealousy at Your Feet.' That letter was signed Georgina, which I seem to remember as dahlia in German, and that of course made the whole thing perfectly clear. I wish I could remember the meaning of dahlia, but alas, that eludes me. My memory is not what it was."

"At any rate, it didn't mean 'Death.' "

"No, indeed. Horrible, is it not? There are very sad things in the world."

"There are," said Mrs. Bantry with a sigh. "It's lucky one has flowers and one's friends."

"She puts us last, you observe," said Dr. Lloyd.

"A man used to send me purple orchids every night to the theater," said Jane dreamily.

" 'I Await Your Favours'—that's what that means," said Miss Marple brightly.

Sir Henry gave a peculiar sort of cough and turned his head away.
Miss Marple gave a sudden exclamation.
"I've remembered. Dahlias mean 'Treachery and Misrepresentation.' "
"Wonderful," said Sir Henry. "Absolutely wonderful."
And he sighed.

❦ ❦ ❦

Silver Blaze

SIR ARTHUR CONAN DOYLE

"I am afraid, Watson, that I shall have to go," said Holmes as we sat down together to our breakfast one morning.

"Go! Where to?"

"To Dartmoor; to King's Pyland."

I was not surprised. Indeed, my only wonder was that he had not already been mixed up in this extraordinary case, which was the one topic of conversation through the length and breadth of England. For a whole day my companion had rambled about the room with his chin upon his chest and his brows knitted, charging and recharging his pipe with the strongest black tobacco, and absolutely deaf to any of my questions or remarks. Fresh editions of every paper had been sent up by our news agent, only to be glanced over and tossed down into a corner. Yet, silent as he was, I knew perfectly well what it was over which he was brooding. There was but one problem before the public which could challenge his powers of analysis, and that was the singular disappearance of the favourite for the Wessex Cup, and the tragic murder of its trainer. When, therefore, he suddenly announced his intention of setting out for the scene of the drama, it was only what I had both expected and hoped for.

"I should be most happy to go down with you if I should not be in the way," said I.

"My dear Watson, you would confer a great favour upon me by coming. And I think that your time will not be misspent, for there are points about the case which promise to make it an absolutely unique one. We have, I think, just time to catch our train at Paddington, and I will go further into the matter upon our journey. You would oblige me by bringing with you your very excellent field-glass."

And so it happened that an hour or so later I found myself in the

corner of a first-class carriage flying along en route for Exeter, while
Sherlock Holmes, with his sharp, eager face framed in his ear-flapped
travelling-cap, dipped rapidly into the bundle of fresh papers which he
had procured at Paddington. We had left Reading far behind us before
he thrust the last one of them under the seat and offered me his cigar-
case.

"We are going well," said he, looking out of the window and glancing
at his watch. "Our rate at present is fifty-three and a half miles an
hour."

"I have not observed the quarter-mile posts," said I.

"Nor have I. But the telegraph posts upon this line are sixty yards
apart, and the calculation is a simple one. I presume that you have
looked into this matter of the murder of John Straker and the disappearance of Silver Blaze?"

"I have seen what the *Telegraph* and the *Chronicle* have to say."

"It is one of those cases where the art of the reasoner should be used
rather for the sifting of details than for the acquiring of fresh evidence.
The tragedy has been so uncommon, so complete, and of such personal
importance to so many people that we are suffering from a plethora of
surmise, conjecture, and hypothesis. The difficulty is to detach the
framework of fact—of absolute undeniable fact—from the embellish-
ments of theorists and reporters. Then, having established ourselves
upon this sound basis, it is our duty to see what inferences may be
drawn and what are the special points upon which the whole mystery
turns. On Tuesday evening I received telegrams from both Colonel Ross,
the owner of the horse, and from Inspector Gregory, who is looking
after the case, inviting my coöperation."

"Tuesday evening!" I exclaimed. "And this is Thursday morning. Why
didn't you go down yesterday?"

"Because I made a blunder, my dear Watson—which is, I am afraid, a
more common occurrence than anyone would think who only knew me
through your memoirs. The fact is that I could not believe it possible
that the most remarkable horse in England could long remain concealed,
especially in so sparsely inhabited a place as the north of Dartmoor.
From hour to hour yesterday I expected to hear that he had been found,
and that his abductor was the murderer of John Straker. When, however,
another morning had come and I found that beyond the arrest of young

Fitzroy Simpson nothing had been done, I felt that it was time for me to take action. Yet in some ways I feel that yesterday has not been wasted."

"You have formed a theory, then?"

"At least I have got a grip of the essential facts of the case. I shall enumerate them to you, for nothing clears up a case so much as stating it to another person, and I can hardly expect your coöperation if I do not show you the position from which we start."

I lay back against the cushions, puffing at my cigar, while Holmes, leaning forward, with his long, thin forefinger checking off the points upon the palm of his left hand, gave me a sketch of the events which had led to our journey.

"Silver Blaze," said he, "is from the Somomy stock and holds as brilliant a record as his famous ancestor. He is now in his fifth year and has brought in turn each of the prizes of the turf to Colonel Ross, his fortunate owner. Up to the time of the catastrophe he was the first favourite for the Wessex Cup, the betting being three to one on him. He has always, however, been a prime favourite with the racing public and has never yet disappointed them, so that even at those odds enormous sums of money have been laid upon him. It is obvious, therefore, that there were many people who had the strongest interest in preventing Silver Blaze from being there at the fall of the flag next Tuesday.

"The fact was, of course, appreciated at King's Pyland, where the colonel's training stable is situated. Every precaution was taken to guard the favourite. The trainer, John Straker, is a retired jockey who rode in Colonel Ross's colours before he became too heavy for the weighing-chair. He has served the colonel for five years as jockey and for seven as trainer, and has always shown himself to be a zealous and honest servant. Under him were three lads, for the establishment was a small one, containing only four horses in all. One of these lads sat up each night in the stable, while the others slept in the loft. All three bore excellent characters. John Straker, who is a married man, lived in a small villa about two hundred yards from the stables. He has no children, keeps one maidservant, and is comfortably off. The country round is very lonely, but about half a mile to the north there is a small cluster of villas which have been built by a Tavistock contractor for the use of invalids and others who may wish to enjoy the pure Dartmoor air. Tavistock itself lies two miles to the west while across the moor, also about two miles distant, is the larger training establishment of Mapleton, which belongs to Lord Backwater and is managed by Silas Brown. In every other direction the moor is a complete wilderness, inhabited only by a few roaming gypsies. Such was the general situation last Monday night when the catastrophe occurred.

"On that evening the horses had been exercised and watered as usual, and the stables were locked up at nine o'clock. Two of the lads walked up to the trainer's house, where they had supper in the kitchen, while the third, Ned Hunter, remained on guard. At a few minutes after nine the maid, Edith Baxter, carried down to the stables his supper, which consisted of a dish of curried mutton. She took no liquid, as there was a water-tap in the stables, and it was the rule that the lad on duty should drink nothing else. The maid carried a lantern with her, as it was very dark and the path ran across the open moor.

"Edith Baxter was within thirty yards of the stables when a man appeared out of the darkness and called to her to stop. As she stepped into the circle of yellow light thrown by the lantern she saw that he was a person of gentlemanly bearing, dressed in a grey suit of tweeds, with a cloth cap. He wore gaiters and carried a heavy stick with a knob to it. She was most impressed, however, by the extreme pallor of his face and by the nervousness of his manner. His age, she thought, would be rather over thirty than under it.

" 'Can you tell me where I am?' he asked. 'I had almost made up my mind to sleep on the moor when I saw the light of your lantern.'

" 'You are close to the King's Pyland training stables,' said she.

" 'Oh, indeed! What a stroke of luck!' he cried. 'I understand that a stable-boy sleeps there alone every night. Perhaps that is his supper which you are carrying to him. Now I am sure that you would not be too proud to earn the price of a new dress, would you?' He took a piece of white paper folded up out of his waistcoat pocket. 'See that the boy has this tonight, and you shall have the prettiest frock that money can buy.'

"She was frightened by the earnestness of his manner and ran past him to the window through which she was accustomed to hand the meals. It was already opened, and Hunter was seated at the small table inside. She had begun to tell him of what had happened when the stranger came up again.

" 'Good evening,' said he, looking through the window. 'I wanted to have a word with you.' The girl has sworn that as he spoke she noticed the corner of the little paper packet protruding from his closed hand.

" 'What business have you here?' asked the lad.

" 'It's business that may put something into your pocket,' said the other. 'You've two horses in for the Wessex Cup—Silver Blaze and Bayard. Let me have the straight tip and you won't be a loser. Is it a fact that at the weights Bayard could give the other a hundred yards in five furlongs, and that the stable have put their money on him?'

" 'So, you're one of those damned touts!' cried the lad. 'I'll show you how we serve them in King's Pyland.' He sprang up and rushed across the stable to unloose the dog. The girl fled away to the house, but as she ran she looked back and saw that the stranger was leaning through the window. A minute later, however, when Hunter rushed out with the hound he was gone, and though he ran all round the buildings he failed to find any trace of him."

"One moment," I asked. "Did the stable-boy, when he ran out with the dog, leave the door unlocked behind him?"

"Excellent, Watson, excellent!" murmured my companion. "The importance of the point struck me so forcibly that I sent a special wire to Dartmoor yesterday to clear the matter up. The boy locked the door before he left it. The window, I may add, was not large enough for a man to get through.

"Hunter waited until his fellow-grooms had returned, when he sent a message to the trainer and told him what had occurred. Straker was excited at hearing the account, although he does not seem to have quite realized its true significance. It left him, however, vaguely uneasy, and Mrs. Straker, waking at one in the morning, found that he was dressing. In reply to her inquiries, he said that he could not sleep on account of his anxiety about the horses, and that he intended to walk down to the stables to see that all was well. She begged him to remain at home, as she could hear the rain pattering against the window, but in spite of her entreaties he pulled on his large mackintosh and left the house.

"Mrs. Straker awoke at seven in the morning to find that her husband had not yet returned. She dressed herself hastily, called the maid, and set off for the stables. The door was open; inside, huddled together upon a chair, Hunter was sunk in a state of absolute stupor, the favourite's stall was empty, and there were no signs of his trainer.

"The two lads who slept in the chaff-cutting loft above the harness-room were quickly aroused. They had heard nothing during the night, for they are both sound sleepers. Hunter was obviously under the influence of some powerful drug, and as no sense could be got out of him, he was left to sleep it off while the two lads and the two women ran out in search of the absentees. They still had hopes that the trainer had for some reason taken out the horse for early exercise, but on ascending the knoll near the house, from which all the neighbouring moors were visible, they not only could see no signs of the missing favourite, but they perceived something which warned them that they were in the presence of a tragedy.

"About a quarter of a mile from the stables John Straker's overcoat was flapping from a furze-bush. Immediately beyond there was a bowl-shaped depression in the moor, and at the bottom of this was found the dead body of the unfortunate trainer. His head had been shattered by a savage blow from some heavy weapon, and he was wounded on the thigh, where there was a long, clean cut, inflicted evidently by some very sharp instrument. It was clear, however, that Straker had defended himself vigorously against his assailant, for in his right hand he held a small knife, which was clotted with blood up to the handle, while in his left he clasped a red-and-black silk cravat, which was recognized by the maid as having been worn on the preceding evening by the stranger who had visited the stables. Hunter, on recovering from his stupor, was also quite positive as to the ownership of the cravat. He was equally certain that the same stranger had, while standing at the window, drugged his curried mutton, and so deprived the stables of their watchman. As to the missing horse, there were abundant proofs in the mud which lay at the bottom of the fatal hollow that he had been there at the time of the struggle. But from that morning he has disappeared, and although a large reward has been offered, and all the gypsies of Dartmoor are on the alert, no news has come of him. Finally, an analysis has shown that the remains of his supper left by the stable-lad contained an appreciable quantity of powdered opium, while the people at the house partook of the same dish on the same night without any ill effect.

"Those are the main facts of the case, stripped of all surmise, and stated as baldly as possible. I shall now recapitulate what the police have done in the matter.

"Inspector Gregory, to whom the case has been committed, is an extremely competent officer. Were he but gifted with imagination he might rise to great heights in his profession. On his arrival he promptly found and arrested the man upon whom suspicion naturally rested. There was little difficulty in finding him, for he inhabited one of those villas which I have mentioned. His name, it appears, was Fitzroy Simpson. He was a man of excellent birth and education, who had squandered a fortune upon the turf, and who lived now by doing a little quiet and genteel book-making in the sporting clubs of London. An examination of his betting-book shows that bets to the amount of five thousand pounds had been registered by him against the favourite. On being arrested he volunteered the statement that he had come down to Dartmoor in the hope of getting some information about the King's Pyland horses, and also about Desborough, the second favourite, which was in charge of Silas Brown at the Mapleton stables. He did not attempt to deny that he had acted as described upon the evening before, but declared that he had no sinister designs and had simply wished to obtain first-hand information. When confronted with his cravat he turned very pale and was utterly unable to account for its presence in the hand of the murdered man. His wet clothing showed that he had been out in the storm of the night before, and his stick, which was a penang-lawyer weighted with lead, was just such a weapon as might, by repeated blows, have inflicted the terrible injuries to which the trainer had succumbed. On the other hand, there was no wound upon his person, while the state of Straker's knife would show that one at least of his assailants must bear his mark upon him. There you have it all in a nutshell, Watson, and if you can give me any light I shall be infinitely obliged to you."

I had listened with the greatest interest to the statement which Holmes, with characteristic clearness, had laid before me. Though most of the facts were familiar to me, I had not sufficiently appreciated their relative importance, nor their connection to each other.

"Is it not possible," I suggested, "that the incised wound upon Straker may have been caused by his own knife in the convulsive struggles which follow any brain injury?"

"It is more than possible: it is probable," said Holmes. "In that case one of the main points in favour of the accused disappears."

"And yet," said I, "even now I fail to understand what the theory of the police can be."

"I am afraid that whatever theory we state has very grave objections to it," returned my companion. "The police imagine, I take it, that this

Fitzroy Simpson, having drugged the lad, and having in some way obtained a duplicate key, opened the stable door and took out the horse, with the intention, apparently, of kidnapping him altogether. His bridle is missing, so that Simpson must have put this on. Then, having left the door open behind him, he was leading the horse away over the moor when he was either met or overtaken by the trainer. A row naturally ensued. Simpson beat out the trainer's brains with his heavy stick without receiving any injury from the small knife which Straker used in self-defence, and then the thief either led the horse on to some secret hiding-place, or else it may have bolted during the struggle, and be now wandering out on the moors. That is the case as it appears to the police, and improbable as it is, all other explanations are more improbable still. However, I shall very quickly test the matter when I am once upon the spot, and until then I cannot really see how we can get much further than our present position."

It was evening before we reached the little town of Tavistock, which lies, like the boss of a shield, in the middle of the huge circle of Dartmoor. Two gentlemen were awaiting us in the station—the one a tall, fair man with lion-like hair and beard and curiously penetrating light blue eyes; the other a small, alert person, very neat and dapper, in a frock-coat and gaiters, with trim little side-whiskers and an eyeglass. The latter was Colonel Ross, the well-known sportsman; the other, Inspector Gregory; a man who was rapidly making his name in the English detective service.

"I am delighted that you have come down, Mr. Holmes," said the colonel. "The inspector here has done all that could possibly be suggested, but I wish to leave no stone unturned in trying to avenge poor Straker and in recovering my horse."

"Have there been any fresh developments?" asked Holmes.

"I am sorry to say that we have made very little progress," said the inspector. "We have an open carriage outside, and as you would no doubt like to see the place before the light fails, we might talk it over as we drive."

A minute later we were all seated in a comfortable landau and were rattling through the quaint old Devonshire city. Inspector Gregory was full of his case and poured out a stream of remarks, while Holmes threw in an occasional question or interjection. Colonel Ross leaned back with his arms folded and his hat tilted over his eyes, while I listened with interest to the dialogue of the two detectives. Gregory was formulating his theory, which was almost exactly what Holmes had foretold in the train.

"The net is drawn pretty close round Fitzroy Simpson," he remarked, "and I believe myself that he is our man. At the same time I recognize that the evidence is purely circumstantial, and that some new development may upset it."

"How about Straker's knife?"

"We have quite come to the conclusion that he wounded himself in his fall."

"My friend Dr. Watson made that suggestion to me as we came down. If so, it would tell against this man Simpson."

"Undoubtedly. He has neither a knife nor any sign of a wound. The evidence against him is certainly very strong. He had a great interest in the disappearance of the favourite. He lies under suspicion of having poisoned the stable-boy; he was undoubtedly out in the storm; he was armed with a heavy stick, and his cravat was found in the dead man's hand. I really think we have enough to go before a jury."

Holmes shook his head. "A clever counsel would tear it all to rags," said he. "Why should he take the horse out of the stable? If he wished to injure it, why could he not do it there? Has a duplicate key been found in his possession? What chemist sold him the powdered opium? Above all, where could he, a stranger to the district, hide a horse, and such a horse as this? What is his own explanation as to the paper which he wished the maid to give to the stableboy?"

"He says that it was a ten-pound note. One was found in his purse. But your other difficulties are not so formidable as they seem. He is not a stranger to the district. He has twice lodged at Tavistock in the summer. The opium was probably brought from London. The key, having served its purpose, would be hurled away. The horse may be at the bottom of one of the pits or old mines upon the moor."

"What does he say about the cravat?"

"He acknowledges that it is his and declares that he had lost it. But a new element has been introduced into the case which may account for him leading the horse from the stable."

Holmes pricked up his ears.

"We have found traces which show that a party of gypsies encamped on Monday night within a mile of the spot where the murder took place.

On Tuesday they were gone. Now, presuming that there was some understanding between Simpson and these gypsies, might he not have been leading the horse to them when he was overtaken, and may they not have him now?"

"It is certainly possible."

"The moor is being scoured for these gypsies. I have also examined every stable and outhouse in Tavistock, and for a radius of ten miles."

"There is another training-stable quite close, I understand?"

"Yes, and that is a factor which we must certainly not neglect. As Desborough, their horse, was second in the betting, they had an interest in the disappearance of the favourite. Silas Brown, the trainer, is known to have had large bets upon the event, and he was no friend to poor Straker. We have, however, examined the stables, and there is nothing to connect him with the affair."

"And nothing to connect this man Simpson with the interests of the Mapleton stables?"

"Nothing at all."

Holmes leaned back in the carriage, and the conversation ceased. A few minutes later our driver pulled up at a neat little red-brick villa with overhanging eaves which stood by the road. Some distance off, across a paddock, lay a long grey-tiled outbuilding. In every other direction the low curves of the moor, bronze-coloured from the fading ferns, stretched away to the sky-line, broken only by the steeples of Tavistock, and by a cluster of houses away to the westward which marked the Mapleton stables. We all sprang out with the exception of Holmes, who continued to lean back with his eyes fixed upon the sky in front of him, entirely absorbed in his own thoughts. It was only when I touched his arm that he roused himself with a violent start and stepped out of the carriage.

"Excuse me," said he, turning to Colonel Ross, who had looked at him in some surprise. "I was day-dreaming." There was a gleam in his eyes and a suppressed excitement in his manner which convinced me, used as I was to his ways, that his hand was upon a clue, though I could not imagine where he had found it.

"Perhaps you would prefer at once to go on to the scene of the crime, Mr. Holmes?" said Gregory.

"I think that I should prefer to stay here a little and go into one or two questions of detail. Straker was brought back here, I presume?"

"Yes, he lies upstairs. The inquest is to-morrow."

"He has been in your service some years, Colonel Ross?"

"I have always found him an excellent servant."

"I presume that you made an inventory of what he had in his pockets at the time of his death, Inspector?"

"I have the things themselves in the sitting-room if you would care to see them."

"I should be very glad." We all filed into the front room and sat round the central table while the inspector unlocked a square tin box and laid a small heap of things before us. There was a box of vestas, two inches of tallow candle, an A D P brier-root pipe, a pouch of sealskin with half an ounce of long-cut Cavendish, a silver watch with a gold chain, five sovereigns in gold, an aluminum pencil-case, a few papers, and an ivory-handled knife with a very delicate, inflexible blade marked Weiss & Co., London.

"This is a very singular knife," said Holmes, lifting it up and examining it minutely. "I presume, as I see blood-stains upon it, that it is the one which was found in the dead man's grasp. Watson, this knife is surely in your line?"

"It is what we call a cataract knife," said I.

"I thought so. A very delicate blade devised for very delicate work. A strange thing for a man to carry with him upon a rough expedition, especially as it would not shut in his pocket."

"The tip was guarded by a disc of cork which we found beside his body," said the inspector. "His wife tells us that the knife had lain upon the dressing-table, and that he had picked it up as he left the room. It was a poor weapon, but perhaps the best that he could lay his hands on at the moment."

"Very possibly. How about these papers?"

"Three of them are receipted hay-dealers' accounts. One of them is a letter of instructions from Colonel Ross. This other is a milliner's account for thirty-seven pounds fifteen made out by Madame Lesurier, of Bond Street, to William Derbyshire. Mrs. Straker tells us that Derbyshire was a friend of her husband's, and that occasionally his letters were addressed here."

"Madame Derbyshire had somewhat expensive tastes," remarked Holmes, glancing down the account. "Twenty-two guineas is rather heavy for a single costume. However, there appears to be nothing more to learn, and we may now go down to the scene of the crime."

As we emerged from the sitting-room a woman, who had been waiting in the passage, took a step forward and laid her hand upon the inspector's sleeve. Her face was haggard and thin and eager, stamped with the print of a recent horror.

"Have you got them? Have you found them?" she panted.

"No, Mrs. Straker. But Mr. Holmes here has come from London to help us, and we shall do all that is possible."

"Surely I met you in Plymouth at a garden-party some little time ago, Mrs. Straker?" said Holmes.

"No, sir; you are mistaken."

"Dear me! Why, I could have sworn to it. You wore a costume of dove-coloured silk with ostrich-feather trimming."

"I never had such a dress, sir," answered the lady.

"Ah, that quite settles it," said Holmes. And with an apology he followed the inspector outside. A short walk across the moor took us to the hollow in which the body had been found. At the brink of it was the furze-bush upon which the coat had been hung.

"There was no wind that night, I understand," said Holmes.

"None, but very heavy rain."

"In that case the overcoat was not blown against the furze-bushes, but placed there."

"Yes, it was laid across the bush."

"You fill me with interest. I perceive that the ground has been trampled up a good deal. No doubt many feet have been here since Monday night."

"A piece of matting has been laid here at the side, and we have all stood upon that."

"Excellent."

"In this bag I have one of the boots which Straker wore, one of Fitzroy Simpson's shoes, and a cast horseshoe of Silver Blaze."

"My dear Inspector, you surpass yourself!" Holmes took the bag, and, descending into the hollow, he pushed the matting into a more central position. Then stretching himself upon his face and leaning his chin upon his hands, he made a careful study of the trampled mud in front of him. "Hullo!" said he suddenly. "What's this?" It was a wax vesta,

half burned, which was so coated with mud that it looked at first like a
little chip of wood.

"I cannot think how I came to overlook it," said the inspector with
an expression of annoyance.

"It was invisible, buried in the mud. I only saw it because I was
looking for it."

"What! you expected to find it?"

"I thought it not unlikely."

He took the boots from the bag and compared the impressions of
each of them with marks upon the ground. Then he clambered up to the
rim of the hollow and crawled about among the ferns and bushes.

"I am afraid that there are no more tracks," said the inspector. "I
have examined the ground very carefully for a hundred yards in each
direction."

"Indeed!" said Holmes, rising. "I should not have the impertinence to
do it again after what you say. But I should like to take a little walk over
the moor before it grows dark that I may know my ground to-morrow,
and I think that I shall put this horseshoe into my pocket for luck."

Colonel Ross, who had shown some signs of impatience at my companion's quiet and systematic method of work, glanced at his watch. "I
wish you would come back with me, Inspector," said he. "There are
several points on which I should like your advice, and especially as to
whether we do not owe it to the public to remove our horse's name
from the entries for the cup."

"Certainly not," cried Holmes with decision. "I should let the name
stand."

The colonel bowed. "I am very glad to have had your opinion, sir,"
said he. "You will find us at poor Straker's house when you have finished your walk, and we can drive together into Tavistock."

He turned back with the inspector, while Holmes and I walked slowly
across the moor. The sun was beginning to sink behind the stable of
Mapleton, and the long, sloping plain in front of us was tinged with
gold, deepening into rich, ruddy browns where the faded ferns and
brambles caught the evening light. But the glories of the landscape were
all wasted upon my companion, who was sunk in the deepest thought.

"It's this way, Watson," said he at last. "We may leave the question of
who killed John Straker for the instant and confine ourselves to finding
out what has become of the horse. Now, supposing that he broke away

during or after the tragedy, where could he have gone to? The horse is a very gregarious creature. If left to himself his instincts would have been either to return to King's Pyland or go over to Mapleton. Why should he run wild upon the moor? He would surely have been seen by now. And why should gypsies kidnap him? These people always clear out when they hear of trouble, for they do not wish to be pestered by the police. They could not hope to sell such a horse. They would run a great risk and gain nothing by taking him. Surely that is clear."

"Where is he, then?"

"I have already said that he must have gone to King's Pyland or to Mapleton. He is not at King's Pyland. Therefore he is at Mapleton. Let us take that as a working hypothesis and see what it leads us to. This part of the moor, as the inspector remarked, is very hard and dry. But it falls away towards Mapleton, and you can see from here that there is a long hollow over yonder, which must have been very wet on Monday night. If our supposition is correct, then the horse must have crossed that, and there is the point where we should look for his tracks."

We had been walking briskly during this conversation, and a few more minutes brought us to the hollow in question. At Holmes's request I walked down the bank to the right, and he to the left, but I had not taken fifty paces before I heard him give a shout and saw him waving his hand to me. The track of a horse was plainly outlined in the soft earth in front of him, and the shoe which he took from his pocket exactly fitted the impression.

"See the value of imagination," said Holmes. "It is the one quality which Gregory lacks. We imagined what might have happened, acted upon the supposition, and find ourselves justified. Let us proceed."

We crossed the marshy bottom and passed over a quarter of a mile of dry, hard turf. Again the ground sloped, and again we came on the tracks. Then we lost them for half a mile, but only to pick them up once more quite close to Mapleton. It was Holmes who saw them first, and he stood pointing with a look of triumph upon his face. A man's track was visible beside the horse's.

"The horse was alone before," I cried.

"Quite so. It was alone before. Hullo, what is this?"

The double track turned sharp off and took the direction of King's Pyland. Holmes whistled, and we both followed along after it. His eyes were on the trail, but I happened to look a little to one side and saw to my surprise the same tracks coming back again in the opposite direction.

"One for you, Watson," said Holmes when I pointed it out. "You have saved us a long walk, which would have brought us back on our own traces. Let us follow the return track."

We had not to go far. It ended at the paving of asphalt which led up to the gates of the Mapleton stables. As we approached, a groom ran out from them.

"We don't want any loiterers about here," said he.

"I only wished to ask a question," said Holmes, with his finger and thumb in his waistcoat pocket. "Should I be too early to see your master, Mr. Silas Brown, if I were to call at five o'clock to-morrow morning?"

"Bless you, sir, if anyone is about he will be, for he is always the first stirring. But here he is, sir, to answer your questions for himself. No, sir, no, it is as much as my place is worth to let him see me touch your money. Afterwards, if you like."

As Sherlock Holmes replaced the half-crown which he had drawn from his pocket, a fierce-looking elderly man strode out from the gate with a hunting-crop swinging in his hand.

"What's this, Dawson!" he cried. "No gossiping! Go about your business! And you, what the devil do you want here?"

"Ten minutes' talk with you, my good sir," said Holmes in the sweetest of voices.

"I've no time to talk to every gadabout. We want no strangers here. Be off, or you may find a dog at your heels."

Holmes leaned forward and whispered something in the trainer's ear. He started violently and flushed to the temples.

"It's a lie!" he shouted. "An infernal lie!"

"Very good. Shall we argue about it here in public or talk it over in your parlour?"

"Oh, come in if you wish to."

Holmes smiled. "I shall not keep you more than a few minutes, Watson," said he. "Now, Mr. Brown, I am quite at your disposal."

It was twenty minutes, and the reds had all faded into greys before Holmes and the trainer reappeared. Never have I seen such a change as had been brought about in Silas Brown in that short time. His face was ashy pale, beads of perspiration shone upon his brow, and his hands shook until the hunting-crop wagged like a branch in the wind. His bullying, overbearing manner was all gone too, and he cringed along at my companion's side like a dog with its master.

"Your instructions will be done. It shall all be done," said he.

"There must be no mistake," said Holmes, looking round at him. The other winced as he read the menace in his eyes.

"Oh, no, there shall be no mistake. It shall be there. Should I change it first or not?"

Holmes thought a little and then burst out laughing. "No, don't," said he, "I shall write to you about it. No tricks, now, or—"

"Oh, you can trust me, you can trust me!"

"Yes, I think I can. Well, you shall hear from me to-morrow." He turned upon his heel, disregarding the trembling hand which the other held out to him, and we set off for King's Pyland.

"A more perfect compound of the bully, coward, and sneak than Master Silas Brown I have seldom met with," remarked Holmes as we trudged along together.

"He has the horse, then?"

"He tried to bluster out of it, but I described to him so exactly what his actions had been upon that morning that he is convinced that I was watching him. Of course you observed the peculiarly square toes in the impressions, and that his own boots exactly corresponded to them. Again, of course no subordinate would have dared to do such a thing. I described to him how, when according to his custom he was the first down, he perceived a strange horse wandering over the moor. How he went out to it, and his astonishment at recognizing, from the white forehead which has given the favourite its name, that chance had put in his power the only horse which could beat the one upon which he had put his money. Then I described how his first impulse had been to lead him back to King's Pyland, and how the devil had shown him how he could hide the horse until the race was over, and how he had led it back and concealed it at Mapleton. When I told him every detail he gave it up and thought only of saving his own skin."

"But his stables had been searched?"

"Oh, an old horse-faker like him has many a dodge."

"But are you not afraid to leave the horse in his power now, since he has every interest in injuring it?"

"My dear fellow, he will guard it as the apple of his eye. He knows that his only hope of mercy is to produce it safe."

"Colonel Ross did not impress me as a man who would be likely to show much mercy in any case."

"The matter does not rest with Colonel Ross. I follow my own methods and tell as much or as little as I choose. That is the advantage of being unofficial. I don't know whether you observed it, Watson, but the colonel's manner has been just a trifle cavalier to me. I am inclined now to have a little amusement at his expense. Say nothing to him about the horse."

"Certainly not without your permission."

"And of course this is all quite a minor point compared to the question of who killed John Straker."

"And you will devote yourself to that?"

"On the contrary, we both go back to London by the night train."

I was thunderstruck by my friend's words. We had only been a few hours in Devonshire, and that he should give up an investigation which he had begun so brilliantly was quite incomprehensible to me. Not a word more could I draw from him until we were back at the trainer's house. The colonel and the inspector were awaiting us in the parlour.

"My friend and I return to town by the night-express," said Holmes. "We have had a charming little breath of your beautiful Dartmoor air."

The inspector opened his eyes, and the colonel's lip curled in a sneer. "So you despair of arresting the murderer of poor Straker," said he.

Holmes shrugged his shoulders. "There are certainly grave difficulties in the way," said he. "I have every hope, however, that your horse will start upon Tuesday, and I beg that you will have your jockey in readiness. Might I ask for a photograph of Mr. John Straker?"

The inspector took one from an envelope and handed it to him.

"My dear Gregory, you anticipate all my wants. If I might ask you to wait here for an instant, I have a question which I should like to put to the maid."

"I must say that I am rather disappointed in our London consultant," said Colonel Ross bluntly as my friend left the room. "I do not see that we are any further than when he came."

"At least you have his assurance that your horse will run," said I.

"Yes, I have his assurance," said the colonel with a shrug of his shoulders. "I should prefer to have the horse."

I was about to make some reply in defence of my friend when he entered the room again.

"Now, gentlemen," said he, "I am quite ready for Tavistock."

As we stepped into the carriage one of the stable-lads held the door open for us. A sudden idea seemed to occur to Holmes, for he leaned forward and touched the lad upon the sleeve.

"You have a few sheep in the paddock," he said. "Who attends to them?"

"I do, sir."

"Have you noticed anything amiss with them of late?"

"Well, sir, not of much account, but three of them have gone lame, sir."

I could see that Holmes was extremely pleased, for he chuckled and rubbed his hands together.

"A long shot, Watson, a very long shot," said he, pinching my arm. "Gregory, let me recommend to your attention this singular epidemic among the sheep. Drive on, coachman!"

Colonel Ross still wore an expression which showed the poor opinion which he had formed of my companion's ability, but I saw by the inspector's face that his attention had been keenly aroused.

"You consider that to be important?" he asked.

"Exceedingly so."

"Is there any point to which you would wish to draw my attention?"

"To the curious incident of the dog in the night-time."

"The dog did nothing in the night-time."

"That was the curious incident," remarked Sherlock Holmes.

Four days later Holmes and I were again in the train, bound for Winchester to see the race for the Wessex Cup. Colonel Ross met us by appointment outside the station, and we drove in his drag to the course beyond the town. His face was grave, and his manner was cold in the extreme.

"I have seen nothing of my horse," said he.

"I suppose that you would know him when you saw him?" asked Holmes.

The colonel was very angry. "I have been on the turf for twenty years and never was asked such a question as that before," said he. "A child would know Silver Blaze with his white forehead and his mottled off-foreleg."

"How is the betting?"

"Well, that is the curious part of it. You could have got fifteen to one yesterday, but the price has become shorter and shorter, until you can hardly get three to one now."

"Hum!" said Holmes. "Somebody knows something, that is clear."

As the drag drew up in the enclosure near the grandstand I glanced at the card to see the entries.

Wessex Plate [it ran] 50 sovs. each h ft with 1000 sovs. added, for four and five year olds. Second, £300. Third, £200. New course (one mile and five furlongs).

1. Mr. Heath Newton's The Negro. Red cap. Cinnamon jacket.
2. Colonel Wardlaw's Pugilist. Pink cap. Blue and black jacket.
3. Lord Backwater's Desborough. Yellow cap and sleeves.
4. Colonel Ross's Silver Blaze. Black cap. Red jacket.
5. Duke of Balmoral's Iris. Yellow and black stripes.
6. Lord Singleford's Rasper. Purple cap. Black sleeves.

"We scratched our other one and put all hopes on your word," said the colonel. "Why, what is that? Silver Blaze favourite?"

"Five to four against Silver Blaze!" roared the ring. "Five to four against Silver Blaze! Five to fifteen against Desborough! Five to four on the field!"

"There are the numbers up," I cried. "They are all six there."

"All six there? Then my horse is running," cried the colonel in great agitation. "But I don't see him. My colours have not passed."

"Only five have passed. This must be he."

As I spoke a powerful bay horse swept out from the weighing enclosure and cantered past us, bearing on its back the well-known black and red of the colonel.

"That's not my horse," cried the owner. "That beast has not a white hair upon its body. What is this that you have done, Mr. Holmes?"

"Well, well, let us see how he gets on," said my friend imperturbably. For a few minutes he gazed through my field-glass. "Capital! An excellent start!" he cried suddenly. "There they are, coming round the curve!"

From our drag we had a superb view as they came up the straight. The six horses were so close together that a carpet could have covered them, but halfway up the yellow of the Mapleton stable showed to the front. Before they reached us, however, Desborough's bolt was shot, and the colonel's horse, coming away with a rush, passed the post a good six lengths before its rival, the Duke of Balmoral's Iris making a bad third.

"It's my race, anyhow," gasped the colonel, passing his hand over his eyes. "I confess that I can make neither head nor tail of it. Don't you think that you have kept up your mystery long enough, Mr. Holmes?"

"Certainly, Colonel, you shall know everything. Let us all go round and have a look at the horse together. Here he is," he continued as we made our way into the weighing enclosure, where only owners and their friends find admittance. "You have only to wash his face and his leg in spirits of wine, and you will find that he is the same old Silver Blaze as ever."

"You take my breath away!"

"I found him in the hands of a faker and took the liberty of running him just as he was sent over."

"My dear sir, you have done wonders. The horse looks very fit and well. It never went better in its life. I owe you a thousand apologies for having doubted your ability. You have done me a great service by recovering my horse. You would do me a greater still if you could lay your hands on the murderer of John Straker."

"I have done so," said Holmes quietly.

The colonel and I stared at him in amazement. "You have got him! Where is he, then?"

"He is here."

"Here! Where?"

"In my company at the present moment."

The colonel flushed angrily. "I quite recognize that I am under obligations to you, Mr. Holmes," said he, "but I must regard what you have just said as either a very bad joke or an insult."

Sherlock Holmes laughed. "I assure you that I have not associated you with the crime, Colonel," said he. "The real murderer is standing immediately behind you." He stepped past and laid his hand upon the glossy neck of the thoroughbred.

"The horse!" cried both the colonel and myself.

"Yes, the horse. And it may lessen his guilt if I say that it was done in self-defence, and that John Straker was a man who was entirely unworthy of your confidence. But there goes the bell, and as I stand to win a little on this next race, I shall defer a lengthy explanation until a more fitting time."

We had a corner of a Pullman car to ourselves that evening as we whirled back to London, and I fancy that the journey was a short one to Colonel Ross as well as to myself as we listened to our companion's narrative of the events which had occurred at the Dartmoor training-stables upon that Monday night, and the means by which he had unravelled them.

"I confess," said he, "that any theories which I had formed from the newspaper reports were entirely erroneous. And yet there were indications there, had they not been overlaid by other details which concealed their true import. I went to Devonshire with the conviction that Fitzroy Simpson was the true culprit, although, of course, I saw that the evidence against him was by no means complete. It was while I was in the carriage, just as we reached the trainer's house, that the immense significance of the curried mutton occurred to me. You may remember that I was distrait and remained sitting after you had all alighted. I was marvelling in my own mind how I could possibly have overlooked so obvious a clue."

"I confess," said the colonel, "that even now I cannot see how it helps us."

"It was the first link in my chain of reasoning. Powdered opium is by no means tasteless. The flavour is not disagreeable, but it is perceptible. Were it mixed with any ordinary dish the eater would undoubtedly detect it and would probably eat no more. A curry was exactly the medium which would disguise this taste. By no possible supposition could this stranger, Fitzroy Simpson, have caused curry to be served in the trainer's family that night, and it is surely too monstrous a coincidence to suppose that he happened to come along with powdered opium upon the very night when a dish happened to be served which would disguise the flavour. That is unthinkable. Therefore Simpson became eliminated from the case, and our attention centres upon Straker and his wife, the only two people who could have chosen curried mutton for supper that night. The opium was added after the dish was set aside for the stable-boy, for the others had the same for supper with no ill effects. Which of them, then, had access to that dish without the maid seeing them?

"Before deciding that question I had grasped the significance of the silence of the dog, for one true inference invariably suggests others. The Simpson incident had shown me that a dog was kept in the stables, and yet, though someone had been in and had fetched out a horse, he had not barked enough to arouse the two lads in the loft. Obviously the midnight visitor was someone whom the dog knew well.

"I was already convinced, or almost convinced, that John Straker went down to the stables in the dead of the night and took out Silver Blaze. For what purpose? For a dishonest one, obviously, or why should he drug his own stable-boy? And yet I was at a loss to know why. There have been cases before now where trainers have made sure of great sums of money by laying against their own horses through agents and then preventing them from winning by fraud. Sometimes it is a pulling jockey. Sometimes it is some surer and subtler means. What was it here? I hoped that the contents of his pockets might help me to form a conclusion.

"And they did so. You cannot have forgotten the singular knife which was found in the dead man's hand, a knife which certainly no sane man would choose for a weapon. It was, as Dr. Watson told us, a form of knife which is used for the most delicate operations known in surgery. And it was to be used for a delicate operation that night. You must know, with your wide experience of turf matters, Colonel Ross, that it is possible to make a slight nick upon the tendons of a horse's ham, and to do it subcutaneously, so as to leave absolutely no trace. A horse so treated would develop a slight lameness, which would be put down to a strain in exercise or a touch of rheumatism, but never to foul play."

"Villain! Scoundrel!" cried the colonel.

"We have here the explanation of why John Straker wished to take the horse out on to the moor. So spirited a creature would have certainly roused the soundest of sleepers when it felt the prick of the knife. It was absolutely necessary to do it in the open air."

"I have been blind!" cried the colonel. "Of course that was why he needed the candle and struck the match."

"Undoubtedly. But in examining his belongings I was fortunate enough to discover not only the method of the crime but even its motives. As a man of the world, Colonel, you know that men do not carry other people's bills about in their pockets. We have most of us quite enough to do to settle our own. I at once concluded that Straker was leading a double life and keeping a second establishment. The nature of the bill showed that there was a lady in the case, and one who had expensive tastes. Liberal as you are with your servants, one can hardly expect that they can buy twenty-guinea walking dresses for their ladies. I questioned Mrs. Straker as to the dress without her knowing it, and having satisfied myself that it had never reached her, I made a note of the milliner's address and felt that by calling there with Straker's photograph I could easily dispose of the mythical Derbyshire.

"From that time on all was plain. Straker had led out the horse to a hollow where his light would be invisible. Simpson in his flight had dropped his cravat, and Straker had picked it up—with some idea, perhaps, that he might use it in securing the horse's leg. Once in the hollow, he had got behind the horse and had struck a light; but the creature, frightened at the sudden glare, and with the strange instinct of animals feeling that some mischief was intended, had lashed out, and the steel shoe had struck Straker full on the forehead. He had already, in spite of the rain, taken off his overcoat in order to do his delicate task, and so, as he fell, his knife gashed his thigh. Do I make it clear?"

"Wonderful!" cried the colonel. "Wonderful! You might have been there!"

"My final shot was, I confess, a very long one. It struck me that so astute a man as Straker would not undertake this delicate tendon-nicking without a little practice. What could he practice on? My eyes fell upon the sheep, and I asked a question which, rather to my surprise, showed that my surmise was correct.

"When I returned to London I called upon the milliner, who had recognized Straker as an excellent customer of the name of Derbyshire, who had a very dashing wife, with a strong partiality for expensive dresses. I have no doubt that this woman had plunged him over head and ears in debt, and so led him into this miserable plot."

"You have explained all but one thing," cried the colonel. "Where was the horse?"

"Ah, it bolted, and was cared for by one of your neighbours. We must have an amnesty in that direction, I think. This is Clapham Junction, if I am not mistaken, and we shall be in Victoria in less than ten minutes. If you care to smoke a cigar in our rooms, Colonel, I shall be happy to give you any other details which might interest you."

✻ ✻ ✻

The Adventure
of the Suffering Ruler

H. R. F. KEATING

It was in the early autumn of 1896 that, returning one day from visiting by train a patient in Hertfordshire and being thus in the vicinity of Baker Street, I decided to call on Sherlock Holmes, whom I had not seen for several weeks. I found him, to my dismay, in a sad state. Although it was by now late afternoon he was still in his dressing-gown lounging upon the sofa in our old sitting-room, his violin lying on the floor beside him and the air musty with cold tobacco smoke from the neglected pipe left carelessly upon the sofa arm. I glanced at once to the mantelpiece where there lay always that neat morocco case which contained the syringe. It was in its customary place, but, when under pretence of examining the familiar bullet-marked letters 'VR' on the wall above, I stepped closer, I saw that it lay upon the envelope of a letter postmarked only two days earlier.

"Well, Holmes," I said, jovially as I could, "I see that your bullet holes of yore are still here."

"It would be strange indeed, Watson, had they disappeared," my old friend answered, with somewhat more fire than he had earlier greeted me.

He laughed then in a melancholy enough fashion.

"Yet I could wish that they had vanished between one night and the next morning," he added. "It would at least provide my mind with some matter to work upon."

My spirits sank at the words. Holmes had always needed stimulation, and if no problem was there to arouse his mind a seven per cent solution of cocaine awaited.

"But have you no case on hand?" I asked.

"Some trifling affairs," Holmes replied. "A commission for the Shah of Persia, a little question of missing securities in Pittsburgh. Nothing to engage my full attention. But, you, my dear Watson, how is it that you have been visiting a patient in Hertfordshire?"

I turned to my old friend in astonishment. I had said nothing of the reason for my being in the vicinity.

"Oh, come, doctor," he said. "Do I have to explain to you once again the simple signs that tell me such things? Why, they are written on your person as clearly as if you carried a newspaper billboard proclaiming them."

"I dare say they may be, Holmes. But beyond the fact that Baker Street station serves that particular county and that I nowadays visit you chiefly when I chance to be in the locality, I cannot see how this time you can know so much of my business."

"And yet the moment you removed your gloves the characteristic pungent odour of iodoform was heavy in the air, indicating beyond doubt that your excursion had been on a professional matter. While your boots are dust-covered to the very tops, which surely means that you travelled for some little time on a country lane."

I glanced down at my boots. The evidence was all too plain to see.

"Well, yes," I admitted. "I did receive this morning a request to visit a gentleman living near Rickmansworth whose condition was causing him anxiety. An unhealed lesion on the abdomen complicated by brain fever, but I have high hopes of a good recovery."

"My dear Watson, under your care who can doubt of that? But I am surprised to hear that your practice now extends to the remote Hertfordshire countryside."

I smiled.

"No, no. I assure you none other of my patients necessitates any journey longer than one performed easily in a hansom."

"And yet you have just been down to Hertfordshire?"

"Yes. I was called on this morning by the manservant of a certain Mr. Smith, a trusted fellow, I gathered, though of European origin. He told me that his master had instructed him to seek out a London doctor and to request a visit as soon as possible. Apparently, Mr. Smith has a somewhat morbid fear of any of his close neighbours knowing that he is ill and so prefers a physician from a distance, even if the visit means a considerably greater financial outlay."

"You were well remunerated then?"

"I think I may say, handsomely so."

"I am not surprised to hear it."

"No, there, Holmes, you are at fault. My services were not asked for because of any particular reputation I may have. In fact, the manservant happened to be in my neighbourhood upon some other errand and, so I understand, simply saw my brass plate and rang at my door."

Holmes raised himself upon one elbow on the sofa. His eyes seemed to me to shine now with a healthier light.

"You misunderstand me, Watson. You had already indicated that your services were called upon more or less by chance. But what I was saying was that the size of your fee did not surprise me, since it is clearly evident that you were required for a quality quite other than your medical attainments."

"Indeed?" I answered, a little nettled I must confess. "And what quality had you in mind?"

"Why, distance, my dear fellow. The distance between medical adviser and patient, and the complete discretion that follows from that."

"I am by no means sure that I understand."

"No? Yet the matter is simple enough. A person living in a remote country house, a gentleman for whom monetary considerations have little weight, sends a trusted servant to obtain the immediate services of a London doctor, of any London doctor more or less, and you expect me to be surprised that you received a fee altogether out of the ordinary?"

"Well, Holmes," I replied, "I will not disguise that my remuneration was perhaps excessive. But my patient evidently is a wealthy man and one prey to nervous fears. He trusts, too, to receive my continuing attentions from week to week. The situation does not strike me as being very much out of the ordinary."

"No, Watson? But I tell you that it is out of the ordinary. The man you attended this afternoon is no ordinary man, you may take my word for that."

"Well, if you say so, Holmes, if you say so," I replied.

Yet I could not but think that for once my old friend had read too much into the circumstances, and I quickly sought for some other subject of conversation, being much relieved when Holmes too seemed disinclined to pursue a matter in which he might be thought to have me at a disadvantage. The remainder of the visit passed pleasantly enough, and I had the satisfaction of leaving Holmes looking a good deal more brisk and cheerful than he had done upon my arrival.

I went down to Hertfordshire again a week later and found my patient already much better for the treatment I had prescribed. I was hopeful enough, indeed, to feel that another two or three weeks of the same regimen, which included plenty of rest and a light diet, would see the illness through.

It was just as I stepped back from the bed after concluding my examination, however, that out of the corner of my eye I detected a sharp movement just outside the window. I was so surprised, since there was no balcony outside, that something of my alarm must have communicated itself to my patient who at once demanded, with the full querulousness of his indisposition, what it was that I had seen.

"I thought I saw a man out there, a glimpse of a face, dark brown and wrinkled," I answered without premeditation, so disturbed was I by an aura of malignancy I had been aware of even from my brief sight of that visage.

But I quickly sought to counteract any anxiety I might have aroused in my already nervous patient.

"Yet it can hardly have been a man," I said. "It was more likely a bird perching momentarily in the ivy."

"No, no," Mr. Smith said, in sharp command. "A face. A burglar. I always knew this house was unsafe. After him doctor, after him. Lay him by the heels. Catch him. Catch him."

I thought it best at least to make pretence of obeying the peremptory order. There would be little hope of calming my patient unless I made an excursion into the garden.

I hurried out of the room and down the stairs, calling to the manservant, who, I had gathered, was the sole other occupant of the house. But he evidently must have been in the kitchens or elsewhere out of hearing since I had no reply. I ran straight out of the front door and looked about me. At once, down at the far side of the garden, I detected a movement behind a still leaf-clad beech hedge. I set out at a run.

Holmes had been right, I thought, as swiftly and silently I crossed a large, damp-sodden lawn. My patient must be a man of mystery if he was being spied upon by daylight in this daring fashion. His cries of alarm over a burglary must, then, be false. No ordinary burglar, surely, would seek to enter a house by broad day.

My quarry had by now gone slinking along the far side of the beech hedge to a point where I lost sight of him behind a dense rhododendron shrubbery. But I was running on a course to cut him off, and I made no doubt that before long I would have the rogue by the collar.

Indeed, as soon as I had rounded the dense clump of rhododendrons, I saw a small wicket gate in the hedge ahead with the figure of the man who had been spying on my patient only just beyond. He appeared from his garb to be a gypsy. In a moment I was through the gate, and in another moment I had him by the arm.

"Now, you villain," I cried. "We shall have the truth of it."

But even before the man had had time to turn in my grasp I heard from behind me the sound of sudden, wild, grim, evil laughter. I looked back. Peering at the two of us from the shelter of the rhododendrons was that same brown, wrinkled face I had glimpsed looking in at my patient's window. I loosened my grip on the gypsy, swung about and once more set out in pursuit.

This time I did not have so far to go. No sooner had I reached the other side of the shrubbery than I came face to face with my man. But he was my man no longer. He wore the same nondescript clothes that I had caught sight of among the brittle rhododendron leaves and his face was still brown-coloured. But that look of hectic evil in it had vanished clear away and in its place were the familiar features of my friend, Sherlock Holmes.

"I am sorry, Watson, to have put you to the trouble of two chases in one afternoon," he said. "But I had to draw you away from that fellow before revealing myself."

"Holmes," I cried. "Then it was you at the window up there?"

"It was, doctor. I knew that it was imperative that I myself should take a good look at this mysterious patient of yours, and so I took the liberty of following you, knowing that this was your day for visiting the case. But you were a little too quick for me in the end, my dear fellow, and I had to beat a more hurried retreat than I altogether cared to."

"Yes, but all the same, Holmes," I said. "You cannot have had any good reason to suppose that it was necessary to spy upon my patient in that manner."

"No good reason, doctor? Why, I should have thought the third finger of his right hand was reason enough, were there no other."

"The third finger of his right hand?"

"Why, yes, my dear fellow. Surely you are not going to tell me that you noticed nothing about that? Come, I was at that window for little more than three or four minutes and I had grasped its significance long before you turned and saw me."

"Now that I think about it," I replied, "my patient does wear a finger-stall on the third finger of his right hand. Some trifling injury, I suppose. It certainly could in no way contribute to his condition."

"I never suggested that it did, doctor. I am sure you know your business better than that. Trust me, then, to know mine."

"But does his concealing that finger have some significance?" I asked.

"Of course it does. Tell me, what does a man customarily wear upon his third finger?"

"A ring, I suppose. But that would not be upon the right hand, surely?"

"Yes, Watson, a ring. You have arrived at the point with your customary perspicacity. But why should a man wish to conceal a particular ring? Tell me that."

"Holmes, I cannot. I simply cannot."

"Because the ring has a particular meaning. And who is it who would wear a ring of that nature? Why, a monarch, of course. I tell you that man in bed there is a king, and he is hiding for some good reason. There can scarcely be any doubt about that."

To my mind, there was at least room for a measure of disagreement with this conclusion. Smith was perhaps a name that anyone wishing to live anonymously might take, but certainly my patient had shown not the least trace of a foreign accent, as he was surely likely to do if he were the ruler of one of the lesser European states whose appearance, especially since he wore a full beard, might be unknown to me. Yet he did have a manservant of European origin, though here again this was not an altogether uncommon circumstance for a single English gentleman who might be something of a traveller. I would have liked to put all these doubts and queries to my friend, but from the moment that he had told me what he had deduced from my patient's concealed finger he lapsed into one of those moods of silence well familiar to me, and for the whole of our journey back to London he uttered scarcely a word, little more than to say to me at the station in Hertfordshire that he had a number of telegrams which he needed urgently to despatch.

I was curious enough, however, to find an opportunity of visiting Baker Street again next day. But, though I found Holmes fully dressed and a great deal more alert than on my last visit, I was unable to obtain from him any hint about the direction of his inquiries. All he would do was to talk, with that vivacity of spirit which he could display whenever the mood took him, about a bewildering variety of subjects, the paintings of the Belgian artist, Ensor, the amorous adventures of Madame Sand, the activities of the Russian nihilists, the gravity of the political situation in Illyria. None was a matter on which I felt myself particularly informed, yet on each Holmes, it seemed, had a fund of knowledge. At length I went back to my medical round not one whit better able to decide whether my Hertfordshire patient was no more than the nervous Englishman, Mr. Smith, whom he seemed to be, or in truth some foreign potentate sheltering under that pseudonym in the safety of the Queen's peace.

The following morning, however, I received a telegram from Holmes requesting me to meet him at his bank in Oxford Street at noon "in re the hidden finger." I was, you can be sure, at the appointed place at the appointed hour, and indeed a good few minutes beforehand.

Holmes arrived exactly to time.

"Now, my good fellow," he said, "if you will do me the kindness of walking a few yards along the street with me, I think I can promise you a sight that will answer a good many of the questions which I have no doubt have been buzzing in your head these past few days."

In silence we made our way together along the busy street. I could not refrain from glancing to left and right at the passers-by, at the cabs, carriages and vans in the roadway and at the glittering shopfronts in an endeavour to see what it was that Holmes wished to show me. But my efforts were in vain. Nothing that I saw roused the least spark in my mind.

Then abruptly Holmes grasped my arm. I came to a halt.

"Well?" my companion demanded.

"My dear fellow, I am not at all clear what it is to which you are directing my attention."

Holmes gave a sigh of frank exasperation.

"The window, Watson. The shop window directly before you."

I looked at the window. It was that of a photographer's establishment, the whole crowded with numerous likenesses of persons both known and unknown.

"Well?" Holmes demanded yet more impatiently.

"It is one of these photographs you wish me to see?" I asked.

"It is, Watson, it is."

I looked at them again, actors and actresses, the beauties of the day, well-known political figures.

"No," I said, "I cannot see any particular reason for singling out one of these pictures above any of the others. Is that what you wish me to do?"

"Watson, look. In the second row, the third from the left."

"The Count Palatine of Illyria," I read on the card below the portrait which Holmes had indicated.

"Yes, yes. And you see nothing there?"

Once more I gave the photograph my full attention.

"Nothing," I answered at last.

"Not the very clear likeness between the ruler of that troubled state and a certain Mr. Smith at present recovering from illness in Hertfordshire?"

I examined the portrait anew.

"Yes," I agreed eventually. "There is a likeness. The beards have a good deal in common, and perhaps the general cast of the countenances."

"Exactly."

From an inner pocket Holmes now drew a newspaper cutting.

"*The Times*," he said. "Of yesterday's date. Read it carefully."

I read, and when I had done so looked up again at Holmes in bewilderment.

"But this is a report of the Count Palatine appearing on the balcony of his palace and being greeted with enthusiasm by a vast crowd," I said. "So, Holmes, how can this man in the photograph be my patient down in Hertfordshire but two days ago?"

"Come, Watson, the explanation is childishly simple."

I felt a little aggrieved and spoke more sharply than I might have done in reply.

"It seems to me, I must say, that the sole explanation is merely that my patient and the Count Palatine of Illyria are not one and the same person."

"Nonsense, Watson. The likeness is clear beyond doubt, and nor is the explanation in any way obscure. It is perfectly plain that the man glimpsed at a distance by the crowd in Illyria is a double for the Count Palatine. The situation there, you know, is decidedly grave. There is the most dangerous unrest. If it were widely known that the Count was not at the helm in his country, the republican element would undoubtedly make an attempt to seize power, an attempt, let me tell you, that would in all likelihood be successful. However, you and I know that the Count is seriously ill and is living in Hertfordshire, under your excellent care, my dear Watson. So the solution is obvious. With the connivance of his close circle the Count has arranged for a substitute to make occasional public appearances in his stead in circumstances under which he will not easily be identified."

"Yes, I suppose you must be right, Holmes," I said. "It certainly seems a complex and extraordinary business though. Yet your account does appear to connect all the various elements."

"It connects them indeed," Holmes replied. "But I think for the time being we can assure ourselves that all is well. Do me the kindness, however, doctor, to let me know as soon as there is any question of the Count becoming fit enough to resume his full powers."

It was, in fact, no later than the following week that I was able to give Holmes the reassuring news he had asked for. I had found my patient very far along the road to recovery, and though, not wishing to let him know that Holmes had penetrated his secret, I had not said to him that quite soon he would be ready to travel, I had left his bedside with that thought in my mind. In consequence I went from the station at Baker Street on my return directly to our old rooms.

"He is distinctly better then?" Holmes asked me.

"Very much so, I am happy to say. The lassitude that originally gave me cause for anxiety has almost completely passed away."

"Bad. Very bad, Watson."

"But surely, Holmes . . ."

"No, Watson, I tell you if the Count's enemies should gain any inkling of the fact that he is likely to be able to return to Illyria in the near future, they will stop at nothing to make sure that he never crosses the Channel."

"But, Holmes, how can they know that he is not in Illyria? You yourself showed me that extract from *The Times.*"

"I dare say, Watson. Yet an illusion of that sort cannot be kept up indefinitely. No doubt the conspirators watch every appearance the supposed Count makes upon the Palace balcony. At any time some small error on the part of the substitute may give the game away. Very possibly that error has been already made and suspicions have been aroused. Remember that I myself was not the only spy you caught down in Hertfordshire a fortnight ago."

"The gypsy, Holmes? But I thought he was no more after all than a passing gypsy."

"Quite possibly he was, Watson. Yet did it not strike you as curious that the fellow was skulking in the grounds of the house?"

"Well, I had supposed that he had in fact never penetrated the garden itself."

"Indeed, Watson? Then it is perhaps as well that I have taken an interest in the matter. We should not wish the Count Palatine to fail to reach his homeland in safety. You have said nothing of his rapid recovery to anybody but myself?"

"Of course not, Holmes. Of course not."

Yet just one week later as, making what I hoped might be my last visit into Hertfordshire, I approached my mysterious patient's residence I was reminded with sudden shame that I had in fact spoken about his recovery outside the house the previous week when I had been talking to the manservant who had driven me back to the station in the dog-cart, and I recalled too that I had spoken in tones deliberately loud and clear so as to make sure that I was understood by this foreigner. I was debating with myself whether those words of mine could perhaps have been overheard then by some lurker, when my eye was caught by just such a person within some fifty yards of the gate of the house itself, an individual who seemed by his dress to be a seaman. But what was a seaman doing here in Hertfordshire, so far from the sea?

I decided that it was my duty now at least to deliver an oblique warning to the Count Palatine's faithful manservant, even though I still did not wish to disclose that I knew through Holmes whom he served. I succeeded, I hope, in giving him some general advice about the dangers of burglars in the neighbourhood, advice which I hoped would alert him without betraying what Holmes and I alone knew. I was relieved, too, when my patient, having declared his intention of visiting a Continental spa now that he felt so much better, asked if his servant could collect from me a supply of a nerve tonic I had prescribed sufficient to last him for a number of weeks. I gladly arranged for the man to come to me next day for the purpose, thinking that I could in this way get the latest tidings before the Count Palatine—if indeed this were the Count Palatine—left our shores.

My anxieties over the lurking seaman I had noticed by the house gate proved fully justified when the manservant called on me the day afterwards. He reported that he had encountered this very fellow in the garden at dusk the night before, and that he had given him a thorough beating before chasing him from the premises. I decided it would be as well to visit Holmes and report on the favourable turn to the situation. It ought, I believed, to assuage any fears he might have. Instead therefore of returning home to lunch I called in at my club, which lies between my house and Baker Street, to take some refreshment there.

It was while I was hastily consuming a boiled fowl and half a bottle of Montrachet that the place next to me at the table was taken by an old acquaintance, Maltravers Bressingham, the big-game hunter. I enquired whether he had been in Africa.

"Why, no, my dear fellow," he replied. "I have been shooting nearer home. In Illyria, in fact. There is excellent sport to be had in the wild boar forests there, you know."

"Indeed?" I answered. "And were you not disturbed by the state of the country? I understand the situation there is somewhat turbulent."

"Turbulent?" Bressingham said, in tones of considerable surprise. "My dear fellow, I assure you that there are positively no signs of unrest at all. I spent a week in the capital, you know, and society there is as calm and as full of enjoyment as one could wish."

"Is it indeed?" I said. "I believed otherwise, but it must be that I have been misinformed."

Sadly puzzled, I left the club and took a hansom for Baker Street. I found Holmes in bed. I was more dismayed at this than I can easily say. A fortnight before, when I had first called on him after a period of some weeks, he had been lying on the sitting-room sofa certainly and in a condition I did not at all like to see. But his state now seemed a good deal more grave. Was that indomitable spirit at last to succumb totally to the sapping weakness which lay for ever ready to emerge when there was nothing to engage the powers of his unique mind? Was the world to be deprived of his services because it held nothing that seemed to him a worthy challenge?

"Holmes, my dear fellow," I said. "What symptoms affect you? Confide in me, pray, as a medical man."

In response I got at first no more than a deep groan. But I persisted, and at length Holmes answered, with a touch of asperity in his voice which I was not wholly displeased to hear.

"Nothing is wrong, Watson. Nothing. This is the merest passing indisposition. I do not require your professional services."

"Very well, my dear fellow. Then let me tell you of events down in Hertfordshire. I trust they will bring you not a little comfort."

But even as I spoke those words, my heart failed me. Certainly I had what had seemed glad tidings from Hertfordshire. But my news was of the foiling of an apparent attempt on the Count Palatine of Illyria, a ruler whom I had believed, on Holmes's authority, to be needed urgently in a country prey to severe unrest. Yet I had heard not half an hour before from an eye-witness of impeccable antecedents that there was no unrest whatsoever in Illyria, and if that were so was not the whole of Holmes's view of the situation a matter for doubt?

Yet I had broached the subject and must continue.

"I happened on my final visit to our friend, Mr. Smith, the day before yesterday to notice lurking near the gates of the house a person dressed as a seaman," I said.

Holmes in answer gave a groan yet louder than any before. It caused me to pause a little before continuing once more, in an altogether less assured manner.

"I considered it my duty, Holmes, to warn Mr. Smith's manservant of the presence of that individual, and to hint in general terms that the fellow might be some sort of burglar intent on the premises."

Another deep groan greeted this information. Yet more falteringly I resumed.

"This morning, my dear chap, the manservant called to collect from me a quantity of nerve tonic that I had prepared for his master, and he told me that he had surprised just such a mysterious seaman in the grounds of the house last evening and that he had—"

Here my hesitant account abruptly concluded. Holmes had given vent to yet another appalling groan, and I was able to see, too, that he was holding his body under the bedclothes in an altogether unnaturally stiff position.

A silence fell. In the quiet of the bedroom I could hear distinctly the buzzing of a bluebottle fly beating itself hopelessly against the window panes. At last I spoke again.

"Holmes. My dear old friend. Holmes. Tell me, am I right in my guess? Holmes, are you suffering from the effects of a thorough thrashing?"

Another silence. Once more I became aware of the useless buzzings of the fly upon the pane. Then Holmes answered.

"Yes, Watson, it is as you supposed."

"But, my dear fellow, this is truly appalling. My action in warning that manservant resulted in your suffering injury. Can you forgive me?"

"The injury I can forgive," Holmes answered. "The insult I suffered at the hands of that fellow I can forgive you, Watson, as I can forgive the man his unwitting action. But those who were its cause I cannot forgive. They are dangerous men, my friend, and at all costs they must be prevented from wreaking the harm they intend."

I could not in the light of that answer bring myself to question in the least whether the men to whom Holmes had pointed existed, however keenly I recalled Maltravers Bressingham's assertion that all was quiet in Illyria.

"Holmes," I asked instead, "have you then some plan to act against these people?"

"I would be sadly failing in my duty, Watson, had I not taken the most stringent precautions on behalf of the Count Palatine, and I hope you have never found me lacking in that."

"Indeed I have not."

"Very well then. During the hours of daylight I think we need not fear too much. They are hardly likely to make an attempt that might easily be thwarted by a handful of honest English passers-by. And in any case I have telegraphed the Hertfordshire police and given them a proper warning. But it is tonight, Watson, that I fear."

"The Count's last night in England, Holmes, if indeed . . ."

I bit back the qualifying phrase it had been on the tip of my tongue to add. Common sense dictated that the terrible situation Holmes foresaw was one that could not occur. Yet on many occasions before I had doubted him and he had in the outcome been proved abundantly right. So now I held my peace.

Holmes with difficulty raised himself up in the bed.

"Watson," he said, "tonight as never before I shall require your active assistance. We must both keep watch. There is no other course open to me. But I fear I myself will be but a poor bruised champion should the affair come to blows. Will you assist me then? Will you bring that old Service revolver of yours and fight once more on the side of justice?"

"I will, Holmes, I will."

What else could I have said?

The hour of dusk that autumn evening found us taking up our watch in Hertfordshire in that same thick rhododendron shrubbery where Holmes had hidden in the disguise of an old, wrinkled, brown-faced fellow at the beginning of this singular adventure. But where he had from deep within that leafy place of concealment looked out at the mellow brightness of afternoon, we now needed to step only a foot or two in among the bushes to be quite concealed and we looked out at a scene soon bathed in serene moonlight.

All was quiet. No feet trod the path beyond the beech hedge. In the garden no bird hopped to and fro, no insect buzzed. Up at the house, which beneath the light of the full moon we had under perfect observation, two lighted windows only showed how things lay, one high up from behind the drawn curtains of the bedroom where I had visited my mysterious patient, another low down, coming from the partly sunken windows of the kitchen where doubtless the manservant was preparing the light evening repast I myself had recommended.

Making myself as comfortable as I could and feeling with some pleasure the heavy weight of the revolver in my pocket, I set myself to endure a long vigil. By my side Holmes moved from time to time, less able than on other such occasions in the past to keep perfectly still, sore as were his limbs from the cudgel wielded, with mistaken honesty, by that European manservant now busy at the stove.

Our watch, however, was to be much shorter than I had expected.

Scarcely half an hour had passed when, with complete unexpectedness, the quiet of the night was broken by a sharp voice from behind us.

"Stay where you are. One move and I would shoot."

The voice I recognized in an instant from the strength of its foreign accent. It was that of Mr. Smith's loyal servant. Taking care not to give him cause to let loose a blast from the gun I was certain he must be aiming at our backs, I spoke up as calmly as I could.

"I am afraid that not for the first time your zeal has betrayed you," I said. "Perhaps you will recognize my voice, as I have recognized yours. I am Dr. Watson, your master's medical attendant. I am here with my friend, Mr. Sherlock Holmes, of whom perhaps you have heard."

"It is the doctor?"

Behind me, as I remained still as a statue, I heard the crunching of the dried leaves underfoot and a moment later the manservant's face was thrust into mine.

"Yes," he said, "it is you. Good. I was keeping guard because of the many rogues there are about here, and I saw in the bushes a movement I did not like. But it is you and your friend only. That is good."

"You did well," Holmes said to him. "I am happy to think that the Count has another alert watcher over him besides ourselves."

"The Count?" said the servant. "What Count is this?"

"Why, man, your master. There is no need for pretence between the three of us. Dr. Watson and I are well aware that the man up in the house there is no Mr. Smith, but none other than the Count Palatine of Illyria."

Holmes's voice had dropped as he pronounced the name, but his secrecy was greeted in an altogether astonishing manner. The gruff manservant broke into rich and noisy laughter.

"Mr. Smith, my Mr. Smith the Count Palatine of Illyria?" he choked out at last. "Why, though my master has travelled much, and though I began to serve him while he was in Austria, he has never so much as set foot in Illyria. Of that I can assure you, gentlemen, and as to being the Count Palatine . . ."

Again laughter overcame him, ringing loudly into the night air.

I do not know what Holmes would have done to silence the fellow, or what attitude he would have taken to this brazen assertion. For at that moment another voice made itself heard, a voice somewhat faint and quavering coming from up beside the house.

"What is this? What is going on there? Josef, is that you?"

It was my patient, certainly recovered from his nervous indisposition enough to venture out to see why there was such a hullabaloo in his grounds.

"Sir, it is the doctor and, sir, a friend of his, a friend with a most curious belief."

At the sound of his servant's reassuring voice my patient began to cross the lawn towards us. As he approached, Sherlock Holmes stepped from the shrubbery and went to meet him, his figure tall and commanding in the silvery moonlight. The two men came together in the full middle of the lawn.

"Good evening," Holmes's voice rang clear. "Whom have I the honour of addressing?"

As he spoke he thrust out a hand in greeting. My patient extended his own in reply. But then, with a movement as rapid as that of a striking snake, Holmes, instead of taking the offered hand and clasping it, seized its third finger, covered as always with its leather finger-stall, and jerked the protective sheath clean away.

There in the bright moonlight I saw for the first time the finger that had hitherto always been concealed from me. It wore no heavy royal signet ring, as indeed was unlikely on a finger of the right hand. It was instead curiously withered, a sight that to anyone other than a medical man might have been considered a little repulsive.

"You are not the Count Palatine of Illyria?" Holmes stammered then, more disconcerted than I had ever seen him in the whole of our long friendship.

"The Count Palatine of Illyria?" Mr. Smith replied. "I assure you, my dear sir, I am far from being such a person. Whatever put a notion like that into your head?"

It was not until the last train of the day returning us to London was at the outskirts of the city that Holmes spoke to me.

"How often have I told you, Watson," he said, "that one must take into account all the factors relevant to a particular situation before making an assessment? A good many dozen times, I should say. So it was all the more reprehensible of me deliberately to have imported a factor into the Hertfordshire business that was the product, not of the simple truth, but of my own over-willing imagination. My dear fellow, I must tell you that there were no reports of unrest in Illyria."

"I knew it, Holmes. I had found out quite by chance."

"And you said nothing?"

"I trusted you, as I have trusted you always."

"And as, until now, I hope I have been worthy of your trust. But inaction has always been the curse of me, my dear fellow. It was the lack of stimulus that drove me to deceit now. You were right about your patient from the start. He never was other than a man with a not unusual nervousness of disposition. You were right, Watson, and I was wrong."

I heard the words. But I wished then, as I wish again now with all the fervour at my command, that they had never been uttered, that they had never needed to be uttered.

※ ※ ※

Rats!

DOROTHY J. CANNELL

Package for Miss Gilda Sweet," croaked the delivery boy looking more like the Artful Dodger than the representative of a posh London store. Gilda didn't notice. She was never one for character analysis when presented with a large white box with an orchid pinned on top.

"Ms. Sweet," she snipped, not because she was a die-hard feminist, but because the title "Miss" smacked of whey-faced spinsters in fuzz-ball cardigans, and women who had never engaged in a bit of slap-and-tickle with some rich old geezer at a swanky restaurant table or been the star turn at the Moose Men's Monthly Meeting.

Gilda didn't hear the delivery boy's mumbled apology. Out came her hungry little hands to grab the package and fondle its private parts. With a duck and a nervous titter the lad was already backing away. Goodie! She wouldn't have to tip him. Banging the door of her bed-sitter shut, she leaned against it—her spun-silver hair drifting about her face like a nun's veil, her candy-coated lips sliding into a kitty cat smile. Old Fred had come through.

When it came to life under the sheets, Mr. Bug-A-Boo (he owned a pest control business) was nothing to brag about. Gilda had known poodles who could do more tricks. Her last Sugar Daddy, Ernie the Insurance Man, had at least made "faking it" a piece of cake. So why did she bother with Fred? Simple. He was blessed with that most useful of pot-bellied virtues—a guilty conscience. And guilt, bless it, meant peace offerings for the two women in his life. A promise to attend church regularly and a new toaster for Wifey, and for The Other Woman something shamefully expensive.

Poor Fred! He had made it clear from the moment he first stepped out of his trousers that he felt lousy about cheating on his wife, who suffered from a terminal case of corns, and even worse about being hardly able to wait to get started. At thirty-something, Gilda had lost her virginity more times than she could count, but she had retained her wide-eyed innocence.

"I don't feel right about this, Poochy Poo! My mother would kill me if she knew! And there's your wife . . ."

"Don't you worry your pretty little head about her," red faced and perspiring Fred was by then down to his socks. "The old girl'll be glad of some early nights. She's always going on about how she's not up to lovey-dovey after working day in and day out, shoulder to shoulder with me in the business."

"You mean it Cuddly-Wuddles? She really wouldn't mind?" Gilda wasn't much surprised when, instead of answering Fred kissed the pout from her lips. The old goat hadn't believed a word he had said; but during the course of the following weeks Gilda often thought, between stifled yawns, that Wifey had reason to thank her for taking over the night shift. So much for gratitude! The day arrived when she answered the hysterical ringing of the telephone to be assaulted by a woman's voice.

"Don't lie to me you, slut! I know you've been sneaking around with my husband! Here's me, stuck at home washing his stinking socks and . . ." Yack! Yack! Gilda didn't bother to ask how Wifey had found out. The woman probably has eyes in the back of her head, along with two noses and half a dozen chins. Hooking the telephone over her shoulder, Gilda allowed the tinny voice to burble and burp as she stared into the mirror over the mantelpiece. If her roots were coming in already she'd give Fernando's the heave-ho and go over to Hair Flair. She'd heard that the bloke who owned the place looked like Rhett Butler. Cripes, she was bored with Fred, and even more bored with his better half.

Gilda returned the receiver to her ear and swayed to the beat, while the mirror caught a flash of the blood red garnet stone on her right hand as she flicked an eyebrow into shape. She owed the ring to Leo the Undertaker. Now there was a character! She'd felt quite creepy when she realized where he'd got the jewelry he'd given her. Why did a straight-forward girl like her always land men with such dreary jobs? There had been Al the Allergist who had made a present to her of all those shots, which hadn't done diddle. She still couldn't smell a skunk if it sat on her shadow. And, speaking of vermin, there was Fred—the small game hunter. Yuck! Maybe he and Wifey were made for each other. The telephone voice kept ranting on about the new accounts she had built up and how she had never shirked the dirty work, crawling around in dank, dark cellars, vacuuming up the creepy crawlies. Revolting! Yawning as loud as she could, Gilda had hung up, blotting out Wifey's feeble-minded threat—"You won't get away with playing fast and loose with my husband, I'll make you pay if it's the last thing I . . ."

Silly woman. The one to pay would be bald, panting Fred in his too tight army shirt and plastic shoes. As was only right and proper, he was horribly upset when he came around that night and was told by Gilda that they "were discovered." Allowing her gauzy black peignoir to slide off her sugar-white shoulder she explained tearfully that she must end their wild and wonderful affair. Fred would have to forget her and their passion filled nights and return to Mrs. Flannel Nightgown. "I'm sorry Pudgikins!" Raising her tear smudged lashes. "Nothing could persuade me to come between you and such a treasure."

Nothing that is except a handsome inducement. Gilda had always prided herself on not being an intellectual, but she knew her subject— men. And she felt certain it would not be long before Fred went shopping. The purchase might be sent as a parting gift—"It's a bugger, Sugar Bun! But I've got to go back to the old girl in case she takes her life!" Or it might be sent in hopes of maintaining the status quo—"I just need a little time Baby Cheeks. I know we can work things out . . ."

She had her uneasy moments when a couple of days passed without the arrival of a gift-wrapped overture but the suspense was now ended. Tossing the orchid on the floor, Gilda opened the box to discover a fur jacket folded voluptuously between transparent layers of tissue. A pity it wasn't a full-length jobbie. Half a coat was better than none perhaps, but it also paid for only half the fun. From now on there would be none of those little extras Fred had come to enjoy—assuming, that is, that he planned on continuing their affair, rather than bunking home to Mother, as he undoubtedly called the little woman.

Shrugging, Gilda went into the bedroom, stepped into a pair of high-heeled black satin shoes she had left kicked by the dressing table and slipped her arms into the jacket. Irritation supplanted glee when she brushed a hand down one sleeve. The fur was coarse, almost bristling.

Fred, like a lot of money-making blokes, had no class. Still the jacket did look good on her.

Gilda swayed this way and that before the mirror, lifting her silver blonde hair on top of her head and arching her neck. The colour of the jacket wasn't anything great—your basic brown. She would have preferred a foxy red or something that didn't look quite so recently dead. On the other hand, the fit was good, excellently tapered and the skins matched perfectly. Flipping one side open, Gilda inspected the lining of rich crimson silk, daintily stitched. The jacket was hand sewn! So perhaps old Fred wasn't such a tight wad after all. The harsh quality of the fur was probably characteristic of some rare weasel, that wouldn't be caught drinking at the same watering hole as a mink.

Somewhat mollified, Gilda lifted the box off the bed and found the note lying under the tissue paper. Well, what had we here? Was she about to be dumped? Or was this Fred's plea for one more chance to prove his sweaty devotion. Unfolding the sheet of paper, Gilda read: "My darling Sugar Puss, I'm down on my knees—begging you to meet me at The Dockside Inn at eight tonight, love Kissy Lips." Honestly, the man had a vocabulary that would have made a toddler blush! If she'd had anything better to do that evening, Gilda might have decided not to show up. Fred mustn't think she could be bought back too easily. Besides, her car was having its annual checkup at the garage and taxis cost an arm and both legs these days. Gilda had an ingrained aversion to spending her own money. Still, The Dockside—besides being sufficiently off the beaten track to suit Fred's newly aroused sense of caution, served food that was out of this world.

Dropping the note on the floor, Gilda took another survey in the mirror and the urge to show off the fur jacket won out. She could always take the bus and tell Fred she'd forked out her last five quid paying the taxi. Sometimes it seemed to Gilda that a girl just couldn't lose.

The first person privileged to see her in all her finery was Mrs. Humbles from across the hall—walking her fat Siamese on its licorice thin lead towards the lift.

"My, aren't we all gussied up today." The old hag pushed the ground floor button, her cow eyes sparkling interest behind the tortoise-shell glasses. The cat at her heels hissed sharply, slaking out a paw, to catch at Gilda's stocking.

"Now, isn't he the naughty one!" Mrs. Humbles' voice held a blend of embarrassment and pride. "Fing Choo is jealous because he thinks your fur coat is smarter than his."

Gilda backed away from the beastly animal. He must be remembering how she had thrown water on him that time when he followed her into the bedsitter.

"Silly boy," Mrs. Humbles gave a rasping chuckle. "Yours is the real thing, my puss." The cat lunged on its lead.

"Why don't you get him checked for rabies?" Gilda whipped the jacket tightly around her and was out the lift the moment the doors opened. She did not have to wait long in the misting rain for the bus that stopped just across the road from her building. The bus driver, a burly Fred type, gave her the eye as she took her seat. Gilda was in her element. The snooty expressions on the faces of the two women seated opposite didn't bother her one bit. Talk about jealous cats! Gilda stroked the fur collar up against her neck and smiled her pastel pink smile.

It was almost dark when she got off the bus at the docks. She was the only person to do so and her footsteps were instantly deadened by the blared honking of tug boats and barges. Giant warehouses loomed all around her and the stench of salt and tar seeped up her pretty little nostrils. She could taste the rank bite of seaweed and raw fish as she scuttled along on her high heels. The Dockside Inn was right on the waterfront. She remembered the general direction, knew she had to pass down a narrow alley and cross a gravel stretch that would become the parking lot. Gilda quickened her pace even though she told herself that she wasn't hearing footsteps. She was in the alley now. Somewhere, out of eyeshot—a shuffle, then silence.

Gilda turned to check if someone were behind her and saw only a pair of dustbins standing perfectly still. What a ninny she was to be nervous! Even if some boozy old tramp were hard on her heels she had nothing to worry about. No man would get the better of her. Ernie the Insurance Man was a heavy weight boxer and he had taught her how to pack a punch. It was only the wind, feeling its way inside her clothes, that made her shiver. But damn Fred, anyway! He could have met her in a taxi.

Twin pinpricks of light flashed yellow in the dark. And something yowled thinly, before moving smoothly up behind her. A cat! Nothing but a skinny old cat. Gilda lashed out with her high heel. One scratch and she would be laid up with blood poisoning for a week. This was no pampered puss like Mrs. Humbles' Fing Choo. And to think she had made that crack in the lift about rabies injections! Her victim sprang back, spitting viciously.

As if in answer to its call other feline forms emerged from doorways and from behind the dustbins, slithering silently into a multi-coloured huddle. The pinpricks of light merged into an amber glare. The individual growls swelled to a rasping roar.

"Nice kitties, pretty kitties!" Gilda cooed.

Ivory teeth nipped teasingly at the hem of her skirt. Some of the amber eyes smiled back at her while others simply stared—steadily, patiently, expectantly.

She began to run and, thrilling to the chase, the cats followed close about her ankles, snipping and slashing. Between one breath and the next they had her surrounded. It was as if every feline for miles around had showed up to join the navy.

Gilda emerged into the open gravel area. The Dockside Inn was only a few yards away. So close. She ran faster and the cats did likewise. They were swarming around her—purring with warm wet pleasure. Baby blue eyes glazed with terror, she yelled for help and suddenly she saw her—a solid, salt-of-the-earth woman standing in front of the Inn, right next to the sign that read—CLOSED FOR REMODELLING. Nice woman. She was smiling as she limped forward. And then Gilda knew. The woman had corns. Poor Wifey, who had always been too busy working side by side with Fred—mastering all that was to be known about pest control—to have time for pedicures.

"Miss Gilda Sweet?" Wifey inquired pleasantly—with the merest emphasis on the word "Miss"—to the single woman who'd had her knees squeezed under many a restaurant table, but had never found a man willing to put a wedding ring on her finger. "I am pleased," she said with a contented sigh, "to see you wearing the jacket, and don't worry—it didn't cost me a penny. Having suitable fur on hand when needed is just one of the perks of my job."

Eyes everywhere. Amber eyes were glowing good as gold as the pretty kitties closed in for the kill.

❧ ❧ ❧

The Convolvulus Clock

RUTH RENDELL

Is that your own hair, dear?"

Sibyl only laughed. She made a roguish face.

"I didn't think it could be," said Trixie. "It looks so thick."

"A woman came up to me in the street the other day," said Sibyl, "and asked me where I had my hair set. I just looked at her. I gave a tiny little tip to my wig like this. You should have seen her face."

She gave another roar of laughter. Trixie smiled austerely. She had come to stay with Sibyl for a week and this was her first evening. Sibyl had bought a cottage in Devonshire. It was two years since Trixie had seen Sibyl and she could detect signs of deterioration. What a pity that was! Sibyl inquired after the welfare of the friends they had in common. How was Mivvy? Did Trixie see anything of the Fishers? How was Poppy?

"Poppy is beginning to go a bit funny," said Trixie.

"How do you mean, funny?"

"You know. Funny. Not quite *compos mentis* anymore."

Sibyl of all people ought to know what going funny meant, thought Trixie.

"We're none of us getting any younger," said Sibyl, laughing.

Trixie didn't sleep very well. She got up at five and had her bath so as to leave the bathroom clear for Sibyl. At seven she took Sibyl a cup of tea. She gave a little scream and nearly dropped the tray.

"Oh, my conscience! I'm sorry, dear, but I thought that was a squirrel on your chest of drawers. I thought it must have come in through the window."

"What on earth was that noise in the middle of the night?" When Sibyl wasn't laughing she could be downright peevish. She looked a hundred without her wig. "It woke me up—I thought the tank was overflowing."

"The middle of the night! I like that! The sun had been up a good hour, I'm sure. I was just having my bath so as not to be a nuisance."

They went out in Sibyl's car. They had lunch in Dawlish and tea in Exmouth. The following day they went out early and drove across Dartmoor. When they got back there was a letter on the mat for Trixie from Mivvy, though Trixie had only been away two days. On Friday Sibyl said they would stay at home and have a potter about the village. The church was famous—the Manor House gardens were open to the public and there was an interesting small gallery where an exhibition was on. She started to get the car out but Trixie said why couldn't they walk, it could hardly be more than a mile. Sibyl said it was just under two miles but she agreed to walk if Trixie really wanted to. Her knee hadn't been troubling her quite so much lately.

"The gallery is called Artifacts," said Sibyl. "It's run by a very nice young couple."

"A husband-and-wife team?" asked Trixie, very modern.

"Jimmy and Judy they're called. I don't think they are actually married."

"Oh, my conscience, Sibyl, how can one be 'actually' married? Surely one is either married or not?" Trixie herself had been married once, long ago, for a short time. Sibyl had never been married and neither had Mivvy or Poppy. Trixie thought that might have something to do with their going funny. "Thankfully, I'm broad-minded. I shan't say anything. I think I can see a seat ahead in that bus shelter. Would you like a little sit-down before we go on?"

Sibyl got her breath back and they walked on more slowly. The road passed between high hedges on high banks dense with wild flowers. It crossed a stream by a hump-backed bridge, where the clear brown shallow water rippled over a bed of stones. The church appeared with granite nave and tower, standing on an eminence and approached, Sibyl said, by fifty-three steps. Perhaps they should go to Artifacts first?

The gallery was housed in an ancient building with bow windows and a front door set under a Georgian portico. When the door was pushed open, a bell tinkled to summon Jimmy or Judy. This morning, however, they needed no summoning for both were in the first room, Judy dusting the dollhouse and Jimmy doing something to the ceiling spotlights.

Sibyl introduced Trixie to them and Trixie was very gracious towards Judy, making no difference in her manner than she would have if the young woman had been properly married and worn a wedding ring.

Trixie was agreeably surprised by the objects in the exhibition and by the items Jimmy and Judy had for sale. She had not expected such a high standard. What she admired most particularly were the small pictures of domestic interiors done in embroidery, the patchwork quilts, and the blown-glass vases in colors of mother-of-pearl and butterfly wings. What she liked best of all and wanted to have was a clock.

There were four of these clocks, all different. The cases were ceramic, plain and smooth or made in a trelliswork, glazed in blues and greens, painted with flowers or the moon and stars, each incorporating a gilt-rimmed face and quartz movement. Trixie's favorite was blue, with a green trellis over the blue, a convolvulus plant with green leaves and pale-pink trumpet flowers climbing the trellis, and a gilt rim 'round the face of the clock, which had hands of gilt and blue.

The convolvulus reminded her of the pattern on her best china tea service. All the clocks had price cards beside them and red discs stuck to the cards.

"I should like to buy this clock," Trixie said to Judy.

"I'm terribly sorry but it's sold."

"Sold?"

"All the clocks were sold at the private view. Roland Elm's work is tremendously popular. He can't make enough of these clocks and he refuses to take orders."

"I still don't understand why I can't buy this one," said Trixie. "This is a shop, isn't it?"

Sibyl had put on her peevish look. "You can see the red sticker, can't you? You know what that means."

"I know what it means at the Royal Academy but hardly here surely."

"I really do wish I could sell it to you," said Judy, "but I can't."

Trixie lifted her shoulders. She was very disappointed and wished she hadn't come. She had been going to buy Sibyl a pear carved from polished pearwood but now she thought better of it. The church also was a letdown—dark, poky, and smelling of mold.

"Things have come to a pretty pass when shopkeepers won't sell their goods to you because they're upset by your manner."

"Judy wasn't upset by your manner," said Sibyl, puffing. "It's more than her reputation is worth to sell you something she's already sold."

"Reputation! I like that!"

"I mean reputation as a gallery owner. Artifacts is quite highly regarded 'round here."

"You would have thought she and her—well, partner—would be glad of sixty-two pounds. I don't suppose they have two halfpennies to bless themselves with."

What Sibyl would have thought was never known, for she was too out of breath to utter and when they got home had to lie down.

Next morning, another letter came from Mivvy.

"Nothing to say for herself, of course," said Trixie at breakfast.

"Practically a carbon copy of Thursday's. She's going very funny. Do you know she told me sometimes she writes fifty letters in a week? God bless your pocket, I said, it's fortunate you can afford it."

They went to Princetown in Sibyl's car and Widecombe-in-the-Moor. Trixie sent postcards to Mivvy, Poppy, the Fishers, and the woman who came in to clean and water the plants in the greenhouse. She would have to buy some sort of present for Sibyl before she left. A plant would have done, only Sibyl didn't like gardening. They went to a bird sanctuary and looked at some standing stones of great antiquity. Trixie was going home on Tuesday afternoon.

On Tuesday morning, another letter arrived from Mivvy all about the Fishers going to see the Queen Mother open a new arts center in Leighton Buzzard. The Fishers were crazy about the Queen Mother, watched for her engagements in advance, and went wherever she went within a radius of 150 miles in order just to catch a glimpse of her. Once they had been at the front of the crowd and the Queen Mother had shaken hands with Dorothy Fisher.

"We're none of us getting any younger," said Sibyl, giggling.

"Well, my conscience, I know one thing," said Trixie. "The days have simply flown past while I've been here."

"I'm glad you've enjoyed yourself."

"Oh, I have, dear—only it would please me to see you a little less frail."

* * *

Trixie walked to the village on her own. Since she couldn't think of anything else, she was going to have to buy the pearwood pear for Sibyl. It was a warm sunny morning, one of the best days she'd had, and the front door of Artifacts stood open to the street. The exhibition was still on and the clocks (and their red "sold" discs) still there. A shaft of sunlight streamed across the patchwork quilts onto the Georgian doll-house. There was no sign of Jimmy and Judy. The gallery was empty but for herself.

Trixie closed the door and opened it to make the bell ring. She picked up one of the pearwood pears and held it out in front of her on the palm of her hand. She held it at arm's length the way she did when she had helped herself to an item in the supermarket just so there couldn't be the slightest question of anyone suspecting her of shoplifting. No one came. Trixie climbed the stairs, holding the pearwood pear out in front of her and clearing her throat to attract attention. There was no one upstairs. A blue Persian cat lay sleeping on a shelf between a ginger jar and a mug with an owl on it. Trixie descended. She closed the front door and opened it to make the bell ring. Jimmy and Judy must be a heedless pair, she thought. Anyone could walk in here and steal the lot.

Of course, she could just take the pearwood pear and leave a five-pound note to pay for it. It cost four pounds seventy-five. But why should she make Jimmy and Judy a present of twenty-five pee just because they were too idle to serve her? Then she remembered that when she had been here with Sibyl a door at the end of the passage had been open, and through that door one could see the garden where there was a display of terra-cotta pots. It was probable Jimmy and Judy were out there, showing the pots to a customer.

Trixie went through the second room and down the passage. The door to the garden was just ajar and she pushed it open. On the lawn, in a cane chair, Judy lay fast asleep. A ledger had fallen off her lap and lay on the grass alongside a heap of books. Guides to the management of tax they were and some which looked like the gallery account-books. It reminded Trixie of Poppy, who was always falling asleep in the daytime —most embarrassingly sometimes, at the table or even while waiting for a bus. Judy had fallen asleep over her bookkeeping. Trixie coughed. She said "Excuse me" very loudly and repeated it, but Judy didn't stir.

What a way to run a business! It would serve them right if someone walked in and cleared their shop. It would teach them a lesson. Trixie pulled the door closed behind her. She found herself tiptoeing as she walked back along the passage and through the second room. In the first room she took the ceramic clock with the convolvulus on it off the shelf and put it into her bag and she took the card with the red sticker on it, too, so as not to attract attention to the clock's absence. The pearwood pear she replaced among the other carved fruit.

The street outside seemed deserted. Trixie's heart was beating rather fast. She went across the road into the little newsagent's and gift shop and bought Sibyl a teacloth with a map of Devonshire on it. At the door, as she was coming out again, she saw Jimmy coming along the street towards the gallery with a bag of groceries under one arm and two pints of milk nestled in the other. Trixie stayed where she was until he had gone into Artifacts.

She didn't much fancy the walk back but there was no help for it. When she got to the bridge over the stream, she heard hooves behind her and for a second or two had a feeling she was pursued by men on horseback—but it was only a girl who passed her, riding a fat white pony.

Sibyl laughed when she saw the teacloth and said it was a funny thing to give someone who *lived* in Devonshire. Trixie felt nervous and couldn't eat her lunch. Jimmy and Judy would have missed the clock by now and the newsagent would have remembered a furtive-looking woman skulking in his doorway and described her to them and soon the police would come. If only Sibyl would hurry with the car! She moved so slowly time had no meaning for her. At this rate, Trixie wouldn't even catch her train at Exeter.

She did catch it—just. Sibyl's car had been followed for several miles of the way by police in a Rover with a blue lamp on top and Trixie's heart had been in her mouth. Why had she done it? What had possessed her to take something she hadn't paid for, she who when shopping in supermarkets held seventeen-pee pots of yogurt at arm's length?

Now she was safely in the train rushing towards Paddington, she began to see things in a different light. She would have paid for that clock if they had let her. What did they expect if they refused to sell things they had on sale? And what *could* they expect if they went to sleep leaving their shop unattended?

For a few moments she had a nasty little qualm that the police might be waiting for her outside her own door but they weren't. Inside all was as it should be, all was as she had left it except that Poppy had put a pint of milk in the fridge and someone had arranged dahlias in a vase. Not Poppy—she wouldn't know a dahlia from a runner bean.

That would be just the place for the clock, on the wall bracket where at present stood a photograph of herself and Dorothy Fisher at Broadstairs in 1949. Trixie put the photograph away in a drawer and the clock where the photograph had been. It looked nice. If transformed a rather dull corner of the room. Trixie put one of the cups from her tea service beside it and it was amazing how well they matched.

Mivvy came 'round first thing in the morning. Before letting her in, Trixie quickly snatched the clock off the shelf and thrust it inside the drawer with the photograph. It seemed so *exposed* up there—it seemed to tell its history in every tiny tick.

"How did you find Sibyl?"

Trixie wanted to say, I went in the train to Exeter and got out at the station and there was Sibyl waiting for me in her car. Only if you started mocking poor Mivvy where would you end? "Very frail, I thought she was going a bit funny."

"I must drop her a line." Mivvy always spoke as if her letters held curative properties. Receiving one of them would set you up for the winter.

After she had gone, Trixie considered replacing the clock on the shelf but thought better of it. Let it stay in the drawer for a bit. She had read of South American millionaires who have Old Masters stolen for them which they can never show but are obliged, for fear of discovery, to keep hidden away forever in dark vaults.

Just before Christmas a letter came from Sibyl. They always sent each other Christmas letters. As Trixie said, if you can't get around to writing the rest of the year, at least you can at Christmas. Mivvy wrote hundreds. Sibyl didn't mention the theft of the clock or indeed mention the gallery at all. Trixie wondered why not. The clock was still in the drawer. Sometimes she lay awake in the night thinking about it, fancying she could hear its tick through the solid mahogany of the drawer, through the ceiling and the bedroom floorboards.

It was curious how she had taken a dislike to the convolvulus tea service. One day she found herself wrapping it in tissue paper and putting it away in the cupboard under the stairs. She took down all the trelliswork 'round the front door and put up wires for the clematis instead. In March she wrote to Sibyl to inquire if there was a new exhibition on at Artifacts. Sibyl didn't answer for weeks. When she did, she told Trixie that months and months back one of those ceramic clocks had been stolen from the gallery and a few days later an embroidered picture had also gone and furniture out of the dollhouse. Hadn't Sibyl mentioned it before? She thought she had but she was getting so forgetful these days.

Trixie took the clock out of the drawer and put it on the shelf. Because she knew she couldn't be found out, she began to feel she hadn't done anything wrong. The Fishers were bringing Poppy 'round for a cup of tea. Trixie started unpacking the convolvulus tea service.

But she lost her nerve when she heard Gordon Fisher's car door slam and she put the clock away again. If she were caught now she might get blamed for the theft of the picture and the dollhouse furniture as well. They would say she had sold those things, and how could she prove she hadn't?

Poppy fell asleep halfway through her second buttered scone. "She gets funnier every time I see her," Trixie said. "Sad, really. Sibyl's breaking up, too. She'll forget her own name next. You should see her letters. I'll just show you the last one." Then she remembered she couldn't do that, it wouldn't be wise, so she had to pretend she'd mislaid it.

"Will you be going down there again this year, dear?" said Dorothy.

"Oh, I expect so. You know how it is, you get to the stage of thinking it may be the last time."

Poppy woke up with a snort, said she hadn't been asleep, and finished her scone.

Gordon asked Trixie, "Would you like to come with us and see Her Majesty open the new leisure complex in Rayleigh on Monday?"

Trixie declined. The Fishers went off to do their shopping, leaving Poppy behind. She was asleep again. She slept till six and, waking, asked

Trixie if she had put something in her tea. It was most unusual, she said, for her to nod off like that. Trixie walked her back to the bus stop because the traffic whipped along there so fast you had to have your wits about you and drivers didn't respect zebra crossings the way they used to. Trixie marched across on the stripes, confident as a lollipop lady but without the lollipop, taking her life in her hands instead.

She wrote to Sibyl that she would come to Devonshire at the end of July, thinking that while there it might be best to make some excuse to avoid going near Artifacts. The clock was still in the drawer but wrapped up now in a piece of old flannel. Trixie had taken a dislike to seeing the color of it each time she opened the drawer. She had a summer dress that color and she wondered why she had ever bought it—it didn't flatter her, whatever it might do for the Queen Mother. Dorothy could have it for her next jumble sale.

Walking back from posting a letter, Mivvy fell over and broke her ankle. It was weeks getting back to normal. Well, you had to face it, it was never going to be *normal*. You wouldn't be exaggerating, Trixie wrote to Sibyl, if you said that obsession of hers for writing letters had crippled her for life. Sibyl wrote back to say she was looking forward to the last week of July and what did Trixie think had happened? They had caught the thief of the pieces from Artifacts trying to sell the picture to a dealer in Plymouth! He had said in court he hadn't taken the clock but you could imagine how much credence the magistrate placed on that!

Trixie unwrapped the clock and put it on the shelf. Next day she got the china out. She wondered why she had been so precipitate in pulling all that trellis off the wall—it looked a lot better than strands of wire on metal hooks.

Mivvy came round in a taxi, hobbling up the path on two sticks, refusing the offer of the taxi driver's arm. "You'll be off to Sibyl's in a day or two, will you, dear?"

Trixie didn't know how many times she had told her not till Monday week. She was waiting for Mivvy to notice the clock but at this rate she was going to have to wait till Christmas.

"What do you think of my clock?"

"What, up there? Isn't that your Wedgwood coffee pot, dear?"

Trixie had to get it down. She thrust it under Mivvy's nose and started explaining what it was.

But Mivvy knew already. "Of course I know it's a clock, dear. It's not the first time I've seen one of these. Oh my goodness, no. The young man who makes these, he's a friend of my nephew Tony. They were at art school together. Let me see, what's his name? It will come to me in a minute. A tree, isn't it? Oak? Ash? Peter Oak? No, Elm is his name. Something Elm. Roland Elm."

Trixie said nothing. The glazed surface of the clock felt very cold against the skin of her hands.

"He never makes them to order, you know. He just makes a limited number for a few selected galleries. Tony told me that. Where did you get yours, I wonder?"

Trixie said nothing. There was worse coming and she waited for it.

"Not around here, I'm sure. I know there are only two or three places in the country they go to. It will come to me in a minute. I shall be writing to Tony tomorrow and I'll mention about you having one of Richard's—no, I mean Raymond's, that is, Roland's, clocks. I always write to him on Tuesdays. Tuesday is his day. I'll mention you've got one with bindweed on it. They're all different, you know. He never makes two alike."

"It's convolvulus, not bindweed," said Trixie. "I'd rather you didn't write to Tony about it if you don't mind."

"Oh, but I'd like to mention it, dear. Whyever not? I won't mention your name if you don't want me to. I'll just say that lady who goes down to stay with Auntie Sibyl in Devonshire."

Trixie said she would walk with Mivvy up to the High Street. It was hopeless trying to get a taxi outside here. She fetched Mivvy's two sticks. "You take my arm and I'll hold your other stick."

The traffic whipped along over the zebra crossing. You were at the mercy of those drivers, Trixie said, it was a matter of waiting till they condescended to stop. "Don't you set foot on those stripes till they stop," she said to Mivvy.

Mivvy didn't, so the cars didn't stop. A container lorry, a juggernaut, came thundering along, but a good way off still. Trixie thought it was going much too fast.

"Now if we're quick," she said. "Run for it!"

Startled by the urgency in her voice, Mivvy obeyed, or tried to obey, as Trixie dropped her arm and gave her a little push forward. The lorry's brakes screamed like people being tortured and Trixie jumped back, screaming herself, covering her face with her hands so as not to see Mivvy under those giant wheels.

Dorothy Fisher said she quite understood Trixie would still want to go to Sibyl's for her holiday. It was the best thing in the world for her— a rest, a complete change, a chance to forget.

Trixie went down by train on the day after the funeral. She had the clock in her bag with her, wrapped first in tissue paper and then in her sky-blue dress. The first opportunity that offered itself she would take the clock back to Artifacts and replace it on the shelf she had taken it from. This shouldn't be too difficult. The clock was a dangerous possession, she could see that, like one of those notorious diamonds that carry a curse with them. Pretty though it was, it was an *unlucky* clock that had involved her in trouble from the time she had first taken it.

There was no question of walking to Artifacts this time. Sibyl was too frail for that. She had gone downhill a lot since last year, and symptomatic of her deterioration was her exchange of the grey wig for a lilac-blue one. They went in the car, though Trixie was by no means sure Sibyl was safe at the wheel.

As soon as they walked into the gallery, Trixie saw that she had no hope of replacing the clock without being spotted. There was a desk in the first room now, with a plump smiling lady sitting at it that Sibyl said was Judy's mother. Trixie thought that amazing—a mother not minding her daughter cohabiting with a man she wasn't married to. Living with a daughter living in sin, you might put it. Jimmy was in the second room, up on a ladder doing something to the window catch.

"They're having upstairs remodeled," said Sibyl. "You can't go up there." And when Trixie tried to make her way towards the garden door, "You don't want to be had up for trespassing, do you?" She winked at Judy's mother. "We're none of us getting any younger when all's said and done, are we?"

They went back to Sibyl's, the clock still in Trixie's bag. It seemed to have grown heavier. She could hear it ticking through the leather and the folds of the sky-blue dress. In the afternoon when Sibyl lay down on the sofa for her rest, the lilac wig stuck on top of a Poole pottery vase, Trixie went out for a walk, taking the clock with her.

She came to the hump-backed bridge over the stream where the water was very low, for it had been a dry summer. She unwrapped the clock and dropped it over the low parapet into the water. It cracked, but the trelliswork and the convolvulus remained intact and the movement continued to move and to tick as well, for all Trixie knew. The blue and green, the pink flowers and the gilt gleamed through the water like some exotic iridescent shell.

Trixie went down the bank. She took off her shoes and waded into the water. It was surprisingly cold. She picked up a large flat stone and beat at the face of the clock with it. She beat with unrestrained fury, gasping and grunting at each blow. The green trellis and the blue sky, the glass face and the pink flowers, all shattered. But they were still there, bright jewel-like shards, for all to see who came this way across the bridge.

Squatting down, Trixie scooped up handfuls of pebbles and buried the pieces of clock under them. With her nails, she dug a pit in the bed of the stream and pushed the colored fragments into it, covering them with pebbles. Her hands were bleeding, her knees were bruised, and her dress was wet. In spite of her efforts, the bed of the stream was still spread with ceramic chips and broken glass and pieces of gilt metal. Trixie began to sob and crawl from side to side of the stream, ploughing her hands through the blue and green and gold gravel, and it was there that one of Sibyl's neighbors found her as he was driving home over the bridge.

He lifted her up and carried her to his car.

"Tick-tock," said Trixie. "Tick-tock. Convolvulus clock."

* * *

Fair and Square

MARGARET YORKE

Mrs. Ford stepped aboard the *S.S. Sphinx*, treading carefully along the ridged gangplank, her stick before her. It would be unfortunate if she were to stumble and injure herself before her holiday had properly begun.

Her holiday.

Mrs. Ford had developed the custom of avoiding some bleak winter weeks by going abroad. While ostensibly seeking the sun, she sought to give her family some relief from having to be concerned for her. She tried hard not to be a burden to her middle-aged sons and daughters and their spouses.

She had been cruising before. She had also stayed in large impersonal hotels in the Algarve and Majorca, where it was possible to spend long winter weeks at low cost, enduring a sense of isolation among uncongenial fellow weather refugees. On her cruise, Mrs. Ford knew she could expect near insolence from certain stewards because she was a woman travelling alone. With luck, this would be counterbalanced by extra thoughtfulness from others because of her age.

Her cabin steward would be an important person in her life, and she had learned to tip in advance as a guarantee of service and her morning tea on time. There would be patient tolerance from couples who were her children's contemporaries; they would wait while she negotiated stairways and would help her in and out of buses on sightseeing excursions ashore. Older passengers in pairs would be too near her in age and too fragile themselves to spare her time or energy, and the wives would see her as an alarming portent of their own future.

There would be plenty of older spinster ladies in cheerful groups or intimately paired. Eleanor Ford would not want to join any such coterie.

The best times would be if the sun shone while the ship was at sea.

Then, in a sheltered corner, she would read or do her tapestry while others played bridge or bingo or went to keep-fit classes. She would have her hair done once a week or so, which would help to pass the time. She hoped she had brought enough minor medications to last the voyage. The ship's shop would certainly sell travel souvenirs and duty-free scents and watches but might be short on tissues, indigestion remedies, and such.

Each night Mrs. Ford would wash her underthings and stockings and hang them near the air-conditioning to dry by morning. For bigger garments she would be obliged to use the laundry service. She would go on most of the shore excursions, though they tired her and she had been to all the ports before, because to stay on board would be to mean she had abandoned all initiative. She would send postcards to her smaller grandchildren and write letters to her sons and daughters.

She would long for home and her warm flat with all her possessions round her and her dull routine—yet this morning she had been pleased, leaving it in driving sleet, at the prospect of escaping to the sun. Most people would envy her, she told herself, wondering which of her fellow-passengers, who had looked so drab waiting at the airport, would, by the whim of the head steward, be her table companions throughout the cruise. She had requested the second sitting and been assured by the shipping office that this wish would be granted—otherwise what did you do in the evening after an early meal? As it was, Mrs. Ford would be able to go to bed almost at once when dinner was over with a book from the ship's library, which was likely to be one of the best features of the vessel.

Her cabin was amidships, the steadiest place in bad weather, and not below the dance-floor, where she might hear the band, nor the swimming pool, where the water might splosh to and fro noisily if the ship rolled. She had been able to control these points when booking. What she could do nothing about was her neighbours. They might be rowdy, reeling in at all hours from the discotheque, or waking early and chattering audibly about their operations or their love lives—Mrs. Ford had overheard some amazing stories on other voyages.

As she unpacked, she thought briefly about Roger, her husband, who had died six years ago. He had been gentle and kind, and she had been lucky in her long life with him. He had left her well provided for, so that even now, with inflation what it was, she could live in modest comfort and put aside enough funds for such an annual trip. She had so nearly not married Roger, for it was Michael whom she had really loved, so long ago. Setting Roger's photograph on her dressing-table, she tried to picture Michael, but it was difficult. She seldom thought of him after all this time.

That night, climbing into her high narrow bunk, she had a little weep. It was like the first night away at school, she thought, when you didn't yet know the other pupils or your way around. It would all be better in a day or two.

In the morning she had breakfast in her cabin. The ship had sailed at midnight, and beyond the window the sun shone on a gently rolling sea. Mrs. Ford had taken a sleeping pill the night before, and so she felt rather heavy-headed, but her spirits lifted. She would find a place on deck in the sun.

On the way, she stopped at the library and selected several thrillers and a life of Lord Wavell, which should be interesting. She found a vacant chair on a wide part of the promenade deck and settled down, wrapped in her warm coat. After a while, in the sunlight, she slept.

The voice woke her.

"You're not playing properly," it charged. "Those aren't the right rules."

Mrs. Ford's heart thumped and she sat upright in her chair, carried back by the sound to when she was twelve years old. She was playing hopscotch with Mary Hopkins, and Phyllis Burton had come to loom over them threateningly—large, confident, and two years older, disturbing their game.

"This is how *we* play," came the present-day response, in a male voice, from the deck quoit player now being challenged on the wide deck near Mrs. Ford's chair.

"They're not the right rules," the voice that was so like Phyllis's insisted. "Look, this is how you should throw."

Long years ago Mrs. Ford's tennis racket had been seized from her grasp and a scorching service delivered by Phyllis Burton. "You played a footfault," she had accused—and later, umpiring a junior match, she had given several footfaults against Eleanor Luton, as Mrs. Ford was then, in a manner that seemed unjust at the time and did so still. All through Mrs. Ford's schooldays, Phyllis Burton's large presence had loomed and intervened, interfered and patronized, mocked and derided.

She was good at everything, but though she was older she was in the same form as Mrs. Ford. She wasn't a dunce, however—it was Eleanor who was a swot, younger than everyone else in her form. In the library she was unmolested; her head in a book, she could escape the pressures of community life she found hard to endure. Eleanor was no joiner, and neither was she a leader—it was Phyllis who became, in time, head girl.

There came the sound of a quoit, thudding.

Mrs. Ford opened her eyes and saw large buttocks before her, shrouded in navy linen, as their owner stooped to throw.

"We enjoy how we play," said a female voice, but uncertainly.

"Things should always be done the right way," said the owner of the navy-blue buttocks, straightening up.

In memory, young Eleanor in her new VAD uniform stooped over a hospital bed to pull at a wrinkled sheet and make her patient feel easier. Phyllis, with two years' experience, told her to strip the bed and make it up over again, although this meant moving the wounded man and causing him pain.

"But the patient—"

"He'll be much more comfortable in the end, it's for his own good," Phyllis had said. And stood there while it was done, not helping, although two could make a bed much more easily than one.

Phyllis had contrived that Eleanor was kept busy with bedpans and scrubbing floors after that, until more junior nurses arrived and she had to be permitted to undertake other tasks.

Michael had been a patient in the hospital. He'd had a flesh wound in the thigh and was young and shocked by what he had seen and suffered in the trenches. He and Eleanor had gone for walks together as he grew stronger. When he cast away his crutches, he took her arm for support —and still held it when he could walk alone. They strolled in the nearby woods, and had tea in the local town. Phyllis saw them once and told Eleanor so, and soon after that Eleanor was switched to night duty so that she scarcely saw Michael again before he went back to the front. She didn't receive a single letter from him, and after months of waiting, although she never saw his name on the casualty lists, she decided he had been killed.

Later she met Roger, who was large and kind and protected her from the harshest aspects of life for so many years, leaving her all the more ill-prepared to battle alone, as now she must.

"Games are no fun unless you play fair and square," said the sturdy woman with Phyllis's voice.

Mrs. Ford looked away from her and saw a thin girl in white pants and a red sweater and a young man in an arran pullover and clean new jeans—the deck quoit players. The older woman was leaving, walking away, but the damage was done.

"Come on, Iris, your turn," said the man.

"No, I don't want to play any more," the girl said.

That had happened long ago too. Eleanor had not wanted to play games after Phyllis Burton's derisive interventions.

There was some murmuring between the two. The man put his arm round Iris's shoulders but she flung it off and, head down, mooched off along the deck, disappearing eventually round the corner. The man watched her go, then moved to the rail and leaned over it, gazing at the water.

Mrs. Ford was trembling. The woman was so like Phyllis, whom she hadn't heard of since "their" war, so long ago. Strange that someone else should waken her memory. Phyllis, if she were still alive, must be well over eighty now—eighty-four, in fact—and this woman was what? Getting on for sixty? It was hard to tell these days.

Mrs. Ford found it difficult to settle back down after that, and spent a restless day.

Proper table allocations, not prepared the night before when seating had been informal as passengers arrived, had now been made, and Mrs. Ford was pleasantly surprised to find that she was at the doctor's table, with two couples past retirement age and a younger pair. The doctor was also young, reminding Mrs. Ford of her eldest grandson, who was thirty-five. She didn't know that her elder son, that grandson's father, now chairman of a group of companies, had personally visited the shipping office to request special attention for his mother, particularly a congenial place for meals. He and his wife had been on a cruise the year before—their first—and had seen for themselves what Mrs. Ford's fate could be. Her children all loved their timid mother and respected her desire to maintain her independence—and, far from relaxing about her when she went away, they worried. On a ship, however, there was con-

stant attention at hand, a doctor immediately available, and swift com-
munication in an emergency.

Mrs. Ford felt happy sitting next to the doctor, waiting for her soup.
She would eat three courses merely, waiting while others ate their way
through the menu like schoolboys on a binge. The doctor told her he
was having a year at sea before moving, in a few months' time, into
general practice. It was a chance to see the world, he said.

He was a tall blond young man with an easy manner and he liked old
ladies, who were often valiant, building walls of reserve around themselves as a defence against pity. Mrs. Ford, he saw, was one like that.
There were others who thought great age allowed them licence to be
rude, and took it, and the doctor liked them too for he admired their
spirit. He ordered wine for the whole table and Mrs. Ford saw the other
three men nod in agreement; they would all take their turn to buy it and
so must she. This had happened to her before and it was always difficult
to insist, as she must if she intended to accept their hospitality. She liked
a glass of wine.

Phyllis Burton, if she were a widow, would have no difficulty in dealing with such a problem. She would, early on, establish ascendancy over
the whole table.

After all these years, here was Phyllis Burton in her mind, and just
because of the dogmatic woman on the deck this morning.

Conversation flowed. The doctor asked about Mrs. Ford's family and
listened with apparent interest to her account of her grandchildren's
prowess in various activities. It was acceptable to brag of their accom-
plishments, but not of one's children's successes, Mrs. Ford had learned.
Everyone disclosed where they lived and if they had cruised before—or,
failing that, what other countries they had visited. Both retired couples
had been to the Far East, the younger pair to Florida. The doctor revealed that he was unmarried, but his face briefly clouded—then he
went on to describe the ship making black smoke off Mykonos (such a
white island!) due to some engine maintenance requirement. He
laughed. It had looked bad from the boats taking the passengers ashore.

Mrs. Ford had enjoyed her meal. The passenger list was in her cabin
when she returned after dinner but she didn't look at it. She read about
Lord Wavell, falling asleep over him and waking later with her spectacles
still on. Then, with the light out and herself neatly tucked under the

bedclothes, she dreamed about Michael. They were walking in the woods near the hospital, holding hands, and he kissed her sweetly, as he had so long ago, her first kiss from an adult male, right-seeming, making it easy when afterwards Roger came along.

She woke in the morning a little disturbed by the dream, but rested.

The next night the captain held his welcoming party, and at it Mrs. Ford, hovering on the animated fringe of guests, saw the doctor talking to a pretty girl in a flame-coloured dress. She saw them together again in Athens, setting off to climb the Acropolis.

Mrs. Ford decided not to attempt the ascent—she had been up there with Roger on a night of the full moon and preferred to hold that memory rather than one of a heated scramble that would exhaust her. She waited in a tourist pavilion by the bus park, drinking coffee, till the groups from the ship returned. This time the doctor was alone. With her far-sighted eyes, Mrs. Ford peered about for the girl but did not see her.

Then she heard the voice again.

"What a clumsy girl you are. I don't know why you can't look where you're going," it said, in Phyllis's tones. "Look at your trousers—they're ruined. Scrambling about like a child up there!"

"I'm sorry, Mummy." Mrs. Ford heard the tight high-pitched reply of someone in a state of tension. "I slipped. It will wash out."

Mrs. Ford, on her way to coach number four, glanced round. The tourists wouldn't pause for coffee—meals were paid for on the tour and they were returning to the ship for lunch before taking other excursions before the *Sphinx* sailed that night. Behind her she saw a tall, well built woman with carefully coiffed iron-grey hair in a tweed skirt, sensible shoes, and an expensive pigskin jacket. Beside her was the girl Mrs. Ford had witnessed talking to the doctor, her blonde hair caught back in a slide at the nape of her neck. On her pale trousers there was a long, dirty smear.

It was to the mother, however, that Mrs. Ford's eyes were drawn. Just so might Phyllis Burton have looked in middle age.

That evening Mrs. Ford consulted the passenger list with a pencil, reading it with care to winnow out the mothers and daughters travelling together. The father might be present too, unobserved so far by Mrs. Ford. She marked several family groups with a question mark. There were no Burtons. Of course not. But the resemblance was so uncanny, she would have to find out who the woman was.

* * *

In the end it was easy.

The next day the sun shone brightly and the sea was calm. Mrs. Ford decided to climb higher in the ship than she had been hitherto and explore the sports deck in search of a quiet corner where she could sit in the sun. Stick hooked over her arm, a hand on the rail, she slowly ascended the companionway and walked along the deck to a spot where it widened out and some chairs were placed. In one sat the blonde girl. Beside her was an empty chair.

"Is this anyone's place?" Mrs. Ford inquired, and the girl, who had been gazing out to sea, turned with a slight start. A smile of great sweetness spread over her face and, confused, Mrs. Ford was again in a wood, long ago, with Michael.

"No—oh, please, let me help you," the girl said, and, springing up, she put a hand under Mrs. Ford's elbow to help her into the low chair. "They're difficult, aren't they? These chairs, I mean. Such a long way down."

"Yes," agreed Mrs. Ford, gasping slightly. "But getting up is harder."

"I know. We found it with my grandfather," the girl said. "But now he's got his own chair for the garden—it's higher, and he can manage."

"Your grandfather?" Mrs. Ford wanted the girl to talk while she caught her breath.

"He's lived with us since my grandmother died—before I was born," said the girl. "He's still quite spry, but a bit forgetful. He's a lamb."

"And are you like him?" She was, Mrs. Ford knew.

The girl laughed.

"Forgetful, you mean?" she said. "Maybe I am—Mummy always says I'm so clumsy and careless. But then, she's so terribly well organized herself. Granny was the same, Grandpa says. She always knew what to do and made instant decisions."

Roger had always known what to do and make quick, if not instant, decisions, Mrs. Ford reflected. "I dither a bit myself," she declared. "I miss my husband a great deal. He cared for me so."

"That must have been wonderful," said the girl, seeming quite unembarrassed by this confidence.

They sat there in the sunshine, gently chatting. The girl's mother was having her hair done, she said. They were cruising together—her mother had had severe bronchitis during the winter and it had seemed a good idea to seek the sun. Her father couldn't get away and so she had come instead. What girl would refuse a chance like this? Her mother had a great desire to see the Pyramids and that would be the high point of the trip for them.

"But you've travelled before?" Mrs. Ford asked. Her elder grandchildren, this child's generation, were always whizzing about the globe.

Mummy hadn't liked her going off just with friends, the girl said, but she *had* been to France to learn the language. There had been family holidays in Corsica, which she loved. They rented a villa. She had two brothers, both older than herself.

"What are their names?" asked Mrs. Ford, still feeling her way. She didn't know the girl's yet.

"Michael's the eldest—he's called after my grandfather," said the girl. "The other one's William, after Daddy."

Mrs. Ford's gently beating old heart began to thump unevenly. Should she say she had known a Michael, long ago? But the girl was going on, needing no prompting.

"Aren't names funny?" she said. "I'm glad I wasn't called after Mummy—her name's Phyllis, after her mother. It would be confusing to have two Phyllis Carters, wouldn't it?"

"I suppose it would," Mrs. Ford agreed, and now bells seemed to be ringing in her head, for her Michael's surname had been Carter.

"I'm called after someone else Grandfather knew," said the girl. "It's quite romantic, really. There was this nurse he met in the war—the first war, you remember."

"Yes, my dear, I do," said Mrs. Ford.

"She was very young and shy and kept being ticked off by this older, bossier nurse, Grandfather said. When he went back to France he wrote her lots of letters, but she never answered. Wasn't that sad? I'm named after her. Her name was Eleanor."

"Oh," said Mrs. Ford faintly, and her head spun. Letters?

"She must have married someone else or something," said the girl. "Or even died. All the letters were sent back to Grandfather. Mummy found them when she helped him clear up after Granny died, in her desk, locked up. She burned them without telling Grandfather. It would only have upset him."

"Yes, I suppose it would," said Mrs. Ford. There was just one fact that must be confirmed. "Your grandmother?" she asked.

"Grandfather married another nurse," said the girl. "Mummy's exactly like her, he says."

Mrs. Ford took it in. All those years ago Phyllis Burton had intercepted letters meant for her. Why? Because she wanted Michael for herself, or because she sought, as always, to despoil?

"And have you uncles and aunts?" she asked at last.

"No, there was only Mummy," the girl replied.

So Phyllis had managed just one child, and had died before this grandchild had been born, while Mrs. Ford, with two sons and two daughters, had survived into great age. And Michael had never forgotten, for this girl bore her name.

She could cope with no more today.

"What a nice little chat we've had," she said. "We'll be meeting again." She began to struggle up from her chair and the girl rose again to help her.

In the days that followed they talked more. Seeing them together, the mother would walk past, but if Eleanor was talking to any man among the passengers, or a ship's officer, the mother would break in upon them at once.

In Mrs. Ford's mind the generations grew confused and there were moments when she imagined it was this confident, domineering woman who had been so perfidious all those years ago, stealing letters meant for another, not this woman's long-dead mother. At night Mrs. Ford shed tears for the young girl that had been herself, waiting for letters that never came and in the end giving up.

But she'd had a long, full, and happy life afterwards. And Michael hadn't persevered—hadn't tried to find her after the war. Perhaps Phyllis had already made sure of him; she'd borne him just one child.

On deck, Mrs. Ford heard Eleanor being admonished.

"A ship's doctor won't do," came that dominant tone. "I've plans for you, and they don't include this sort of thing at all. It stops the instant you leave the ship, do you hear?"

Eleanor told Mrs. Ford about it later.

"He's a widower. His wife died in a car crash when she was pregnant," she said. "But it isn't just that. Mummy wants me to marry an earl, if she can find one, or at least some sort of tycoon, like Daddy."

"It's early days. You don't really know each other," said Mrs. Ford.

"I know, but he's only doing a short spell in the ship, then he's going into general practice. We could get better acquainted then, couldn't we?"

"Yes," agreed Mrs. Ford.

"And as for earls and tycoons—" Eleanor put scorn in her voice.

She'd learned typing and done a Cordon Bleu cooking course, Eleanor said. She'd wanted to be a nurse, but Mummy hadn't approved. The girl seemed docile and subdued—too much so, Mrs. Ford thought.

Michael Carter, she remembered, had seemed to have plenty of money, though neither had thought about things like that, when during that long-ago war they took their quiet walks and had tea in a café. Phyllis Burton might have destroyed the innocent budding romance simply because that was her way, but she wouldn't have married Michael unless he had been what was called, in those days, "a catch." She'd have made sure of the same for her daughter—and the daughter was repeating the pattern now.

"You're of age," Mrs. Ford said. "Make your own decisions."

Later the mother spoke to her. It was eerie, hearing that voice from the past urging her, since she had become friendly with Eleanor, to warn her against the doctor.

"But why?" Mrs. Ford asked. "He seems such a nice young man."

"Think of her future," the girl's mother said. "She can do better than that."

"He'd look after her," Mrs. Ford said, and she knew that he would. The girl was timid and lacking in confidence; the doctor, experienced and quite a lot older, would make her feel safe, as she had felt with Roger. "It depends on what you think is important," she said, rather bravely for her, and Eleanor's mother soon left, quite annoyed.

Mrs. Ford smiled to herself and stitched on at her *gros point*. She'd help the young pair if she could. Nowadays, as she knew from her own family, people tried things out before making a proper commitment, and though such a system had, in her view, disadvantages, there were also points in its favour.

Mrs. Ford did not go to Cairo. The drive was a long one from Alexandria, and she'd been before—stayed with Roger at Mena House, in fact, years ago. She spent the day quietly in Alexandria. The doctor, she knew, had gone on the trip in case a passenger fell ill, as might easily happen. That evening he said that someone had fainted, but nothing more serious had occurred.

The next day was spent at sea, giving people a chance to recover from the most tiring expedition of the voyage. Among those sleeping on chairs on deck, Mrs. Ford saw Eleanor's mother. Her mouth was a little agape and her spectacles were still on her nose. In her hand she held an open book. Perhaps she was not as robust as she seemed, Mrs. Ford mused—her own mother, after all, the Phyllis of Mrs. Ford's youth, had not survived late middle age.

On the upper deck, Eleanor and the doctor were playing deck tennis. Mrs. Ford, seeing them, smiled to herself as she walked away. Youth was resilient.

Several days later the *Sphinx* anchored off Nauplia. The weather was fine, though a haze hung over the distant mountains and there was snow on the highest peak, rare for this area. Mrs. Ford stood in line to disembark by the ship's launches with the other passengers going ashore. Stalwart ship's officers would easily help her aboard and she quite enjoyed feeling a firm grasp on her arm as she stepped over the gunwale into the boat.

A row of coaches waited on the quay. Mrs. Ford allowed herself to be directed into one. She would enjoy today, for while Mycenae, their first stop, was a dramatic, brooding place, holding an atmosphere redolent of tragedy, Epidaurus, in its perfect setting, was a total contrast. They drove past groves of orange trees laden with fruit. The almond trees were in bloom and the grass, which later in the year would be bleached by the heat of the sun, was a brilliant green.

The haze had lifted when the coach stopped at Epidaurus. Mrs. Ford debated whether to go straight to the stadium, which so few tours allowed time to visit and where it would be peaceful and cool, but in the end, walking among the pines and inhaling their scent, she decided to visit it again.

She walked past the group from her coach as, like docile children, they clustered around their guide and, sauntering on, using her stick, she turned up the track to the left of the theatre where the ascent was easier than up the steep steps.

At the top she turned to the right and entered the vast semicircle of stone. She moved inwards a little and sat down, gazing about her, sighing with pleasure. Below stood her group; she had plenty of time to rest and enjoy her surroundings.

The sun was quite strong now and she sat thinking of very little except her present contentment. A guide below began the acoustic demonstration, scrabbling his feet in the dust, jingling keys, lighting a match. Mrs. Ford had seen it all before. Then her eye caught a flash of bright blue lower down—young Eleanor's sweater. She was almost at the bottom of the auditorium and with her was a tall young man easily discerned by Mrs. Ford's farsighted eyes to be the ship's doctor. They were absorbed as much with each other as with the scenery, Mrs. Ford thought as she watched them together.

Then a voice behind her called loudly.

"Eleanor!" she heard. "Eleanor! Come here at once!"

Mrs. Ford reacted instinctively to the sound of her name and she turned. Her pulse was beating fast and she felt her nerves tighten with fear. Since her youth no one had talked to her in such a tone.

Down the steep steps of the aisle between the seats, Phyllis's daughter, whose name was also Phyllis, came boldly towards her, striding with purpose, Phyllis the malevolent, Phyllis the destroyer. Mrs. Ford's grip on her stick, which was resting across her knees, tightened as the lumbering figure in its sensible skirt and expensive jacket approached. Her pace did not slacken as she drew near, Mrs. Ford knew with a part of her mind that it was not she but her young namesake below who was the target of the imperious summons.

She acted spontaneously. She slid her walking stick out across the aisle, handle foremost, as Phyllis drew level, and by chance, not deliberate design, the hooked end caught round the woman's leg. Mrs. Ford tightened her grasp with both hands and hung on, but the stick was pulled from her grip as the hurrying woman stumbled and fell.

She didn't fall far—she was too bulky and the stairway too narrow—but she came to rest some little way below Mrs. Ford and lay quite still. No one noticed at first, for there were shouts and cries filling the air from tourists testing the amplification of the theatre and attention was focused below.

Mrs. Ford's pulse had begun to steady by the time people began to gather around the body. Her stick lay at the side of the aisle. She retrieved it quite easily. She returned to her coach by the same way she had come, away from all the commotion, and was driven back to Nauplia where the ship waited at anchor.

There was talk in the coach.

"Some woman tripped and fell."

"It's dangerous. You'd think there'd be a rope."

"People should look where they're going."

"She must have been wearing unsuitable shoes."

The doctor was not at the table for dinner that night, and over the loudspeaker the captain announced that though sailing had been delayed this would not interfere with the rest of the timetable—the next port would be reached as planned.

Mrs. Ford's table companions related various versions of what had happened ashore to cause the delay. The woman, Eleanor's mother, had stumbled in the theatre at Epidaurus and in falling had hit her head against a projecting stone, dying at once. Someone else thought she'd had a stroke or a heart attack and that this had caused her to fall, for she was a big woman and florid of face. The Greeks had taken over, since the accident had happened ashore, and the formalities were therefore their concern.

"Terrible for the daughter," someone remarked. "Such a shock."

"The father's flying out," someone else said.

Mrs. Ford ate her sole meunière. She had only wanted to stop Phyllis from interfering. Hadn't she?

Her son, meeting her at the airport some days later, found his mother looking well and rested. He knew about the accident—it had been reported in the newspapers.

"What a terrible thing to happen," he said. "It must have been most distressing. Poor woman."

"Well, she saw the Pyramids," Mrs. Ford replied.

What a heartless response, thought her son in surprise, and looked at his gentle mother, astonished.

The Uninvited

MICHAEL GILBERT

M r. Calder was silent, solitary and generous with everything, from a basket of cherries or mushrooms, to efficient first aid to a child who had tumbled. The children liked him. But their admiration was reserved for his dog.

The great, solemn, sagacious Rasselas was a deerhound. He had been born in the sunlight. His coat was the color of dry sherry, his nose was blue-black and his eyes shone like worked amber. From the neat tufts at his heels to the top of his dome-shaped head, there was a royalty about him. He had lived in courts and consorted on his own terms with other princes.

Mr. Calder's cottage stood at the top of a fold in the Kentish Downs. The road curled up to it from Lamperdown, in the valley. First it climbed slowly between woods, then forked sharply left and rose steeply, coming out onto the plateau, rounded and clear as a bald pate. The road served only the cottage, and stopped in front of its gate.

Beyond the house, there were paths which led through the home fields and into the woods beyond, woods full of primroses, bluebells, pheasant's eggs, chestnuts, hollow trees and ghosts. The woods did not belong to Mr. Calder. They belonged, in theory, to a syndicate of businessmen from the Medway towns, who came at the week ends, in autumn and winter, to kill birds. When the sound of their shooting brakes announced their arrival, Mr. Calder would call Rasselas indoors. At all other times, the great dog roamed freely in the garden and in the three open fields which formed Mr. Calder's domain. But he never went out of sight of the house, nor beyond the sound of his master's voice.

The children said that the dog talked to the man, and this was perhaps not far from the truth. Before Mr. Calder came, the cottage had been inhabited by a bad-tempered oaf who had looked on himself as custodian for the Medway sportsmen, and had chased and harried the children who, in their turn, had become adept at avoiding him.

When Mr. Calder first came, they had spent a little time in trying him, before finding him harmless. Nor had it taken them long to find out something else. No one could cross the plateau unobserved, small though he might be and quietly though he might move. A pair of sensitive ears would have heard, a pair of amber eyes would have seen; and Rasselas would pad in at the open door and look enquiringly at Mr. Calder who would say, "Yes, it's the Lightfoot boys and their sister. I saw them, too." And Rasselas would stalk out and lie down again in his favorite day bed, on the sheltered side of the woodpile.

Apart from the children, visitors to the cottage were a rarity. The postman wheeled his bicycle up the hill once a day; delivery vans appeared at their appointed times; the fish man on Tuesdays, the grocer on Thursdays, the butcher on Fridays. In the summer, occasional hikers wandered past, unaware that their approach, their passing, and their withdrawal had all been reported to the owner of the cottage.

Mr. Calder's only regular visitor was Mr. Behrens, the retired schoolmaster, who lived in the neck of the valley, two hundred yards outside Lamperdown Village, in a house which had once been the Rectory. Mr. Behrens kept bees, and lived with his aunt. His forward-stooping head, his wrinkled, brown skin, blinking eyes and cross expression made him look like a tortoise which has been roused untimely from its winter sleep.

Once or twice a week, summer and winter, Mr. Behrens would get out his curious tweed hat and his iron-tipped walking stick, and would go tip-tapping up the hill to have tea with Mr. Calder. The dog knew and tolerated Mr. Behrens, who would scratch his ears and say, "Rasselas. Silly name. *You* came from Persia, not Abyssinia." It was believed that the two old gentlemen played backgammon.

There were other peculiarities about Mr. Calder's menage which were not quite so very apparent to the casual onlooker.

When he first took over the house, some of the alterations he had asked for had caused Mr. Benskin, the builder, to scratch his head. Why, for instance, had he wanted one perfectly good southern-facing window filled in, and two more opened, on the north side of the house?

Mr. Calder had been vague. He said that he liked an all-round view and plenty of fresh air. In which case, asked Mr. Benskin, why had he insisted on heavy shutters on all downstairs windows and a steel plate behind the woodwork of the front and back doors?

There had also been the curious matter of the telephone line. When Mr. Calder had mentioned that he was having the telephone installed, Mr. Benskin had laughed. The post office, overwhelmed as they were with post-war work, were hardly likely to carry their line of poles a full mile up the hill for one solitary cottage. But Mr. Benskin had been wrong, and on two counts. Not only had the post office installed a telephone, with surprising promptness, but they had actually dug a trench and brought it in underground.

When this was reported to him, Mr. Benskin had told the public ear of the Golden Lion that he had always known there was something odd about Mr. Calder.

"He's an inventor," he said. "To my mind, there's no doubt that's what he is. An inventor. He's got government support. Otherwise, how'd he get a telephone line laid like that?"

Had Mr. Benskin been able to observe Mr. Calder getting out of bed in the morning, he would have been fortified in his opinion. For it is a well-known fact that inventors are odd, and Mr. Calder's routine on rising was very odd indeed.

Summer and winter, he would wake half an hour before dawn. He turned on no electric light. Instead, armed with a big torch, he would pad downstairs, the cold nose of Rasselas a few inches behind him, and make a minute inspection of the three ground-floor rooms. On the edges of the shutters were certain tiny, thread-like wires, almost invisible to the naked eye. When he had satisfied himself that these were in order, Mr. Calder would return upstairs and get dressed.

By this time, day was coming up. The darkness had withdrawn across the bare meadows and chased the ghosts back into the surrounding woods. Mr. Calder would take a pair of heavy naval binoculars from his dressing table, and, sitting back from the window, would study with care the edges of his domain. Nothing escaped his attention: a wattle hurdle blocking a path; a bent sapling at the edge of the glade; a scut of fresh earth in the hedge. The inspection was repeated from the window on the opposite side.

Then, whistling softly to himself, Mr. Calder would walk downstairs to cook breakfast for himself and for Rasselas.

The postman, who arrived at eleven o'clock, brought the newspapers with the letters. Perhaps because he lived alone and saw so few people, Mr. Calder seemed particularly fond of his letters and papers. He opened them with a loving care which an observer might have found ludicrous. His fingers caressed the envelope, or the wrapping paper, very gently, as a man will squeeze a cigar. Often he would hold an envelope up to the light as if he could read, through the outer covering, the message inside. Sometimes, he would even weigh an envelope in the delicate letter scales which he kept on top of his desk between a stuffed seagull and a night-scented jasmine in a pot.

On a fine morning in May, when the sun was fulfilling, in majesty, the promise of a misty dawn, Mr. Calder unfolded his copy of the *Times*, turned, as was his custom, to the foreign news pages, and started to read.

He had stretched his hand out toward his coffee cup when he stopped. It was a tiny check, a break in the natural sequence of his actions, but it was enough to make Rasselas look up. Mr. Calder smiled reassuringly at the dog. His hand resumed its movement, picked up the cup, carried it to his mouth. But the dog was not easy.

Mr. Calder read, once more, the five-line item which had caught his attention. Then he glanced at his watch, went across to the telephone, dialed a Lamperdown number and spoke to Jack, at the garage which also ran a taxi service.

"Just do it if we hurry," said Jack. "No time to spare. I'll come right up."

While he waited for the taxi, Mr. Calder first telephoned Mr. Behrens, to warn him that they might have to postpone their game of backgammon. Then he spent a little time telling Rasselas that he was leaving him in charge of the cottage, but that he would be back before dark. Rasselas swept the carpet with his feathery tail, and made no attempt to follow Mr. Calder when Jack's Austin came charging up the hill and reversed in front of the cottage gate.

In the end, the train was ten minutes late at the junction, and Mr. Calder caught it with ease.

He got out at Victoria, walked down Victoria Street, turned to the right, opposite the open space where the Colonial Office used to stand, and to the right again into the Square. In the southwest corner stands the Westminister branch of the London and Home Counties Bank.

Mr. Calder walked into the bank. The head cashier, Mr. Macleod, nodded gravely to him and said, "Mr. Fortescue is ready. You can go straight in."

"I'm afraid the train was late," said Mr. Calder. "We lost ten minutes at the junction, and never caught it up."

"Trains are not as reliable now as they used to be," agreed Mr. Macleod.

A young lady from a nearby office had just finished banking the previous day's takings. Mr. Macleod was watching her out of the corner of his eye until the door had shut behind her. Then he said, with exactly the same inflection, but more softly, "Will it be necessary to make any special arrangements for your departure?"

"Oh, no, thank you," said Mr. Calder. "I took all the necessary precautions."

"Fine," said Mr. Macleod.

He held open the heavy door, paneled in sham walnut in the style affected by pre-war bank designers, ushered Mr. Calder into the anteroom and left him there for a few moments, in contemplation of its only ornament, a reproduction, in a massive gilt frame, of Landseer's allegory "The Tug of War." Thrift and Industry appeared to be gaining a hard-fought victory over Luxury and Extravagance.

Then the head cashier reappeared and held open the door for Mr. Calder.

Mr. Fortescue, who came forward to greet him, would have been identified in any company as a bank manager. It was not only the conventional dress, the square, sagacious face, the suggestion that as soon as his office door closed behind him, he would extract an old pipe and push it into his discreet but friendly mouth. It was more than that. It was the bearing, the balance, the air of certainty and stability in a dubious and unstable world, which sits upon a man when he is the representative of a corporation with a hundred million pounds of disclosed assets.

"Nice to see you," he said. "Grab a chair. Any trouble on the way up?"

"No trouble," said Mr. Calder. "I don't think anything can start for another two or three weeks."

"They might have post-dated the item to put you off your guard." He picked up his own copy of the *Times* and re-read the four and a half lines of print which recorded that Colonel Josef Weinleben, the international expert on bacterial antibodies, had died in Klagenfurt as the result of an abdominal operation.

"No," said Calder. "He wanted me to read it, and sweat."

"It would be the established procedure to organize his own 'death' before setting on a serious mission," Mr. Fortescue agreed. He picked up a heavy paper knife and tapped thoughtfully with it on the desk. "But it could be true, this time. Weinleben must be nearly sixty."

"He's coming," said Mr. Calder. "I can feel it in my bones. It may even be true that he's ill. If he was dying, he'd like to take me along with him."

"What makes you so sure?"

"I tortured him," said Mr. Calder. "And broke him. He'd never forget."

"No," said Mr. Fortescue. He held the point of the paper knife toward the window, sighting down it as if it had been a pistol. "No. I think very likely you're right. We'll try to pick him up at the port, and tag him. But we can't guarantee to stop him getting in. If he tries to operate, of course, he'll have to show his hand. You've got your permanent cover. Do you want anything extra?"

He might, thought Mr. Calder, have been speaking to a customer. You've got your normal overdraft. Do you want any extra accommodation, Mr. Calder? The bank is here to serve you. There was something at the same time ridiculous and comforting in treating life and death as though they were entries in the same balance sheet.

"I'm not at all sure that I want you to stop him," he said. "We aren't at war. You could only deport him. It might be more satisfactory to let him through."

"Do you know," said Mr. Fortescue, "the same thought had occurred to me."

Mrs. Farmer, who kept the Seven Gables Guest House, between Aylesford and Bearsted, considered Mr. Wendon a perfect guest. His passport and the card which he had duly filled in on arrival showed him to be a Dutchman; but his English, though accented in odd places, was colloquial and fluent. An upright, red-faced, gray-haired man, he was particularly nice with Mrs. Farmer's two young children. Moreover, he gave no trouble. He was—and this was a sovereign virtue in Mrs. Farmer's eyes—methodical and predictable.

Every morning, in the endless succession of the fine days which heralded that summer, he would go out walking, clad in aged but respectable tweed, field glasses over one shoulder, a small knapsack on the other for camera, sandwiches, and thermos flask. And in the evenings, he would sit in the lounge, drinking a single glass of schnapps as an aperitif before dinner, and entertaining Tom and Rebecca with accounts of the birds he had observed that day. It was difficult to imagine, seeing him sitting there, gentle, placid, and upright, that he had killed men and women—and children, too—with his own well-kept hands. But then Mr. Wendon, or Weinleben, or Weber, was a remarkable man.

On the tenth day of his stay, he received a letter from Holland. Its contents seemed to cause him some satisfaction, and he read it twice before putting it away in his wallet. The stamps he tore off, giving them to Mrs. Farmer for Tom.

"I may be a little late this evening," he said. "I am meeting a friend at Maidstone. Don't keep dinner for me."

That morning, he packed his knapsack with particular care and caught the Maidstone bus at Aylesford crossroads. He had said that he was going to Maidstone and he never told unnecessary lies.

After that, his movements became somewhat complicated, but by four o'clock, he was safely ensconced in a dry ditch to the north of the old Rectory at Lamperdown. Here he consumed a biscuit, and observed the front drive of the house.

At a quarter past four, Jack arrived with his taxi and Mr. Behren's aunt came out, wearing, despite the heat of the day, coat and gloves and a rather saucy scarf, and was installed in the back seat. Mr. Behrens handed in her shopping basket, waved goodbye, and retired into the house.

Five minutes later, Mr. Wendon was knocking at the front door. Mr. Behrens opened it, and blinked when he saw the gun in his visitor's hand.

"I must ask you to turn around and walk in front of me," said Mr. Wendon.

"Why should I?" said Mr. Behrens. He sounded more irritated than alarmed.

"If you don't, I shall shoot you," said Mr. Wendon. He said it exactly as if he meant it and pushed Mr. Behrens toward a door.

After a moment, Mr. Behrens wheeled about, and asked, "Where now?"

"That looks the sort of place I had in mind," said Mr. Wendon. "Open the door and walk in. But quite slowly."

It was a small, dark room, devoted to hats, coats, sticks, old tennis rackets, croquet mallets, bee veils, and such.

"Excellent," said Mr. Wendon. He helped himself to the old-fashioned tweed hat and the iron-tipped walking stick which Mr. Behrens carried abroad with him on all his perambulations of the countryside. "A small window, and a stout, old door. What could be better?"

Still watching Mr. Behrens closely, he laid the hat and stick on the hall table, dipped his left hand into his own coat pocket and brought out a curious-looking metal object.

"You have not, perhaps, seen one of these before? It works on the same principle as a Mills grenade, but is six times as powerful and is incendiary as well as explosive. When I shut this door, I shall bolt it and hang the grenade from the upturned bolt. The least disturbance will dislodge it. It is powerful enough to blow the door down."

"All right," said Mr. Behrens. "But get on with it. My sister will be back soon."

"Not until eight o'clock, if she adheres to last week's arrangements," said Mr. Wendon quite knowingly.

He closed the door, shot the bolts, top and bottom, and suspended the grenade with artistic care from the top one.

Mr. Calder had finished his tea by five o'clock, and then shortly afterward strolled down to the end of the paddock, where he was repairing the fence. Rasselas lay quietly in the lee of the wood pile. The golden afternoon turned imperceptibly toward evening.

Rasselas wrinkled his velvet muzzle to dislodge a fly. On one side, he could hear Mr. Calder digging with his mattock into the hilltop chalk and grunting as he dug. Behind, some four fields away, a horse, fly-plagued, with kicking its heels and bucking. Then, away to his left, he located a familiar sound. The clink of an iron-tipped walking stick on stone.

Rasselas liked to greet the arrival of this particular friend of his master, but he waited, with dignity, until the familiar tweed had come into view. Then he unfolded himself and trotted gently out into the road.

So strong was the force of custom, so disarming were the familiar and expected sight and sound, that even Rasselas' five senses were lulled. But his instinct was awake. The figure was still a dozen paces off and advancing confidently, when Rasselas stopped. His eyes searched the figure. Right appearance, right hat, right noises. But wrong gait. Quicker, and more purposeful than their old friend. And, above all, wrong smell.

The dog hackled, then crouched as if to jump. But it was the man who jumped. He leaped straight at the dog, his hand came out from under his coat and the loaded stick hissed through the air with brutal force. Rasselas was still moving, and the blow missed his head, but struck him full on the back of the neck. He went down without a sound.

Mr. Calder finished digging the socket for the corner post he was planting, straightened his back and decided that he would fetch the brush and creosote from the house. As he came out of the paddock, he saw the great dog lying in the road.

He ran forward and knelt in the dust. There was no need to look twice.

He hardly troubled to raise his eyes when a voice which he recognized spoke from behind him.

"Keep your hands in sight," said Colonel Weinleben, "and try not to make any sudden or unexpected move."

Mr. Calder got up.

"I suggest we move back into the house," said the colonel. "We shall be more private there. I should like to devote at least as much attention to you as you did to me on the last occasion we met."

Mr. Calder seemed hardly to be listening. He was looking down at the crumpled, empty, tawny skin, incredibly changed by the triviality of life's departure. His eyes were full of tears.

"You killed him," he said.

"As I shall shortly kill you," said the colonel. And as he spoke, he spun round like a startled marionette, took a stiff pace forward and fell, face downward.

Mr. Calder looked at him incuriously. From the shattered hole in the side of his head, dark blood ran out and mixed with the white dust. Rasselas had not bled at all. He was glad of that tiny distinction between the two deaths.

It was Mr. Behrens who had killed Colonel Weinleben, with a single shot from a .312 rifle, fired from the edge of the wood. The rifle was fitted with a telescopic sight, but the shot was a fine one, even for an excellent marksman such as Mr. Behrens.

He'd run for nearly a quarter of a mile before firing it; he had to get into position very quickly, and he had only just been able to see the colonel's head over the top of an intervening hedge.

He burst through this hedge now, saw Rasselas, and started to curse.

"It wasn't your fault," said Mr. Calder. He was sitting in the road, the dog's head in his lap.

"If I'm meant to look after you, I ought to look after you properly," said Mr. Behrens. "Not let myself be jumped by an amateur like that. I hadn't reckoned on him blocking the door with a grenade. I had to break out of the window, and it took me nearly half an hour."

"We've a lot to do," said Mr. Calder. He got stiffly to his feet and went to fetch a spade.

Between them they dug a deep grave, behind the wood pile, and laid the dog in it, and filled it in, and patted the earth into a mound. It was a fine resting place, looking out southward over the feathery tops of the trees, across the Weald of Kent. A resting place for a prince.

Colonel Weinleben they buried later, with a good deal more haste and less ceremony, in the wood. He was the illegitimate son of a cobbler from Mainz and greatly inferior to the dog, both in birth and breeding.

⚜ ⚜ ⚜

The Black Cliffs

JOAN AIKEN

It was cold on the crossing, but calm; a sea nip in the air. Dark had fallen already by the time the two Americans boarded the ferry, but in spite of this they stayed on deck most of the way over to Rosslare, watching while the sky merged with the sea and then, by degrees, became pounced at irregular intervals by large brilliant white stars. Irving murmured this phrase aloud.

"*Pounced?*" Charley said. "What sort of crazy word's that, Irv? *Pounced* with stars? How can the sky be pounced with stars?"

"It comes from Latin," Irving answered absently, "Meaning to punch, or pierce with claws—from which you get pounce-work, decoration by perforations; it's the same word as puncture—which used to mean a sudden swoop with intent to seize."

"Hey, Irv, what a hell of a lot you know," Charley exclaimed admiringly. "A sudden swoop with intent to seize—like this, hey?"

And he grabbed his friend with rough, jocular affection.

"Watch out—you'll have us over the rail!" Irving cast a quick glance towards the open lounge door, where half a dozen other passengers were standing with their drinks, admiring the luminosity of the sky. If those people had not been there . . . the rail was not very high. But they *were* there; and Irving said to Charley, hardly troubling to keep the acid from his voice, "You'll have to remember not to be too demonstrative on the other side. The Irish may not like it."

"Oh, rats, Irv. Why ever not?"

"And *don't* call me *Irv*."

Irving Christopher St. John his full and distinguished name was, lately dignified by the addition of Professor. He had discovered, also, that on this side of the Atlantic the surname became even more aristocratic by being pronounced Sinjun; he had determined to adopt this usage forthwith. He did not think he would be able to bear it if Charley persisted in referring to him as "My friend Irv Saint John."

"Sorry, Bimbo," Charley said humbly. "I'll try to remember."

A flitting shaft of light from the swinging door briefly outlined Charley's hopelessly plebeian, undistinguished face, the shiny balding brow, with a straw-colored wavy cowlick hopefully and thinly spread over it, the doglike pleading eyes fixed on those of his friend, who made so little attempt, these days, to conceal irritation and boredom.

"Oh, let's go and eat before those louts mop up every crumb of food on the boat."

Two coachloads of Irish sports fans were returning homewards from an international match at Wembley. They wore colored paper caps, sang and laughed uproariously, and had queued up ten deep for Guinness the moment the bar showed signs of opening. Now some of them were singing "In Dublin's Fair City," strewn like wreckage from a storm all over the lounge, while clumps of others moved purposefully in the direction of the cafeteria, clutching two glasses of drink apiece. Nothing but fish and chips remained by the time Irving and Charley joined the line at the counter.

It was like that all the way over—vomit in the lavatories, empty beer cans rolling about the floor. When the ferry berthed and passengers went down to the enclosed car-deck to drive off, there ensued an endless, claustrophobic wait, because some drunken sportsman was lost in oblivion, curled up sleeping off the chagrin of his team's defeat, and could not be found to shift his car from the foot of the ramp. Irving, at the wheel of their rented automobile in the stuffy, clanging cave, which vibrated furiously with the sound of motors being irritably revved and was humid with exhaust fumes, could have screamed with exasperation at the delay; one more interruption to his plan, he felt, and he might lose all control, go berserk, do something crazy and irremediable.

Just let us get to the west coast, he thought.

At last they were off, proceeding fast but cautiously through the misty Irish night.

"It's so late now, what's the point of stopping at a hotel?" Irving said. "We'd only get half the night we'd paid for, it would be a waste of money. Why don't we just travel straight on, across to the other side? The middle of Ireland's a bore, anyway, might as well get through it in the dark. I don't mind driving if you want to sleep."

Charley, of course, was perfectly agreeable to this plan, but insisted that he must do a stint as well.

"Anything you say, Irv. I'll take the first spell if you like."

"No, I'll do first spell. I'm wide awake now, don't feel as if I could ever sleep again. You take a nap."

"Sure? Certain sure? Okay—if you say so, Bimbo," Charley replied biddably, wound his seat back, and wrapped himself in the blanket they had brought with them. They planned to camp if the weather proved suitable; otherwise stay at farms, hotels, bed-and-breakfast places, whatever offered. The project was to see the sights of the west coast, make leisurely search for Irving's ancestors (supposed to have originated from a small town called Lismaley in County Clare), and then return at a relaxed pace towards Dublin, where Irving was shortly to commence on a year's exchange from Chicago University, teaching American literature at Trinity College. A pleasant, peaceful program; they had two weeks of leisure.

In the first place, Irving had not intended Charley to come to Dublin.

"I really think it would be better, Charley, if you didn't. A year's not so long. And it would be good for you to be on your own. Give you time to get down to some course of study."

Charley had simply not taken him seriously.

"Oh, come on, Bimbo, you've got to be kidding! Not come to Dublin? Are you crazy? Why, I'm living for the day. Want to see the Ould Country." (Charley's ancestors had come from Sweden.) "I won't be in your hair, though, pal. Don't you worry about little old Charley."

"But what will you do with yourself?"

"Don't you fret about old Chas. I'll find myself some job—soda jerk in a drugstore or sump'n."

"*Chemist,*" Irving said irritably.

"Chemist, okay, or a laundromat, or any old thing. I can always find a job," Charley said with simple pride, and it was true, he could; prepared to turn his hand to anything, with a nonexistent threshold to boredom, he could work on a lathe, a production belt, mind babies, deliver groceries. Tolerant, good-tempered, dull, he was happy performing any task, however menial.

At one time this had seemed an asset; he was endlessly hardworking and useful, had painted Irving's apartment, spent hours sanding down

furniture or pasting up wallpaper. Now all this dumb docility and re-
fusal to take offense merely added to the aggravation.

A misty hunter's moon rose behind them. Irving drove on and on, his
lips compressed. The road held no other traffic. For miles they passed
no dwelling; untidy hedges, garlanded with late hay brushed from farm
wagons, reeled by endlessly on either side.

Charley slept the sleep of the innocent. Mouth open, gently snoring,
he lay childishly curled under the blanket, his heavy-boned frame utterly
relaxed in the security of knowing that his friend was driving.

And Irving, brows knit, drove on through Wexford and County Cork
and Limerick. Long obsessive analysis of his problem had not made its
solution any plainer beyond a certain vague urge; he simply told himself
over and over that he had to get rid of Charley. This stultification, this
prison life, could not continue. He was not going to have his new colleagues in Dublin form their first impressions of him as Charley's friend,
Charley's patron. In the hugeness of Chicago, okay; the chaos of such a
city made all lives anonymous and therefore free. But he had sensed
instantly on his preliminary visit to Dublin that here was a small, observant, bright-eyed, talkative community, ready to pounce on anybody's
foibles, discuss them at length, and pronounce on them either with
prudish disapproval or ribald indulgence. Irving could not stomach the
prospect of either attitude. No, there had to be a clean break, and Charley must be brought to accept this.

Morning found them well across to the west. They breakfasted in
Limerick, a grey, lively town, set about with spires of churches. Charley
grumbled that he could not understand a word the Irish said, but Irving
was delighted by their conversation and asked frequent questions in order to elicit the absurd, poetic torrent of speech that flowed so readily
on any and every topic.

"Yerrah, sir! And is it the back end of Erin ye would be visiting? And
how do ye ever hope to get to a little ramscramble place like Lismaley—
and that from here, might I ask? I'd say it couldn't be done! Ye'd do
better to remain in Limerick—faith, for all know 'tis the finest town in
the west, and let ye enjoy yourselves while ye may!"

Despite this advice, by mid-morning they were off again, skirting the
northern shores of the Shannon estuary. Beneath his preoccupations,
Irving found himself enjoying this peaceful small country—the hazel

and fuchsia hedges, the lonely silences, the weed-wrapped rocks by the shore, swans and gulls amiably competing on the tidal waters. But Charley's presence became more than ever an irritant.

How could I have borne his conversation for so long? Irving demanded of himself, listening in disgust to the sophomoric jokes, the inane comments on roadside objects, the pointless questions.

"Why are the Irish villages so poor-looking? Why don't they ever fix up their ruined churches—that must be the sixth we passed since lunch. Why aren't there any factories in Ireland?"

Charley was a hopeless map-reader, and signposts confused him; he could never be brought to understand the principle whereby a sign coupling two places that lay in diametrically opposite directions must indicate a fork in the road ahead. "But, Irv, how can it lead to *both* Dublin and Kilkee? Dublin's way over on the east, and Kilkee ought to be ahead of us."

In consequence they were continually lost and had to keep pulling up to study the map. Oh, for a companion who would understand this journey, Irving thought ragingly, and then asked himself what kind of a companion that would be? Some quiet, undemonstrative intelligence, somebody who knew the land and could expound it, not this vacuum of ignorance and ill-considered pawky humor.

"Gee, I'm hungry, I could eat a horse, Bimbo," Charley suddenly burst out in the late afternoon. "Aren't *you* hungry, Bimbo? What say we start looking for somewhere to stay the night?"

"Why didn't you suggest that in Killane?" Irving demanded coldly.

"Oh, no, Irv. That was a dismal hole. Not a decent-looking joint in the whole dump."

Irving had been rather taken by Killane, a mysterious little port, silent as death, not a human to be seen in the whole length of its immensely wide main street leading down to a couple of apparently disused warehouses. If he had not been so anxious to press on, he would have liked to investigate it further. But, like some migrating bird, he was feverishly anxious to continue, to keep moving, not to rest for a moment on the road, to reach the point where the land came to an abrupt stop.

"Well, there's plainly not much chance of finding a bed round *here*," he said.

Charley was driving and they were in the process of traversing an immense tract of brown peat-bog, from which the top layer had been

cut out at intervals in black strips and piled up in black heaps—a deso-
late, gloomy stretch of country.

"What do they *want* with all that peat?" Charley wondered.

Another hour's driving brought them at length to a melancholy,
strung-out, scattered village called Ballybaha: slate-roofed, one-storey
houses behind fuchsia hedges, at long distances apart, with an occasional
view of the ocean behind tufted sand-dunes in the distance.

"Who'd want to live here?" demanded Charley in disgust. "Why
aren't there any pretty villages like we saw in England? Thatch? Tudor
cottages?"

"The Irish were too poor," Irving pointed out. "They were living in
mud huts when the English were building those Tudor cottages—and
the Irish were paying them taxes. The only peasant artifacts left over
from those times—the only things that didn't get worn out with constant use—are the things that fell into bogs."

Bogs! he suddenly thought. Why didn't they occur to me? But the
summer had been a cold, unusually dry one; the bogs they crossed
seemed baked into a substance like dark fruitcake. Besides, a bog is too
indefinite, its embrace is incomplete; what it takes it may give back
again. Whereas ahead, on ahead . . .

"There's a bed-and-breakfast place!" said Charley in triumph.

"Well? Will it do for you?" Irving coldly inquired.

"Oh, sure. Anything will do for *me,* you know that, Irv." Charley's
placid humor was unimpaired. He ran the car off the road onto an earth
patch in front of the largish bungalow whose sign announced INISHKEEN
GUESTHOUSE. SELECT BED AND BREAKFAST. HOLIDAY ACCOMMODATION.

"*Select*—whatever can they mean by that, Bimbo?"

"Suitable for distinguished strangers such as ourselves. Give us the
key and I'll get out the bags."

But Charley insisted on doing that—as he always did. Watching him,
stooped, red-faced, with his head under the boot lid, Irving had a wild
wish to leap back into the car and drive off, leaving him stranded in
Ballybaha.

The quiet, genteel, sad lady who ran the Inishkeen Guesthouse received them without comment, and promised a meal at seven. "Till
then, if ye should wish for a drink, they'll be glad to accommodate ye at
the Anglers' Arms."

Accordingly, since the guesthouse bedroom was tiny and the lounge dismal, the two travelers later strolled along the usual wide, empty, dusty street to a dour-looking establishment by the crossroads in the middle of the village. On their way they were startled to observe, not far from the customary grey fragment of ecclesiastical ruin, a shatteringly avant-garde contemporary structure, apparently the modern church replacing the ruin. It was hexagonal in shape, low, presumably to hug the windswept ground, but with a curiously peaked and angled roof made of pink slate. It had narrow slit windows, like those of a frontier-post, and a short prong in the middle of the roof.

Like an aerial, Irving thought, to get in touch with the upper regions.

Charley said predictably, "Hey, man, what a crazy building! Is that a *church?* Looks like those folded paper boats we used to make as kids—know what I mean?"

Irving did know, but said, "I never played with paper boats."

"Want to go have a look-see?"

"I'd sooner have a drink. It would be too dark to see much, anyway."

"Okay, Bimbo—you're right, as usual."

At such an early hour, they were the only drinkers in the bar and had all the white-haired landlord's friendly attention. Thomas Roche, his name was, he told them, and happy he was indeed to meet travellers from the other side of the Atlantic. To be sure, his own brother was in Boston and his cousin in Cleveland but he himself hadn't crossed the water, and what could he be bringing them? Charley, only an occasional drinker—he usually stuck to Coke—chose sherry, which looked appalling. Irving had whisky. Its fine dryness put heart into him, and he politely congratulated the landlord on the remarkable modern church, so unusual for such a small community. To their surprise, Mr. Roche's face darkened.

"Well ye may say it is a remarkable building, and the heart's blood of the whole village draining away into it, year after year!"

He was evidently bursting to talk about it, and a few questions brought out the whole story: how when the old church finally collapsed in a winter gale five years ago the priest, Father Hegarty, fetched down an architect all the way of the road from Dublin give them an estimate—the architect was a friend of his, d'ye see?—and how this fine fellow, with a tongue as long as his yard-measure, managed to throw a spell over the whole congregation so that they believed him when he said that for twenty thousand he could build them the finest church in the west of Ireland. "Twenty thousand! Long will his soul weep in purgatory for that lie! Faith, you'd think they were all bewitched that believed him!"

"How many inhabitants in the village?"

"Three hundred, if that."

"So what happened?"

"So his lordship the Bishop accepted the plan and the work went forward. A grand job they were doing! Only it took three years longer than was estimated, and cost five times as much. And the troubles that ensued in the course of the building ye'd never credit! Twice the steeple fell down, till they were under the necessity of settling for the thing you see. Three times the foundations sank under them. Glory be, and them wondering if the church would ever be finished before Judgment Day! And when at last finished it was, what do you think? They found Father Hegarty's fine friend had forgotten to install any heating, so it all had to be pulled apart again."

"Is it really finished now?" asked Irving.

" 'Tis, 'tis, for what it's worth. And it barely sufficient in size now for all the summer visitors, and in wintertime the tremendous noise of clangs and rumblings made by the costly heating-system will often be drowning out Father Hegarty's voice—and yet for all of that, more often than not you can freeze half out of your skin before Mass is finished. And as for paying off the great debt that it has incurred on the village, we shall be waiting to do that until our children's children are bringing home their wages, and isn't that an iniquitous thing? What a burden to lay on the poor people!"

Mr. Roche's eyes flashed angrily. The two Americans began to understand that if Father Hegarty constituted the chief spiritual power in the village, Mr. Roche the innkeeper was his main temporal opponent. He went on, talking faster and faster, to tell them how the money was dragged out of the villagers in dribs and drabs for the church fund, how if this one sold a load of hay, or that one got a good price for a few fish, Father Hegarty would be round in a flash to demand an extra contribution. " 'Tis an imposition, so it is, are ye not in agreement with me?"

Irving, who had begun to be bored by the topic some time back, said smoothly that indeed it did seem a great waste, but he believed they must be going back to the guesthouse now, for Mrs. Kelleher would have their supper waiting.

"Come back after, and I'll be telling ye more."

God forbid, Irving thought. He explained that they had to make up for a sleepless night, and they escaped. Charley, surprisingly, looked a little mulish.

"You didn't *want* to stay and hear him ranting on about the wrongs of the parishioners?" Irving asked when they were out in the wide, empty road.

"It was interesting. Those conniving monsters of priests really screw the people," Charley grumbled. "They have it all their own way—"

He pursued this theme all the way back to the guesthouse. Irving, with his chin on his chest and hands thrust into his pockets, paid little heed. Soon, now, he was thinking. And his mind expanded to embrace the image of the cliffs ahead, the Cliffs of Scath, where the land comes to a sudden stop, as if sheared off by a guillotine. Nine hundred feet of vertical black rock. The Great Wall of Thomond. That is the place. To-morrow. Enough of this.

That night he slept uneasily, tossing from side to side in the narrow chilly bed; Charley, across the room, snored peacefully on his back, clenched fists flung above his head like a baby. Such rest as Irving had was broken by dreams: he was struggling to build a great stone tower, but lumps of rock kept coming loose in the gale that was blowing and thundered down menacingly around him. Then the whole tower began to sway from side to side overhead. He managed to wake himself just in time before the unstable structure fell and crushed him. Awake, he found that a real gale had blown up. How would that affect his intentions? All to the good, he decided vaguely—nobody goes sightseeing in a gale. And he fell at last into a heavy sleep.

When he woke he found Charley already up, shaving and whistling to himself. This habit of tuneless whistling, half under his breath, usually flung Irving into a frenzy of irritation, but today he was able to bear it, thinking: the last time.

After they had breakfasted and paid their bill, Charley insisted on walking along to inspect the new church.

"What's the point of that? You *know* all about it already." Irving was in a fever of impatience to be off.

"After all he said, I'd like to *see* it, Irv. Hell, you're always saying why don't I take an interest in things?"

"Interest in things that *matter*, for pete's sake!"

"Well, this matters to me," Charley said doggedly. Reluctantly, Irving accompanied him. By now the gale had blown out. Wet leaves, fuchsia twigs, and wisps of hay littered the ground; a heavy damp mist lay in the air. We shan't be able to see the Aran Isles, Irving thought regretfully.

In front of the church, they discovered a tall, black-robed figure, sweeping up the storm's debris from the cobbled approach path. This must be the wicked Father Hegarty, Irving thought, the despoiler of the people. It will be interesting to see how Charley deals with him.

Straightening from his task, the priest gave them an assessing glance and a polite smile. He was a strongly built man—in his forties perhaps —with a bland unreadable face and a pair of shrewd grey eyes, rather small, set close to his nose. He seemed very much at ease with himself, and who'd wonder, Irving thought. Look what he has achieved. It would be interesting to know, though, what official process brought him here; he looks such a capable man, wasted in this tiny parish. Don't they send priests to such remote spots for disciplinary reasons?

"Good morning, Father," he said. "We were impressed by your church last night and thought we'd like to take a closer look in daylight."

"You are welcome, the both of you." His eye swept over them.

What did he make of two such ill-assorted friends? Fidgety under the priest's intent scrutiny, Irving was glad to move inside the church and observe its expected banalities: the mock-Byzantine mosaics, angular Stations of the Cross, gaudy abstract window-glass, the jazzy geometric chandeliers, the concrete crucifix with its caricature of a Christ. There was a shrill, self-conscious air about the whole interior, he thought, like a girl with her first lipstick and cigarette, hoping to shock her mother.

And there was something else, too. Something out of proportion. Something strange, mocking, *wrong* . . .

Charley, needless to say, seemed highly impressed by it. Prowling about, looking at everything.

"Wow!" he muttered. "They sure got their money's worth, even if they did have to pay through the nose for it."

"It's a dreary, phony mess. And worse. There's something the matter with it. Let's get out of here."

Irving strode toward the door without attempting to conceal the disgust the place aroused in him. Regrettably, at this moment, the priest came in and, after saluting the altar, asked what they thought of the building.

"Very striking," Irving said. Father Hegarty gave him a quick glance.

Charley burst out, "It's a great building, sir—I'll say that for it! Only, be honest now—was it really worth squeezing all the dough out of those poor people for? Wouldn't a plain wooden drill-hall have done just as well, and then the kids could use it on wet days for volleyball or something?"

Irving wished he had been close enough to give Charley a kick. But the priest was not in the least offended. Evidently quite accustomed to this criticism, he remained perfectly amiable and bland in the discussion that followed, while Charley became more and more impassioned. Irving, refusing to become involved, stood aside, smiling faintly with his brows raised, while Charley, as might have been expected, soon found himself driven into a corner by Father Hegarty's trained powers of disputation.

"After all, what else would the people be spending their money on? Is it not best to devote your wealth to the glory of God?"

There was something ironic about his smile.

"A few comforts—diversions—in this back-of-beyond spot," Charley muttered.

"And fifty years from now, what would remain of those same comforts and pleasures? Who will remember that Mrs. O'Brien once had a TV set? But this church will endure from generation to generation."

Will it? Irving wondered skeptically.

"Do you not think the builders of Chartres, of Burgos, of St. Peter's, gave up a few comforts and pleasures in their day—and were justified by the result?"

"Oh, come on, Father, you can hardly compare—" Irving unwisely put in, and received such a razor-keen sideways glance from the small grey eyes that he fell silent. *And what in heaven's name was that little thing on the priest's watchchain?*

Father Hegarty said smoothly, "We can only do our best and hope it will meet the approval of future generations. And of our Lord. But now, tell me about yourselves. I can see at once what you are—" He allowed a fractionary pause and added, "You have the air of academics, am I not right?"

"Oh, sure, my pal's a professor," Charley said, again eager as a friendly dog. "He's going to teach for a year at Dublin College—"

"Is that so now? From Chicago University? And ye'll be spending a year in Dublin? Aren't you the lucky pair? And Professor St. John—" Father Hegarty pronounced it Sinjun "—will be searching for records of his forebears. That's very interesting. So we may hope to see more of you in these parts?"

"Possibly," said Irving, forming a private resolve that he personally would never again set foot in the village of Ballybaha. Something in Father Hegarty's questions made him profoundly uncomfortable: a touch of slightly patronizing amusement, as if the priest were saying, "Don't think for a moment you can fool me—I have you taped."

But I have you taped, too, Irving thought.

"And now you must sign our visitors' book."

Charley immediately wrote his name and tucked a pound into the offertory box. Irving managed to avoid doing so, as Charley remarked naïvely, "You weren't offended by the argument, sir?"

"Indeed, no! It's always a pleasure to talk to visitors—though little enough time I have for it. And where are you off to now, may I ask?"

"Oh, we're going to Lismaley," Charley said. "But first Irv here wants to take in the Cliffs of Scath. Not me! I've no head for heights."

"Is that so? Well, I hope the visibility improves for you. The cliffs can be a grand sight. Now I must be off with myself—I've twenty or more calls to make. I cover as much as fifty miles in a day—"

He had walked them to the gate and nodded a courteous goodbye as he mounted his bicycle, which had been leaning against the churchyard wall, and rode away.

"Quite an okay guy, really, wasn't he?" Charley remarked.

Irving said coldly, "It's my opinion that he's a warlock."

"Always kidding, Irv." Charley guffawed and slapped his friend's shoulder.

Driving north along the coast, as the sea-mist came and went, they began from time to time to get glimpses of their objective. From the height of a headland, the panoramic vista of the curved coast ahead was interrupted by a thick black bar across the horizon abruptly cut off in the middle, like an arm ending in a clenched fist. A black arm.

"Good grief," Charley muttered, peering ahead. "And that's a *cliff*? How far is it now?"

"Oh, twenty miles maybe."

"Do we really have to go there, Irv? I never was too keen on the Empire State Building—"

"Certainly we have to go. Those cliffs are one of the outstanding features of the whole country."

"Well, okay. Hey," Charley said, reverting to a more cheerful topic, "that priest really wasn't a bad guy, was he? He didn't get mad because I disagreed with him."

"It's his job not to. Besides, he wanted your money. It wasn't in his interest to antagonize you."

"Yeah, I guess," Charley said slowly. "To him we were rich Yanks. He seemed to know all about professors' salaries in American universities, didn't he? D'you think he really has a cousin at Chicago University?"

"Oh, very likely. Irish families are huge."

"You should have given him a donation, Irv."

"Why? I'm not obliged to subscribe to his meretricious church."

"If you think it's got merit, why not subscribe?"

"*Meretricious*, Charley, means phony."

"Oh, really?"

Irving did not trouble to voice his real feelings about the building and its use.

Road signs in Gothic now began directing them to the Cliffs of Scath.

"I wonder what Scath means?" said Charley idly.

"She was the Queen of Darkness," Irving briefly replied.

Another half hour's driving brought them to the official car-park for the cliffs. It was, as Irving had hoped, empty; the weather had turned wet, and in any case the holiday season was over. The seaward end of the car park lay quite close to the edge of the cliff. An arrow indicated the gift-shop but Irving was pleased to see a sign had been pasted over it which said, "Closed for the winter."

"What say we have lunch before we look at the cliff?" Charley said. He was sweating slightly.

He ran a hand up over his smooth shiny forehead. "You know how I feel about high drops, Bimbo—I guess I could take it better on a hard-boiled egg."

"Hell, Charley! We wasted such a lot of time already cashing checks in that wretched little bank—"

"Please, Irv."

"All right."

At least, Irving thought, it would be for the last time.

The mist was too thick, damp, and cold for lunching on the grass. They sat uncomfortably in the car, munching the hard-boiled eggs and sodabread Mrs. Kelleher had put up for them. Irving's raging impatience nearly choked him. At any minute somebody might arrive and spoil his chance. Though in this weather it was not too probable.

For dessert Charley produced a couple of chocolate bars he had bought in the village—he had a childlike fondness for sweet things.

"Want a bite, Irv? No? Sure?"

He had bought a Madeira cake, too, and hacked at it with a plastic knife purloined from the ferry cafeteria, grumbling, as he had all the way across Ireland, "Why in God's name, Irv, didn't you remind me to bring my Swiss army knife? That's what we need. This thing's no damn good."

That's another thing I shan't have to hear again, Irving thought detachedly.

He glanced down at the zigzags of the empty road leading up to the car park and said, "Come on, Charley—I think the mist's lifting a bit. We'll be able to see the Aran Islands in a minute. Put that stuff in the trunk and let's go."

Charley, rather slowly, rather reluctantly, packed the remains of the meal together into the plastic bag, walked round to the rear of the car, and raised the lid of the luggage compartment.

"Stick it well in between the bags," Irving said. "I can't stand loose milk bottles rolling around in the back while I'm driving."

He judged his moment carefully, as Charley began to withdraw his head and shoulders after obeying this order, and brought the trunk lid crashing down with all his force, so that the sharp edge took Charley exactly on the dome of his head, splitting it as if it had been one of the hard-boiled eggs they had just eaten.

Irving had ready a large polythene bag. With a quick glance round—

still no car in view or audible—he slipped the bag over Charley's head and then, hoisting the body with difficulty—not far to take it, thank goodness—staggered to where the cliff-edge was barricaded off by a rampart of earth, reinforced all along by massive rock paving-slabs, set upright against it. Rolling Charley over this parapet was not too hard. In one spot it was only about three feet high—he had marked the best point while they were eating lunch. From there to the real brink was only the width of a narrow sheep track.

He thrust the body over and saw it recede to what seemed an infinite depth before it passed the curve of the cliff to vanish completely. The black, silky sea, visible from moment to moment in the mist, lay so far below that no sound, no splash, came back to him—even the sound of the waves was audible up here only as the faintest sigh.

Briskly, Irving dusted his hands on a clump of sea-thrift, stepped back over the earth-and-rock rampart, and walked across to the rented car. A wipe with a tissue and the boot lid—beaded over already with raindrops—showed no trace. The tissue could be burned later. What about Charley's bag? Should that follow its owner over the cliff? No, he decided; he would think of some other way to dispose of it.

He shut down the lid and, turning, was badly discomposed to see the black-robed figure of Father Hegarty walking slowly up the last section of the hill, wheeling his bicycle.

"Quite a stiff climb, that," the priest remarked, nodding backward toward the road behind him.

"Surely your pastoral visits don't bring you up here, Father?" Irving said, unsticking his tongue from the roof of his mouth. Where the *devil* had the man sprung from, so suddenly? Had he been concealed by one of the bends in the road? And what—if anything—could he have seen?

"No. But I have a couple of parishioners living not far inland from here. Once in a way I take a notion to come by and wonder at God's handiwork in this mighty place. Your visit put it in my mind to do so. Did it ever occur to you, I wonder now, to ask yourself where the rest of the cliff went?"

Irving echoed stupidly, "The rest of the cliff?"

"We see this great broken edge—like a sliced loaf. What did God do with the other half?"

"Could the Aran Islands be the bit that fell off?" Irving suggested vaguely, glancing out to sea. But the mist had thickened again—no islands were visible.

"And—speaking of the other half—where is your young friend? Not over the cliff, I trust?" Father Hegarty said playfully.

"Oh—" Irving had had time to take breath now, and felt calmer. "We decided to go different ways. He caught a bus."

"Is that so, now?" Father Hegarty's slow words and cold glance were like a bowlful of icy sea mist between the shoulderblades. The priest added with seeming irrelevance, "Since I am so lucky as to meet you again, might I mention that, back there in the church, you perhaps forgot to give us a donation for our church fund? Your young friend was so generous that I am sure it was nothing more than forgetfulness on your part—"

"Oh, right—I believe I did forget. Sure—a couple of pounds. Naturally I'd be glad—"

Irving dug with wet, shaking hands in his back pocket.

"*Well*, now—I was thinking of something more in the nature of a regular subscription," Father Hegarty said gravely. "We won't trouble about the details at present—I'll be in touch with you later. You need not give me your Dublin address—I've a cousin in the English department at Trinity. I'll tell him to look you up. A fine young fellow he is—you'll take to him, I'm sure. Bless me! look at the time—I must be getting on with my visits."

And, throwing a leg over his bicycle, the priest rode off downhill, disappearing into the mist as silently as if he had flown away on black wings.

The Dream is Better

JULIAN SYMONS

I

Andrew Blood's Manuscript

I think of the misery of the past and the peace of the present. I think of the women who almost blasted my life, Jean and Olga, and then of Helen, who has brought me happiness.

In retrospect, the past seems to have been nothing but a series of defeats and humiliations. I know the need to put them down on paper. Helen is here today and sits on the other side of the room. I tell her of my intention and she approves with the serenity that is her nature. Jean and Olga were furious, frantic, and deceitful. I had thought that to be the nature of all women except my mother, but Helen has shown me otherwise. She brings to my mind Edgar Allan Poe's lines:

> "Helen, thy beauty is to me
> Like those Nicean barks of yore,
> That gently, o'er a perfumed sea,
> The weary, wayworn wanderer bore
> To his own native shore."

With Helen I am at peace. It is not my fault that such peace has been reached through travail and through blood. The last may be thought appropriate, since my name is Andrew John Blood.

My father was an inspector in the revenue service, what is sometimes called an income-tax collector, although of course he did not collect taxes in person but was responsible only for assessing the sums owing and sending out the necessary notices. The occupation is respectable but not popular, and boys at school would jeer at me because of it. The combination of my surname and my father's occupation led them to call me bloodsucker.

"Watch out, don't let him get near you, he'll suck your blood!" they would cry. "My dad says it's what his dad does for a living!" They would go on to make sucking noises, so that often I ran home in tears. My mother comforted me and said that they were only teasing.

It would have been useless to speak to my father. He had only two interests in life, his work and his stamp collection. He was especially concerned with Nineteenth Century stamps of Chile, Peru, and Ecuador, and engaged in long correspondence about them. Once, when I was making a drawing, I knocked over the India ink I was using and ruined several pages of stamps. He showed no outward anger but afterwards had as little to do with me as possible. I have affections—yes, indeed I have affections, and of the purest kind—but I could feel no emotion when he stepped absentmindedly off the pavement one day (his mind perhaps on some Peruvian stamp issue), was knocked over by a lorry and instantly killed. After the funeral my mother said that I must be the man of the house and look after her now. I was thirteen years old.

What can I say about Mother? Her photograph, in an old-fashioned silver frame, is on the table at which I write. Her head is a little to one side, and she has the wistful and apologetic expression that I remember so well. Looking at the photograph, I see that she was a pretty woman. I was always said to look like her and be a pretty child, but this never occurred to me at the time, I suppose because for years I was so close to her.

I was an only child and she fussed over me, making sure that I always had clean linen, cooking and washing up, keeping my bedroom tidy and making the bed. Even when I got my first job as an apprentice draughtsman in a big engineering firm (I had always been good at making neat accurate drawings), I never had to dry a plate or a dish, and never hung up a jacket or put away a pair of shoes. My mother had said that I must look after her, but what she meant was that with my father gone she would have more time to look after me. We were constant companions and needed nobody else.

We lived in a small town in the southeast of England. Our house was about forty years old, with a bow window in front, a living room, dining room, and three bedrooms. It was a replica of the others in the road, for they had all been built at the same time. Here I lived for the first thirty years of my life.

Looking back on that time, which seems very long ago, I cannot say I was unhappy. I enjoyed my work in the drawing office of my firm. I bought a small car and used it to take Mother for a spin in the country and dinner at a little country inn, or to go with her to the town repertory theatre. She was fond of a good play.

Occasionally, late at night in my room, I wrote poems about girls, visionary girls who were an ideal for me as they were for Poe. In no way did they resemble the coarse creatures I met at the office, with their constant giggling and their vulgar jokes. Such girls were no worse than the men, but I expected that they would be better.

I was twenty-seven years of age when I met Jean.

My mother liked to go to the Conservative Party bazaar. This was held during the summer, in the grounds of Ampleton House, home of Lord and Lady Ampleton. The stalls were erected on the big central lawn, but there were tree-lined avenues on either side, down which one could walk, with little paths off them that led to cunningly created arbors and small waterfalls.

It was an enchanting place. Of course, Mother expected me to accompany her but, once arrived, she soon found people she knew and on this occasion immediately met Mrs. Wilson, the Party secretary. I knew that she was occupied for at least half an hour, so that I was free to wander. I walked down one of the avenues, and then stood still at the vision I saw at the other end of it.

The avenue sloped upwards and the girl I saw was at the top of the slope, so that she was outlined against the blue sky. Her figure was slim and elegant, her bright golden hair was shoulder length, and her distant profile—for she was turned away from me—looked exquisitely delicate. I made no approach to her, for at that moment all I wanted was to keep this perfection in my memory. But she began to move towards me and to my surprise smiled and waved a hand. When we were a yard or two apart, she spoke to me by name and told me that she was Jean Merton.

She laughed, a low musical sound. "You won't know me but I've heard a lot about you. I'm Mrs. Wilson's niece."

When seen so close she lacked the perfection of beauty I had imagined from a distance, but there was a charm and eagerness about her that overwhelmed me. Her eyes danced with pleasure and she said out-right how delighted she was to meet me.

"Aunt Wilson would bring me along, though I knew it would be an awful drag. But now it's different. Come and help me buy jam and honey—I said I'd take some back. And I've got to get a bit of something or other for my younger sister, Nancy. She likes bright and gaudy bits of jewelry." She took my hand as though that was the most natural thing in the world, and it seemed natural to me also.

We bought half a dozen things at the fair, including a one-eyed ele-phant Jean said she must have because he looked so pathetic, and by the time we found Mrs. Wilson and my mother I knew I was in love. If you think that is ridiculous you fail to understand the spell that may be cast by beauty. I had learned various facts about Jean—that she had some sort of secretarial job, was four years younger than me, and so on—but they were unimportant. She was the most beautiful person I had ever seen, and I wanted to be with her always.

I said something of this to my mother when we returned home. She listened with a smile that changed to a frown. When I had done, she said, "Andrew, you are twenty-seven years old. How many girls have you taken out?"

"None. There was nobody I liked."

"Your father died before telling you things you should have known. And then, perhaps I have been selfish. I had hoped we would always be together until—" Her voice faltered. I told her that of course I would never leave her, but she continued.

"You are an unworldly boy, a dreamer. That has always been so, and I would not wish you different. From what I hear, I am not sure that Jean Merton is the right girl for you. Perhaps there is no right girl. You may find that girls are not like your dreams, that always the dream is better."

I hardly listened. I had already arranged to take Jean to a concert the following evening.

In the following days I took Jean to the concert, to a traveling art exhibition that had come to our Town Hall, and to the cinema—a film with Woody Allen she wanted to see. After the film we went to dinner at the Venezia, which was said to be the best restaurant in town. I cannot remember what we ate and drank. There remains in my mind only the vision of her on the other side of the table, her laugh, her flickering fingers as she made a point about the film, her hair shining gold, whether in daylight at the art exhibition or in the subdued light of the Venezia.

Her family home was a little way outside town. She did not live there but in a small block of flats near the town center. When I took her back that night she invited me in, saying that she had a bottle of cognac. I said that I had drunk both a glass of sherry and some wine.

"Don't be so stuffy, Andrew. Come up anyway."

The apartment was small, a bed-sitting room, kitchenette and bath. She poured the brandy, then came and sat beside me.

"Andrew."

"Yes?"

"You like me, don't you? If you like me, kiss me." I put an arm round her and our lips met, hers pressed against mine.

"I shall begin to think you don't like me," she murmured, and the words seemed to break the bond that had kept me almost silent. I said that liking was not the word, that for me she was a thing of beauty, and that beautiful things should be worshipped. She ran a hand through my hair and said that I was a funny boy, she'd never met anybody like me.

I drove home that night in a daze. On the following night I asked Jean to marry me.

We had spent part of the evening in the lounge bar of the County Hotel. Jean liked sitting in pubs and bars, saying that they had a wonderful atmosphere. She was fond of a drink called a whiskey sour, which looked pleasant but seemed to me to have a curious taste. I thought that she both drank and smoked too much.

That night she seemed nervous, lighting cigarettes and putting them out half-smoked. I asked what was the matter and she said that her work was boring—sometimes she felt she couldn't face it for another day.

At that I spoke. The words came out of their own volition. "Why not give it up?"

"What do you mean?"

"Give it up. Marry me."

I put down the pen now and visualize the scene clearly—a scene utterly remote from this little room. The bar was dim, with purple-shaded wall lights. Canned music played softly. Jean's features were slightly blurred, in a way that enhanced her beauty. Her gaze looked beyond me, as though she saw our future together. She said nothing, and I was content to let the moment rest.

Then a man's voice spoke from behind my left ear "Who's this?" it said.

"Jerry," Jean said. "Jerry Wilson, this is Andrew Blood. Andrew has just asked me to marry him." The man gave a kind of snort. "And I've said yes," she told him.

"Don't be bloody stupid." The man took his hands out of his pockets. They were large and covered with hair, like a monkey's. He used obscene words to her, words I shall not write down, and was gone.

I should have known the truth then, although I could not have imagined all of it. Jean said that the man was somebody she used to know and that he was really rather awful. She also said again that she would marry me.

"You are making a mistake," my mother said when I told her. "I don't say that only because I shall miss you. She is not Miss Right. I could tell you things I have heard—"

I refused to listen to them.

We went together to buy the engagement ring, a simple circle of diamonds. I met her father and mother. He was a farmer and evidently well-to-do. They were polite to me, but seemed to greet the news with some reserve, which was a matter of indifference to me.

I have never cared for other people or felt the need of friends, having always been content with life at home, but I told my colleagues in the drawing office. There were congratulations, mixed with the kind of jokes I dislike, although I endured them. The department manager called me in, congratulated me, said that they were pleased with my work and that my salary would be raised. He said also that he and the rest of them hoped to meet my future wife. I made some reply, I don't know what. I had no wish that Jean should meet any of them. My private life had nothing to do with my work.

The engagement was announced in the local paper. I saw Jean most evenings and she often came to lunch on Sunday. Mother was an excellent cook, took special pains with these lunches, and was polite to Jean, but I could see it was all on the surface.

Jean said more than once that Mother didn't like her.

"She doesn't want to lose her pretty baby boy. And she thinks I smoke too much—I can see her counting the number of cigarettes each time I light one." Of course I said that wasn't true, although I knew there was something in it. "And she expects to be paid compliments every time she cooks a meal. I can cook, you know. I'll make dinner for us tomorrow night."

And she did. Each of the courses was from a recipe originated by a great chef and had some complicated sauce or dressing. I really preferred Mother's simpler cooking, but of course I said everything was wonderful. Afterwards we sat on the sofa. I kissed her, and within a few moments she made a suggestion to me which, again, I shall not write down, accompanying it with physical actions. I said as gently as possible that I did not care for or approve that kind of thing, certainly not until we were married.

She lay back and stared at me. I could see that she was angry, but anger made her more beautiful than ever. She said I had better go home, and I left her.

I heard nothing from her after that. I telephoned her office and was told that she was on a week's holiday. I rang the flat but there was no reply.

When the week had passed, she called and said that she would like to see me. The place was the lounge of the County Hotel, where I had proposed to her. When I arrived she was already there, a whisky sour in front of her. She pushed a little box across to me.

"One ring, returned," she said. "Engagement finished."

I stared at her unbelievingly.

"It was a mistake. I should never have said yes. You want to know why I did? You'll hardly believe it in these days of the pill—or perhaps you've never heard of the pill, I'd forgotten what you're like—but Jerry had got me pregnant. He didn't want the kid and I did, or I thought so. So when you turned up I said yes. I was going to try to make you believe the kid was yours, but there wasn't much chance of that, was there? I don't think I could have gone through with it anyway, but it doesn't matter now. I had an abortion. Jerry and I are getting married."

I took the ring and looked at it wonderingly. I could feel tears forming in my eyes, tears not of self-pity but of regret at losing so much beauty. Jean finished her drink.

"It would never have done, and you must know that. I like the way you look, but you don't really need anyone but your mother."

That was the end of it. I told Mother that the engagement was broken. She said that she was pleased for my sake and with her wonderful discretion never uttered another word about it. I sold the ring back for half what I paid for it. There were jokes at the office, but I ignored them and after a while they stopped. I have said already that I had no close friends.

Mother and I settled down to our old life together. She said sometimes that Miss Right would come along one day, although she hoped it would be after she had gone. Sometimes she added that this might not be long. I told her not to talk like that and paid no attention to what she said.

Then one day, nearly two years after the parting from Jean, I came home and found Mother dead. It seemed that she had a heart condition of which she had never told me. She had gone upstairs to lie down in the afternoon, as she often did, and had passed out of life without pain.

I was stunned. In the days and weeks that followed I realized how much I had depended upon her for everything. I knew I must change my life. I sold the house, got rid of the furniture and most of Mother's possessions, although I could not bring myself to dispose of some things, like her jewelry. That was a terrible time and I cannot write more about it.

The doctor was concerned for me and said that I should go away to recover from the shock. I did so, and found Helen. Again, I shall not write about this. When I returned I bought an apartment and lived there contentedly. Through Helen I have learned to cook, to wash and iron clothes, and through her the flat is kept in a way that would have made Mother proud. I never spoke of her to the people I worked with, feeling it was better so.

So passed weeks, and months. I have made what happened sound sudden but it was gradual. I recovered from the shocks of Jean's betrayal and Mother's death, like somebody slowly emerging from severe illness who becomes a little stronger each day. With Helen's help I recovered my serenity so that the past was wiped out as though it had never been.

And then Olga entered my life—Olga from central Europe, Olga Kreisky.

Olga's parents had been refugees who came to this country just before the war, and although she was born in England she spoke with a distinct foreign accent. She had some architectural training and came to the office as a draughtsman. She was a large woman, large in a way that people call motherly, although my mother had been fine-boned and delicate, as I am.

Olga was, I suppose, about my own age, although because of her size she seemed to me older. I do not know why she should have taken an interest in me, but she did so from the beginning. She would sit at the same table with me in the canteen and would say that I did not eat enough, I should have ordered the batter pudding or the macaroni and cheese. I would reply that I was not hungry and in any case did not care for starchy foods.

"But you are so thin, And-rew"—almost from the start she called me Andrew, dwelling lovingly on the name. "You should put flesh on your bones. It is because you cook for yourself, that is not good. A man on his own never eats properly."

She told me she lived with her sister, who would be getting married soon. "Then I am on my own too, but never fear, I shall go on making my soups and puddings, and my schnitzels. You must come round, And-rew, and I cook for you my special wiener schnitzel. You will not feel hungry afterwards, I can tell you." She laughed heartily and her plump cheeks wobbled.

Mother taught me always to be polite and I hope I have not forgotten my manners. I said I had a poor digestion and must be very careful. She said she knew of many special health foods and she could prepare those too. I stopped using the canteen, but it did not free me from her. She would come over to my drawing board to see what I was working on and, leaning over so that I felt the pressure of her bosom, praise my skill and neatness.

She made sure that she left the office when I did, and at first I made the foolish mistake of giving her a lift in my car, with the result that I was invited indoors to meet her sister. She introduced me as "My dear friend And-rew" and her sister Nadia said she had heard much about me. How could she have done when there was nothing to hear? I stopped driving to work in the car.

Olga wanted to see my flat, saying she was sure it needed a woman's touch. I avoided giving her the address. I knew it would be disastrous for her to meet Helen. I had to endure a great deal of what I believe is called "ribbing" about Olga at the office. I said nothing, I showed my supreme indifference, both to the dolts surrounding me and to Olga, but Olga's skin was hippopotamus-thick. She began to bring pies and sandwiches to the office, insisting that we share them for lunch. I did not know how to refuse without rudeness. I nearly told her of Helen at home, who would prepare anything I wished, but refrained.

The strain on my nerves grew. I thought of changing my job, but feared that Olga might follow me elsewhere. Her round fat face, her huge udders, the whole bulk of her began to obsess me. I had nightmares in which the weight of her flesh bore me down, so that I wriggled unavailingly beneath her. Yet I could not have imagined the nightmare that happened.

I had returned from work at the usual time, looking forward to my evening at home with Helen. A steak and salad, cheese and coffee, then an hour or two in front of the television. When the bell rang, Helen answered it. That was a mistake, for outside stood Olga, her arms full of brown paper parcels. It was dark in the hall, so that at first she did not see she was speaking to Helen.

"And-rew, I have been a naughty girl. You will not tell me your address, it is not in the phonebook, but I get it from the accounts department. But you forgive me, And-rew, when you see what I have here for us to eat. There is smoked salmon and then a special Hungarian sausage with noodles—"

At that moment she realized she was talking to Helen. And she began to laugh.

Her laughter roused me to fury. If she had not laughed I might have told her just to go away. But she laughed, this fat European cow laughed at my Helen. I pulled her inside the door and then towards the kitchen. She dropped the groceries. Then we were in the kitchen. I took the knife with which I had been trimming the steak and plunged it into the fat creature who had insulted Helen.

I cannot say what else I did with the knife. I was sane before the action, I am perfectly sane now, but I admit that for those moments I was mad. Mad, but greatly provoked. I do not excuse my action, yet surely all must agree that I was greatly provoked. When it was over, and the screaming had stopped, I looked at the thing on the floor and saw blood, blood everywhere. I felt that this was something ordained, that I had fulfilled my name. There had been eggs among the groceries and they had broken, so that in one place the yellow egg yolks were mixed with the red blood. When the police came I was trying to clear up the mess on the kitchen floor.

Such are the events that brought me to this room. I have set them down at Dr. Glasser's suggestion, and should like to add that I am happy to have retired from the world and grateful for the opportunity to live here and to receive visits from Helen.

II
The Ironies of Dr. Glasser

Dr. Glasser's office was large and square. The walls were white and covered with framed certificates testifying to the doctor's psychiatric eminence. In person the doctor was tall, with an aquiline nose and a fine head of grey hair. There was something ironical in his gaze and in his manner, as though he found the world even more absurd than he had expected.

His visitor—small, tubby, with innocent eyes behind gold-rimmed spectacles—was named Johnson. He was a vice-president of the Mental Patients' Reform League. He put down the sheets of paper, which were written in a neat and elegant hand.

"Most interesting. And remarkably coherent, it seems to me."

"Yes, Andrew is perfectly coherent. It is a classic case, textbook material." Dr. Glasser steepled his fingers and looked up at the ceiling, as though he were lecturing. "The child is ignored by the father, attachment to the mother becomes total. Every woman met is seen not as a real person but in terms of the mother. Because of the incest taboo the sex act cannot be contemplated with any woman, they must all be remade in the mother's image. The experience with Jean was unfortunate, but it would have been much the same with any woman who desired sexual relations. For the reasons I have given, the sex act fills Andrew with horror."

Mr. Johnson moved uneasily. "I understand. But my point is—"

Dr. Glasser in flow was not easily checked. "He rejects it with violence. The injuries inflicted on poor Olga Kreisky were savage, far more than is indicated in the manuscript. There were mutilations."

"Very distressing. But all this was several years ago."

"Six years."

"As you know, the League's concern is that far too many patients are kept in homes, when they would be perfectly capable of leading normal lives. I understand Andrew still makes technical drawings."

"He does indeed. Very good ones."

"So that he is obviously capable of work. From his record, his behavior here has been exemplary. If he were let out on condition that he lives with this Helen, who I suppose might be called a mother-substitute, and to whom he is evidently devoted, would he be a danger to the community? But first, would you agree that Helen is a mother-substitute?"

The doctor turned his ironical gaze on Mr. Johnson. "I would."

"And would he be a danger to other people?"

"Perhaps not."

Mr. Johnson took off his glasses, polished them, and said earnestly, "Only perhaps? You agreed that his behavior has been exemplary."

"I did."

"Then why should he not be released?"

"Suppose somebody else insulted Helen?"

Mr. Johnson was taken aback. "Why should that happen? Helen has been remarkably faithful to him—she is clearly devoted. I understand from the document that she pays visits. Perhaps they might marry."

Dr. Glasser sighed. "Come along, Mr. Johnson. We will speak to this exemplary patient."

They left the room, took a lift, walked down a corridor, then down another at right angles to it. On either side were doors with names on them. The doors had keyholes but lacked handles. In a room between the corridors four male nurses sat playing cards. Little Mr. Johnson was uneasily conscious that they were all big men. The doctor spoke to one of them, who accompanied them. He opened one of the doors with a key from a bunch at his waist and said, "Andrew, here's Dr. Glasser to see you."

They entered a small sitting room, simply furnished. Several drawings were pinned up on the walls, some machinery, one of Dr. Glasser, and two of a woman Mr. Johnson supposed to be Helen. A man who sat reading in an armchair put down his book. He was small and had neat, almost doll-like features. "Good afternoon, Doctor."

"Andrew, this is Mr. Johnson from the Mental Patients' Reform League. He enjoyed your manuscript."

"Did you really? I'm so pleased." A smile touched the neat features. "It's all true, you know, every word. I was provoked, but I did very wrong. Just for the moment I went mad, although I am perfectly sane now, have been for years. Look at what I'm reading." He held up the book. "*Persuasion,* Jane Austen. I like to read about the past, it's so much more civilized than the present."

Mr. Johnson asked in his earnest way, "Supposing you were released, would you like that?" Andrew Blood considered, then nodded. "You would take a job, use your technical skills?" Another nod. "And live with Helen? Perhaps get married?"

A look of uncertainty, even alarm, touched the neat features. Andrew Blood looked questioningly at the doctor, who said softly, "If Helen is here, Andrew, we'd be delighted to meet her."

The uncertain look was replaced by a charming smile. Andrew jumped up and went to an inner room. The nurse began to say something, but was checked by Dr. Glasser. It was perhaps no more than two or three minutes, although it seemed longer to Mr. Johnson, before the figure appeared in the doorway.

It was small and wore a wig of grey hair, permanently waved. The face below it was that of Andrew Blood, but it had been powdered to a dead whiteness and lipstick crudely applied so that it looked like a clown's face. The figure wore an oatmeal-colored twin set with a rope of imitation pearls round the neck and high-heeled shoes. It came mincingly across the room, held out a ringed hand, and said in a falsetto voice, "How do you do?"

The figure was ludicrous in itself, but it was the words and the falsetto voice that broke Mr. Johnson's composure. He was unable to refrain from laughter. The sounds were loud in the little room, and although he put a hand over his mouth laughter continued to bubble up.

That was one moment. In the next he was on the floor, hands were tearing at his face and throat, a high voice was screaming abuse. His face had been badly scratched and his spectacles knocked off, although not broken, before the doctor and nurse managed to pull the figure off him.

Back in the office Dr. Glasser poured a tot of whiskey and apologized. "Forgive me for practising that little deceit. I should have told you that Andrew was Helen, but I thought visual evidence would be more convincing. Of course, I could not know that you would laugh. That was an insult to Helen, and Andrew was outraged by it, as he was when Olga Kreisky laughed."

"And Helen is—"

"Hardly Poe's Helen, as you will have gathered from her appearance. Helen was the name of Andrew's mother. She was the center of his life, and when she died he recreated her. Those were some of her old clothes. Andrew said in the manuscript that he could not bring himself to dispose of them. He is a small neat man, and they fit him reasonably well.

"I told you it was a classic case and so it is, not of transvestism but of personality transfer. It occurs only among those who cannot face the physical aspects of life. Mrs. Blood understood that when she told him there might be no right girl for him, that he would always be one of those for whom the dream is better."

✻　✻　✻

Behind the Locked Door

PETER LOVESEY

Sometimes when the shop was quiet Braid would look up at the ceiling and give a thought to the locked room overhead. He was mildly curious, no more. If the police had not taken an interest he would never have done anything about it.

The Inspector appeared one Wednesday soon after eleven, stepping in from Leadenhall Street with enough confidence about him to show he was no tourist. Neither was he in business; it is one of the City's most solemn conventions that between ten and four nobody is seen on the streets in a coat. This one was a brown imitation-leather coat, categorically not City at any hour.

Gaunt and pale, a band of black hair trained across his head to combat baldness, the Inspector stood back from the counter, not interested in buying cigarettes, waiting rather, one hand in a pocket of the coat, the other fingering his woolen tie, while the last genuine customer named his brand and took his change.

When the door was shut he came a step closer and told Braid, "I won't take up much of your time. Detective Inspector Gent, C.I.D." The hand that had been in the pocket now exhibited a card. "Routine inquiry. You are Frank Russell Braid, the proprietor of this shop?"

Braid nodded, and moistened his lips. He was perturbed at hearing his name articulated in full like that, as if he were in court. He had never been in trouble with the police, had never done a thing he was ashamed of. Twenty-seven years he had served the public loyally over this counter. He had not received a single complaint he could recollect, or made one. From the small turnover he achieved he had always paid whatever taxes the government imposed.

Some of his customers—bankers, brokers, accountants—made fortunes and talked openly of tax dodges. That was not Frank Braid's way.

He believed in fate. If it was decreed that he should one day be rich, it would happen. Meanwhile he would continue to retail cigarettes and tobacco honestly and without regret.

"I believe you also own the rooms upstairs, sir?"

"Yes."

"There is a tenant, I understand."

So Messiter had been up to something. Braid clicked his tongue, thankful that the suspicion was not directed his way, yet irritated at being taken in. From the beginning Messiter had made a good impression. The year of his tenancy had seemed to confirm it. An educated man, decently dressed, interesting to talk to, and completely reliable with the rent. This was a kick in the teeth.

"His name, sir?"

"Messiter." With deliberation Braid added, "Norman Henry Messiter."

"How long has Mr. Messiter been a lodger here?"

" 'Lodger' isn't the word. He uses the rooms as a business address. He lives in Putney. He started paying rent in September last year. That would be thirteen months, wouldn't it?"

It was obvious from the Inspector's face that this was familiar information. "Is he upstairs this morning, sir?"

"No. I don't see a lot of Mr. Messiter. He calls on Tuesdays and Fridays to collect the mail."

"Business correspondence?"

"I expect so. I don't examine it."

"But you know what line Mr. Messiter is in?" It might have been drugs from the way the Inspector put the question.

"He deals in postage stamps."

"It's a stamp shop upstairs?"

"No. It's all done by correspondence. This is simply the address he uses when he writes to other dealers."

"Odd," the Inspector commented. "I mean, going to the expense of renting rooms when he could just as easily carry on the business from home."

Braid would not be drawn. He would answer legitimate questions, but he was not going to volunteer opinions. He busied himself tearing open a carton of cigarettes.

"So it's purely for business?" the Inspector resumed. "Nothing happens up there?"

That started Braid's mind racing. Nothing *happens* . . . ? What did they suspect? Orgies? Blue films?

"It's an unfurnished flat," he said. "Kitchen, bathroom, and living room. It isn't used."

At that the Inspector rubbed his hands. "Good. In that case you can show me over the place without intruding on anyone's privacy."

It meant closing for a while, but most of his morning regulars had been in by then.

"Thirteen months ago you first met Mr. Messiter," the Inspector remarked on the stairs.

Strictly it was untrue. As it was not put as a question, Braid made no response.

"Handsome set of banisters, these, Mr. Braid. Individually carved, are they?"

"The building is at least two hundred years old," Braid told him, grateful for the distraction. "You wouldn't think so to look at it from Leadenhall Street. You see, the front has been modernized. I wouldn't mind an old-fashioned front if I were selling silk hats or umbrellas, but cigarettes—"

"Need a more contemporary display," the Inspector cut in as if he had heard enough. "Was it thirteen months ago you first met Mr. Messiter?"

Clearly this had some bearing on the police inquiry. It was no use prevaricating. "In point of fact, no. More like two years." As the Inspector's eyebrows peaked in interest, Braid launched into a rapid explanation. "It was purely in connection with the flat. He came in here one day and asked if it was available. Just like that, without even looking over the place. At the time I had a young French couple as tenants. I liked them and I had no intention of asking them to leave. Besides, I know the law. You can't do that sort of thing. I told Mr. Messiter. He said he liked the location so much that he would wait till they moved out, and to show good faith he was ready to pay the first month's rent as a deposit."

"Without even seeing inside?"

"It must seem difficult to credit, but that was how it was," said Braid. "I didn't take the deposit, of course. Candidly, I didn't expect to see him again. In my line of business you sometimes get people coming in off the street simply to make mischief. Well, the upshot was that he *did* come back—repeatedly. I must have seen the fellow once a fortnight for the next eleven months. I won't say I understood him any better, but at least I knew he was serious. So when the French people eventually went back to Marseilles, Mr. Messiter took over the flat." By now they were standing on the bare boards of the landing. "The accommodation is unfurnished," he said in explanation. "I don't know what you hope to find."

If Inspector Gent knew, he was not saying. He glanced through the open door of the bathroom. The place had the smell of disuse.

He reverted to his theme. "Strange behavior, waiting all that time for a flat he doesn't use." He stepped into the kitchen and tried a tap. Water the color of weak tea spattered out. "No furniture about," he went on. "You must have thought it was odd, his not bringing in furniture."

Braid made no comment. He was waiting by the door of the locked room. This, he knew, was where the interrogation would begin in earnest.

"What's this—the living room?" the Inspector asked. He came to Braid's side and tried the door. "Locked. May I have the key, Mr. Braid?"

"That isn't possible, I'm afraid. Mr. Messiter changed the lock. We—er—came to an agreement."

The Inspector seemed unsurprised. "Paid some more on the rent, did he? I wonder why." He knelt by the door. "Strong lock. Chubb mortice. No good trying to open that with a piece of wire. How did he justify it, Mr. Braid?"

"He said it was for security."

"It's secure, all right." Casually, the Inspector asked, "When did you last see Mr. Messiter?"

"Tuesday." Braid's stomach lurched. "You don't suspect he is—"

"Dead in there? No, sir. Messiter is alive, no doubt of that. Active, I would say." He grinned in a way Braid found disturbing. "But I wouldn't care to force this without a warrant. I'll be arranging that. I'll be back." He started downstairs.

"Wait," said Braid, going after him. "As the landlord, I think I have the right to know what you suspect is locked in that room."

"Nothing dangerous or detrimental to health, sir," the Inspector told him without turning his head. "That's all you need to know. You trusted

Messiter enough to let him install his own lock, so with respect you're in no position to complain about rights."

After the Inspector had left, Braid was glad he had not been stung into a response he regretted; but he was angry, and his anger refused to be subdued through the rest of the morning and afternoon. It veered between the Inspector, Messiter, and himself. He recognized now his mistake in agreeing to a new lock, but to be rebuked like a gullible idiot was unjust. Messiter's request had seemed innocent enough at the time.

Well, to be truthful, it had crossed Braid's mind that what was planned could be an occasional afternoon up there with a girl, but he had no objection to that if it was discreet. He was not narrow-minded. In its two centuries of existence the room must have seen some passion. But crime was quite another thing, not to be countenanced.

He had trusted Messiter, been impressed by his sincerity. The man had seemed genuinely enthusiastic about the flat, its old-world charm, the high corniced ceilings, the solid doors. To wait, as he had, nearly a year for the French people to leave had seemed a commitment, an assurance of good faith.

It was mean and despicable. Whatever was locked in that room had attracted the interest of the police. Messiter must have known this was a possibility when he took the rooms. He had cynically and deliberately put at risk the reputation of the shop. Customers were quick to pick up the taint of scandal. When this got into the papers, years of goodwill and painstaking service would go down the drain.

That afternoon, when Braid's eyes turned to the ceiling, he was not merely curious about the locked room. He was asking questions. Angry, urgent questions.

By six, when he closed, the thing had taken a grip on his mind. He had persuaded himself he had a right to know the extent of Messiter's deceit. Dammit, the room belonged to Braid. He would not sleep without knowing what was behind that locked door.

And he had thought of a way of doing it.

In the back was a wooden ladder about nine feet long. Years before, when the shop was a glover's, it had been used to reach the high shelves behind the counter. Modern shop design kept everything in easy reach. Where gloves had once been stacked in white boxes were displays of Marlboro country and the pure gold of Benson and Hedges. One morning in the summer he had taken the ladder outside the shop to investigate the working of the awning, which was jammed. Standing several rungs from the top he had been able to touch the ledge below the window of the locked room.

The evening exodus was over, consigning Leadenhall Street to surrealistic silence, when Braid propped the ladder against the shopfront. The black marble and dark-tinted glass of banks and insurance buildings glinted funereally in the streetlights, only the brighter windows of the Bull's Head at the Aldgate end indicating, as he began to climb, that life was there. If anyone chanced to pass that way and challenge him, he told himself, he would inform them with justification that the premises were his own and he was simply having trouble with a lock.

He stepped onto the ledge and drew himself level with the window, which was of the sash type. By using a screwdriver he succeeded in slipping aside the iron catch. The lower section was difficult to move, but once he had got it started it slid easily upward. He climbed inside and took out a flashlight.

The room was empty.

Literally empty. No furniture, no curtains, no carpet. Bare floorboards, ceiling, and walls with paper peeled away in several places.

Uncomprehending, he beamed the flashlight over the floorboards. They had not been disturbed in months. He examined the skirting board, the plaster cornice, and the window sill. He could not see how anything could be hidden here. The police were probably mistaken about Messiter. And so was he. With a sense of shame he climbed out of the window and drew it down.

On Friday, Messiter came in about eleven as usual, relaxed, indistinguishable in dress from the stockbrokers and bankers: dark suit, old boys' tie, shoes gleaming. With a smile he peeled a note from his wallet and bought his box of five Imperial Panatellas, a ritual that from the beginning had signaled goodwill toward his landlord. Braid sometimes wondered if he actually smoked them. He did not carry conviction as a smoker of cigars. He was a quiet man, functioning best in private conversations. Forty-seven by his own admission, he looked ten years younger, dark-haired with brown eyes that moistened when he spoke of things that moved him.

"Any letters for me, Mr. Braid?"

"Five or six." Braid took them from the shelf behind him.

"How is business?"

"No reason to complain," Messiter said, smiling. "My work is my hobby, and there aren't many lucky enough to say that. And how is the world of tobacco? Don't tell me. You'll always do a good trade here, Mr. Braid. All the pressures—you can see it in their faces. They need the weed and always will." Mildly he inquired, "Nobody called this week asking for me, I suppose?"

Braid had not intended saying anything, but Messiter's manner disarmed him. That and the shame he felt at the suspicions he had harbored impelled him to say, "Actually there *was* a caller. I had a detective in here—when was it?—Wednesday—asking about you. It was obviously a ridiculous mistake."

He described Inspector Gent's visit without mentioning his own investigation afterward with the ladder. "Makes you wonder what the police are up to these days," he concluded. "I believe we're all on the computer at Scotland Yard now. This sort of thing is bound to happen."

"You trust me, Mr. Braid. I appreciate that," Messiter said, his eyes starting to glisten. "You took me on trust from the beginning."

"I'm sure you aren't stacking stolen goods upstairs, if that's what you mean," Braid told him with sincerity.

"But the Inspector was not so sure?"

"He said something about a search warrant. Probably by now he has realized his mistake. I don't expect to see him again."

"I wonder what brought him here," Messiter said, almost to himself.

"I wouldn't bother about it. It's a computer error."

"I don't believe so. What did he say about the lock I fitted on the door, Mr. Braid?"

"Oh, at the time he seemed to think it was quite sinister." He grinned. "Don't worry—it doesn't bother me at all. You consulted me about it and you pay a pound extra a week for it, so who am I to complain? What you keep in there—if anything—is your business." He chuckled in a way intended to reassure. "That detective carried on as if you had a fortune hidden away in there."

"Oh, but I have."

Braid felt a pulse throb in his temple.

"It's high time I told you," said Messiter serenely. "I suppose I should apologize for not saying anything before. Not that there's anything criminal, believe me. Actually it's a rather remarkable story. I'm a philatelist, as you know. People smile at that and I don't blame them. Whatever name you give it, stamp collecting is a hobby for kids. In the business we're a little sensitive on the matter. We dignify it with its own technology—dies and watermarks and so forth—but I've always suspected this is partly to convince ourselves that the whole thing is serious and important.

"Well, it occurred to me four or five years ago that there was a marvelous way of justifying stamp collecting to myself and that was by writing a book about stamps. You must have heard of Rowland Hill, the fellow who started the whole thing off?"

"The Penny Post?"

Messiter nodded. "1840—the world's first postage stamps, the One-Penny Black and the Twopence Blue. My idea was not to write a biography of Hill—that's been done several times over by cleverer writers than I am—but to analyze the way his idea caught on. The response of the Victorian public was absolutely phenomenal, you know. It's all in the newspapers of the period. I went to the Newspaper Library at Colindale to do my research. I spent weeks over it."

Messiter's voice conveyed not fatigue at the memory, but excitement. "There was so much to read. Reports of Parliament. Letters to the Editor. Special articles describing the collection and delivery of the mail." He paused, pointing a finger at Braid. "You're wondering what this has to do with the room upstairs. I'll tell you. Whether it was providence or pure good luck I wouldn't care to say, but one afternoon in that Newspaper Library I turned up *The Times* for a day in May 1841, and my eye was caught—riveted, I should say—by an announcement in the Personal Column on the front page."

Messiter's hand went to his pocket and withdrew his wallet. From it he took a folded piece of paper. "This is what I saw."

Braid took it from him, a photostat of what was unquestionably a column of old newspaper type. The significant words had been scored round in ballpoint.

A Young Lady, being desirous of covering her dressing-room with cancelled postage stamps, has been so far encouraged in her wish by private friends as to have succeeded in collecting 16,000. These, however, being insufficient, she will be greatly obliged if any good-natured person who may have these otherwise worthless little articles at their disposal, would assist her in her whimsical project. Address to Miss E. D., Mr. Butt's, Glover, Leadenhall Street.

Braid made the connection instantly.

His throat went dry. He read it again. And again.

"You understand?" said Messiter. "It's a stamp man's dream—a room literally papered with Penny Blacks!"

"But this was—"

"1841. Right. More than a century ago. Have you ever looked through a really old newspaper? It's quite astonishing how easy it is to get caught up in the immediacy of the events. When I read that announcement, I could see that dressing room vividly in my imagination—chintz curtains, gas brackets, brass bedstead, washstand and mirror. I could see Miss E. D. with her paste pot and brush assiduously covering the wall with stamps.

"It was such an exciting idea that it came as a jolt to realize that it all had happened so long ago that Miss E. D. must have died about the turn of the century. And what of her dressing room? That, surely, must have gone, if not in the Blitz, then in the wholesale rebuilding of the City. My impression of Leadenhall Street was that the banks and insurance companies had lined it from end to end with gleaming office buildings five stories high. Even if by some miracle the shop that had been Butt's the Glover's *had* survived, and Miss E. D.'s room *had* been over the shop, common sense told me that those stamps must long since have been stripped from the walls."

He paused and lighted a cigar. Braid waited, his heart pounding.

"Yet there was a possibility, remote but tantalizing and irresistible, that someone years ago redecorated the room by papering *over* the stamps. Any decorator will tell you they sometimes find layer on layer of wallpaper. Imagine peeling back the layers to find thousands of Penny Blacks and Twopence Blues unknown to the world of philately! These days the commonest ones are catalogued at ten pounds or so, but find some rarities—inverted watermarks, special cancellations—and you could be up to five hundred pounds a stamp. Maybe a thousand pounds. Mr. Braid, I don't exaggerate when I tell you the value of such a room could run to half a million pounds. Half a million for what that young lady in her innocence called 'worthless little articles'!"

As if he read the thought, Messiter said, "It was my discovery. I went to a lot of trouble. Eventually I found the *Post Office Directory* for 1845 in the British Library. The list of residents in Leadenhall Street included a glover by the name of Butt."

"So you got the number of this shop?" Messiter nodded. "And when you came to Leadenhall Street, here it was, practically the last pre-Victorian building this side of Lloyd's?"

Messiter drew on his cigar, scrutinizing Braid.

"All those stamps," Braid whispered. "Twenty-seven years I've owned this shop and the flat without knowing that in the room upstairs was a fortune. It took you to tell me that."

"Don't get the idea it was easy for me," Messiter pointed out. "Remember I waited practically a year for those French people to move out. That was a test of character, believe me, not knowing what I would find when I took possession."

Strangely, Braid felt less resentment toward Messiter than the young Victorian woman who had lived in this building, *his* building, and devised a pastime so sensational in its consequence that his own walls mocked him.

Messiter leaned companionably across the counter. "Don't look so shattered, chum. I'm not the rat you take me for. Why do you think I'm telling you this?"

Braid shrugged. "I really couldn't say."

"Think about it. As your tenant, I did nothing underhanded. When I took the flat, didn't I raise the matter of redecoration? You said I was free to go ahead whenever I wished. I admit you didn't know then that the walls were covered with Penny Blacks, but I wasn't certain myself till I peeled back the old layers of paper. What a moment that was!"

He paused, savoring the recollection. "I've had a great year thanks to those stamps. In fact, I've set myself up for some time to come. Best of all, I had the unique experience of finding that room." He flicked ash from the cigar. "I estimate there are still upwards of twenty thousand stamps up there, Mr. Braid. In all justice, they belong to you."

Braid stared in amazement.

"I'm serious," Messiter went on. "I've made enough to buy a place in the country and write my book. The research is finished. That's been my plan for years, to earn some time, and I've done it. I want no more."

Frowning, Braid said, "I don't understand why you're doing this. Is it because of the police? You said there was nothing dishonest."

"And I meant it, but you are right, Mr. Braid. I am a little shaken to hear of your visit from the Inspector."

"What do you mean?"

Messiter asked obliquely, "When you read your newspaper, do you ever bother with the financial pages?"

Braid gave him a long look. Messiter held his stare.

"If it really has any bearing on this, the answer is no. I don't have much interest in the stock market. Nor any capital to invest," he added.

"Just as well in these uncertain times," Messiter commented. "Blue-chip investments have been hard to find these last few years. That's why people have been putting their money into other things. Art, for instance. A fine work of art holds its value in real terms even in a fluctuating economy. So do jewelry and antiques. And old postage stamps, Mr. Braid. Lately a lot of money has been invested in old stamps."

"That I can understand."

"Then you must also understand that information such as this"—he put his hand on the photostat between them—"is capable of causing flutters of alarm. Over the last year or so I have sold to dealers a number of early English stamps unknown to the market. These people are not fools. Before they buy a valuable stamp, they like to know the history of its ownership. I have had to tell them my story and show them the story in *The Times*. That's all right. Generally they need no more convincing. But do you understand the difficulty? It's the prospect of twenty thousand Penny Blacks and Twopence Blues unknown to the stamp world shortly coming onto the market. Can you imagine the effect?"

"I suppose it will reduce the value of those stamps people already own."

"Precisely. The rarities will not be so rare. Rumors begin, and it isn't long before there is a panic and stamp prices tumble."

"Which is when the sharks move in," said Braid. "I see it now. The police probably suspect the whole thing is a fraud."

Messiter gave a nod.

"But you and I know it isn't a fraud," Braid went on. "We can show them the room. I still don't understand why you are giving it up."

"I told you the reason. I always planned to write my book. And there is something else. It's right to warn you that there is sure to be publicity over this. Newspapers, television—this is the kind of story they relish, the unknown Victorian girl, the stamps undiscovered for over a century. Mr. Braid, I value my privacy. I don't care for my name being printed in the newspapers. It will happen, I'm sure, but I don't intend to be around when it does. That's why I am telling nobody where I am going. After the whole thing has blown over, I'll send you a forwarding address, if you would be so kind—"

"Of course, but—"

A customer came in, one of the regulars. Braid gave him a nod and wished he had gone to the kiosk up the street.

Messiter picked up the conversation. "Was it a month's notice we agreed? I'll see that my bank settles the rent." He took the keys of the flat from his pocket and put them on the counter with the photostat. "For you. I won't need these again." Putting a hand on Braid's arm, he added, "Some time we must meet and have a drink to Miss E. D.'s memory."

He turned and left the shop and the customer asked for 20 Rothmans. Braid lifted his hand in a belated salute through the shop window and returned to his business. More customers came in. Fridays were always busy with people collecting their cigarettes for the weekend. He was thankful for the activity. It compelled him to adjust by degrees and accept that he was now a rich man. Unlike Messiter, he would not object to the story getting into the press. Some of these customers who had used the shop for years and scarcely acknowledged him as a human being would choke on their toast and marmalade when they saw his name one morning in *The Times*.

It satisfied him most to recover what he owned. When Messiter had disclosed the secret of the building, it was as if the 27 years of Braid's tenure were obliterated. The place was full of Miss E. D. That young lady —she would always be young—had in effect asserted her prior claim. He had doubted if he would ever again believe the building was truly his own. But now that her "whimsical project" had been ceded to him, he was going to take pleasure in dismantling the design, stamp by stamp, steadily accumulating a fortune Miss E. D. had never supposed would accrue. Vengeful it might be, but it would exorcise her from the building that belonged to him.

Ten minutes before closing time Inspector Gent entered the shop. As before, he waited for the last customer to leave.

"Sorry to disturb you again, sir. I have that warrant now."

"You won't need it," Braid cheerfully told him. "I have the key. Mr. Messiter was here this morning." He started to recount the conversation.

"Then I suppose he took out his cutting from *The Times*," put in the Inspector.

"You *know* about that?"

"Do I?" he said caustically. "The man has been round just about every stamp shop north of Birmingham telling the tale of that young woman and the Penny Blacks on her dressing-room wall."

Braid frowned. "There's nothing dishonest in that. The story really did appear in *The Times,* didn't it?"

"It did, sir. We checked. And this *is* the address mentioned." The Inspector eyed him expressionlessly. "The trouble is that the Penny Blacks our friend Messiter has been selling in the north aren't off any dressing-room wall. He buys them from a dealer in London, common specimens, about ten pounds each one. Then he works on them."

"Works on them? What do you mean?"

"Penny Blacks are valued according to the plates they were printed from, sir. There are distinctive markings on each of the plates, most particularly in the shape of the guide letters that appear in the corners. The stamps Messiter has been selling are doctored to make them appear rare. He buys a common Plate 6 stamp in London, touches up the guide letters, and sells it to a Manchester dealer as a Plate 11 stamp for seventy-five pounds. As it's catalogued at more than twice that, the dealer thinks he has a bargain. Messiter picks his victims carefully: generally they aren't specialists in early English stamps, but almost any dealer is ready to look at a Penny Black in case it's a rare one."

Braid shook his head. "I don't understand this at all. Why should Messiter have needed to resort to forgery? There are twenty thousand stamps upstairs."

"Have you seen them?"

"No, but the newspaper story—"

"That fools everyone, sir."

"You said it was genuine."

"It is. And the idea of a roomful of Penny Blacks excites people's imagination. They *want* to believe it. That's the secret of all the best confidence tricks. Now why do you suppose Messiter had a mortice lock fitted on that room? You thought it was because the contents were worth a fortune? Has it occurred to you as a possibility that he didn't want anyone to know there was nothing there?"

Braid's dream disintegrated.

"It stands to reason, doesn't it," the Inspector went on, "that the stamps were ripped off the wall generations ago? When Messiter found empty walls, he couldn't abandon the idea. It had taken a grip on him. That young woman who thought of papering her wall with stamps could never have supposed she would be responsible over a century later for turning a man to crime."

The Inspector held out his hand. "If I could have that key, sir, I'd like to see the room for myself." Braid followed the Inspector upstairs and watched him unlock the door. They entered the room.

"I don't mind admitting I have a sneaking admiration for Messiter," the Inspector said. "Imagine the poor beggar coming in here at last after going to all the trouble he did to find the place. Look, you can see where he peeled back the wallpaper layer by layer"—gripping a furl of paper, he drew it casually aside—"to find absolutely—" He stopped. "My God!"

The stamps were there, neatly pasted in rows.

Braid said nothing, but the blood slowly drained from his face.

Miss E. D.'s scheme of interior decoration had been more ambitious than anyone expected. She had diligently inked over every stamp with red, purple, or green ink—to form an intricate mosaic of colors. Originally Penny Blacks or Twopence Blues, Plate 6 or Plate 11, they were now as she had described them in *The Times*—"worthless little articles."

❅　❅　❅

The Invisible Man

G. K. CHESTERTON

In the cool blue twilight of two steep streets in Camden Town, the shop at the corner, a confectioner's, glowed like the butt of a cigar. One should rather say, perhaps, like the butt of a firework, for the light was of many colours and some complexity, broken up by many mirrors and dancing on many gilt and gaily-coloured cakes and sweet-meats. Against this one fiery glass were glued the noses of many gutter-snipes, for the chocolates were all wrapped in those red and gold and green metallic colours which are almost better than chocolate itself; and the huge white wedding-cake in the window was somehow at once re-mote and satisfying, just as if the whole North Pole were good to eat. Such rainbow provocations could naturally collect the youth of the neighbourhood up to the ages of ten or twelve. But this corner was also attractive to youth at a later stage; and a young man, not less than twenty-four, was staring into the same shop window. To him, also, the shop was of fiery charm, but this attraction was not wholly to be ex-plained by chocolates; which, however, he was far from despising.

He was a tall, burly, red-haired young man, with a resolute face but a listless manner. He carried under his arm a flat, grey portfolio of black-and-white sketches, which he had sold with more or less success to pub-lishers ever since his uncle (who was an admiral) had disinherited him for Socialism, because of a lecture which he had delivered against that economic theory. His name was John Turnbull Angus.

Entering at last, he walked through the confectioner's shop to the back room, which was a sort of pastry-cook restaurant, merely raising his hat to the young lady who was serving there. She was a dark, elegant, alert girl in black, with a high colour and very quick, dark eyes; and after the ordinary interval she followed him into the inner room to take his order.

His order was evidently a usual one. "I want, please," he said with precision, "one halfpenny bun and a small cup of black coffee." An instant before the girl could turn away he added, "Also, I want you to marry me."

The young lady of the shop stiffened suddenly and said, "Those are jokes I don't allow."

The red-haired young man lifted grey eyes of an unexpected gravity.

"Really and truly," he said, "it's as serious—as serious as the half-penny bun. It is expensive, like the bun; one pays for it. It is indigestible, like the bun. It hurts."

The dark young lady had never taken her dark eyes off him, but seemed to be studying him with almost tragic exactitude. At the end of her scrutiny she had something like the shadow of a smile, and she sat down in a chair.

"Don't you think," observed Angus, absently, "that it's rather cruel to eat these halfpenny buns? They might grow up into penny buns. I shall give up these brutal sports when we are married."

The dark young lady rose from her chair and walked to the window, evidently in a state of strong but not unsympathetic cogitation. When at last she swung round again with an air of resolution she was bewildered to observe that the young man was carefully laying out on the table various objects from the shop window. They included a pyramid of highly coloured sweets, several plates of sandwiches, and the two decant-ers containing that mysterious port and sherry which are peculiar to pastry-cooks. In the middle of this neat arrangement he had carefully let down the enormous load of white sugared cake which had been the huge ornament of the window.

"What on earth are you doing?" she asked.

"Duty, my dear Laura," he began.

"Oh, for the Lord's sake, stop a minute," she cried, "and don't talk to me in that way. I mean, what is all that?"

"A ceremonial meal, Miss Hope."

"And what is *that*?" she asked impatiently, pointing to the mountain of sugar.

"The wedding-cake, Mrs. Angus," he said.

The girl marched to that article, removed it with some clatter, and put it back in the shop window; she then returned, and, putting her elegant elbows on the table, regarded the young man not unfavourably but with considerable exasperation,

"You don't give me any time to think," she said.

"I'm not such a fool," he answered; "that's my Christian humility."

She was still looking at him; but she had grown considerably graver behind the smile.

"Mr. Angus," she said steadily, "before there is a minute more of this nonsense I must tell you something about myself as shortly as I can."

"Delighted," replied Angus gravely. "You might tell me something about myself, too, while you are about it."

"Oh, do hold your tongue and listen," she said. "It's nothing that I'm ashamed of, and it isn't even anything that I'm specially sorry about. But what would you say if there were something that is no business of mine and yet is my nightmare?"

"In that case," said the man seriously, "I should suggest that you bring back the cake."

"Well, you must listen to the story first," said Laura, persistently. "To begin with, I must tell you that my father owned the inn called the 'Red Fish' at Ludbury, and I used to serve people in the bar."

"I have often wondered," he said, "why there was a kind of a Christian air about this one confectioner's shop."

"Ludbury is a sleepy, grassy little hole in the Eastern Counties, and the only kind of people who ever came to the 'Red Fish' were occasional commercial travellers, and for the rest, the most awful people you can see, only you've never seen them. I mean little, loungy men, who had just enough to live on and had nothing to do but lean about in bar-rooms and bet on horses, in bad clothes that were just too good for them. Even these wretched young rotters were not very common at our house; but there were two of them that were a lot too common—common in every sort of way. They both lived on money of their own, and were wearisomely idle and overdressed. But yet I was a bit sorry for them, because I half believe they slunk into our little empty bar because each of them had a slight deformity; the sort of thing that some yokels laugh at. It wasn't exactly a deformity either; it was more an oddity. One of them was a surprisingly small man, something like a dwarf, or at least like a jockey. He was not at all jockeyish to look at, though; he had a round black head and a well-trimmed black beard, bright eyes like a bird's; he jingled money in his pockets; he jangled a great gold watch chain; and he never turned up except dressed just too much like a gentleman to be one. He was no fool though, though a futile idler; he was curiously clever at all kinds of things that couldn't be the slightest use; a sort of impromptu conjuring; making fifteen matches set fire to each other like a regular firework; or cutting a banana or some such thing into a dancing doll. His name was Isidore Smythe; and I can see him still, with his little dark face, just coming up to the counter, making a jumping kangaroo out of five cigars.

"The other fellow was more silent and more ordinary; but somehow he alarmed me much more than poor little Smythe. He was very tall and slight, and light-haired; his nose had a high bridge, and he might almost have been handsome in a spectral sort of way; but he had one of the most appalling squints I have ever seen or heard of. When he looked straight at you, you didn't know where you were yourself, let alone what he was looking at. I fancy this sort of disfigurement embittered the poor chap a little; for while Smythe was ready to show off his monkey tricks anywhere, James Welkin (that was the squinting man's name) never did anything except soak in our bar parlour, and go for great walks by himself in the flat, grey country all round. All the same, I think Smythe, too, was a little sensitive about being so small, though he carried it off more smartly. And so it was that I was really puzzled, as well as startled, and very sorry, when they both offered to marry me in the same week.

"Well, I did what I've since thought was perhaps a silly thing. But, after all, these freaks were my friends in a way; and I had a horror of their thinking I refused them for the real reason, which was that they were so impossibly ugly. So I made up some gas of another sort, about never meaning to marry anyone who hadn't carved his way in the world. I said it was a point of principle with me not to live on money that was just inherited like theirs. Two days after I had talked in this well-meaning sort of way, the whole trouble began. The first thing I heard was that both of them had gone off to seek their fortunes, as if they were in some silly fairy tale.

"Well, I've never seen either of them from that day to this. But I've had two letters from the little man called Smythe, and really they were rather exciting."

"Ever heard of the other man?" asked Angus.

"No, he never wrote," said the girl, after an instant's hesitation. "Smythe's first letter was simply to say that he had started out walking with Welkin to London; but Welkin was such a good walker that the little man dropped out of it, and took a rest by the roadside. He happened to be picked up by some travelling show, and, partly because he was nearly a dwarf, and partly because he was really a clever little wretch, he got on quite well in the show business, and was soon sent up to the Aquarium, to do some tricks that I forget. That was his first letter. His second was much more of a startler, and I only got it last week."

The man called Angus emptied his coffee-cup and regarded her with mild and patient eyes. Her own mouth took a slight twist of laughter as she resumed, "I suppose you've seen on the hoardings all about this 'Smythe's Silent Service'? Or you must be the only person that hasn't. Oh, I don't know much about it, it's some clockwork invention for doing all the housework by machinery. You know the sort of thing: 'Press a Button—A Butler who Never Drinks.' 'Turn a Handle—Ten Housemaids who Never Flirt.' You must have seen the advertisements. Well, whatever these machines are, they are making pots of money; and they are making it all for that little imp whom I knew down in Ludbury. I can't help feeling pleased the poor little chap has fallen on his feet; but the plain fact is, I'm in terror of his turning up any minute and telling me he's carved his way in the world—as he certainly has."

"And the other man?" repeated Angus with a sort of obstinate quietude.

Laura Hope got to her feet suddenly. "My friend," she said, "I think you are a witch. Yes, you are quite right. I have not seen a line of the other man's writing; and I have no more notion than the dead of what or where he is. But it is of him that I am frightened. It is he who is all about my path. It is he who has half driven me mad. Indeed, I think he has driven me mad; for I have felt him where he could not have been, and I have heard his voice when he could not have spoken."

"Well, my dear," said the young man, cheerfully, "if he were Satan himself, he is done for now you have told somebody. One goes mad all alone, old girl. But when was it you fancied you felt and heard our squinting friend?"

"I heard James Welkin laugh as plainly as I hear you speak," said the girl, steadily. "There was nobody there, for I stood just outside the shop at the corner, and could see down both streets at once. I had forgotten how he laughed, though his laugh was as odd as his squint. I had not thought of him for nearly a year. But it's a solemn truth that a few seconds later the first letter came from his rival."

"Did you ever make the spectre speak or squeak, or anything?" asked Angus, with some interest.

Laura suddenly shuddered, and then said, with an unshaken voice, "Yes. Just when I had finished reading the second letter from Isidore Smythe announcing his success, just then, I heard Welkin say, 'He shan't have you, though.' It was quite plain, as if he were in the room. It is awful, I think I must be mad."

"If you really were mad," said the young man, "you would think you must be sane. But certainly there seems to me to be something a little rum about this unseen gentleman. Two heads are better than one—I spare you allusions to any other organs—and really, if you would allow me, as a sturdy, practical man, to bring back the wedding-cake out of the window——"

Even as he spoke, there was a sort of steely shriek in the street outside, and a small motor, driven at devilish speed, shot up to the door of the shop and stuck there. In the same flash of time a small man in a shiny top hat stood stamping in the outer room.

Angus, who had hitherto maintained hilarious ease from motives of mental hygiene, revealed the strain of his soul by striding abruptly out of the inner room and confronting the new-comer. A glance at him was quite sufficient to confirm the savage guesswork of a man in love. This very dapper but dwarfish figure, with the spike of black beard carried insolently forward, the clever unrestful eyes, the neat but very nervous fingers, could be none other than the man just described to him: Isidore Smythe, who made dolls out of banana skins and match-boxes; Isidore Smythe, who made millions out of undrinking butlers and unflirting housemaids of metal. For a moment the two men, instinctively understanding each other's air of possession, looked at each other with that curious cold generosity which is the soul of rivalry.

Mr. Smythe, however, made no allusion to the ultimate ground of their antagonism, but said simply and explosively, "Has Miss Hope seen that thing on the window?"

"On the window?" repeated the staring Angus.

"There's no time to explain other things," said the small millionaire shortly. "There's some tomfoolery going on here that has to be investigated."

He pointed his polished walking-stick at the window, recently depleted by the bridal preparations of Mr. Angus; and that gentleman was astonished to see along the front of the glass a long strip of paper pasted, which had certainly not been on the window when he looked through it some time before. Following the energetic Smythe outside into the street, he found that some yard and a half of stamp paper had been carefully gummed along the glass outside, and on this was written in straggly characters, "If you marry Smythe, he will die."

"Laura," said Angus, putting his big red head into the shop, "you're not mad."

"It's the writing of that fellow Welkin," said Smythe gruffly. "I haven't seen him for years, but he's always bothering me. Five times in the last fortnight he's had threatening letters left at my flat, and I can't even find out who leaves them, let alone if it is Welkin himself. The porter of the flats swears that no suspicious characters have been seen, and here he has pasted up a sort of dado on a public shop window, while the people in the shop——"

"Quite so," said Angus modestly, "while the people in the shop were having tea. Well, sir, I can assure you I appreciate your common sense in dealing so directly with the matter. We can talk about other things afterwards. The fellow cannot be very far off yet, for I swear there was no paper there when I went last to the window, ten or fifteen minutes ago. On the other hand, he's too far off to be chased, as we don't even know the direction. If you'll take my advice, Mr. Smythe, you'll put this at once in the hands of some energetic inquiry man, private rather than public. I know an extremely clever fellow, who has set up in business five minutes from here in your car. His name's Flambeau, and though his youth was a bit stormy, he's a strictly honest man now, and his brains are worth money. He lives in Lucknow Mansions, Hampstead."

"That is odd," said the little man, arching his black eyebrows. "I live, myself, in Himylaya Mansions, round the corner. Perhaps you might care to come with me; I can go to my rooms and sort out these queer Welkin documents, while you run round and get your friend the detective."

"You are very good," said Angus politely. "Well, the sooner we act the better."

Both men, with a queer kind of impromptu fairness, took the same sort of formal farewell of the lady, and both jumped into the brisk little car. As Smythe took the handles and they turned the great corner of the street, Angus was amused to see a gigantesque poster of "Smythe's Silent Service," with a picture of a huge headless iron doll, carrying a saucepan with the legend, "A Cook who is Never Cross."

"I use them in my own flat," said the little black-bearded man, laughing, "partly for advertisements, and partly for real convenience. Honestly, and all above board, those big clockwork dolls of mine do bring your coals or claret or a timetable quicker than any live servants I've ever known, if you know which knob to press. But I'll never deny, between ourselves, that such servants have their disadvantages, too."

"Indeed?" said Angus; "is there something they can't do?"

"Yes," replied Smythe coolly; "they can't tell me who left those threatening letters at my flat."

The man's motor was small and swift like himself; in fact, like his domestic service, it was of his own invention. If he was an advertising quack, he was one who believed in his own wares. The sense of something tiny and flying was accentuated as they swept up long white curves of road in the dead but open daylight of evening. Soon the white curves came sharper and dizzier; they were upon ascending spirals, as they say in the modern religions. For, indeed, they were cresting a corner of London which is almost as precipitous as Edinburgh, if not quite so picturesque. Terrace rose above terrace, and the special tower of flats they sought, rose above them all to almost Egyptian height, gilt by the level sunset. The change, as they turned the corner and entered the crescent known as Himylaya Mansions, was as abrupt as the opening of a window; for they found that pile of flats sitting above London as above a green sea of slate. Opposite to the mansions, on the other side of the gravel crescent, was a bushy enclosure more like a steep hedge or dyke than a garden, and some way below that ran a strip of artificial water, a sort of canal, like the moat of that embowered fortress. As the car swept round the crescent it passed, at one corner, the stray stall of a man selling chestnuts; and right away at the other end of the curve, Angus could see a dim blue policeman walking slowly. These were the only human shapes in that high suburban solitude; but he had an irrational sense that they expressed the speechless poetry of London. He felt as if they were figures in a story.

The little car shot up to the right house like a bullet, and shot out its owner like a bomb shell. He was immediately inquiring of a tall commissionaire in shining braid, and a short porter in shirt sleeves, whether anybody or anything had been seeking his apartments. He was assured that nobody and nothing had passed these officials since his last inquiries; whereupon he and the slightly bewildered Angus were shot up in the lift like a rocket, till they reached the top floor.

"Just come in for a minute," said the breathless Smythe. "I want to show you those Welkin letters. Then you might run round the corner and fetch your friend." He pressed a button concealed in the wall, and the door opened of itself.

It opened on a long, commodious ante-room, of which the only arresting features, ordinarily speaking, were the rows of tall half-human mechanical figures that stood up on both sides like tailors' dummies. Like tailors' dummies they were headless; and like tailors' dummies they had a handsome unnecessary humpiness in the shoulders, and a pigeon-breasted protuberance of chest; but barring this, they were not much more like a human figure than any automatic machine at a station that is about the human height. They had two great hooks like arms, for carrying trays; and they were painted pea-green, or vermilion, or black for convenience of distinction; in every other way they were only automatic machines and nobody would have looked twice at them. On this occasion, at least, nobody did. For between the two rows of these domestic dummies lay something more interesting than most of the mechanics of the world. It was a white, tattered scrap of paper scrawled with red ink; and the agile inventor had snatched it up almost as soon as the door flew open. He handed it to Angus without a word. The red ink on it actually was not dry, and the message ran, "If you have been to see her today, I shall kill you."

There was a short silence, and then Isidore Smythe said quietly, "Would you like a little whiskey? I rather feel as if I should."

"Thank you; I should like a little Flambeau," said Angus, gloomily. "This business seems to me to be getting rather grave. I'm going round at once to fetch him."

"Right you are," said the other, with admirable cheerfulness. "Bring him round here as quick as you can."

But as Angus closed the front door behind him he saw Smythe push back a button, and one of the clockwork images glided from its place and slid along a groove in the floor carrying a tray with syphon and decanter. There did seem something a trifle weird about leaving the little man alone among those dead servants, who were coming to life as the door closed.

Six steps down from Smythe's landing the man in shirt sleeves was doing something with a pail. Angus stopped to extract a promise, fortified with a prospective bribe, that he would remain in that place until the return with the detective, and would keep count of any kind of stranger coming up those stairs. Dashing down to the front hall he then laid similar charges of vigilance on the commissionaire at the front door, from whom he learned the simplifying circumstances that there was no back door. Not content with this, he captured the floating policeman and induced him to stand opposite the entrance and watch it; and finally paused an instant for a pennyworth of chestnuts, and an inquiry as to the probable length of the merchant's stay in the neighbourhood.

The chestnut seller, turning up the collar of his coat, told him he should probably be moving shortly, as he thought it was going to snow. Indeed, the evening was growing grey and bitter, but Angus, with all his eloquence, proceeded to nail the chestnut man to his post.

"Keep yourself warm on your own chestnuts," he said earnestly. "Eat up your whole stock; I'll make it worth your while. I'll give you a sovereign if you'll wait here till I come back, and then tell me whether any man, woman, or child has gone into that house where the commissionaire is standing."

He then walked away smartly, with a last look at the besieged tower.

"I've made a ring round that room, anyhow," he said. "They can't all four of them be Mr. Welkin's accomplices."

Lucknow Mansions were, so to speak, on a lower platform of that hill of houses, of which Himylaya Mansions might be called the peak. Mr. Flambeau's semi-official flat was on the ground floor, and presented in every way a marked contrast to the American machinery and cold hotel-like luxury of the flat of the Silent Service. Flambeau, who was a friend of Angus, received him in a rococo artistic den behind his office, of which the ornaments were sabres, harquebuses, Eastern curiosities, flasks of Italian wine, savage cooking-pots, a plumy Persian cat, and a small dusty-looking Roman Catholic priest, who looked particularly out of place.

"This is my friend Father Brown," said Flambeau. "I've often wanted you to meet him. Splendid weather, this; a little cold for Southerners like me."

"Yes, I think it will keep clear," said Angus, sitting down on a violet-striped Eastern ottoman.

"No," said the priest quietly, "it has begun to snow."

And, indeed, as he spoke, the first few flakes, foreseen by the man of chestnuts, began to drift across the darkening windowpane.

"Well," said Angus heavily. "I'm afraid I've come on business, and rather jumpy business at that. The fact is, Flambeau, within a stone's throw of your house is a fellow who badly wants your help; he's perpetually being haunted and threatened by an invisible enemy—a scoundrel whom nobody has even seen." As Angus proceeded to tell the whole tale of Smythe and Welkin, beginning with Laura's story, and going on with his own, the supernatural laugh at the corner of two empty streets, the strange distinct words spoken in an empty room, Flambeau grew more and more vividly concerned, and the little priest seemed to be left out of it, like a piece of furniture. When it came to the scribbled stamp paper pasted on the window, Flambeau rose, seeming to fill the room with his huge shoulders.

"If you don't mind," he said, "I think you had better tell me the rest on the nearest road to this man's house. It strikes me, somehow, that there is no time to be lost."

"Delighted," said Angus, rising also, "though he's safe enough for the present, for I've set four men to watch the only hole to his burrow."

They turned out into the street, the small priest trundling after them with the docility of a small dog. He merely said, in a cheerful way, like one making conversation, "How quick the snow gets thick on the ground."

As they threaded the steep side streets already powdered with silver, Angus finished his story; and by the time they reached the crescent with the towering flats, he had leisure to turn his attention to the four sentinels. The chestnut seller, both before and after receiving a sovereign, swore stubbornly that he had watched the door and seen no visitor enter. The policeman was even more emphatic. He said he had had experience of crooks of all kinds; in top hats and in rags; he wasn't so green as to expect suspicious characters to look suspicious; he looked out for anybody, and, so help him, there had been nobody. And when all three men gathered round the gilded commissionaire, who still stood smiling astride of the porch, the verdict was more final still.

"I've got a right to ask any man, duke or dustman, what he wants in these flats," said the genial and gold-laced giant, "and I'll swear there's been nobody to ask since this gentleman went away."

The unimportant Father Brown, who stood back, looking modestly at the pavement, here ventured to say meekly, "Has nobody been up and down stairs, then, since the snow began to fall? It began while we were all round at Flambeau's."

"Nobody's been in here, sir, you can take it from me," said the official, with beaming authority.

"Then I wonder what that is?" said the priest, and stared at the ground blankly like a fish.

The others all looked down also; and Flambeau used a fierce exclamation and a French gesture. For it was unquestionably true that down the middle of the entrance guarded by the man in gold lace, actually between the arrogant, stretched legs of that colossus, ran a stringy pattern of grey footprints stamped upon the white snow.

"God!" cried Angus involuntarily, "the Invisible Man!"

Without another word he turned and dashed up the stairs, with Flambeau following; but Father Brown still stood looking about him in the snow-clad street as if he had lost interest in his query.

Flambeau was plainly in a mood to break down the door with his big shoulders; but the Scotchman, with more reason, if less intuition, fumbled about on the frame of the door till he found the invisible button; and the door swung slowly open.

It showed substantially the same serried interior; the hall had grown darker, though it was still struck here and there with the last crimson shafts of sunset, and one or two of the headless machines had been moved from their places for this or that purpose, and stood here and there about the twilit place. The green and red of their coats were all darkened in the dusk; and their likeness to human shapes slightly increased by their very shapelessness. But in the middle of them all, exactly where the paper with the red ink had lain, there lay something that looked like red ink spilt out of its bottle. But it was not red ink.

With a French combination of reason and violence Flambeau simply said "Murder!" and, plunging into the flat, had explored every corner and cupboard of it in five minutes. But if he expected to find a corpse he found none. Isidore Smythe was not in the place, either dead or alive. After the most tearing search the two men met each other in the outer hall, with streaming faces and staring eyes. "My friend," said Flambeau, talking French in his excitement, "not only is your murderer invisible, but he makes invisible also the murdered man."

Angus looked round at the dim room full of dummies, and in some Celtic corner of his Scotch soul a shudder started. One of the life-size dolls stood immediately overshadowing the blood stain, summoned, perhaps, by the slain man an instant before he fell. One of the high-shouldered hooks that served the thing for arms, was a little lifted, and Angus had suddenly the horrid fancy that poor Smythe's own iron child had struck him down. Matter had rebelled, and these machines had killed their master. But even so, what had they done with him?

"Eaten him?" said the nightmare at his ear; and he sickened for an instant at the idea of rent, human remains absorbed and crushed into all that acephalous clockwork.

He recovered his mental health by an emphatic effort, and said to Flambeau, "Well, there it is. The poor fellow has evaporated like a cloud and left a red streak on the floor. The tale does not belong to this world."

"There is only one thing to be done," said Flambeau, "whether it belongs to this world or the other. I must go down and talk to my friend."

They descended, passing the man with the pail, who again asserverated that he had let no intruder pass, down to the commissionaire and the hovering chestnut man, who rigidly reasserted their own watchfulness. But when Angus looked round for his fourth confirmation he could not see it, and called out with some nervousness, "Where is the policeman?"

"I beg your pardon," said Father Brown; "that is my fault. I just sent him down the road to investigate something—that I just thought worth investigating."

"Well, we want him back pretty soon," said Angus abruptly, "for the wretched man upstairs has not only been murdered, but wiped out."

"How?" asked the priest.

"Father," said Flambeau, after a pause, "upon my soul I believe it is more in your department than mine. No friend or foe has entered the house, but Smythe is gone, as if stolen by the fairies. If that is not supernatural, I——"

As he spoke they were all checked by an unusual sight; the big blue policeman came round the corner of the crescent, running. He came straight up to Brown.

"You're right, sir," he panted, "they've just found poor Mr. Smythe's body in the canal down below."

Angus put his hand wildly to his head. "Did he run down and drown himself?" he asked.

"He never came down, I'll swear," said the constable, "and he wasn't drowned either, for he died of a great stab over the heart."

"And yet you saw no one enter?" said Flambeau in a grave voice.

"Let us walk down the road a little," said the priest.

As they reached the other end of the crescent he observed abruptly, "Stupid of me! I forgot to ask the policeman something. I wonder if they found a light brown sack."

"Why a light brown sack?" asked Angus, astonished.

"Because if it was any other coloured sack, the case must begin over again," said Father Brown; "but if it was a light brown sack, why, the case is finished."

"I am pleased to hear it," said Angus with hearty irony. "It hasn't begun, so far as I am concerned."

"You must tell us all about it," said Flambeau with a strange heavy simplicity, like a child.

Unconsciously they were walking with quickening steps down the long sweep of road on the other side of the high crescent, Father Brown leading briskly, though in silence. At last he said with an almost touching vagueness, "Well, I'm afraid you'll think it so prosy. We always begin at the abstract end of things, and you can't begin this story anywhere else.

"Have you ever noticed this—that people never answer what you say? They answer what you mean—or what they think you mean. Suppose one lady says to another in a country house, 'Is anybody staying with you?' the lady doesn't answer 'Yes; the butler, the three footmen, the parlourmaid, and so on,' though the parlourmaid may be in the room, or the butler behind her chair. She says 'There is *nobody* staying with us,' meaning nobody of the sort you mean. But suppose a doctor inquiring into an epidemic asks, 'Who is staying in the house?' then the lady will remember the butler, the parlourmaid, and the rest. All language is used like that; you never get a question answered literally, even when you get it answered truly. When those four quite honest men said that no man had gone into the Mansions, they did not really mean that *no man* had gone into them. They meant no man whom they could suspect of being your man. A man did go into the house, and did come out of it, but they never noticed him."

"An invisible man?" inquired Angus, raising his red eyebrows.

"A mentally invisible man," said Father Brown.

A minute or two after he resumed in the same unassuming voice, like a man thinking his way. "Of course you can't think of such a man, until you do think of him. That's where his cleverness comes in. But I came to think of him through two or three little things in the tale Mr. Angus told us. First, there was the fact that this Welkin went for long walks. And then there was the vast lot of stamp paper on the window. And then, most of all, there were the two things the young lady said—things that couldn't be true. Don't get annoyed," he added hastily, noting a sudden movement of the Scotchman's head; "she thought they were true. A person *can't* be quite alone in a street a second before she receives a letter. She can't be quite alone in a street when she starts reading a letter just received. There must be somebody pretty near her; he must be mentally invisible."

"Why must there be somebody near her?" asked Angus.

"Because," said Father Brown, "barring carrier-pigeons, somebody must have brought her the letter."

"Do you really mean to say," asked Flambeau, with energy, "that Welkin carried his rival's letters to his lady?"

"Yes," said the priest. "Welkin carried his rival's letters to his lady. You see, he had to."

"Oh, I can't stand much more of this," exploded Flambeau. "Who is this fellow? What does he look like? What is the usual get-up of a mentally invisible man?"

"He is dressed rather handsomely in red, blue and gold," replied the priest promptly with precision, "and in this striking, and even showy, costume he entered Himylaya Mansions under eight human eyes; he killed Smythe in cold blood, and came down into the street again carrying the dead body in his arms——"

"Reverend sir," cried Angus, standing still, "are you raving mad, or am I?"

"You are not mad," said Brown, "only a little unobservant. You have not noticed such a man as this, for example."

He took three quick strides forward, and put his hand on the shoulder of an ordinary passing postman who had bustled by them unnoticed under the shade of the trees.

"Nobody ever notices postmen somehow," he said thoughtfully; "yet they have passions like other men, and even carry large bags where a small corpse can be stowed quite easily."

The postman, instead of turning naturally, had ducked and tumbled against the garden fence. He was a lean fair-bearded man of very ordinary appearance, but as he turned an alarmed face over his shoulder, all three men were fixed with an almost fiendish squint.

Flambeau went back to his sabres, purple rugs and Persian cat, having many things to attend to. John Turnbull Angus went back to the lady at the shop, with whom that imprudent young man contrives to be extremely comfortable. But Father Brown walked those snow-covered hills under the stars for many hours with a murderer, and what they said to each other will never be known.

Lamb to the Slaughter

ROALD DAHL

The room was warm and clean, the curtains drawn, the two table lamps alight—hers and the one by the empty chair opposite. On the sideboard behind her, two tall glasses, soda water, whisky. Fresh ice cubes in the Thermos bucket.

Mary Maloney was waiting for her husband to come home from work.

Now and again she would glance up at the clock, but without anxiety, merely to please herself with the thought that each minute gone by made it nearer the time when he would come. There was a slow smiling air about her, and about everything she did. The drop of the head as she bent over her sewing was curiously tranquil. Her skin—for this was her sixth month with child—had acquired a wonderful translucent quality, the mouth was soft, and the eyes, with their new placid look, seemed larger, darker than before.

When the clock said ten minutes to five, she began to listen, and a few moments later, punctually as always she heard the tyres on the gravel outside, and the car door slamming, the footsteps passing the window, the key turning in the lock. She laid aside her sewing, stood up, and went forward to kiss him as he came in.

"Hullo, darling," she said.

"Hullo," he answered.

She took his coat and hung it in the closet. Then she walked over and made the drinks, a strongish one for him, a weak one for herself; and soon she was back again in her chair with the sewing, and he in the other, opposite, holding the tall glass with both his hands, rocking it so the ice cubes tinkled against the side.

For her, this was always a blissful time of day. She knew he didn't want to speak much until the first drink was finished, and she, on her side, was content to sit quietly, enjoying his company after the long hours alone in the house. She loved to luxuriate in the presence of this man, and to feel—almost as a sunbather feels the sun—that warm male glow that came out of him to her when they were alone together. She loved him for the way he sat loosely in a chair, for the way he came in a door, or moved slowly across the room with long strides. She loved the intent, far look in his eyes when they rested on her, the funny shape of the mouth, and especially, the way he remained silent about his tired-ness, sitting still with himself until the whisky had taken some of it away.

"Tired, darling?"

"Yes," he said. "I'm tired." And as he spoke, he did an unusual thing. He lifted his glass and drained it in one swallow although there was still half of it, at least half of it, left. She wasn't really watching him but she knew what he had done because she heard the ice cubes falling back against the bottom of the empty glass when he lowered his arm. He paused a moment, leaning forward in the chair, then he got up and went slowly over to fetch himself another.

"I'll get it!" she cried, jumping up.

"Sit down," he said.

When he came back, she noticed that the new drink was dark amber with the quantity of whisky in it.

"Darling, shall I get your slippers?"

"No."

She watched him as he began to sip the dark yellow drink, and she could see little oily swirls in the liquid because it was so strong.

"I think it's a shame," she said, "that when a policeman gets to be as senior as you, they keep him walking about on his feet all day long."

He didn't answer, so she bent her head again and went on with her sewing; but each time he lifted the drink to his lips, she heard the ice cubes clicking against the side of the glass.

"Darling," she said. "Would you like me to get you some cheese? I haven't made any supper because it's Thursday."

"No," he said.

"If you're too tired to eat out," she went on, "it's still not too late. There's plenty of meat and stuff in the freezer, and you can have it right here and not even move out of the chair."

Her eyes waited on him for an answer, a smile, a little nod, but he made no sign.

"Anyway," she went on, "I'll get you some cheese and crackers first."

"I don't want it," he said.

She moved uneasily in her chair, the large eyes still watching his face. "But you *must* have supper. I can easily do it here. I'd like to do it. We can have lamb chops. Or pork. Anything you want. Everything's in the freezer."

"Forget it," he said.

"But, darling, you *must* eat! I'll fix it anyway, and then you can have it or not, as you like."

She stood up and placed her sewing on the table by the lamp.

"Sit down," he said. "Just for a minute, sit down."

It wasn't till then that she began to get frightened.

"Go on," he said. "Sit down."

She lowered herself back slowly into the chair, watching him all the time with those large, bewildered eyes. He had finished the second drink and was staring down into the glass, frowning.

"Listen," he said, "I've got something to tell you."

"What is it, darling? What's the matter?"

He had become absolutely motionless, and he kept his head down so that the light from the lamp beside him fell across the upper part of his face, leaving the chin and mouth in shadow. She noticed there was a little muscle moving near the corner of his left eye.

"This is going to be a bit of a shock to you, I'm afraid," he said. "But I've thought about it a good deal and I've decided the only thing to do is tell you right away. I hope you won't blame me too much."

And he told her. It didn't take long, four or five minutes at most, and she sat very still through it all, watching him with a kind of dazed horror as he went further and further away from her with each word.

"So there it is," he added. "And I know it's kind of a bad time to be telling you, but there simply wasn't any other way. Of course I'll give you money and see you're looked after. But there needn't really be any fuss. I hope not anyway. It wouldn't be very good for my job."

Her first instinct was not to believe any of it, to reject it all. It occurred to her that perhaps he hadn't even spoken, that she herself had imagined the whole thing. Maybe, if she went about her business and acted as though she hadn't been listening, then later, when she sort of woke up again, she might find none of it had ever happened.

"I'll get the supper," she managed to whisper, and this time he didn't stop her.

When she walked across the room she couldn't feel her feet touching the floor. She couldn't feel anything at all—except a slight nausea and a desire to vomit. Everything was automatic now—down the stairs to the cellar, the light switch, the deep freeze, the hand inside the cabinet taking hold of the first object it met. She lifted it out, and looked at it. It was wrapped in paper, so she took off the paper and looked at it again.

A leg of lamb.

All right then, they would have lamb for supper. She carried it upstairs, holding the thin bone-end of it with both her hands, and as she went through the living-room, she saw him standing over by the window with his back to her, and she stopped.

"For God's sake," he said, hearing her, but not turning round. "Don't make supper for me. I'm going out."

At that point, Mary Maloney simply walked up behind him and without any pause she swung the big frozen leg of lamb high in the air and brought it down as hard as she could on the back of his head.

She might just as well have hit him with a steel club.

She stepped back a pace, waiting, and the funny thing was that he remained standing there for at least four or five seconds, gently swaying. Then he crashed to the carpet.

The violence of the crash, the noise, the small table overturning, helped bring her out of the shock. She came out slowly, feeling cold and surprised, and she stood for a while blinking at the body, still holding the ridiculous piece of meat tight with both hands.

All right, she told herself. So I've killed him.

It was extraordinary, now, how clear her mind became all of a sudden. She began thinking very fast. As the wife of a detective, she knew quite well what the penalty would be. That was fine. It made no difference to her. In fact, it would be a relief. On the other hand, what about the child? What were the laws about murderers with unborn children? Did they kill them both—mother and child? Or did they wait until the tenth month? What did they do?

Mary Maloney didn't know. And she certainly wasn't prepared to take a chance.

She carried the meat into the kitchen, placed it in a pan, turned the oven on high, and shoved it inside. Then she washed her hands and ran upstairs to the bedroom. She sat down before the mirror, tidied her face, touched up her lips and face. She tried a smile. It came out rather peculiar. She tried again.

"Hullo Sam," she said brightly, aloud.

The voice sounded peculiar too.

"I want some potatoes please, Sam. Yes, and I think a can of peas."

That was better. Both the smile and the voice were coming out better now. She rehearsed it several times more. Then she ran downstairs, took her coat, went out the back door, down the garden, into the street.

It wasn't six o'clock yet and the lights were still on in the grocery shop.

"Hullo Sam," she said brightly, smiling at the man behind the counter.

"Why, good evening, Mrs. Maloney. How're *you?*"

"I want some potatoes please, Sam. Yes, and I think a can of peas."

The man turned and reached up behind him on the shelf for the peas.

"Patrick's decided he's tired and doesn't want to eat out tonight," she told him. "We usually go out Thursdays, you know, and now he's caught me without any vegetables in the house."

"Then how about meat, Mrs. Maloney?"

"No, I've got meat, thanks. I got a nice leg of lamb, from the freezer."

"Oh."

"I don't much like cooking it frozen, Sam, but I'm taking a chance on it this time. You think it'll be all right?"

"Personally," the grocer said, "I don't believe it makes any difference. You want these Idaho potatoes?"

"Oh yes, that'll be fine. Two of those."

"Anything else?" The grocer cocked his head on one side, looking at her pleasantly. "How about afterwards? What you going to give him for afterwards?"

"Well—what would you suggest, Sam?"

The man glanced around his shop. "How about a nice big slice of cheesecake? I know he likes that."

"Perfect," she said. "He loves it."

And when it was all wrapped and she had paid, she put on her brightest smile and said, "Thank you, Sam. Good night."

"Good night, Mrs. Maloney. And thank *you*."

And now, she told herself as she hurried back, all she was doing now, she was returning home to her husband and he was waiting for his supper; and she must cook it good, and make it as tasty as possible because the poor man was tired; and if, when she entered the house, she happened to find anything unusual, or tragic, or terrible, then naturally it would be a shock and she'd become frantic with grief and horror. Mind you, she wasn't *expecting* to find anything. She was just going home with the vegetables. Mrs. Patrick Maloney going home with the vegetables on Thursday evening to cook supper for her husband.

That's the way, she told herself. Do everything right and natural. Keep things absolutely natural and there'll be no need for any acting at all.

Therefore, when she entered the kitchen by the back door, she was humming a little tune to herself and smiling.

"Patrick!" she called. "How are you, darling?"

She put the parcel down on the table and went through into the living-room; and when she saw him lying there on the floor with his legs doubled up and one arm twisted back underneath his body, it really was rather a shock. All the old love and longing for him welled up inside her, and she ran over to him, knelt down beside him, and began to cry her heart out. It was easy. No acting was necessary.

A few minutes later she got up and went to the phone. She knew the number of the police station, and when the man at the other end answered, she cried to him, "Quick! Come quick! Patrick's dead!"

"Who's speaking?"

"Mrs. Maloney. Mrs. Patrick Maloney."

"You mean Patrick Maloney's dead?"

"I think so," she sobbed. "He's lying on the floor and I think he's dead."

"Be right over," the man said.

The car came very quickly, and when she opened the front door, two policemen walked in. She knew them both—she knew nearly all the men at that precinct—and she fell right into Jack Noonan's arms, weeping hysterically. He put her gently into a chair, then went over to join the other one, who was called O'Malley, kneeling by the body.

"Is he dead?" she cried.

"I'm afraid he is. What happened?"

Briefly, she told her story about going out to the grocer and coming back to find him on the floor. While she was talking, crying and talking, Noonan discovered a small patch of congealed blood on the dead man's head. He showed it to O'Malley who got up at once and hurried to the phone.

Soon, other men began to come into the house. First a doctor, then two detectives, one of whom she knew by name. Later, a police photographer arrived and took pictures, and a man who knew about fingerprints. There was a great deal of whispering and muttering beside the corpse, and the detectives kept asking her a lot of questions. But they always treated her kindly. She told her story again, this time right from the beginning, when Patrick had come in, and she was sewing, and he was tired, so tired he hadn't wanted to go out for supper. She told how she'd put the meat in the oven—"it's there now, cooking"—and how she'd slipped out to the grocer for vegetables, and come back to find him lying on the floor.

"Which grocer?" one of the detectives asked.

She told him, and he turned and whispered something to the other detective who immediately went outside into the street.

In fifteen minutes he was back with a page of notes and there was more whispering, and through her sobbing she heard a few of the whispered phrases—". . . acted quite normal . . . very cheerful . . . wanted to give him a good supper . . . peas . . . cheesecake . . . impossible that she . . ."

After a while, the photographer and the doctor departed and two other men came in and took the corpse away on a stretcher. Then the fingerprint man went away. The two detectives remained, and so did the two policemen. They were exceptionally nice to her, and Jack Noonan asked if she wouldn't rather go somewhere else, to her sister's house perhaps, or to his own wife who would take care of her and put her up for the night.

No, she said. She didn't feel she could move even a yard at the moment. Would they mind awfully if she stayed just where she was until she felt better? She didn't feel too good at the moment, she really didn't.

Then hadn't she better lie down on the bed? Jack Noonan asked.

No, she said, she'd like to stay right where she was, in this chair. A little later perhaps, when she felt better, she would move.

So they left her there while they went about their business, searching the house. Occasionally one of the detectives asked her another question. Sometimes Jack Noonan spoke to her gently as he passed by. Her husband, he told her, had been killed by a blow on the back of the head administered with a heavy blunt instrument, almost certainly a large piece of metal. They were looking for the weapon. The murderer may have taken it with him, but on the other hand he may've thrown it away or hidden it somewhere on the premises.

"It's the old story," he said. "Get the weapon, and you've got the man."

Later, one of the detectives came up and sat beside her. Did she know, he asked, of anything in the house that could've been used as the weapon? Would she mind having a look around to see if anything was missing—a very big spanner, for example, or a heavy metal vase.

They didn't have any heavy metal vases, she said.

"Or a big spanner?"

She didn't think they had a big spanner. But there might be some things like that in the garage.

The search went on. She knew that there were other policemen in the garden all around the house. She could hear their footsteps on the gravel outside, and sometimes she saw the flash of a torch through a chink in the curtains. It began to get late, nearly nine she noticed by the clock on the mantel. The four men searching the rooms seemed to be growing weary, a trifle exasperated.

"Jack," she said, the next time Sergeant Noonan went by. "Would you mind giving me a drink?"

"Sure I'll give you a drink. You mean this whisky?"

"Yes, please. But just a small one. It might make me feel better."

He handed her the glass.

"Why don't you have one yourself," she said. "You must be awfully tired. Please do. You've been very good to me."

"Well," he answered. "It's not strictly allowed, but I might take just a drop to keep me going."

One by one the others came in and were persuaded to take a little nip of whisky. They stood around rather awkwardly with the drinks in their hands, uncomfortable in her presence, trying to say consoling things to her. Sergeant Noonan wandered into the kitchen, came out quickly and said, "Look, Mrs. Maloney. You know that oven of yours is still on, and the meat still inside."

"Oh *dear* me!" she cried. "So it is!"

"I better turn it off for you, hadn't I?"

"Will you do that, Jack? Thank you so much."

When the sergeant returned the second time, she looked at him with her large, dark eyes. "Jack Noonan," she said.

"Yes?"

"Would you do me a small favour—you and these others?"

"We can try, Mrs. Maloney."

"Well," she said. "Here you all are, and good friends of dear Patrick's too, and helping to catch the man who killed him. You must be terribly hungry by now because it's long past your supper time, and I know Patrick would never forgive me, God bless his soul, if I allowed you to remain in his house without offering you decent hospitality. Why don't you eat up that lamb that's in the oven? It'll be cooked just right by now."

"Wouldn't dream of it," Sergeant Noonan said.

"Please," she begged. "Please eat it. Personally I couldn't touch a thing, certainly not what's been in the house when he was here. But it's all right for you. It'd be a favour to me if you'd eat it up. Then you can go on with your work again afterwards."

There was a good deal of hesitating among the four policemen, but they were clearly hungry, and in the end they were persuaded to go into the kitchen and help themselves. The woman stayed where she was, listening to them through the open door, and she could hear them speaking among themselves, their voices thick and sloppy because their mouths were full of meat.

"Have some more, Charlie?"

"No. Better not finish it."

"She *wants* us to finish it. She said so. Be doing her a favour."

"Okay then. Give me some more."

"That's the hell of a big club the guy must've used to hit poor Patrick," one of them was saying. "The doc says his skull was smashed all to pieces just like from a sledge-hammer."

"That's why it ought to be easy to find."

"Exactly what I say."

"Whoever done it, they're not going to be carrying a thing like that around with them longer than they need."

One of them belched.

"Personally, I think it's right here on the premises."

"Probably right under our very noses. What you think, Jack?"

And in the other room, Mary Maloney began to giggle.

✿ ✿ ✿

Madame Sara

L. T. MEADE & ROBERT EUSTACE

Everyone in trade and a good many who are not have heard of Werner's Agency, the Solvency Inquiry Agency of all British trade. Its business is to know the financial condition of all whole-sale and retail firms, from Rothschild's to the smallest sweetstuff shop in Whitechapel. I do not say that every firm figures on its books, but by methods of secret inquiry it can discover the status of any firm or individual. It is the great safeguard to British trade and prevents much fraudulent dealing.

Of this agency I, Dixon Druce, was appointed manager in 1890. Since then I have met queer people and seen strange sights, for men do curious things for money in this world.

It so happened that in June, 1899, my business took me to Madeira on an inquiry of some importance. I left the island on the 14th of the month by the *Norham Castle* for Southampton. I got on board after dinner. It was a lovely night, and the strains of the band in the public gardens of Funchal came floating across the star-powdered bay through the warm, balmy air. Then the engine bells rang to "Full speed ahead," and, flinging a farewell to the fairest island on earth, I turned to the smoking-room in order to light my cheroot.

"Do you want a match, sir?"

The voice came from a slender, young-looking man who stood near the taffrail. Before I could reply he had struck one and held it out to me.

"Excuse me," he said, as he tossed it overboard, "but surely I am addressing Mr. Dixon Druce?"

"You are, sir," I said, glancing keenly back at him, "but you have the advantage of me."

"Don't you know me?" he responded. "Jack Selby, Hayward's House, Harrow, 1879."

"By Jove! so it is," I cried.

Our hands met in a warm clasp, and a moment later I found myself sitting close to my old friend, who had fagged for me in the bygone days, and whom I had not seen from the moment when I said good-bye to the "Hill" in the grey mist of a December morning twenty years ago. He was a boy of fourteen then, but nevertheless I recognised him. His face was bronzed and good-looking, his features refined. As a boy Selby had been noted for his grace, his well-shaped head, his clean-cut features; these characteristics still were his, and although he was now slightly past his first youth he was decidedly handsome. He gave me a quick sketch of his history.

"My father left me plenty of money," he said, "and The Meadows, our old family place, is now mine. I have a taste for natural history; that taste took me two years ago to South America. I have had my share of strange adventures, and have collected valuable specimens and trophies. I am now on my way home from Para, on the Amazon, having come by a Booth boat to Madeira and changed there to the Castle Line. But why all this talk about myself?" he added, bringing his deck-chair a little nearer to mine. "What about your history, old chap? Are you settled down with a wife and kiddies of your own, or is that dream of your school days fulfilled, and are you the owner of the best private laboratory in London?"

"As to the laboratory," I said, with a smile, "you must come and see it. For the rest I am unmarried. Are you?"

"I was married the day before I left Para, and my wife is on board with me."

"Capital," I answered. "Let me hear all about it."

"You shall. Her maiden name was Dallas; Beatrice Dallas. She is just twenty now. Her father was an Englishman and her mother a Spaniard; neither parent is living. She has an elder sister, Edith, nearly thirty years of age, unmarried, who is on board with us. There is also a step-brother, considerably older than either Edith or Beatrice. I met my wife last year in Para, and at once fell in love. I am the happiest man on earth. It goes without saying that I think her beautiful, and she is also very well off. The story of her wealth is a curious one. Her uncle on the mother's side was an extremely wealthy Spaniard, who made an enormous fortune in Brazil out of diamonds and minerals; he owned several mines. But it is supposed that his wealth turned his brain. At any rate, it seems to have done so as far as the disposal of his money went. He divided the yearly profits and interest between his nephew and his two nieces, but declared that the property itself should never be split up. He has left the whole of it to that one of the three who should survive the others. A perfectly insane arrangement, but not, I believe, unprecedented in Brazil."

"Very insane," I echoed. "What was he worth?"

"Over two million sterling."

"By Jove!" I cried, "what a sum! But what about the half-brother?"

"He must be over forty years of age, and is evidently a bad lot. I have never seen him. His sisters won't speak to him or have anything to do with him. I understand that he is a great gambler; I am further told that he is at present in England, and, as there are certain technicalities to be gone through before the girls can fully enjoy their incomes, one of the first things I must do when I get home is to find him out. He has to sign certain papers, for we sha'n't be able to put things straight until we get his whereabouts. Some time ago my wife and Edith heard that he was ill, but dead or alive we must know all about him, and as quickly as possible."

I made no answer, and he continued:

"I'll introduce you to my wife and sister-in-law to-morrow. Beatrice is quite a child compared to Edith, who acts towards her almost like a mother. Bee is a little beauty, so fresh and round and young-looking. But Edith is handsome, too, although I sometimes think she is as vain as a peacock. By the way, Druce, this brings me to another part of my story. The sisters have an acquaintance on board, one of the most remarkable women I have ever met. She goes by the name of Madame Sara, and knows London well. In fact, she confesses to having a shop in the Strand. What she has been doing in Brazil I do not know, for she keeps all her affairs strictly private. But you will be amazed when I tell you what her calling is."

"What?" I asked.

"A professional beautifier. She claims the privilege of restoring youth to those who consult her. She also declares that she can make quite ugly people handsome. There is no doubt that she is very clever. She knows a little bit of everything, and has wonderful recipes with regard to medicines, surgery, and dentistry. She is a most lovely woman herself, very fair, with blue eyes, an innocent, childlike manner, and quantities of rippling gold hair. She openly confesses that she is very much older than

she appears. She looks about five-and-twenty. She seems to have travelled all over the world, and says that by birth she is a mixture of Indian
and Italian, her father having been Italian and her mother Indian. Accompanying her is an Arab, a handsome, picturesque sort of fellow, who
gives her the most absolute devotion, and she is also bringing back to
England two Brazilians from Para. This woman deals in all sorts of
curious secrets, but principally in cosmetics. Her shop in the Strand
could, I fancy, tell many a strange history. Her clients go to her there,
and she does what is necessary for them. It is a fact that she occasionally
performs small surgical operations, and there is not a dentist in London
who can vie with her. She confesses quite naïvely that she holds some
secrets for making false teeth cling to the palate that no one knows
of. Edith Dallas is devoted to her—in fact, her adoration amounts to
idolatry."

"You give a very brilliant account of this woman," I said. "You must
introduce me to-morrow."

"I will," answered Jack, with a smile. "I should like your opinion of
her. I am right glad I have met you, Druce, it is like old times. When we
get to London I mean to put up at my town house in Eaton Square for
the remainder of the season. The Meadows shall be re-furnished, and
Bee and I will take up our quarters some time in August; then you must
come and see us. But I am afraid before I give myself up to mere pleasure I must find that precious brother-in-law, Henry Joachim Silva."

"If you have any difficulty apply to me," I said. "I can put at your
disposal, in an unofficial way, of course, agents who would find almost
any man in England, dead or alive."

I then proceeded to give Selby a short account of my own business.

"Thanks," he said, presently, "that is capital. You are the very man we
want."

The next morning after breakfast Jack introduced me to his wife and
sister-in-law. They were both foreign-looking, but very handsome, and
the wife in particular had a graceful and uncommon appearance.

We had been chatting about five minutes when I saw coming down
the deck a slight, rather small woman, wearing a big sun hat.

"Ah, Madame," cried Selby, "here you are. I had the luck to meet an
old friend on board—Mr. Dixon Druce—and I have been telling him all
about you. I should like you to know each other. Druce, this lady is

Madame Sara, of whom I have spoken to you. Mr. Dixon Druce—Madame Sara."

She bowed gracefully and then looked at me earnestly. I had seldom seen a more lovely woman. By her side both Mrs. Selby and her sister seemed to fade into insignificance. Her complexion was almost dazzlingly fair, her face refined in expression, her eyes penetrating, clever, and yet with the innocent, frank gaze of a child. Her dress was very simple; she looked altogether like a young, fresh, and natural girl.

As we sat chatting lightly and about commonplace topics, I instinctively felt that she took an interest in me even greater than might be evinced from an ordinary introduction. By slow degrees she so turned the conversation as to leave Selby and his wife and sister out, and then as they moved away she came a little nearer, and said in a low voice:

"I am very glad we have met, and yet how odd this meeting is! Was it really accidental?"

"I do not understand you," I answered.

"I know who you are," she said, lightly. "You are the manager of Werner's Agency; its business is to know the private affairs of those people who would rather keep their own secrets. Now, Mr. Druce, I am going to be absolutely frank with you. I own a small shop in the Strand —it is a perfumery shop—and behind those innocent-looking doors I conduct that business which brings me in gold of the realm. Have you, Mr. Druce, any objection to my continuing to make a livelihood in perfectly innocent ways?"

"None whatever," I answered. "You puzzle me by alluding to the subject."

"I want you to pay my shop a visit when you come to London. I have been away for three or four months. I do wonders for my clients, and they pay me largely for my services. I hold some perfectly innocent secrets which I cannot confide to anybody. I have obtained them partly from the Indians and partly from the natives of Brazil. I have lately been in Para to inquire into certain methods by which my trade can be improved."

"And your trade is——?" I said, looking at her with amusement and some surprise.

"I am a beautifier," she said, lightly. She looked at me with a smile. "You don't want me yet, Mr. Druce, but the time may come when even you will wish to keep back the infirmities of years. In the meantime can you guess my age?"

"I will not hazard a guess," I answered.

"And I will not tell you. Let it remain a secret. Meanwhile, understand that my calling is quite an open one, and I do hold secrets. I should advise you, Mr. Druce, even in your professional capacity, not to interfere with them."

The childlike expression faded from her face as she uttered the last words. There seemed to ring a sort of challenge in her tone. She turned away after a few moments and I rejoined my friends.

"You have been making acquaintance with Madame Sara, Mr. Druce," said Mrs. Selby. "Don't you think she is lovely?"

"She is one of the most beautiful women I have ever seen," I answered, "but there seems to be a mystery about her."

"Oh, indeed there is," said Edith Dallas, gravely.

"She asked me if I could guess her age," I continued. "I did not try, but surely she cannot be more than five-and-twenty."

"No one knows her age," said Mrs. Selby, "but I will tell you a curious fact, which, perhaps, you will not believe. She was bridesmaid at my mother's wedding thirty years ago. She declares that she never changes, and has no fear of old age."

"You mean that seriously?" I cried. "But surely it is impossible?"

"Her name is on the register, and my mother knew her well. She was mysterious then, and I think my mother got into her power, but of that I am not certain. Anyhow, Edith and I adore her, don't we, Edie?"

She laid her hand affectionately on her sister's arm. Edith Dallas did not speak, but her face was careworn. After a time she said, slowly:

"Madame Sara is uncanny and terrible."

There is, perhaps, no business imaginable—not even a lawyer's—that engenders suspicions more than mine. I hate all mysteries—both in persons and things. Mysteries are my natural enemies; I felt now that this woman was a distinct mystery. That she was interested in me I did not doubt, perhaps because she was afraid of me.

The rest of our voyage passed pleasantly enough. The more I saw of Mrs. Selby and her sister the more I liked them. They were quiet, simple, and straightforward. I felt sure that they were both as good as gold.

We parted at Waterloo, Jack and his wife and her sister going to Jack's house in Eaton Square, and I returning to my quarters in St. John's

Wood. I had a house there, with a long garden, at the bottom of which was my laboratory, the laboratory that was the pride of my life, it being, I fondly considered, the best private laboratory in London. There I spent all my spare time making experiments and trying this chemical combination and the other, living in hopes of doing great things some day, for Werner's Agency was not to be the end of my career. Nevertheless, it interested me thoroughly, and I was not sorry to get back to my commercial conundrums.

The next day, just before I started to go to my place of business, Jack Selby was announced.

"I want you to help me," he said. "I have been already trying in a sort of general way to get information about my brother-in-law, but all in vain. There is no such person in any of the directories. Can you put me on the road to discovery?"

I said I could and would if he would leave the matter in my hands.

"With pleasure," he replied. "You see how we are fixed up. Neither Edith nor Bee can get money with any regularity until the man is found. I cannot imagine why he hides himself."

"I will insert advertisements in the personal columns of the newspapers," I said, "and request anyone who can give information to communicate with me at my office. I will also give instructions to all the branches of my firm, as well as to my head assistants in London, to keep their eyes open for any news. You may be quite certain that in a week or two we shall know all about him."

Selby appeared cheered at this proposal, and, having begged of me to call upon his wife and her sister as soon as possible, took his leave.

On that very day advertisements were drawn up and sent to several newspapers and inquiry agents; but week after week passed without the slightest result. Selby got very fidgety at the delay. He was never happy except in my presence, and insisted on my coming, whenever I had time, to his house. I was glad to do so, for I took an interest both in him and his belongings, and as to Madame Sara I could not get her out of my head. One day Mrs. Selby said to me:

"Have you ever been to see Madame? I know she would like to show you her shop and general surroundings."

"I did promise to call upon her," I answered, "but have not had time to do so yet."

"Will you come with me to-morrow morning?" asked Edith Dallas, suddenly.

She turned red as she spoke, and the worried, uneasy expression became more marked on her face. I had noticed for some time that she had been looking both nervous and depressed. I had first observed this peculiarity about her on board the *Norham Castle*, but, as time went on, instead of lessening it grew worse. Her face for so young a woman was haggard; she started at each sound, and Madame Sara's name was never spoken in her presence without her evincing almost undue emotion.

"Will you come with me?" she said, with great eagerness.

I immediately promised, and the next day, about eleven o'clock, Edith Dallas and I found ourselves in a hansom driving to Madame Sara's shop. We reached it in a few minutes, and found an unpretentious little place wedged in between a hosier's on one side and a cheap print-seller's on the other. In the windows of the shop were pyramids of perfume bottles, with scintillating facet stoppers tied with coloured ribbons. We stepped out of the hansom and went indoors. Inside the shop were a couple of steps, which led to a door of solid mahogany.

"This is the entrance to her private house," said Edith, and she pointed to a small brass plate, on which was engraved the name—"Madame Sara, Parfumeuse."

Edith touched an electric bell and the door was immediately opened by a smartly-dressed page-boy. He looked at Miss Dallas as if he knew her very well, and said:

"Madame is within, and is expecting you, miss."

He ushered us both into a quiet-looking room, soberly but handsomely furnished. He left us, closing the door. Edith turned to me.

"Do you know where we are?" she asked.

"We are standing at present in a small room just behind Madame Sara's shop," I answered. "Why are you so excited, Miss Dallas? What is the matter with you?"

"We are on the threshold of a magician's cave," she replied. "We shall soon be face to face with the most marvellous woman in the whole of London. There is no one like her."

"And you—fear her?" I said, dropping my voice to a whisper.

She started, stepped back, and with great difficulty recovered her composure. At that moment the page-boy returned to conduct us through a series of small waiting-rooms, and we soon found ourselves in the presence of Madame herself.

"Ah!" she said, with a smile. "This is delightful. You have kept your word, Edith, and I am greatly obliged to you. I will now show Mr. Druce some of the mysteries of my trade. But understand, sir," she added, "that I shall not tell you any of my real secrets, only as you would like to know something about me you shall."

"How can you tell I should like to know about you?" I asked.

She gave me an earnest glance which somewhat astonished me, and then she said:

"Knowledge is power; don't refuse what I am willing to give. Edith, you will not object to waiting here while I show Mr. Druce through my rooms. First observe this room, Mr. Druce. It is lighted only from the roof. When the door shuts it automatically locks itself, so that any intrusion from without is impossible. This is my sanctum sanctorum—a faint odour of perfumes pervades the room. This is a hot day, but the room itself is cool. What do you think of it all?"

I made no answer. She walked to the other end and motioned to me to accompany her. There stood a polished oak square table, on which lay an array of extraordinary-looking articles and implements—stoppered bottles full of strange medicaments, mirrors, plane and concave, brushes, sprays, sponges, delicate needle-pointed instruments of bright steel, tiny lancets, and forceps. Facing this table was a chair, like those used by dentists. Above the chair hung electric lights in powerful reflectors, and lenses like bull's-eye lanterns. Another chair, supported on a glass pedestal, was kept there, Madame Sara informed me, for administering static electricity. There were dry-cell batteries for the continuous currents and induction coils for Faradic currents. There were also platinum needles for burning out the roots of hairs.

Madame took me from this room into another, where a still more formidable array of instruments were to be found. Here were a wooden operating table and chloroform and ether apparatus. When I had looked at everything, she turned to me.

"Now you know," she said. "I am a doctor—perhaps a quack. These are my secrets. By means of these I live and flourish."

She turned her back on me and walked into the other room with the light, springy step of youth. Edith Dallas, white as a ghost, was waiting for us.

"You have done your duty, my child," said Madame. "Mr. Druce has seen just what I want him to see. I am very much obliged to you both. We shall meet to-night at Lady Farringdon's 'At-home.' Until then, farewell."

When we got into the street and were driving back again to Eaton Square, I turned to Edith.

"Many things puzzle me about your friend," I said, "but perhaps none more than this. By what possible means can a woman who owns to being the possessor of a shop obtain the *entrée* to some of the best houses in London? Why does Society open her doors to this woman, Miss Dallas?"

"I cannot quite tell you," was her reply. "I only know the fact that wherever she goes she is welcomed and treated with consideration, and wherever she fails to appear there is a universally expressed feeling of regret."

I had also been invited to Lady Farringdon's reception that evening, and I went there in a state of great curiosity. There was no doubt that Madame interested me. I was not sure of her. Beyond doubt there was a mystery attached to her, and also, for some unaccountable reason, she wished both to propitiate and defy me. Why was this?

I arrived early, and was standing in the crush near the head of the staircase when Madame was announced. She wore the richest white satin and quantities of diamonds. I saw her hostess bend towards her and talk eagerly. I noticed Madame reply and the pleased expression that crossed Lady Farringdon's face. A few minutes later a man with a foreign-looking face and long beard sat down before the grand piano. He played a light prelude and Madame Sara began to sing. Her voice was sweet and low, with an extraordinary pathos in it. It was the sort of voice that penetrates to the heart. There was an instant pause in the gay chatter. She sang amidst perfect silence, and when the song had come to an end there followed a *furore* of applause. I was just turning to say something to my nearest neighbour when I observed Edith Dallas, who was standing close by. Her eyes met mine; she laid her hand on my sleeve.

"The room is hot," she said, half panting as she spoke. "Take me out on the balcony."

I did so. The atmosphere of the reception-rooms was almost intolerable, but it was comparatively cool in the open air.

"I must not lose sight of her," she said, suddenly.

"Of whom?" I asked, somewhat astonished at her words.

"Of Sara."

"She is there," I said. "You can see her from where you stand."

We happened to be alone. I came a little closer.

"Why are you afraid of her?" I asked.

"Are you sure that we shall not be heard?" was her answer.

"Certain."

"She terrifies me," were her next words.

"I will not betray your confidence, Miss Dallas. Will you not trust me? You ought to give me a reason for your fears."

"I cannot—I dare not; I have said far too much already. Don't keep me, Mr. Druce. She must not find us together."

As she spoke she pushed her way through the crowd, and before I could stop her was standing by Madame Sara's side.

The reception in Portland Place was, I remember, on the 26th of July. Two days later the Selbys were to give their final "At-home" before leaving for the country. I was, of course, invited to be present, and Madame was also there. She had never been dressed more splendidly, nor had she ever before looked younger or more beautiful. Wherever she went all eyes followed her. As a rule her dress was simple, almost like what a girl would wear, but to-night she chose rich Oriental stuffs made of many colours, and absolutely glittering with gems. Her golden hair was studded with diamonds. Round her neck she wore turquoise and diamonds mixed. There were many younger women in the room, but not the youngest nor the fairest had a chance beside Madame. It was not mere beauty of appearance, it was charm—charm which carries all before it.

I saw Miss Dallas, looking slim and tall and pale, standing at a little distance. I made my way to her side. Before I had time to speak she bent towards me.

"Is she not divine?" she whispered. "She bewilders and delights everyone. She is taking London by storm."

"Then you are not afraid of her to-night?" I said.

"I fear her more than ever. She has cast a spell over me. But listen, she is going to sing again."

I had not forgotten the song that Madame had given us at the Farringdons', and stood still to listen. There was a complete hush in the room. Her voice floated over the heads of the assembled guests in a dreamy Spanish song. Edith told me that it was a slumber song, and that Madame boasted of her power of putting almost anyone to sleep who listened to her rendering of it.

"She has many patients who suffer from insomnia," whispered the girl, "and she generally cures them with that song, and that alone. Ah! we must not talk; she will hear us."

Before I could reply Selby came hurrying up. He had not noticed Edith. He caught me by the arm.

"Come just for a minute into this window, Dixon," he said. "I must speak to you. I suppose you have no news with regard to my brother-in-law?"

"Not a word," I answered.

"To tell you the truth, I am getting terribly put out over the matter. We cannot settle any of our money affairs just because this man chooses to lose himself. My wife's lawyers wired to Brazil yesterday, but even his bankers do not know anything about him."

"The whole thing is a question of time," was my answer. "When are you off to Hampshire?"

"On Saturday."

As Selby said the last words he looked around him, then he dropped his voice.

"I want to say something else. The more I see"—he nodded towards Madame Sara—"the less I like her. Edith is getting into a very strange state. Have you not noticed it? And the worst of it is my wife is also infected. I suppose it is that dodge of the woman's for patching people up and making them beautiful. Doubtless the temptation is overpowering in the case of a plain woman, but Beatrice is beautiful herself and young. What can she have to do with cosmetics and complexion pills?"

"You don't mean to tell me that your wife has consulted Madame Sara as a doctor?"

"Not exactly, but she has gone to her about her teeth. She complained of toothache lately, and Madame's dentistry is renowned. Edith is constantly going to her for one thing or another, but then Edith is infatuated."

As Jack said the last words he went over to speak to someone else, and before I could leave the seclusion of the window I perceived Edith Dallas and Madame Sara in earnest conversation together. I could not help overhearing the following words:

"Don't come to me to-morrow. Get into the country as soon as you can. It is far and away the best thing to do."

As Madame spoke she turned swiftly and caught my eye. She bowed, and the peculiar look, the sort of challenge, she had before given me flashed over her face. It made me uncomfortable, and during the night that followed I could not get it out of my head. I remembered what Selby had said with regard to his wife and her money affairs. Beyond doubt he had married into a mystery—a mystery that Madame Sara knew all about. There was a very big money interest, and strange things happen when millions are concerned.

The next morning I had just risen and was sitting at breakfast when a note was handed to me. It came by special messenger, and was marked "Urgent." I tore it open. These were its contents:

"MY DEAR DRUCE,—A terrible blow has fallen on us. My sister-in-law, Edith, was taken suddenly ill this morning at breakfast. The nearest doctor was sent for, but he could do nothing, as she died half an hour ago. Do come and see me, and if you know any very clever specialist bring him with you. My wife is utterly stunned by the shock.
—Yours, Jack Selby."

I read the note twice before I could realize what it meant. Then I rushed out and, hailing the first hansom I met, said to the man:

"Drive to No. 192, Victoria Street, as quickly as you can."

Here lived a certain Mr. Eric Vandeleur, an old friend of mine and the police surgeon for the Westminster district, which included Eaton Square. No shrewder or sharper fellow existed than Vandeleur, and the present case was essentially in his province, both legally and professionally. He was not at his flat when I arrived, having already gone down to the court. Here I accordingly hurried, and was informed that he was in the mortuary.

For a man who, as it seemed to me, lived in a perpetual atmosphere of crime and violence, of death and coroners' courts, his habitual cheerfulness and brightness of manner were remarkable. Perhaps it was only the reaction from his work, for he had the reputation of being one of the most astute experts of the day in medical jurisprudence, and the most skilled analyst in toxicological cases on the Metropolitan Police staff. Before I could send him word that I wanted to see him I heard a door bang, and Vandeleur came hurrying down the passage, putting on his coat as he rushed along.

"Halloa!" he cried. "I haven't seen you for ages. Do you want me?"

"Yes, very urgently," I answered. "Are you busy?"

"Head over ears, my dear chap. I cannot give you a moment now, but perhaps later on."

"What is it? You look excited."

"I have got to go to Eaton Square like the wind, but come along, if you like, and tell me on the way."

"Capital," I cried. "The thing has been reported, then? You are going to Mr. Selby's, No. 34A; then I am going with you."

He looked at me in amazement.

"But the case has only just been reported. What can you possibly know about it?"

"Everything. Let us take this hansom, and I will tell you as we go along."

As we drove to Eaton Square I quickly explained the situation, glancing now and then at Vandeleur's bright, clean-shaven face. He was no longer Eric Vandeleur, the man with the latest club story and the merry twinkle in his blue eyes: he was Vandeleur the medical jurist, with a face like a mask, his lower jaw slightly protruding and features very fixed.

"This thing promises to be serious," he replied, as I finished, "but I can do nothing until after the autopsy. Here we are, and there is my man waiting for me; he has been smart."

On the steps stood an official-looking man in uniform, who saluted.

"Coroner's officer," explained Vandeleur.

We entered the silent, darkened house. Selby was standing in the hall. He came to meet us. I introduced him to Vandeleur, and he at once led us into the dining-room, where we found Dr. Osborne, whom Selby had called in when the alarm of Edith's illness had been first given. Dr. Osborne was a pale, under-sized, very young man. His face expressed considerable alarm. Vandeleur, however, managed to put him completely at his ease.

"I will have a chat with you in a few minutes, Dr. Osborne," he said; "but first I must get Mr. Selby's report. Will you please tell us, sir, exactly what occurred?"

"Certainly," he answered. "We had a reception here last night, and my sister-in-law did not go to bed until early morning; she was in bad spirits, but otherwise in her usual health. My wife went into her room after she was in bed, and told me later on that she had found Edith in hysterics, and could not get her to explain anything. We both talked about taking her to the country without delay. Indeed, our intention was to get off this afternoon."

"Well?" said Vandeleur.

"We had breakfast about half-past nine, and Miss Dallas came down, looking quite in her usual health, and in apparently good spirits. She ate with appetite, and, as it happened, she and my wife were both helped from the same dish. The meal had nearly come to an end when she jumped up from the table, uttered a sharp cry, turned very pale, pressed her hand to her side, and ran out of the room. My wife immediately followed her. She came back again in a minute or two, and said that Edith was in violent pain, and begged of me to send for a doctor. Dr. Osborne lives just round the corner. He came at once, but she died almost immediately after his arrival."

"You were in the room?" asked Vandeleur, turning to Osborne.

"Yes," he replied. "She was conscious to the last moment, and died suddenly."

"Did she tell you anything?"

"No, except to assure me that she had not eaten any food that day until she had come down to breakfast. After the death occurred I sent immediately to report the case, locked the door of the room where the poor girl's body is, and saw also that nobody touched anything on this table."

Vandeleur rang the bell and a servant appeared. He gave quick orders. The entire remains of the meal were collected and taken charge of, and then he and the coroner's officer went upstairs.

When we were alone Selby sank into a chair. His face was quite drawn and haggard.

"It is the horrible suddenness of the thing which is so appalling," he cried. "As to Beatrice, I don't believe she will ever be the same again. She was deeply attached to Edith. Edith was nearly ten years her senior, and always acted the part of mother to her. This is a sad beginning to our life. I can scarcely think collectedly."

I remained with him a little longer, and then, as Vandeleur did not return, went back to my own house. There I could settle to nothing, and when Vandeleur rang me up on the telephone about six o'clock I hurried off to his rooms. As soon as I arrived I saw that Selby was with him, and the expression on both their faces told me the truth.

"This is a bad business," said Vandeleur. "Miss Dallas has died from swallowing poison. An exhaustive analysis and examination have been made, and a powerful poison, unknown to European toxicologists, has been found. This is strange enough, but how it has been administered is a puzzle. I confess, at the present moment, we are all nonplussed. It certainly was not in the remains of the breakfast, and we have her dying evidence that she took nothing else. Now, a poison with such appalling potency would take effect quickly. It is evident that she was quite well when she came to breakfast, and that the poison began to work towards the close of the meal. But how did she get it? This question, however, I shall deal with later on. The more immediate point is this. The situation is a serious one in view of the monetary issues and the value of the lady's life. From the aspects of the case, her undoubted sanity and her affection for her sister, we may almost exclude the idea of suicide. We must, therefore, call it murder. This harmless, innocent lady is struck down by the hand of an assassin, and with such devilish cunning that no trace or clue is left behind. For such an act there must have been some very powerful motive, and the person who designed and executed it must be a criminal of the highest order of scientific ability. Mr. Selby has been telling me the exact financial position of the poor lady, and also of his own young wife. The absolute disappearance of the step-brother, in view of his previous character, is in the highest degree strange. Knowing, as we do, that between him and two million sterling there stood two lives—*one is taken!*"

A deadly sensation of cold seized me as Vandeleur uttered these last words. I glanced at Selby. His face was colourless and the pupils of his eyes were contracted, as though he saw something which terrified him.

"What has happened once may happen again," continued Vandeleur. "We are in the presence of a great mystery, and I counsel you, Mr. Selby, to guard your wife with the utmost care."

These words, falling from a man of Vandeleur's position and authority on such matters, were sufficiently shocking for me to hear, but for Selby to be given such a solemn warning about his young and beautiful and newly-married wife, who was all the world to him, was terrible indeed. He leant his head on his hands.

"Mercy on us!" he muttered. "Is this a civilized country when death can walk abroad like this, invisible, not to be avoided? Tell me, Mr. Vandeleur, what I must do."

"You must be guided by me," said Vandeleur, "and, believe me, there is no witchcraft in the world. I shall place a detective in your household immediately. Don't be alarmed; he will come to you in plain clothes and will simply act as a servant. Nevertheless, nothing can be done to your wife without his knowledge. As to you, Druce," he continued, turning to me, "the police are doing all they can to find this man Silva, and I ask you to help them with your big agency, and to begin at once. Leave your friend to me. Wire instantly if you hear news."

"You may rely on me," I said, and a moment later I had left the room.

As I walked rapidly down the street the thought of Madame Sara, her shop and its mysterious background, its surgical instruments, its operating-table, its induction coils, came back to me. And yet what could Madame Sara have to do with the present strange, inexplicable mystery?

The thought had scarcely crossed my mind before I heard a clatter alongside the kerb, and turning round I saw a smart open carriage, drawn by a pair of horses, standing there. I also heard my own name. I turned. Bending out of the carriage was Madame Sara.

"I saw you going by, Mr. Druce. I have only just heard the news about poor Edith Dallas. I am terribly shocked and upset. I have been to the house, but they would not admit me. Have you heard what was the cause of her death?"

Madame's blue eyes filled with tears as she spoke.

"I am not at liberty to disclose what I have heard, Madame," I answered, "since I am officially connected with the affair."

Her eyes narrowed. The brimming tears dried as though by magic. Her glance became scornful.

"Thank you," she answered; "your reply tells me that she did not die naturally. How very appalling! But I must not keep you. Can I drive you anywhere?"

"No, thank you."

"Good-bye, then."

She made a sign to the coachman, and as the carriage rolled away turned to look back at me. Her face wore the defiant expression I had seen there more than once. Could she be connected with the affair? The thought came upon me with a violence that seemed almost conviction. Yet I had no reason for it—none.

To find Henry Joachim Silva was now my principal thought. Advertisements were widely circulated. My staff had instructions to make every possible inquiry, with large money rewards as incitements. The collateral branches of other agencies throughout Brazil were communicated with by cable, and all the Scotland Yard channels were used. Still there was no result. The newspapers took up the case; there were paragraphs in most of them with regard to the missing step-brother and the mysterious death of Edith Dallas. Then someone got hold of the story of the will, and this was retailed with many additions for the benefit of the public. At the inquest the jury returned the following verdict:

"We find that Miss Edith Dallas died from taking poison of unknown name, but by whom or how administered there is no evidence to say."

This unsatisfactory state of things was destined to change quite suddenly. On the 6th of August, as I was seated in my office, a note was brought me by a private messenger. It ran as follows:

"Norfolk Hotel, Strand.

"DEAR SIR,—I have just arrived in London from Brazil, and have seen your advertisements. I was about to insert one myself in order to find the whereabouts of my sisters. I am a great invalid and unable to leave my room. Can you come to see me at the earliest possible moment?—Yours,

"*Henry Joachim Silva.*"

In uncontrollable excitement I hastily dispatched two telegrams, one to Selby and the other to Vandeleur, begging of them to be with me, without fail, as soon as possible. So the man had never been in England at all. The situation was more bewildering than ever. One thing, at least, was probable—Edith Dallas's death was not due to her step-brother. Soon after half-past six Selby arrived, and Vandeleur walked in ten minutes later. I told them what had occurred and showed them the letter. In half an hour's time we reached the hotel, and on stating who I was we were shown into a room on the first floor by Silva's private servant. Resting in an arm-chair, as we entered, sat a man; his face was terribly thin. The eyes and cheeks were so sunken that the face had almost the appearance of a skull. He made no effort to rise when we entered, and glanced from one of us to the other with the utmost astonishment. I at once introduced myself and explained who we were. He then waved his hand for his man to retire.

"You have heard the news, of course, Mr. Silva?" I said.

"News! What?" He glanced up to me and seemed to read something in my face. He started back in his chair.

"Good heavens!" he replied. "Do you allude to my sisters? Tell me, quickly, are they alive?"

"Your elder sister died on the 29th of July, and there is every reason to believe that her death was caused by foul play."

As I uttered these words the change that passed over his face was fearful to witness. He did not speak, but remained motionless. His claw-like hands clutched the arms of the chair, his eyes were fixed and staring, as though they would start from their hollow sockets, the colour of his skin was like clay. I heard Selby breathe quickly behind me, and Vandeleur stepped towards the man and laid his hand on his shoulder.

"Tell us what you know of this matter," he said, sharply.

Recovering himself with an effort, the invalid began in a tremulous voice:

"Listen closely, for you must act quickly. I am indirectly responsible for this fearful thing. My life has been a wild and wasted one, and now I am dying. The doctors tell me I cannot live a month, for I have a large aneurism of the heart. Eighteen months ago I was in Rio. I was living fast and gambled heavily. Among my fellow-gamblers was a man much older than myself. His name was José Aranjo. He was, if anything, a greater gambler than I. One night we played alone. The stakes ran high until they reached a big figure. By daylight I had lost to him nearly £200,000. Though I am a rich man in point of income under my uncle's will, I could not pay a twentieth part of that sum. This man knew my financial position, and, in addition to a sum of £5,000 paid down, I gave him a document. I must have been mad to do so. The document was this—it was duly witnessed and attested by a lawyer—that, in the event of my surviving my two sisters and thus inheriting the whole of my uncle's vast wealth, half a million should go to José Aranjo. I felt I was breaking up at the time, and the chances of my inheriting the money were small. Immediately after the completion of the document this man left Rio, and I then heard a great deal about him that I had not previously known. He was a man of the queerest antecedents, partly Indian, partly Italian. He had spent many years of his life amongst the Indians. I heard also that he was as cruel as he was clever, and possessed some wonderful secrets of poisoning unknown to the West. I thought a great deal about this, for I knew that by signing that document I had placed the lives of my two sisters between him and a fortune. I came to Para six weeks ago, only to learn that one of my sisters was married and that both had gone to England. Ill as I was, I determined to follow them in order to warn them. I also wanted to arrange matters with you, Mr. Selby."

"One moment, sir," I broke in, suddenly. "Do you happen to be aware if this man, José Aranjo, knew a woman calling herself Madame Sara?"

"Knew her?" cried Silva. "Very well indeed, and so, for that matter, did I. Aranjo and Madame Sara were the best friends, and constantly met. She called herself a professional beautifier—was very handsome, and had secrets for the pursuing of her trade unknown even to Aranjo."

"Good heavens!" I cried, "and the woman is now in London. She returned here with Mrs. Selby and Miss Dallas. Edith was very much influenced by her, and was constantly with her. There is no doubt in my mind that she is guilty. I have suspected her for some time, but I could not find a motive. Now the motive appears. You surely can have her arrested?"

Vandeleur made no reply. He gave me a strange look, then he turned to Selby.

"Has your wife also consulted Madame Sara?" he asked, sharply.

"Yes, she went to her once about her teeth, but has not been to the shop since Edith's death. I begged of her not to see the woman, and she promised me faithfully she would not do so."

"Has she any medicines or lotions given to her by Madame Sara—does she follow any line of treatment advised by her?"

"No, I am certain on that point."

"Very well, I will see your wife to-night in order to ask her some questions. You must both leave town at once. Go to your country house and settle there. I am quite serious when I say that Mrs. Selby is in the utmost possible danger until after the death of her brother. We must leave you now, Mr. Silva. All business affairs must wait for the present. It is absolutely necessary that Mrs. Selby should leave London at once. Good-night, sir. I shall give myself the pleasure of calling on you to-morrow morning."

We took leave of the sick man. As soon as we got into the street Vandeleur stopped.

"I must leave it to you, Selby," he said, "to judge how much of this matter you will tell to your wife. Were I you I would explain everything. The time for immediate action has arrived, and she is a brave and sensible woman. From this moment you must watch all the foods and liquids that she takes. She must never be out of your sight or out of the sight of some other trustworthy companion."

"I shall, of course, watch my wife myself," said Selby. "But the thing is enough to drive one mad."

"I will go with you to the country, Selby," I said, suddenly.

"Ah!" cried Vandeleur, "that is the best thing possible, and what I wanted to propose. Go, all of you, by an early train to-morrow."

"Then I will be off home at once, to make arrangements," I said. "I will meet you, Selby, at Waterloo for the first train to Cronsmoor to-morrow."

As I was turning away Vandeleur caught my arm.

"I am glad you are going with them," he said. "I shall write to you to-night *re* instructions. Never be without a loaded revolver. Good-night."

By 6:15 the next morning Selby, his wife, and I were in a reserved, locked, first-class compartment, speeding rapidly west. The servants and Mrs. Selby's own special maid were in a separate carriage. Selby's face showed signs of a sleepless night, and presented a striking contrast to the fair, fresh face of the girl round whom this strange battle raged. Her husband had told her everything, and, though still suffering terribly from the shock and grief of her sister's death, her face was calm and full of repose.

A carriage was waiting for us at Cronsmoor, and by half-past nine we arrived at the old home of the Selbys, nestling amid its oaks and elms. Everything was done to make the home-coming of the bride as cheerful as circumstances would permit, but a gloom, impossible to lift, over-shadowed Selby himself. He could scarcely rouse himself to take the slightest interest in anything.

The following morning I received a letter from Vandeleur. It was very short, and once more impressed on me the necessity of caution. He said that two eminent physicians had examined Silva, and the verdict was that he could not live a month. Until his death precautions must be strictly observed.

The day was cloudless, and after breakfast I was just starting out for a stroll when the butler brought me a telegram. I tore it open; it was from Vandeleur.

"Prohibit all food until I arrive. Am coming down," were the words. I hurried into the study and gave it to Selby. He read it and looked up at me.

"Find out the first train and go and meet him, old chap," he said. "Let us hope that this means an end of the hideous affair."

I went into the hall and looked up the trains. The next arrived at Cronsmoor at 10:45. I then strolled round to the stables and ordered a carriage, after which I walked up and down on the drive. There was no doubt that something strange had happened. Vandeleur coming down so suddenly must mean a final clearing up of the mystery. I had just turned round at the lodge gates to wait for the carriage when the sound of wheels and of horses galloping struck on my ears. The gates were swung open, and Vandeleur in an open fly dashed through them. Before I could recover from my surprise he was out of the vehicle and at my side. He carried a small black bag in his hand.

"I came down by special train," he said, speaking quickly. "There is not a moment to lose. Come at once. Is Mrs. Selby all right?"

"What do you mean?" I replied. "Of course she is. Do you suppose that she is in danger?"

"Deadly," was his answer. "Come."

We dashed up to the house together. Selby, who had heard our steps, came to meet us.

"Mr. Vandeleur!" he cried. "What is it? How did you come?"

"By special train, Mr. Selby. And I want to see your wife at once. It will be necessary to perform a very trifling operation."

"Operation!" he exclaimed.

"Yes, at once."

We made our way through the hall and into the morning-room, where Mrs. Selby was busily engaged reading and answering letters. She started up when she saw Vandeleur and uttered an exclamation of surprise.

"What has happened?" she asked.

Vandeleur went up to her and took her hand.

"Do not be alarmed," he said, "for I have come to put all your fears to rest. Now, please, listen to me. When you visited Madame Sara with your sister, did you go for medical advice?"

The colour rushed into her face.

"One of my teeth ached," she answered. "I went to her about that. She is, as I suppose you know, a most wonderful dentist. She examined the tooth, found that it required stopping, and got an assistant, a Brazilian, I think, to do it."

"And your tooth has been comfortable ever since?"

"Yes, quite. She had one of Edith's stopped at the same time."

"Will you kindly sit down and show me which was the tooth into which the stopping was put?"

She did so.

"This was the one," she said, pointing with her finger to one in the lower jaw. "What do you mean? Is there anything wrong?"

Vandeleur examined the tooth long and carefully. There was a sudden rapid movement of his hand, and a sharp cry from Mrs. Selby. With the deftness of long practice, and a powerful wrist, he had extracted the tooth with one wrench. The suddenness of the whole thing, startling as it was, was not so strange as his next movement.

"Send Mrs. Selby's maid to her," he said, turning to her husband; "then come, both of you, into the next room."

The maid was summoned. Poor Mrs. Selby had sunk back in her chair, terrified and half fainting. A moment later Selby joined us in the dining-room.

"That's right," said Vandeleur; "close the door, will you?"

He opened his black bag and brought out several instruments. With one he removed the stopping from the tooth. It was quite soft and came away easily. Then from the bag he produced a small guinea-pig, which he requested me to hold. He pressed the sharp instrument into the tooth, and opening the mouth of the little animal placed the point on the tongue. The effect was instantaneous. The little head fell on to one of my hands—the guinea-pig was dead. Vandeleur was white as a sheet. He hurried up to Selby and wrung his hand.

"Thank Heaven!" he said, "I've been in time, but only just. Your wife is safe. This stopping would hardly have held another hour. I have been thinking all night over the mystery of your sister-in-law's death, and over every minute detail of evidence as to how the poison could have been administered. Suddenly the coincidence of both sisters having had their teeth stopped struck me as remarkable. Like a flash the solution came to me. The more I considered it the more I felt that I was right; but by what fiendish cunning such a scheme could have been conceived and executed is still beyond my power to explain. The poison is very like hyoscine, one of the worst toxic-alkaloids known, so violent in its deadly proportions that the amount that would go into a tooth would cause almost instant death. It has been kept in by a gutta-percha stopping, certain to come out within a month, probably earlier, and most probably during mastication of food. The person would die either immediately or after a very few minutes, and no one would connect a visit to the dentist with a death a month afterwards."

What followed can be told in a very few words. Madame Sara was arrested on suspicion. She appeared before the magistrate, looking innocent and beautiful, and managed during her evidence completely to baffle that acute individual. She denied nothing, but declared that the poison must have been put into the tooth by one of the two Brazilians whom she had lately engaged to help her with her dentistry. She had her suspicions with regard to these men soon afterwards, and had dismissed them. She believed that they were in the pay of José Aranjo, but she could not tell anything for certain. Thus Madame escaped conviction. I was certain that she was guilty, but there was not a shadow of real proof. A month later Silva died, and Selby is now a double millionaire.

The Case of Mr. Foggatt

ARTHUR MORRISON

Almost the only dogmatism that Martin Hewitt permitted himself in regard to his professional methods was one on the matter of accumulative probabilities. Often when I have remarked upon the apparently trivial nature of the clues by which he allowed himself to be guided—sometimes, to all seeming, in the very face of all likelihood —he has replied that two trivialities, pointing in the same direction, became at once, by their mere agreement, no trivialities at all, but enormously important considerations. "If I were in search of a man," he would say, "of whom I knew nothing but that he squinted, bore a birthmark on his right hand, and limped, and I observed a man who answered to the first peculiarity, so far the clue would be trivial, because thousands of men squint. Now, if that man presently moved and exhibited a birthmark on his right hand, the value of that squint and that mark would increase at once a hundred or a thousand fold. Apart they are little; together much. The weight of evidence is not doubled merely; it would be only doubled if half the men who squinted had right-hand birthmarks; whereas, the proportion, if it could be ascertained, would be perhaps more like one in ten thousand. The two trivialities, pointing in the same direction, become very strong evidence. And when the man is seen to walk with a limp, that limp (another triviality), reinforcing the others, brings the matter to the rank of a practical certainty. The Bertillon system of identification—what is it but a summary of trivialities? Thousands of men are of the same height, thousands of the same length of foot, thousands of the same girth of head—thousands correspond in any separate measurement you may name. It is when the measurements are taken *together* that you have your man identified for ever. Just consider how few, if any, of your friends correspond exactly in any two personal peculiarities." Hewitt's dogma received its illustration unexpectedly close at home.

The old house wherein my chambers and Hewitt's office were situated contained, beside my own, two or three more bachelors' dens, in addition to the offices on the ground and first and second floors. At the very top of all, at the back, a fat, middle-aged man, named Foggatt, occupied a set of four rooms. It was only after long residence, by an accidental remark of the housekeeper's, that I learned the man's name, which was not painted on his door or displayed, with all the others, on the wall of the ground-floor porch.

Mr. Foggatt appeared to have few friends, but lived in something as nearly approaching luxury as an old bachelor in chambers can live. An ascending case of champagne was a common phenomenon of the staircase, and I have more than once seen a picture, destined for the top floor, of a sort that went far to awaken green covetousness in the heart of a poor journalist.

The man himself was not altogether prepossessing. Fat as he was, he had a way of carrying his head forward on his extended neck and gazing widely about with a pair of the roundest and most prominent eyes I remember to have ever seen, except in a fish. On the whole, his appearance was rather vulgar, rather arrogant, and rather suspicious, without any very pronounced quality of any sort. But certainly he was not pretty. In the end, however, he was found shot dead in his sitting-room.

It was in this way: Hewitt and I had dined together at my club, and late in the evening had returned to my rooms to smoke and discuss whatever came uppermost. I had made a bargain that day with two speculative odd lots at a book sale, each of which contained a hidden prize. We sat talking and turning over these books while time went unperceived, when suddenly we were startled by a loud report. Clearly it was in the building. We listened for a moment, but heard nothing else, and then Hewitt expressed his opinion that the report was that of a gunshot. Gunshots in residential chambers are not common things, wherefore I got up and went to the landing, looking up the stairs and down.

At the top of the next flight I saw Mrs. Clayton, the housekeeper. She appeared to be frightened, and told me that the report came from Mr. Foggatt's room. She thought he might have had an accident with the pistol that usually lay on his mantelpiece. We went upstairs with her, and she knocked at Mr. Foggatt's door.

There was no reply. Through the ventilating fanlight over the door it could be seen that there were lights within, a sign, Mrs. Clayton maintained, that Mr. Foggatt was not out. We knocked again, much more loudly, and called, but still ineffectually. The door was locked, and an application of the housekeeper's key proved that the tenant's key had been left in the lock inside. Mrs. Clayton's conviction that "something had happened" became distressing, and in the end Hewitt prised open the door with a small poker.

Something *had* happened. In the sitting-room Mr. Foggatt sat with his head bowed over the table, quiet and still. The head was ill to look at, and by it lay a large revolver, of the full-sized Army pattern. Mrs. Clayton ran back toward the landing with faint screams.

"Run, Brett," said Hewitt; "a doctor and a policeman!"

I bounced down the stairs half a flight at a time. "First," I thought, "a doctor. He may not be dead." I could think of no doctor in the immediate neighbourhood, but ran up the street away from the Strand, as being the more likely direction for the doctor, although less so for the policeman. It took me a good five minutes to find the medico, after being led astray by a red lamp at a private hotel, and another five to get back, with a policeman.

Foggatt was dead, without a doubt. Probably had shot himself, the doctor thought, from the powder-blackening and other circumstances. Certainly nobody could have left the room by the door, or he must have passed my landing, while the fact of the door being found locked from the inside made the thing impossible. There were two windows to the room, both of which were shut, one being fastened by the catch, while the catch of the other was broken—an old fracture. Below these windows was a sheer drop of 50ft. or more, without a foot or hand-hold near. The windows in the other rooms were shut and fastened. Certainly it seemed suicide—unless it were one of those accidents that will occur to people who fiddle ignorantly with firearms. Soon the rooms were in possession of the police, and we were turned out.

We looked in at the housekeeper's kitchen, where her daughter was reviving and calming Mrs. Clayton with gin and water.

"You mustn't upset yourself, Mrs. Clayton," Hewitt said, "or what will become of us all? The doctor thinks it was an accident."

He took a small bottle of sewing-machine oil from his pocket and handed it to the daughter, thanking her for the loan.

There was little evidence at the inquest. The shot had been heard, the body had been found—that was the practical sum of the matter. No friends or relatives of the dead man came forward. The doctor gave his opinion as to the probability of suicide or an accident, and the police evidence tended in the same direction. Nothing had been found to indicate that any other person had been near the dead man's rooms on the night of the fatality. On the other hand, his papers, bank-book, etc., proved him to be a man of considerable substance, with no apparent motive for suicide. The police had been unable to trace any relatives, or, indeed, any nearer connections than casual acquaintances, fellow clubmen, and so on. The jury found that Mr. Foggatt had died by accident.

"Well, Brett," Hewitt asked me afterwards, "what do you think of the verdict?"

I said that it seemed to be the most reasonable one possible, and to square with the common-sense view of the case.

"Yes," he replied, "perhaps it does. From the point of view of the jury, and on their information, their verdict was quite reasonable. Nevertheless, Mr. Foggatt did not shoot himself. He was shot by a rather tall, active young man, perhaps a sailor, but certainly a gymnast—a young man whom I think I could identify, if I saw him."

"But how do you know this?"

"By the simplest possible inferences, which you may easily guess, if you will but think."

"But, then, why didn't you say this at the inquest?"

"My dear fellow, they don't want my inferences and conjectures at an inquest, they only want evidence. If I had traced the murderer, of course then I should have communicated with the police. As a matter of fact, it is quite possible that the police have observed and know as much as I do —or more. They don't give everything away at an inquest, you know—it wouldn't do."

"But if you are right, how did the man get away?"

"Come, we are near home now. Let us take a look at the back of the house. He *couldn't* have left by Foggatt's landing-door, as we know; and as he *was* there (I am certain of that), and as the chimney is out of the question—for there was a good fire in the grate—he must have gone out by the window. Only one window is possible—that with the broken catch—for all the others were fastened inside. Out of that window, then, he went."

"But how? The window is 50ft. up."

"Of course it is. But why *will* you persist in assuming that the only way of escape by a window is downward? See, now, look up there. The window is at the top-floor, and it has a very broad sill. Over the window is nothing but the flat face of the gable-end; but to the right, and a foot or two above the level of the top of the window, an iron gutter ends. Observe, it is not of lead composition, but a strong iron gutter, supported, just at its end, by an iron bracket. If a tall man stood on the end of the window-sill, steadying himself by the left hand and leaning to the right, he could just touch the end of this gutter with his right hand—the full stretch, toe to finger, is 7ft. 3in.; I have measured it. An active gymnast, or a sailor, could catch the gutter with a slight spring, and by it draw himself upon the roof. You will say he would have to be *very* active, dexterous, and cool. So he would. And that very fact helps us, because it narrows the field of inquiry. We know the sort of man to look for. Because, being certain (as I am) that the man was in the room, I *know* that he left in the way I am telling you. He must have left in some way, and all the other ways being impossible, this alone remains, difficult as the feat may seem. The fact of his shutting the window behind him further proves his coolness and address at so great a height from the ground."

All this was very plain, but the main point was still dark.

"You say you *know* that another man was in the room," I said; "how do you know that?"

"As I said, by an obvious inference. Come now, you shall guess how I arrived at that inference. You often speak of your interest in my work, and the attention with which you follow it. This shall be a simple exercise for you. You saw everything in the room as plainly as I myself. Bring the scene back to your memory, and think over the various small objects littering about, and how they would affect the case. Quick observation is the first essential for my work. Did you see a newspaper, for instance?"

"Yes. There was an evening paper on the floor, but I didn't examine it."

"Anything else?"

"On the table there was a whisky decanter, taken from the tantalus stand on the sideboard, and one glass. That, by-the-bye," I added, "looked as though only one person were present."

"So it did, perhaps, although the inference wouldn't be very strong. Go on."

"There was a fruit-stand on the sideboard, with a plate beside it, containing a few nutshells, a piece of apple, a pair of nutcrackers, and, I think, some orange peel. There was, of course, all the ordinary furniture, but no chair pulled up to the table except that used by Foggatt himself. That's all I noticed, I think. Stay—there was an ash-tray on the table, and a partly-burned cigar near it—only one cigar, though."

"Excellent—excellent, indeed, as far as memory and simple observation go. You saw everything plainly, and you remember everything. Surely *now* you know how I found out that another man had just left?"

"No, I don't; unless there were different kinds of ash in the ash-tray."

"That is a fairly good suggestion, but there were not—there was only a single ash, corresponding in every way to that on the cigar. Don't you remember anything that I did as we went downstairs?"

"You returned a bottle of oil to the housekeeper's daughter, I think."

"I did. Doesn't that give you a hint? Come, you surely have it now?"

"I haven't."

"Then I shan't tell you; you don't deserve it. Think, and don't mention the subject again till you have at least one guess to make. The thing stares you in the face—you see it, you remember it, and yet you *won't* see it. I won't encourage your slovenliness of thought, my boy, by telling you what you can know for yourself if you like. Good-bye—I'm off now. There is a case in hand I can't neglect."

"Don't you propose to go further into this, then?"

Hewitt shrugged his shoulders. "I'm not a policeman," he said. "The case is in very good hands. Of course, if anybody comes to me to do it as a matter of business, I'll take it up. It's very interesting, but I can't neglect my regular work for it. Naturally, I shall keep my eyes open and my memory in order. Sometimes these things come into the hands by themselves, as it were; in that case, of course, I am a loyal citizen, and ready to help the law. *Au revoir.*"

I am a busy man myself, and thought little more of Hewitt's conundrum for some time—indeed, when I did think, I saw no way to the answer. A week after the inquest I took a holiday (I had written my nightly leaders regularly every day for the past five years), and saw no more of Hewitt for six weeks. After my return, with still a few days of leave to run, one evening we together turned into Luzatti's, off Coventry Street, for dinner.

"I have been here several times lately," Hewitt said; "they feed you very well. No, not that table"—he seized my arm as I turned to an unoccupied corner—"I fancy it's draughty." He led the way to a longer table where a dark, lithe, and (as well as could be seen) tall young man already sat, and took chairs opposite him.

We had scarcely seated ourselves before Hewitt broke into a torrent of conversation on the subject of bicycling. As our previous conversation had been of a literary sort, and as I had never known Hewitt at any other time to show the slightest interest in bicycling, this rather surprised me. I had, however, such a general outsider's grasp of the subject as is usual in a journalist-of-all-work, and managed to keep the talk going from my side. As we went on I could see the face of the young man opposite brighten with interest. He was a rather fine-looking fellow, with a dark though very clear skin, but had a hard, angry look of eye, a prominence of cheek-bone, and a squareness of jaw that gave him a rather uninviting aspect. As Hewitt rattled on, however, our neighbour's expression became one of pleasant interest merely.

"Of course," Hewitt said, "we've a number of very capital men just now, but I believe a deal in the forgotten riders of five, ten, and fifteen years back. Osmond, I believe, was better than any man riding now, and I think it would puzzle some of them to beat Furnivall as he was at his best. But poor old Cortis—really, I believe he was as good as anybody. Nobody ever beat Cortis—except—let me see—I think somebody beat Cortis once—who was it, now? I can't remember."

"Liles," said the young man opposite, looking up quickly.

"Ah, yes—Liles it was; Charley Liles. Wasn't it a championship?"

"Mile championship, 1880; Cortis won the other three, though."

"Yes, so he did. I saw Cortis when he first broke the old 2.46 mile record." And straightway Hewitt plunged into a whirl of talk of bicycles, tricycles, records, racing cyclists, Hillier and Synyer and Noel Whiting, Taylerson and Appleyard; talk wherein the young man opposite bore an animated share, while I was left in the cold.

Our new friend, it seemed, had himself been a prominent racing bicyclist a few years back, and was presently, at Hewitt's request, exhibiting a neat gold medal that hung at his watch-guard. That was won, he explained, in the old tall bicycle days, the days of bad tracks, when every racing cyclist carried cinder scars on his face from numerous accidents. He pointed to a blue mark on his forehead, which, he told us, was a track scar, and described a bad fall that had cost him two teeth, and broken others. The gaps among his teeth were plain to see as he smiled.

Presently the waiter brought dessert, and the young man opposite took an apple. Nutcrackers and a fruit-knife lay on our side of the stand, and Hewitt turned the stand to offer him the knife.

"No, thanks," he said, "I only polish a good apple, never peel it. It's a mistake except with thick-skinned, foreign ones."

And he began to munch the apple as only a boy or a healthy athlete can. Presently he turned his head to order coffee. The waiter's back was turned, and he had to be called twice. To my unutterable amazement Hewitt reached swiftly across the table, snatched the half-eaten apple from the young man's plate and pocketed it; gazing immediately, with an abstracted air, at a painted Cupid on the ceiling.

Our neighbour turned again, looked doubtfully at his plate and the tablecloth about it, and then shot a keen glance in the direction of Hewitt. He said nothing, however, but took his coffee and his bill, deliberately drank the former, gazing quietly at Hewitt as he did it, paid the latter, and left.

Immediately Hewitt was on his feet and, taking an umbrella which stood near, followed. Just as he reached the door he met our late neighbour, who had turned suddenly back.

"Your umbrella, I think?" Hewitt asked, offering it.

"Yes, thanks." But the man's eye had more than its former hardness, and his jaw-muscles tightened as I looked. He turned and went. Hewitt came back to me. "Pay the bill," he said, "and go back to your rooms; I will come on later: I must follow this man—it's the Foggatt case." As he went out I heard a cab rattle away, and immediately after it another.

I paid the bill and went home. It was ten o'clock before Hewitt turned up, calling in at his office below on his way up to me.

"Mr. Sidney Mason," he said, "is the gentleman the police will be wanting tomorrow, I expect, for the Foggatt murder. He is as smart a man as I remember ever meeting, and has done me rather neatly twice this evening."

"You mean the man we sat opposite at Luzatti's, of course?"

"Yes, I got his name, of course, from the reverse of that gold medal he was good enough to show me. But I fear he has bilked me over the address. He suspected me, that was plain, and left his umbrella by way of experiment, to see if I were watching him sharply enough to notice the circumstance, and to avail myself of it to follow him. I was hasty and fell into the trap. He cabbed it away from Luzatti's, and I cabbed it after him. He has led me a pretty dance up and down London to-night, and two cabbies have made quite a stroke of business out of us. In the end he entered a house of which, of course, I have taken the address, but I expect he doesn't live there. He is too smart a man to lead me to his den; but the police can certainly find something of him at the house he went in at—and, I expect, left by the back way. By the way, you never guessed that simple little puzzle as to how I found that this *was* a murder, did you? You see it now, of course?"

"Something to do with that apple you stole, I suppose?"

"Something to do with it? I should think so, you worthy innocent. Just ring your bell—we'll borrow Mrs. Clayton's sewing-machine oil again. On the night we broke into Foggatt's room you saw the nutshells and the bitten remains of an apple on the sideboard, and you remembered it; and yet you couldn't see that in that piece of apple possibly lay an important piece of evidence. Of course, I never expected you to have arrived at any conclusion, as I had, because I had ten minutes in which to examine that apple, and to do what I did with it. But at least you should have seen the possibility of evidence in it.

"First, now, the apple was white. A bitten apple, as you must have observed, turns of a reddish-brown colour if left to stand long. Different kinds of apples brown with different rapidities, and the browning always begins at the core. This is one of the twenty thousand tiny things that few people take the trouble to notice, but which it is useful for a man in my position to know. A russet will brown quite quickly. The apple on the sideboard was, as near as I could tell, a Newtown pippin or other apple of that kind, which will brown at the core in from twenty minutes to half an hour, and in other parts in a quarter of an hour more. When we saw it it was white, with barely a tinge of brown about the exposed core. Inference—somebody had been eating it fifteen or twenty minutes before—perhaps a little longer; an inference supported by the fact that it was only partly eaten.

"I examined that apple, and found it bore marks of very irregular teeth. While you were gone I oiled it over, and, rushing down to my rooms, where I always have a little plaster of Paris handy for such work, took a mould of the part where the teeth had left the clearest marks. I then returned the apple to its place, for the police to use if they thought fit. Looking at my mould, it was plain that the person who had bitten that apple had lost two teeth, one at top and one below, not exactly opposite, but nearly so. The other teeth, although they would appear to have been fairly sound, were irregular in size and line. Now the dead man had, as I saw, a very excellent set of false teeth, regular and sharp, with none missing. Therefore it was plain that *somebody else* had been eating that apple. Do I make myself clear?"

"Quite. Go on."

"There were other inferences to be made—slighter, but all pointing the same way. For instance, a man of Foggatt's age does not as a rule munch an unpeeled apple like a schoolboy—inference, a young man, and healthy. Why I came to the conclusion that he was tall, active, a gymnast, and perhaps a sailor, I have already told you, when we examined the outside of Foggatt's window. It was also pretty clear that robbery was not the motive, since nothing was disturbed, and that a friendly conversation had preceded the murder—witness the drinking and the eating of the apple. Whether or not the police noticed these things I can't say. If they had had their best men on they certainly would, I think; but the case, to a rough observer, looked so clearly one of accident or suicide, that possibly they didn't.

"As I said, after the inquest I was unable to devote any immediate time to the case, but I resolved to keep my eyes open. The man to look for was tall, young, strong and active, with a very irregular set of teeth, a tooth missing from the lower jaw just to the left of the centre, and another from the upper jaw a little further still toward the left. He might possibly be a person I had seen about the premises (I have a good memory for faces), or, of course, he possibly might not.

"Just before you returned from your holiday I noticed a young man at Luzatti's whom I remembered to have seen somewhere about the offices in this building. He was tall, young, and so on, but I had a client with me, and was unable to examine him more narrowly—indeed, as I was not exactly engaged on the case, and as there are several tall young men about, I took little trouble. But to-day, finding the same young man with a vacant seat opposite him, I took the opportunity of making a closer acquaintance."

"You certainly managed to draw him out."

"Oh, yes—the easiest person in the world to draw out is a cyclist. The easiest cyclist to draw out is, of course, the novice, but the next easiest is the veteran. When you see a healthy, well-trained looking man, who nevertheless has a slight stoop in the shoulders, and, maybe, a medal on his watch-guard, it is always a safe card to try him first with a little cycle-racing talk. I soon brought Mr. Mason out of his shell, read his name on his medal, and had a chance of observing his teeth—indeed, he spoke of them himself. Now, as I observed just now, there are several tall, athletic young men about, and also there are several men who have lost teeth. But now I saw that this tall and athletic young man had lost exactly *two* teeth—one from the lower jaw, just to the left of the centre, and another from the upper jaw, further still toward the left! Trivialities, pointing in the same direction, became important considerations. More, his teeth were irregular throughout, and, as nearly as I could remember it, looked remarkably like this little plaster mould of mine."

He produced from his pocket an irregular lump of plaster, about three inches long. On one side of this appeared in relief the likeness of two irregular rows of six or eight teeth, minus one in each row, where a deep gap was seen, in the position spoken of by my friend. He proceeded:

"This was enough at least to set me after this young man. But he gave me the greatest chance of all when he turned and left his apple (eaten unpeeled, remember!—another important triviality) on his plate. I'm afraid I wasn't at all polite, and I ran the risk of arousing his suspicions, but I couldn't resist the temptation to steal it. I did, as you saw, and here it is."

He brought the apple from his coat-pocket. One bitten side, placed against the upper half of the mould, fitted precisely, a projection of apple filling exactly the deep gap. The other side similarly fitted the lower half.

"There's no getting behind that, you see," Hewitt remarked. "Merely observing the man's teeth was a guide, to some extent, but this is as plain as his signature or his thumb-impression. You'll never find two men *bite* exactly alike, no matter whether they leave distinct teeth-marks or not. Here, by-the-bye, is Mrs. Clayton's oil. We'll take another mould from this apple, and compare *them*."

He oiled the apple, heaped a little plaster in a newspaper, took my water-jug and rapidly pulled off a hard mould. The parts corresponding to the merely broken places in the apple were, of course, dissimilar; but as to the teeth-marks, the impressions were identical.

"That will do, I think," Hewitt said. "To-morrow morning, Brett, I shall put up these things in a small parcel, and take them round to Bow Street."

"But are they sufficient evidence?"

"Quite sufficient for the police purpose. There is the man, and all the rest—his movements on the day and so forth are simple matters of inquiry; at any rate, that is police business."

I had scarcely sat down to my breakfast on the following morning when Hewitt came into the room and put a long letter before me.

"From our friend of last night," he said; "read it."

This letter began abruptly, and undated, and was as follows:

To Martin Hewitt, Esq.

Sir,—I must compliment you on the adroitness you exhibited this evening in extracting from me my name. The address I was able to balk you of for the time being, although by the time you read this you will probably have found it through the *Law List*, as I am an admitted solicitor. That, however, will be of little use to you, for I am removing myself, I think, beyond the reach even of your abilities of search. I knew you well by sight, and was, perhaps, foolish to allow myself to be drawn as I did. Still, I had no idea that it would be dangerous, especially after seeing you, as a witness with very little to say, at the inquest upon the scoundrel I shot. Your somewhat discourteous seizure of my apple at first amazed me —indeed, I was a little doubtful as to whether you had really taken it— but it was my first warning that you might be playing a deep game against me, incomprehensible as the action was to my mind. I subsequently reflected that I had been eating an apple, instead of taking the drink he first offered me, in the dead wretch's rooms on the night he came to his merited end. From this I assume that your design was in some way to compare what remained of the two apples—although I do not presume to fathom the depths of your detective system. Still, I have heard of many of your cases, and profoundly admire the keenness you exhibit. I am thought to be a keen man myself, but although I was able, to some extent, to hold my own to-night, I admit that your acumen in this case alone is something beyond me.

I do not know by whom you are commissioned to hunt me, nor to what extent you may be acquainted with my connection with the creature I killed. I have sufficient respect for you, however, to wish that you should not regard me as a vicious criminal, and a couple of hours to spare in which to offer you an explanation that may persuade you that such is not altogether the case. A hasty and violent temper I admit possessing; but even now I cannot regret the one crime it has led me into—for it is, I suppose, strictly speaking, a crime. For it was the man Foggatt who made a felon of my father before the eyes of the world, and killed him with shame. It was he who murdered my mother, and none the less murdered her because she died of a broken heart. That he was also a thief and a hypocrite might have concerned me little, but for that.

Of my father I remember very little. He must, I fear, have been a weak and incapable man in many respects. He had no business abilities—in fact, was quite unable to understand the complicated business matters in which he largely dealt. Foggatt was a consummate master of all those arts of financial jugglery that make so many fortunes, and ruin so many others, in matters of company promoting, stocks and shares. He was unable to exercise them, however, because of a great financial disaster in which he had been mixed up a few years before, and which made his name one to be avoided in future. In these circumstances he made a sort of secret and informal partnership with my father, who, ostensibly alone in the business, acted throughout on the directions of Foggatt, understanding as little of what he did, poor, simple man, as a schoolboy would have done. The transactions carried on went from small to large, and, unhappily, from honourable to dishonourable. My father relied on the superior abilities of Foggatt with an absolute trust, carrying out each day the directions given him privately the previous evening, buying, selling, printing prospectuses, signing whatever had to be signed, all with sole responsibility and as sole partner, while Foggatt, behind the scenes, absorbed the larger share of the profits. In brief, my unhappy and foolish father was a mere tool in the hands of the cunning scoundrel who pulled all the wires of the business, himself unseen and irresponsible. At last three companies, for the promotion of which my father was responsible, came to grief in a heap. Fraud was written large over all their history, and while Foggatt retired with his plunder, my father was left to meet ruin, disgrace, and imprisonment. From beginning to end he, and he only, was responsible. There was no shred of evidence to connect Foggatt with the matter, and no means of escape from the net drawn about my father. He lived through three years of imprisonment and then, entirely abandoned by the man who had made use of his simplicity, he died—of nothing but shame and a broken heart.

Of this I knew nothing at the time. Again and again, as a small boy, I remember asking of my mother why I had no father at home, as other boys had—unconscious of the stab I thus inflicted on her gentle heart. Of her my earliest, as well as my latest, memory is that of a pale, weeping woman, who grudged to let me out of her sight.

Little by little I learnt the whole cause of my mother's grief, for she had no other confidant, and I fear my character developed early, for my first coherent remembrance of the matter is that of a childish design to take a table-knife and kill the bad man who had made my father die in prison and caused my mother to cry.

One thing, however, I never knew: the name of that bad man. Again and again, as I grew older, I demanded to know, but my mother always withheld it from me, with a gentle reminder that vengeance was for a greater hand than mine.

I was seventeen years of age when my mother died. I believe that nothing but her strong attachment to myself and her desire to see me safely started in life kept her alive so long. Then I found that through all those years of narrowed means she had contrived to scrape and save a little money—sufficient, as it afterwards proved, to see me through the examinations for entrance to my profession, with the generous assistance of my father's old legal advisers, who gave me my articles, and who have all along treated me with extreme kindness.

For most of the succeeding years my life does not concern the matter in hand. I was a lawyer's clerk in my benefactors' service, and afterwards a qualified man among their assistants. All through, the firm were careful, in pursuance of my poor mother's wishes, that I should not learn the name or whereabouts of the man who had wrecked her life and my father's. I first met the man himself at the Clifton Club, where I had gone with an acquaintance who was a member. It was not till afterwards that I understood his curious awkwardness on that occasion. A week later I called (as I have frequently done) at the building in which your office is situated, on business with a solicitor who has an office on the floor above your own. On the stairs I almost ran against Mr. Foggatt. He started and turned pale, exhibiting signs of alarm that I could not understand, and asked me if I wished to see him.

"No," I replied; "I didn't know you lived here. I am after somebody else just now. Aren't you well?"

He looked at me rather doubtfully, and said he was *not* very well.

I met him twice or thrice after that, and on each occasion his manner grew more friendly, in a servile, flattering, and mean sort of way—a thing unpleasant enough in anybody, but doubly so in the intercourse of a man with another young enough to be his own son. Still, of course, I treated the man civilly enough. On one occasion he asked me into his rooms to look at a rather fine picture he had lately bought, and observed casually, lifting a large revolver from the mantelpiece:

"You see I am prepared for any unwelcome visitors to my little den! He! he!" Conceiving him, of course, to refer to burglars, I could not help wondering at the forced and hollow character of his laugh. As we went down the stairs he said, "I think we know one another pretty well now, Mr. Mason, eh? And if I could do anything to advance your professional prospects I should be glad of the chance, of course. I understand the struggles of a young professional man—he! he!" It was the forced laugh again, and the man spoke nervously. "I think," he added, "that if you will drop in to-morrow evening, perhaps I may have a little proposal to make. Will you?"

I assented, wondering what this proposal could be. Perhaps this eccentric old gentleman was a good fellow, after all, anxious to do me a good turn, and his awkwardness was nothing but a natural delicacy in breaking the ice. I was not so flush of good friends as to be willing to lose one. He might be desirous of putting business in my way.

I went, and was received with a cordiality that even then seemed a little over-effusive. We sat and talked of one thing and another for a long while, and I began to wonder when Mr. Foggatt was coming to the point that most interested me. Several times he invited me to drink and smoke, but long usage to athletic training has given me a distaste for both practices, and I declined. At last he began to talk about myself. He was afraid that my professional prospects in this country were not great, but he had heard that in some of the Colonies—South Africa, for example—young lawyers had brilliant opportunities.

"If you'd like to go there," he said, "I've no doubt, with a little capital, a clever man like you could get a grand practice together very soon. Or you might buy a share in some good established practice. I should be glad to let you have five hundred pounds, or even a little more if that wouldn't satisfy you, and——"

I stood aghast. Why should this man, almost a stranger, offer me five hundred pounds, or even more—"if that wouldn't satisfy" me? What claim had I on him? It was very generous of him, of course, but out of the question. I was at least a gentleman, and had a gentleman's self-respect. Meanwhile he had gone maundering on, in a halting sort of way, and presently let slip a sentence that struck me like a blow between the eyes.

"I shouldn't like you to bear ill-will because of what has happened in the past," he said. "Your late—your late lamented mother—I'm afraid— she had unworthy suspicions—I'm sure—it was best for all parties—your father always appreciated——"

I set back my chair and stood erect before him. This grovelling wretch, forcing the words through his dry lips, was the thief who had made another of my father and had brought to miserable ends the lives of both my parents. Everything was clear. The creature went in fear of me, never imagining that I did not know him, and sought to buy me off; to buy me from the remembrance of my dead mother's broken heart for £500—£500 that he had made my father steal for him. I said not a word. But the memory of all my mother's bitter years, and a savage sense of this crowning insult to myself, took a hold upon me, and I was a tiger. Even then, I verily believe that one word of repentance, one tone of honest remorse, would have saved him. But he drooped his eyes, snuffled excuses, and stammered of "unworthy suspicions" and "no ill-will." I let him stammer. Presently he looked up and saw my face: and fell back in his chair, sick with terror. I snatched the pistol from the mantelpiece, and, thrusting it in his face, shot him where he sat.

My subsequent coolness and quietness surprise me now. I took my hat and stepped toward the door. But there were voices on the stairs. The door was locked on the inside, and I left it so. I went back and quietly opened a window. Below was a clear drop into darkness, and above was plain wall; but away to one side, where the slope of the gable sprang from the roof, an iron gutter ended, supported by a strong bracket. It was the only way. I got upon the sill and carefully shut the window behind me, for people were already knocking at the lobby door. From the end of the sill, holding on by the reveal of the window with one hand, leaning and stretching my utmost, I caught the gutter, swung myself clear, and scrambled on the roof. I climbed over many roofs before I found, in an adjoining street, a ladder lashed perpendicularly against the front of a house in course of repair. This, to me, was an easy opportunity of descent, notwithstanding the boards fastened over the face of the ladder, and I availed myself of it.

I have taken some time and trouble in order that you (so far as I am aware the only human being beside myself who knows me to be the author of Foggatt's death) shall have at least the means of appraising my crime at its just value of culpability. How much you already know of what I have told you I cannot guess. I am wrong, hardened and flagitious, I make no doubt, but I speak of the facts as they are. You see the thing, of course, from your own point of view—I from mine. And I remember my mother.

Trusting that you will forgive the odd freak of a man—a criminal, let us say—who makes a confidant of the man set to hunt him down, I beg leave to be, Sir, your obedient servant,

"Sidney Mason."

I read the singular document through and handed it back to Hewitt. "How does it strike you?" Hewitt asked.

"Mason would seem to be a man of very marked character," I said. "Certainly no fool. And, if his tale is true, Foggatt is no great loss to the world."

"Just so—if the tale is true. Personally, I am disposed to believe it is."

"Where was the letter posted?"

"It wasn't posted. It was handed in with the others from the front door letter-box this morning in an unstamped envelope. He must have dropped it in himself during the night. Paper," Hewitt proceeded, holding it up to the light, "Turkey mill, ruled foolscap. Envelope, blue official shape, Pirie's watermark. Both quite ordinary and no special marks."

"Where do you suppose he's gone?"

"Impossible to guess. Some might think he meant suicide by the expression 'beyond the reach even of your abilities of search,' but I scarcely think he is the sort of man to do that. No, there is no telling. Something may be got by inquiring at his late address, of course; but when such a man tells you he doesn't think you will find him, you may count upon its being a difficult job. His opinion is not to be despised."

"What shall you do?"

"Put the letter in the box with the casts for the police. *Fiat justitia,* you know, without any question of sentiment. As to the apple—I really think, if the police will let me, I'll make you a present of it. Keep it somewhere as a souvenir of your absolute deficiency in reflective observation in this case, and look at it whenever you feel yourself growing dangerously conceited. It should cure you."

This is the history of the withered and almost petrified half-apple that

stands in my cabinet among a number of flint implements and one or
two rather fine old Roman vessels. Of Mr. Sidney Mason we never heard
another word. The police did their best, but he had left not a track
behind him. His rooms were left almost undisturbed, and he had gone
without anything in the way of elaborate preparation for his journey,
and yet without leaving a trace of his intentions.

❦ ❦ ❦

The Case
of the Late Mr. Rewse

ARTHUR MORRISON

Of this case I personally saw nothing beyond the first advent in Hewitt's office of Mr. Horace Bowyer, who put the case in his hands, and then I merely saw Mr. Bowyer's back as I passed down stairs from my rooms. But I noted the case in full detail after Hewitt's return from Ireland, as it seemed to me one not entirely without interest, if only as an exemplar of the fatal case with which a man may unwittingly dig a pit for his own feet—a pit from which there is no climbing out.

A few moments after I had seen the stranger disappear into Hewitt's office, Kerrett brought to Hewitt in his inner room a visitor's slip announcing the arrival on urgent business of Mr. Horace Bowyer. That the visitor was in a hurry was plain from a hasty rattling of the closed wicket in the outer room where Mr. Bowyer was evidently making impatient attempts to follow his announcement in person. Hewitt showed himself at the door and invited Mr. Bowyer to enter, which he did, as soon as Kerrett had released the wicket, with much impetuosity. He was a stout, florid gentleman with a loud voice and a large stare.

"Mr. Hewitt," he said, "I must claim your immediate attention to a business of the utmost gravity. Will you please consider yourself commissioned, wholly regardless of expense, to set aside whatever you may have in hand and devote yourself to the case I shall put in your hands?"

"Certainly not," Hewitt replied with a slight smile. "What I have in hand are matters which I have engaged to attend to, and no mere compensation for loss of fees could persuade me to leave my clients in the lurch, else what would prevent some other gentleman coming here tomorrow with a bigger fee than yours and bribing me away from you?"

"But this—this is a most serious thing, Mr. Hewitt. A matter of life or death—it is indeed!"

"Quite so," Hewitt replied: "but there are a thousand such matters at this moment pending of which you and I know nothing, and there are also two or three more of which you know nothing but on which I am at work. So that it becomes a question of practicability. If you will tell me your business I can judge whether or not I may be able to accept your commission concurrently with those I have in hand. Some operations take months of constant attention; some can be conducted intermittently; others still are a mere matter of a few days—many of hours simply."

"I will tell you then," Mr. Bowyer replied. "In the first place, will you have the kindness to read that? It is a cutting from the *Standard's* column of news from the provinces of two days ago."

Hewitt took the cutting and read as follows:

"The epidemic of small-pox in County Mayo, Ireland, shows few signs of abating. The spread of the disease has been very remarkable considering the widely-scattered nature of the population, though there can be no doubt that the market towns are the centres of infection, and that it is from these that the germs of contagion are carried into the country by people from all parts who resort thither on market days. In many cases the disease has assumed a particularly malignant form, and deaths have been very rapid and numerous. The comparatively few medical men available are sadly overworked, owing largely to the distances separating their different patients. Among those who have succumbed within the last few days is Mr. Algernon Rewse, a young English gentleman who has been staying with a friend at a cottage a few miles from Cullanin, on a fishing excursion."

Hewitt placed the cutting on the table at his side. "Yes?" he said inquiringly. "It is to Mr. Algernon Rewse's death you wish to draw my attention?"

"It is," Mr. Bowyer answered; "and the reason I come to you is that I very much suspect—more than suspect, indeed—that Mr. Algernon Rewse has *not* died by smallpox, but has been murdered—murdered cold-bloodedly, and for the most sordid motives, by the friend who has been sharing his holiday."

"In what way do you suppose him to have been murdered?"

"That I cannot say—that, indeed, I want you to find out, among other things—chiefly perhaps, the murderer himself, who has made off."

"And your own status in the matter," queried Hewitt, "is that of——?"

"I am trustee under a will by which Mr. Rewse would have benefited considerably had he lived but a month or two longer. That circumstance indeed lies rather near the root of the matter. The thing stood thus. Under the will I speak of—that of young Rewse's uncle, a very old friend of mine in his lifetime—the money lay in trust till the young fellow should attain twenty-five years of age. His younger sister, Miss Mary Rewse, was also benefited, but to a much smaller extent. She was to come into her property also on attaining the age of twenty-five, or on her marriage, whichever event happened first. It was further provided that in case either of these young people died before coming into the inheritance, his or her share should go to the survivor. I want you particularly to remember this. You will observe that now, in consequence of young Algernon Rewse's death, barely two months before his twenty-fifth birthday, the whole of the very large property—all personalty, and free from any tie or restriction—which would otherwise have been his, will, in the regular course, pass, on her twenty-fifth birthday, *or on her marriage*, to Miss Mary Rewse, whose own legacy was comparatively trifling. You will understand the importance of this when I tell you that the man whom I suspect of causing Algernon Rewse's death, and who has been his companion on his otherwise lonely holiday, is engaged to be married to Miss Rewse."

Mr. Bowyer paused at this, but Hewitt only raised his eyebrows and nodded.

"I have never particularly liked the man," Mr. Bowyer went on. "He never seemed to have much to say for himself. I like a man who holds up his head and opens his mouth. I don't believe in the sort of modesty that he showed so much of—it isn't genuine. A man can't afford to be genuinely meek and retiring who has his way to make in the world—and he was clever enough to know *that*."

"He is poor, then?" Hewitt asked.

"Oh yes, poor enough. His name, by-the-bye, is Main—Stanley Main —and he is a medical man. He hasn't been practising, except as assistant, since he became qualified, the reason being, I understand, that he couldn't afford to buy a good practice. He is the person who will profit by young Rewse's death—or at any rate, who intended to; but we will see about that. As for Mary, poor girl, she wouldn't have lost her brother for fifty fortunes."

"As to the circumstances of the death, now?"

"Yes, yes, I am coming to that. Young Algernon Rewse, you must know, had rather run down in health, and Main persuaded him that he wanted a change. I don't know what it was altogether, but Rewse seemed to have been having his own little love troubles and that sort of thing, you know. He'd been engaged, I think, or very nearly so, and the young lady died, and so on. Well, as I said, he had run down and got into low health and spirits, and no doubt a change of some sort would have done him good. This Stanley Main always seemed to have a great influence over the poor boy—he was four or five years older than Rewse—and somehow he persuaded him to go away, the two together, to some out-landish wilderness of a place in the West of Ireland for salmon-fishing. It seemed to me at the time rather a ridiculous sort of place to go to, but Main had his way, and they went. There was a cottage—rather a good sort of cottage, I believe, for the district—which some friend of Main's, once a landowner in the district, had put up as a convenient box for salmon-fishing, and they rented it. Not long after they got there this epidemic of small-pox got about in the district—though that, I believe, has had little to do with poor young Rewse's death. All appeared to go well until a day over a week ago, when Mrs. Rewse received this letter from Main." Mr. Bowyer handed Martin Hewitt a letter, written in an irregular and broken hand, as though of a person writing under stress of extreme agitation. It ran thus:—

"My dear Mrs. Rewse,—You will probably have heard through the newspapers—indeed I think Algernon has told you in his letters—that a very bad epidemic of small-pox is abroad in this district. I am deeply grieved to have to tell you that Algernon himself has taken the disease in a rather bad form. He showed the first symptoms to-day (Tuesday), and he is now in bed in the cottage. It is fortunate that I, as a medical man, happen to be on the spot, as the nearest local doctor is five miles off at Cullanin, and he is working and travelling night and day as it is. I have my little medicine chest with me, and can get whatever else is necessary from Cullanin, so that everything is being done for Algernon that is pos-sible, and I hope to bring him up to scratch in good health soon, though of course the disease is a dangerous one. Pray don't unnecessarily alarm yourself, and don't think about coming over here, or anything of that sort. You can do no good, and will only run risk yourself. I will take care to let you know how things go on, so please don't attempt to come. The journey is long and would be very trying to you, and you would have no place to stay at nearer than Cullanin, which is quite a centre of infection. I will write again to-morrow.—Yours most sincerely,

Stanley Main."

Not only did the handwriting of this letter show signs of agitation, but here and there words had been repeated, and sometimes a letter had been omitted. Hewitt placed the letter on the table by the newspaper cutting, and Mr. Bowyer proceeded.

"Another letter followed on the next day," he said, handing it to Hewitt as he spoke; "a short one, as you see, not written with quite such signs of agitation. It merely says that Rewse is very bad, and repeats the former entreaties that his mother will not think of going to him. Hewitt glanced at the letter and placed it with the other, while Mr. Bowyer continued: "Notwithstanding Main's persistent anxiety that she should stay at home, Mrs. Rewse, who was of course terribly worried about her only son, had almost made up her mind, in spite of her very delicate health, to start for Ireland, when she received a third letter announcing Algernon's death. Here it is. It is certainly the sort of letter that one might expect to be written in such circumstances, and yet there seems to me at least a certain air of disingenuousness about the wording. There are, as you see, the usual condolences, and so forth. The disease was of the malignant type, it says, which is terribly rapid in its action, often carrying off the patient even before the eruption has time to form. Then —and this is a thing I wish you especially to note—there is once more a repetition of his desire that neither the young man's mother nor his sister shall come to Ireland. The funeral must take place immediately, he says, under arrangements made by the local authorities, and before they could reach the spot. Now doesn't this obtrusive anxiety of his that no connection of young Rewse's should be near him during his illness, nor even at the funeral, strike you as rather singular?"

"Well, possibly it is: though it may easily be nothing but zeal for the health of Mrs. Rewse and her daughter. As a matter of fact what Main says is very plausible. They could do no sort of good in the circumstances, and might easily run into danger themselves, to say nothing of the fatigue of the journey and general nervous upset. Mrs. Rewse is in weak health, I think you said?"

"Yes, she's almost an invalid in fact; she is subject to heart disease. But tell me now, as an entirely impartial observer, doesn't it seem to you that there is a very forced, unreal sort of tone in all these letters?"

"Perhaps one may notice something of the sort, but fifty things may cause that. The case from the beginning may have been worse than he made it out. What ensued on the receipt of this letter?"

"Mrs. Rewse was prostrated, of course. Her daughter communicated with me as a friend of the family, and that is how I heard of the whole thing for the first time. I saw the letters, and it seemed to me, looking at all the circumstances of the case, that somebody at least ought to go over and make certain that everything was as it should be. Here was this poor young man, staying in a lonely cottage with the only man in the world who had any reason to desire his death, or any profit to gain by it, and he had a very great inducement indeed. Moreover he was a medical man, *carrying his medicine chest with him*, remember, as he says himself in his letter. In this situation Rewse suddenly dies, with nobody about him, so far as there is anything to show, but Main himself. As his medical attendant it would be Main who would certify and register the death, and no matter what foul play might have taken place he would be safe as long as nobody was on the spot to make searching inquiries—might easily escape even then, in fact. When one man is likely to profit much by the death of another a doctor's medicine chest is likely to supply but too easy a means to his end."

"Did you say anything of your suspicions to the ladies?"

"Well—well I hinted perhaps—no more than hinted, you know. But they wouldn't hear of it—got indignant, and 'took on' as people call it, worse than ever, so that I had to smooth them over. But since it seemed somebody's duty to see into the matter a little more closely, and there seemed to be nobody to do it but myself, I started off that very evening by the night mail. I was in Dublin early the next morning and spent that day getting across Ireland. The nearest station was ten miles from Cullanin, and that, as you remember, was five miles from the cottage, so that I drove over on the morning of the following day. I must say Main appeared very much taken aback at seeing me. His manner was nervous and apprehensive, and made me more suspicious than ever. The body had been buried, of course, a couple of days or more. I asked a few rather searching questions about the illness, and so forth, and his answers became positively confused. He had burned the clothes that Rewse was wearing at the time the disease first showed itself, he said, as well as all the bed-clothes, since there was no really efficient means of disinfection at hand. His story in the main was that he had gone off to Cullanin one morning on foot to see about a top joint of a fishing-rod that was to be repaired. When he returned early in the afternoon he found Algernon Rewse sickening of small-pox, at once put him to bed, and there nursed him till he died. I wanted to know, of course, why no other medical man had been called in. He said that there was only one available, and it was doubtful if he could have been got at even a day's notice, so overworked was he; moreover he said this man, with his hurry and over-strain, could never have given the patient such efficient attention as he himself, who had nothing else to do. After a while I put it to him plainly that it would at any rate have been more prudent to have had the body at least inspected by some independent doctor, considering the fact that he was likely to profit so largely by young Rewse's death, and I suggested that with an exhumation order it might not be too late now, as a matter of justice to himself. The effect of that convinced me. The man gasped and turned blue with terror. It was a full minute, I should think, before he could collect himself sufficiently to attempt to dissuade me from doing what I had hinted at. He did so as soon as he could think of—entreated me in fact almost desperately. That decided me. I said that after what he had said, and particularly in view of his whole manner and bearing, I should insist, by every means in my power, on having the body properly examined, and I went off at once to Cullanin to set the telegraph going, and see whatever local authority might be proper. When I returned in the afternoon Stanley Main had packed his bag and vanished, and I have not heard nor seen anything of him since. I stayed in the neighbourhood that day and the next, and left for London in the evening. By the help of my solicitors proper representations were made at the Home Office, and, especially in view of Main's flight, a prompt order was made for exhumation and medical examination preliminary to an inquest. I am expecting to hear that the disinterment has been effected to-day. What I want you to do of course is chiefly find Main. The Irish constabulary in that district are fine big men, and no doubt most excellent in quelling a faction fight or shutting up a shebeen, but I doubt their efficiency in anything requiring much more finesse. Perhaps also you may be able to find out something of the means by which the murder—it is plain it is one—was committed. It is quite possible that Main may have adopted

some means to give the body the appearance, even to a medical man, of
death from small-pox."

"That," Hewitt said, "is scarcely likely, else, indeed, why did he not
take care that another doctor should see the body before the burial? That
would have secured him. But that is not a thing one can deceive a doctor
over. Of course in the circumstances exhumation is desirable, but if the
case *is* one of small-pox, I don't envy the medical man who is to examine. At any rate the business is, I should imagine, not likely to be a
very long one, and I can take it in hand at once. I will leave to-night for
Ireland by the 6.30 train from Euston."

"Very good. I shall go over myself, of course. If anything comes to my
knowledge in the meanwhile, of course I'll let you know."

An hour or two after this a cab stopped at the door, and a young lady
dressed in black sent in her name and a minute later was shown into
Hewitt's room. It was Miss Mary Rewse. She wore a heavy veil, and all
she said she uttered in evidently deep distress of mind. Hewitt did what
he could to calm her, and waited patiently.

At length, she said: "I felt that I must come to you, Mr. Hewitt, and
yet now that I am here I don't know what to say. Is it the fact that Mr.
Bowyer has commissioned you to investigate the circumstances of my
poor brother's death, and to discover the whereabouts of Mr. Main?"

"Yes, Miss Rewse, that is the fact. Can you tell me anything that will
help me?"

"No, no, Mr. Hewitt, I fear not. But it is such a dreadful thing, and
Mr. Bowyer is—I'm afraid he is so much prejudiced against Mr. Main
that I felt I ought to do something—to say something at least to prevent
you entering on the case with your mind made up that he has been
guilty of such an awful thing. He is really quite incapable of it, I assure
you."

"Pray, Miss Rewse," Hewitt replied, "don't allow that apprehension
to disturb you. If Mr. Main is, as you say, incapable of such an act as
perhaps he is suspected of, you may rest assured no harm will come to
him. So far as I am concerned at any rate I enter the case with a perfectly open mind. A man in my profession who accepted prejudices at
the beginning of a case would have very poor results to show indeed. As
yet I have no opinion, no theory, no prejudice, nothing indeed but a
large outline of facts. I shall derive no opinion and no theory from
anything but a consideration of the actual circumstances and evidences

on the spot. I quite understand the relation in which Mr. Main stands in regard to yourself and your family. Have you heard from him lately?"

"Not since the letter informing us of my brother's death."

"Before then?"

Miss Rewse hesitated. "Yes," she said, "we corresponded. But—but there was really nothing—the letters were of a personal and private sort —they were——"

"Yes, yes, of course," Hewitt answered, with his eyes fixed keenly on the veil which Miss Rewse still kept down. "Of course I understand that. Then there is nothing else you can tell me?"

"No, I fear not. I can only implore you to remember that no matter what you may see and hear, no matter what the evidence may be, I am sure, sure, *sure* that poor Stanley could never do such a thing." And Miss Rewse buried her face in her hands.

Hewitt kept his eyes on the lady, though he smiled slightly, and asked, "How long have you known Mr. Main?"

"For some five or six years now. My poor brother knew him at school, though of course they were in different forms, Mr. Main being the elder."

"Were they always on good terms?"

"They were always like brothers."

Little more was said. Hewitt condoled with Miss Rewse as well as he might, and she presently took her departure. Even as she descended the stairs a messenger came with a short note for Mr. Bowyer enclosing a telegram just received from Cullanin. The telegram ran thus:

Body exhumed. Death from shot-wound. No trace of small-pox. Nothing yet heard of Main. Have communicated with coroner.—O'Reilly.

II

Hewitt and Mr. Bowyer travelled towards Mayo together, Mr. Bowyer restless and loquacious on the subject of the business in hand, and Hewitt rather bored thereby. He resolutely declined to offer an opinion on any single detail of the case till he had examined the available evidence, and his occasional remarks on matters of general interest, the scenery and so forth, struck his companion, unused to business of the sort which had occasioned the journey, as strangely cold-blooded and indifferent. Telegrams had been sent ordering that no disarrangement of the contents of the cottage was to be allowed pending their arrival, and Hewitt well knew that nothing more was practicable till the site was reached. At Ballymaine, where the train was left at last, they stayed for the night, and left early the next morning for Cullanin, where a meeting with Dr. O'Reilly at the mortuary had been appointed. There the body lay stripped of its shroud, calm and grey, and beginning to grow ugly, with a scarcely noticeable breach in the flesh of the left breast.

"The wound has been thoroughly cleansed, closed and stopped with a carbolic plug before interment," Dr. O'Reilly said. He was a middle-aged, grizzled man, with a face whereon many recent sleepless nights had left their traces. "I have not thought it necessary to do anything in the way of dissection. The bullet is not present, it has passed clean through the body, between the ribs both back and front, piercing the heart on its way. The death must have been instantaneous."

Hewitt quickly examined the two wounds, back and front, as the doctor turned the body over, and then asked: "Perhaps, Dr. O'Reilly, you have some experience of a gunshot wound before this?"

The doctor smiled grimly. "I think so," he answered, with just enough of brogue in his words to hint his nationality and no more. "I was an army surgeon for a good many years before I came to Cullanin, and saw service in Ashanti and in India."

"Come then," Hewitt said, "you're an expert. Would it have been possible for the shot to have been fired from behind?"

"Oh, no. See! the bullet entering makes a wound of quite a different character from that of the bullet leaving."

"Have you any idea of the weapon used?"

"A large revolver, I should think; perhaps of the regulation size; that is, I should judge the bullet to have been a conical one of about the size fitted to such a weapon—smaller than that from a rifle."

"Can you form an idea of from what distance the shot was fired?"

Dr. O'Reilly shook his head. "The clothes have all been burned," he said, "and the wound has been washed, otherwise one might have looked for powder blackening."

"Did you know either the dead man or Dr. Main personally?"

"Only very slightly. I may say I saw just such a pistol as might cause that sort of wound in his hands the day before he gave out that Rewse had been attacked by small-pox. I drove past the cottage as he stood in the doorway with it in his hand. He had the breach opened, and seemed to be either loading or unloading it—which it was I couldn't say."

"Very good, doctor, that may be important. Now is there any single circumstance, incident or conjecture that you can tell me of in regard to this case that you have not already mentioned?"

Doctor O'Reilly thought for a moment, and replied in the negative. "I heard of course," he said, "of the reported new case of small-pox, and that Main had taken the case in hand himself. I was indeed relieved to hear it, for I had already more on my hands than one man can safely be expected to attend to. The cottage was fairly isolated, and there could have been nothing gained by removal to an asylum—indeed there was practically no accommodation. So far as I can make out nobody seems to have seen young Rewse, alive or dead, after Main had announced that he had the small-pox. He seems to have done everything himself, laying out the body and all, and you may be pretty sure that none of the strangers about was particularly anxious to have anything to do with it. The undertaker (there is only one here, and he is down with the small-pox himself now) was as much overworked as I was myself, and was glad enough to send off a coffin by a market cart and leave the laying out and screwing down to Main, since he had got those orders. Main made out the death certificate himself, and, since he was trebly qualified, everything seemed in order."

"The certificate merely attributed the death to small-pox, I take it, with no qualifying remarks?"

"Small-pox, simply."

Hewitt and Mr. Bowyer bade Dr. O'Reilly good morning, and their car was turned in the direction of the cottage where Algernon Rewse had met his death. At the Town Hall in the market place, however, Hewitt stopped the car and set his watch by the public clock. "This is more than half an hour before London time," he said, "and we mustn't be at odds with the natives about the time."

As he spoke, Dr. O'Reilly came running up breathlessly. "I've just heard something," he said. "Three men heard a shot in the cottage as they were passing, last Tuesday week."

"Where are the men?"

"I don't know at the moment; but they can be found. Shall I set about it?"

"If you possibly can," Hewitt said, "you will help us enormously. Can you send them messages to be at the cottage as soon as they can get there to-day? Tell them they shall have a half-a-sovereign apiece."

"Right, I will. Good-day."

"Tuesday week," said Mr. Bowyer as they drove off; "that was the date of Main's first letter, and the day on which, by his account, Rewse was taken ill. Then if that was the shot that killed Rewse he must have been lying dead in the place while Main was writing those letters reporting his sickness to his mother. The cold-blooded scoundrel!"

"Yes," Hewitt replied, "I think it probable in any case that Tuesday was the day that Rewse was shot. It wouldn't have been safe for Main to write the mother lying letters about the small-pox before. Rewse might have written home in the meantime, or something might have occurred to postpone Main's plans, and then there would be impossible explanations required."

Over a very bad road they jolted on and in the end arrived where the road, now become a mere path, passed a tumble-down old farmhouse.

"This is where the woman lives who cooked and cleaned house for Rewse and Main," Mr. Bowyer said. "There is the cottage, scarce a hundred yards off, a little to the right of the track."

"Well," replied Hewitt, "suppose we stop here and ask her a few questions? I like to get the evidence of all the witnesses as soon as possible. It simplifies subsequent work wonderfully."

They alighted, and Mr. Bowyer roared through the open door and tapped with his stick. In reply to his summons a decent-looking woman of perhaps fifty, but wrinkled beyond her age, and better dressed than any woman Hewitt had seen since leaving Cullanin, appeared from the hinder buildings and curtsied pleasantly.

"Good morning, Mrs. Hurley, good morning," Mr. Bowyer said, "this is Mr. Martin Hewitt, a gentleman from London, who is going to look into this shocking murder of our young friend Mr. Rewse and sift it to the bottom. He would like you to tell him something, Mrs. Hurley."

The woman curtsied again. "An' it's the jintleman is welcome, sor, and doin's as ut is." She had a low, pleasing voice, much in contrast with her unattractive appearance, and characterised by the softest and broadest brogue imaginable. "Will ye not come in? Mother av Hiven! An' thim two livin' together, an' fishin' an' readin' an' all, like brothers! An' trut' ut is he was a foine young jintleman indade, indade!"

"I suppose, Mrs. Hurley," Hewitt said, "you've seen as much of the life of those two gentlemen here as anybody?"

"Treu ut is, sor; none more—nor as much."

"Did you ever hear of anybody being on bad terms with Mr. Rewse—anybody at all, Mr. Main or another?"

"Niver a soul in all Mayo. How could ye? Such a folne young jintleman, an' fair-spoken an' all."

"Tell me all that happened on the day that you heard that Mr. Rewse was ill—Tuesday week."

"In the mornin', sor, 'twas much as ord'nary. I was over there at half afther sivin, an' 'twas half an hour afther that I cud hear the jintlemen dhressin'. They tuk their breakfast—though Mr. Rewse's was a small wan. It was half afther nine that Mr. Main wint off walkin' to Cullanin, Mr. Rewse stayin' in, havin' letthers to write. Half an hour later I came away mesilf. Later than that (it was nigh elivin) I wint across for a pail from the yard, an' then, through the windy as I passed I saw the dear young jintleman sittin' writin' at the table calm an' peaceful—an' saw him no more in this warrl'."

"And after that?"

"Afther that, sor, I came back wid the pail, an' saw nor heard no more till two o'clock, whin Mr. Main came back from Cullanin."

"Did you see him as he came back?"

"That I did, sor, as I stud there nailin' the fence where the pig bruk ut. I'd been there an' had me oi down the road lookin' for him an hour past, expectin' he might be bringin' somethin' for me to cook for their dinner. An' more by token he gave me the toime from his watch, set by the Town Hall clock."

"And was it two o'clock?"

"It was that to the sthroke, an' me own ould clock was right too whin I wint to set ut. An'——"

"One moment; may I see your clock?"

Mrs. Hurley turned and shut an open door which had concealed an old hanging clock. Hewitt produced his watch and compared the time. "Still right I see, Mrs. Hurley," he said; "your clock keeps excellent time."

"It does that, sor, an' nivir more than claned twice by Rafferty since me own father (rest his soul!) lift ut here. 'Tis no bad clock, as Mr. Rewse himsilf said oft an' again; an' I always kape ut by the Town Hall toime. But as I was sayin', Mr. Main came back an' gave me the toime; thin he wint sthraight to his house, an' no more av him I saw till may be half afther three.''

"And then?"

"An' thin, sor, he came across, in a sad takin', wid a letther. 'Take ut,'' sez he, 'an' have ut posted at Cullanin by the first that can get there. Mr. Rewse has the sickness on him awful bad,' he sez, 'an' ye must not be near the place or ye'll take ut. I have him to bed, an' his clothes I shall burn behin' the cottage,' sez he, 'so if ye see smoke ye'll know what ut is. There'll be no docthor wanted. I'm wan mesilf, an' I'll do all for 'um. An' sure I knew him for a docthor ivir since he come. 'The cottage ye shall not come near,' he sez, 'till ut's over one way or another, an' yez can lave whativir av food an' dhrink we want midbetwixt the houses an' go back, an' I'll come and fetch ut. But have the letther posted,' he sez, 'at wanst. 'Tis not contagious,' he sez, 'bein' as I've dishinfected it mesilf. But kape yez away from the cottage.' An' I kept."

"And then did he go back to the cottage at once?"

"He did that, sor, an' a sore stew was he in to all seemin'—white as paper, and much need, too, the murtherin' scutt! An' him always so much the jintleman an' all. Well I saw no more av him that day. Next day he laves another letther wid the dirthy plates there mid-betwixt the houses, an' shouts for ut to be posted. 'Twas for the poor young jintleman's mother, sure, as was the other wan. An' the day afther there was another letther, an' wan for the undhertaker, too, for he tells me it's all over, an' he's dead. An' they buried him next day followin'.''

"So that from the time you went for the pail and saw Mr. Rewse writing, till after the funeral, you were never at the cottage at all?"

"Nivir, sor; an' can ye blame me? Wid children an' Terence himself sick wid bronchitis in this house?"

"Of course, of course, you did quite right—indeed you only obeyed orders. But now think; do you remember on any one of those three days hearing a shot, or any other unusual noise in the cottage?"

"Nivir at all, sor. 'Tis that I've been thryin' to bring to mind these four days. Such may have been, but not that I heard."

"After you went for the pail, and before Mr. Main returned to the house, did Mr. Rewse leave the cottage at all, or might he have done so?"

"He did not lave at all, to my knowledge. Sure he *might* have gone an' he might have come back widout my knowin'. But see him I did not."

"Thank you, Mrs. Hurley. I think we'll go across to the cottage now. If any people come will you send them after us? I suppose a policeman is there?"

"He is, sor. An' the serjint is not far away. They've been in chyarge since Mr. Bowyer wint away last—but shlapin' here."

Hewitt and Mr. Bowyer walked towards the cottage. "Did you notice," said Mr. Bowyer, "that the woman saw Rewse *writing letters?* Now what were those letters, and where are they? He has no correspondents that I know of but his mother and sister, and they heard nothing from him. Is this something else?—some other plot? There is something very deep here."

"Yes," Hewitt replied thoughtfully. "I think our inquiries may take us deeper than we have expected; and in the matter of those letters—yes, I think they may lie near the kernel of the mystery."

Here they arrived at the cottage—an uncommonly substantial structure for the district. It was square, of plain, solid brick, with a slated roof. On the patch of ground behind it there were still signs of the fires, wherein Main had burnt Rewse's clothes and other belongings. And sitting on the window-sill in front was a big member of the R.I.C., soldierly and broad, who rose as they came and saluted Mr. Bowyer.

"Good-day constable," Mr. Bowyer said. "I hope nothing has been disturbed?"

"Not a shtick, sor. Nobody's as much as gone in."

"Have any of the windows been opened or shut?" Hewitt asked.

"This wan was, sor," the policeman said, indicating the one behind him, "when they took away the corrpse, an' so was the next round the corner. 'Tis the bedroom windies they are, an' they opened thim to give ut a bit av air. The other windy behin'—sittin'-room windy—has not been opened."

"Very well," Hewitt answered, "we'll take a look at that unopened window from the inside."

The door was opened and they passed inside. There was a small lobby, and on the left of this was the bedroom with two single beds. The only other room of consequence was the sitting-room, the cottage consisting merely of these, a small scullery and a narrow closet used as a bath-room, wedged between the bedroom and the sitting-room. They made for the single window of the sitting-room at the back. It was an ordinary sash window, and was shut, but the catch was not fastened.

Hewitt examined the catch, drawing Mr. Bowyer's attention to a bright scratch on the grimy brass. "See," he said, "that nick in the catch exactly corresponds with the narrow space between the two frames of the window. And look"—he lifted the bottom sash a little as he spoke—"there is the mark of a knife on the frame of the top sash. Somebody has come in by that window, forcing the catch with a knife."

"Yes, yes!" cried Mr. Bowyer, greatly excited, "and he has gone out that way too, else why is the window shut and the catch not fastened? Why should he do that? What in the world does *this* thing mean?"

Before Hewitt could reply the constable put his head into the room and announced that one Larry Shanahan was at the door, and had been promised half-a-sovereign.

"One of the men who heard a shot," Hewitt said to Mr. Bowyer. "Bring him in, constable."

The constable brought in Larry Shanahan, and Larry Shanahan brought in a strong smell of whisky. He was an extremely ragged person, with only one eye, which caused him to hold his head aside as he regarded Hewitt, much as a parrot does. On his face sun-scorched brown and fiery red struggled for mastery, and his voice was none of the clearest. He held his hat against his stomach with one hand and with the other pulled his forelock.

"An' which is the honourable jintleman," he said, "as do be burrnin' to prisint me wid a bit o' goold?"

"Here I am," said Hewitt, jingling money in his pocket, "and here is the half-sovereign. It's only waiting where it is till you have answered a few questions. They say you heard a shot fired here-about?"

"Faith, an' that I did, sor. 'Twas a shot in this house, indade, no other."

"And when was it?"

"Sure, 'twas in the afthernoon."

"But on what day?"

"Last Tuesday sivin-noight, sor, as I know by rayson av Ballyshiel fair that I wint to."

"Tell me all about it."

"I will, sor. 'Twas pigs I was dhrivin' that day, sor, to Ballyshiel fair from just beyond Cullanin. At Cullanin, sor, I dhropped in wid Danny Mulcahy, that intintioned thravellin' the same way, an' while we tuk a thrifle av a dhrink in comes Dennis Grady, that was to go to Ballyshiel similiarously. An' so we had another thrifle av a dhrink, or maybe a thrifle more, an' we wint togedther, passin' this way, sor, as ye may not know, bein' likely a shtranger. Well, sor, ut was as we were just forninst this place that there came a divil av a bang that makes us shtop simultaneous. 'What's that?' sez Dan. ' 'Tis a gunshot,' sez I, 'an' 'tis in the brick house too.' 'That is so,' sez Dennis; 'nowhere else.' And we lukt at wan another. 'An' what'll we do?' sez I. 'What would yez?' sez Dan; "tis non av our business.' 'That is so,' sez Dennis again, and we wint on. Ut was quare, maybe, but it might aisily be wan av the jintlemen emptyin' a barr'l out o' windy or what not. An'—an' so—an' so——" Mr. Shanahan scratched his ear, "an' so—we wint."

"And do you know at what time this was?"

Larry Shanahan ceased scratching, and seized his ear between thumb and forefinger, gazing severely at the floor with his one eye as he did so, plunged in computation. "Sure," he said, " 'twould be—'twould be— let's see—'twould be—" he looked up, " 'twould be half-past two maybe, or maybe a thrifle nearer three."

"And Main was in the place all the time after two," Mr. Bowyer said, bringing down his fist on his open hand. "That finishes it. We've nailed him to the minute."

"Had you a watch with you?" asked Hewitt.

"Divil of a watch in the company, sor. I made an internal calculation. 'Tis foive mile from Cullanin, and we never lift till near half an hour after the Town Hall clock had struck twelve. 'Twould take us two hours and a thrifle more, considherin' the pigs an' the rough road, an' the distance, an'—an' the thrifle of dhrink." His eye rolled slyly as he said it. "That was my calculation, sor."

Here the constable appeared with two more men. Each had the usual number of eyes, but in other respects they were very good copies of Mr. Shanahan. They were both ragged, and neither bore any violent likeness to a teetotaler. "Dan Mulcahy and Dennis Grady," announced the constable.

Mr. Dan Mulcahy's tale was of a piece with Mr. Larry Shanahan's, and Mr. Dennis Grady's was the same. They had all heard the shot it was plain. What Dan had said to Dennis and what Dennis had said to Larry mattered little. Also they were all agreed that the day was Tuesday by token of the fair. But as to the time of day there arose a disagreement.

" 'Twas nigh soon afther wan o'clock," said Dan Mulcahy.

"Soon afther wan!" exclaimed Larry Shanahan with scorn. "Soon afther your grandmother's pig! 'Twas half afther two at laste. Ut sthruck twelve nigh 'alf an hour before we lift Cullanin. Why, yez heard ut!"

"That I did not. Ut sthruck eleven, an' we wint in foive minutes."

"What fool-talk ye shpake Dan Mulcahy. 'Twas twelve sthruck; I counted ut."

"Thin ye counted wrong. I counted ut, an' 'twas elivin."

"Yez nayther av yez right," interposed Dennis Grady. " 'Twas not elivin when we lift; 'twas not, be the mother av Moses!"

"I wondher at ye, Dennis Grady; ye must have been dhrunk as a Kerry cow," and both Mulcahy and Shanahan turned upon the obstinate Grady, and the dispute waxed clamorous till Hewitt stopped it.

"Come, come," he said, "never mind the time then. Settle that between you after you've gone. Does either of you remember—not calculate, you know, but *remember*—the time you got to Ballyshiel?—the actual time by a clock—not a guess."

Not one of the three had looked at a clock at Ballyshiel.

"Do you remember anything about coming home again?"

They did not. They looked furtively at one another and presently broke into a grin.

"Ah! I see how *that* was," Hewitt said good-humouredly. "That's all now, I think. Come, it's ten shillings each, I think." And he handed over the money. The men touched their forelocks again, stowed away the money and prepared to depart. As they went Larry Shanahan stepped mysteriously back again and said in a whisper, "Maybe the jintlemen wud like me to kiss the book on ut? An' as to the toime——"

"Oh, no thank you," Hewitt laughed. "We take your word for it Mr. Shanahan." And Mr. Shanahan pulled his forelock again and vanished.

"There's nothing but confusion to be got from them," Mr. Bowyer remarked testily. "It's a mere waste of time."

"No, no, not a waste of time," Hewitt replied, "nor a waste of money. One thing is made pretty plain. That is that the shot was fired on Tuesday. Mrs. Hurley never noticed the report, but these three men were close by, and there is no doubt that they heard it. It's the only single thing they agree about at all. They contradict one another over everything else, but they agree completely in that. Of course I wish we could have got the exact time; but that can't be helped. As it is it is rather fortunate that they disagreed so entirely. Two of them are certainly wrong, and perhaps all three. In any case it wouldn't have been safe to trust to mere computation of time by three men just beginning to get drunk, who had no particular reason for remembering. But if by any chance they had agreed on the time we might have been led into a wrong track altogether by taking the thing as fact. But a gunshot is not such a doubtful thing. When three independent witnesses hear a gun-shot together there can be little doubt that a shot has been fired. Now I think you'd better sit down. Perhaps you can find something to read. I'm about to make a very minute examination of this place, and it will probably bore you if you've nothing else to do."

But Mr. Bowyer would think of nothing but the business in hand. "I don't understand that window," he said, shaking his finger towards it as he spoke. "Not at all. Why should Main want to get in and out by a window? He wasn't a stranger."

Hewitt began a most careful inspection of the whole surface of floor, ceiling, walls and furniture of the sitting-room. At the fireplace, he stooped and lifted with great care a few sheets of charred paper from the grate. These he put on the window-ledge. "Will you just bring over that little screen," he asked, "to keep the draught from this burnt paper? Thank you. It looks like letter paper, and thick letter paper, since the ashes are very little broken. The weather has been fine, and there has been no fire in that grate for a long time. These papers have been care-fully burned with a match or a candle."

"Ah! perhaps the letters poor young Rewse was writing in the morn-ing. But what can they tell us?"

"Perhaps nothing—perhaps a great deal." Hewitt was examining the cinders keenly, holding the surface sidways to the light. "Come," he said, "see if I can guess Rewse's address in London. 17 Mountjoy Gardens, Hampstead. Is that it?"

"Yes. Is it there? Can you read it? Show me." Mr. Bowyer hurried across the room, eager and excited.

"You can sometimes read words on charred paper," Hewitt replied, "as you may have noticed. This has curled and crinkled rather too much in the burning, but it is plainly notepaper with an embossed heading, which stands out rather clearly. He has evidently brought some notepa-per with him from home in his trunk. See, you can just see the ink lines crossing out the address; but there's little else. At the beginning of the letter there is 'My d——' then a gap, and then the last stroke of 'M' and the rest of the word 'mother.' 'My dear Mother,' or 'My dearest Mother' evidently. Something follows too in the same line, but that is unreadable. 'My dear Mother and Sister' perhaps. After that there is nothing recognisable. The first letter looks rather like 'W,' but even that is indistinct. It seems to be a longish letter—several sheets, but they are stuck together in the charring. Perhaps more than one letter."

"The thing is plain," Mr. Bowyer said. "The poor lad was writing home, and perhaps to other places, and Main, after his crime, burned the letters, because they would have stultified his own with the lying tale about small-pox."

Hewitt said nothing, but resumed his general search. He passed his hand rapidly over every inch of the surface of everything in the room. Then he entered the bedroom and began an inspection of the same sort there. There were two beds, one at each end of the room, and each inch of each piece of bed linen passed rapidly under his sharp eye. After the bedroom he betook himself to the little bathroom, and then to the scullery. Finally he went outside and examined every board of a close fence that stood a few feet from the sitting-room window, and the brick-paved path lying between.

When it was all over he returned to Mr. Bowyer. "Here is a strange thing," he said. "The shot passed clean through Rewse's body, striking no bones, and meeting no solid resistance. It was a good-sized bullet, as Dr. O'Reilly testifies, and therefore must have had a large charge of powder behind it in the cartridge. After emerging from Rewse's back it *must* have struck something else in this confined place. Yet on nowhere —ceiling, floor, wall nor furniture, can I find the mark of a bullet nor the bullet itself."

"The bullet itself Main might easily have got rid of."

"Yes, but not the mark. Indeed, the bullet would scarcely be easy to get at if it had struck anything I have seen about here; it would have buried itself. Just look round now. Where could a bullet strike in this place without leaving its mark?"

Mr. Bowyer looked round. "Well, no," he said, "nowhere. Unless the window was open and it went out that way."

"Then it must have hit the fence or the brick paving between, and there is no sign of a bullet there," Hewitt replied. "Push the sash, as high as you please, the shot couldn't have passed *over* the fence without hitting the window first. As to the bedroom windows, that's impossible.

Mr. Shanahan and his friends would not only have heard the shot, they would have seen it—which they didn't."

"Then what's the meaning of it?"

"The meaning of it is simply this: either Rewse was shot somewhere else and his body brought here afterwards, or the article, whatever it was, that the bullet struck must have been taken away."

"Yes, of course. It's just another piece of evidence destroyed by Main, that's all. Every step we go we see the diabolical completeness of his plans. But now every piece of evidence missing only tells the more against him. The body alone condemns him past all redemption."

Hewitt was gazing about the room thoughtfully. "I think we'll have Mrs. Hurley over here," he said; "she should tell us if anything is missing. Constable, will you ask Mrs. Hurley to step over here?"

Mrs. Hurley came at once and was brought into the sitting-room. "Just look about you, Mrs. Hurley," Hewitt said, "in this room and everywhere else, and tell me if anything is missing that you can remember was here on the morning of the day you last saw Mr. Rewse."

She looked thoughtfully up and down the room. "Sure, sor," she said, " 'tis all there as ord'nary." Her eyes rested on the mantel-piece and she added at once, "Except the clock, indade."

"Except the clock?"

"The clock ut is, sure. Ut stud on that same mantelpiece on that mornin' as ut always did."

"What sort of clock was it?"

"Just a plain round wan wid a metal case—an American clock they said ut was. But ut kept nigh as good time as me own."

"It *did* keep good time, you say?"

"Faith an' ut did, sor. Mine an' this ran together for weeks wid nivir a minute betune thim."

"Thank you, Mrs. Hurley, thank you; that will do," Hewitt exclaimed, with some excitement in his voice. He turned to Mr. Bowyer. "We must find that clock," he said. "And there's the pistol; nothing has been seen of that. Come, help me search. Look for a loose board."

"But he'll have taken them away with him probably."

"The pistol perhaps—although that isn't likely. The clock, no. It's evidence, man, evidence!" Hewitt darted outside and walked hurriedly round the cottage, looking this way and that about the country adjacent.

Presently he returned. "No," he said, "I think it's more likely in the house." He stood for a moment and thought. Then he made for the fireplace and flung the fender across the floor. All round the hearthstone an open crack extended. "See there!" he exclaimed as he pointed to it. He took the tongs, and with one leg levered the stone up till he could seize it in his fingers. Then he dragged it out and pushed it across the linoleum that covered the floor. In the space beneath lay a large revolver and a common American round nickel-plated clock. "See here!" he cried, "see here!" and he rose and placed the articles on the mantelpiece. The glass before the clock-face was smashed to atoms, and there was a gaping rent in the face itself. For a few seconds Hewitt regarded it as it stood, and then he turned to Mr. Bowyer. "Mr. Bowyer," he said, "we have done Mr. Stanley Main a sad injustice. Poor young Rewse committed suicide. There is proof undeniable," and he pointed to the clock.

"Proof? How? Where? Nonsense, man. Pooh! Ridiculous! If Rewse committed suicide why should Main go to all that trouble and tell all those lies to prove that he died of small-pox? More even that that, what has he run away for?"

"I'll tell you, Mr. Bowyer, in a moment. But first as to this clock. Remember, Main set his watch by the Cullanin Town Hall clock, and Mrs. Hurley's clock agreed exactly. That we have proved ourselves to-day by my own watch. Mrs. Hurley's clock still agrees. *This* clock was always kept in time with Mrs. Hurley's. Main returned at two exactly. Look at the time by that clock—the time when the bullet crashed into and stopped it."

The time was three minutes to one.

Hewitt took the clock, unscrewed the winder and quickly stripped off the back, exposing the works. "See," he said, "the bullet is lodged firmly among the wheels, and has been torn into snags and strips by the impact. The wheels themselves are ruined altogether. The central axle which carries the hands is bent. See there! Neither hand will move in the slightest. That bullet struck the axle and fixed those hands immovably at the moment of the time when Algernon Rewse died. Look at the mainspring. It is less than half run out. Proof that the clock was going when the shot struck it. Main left Rewse alive and well at half-past nine. He did not return till two—when Rewse had been dead more than an hour."

"But then, hang it all! How about the lies and the false certificate, and the bolting?"

"Let me tell you the whole tale, Mr. Bowyer, as I conjecture it to have been. Poor young Rewse was, as you told me, in a bad state of health—thoroughly run down, I think you said. You said something of his engagement and the death of the lady. This pointed clearly to a nervous—a mental upset. Very well. He broods, and so forth. He must go away and find change of scene and occupation. His intimate friend Main brings him here. The holiday has its good effect perhaps, at first, but after a while it gets monotonous, and brooding sets in again. I do not know whether or not you happen to know it, but it is a fact that four-fifths of all persons suffering from melancholia have suicidal tendencies. This may never have been suspected by Main, who otherwise might not have left him so long alone. At any rate he *is* left alone, and he takes the opportunity. He writes a note to Main and a long letter to his mother—an awful, heartbreaking letter, with a terrible picture of the mental agony wherein he was to die—perhaps with a tincture of religious mania in it, and prophesying merited hell for himself in the hereafter. This done, he simply stands up from the table, at which he has been writing, and with his back to the fireplace shoots himself. There he lies till Main returns an hour later. Main finds the door shut and nobody answers his knock. He goes round to the sitting-room window, looks through, and perhaps he sees the body. Anyway he pushes back the catch with his knife, opens the window and gets in, and *then* he sees. He is completely knocked out of time. The thing is terrible. What shall he—what can he do? Poor Rewse's mother and sister dote on him, and his mother is an invalid—heart disease. To let her see that awful letter would be to kill her. He burns the letter, also the note to himself. Then an idea strikes him. Even without the letter the news of her boy's suicide will probably kill the poor old lady. Can she be prevented hearing of it? Of his death she must know—that's inevitable. But as to the manner? Would it not be possible to concoct some kind lie? And then the opportunities of the situation occur to him. Nobody but himself knows of it. He is a medical man, fully qualified, and empowered to give certificates of death. More, there is an epidemic of small-pox in the neighbourhood. What easier, with a little management, than to call the death one by small-pox? Nobody would be anxious to examine too closely the corpse of a small-pox patient. He decides that he will do it. He writes the letter to Mrs. Rewse announcing that her son has the disease, and he forbids Mrs. Hurley to come near the place for fear of infection. He cleans the floor—it is linoleum here, you see, and the stains were fresh—burns the clothes, cleans and stops the wound. At every turn his medical knowledge is of use. He puts the smashed clock and the pistol out of sight under the hearth. In a word he carries out the whole thing rather cleverly, and a terrible few days he must have passed. It never strikes him that he has dug a frightful pit for his own feet. You are suspicious, and you come across. In a perhaps rather peremptory manner you tell him how suspicious his conduct has been. And then a sense of his terrible position comes upon him like a thunderclap. He sees it all. He has deliberately of his own motion destroyed every evidence of the suicide. There is no evidence in the world that Rewse did not die a natural death, except the body, and that you are going to dig up. He sees now (you remind him of it in fact) that *he* is the one man alive who can profit by Rewse's death. And there is the shot body, and there is the false death certificate, and there are the lying letters, and the tales to the neighbours and everything. He has himself destroyed everything that proves suicide. All that remains points to a foul murder and to him as the murderer. Can you wonder at his complete breakdown and his flight? What else in the world could the poor fellow do?"

"Well, well—yes, yes," Mr. Bowyer replied thoughtfully, "it seems very plausible of course. But still, look at probabilities, my dear sir, look at probabilities."

"No, but look at *possibilities*. There is that clock. Get over it if you can. Was there ever a more insurmountable alibi? Could Main possibly be here shooting Rewse and half way between here and Cullanin at the same time? Remember, Mrs. Hurley saw him come back at two, and she had been watching for an hour, and could see more than half a mile up the road."

"Well, yes, I suppose you're right. And what must we do now?"

"Bring Main back. I think we should advertise to begin with. Say, 'Rewse is proved to have died over an hour before you came. All safe. Your evidence is wanted,' or something of that sort. And we must set the telegraph going. The police already are looking for him, no doubt. Meanwhile I will look here for a clue myself."

The advertisement was successful in two days. Indeed Main afterwards said that he was at the time, once the first terror was over, in doubt whether or not it would be best to go back and face the thing out, trusting to his innocence. He could not venture home for money, nor to his bank, for fear of the police. He chanced upon the advertisement as he searched the paper for news of the case, and that decided him. His explanation of the matter was precisely as Hewitt had expected. His only thought till Mr. Bowyer first arrived at the cottage had been to smother the real facts and to spare the feelings of Mrs. Rewse and her daughter, and it was not till that gentleman put them so plainly before him that he in the least realised the dangers of his position. That his fears for Mrs. Rewse were only too well grounded was proved by events, for the poor old lady only survived her son by a month.

These events took place some little while ago, as may be gathered from the fact that Miss Rewse has now been Mrs. Stanley Main for nearly three years.

In the Fog

RICHARD HARDING DAVIS

The Grill is the club most difficult of access in the world. To be placed on its rolls distinguishes the new member as greatly as though he had received a vacant Garter or had been caricatured in *Vanity Fair*.

Men who belong to the Grill Club never mention that fact. If you ask one of them which club he frequents, he will name all save that particular one. He is afraid if he told you he belonged to the Grill that it would sound like boasting.

The Grill Club dates back to the days when Shakespeare's Theatre stood on the present site of the *Times* office. It has a golden grill which Charles the Second presented to the Club, and the original manuscript of "Tom and Jerry in London," which was bequeathed to it by Pierce Egan himself. The members when they write letters at the Club still use sand to blot the ink.

The Grill enjoys the distinction of having without political prejudice blackballed a Prime Minister of each party. At the same sitting at which one of these fell, it elected, on account of his brogue and his bulls, Quiller, the Queen's Counsellor, who was then a penniless barrister.

When Paul Preval, the French artist who came to London by royal command to paint the portrait of the Prince of Wales, was made an honorary member—only foreigners may be honorary members—he said, as he signed his first wine card, "I would rather see my name on that than a picture in the Louvre."

At which Quiller remarked, "That is a devil of a compliment, because the only men who can read their names in the Louvre to-day have been dead fifty years."

On the night after the great fog of 1897 there were five members in the Club, four of them busy with supper, and one reading in front of the fireplace. There is only one room to the Club and one long table. At the far end of the room the fire of the grill glows red, and, when the fat falls, blazes into flame, and at the other there is a broad bow window of diamond panes, which looks down upon the street. The four men at the table were strangers to each other, but as they picked at the grilled bones, and sipped their Scotch-and-sodas, they conversed with such charming animation that a visitor to the Club—which does not tolerate visitors—would have counted them as friends of long acquaintance, certainly not as Englishmen who had met without the form of an introduction and for the first time. But it is the etiquette and tradition of the Grill that whoever enters it must speak with whomever he finds there. It is to enforce this rule that there is but one long table, and whether there are twenty men at it, or two, the waiters, supporting the rule, will place them side by side.

For this reason the four strangers at supper were seated together, with the candles grouped about them and the long length of the table cutting a white path through the outer gloom of the room.

"I repeat," said the gentleman with the black pearl stud, "that the days for romantic adventure and deeds of foolish daring have passed, and that the fault lies with ourselves. Voyages to the Pole I do not catalogue as adventures. That African explorer, young Chetney, who turned up yesterday after he was supposed to have died in Uganda, did nothing adventurous. He made maps and explored the sources of rivers. He was in constant danger, but the presence of danger does not constitute adventure. Were that so, the chemist who studies high explosives or who investigates deadly poisons passes through adventures daily. No, 'adventures are for the adventurous.' But one no longer ventures. The spirit of it died of inertia. We are grown too practical, too just—above all, too sensible. In this room, for instance, members of this Club have, at the sword's point, disputed the proper scanning of one of Pope's couplets. Over so weighty a matter as spilled Burgundy on a gentleman's cuff ten men fought across this table, each with his rapier in one hand and a candle in the other. All ten were wounded. The question of the spilled Burgundy concerned but two of them. The other eight engaged because they were men of 'spirit.' They were, indeed, the first gentlemen of their day. To-night, were you to spill Burgundy on my cuff, were you even to insult me grossly, these gentlemen would not consider it incumbent upon them to kill each other. They would separate us and appear as witnesses against us at Bow Street to-morrow morning. We have here to-night, in the persons of Sir Andrew and myself, an illustration of how the ways have changed."

The men around the table turned and glanced toward the gentleman in front of the fireplace. He was an elderly and somewhat portly person, with a kindly wrinkled countenance, which wore continually a smile of almost childish confidence and good nature. It was a face which the illustrated prints had made intimately familiar. He held a book from him at arm's-length, as though to adjust it to his eyesight, and his brows were knit with interest.

"Now, were this the eighteenth century," continued the gentleman with the black pearl, "when Sir Andrew left the Club to-night I would have him bound and gagged and thrown into a sedan chair. The watch would not interfere, the passers-by would take to their heels, my hired bullies and ruffians would convey him to some lonely spot where we would guard him until morning. Nothing would come of it, except added reputation to myself as a gentleman of adventurous spirit, and possibly an essay in the *Tattler*, with stars for names, entitled, let us say, 'The Budget and the Baronet.' "

"But to what end, sir?" inquired the youngest of the members. "And why Sir Andrew, of all persons—why should you select him for this adventure?"

The gentleman with the black pearl shrugged his shoulders.

"It would prevent him speaking in the House to-night. The Navy Increase Bill," he added gloomily. "It is a Government measure, and Sir Andrew speaks for it. And so great is his influence and so large his following, that if he does"—the gentleman laughed ruefully—"if he does, it will go through. Now, had I the spirit of our ancestors," he exclaimed, "I would bring chloroform from the nearest chemist and drug him in that chair. I would tumble his unconscious form into a hansom cab and hold him prisoner until daylight. If I did, I would save the British taxpayer the cost of five more battleships, some many millions of pounds."

All the gentlemen again turned and surveyed the Baronet with freshened interest. The honorary member of the Grill, whose accent had already betrayed him as an American, laughed softly.

"To look at him now," he said, "one would not guess he was deeply concerned with the affairs of State."

The others nodded silently.

"He has not lifted his eyes from that book since we first entered," added the youngest member. "He surely cannot mean to speak to-night."

"Oh, yes, he will speak," muttered the one with the black pearl moodily. "During these last hours of the session the House sits late, but when the Navy Bill comes up on its third reading he will be in his place —and he will pass it."

The fourth member, a stout and florid gentleman of a somewhat sporting appearance, in a short smoking-jacket and black tie, sighed enviously.

"Fancy one of us being as cool as that, if he knew he had to stand up within an hour and rattle off a speech in Parliament. I'd be in a devil of a funk myself. And yet he is as keen over that book he's reading as though he had nothing before him until bedtime."

"Yes, see how eager he is," whispered the youngest member. "He does not lift his eyes even now when he cuts the pages. It is probably an Admiralty Report, or some other weighty work of statistics which bears upon his speech."

The gentleman with the black pearl laughed morosely.

"The weighty work in which the eminent statesman is so deeply engrossed," he said, "is called *The Great Rand Robbery*. It is a detective novel for sale at all bookstalls."

The American raised his eyebrows in disbelief.

"*The Great Rand Robbery?*" he repeated incredulously. "What an odd taste!"

"It is not a taste, it is his vice," returned the gentleman with the pearl stud. "It is his one dissipation. He is noted for it. You, as a stranger, could hardly be expected to know of this idiosyncrasy. Mr. Gladstone sought relaxation in the Greek poets, Sir Andrew finds his in Gaboriau. Since I have been a member of Parliament I have never seen him in the library without a shilling shocker in his hands. He brings them even into the sacred precincts of the House, and from the Government benches reads them concealed inside his hat. Once started on a tale of murder, robbery, and sudden death, nothing can tear him from it, not even the call of the division bell, nor of hunger, nor the prayers of the party Whip. He gave up his country house because when he journeyed to it in the train he would become so absorbed in his detective stories that he

was invariably carried past his station." The member of Parliament
twisted his pearl stud nervously and bit at the edge of his moustache. "If
it only were the first pages of *The Rand Robbery* that he were reading
now," he murmured bitterly, "instead of the last! With such another
book as that, I swear I could hold him here until morning. There would
be no need of chloroform then to keep him from the House."

The eyes of all were fastened upon Sir Andrew, and they saw with
fascination that with his forefinger he was now separating the last two
pages of the book. The member of Parliament struck the table softly
with his open palm.

"I would give a hundred pounds," he whispered, "if I could place in
his hands at this moment a new story of Sherlock Holmes—a thousand
pounds!" he added wildly. "Five thousand pounds!"

The American observed the speaker sharply, as though the words
bore to him some special application, and then, at an idea which apparently had but just come to him, smiled in great embarrassment.

Sir Andrew ceased reading, but, as though still under the influence of
the book, sat looking blankly into the open fire. For a brief space no one
moved, until the baronet withdrew his eyes and, with a sudden start of
recollection, felt anxiously for his watch. He scanned its face eagerly and
scrambled briskly to his feet.

The voice of the American instantly broke the silence in a high, nervous accent.

"And yet Sherlock Holmes himself," he cried, "could not decipher the
mystery which to-night baffles the police of London."

At these unexpected words, which carried in them something of the
tone of a challenge, the gentlemen about the table started as suddenly as
though the American had fired a pistol in the air, and Sir Andrew halted
abruptly and stood observing him with grave surprise.

The gentleman with the black pearl was the first to recover.

"Yes, yes," he said eagerly, throwing himself across the table. "A mystery that baffles the police of London? I had heard nothing of it. Tell us
at once, pray do—tell us at once."

The American flushed uncomfortably and picked uneasily at the tablecloth.

"No one but the police has heard of it," he murmured, "and they
only through me. It is a remarkable crime, to which, unfortunately, I am
the only person who can bear witness. Because I am the only witness, I

am, in spite of my immunity as a diplomat, detained in London by the
authorities of Scotland Yard. My name," he said, inclining his head politely, "is Sears—Lieutenant Ripley Sears, of the United States Navy, at
present Naval Attaché to the Court of Russia. Had I not been detained
to-day by the police, I would have started this morning for Petersburg."

The gentleman with the black pearl interrupted with so pronounced
an exclamation of excitement and delight that the American stammered
and ceased speaking.

"Do you hear, Sir Andrew?" cried the member of Parliament jubi-
lantly. "An American diplomat halted by our police because he is the
only witness of a most remarkable crime—*the* most remarkable crime, I
believe you said, sir," he added, bending eagerly toward the naval officer,
"which has occurred in London in many years."

The American moved his head in assent and glanced at the two other
members. They were looking doubtfully at him, and the face of each
showed that he was greatly perplexed.

Sir Andrew advanced to within the light of the candles and drew a
chair toward him.

"The crime must be exceptional indeed," he said, "to justify the police in interfering with a representative of a friendly Power. If I were not
forced to leave at once, I should take the liberty of asking you to tell us
the details."

The gentleman with the pearl pushed the chair toward Sir Andrew
and motioned him to be seated.

"You cannot leave us now," he exclaimed. "Mr. Sears is just about to
tell us of this remarkable crime."

He nodded vigorously at the naval officer and the American, after
first glancing doubtfully toward the servants at the far end of the room,
and leaned forward across the table. The others drew their chairs nearer
and bent toward him. The baronet glanced irresolutely at his watch, and
with an exclamation of annoyance snapped down the lid. "They can
wait," he muttered. He seated himself quickly and nodded at Lieutenant
Sears.

"If you will be so kind as to begin, sir," he said impatiently.

"Of course," said the American, "you understand that I am speaking
to gentlemen. The confidences of this Club are inviolate. Until the police
give the facts to the public press, I must consider you my confederates.

You have heard nothing and you know no one connected with this mystery. Even I must remain anonymous."

The gentlemen seated around him nodded gravely.

"Of course," the Baronet assented with eagerness, "of course."

"We will refer to it," said the gentleman with the black pearl, "as 'The Story of the Naval Attaché.'"

The American started his tale:

I arrived in London two days ago, and I engaged a room at the Bath Hotel. I know very few people in London, and even the members of our Embassy were strangers to me. But in Hong Kong I had become great pals with an officer in your Navy, who has since retired, and who is now living in a small house in Rutland Gardens, opposite the Knightsbridge Barracks. I telegraphed him that I was in London, and yesterday morning I received a most hearty invitation to dine with him the same evening at his house. He is a bachelor, so we dined alone and talked over all our old days on the Asiatic Station, and of the changes which had come to us since we had last met there. As I was leaving the next morning for my post at Petersburg, and had many letters to write, I told him, about ten o'clock, that I must get back to the hotel, and he sent out his servant to call a hansom.

For the next quarter of an hour, as we sat talking, we could hear the cab-whistle sounding violently from the doorstep, but apparently with no result.

"It cannot be that the cabmen are on strike," my friend said, as he rose and walked to the window.

He pulled back the curtains and at once called to me.

"You have never seen a London fog, have you?" he asked. "Well, come here. This is one of the best, or, rather, one of the worst, of them." I joined him at the window, but I could see nothing. Had I not known that the house looked out upon the street, I would have believed that I was facing a dead wall. I raised the sash and stretched out my head, but still I could see nothing. Even the light of the street lamps opposite, and in the upper windows of the barracks, had been smothered in the yellow mist. The lights of the room in which I stood penetrated the fog only to the distance of a few inches from my eyes.

Below me the servant was still sounding his whistle, but I could afford to wait no longer, and told my friend that I would try and find the way to my hotel on foot. He objected, but the letters I had to write were for the Navy Department, and, besides, I had always heard that to be out in a London fog was the most wonderful experience, and I was curious to investigate one for myself.

My friend went with me to his front door and laid down a course for me to follow. I was first to walk straight across the street to the brick wall of the Knightsbridge Barracks. I was then to feel my way along the wall until I came to a row of houses set back from the sidewalk. They would bring me to a cross street. On the other side of this street was a row of shops which I was to follow until they joined the iron railings of Hyde Park. I was to keep to the railings until I reached the gates at Hyde Park Corner, where I was to lay a diagonal course across Piccadilly and tack in toward the railings of Green Park. At the end of these railings, going east, I would find the Walsingham and my own hotel.

To a sailor the course did not seem difficult, so I bade my friend good-night and walked forward until my feet touched the wooden paving. I continued upon it until I reached the kerbing of the sidewalk. A few steps further my hands struck the wall of the barracks. I turned in the direction from which I had just come, and saw a square of faint light cut into the yellow fog. I shouted "All right!" and my friend's voice answered, "Good luck to you!" The light from his open door disappeared with a bang, and I was left alone in a dripping, yellow darkness. I have been in the Navy for ten years, but I have never known such a fog as that of last night, not even among the icebergs of Behring Sea. There one could at least see the light of the binnacle, but last night I could not even distinguish the hand by which I guided myself along the barrack wall. At sea, a fog is a natural phenomenon. It is as familiar as the rainbow which follows a storm, it is as proper that a fog should spread upon the waters as that steam shall rise from a kettle. But a fog which springs from the paved streets, that rolls between solid house-fronts, that forces cabs to move at half speed, that drowns policemen and extinguishes the electric lights of the music-hall, that is to me incomprehensible. It is as out of place as a tidal wave on Broadway.

As I felt my way along the wall, I encountered other men who were coming from the opposite direction, and each time when we hailed each other I stepped away from the wall to make room for them to pass. But the third time I did this, when I reached out my hand, the wall had disappeared, and the further I moved to find it the further I seemed to be sinking into space. I had the unpleasant conviction that at any mo-

ment I might step over a precipice. Since I had set out I had heard no
traffic in the street, and now, although I listened some minutes, I could
only distinguish the occasional footfalls of pedestrians. Several times I
called aloud, and once a jocular gentleman answered me, but only to ask
me where I thought he was, and then even he was swallowed up in the
silence. Just above me I could make out a jet of gas which I guessed
came from a street lamp, and I moved over to that, and, while I tried to
recover my bearings, kept my hand on the iron post. Except for this
flicker of gas, no larger than the tip of my finger, I could distinguish
nothing about me. For the rest, the mist hung between me and the
world like a damp and heavy blanket.

I could hear voices, but I could not tell whence they came, and the
scrape of a foot moving cautiously or a muffled cry as someone stumbled were the only sounds that reached me.

I decided that I had best remain where I was until someone took me
in tow, and it must have been for ten minutes that I waited, straining my
ears and hailing distant footfalls. In a house near me some people were
dancing to the music of a Hungarian band. I even fancied I could hear
the windows shake to the rhythm of their feet, but I could not make out
from which part of the compass the sounds came. And sometimes, as
the music rose, it seemed close at my hand, and again, to be floating
high in the air above my head. Although I was surrounded by thousands
of householders—thirteen—I was as completely lost as though I had
been set down by night in the Sahara Desert. There seemed to be no use
in waiting longer for an escort, so I again set out and at once bumped
against a low iron fence. At first I believed this to be an area railing, but
on following it I found that it stretched for a long distance, and that it
was pierced at regular intervals with gates. I was standing uncertainly,
with my hand on one of these, when a square of light suddenly opened
in the night, and in it I saw, as you see a picture thrown by a biograph
in a darkened theatre, a young gentleman in evening dress, and at the
back of him the lights of a hall. I guessed from its elevation and distance
from the sidewalk that this light must come from the door of a house set
back from the street, and I determined to approach it and ask the young
man to tell me where I was. But in fumbling with the lock of the gate I
instinctively bent my head, and when I raised it again the door had
partly closed, leaving only a narrow shaft of light. Whether the young
man had re-entered the house or had left it, I could not tell, but I

hastened to open the gate, and as I stepped forward I found myself upon an asphalt walk. At the same instant there was the sound of quick steps upon the path and someone rushed past me. I called to him, but he made no reply, and I heard the gate click and the footsteps hurrying away upon the sidewalk.

Under other circumstances the young man's rudeness, and his reck-lessness in dashing so hurriedly through the mist, would have struck me as peculiar, but everything was so distorted by the fog that at the mo-ment I did not consider it. The door was still as he had left it, partly open. I went up the path, and after much fumbling found the knob of the door-bell and gave it a sharp pull. The bell answered me from a great depth and distance, but no movement followed from inside the house, and although I pulled the bell again and again I could hear noth-ing save the dripping of the mist about me. I was anxious to be on my way, but unless I knew my way there was little chance of my making any speed, and I was determined that until I learned my bearings I would not venture back into the fog. So I pushed the door open and stepped into the house.

I found myself in a long and narrow hall upon which doors opened from either side. At the end of the hall was a staircase with a balustrade which ended in a sweeping curve. The balustrade was covered with heavy Persian rugs, and the walls of the hall were also hung with them. The door on my left was closed, but the one nearer me on the right was open, and as I stepped opposite to it I saw that it was a sort of reception or waiting room, and that it was empty. The door below it was also open, and with the idea that I would surely find someone there I walked on up the hall. I was in evening dress, and I felt I did not look like a burglar, so I had no great fear that, should I encounter one of the inmates of the house, he would shoot me on sight. The second door in the hall opened into a dining-room. This was also empty. One person had been dining at the table, but the cloth had not been cleared away, and a flickering candle showed half-filled wineglasses and the ashes of cigarettes. The greater part of the room was in complete darkness.

By this time I had grown conscious of the fact that I was wandering about in a strange house, and that apparently I was alone in it. The silence of the place began to try my nerves, and in a sudden, unexplain-able panic I started for the open street. As I turned, I saw a man sitting on a bench which the curve of the balustrade had hidden from me. His eyes were shut and he was sleeping soundly.

The moment before I had been bewildered because I could see no one, but at sight of this man I was much more bewildered.

He was a very large man, a giant in height, with long, yellow hair which hung below his shoulders. He was dressed in a red silk shirt that was belted at the waist and hung outside black velvet trousers which, in turn, were stuffed into high, black boots. I recognised the costume at once as that of a Russian servant in his native livery, but what he could be doing in a private house in Knightsbridge was incomprehensible.

I advanced and touched the man on the shoulder, and, after an effort, he awoke and, on seeing me, sprang to his feet and began bowing rapidly and making deprecatory gestures. I had picked up enough Russian in Petersburg to make out that the man was apologising for having fallen asleep, and I also was able to explain to him that I desired to see his master.

He nodded vigorously and said, "Will the Excellency come this way? The Princess is here."

I distinctly made out the word "Princess," and I was a good deal embarrassed. I had thought it would be easy enough to explain my intrusion to a man; but how a woman would look at it was another matter, and as I followed him down the hall I was somewhat puzzled.

As we advanced he noticed that the front door was standing open, and, giving an exclamation of surprise, hastened toward it and closed it. Then he rapped twice on the door of what was apparently the drawing-room. There was no reply to his knock, and he tapped again, and then timidly, and cringing subserviently, opened the door and stepped inside. He withdrew himself almost at once and stared stupidly at me, shaking his head.

"She is not there," he said. He stood for a moment gazing blankly through the open door and then hastened toward the dining-room. The solitary candle which still burned there seemed to assure him that the room also was empty. He came back and bowed me toward the drawing-room. "She is above," he said; "I will inform the Princess of the Excellency's presence."

Before I could stop him he had turned and was running up the staircase, leaving me alone at the open door of the drawing-room. I decided that the adventure had gone quite far enough, and if I had been able to explain to the Russian that I had lost my way in the fog, and now only wanted to get back into the street again, I would have left the house on the instant.

Of course, when I first rang the bell of the house I had no other expectation than that it would be answered by a parlourmaid who would direct me on my way. I certainly could not then foresee that I would disturb a Russian princess in her boudoir, or that I might be thrown out by her athletic bodyguard. Still, I thought I ought not now to leave the house without making some apology, and, if the worst should come, I could show my card. They could hardly believe that a member of an embassy had any designs upon the hat-rack.

The room in which I stood was dimly lighted, but I could see that, like the hall, it was hung with heavy Persian rugs. The corners were filled with palms, and there was the unmistakable odour in the air of Russian cigarettes and strange, dry scents that carried me back to the bazaars of Vladivostock. Near the front windows was a grand piano, and at the other end of the room a heavily carved screen of some black wood, picked out with ivory. The screen was over-hung with a canopy of silken draperies and formed a sort of alcove. In front of the alcove was spread the white skin of a polar bear, and set on that was one of those low Turkish coffee tables. It held a lighted spirit-lamp and two gold coffee-cups. I had heard no movement from above stairs, and it must have been fully three minutes that I stood waiting, noting these details of the room and wondering at the delay and at the strange silence.

And then, suddenly, as my eye grew more used to the half-light, I saw, projecting from behind the screen as though it were stretched along the back of a divan, the hand of a man and the lower part of his arm. I was as startled as though I had come across a footprint on a deserted island. Evidently the man had been sitting there ever since I had come into the room, even since I had entered the house, and he had heard the servant knocking upon the door. Why he had not declared himself I could not understand, but I supposed that possibly he was a guest, with no reason to interest himself in the Princess's other visitors, or perhaps, for some reason, he did not wish to be observed. I could see nothing of him except his hand, but I had an unpleasant feeling that he had been peering at me through the carving in the screen, and that he was still doing so. I moved my feet noisily on the floor and said tentatively, "I beg your pardon."

There was no reply, and the hand did not stir. Apparently the man was bent upon ignoring me, but as all I wished was to apologise for my intrusion and to leave the house, I walked up to the alcove and peered around it. Inside the screen was a divan piled with cushions, and on the end of it nearer me the man was sitting. He was a young Englishman with light yellow hair and a deeply bronzed face. He was seated with his arms stretched out along the back of the divan, and with his head resting against a cushion. His attitude was one of complete ease. But his mouth had fallen open, and his eyes were set with an expression of utter horror. At the first glance I saw that he was quite dead.

For a flash of time I was too startled to act, but in the same flash I was convinced that the man had met his death from no accident, that he had not died through any ordinary failure of the laws of Nature. The expression on his face was much too terrible to be misinterpreted. It spoke as eloquently as words. It told me that before the end had come he had watched his death approach and threaten him.

I was so sure he had been murdered that I instinctively looked on the floor for the weapon, and, at the same moment, out of concern for my own safety, quickly behind me; but the silence of the house continued unbroken.

I have seen a great number of dead men; I was on the Asiatic Station during the Japanese-Chinese war. I was in Port Arthur after the massacre. So a dead man for the single reason that he is dead does not repel me, and, though I knew that there was no hope that this man was alive, still, for decency's sake, I felt his pulse, and while I kept my ears alert for any sound from the floors above me, I pulled open his shirt and placed my hand upon his heart. My fingers instantly touched upon the opening of a wound, and as I withdrew them I found them wet with blood. he was in evening dress, and in the wide bosom of his shirt I found a narrow slit, so narrow that in the dim light it was scarcely discernible. The wound was no wider than the smallest blade of a pocket-knife, but when I stripped the shirt away from the chest and left it bare, I found that the weapon, narrow as it was, had been long enough to reach his heart. There is no need to tell you how I felt as I stood by the body of this boy (for he was hardly older than a boy), or of the thoughts that came into my head. I was bitterly sorry for this stranger, bitterly indignant at his murderer, and, at the same time, selfishly concerned for my own safety and for the notoriety which I saw was sure to follow. My instinct was to leave the body where it lay and to hide myself in the fog, but I also felt that since a succession of accidents had made me the only witness to a crime, my duty was to make myself a good witness and to assist to establish the facts of this murder.

That it might possibly be a suicide, and not a murder, did not disturb me for a moment. The fact that the weapon had disappeared and the expression on the boy's face were enough to convince at least me that he had had no hand in his own death. I judged it, therefore, of the first importance to discover who was in the house, or, if they had escaped from it, who had been in the house before I entered it. I had seen one man leave it; but all I could tell of him was that he was a young man, that he was in evening dress, and that he had fled in such haste that he had not stopped to close the door behind him.

The Russian servant I had found apparently asleep, and, unless he acted a part with supreme skill, he was a stupid and ignorant boor and as innocent of the murder as myself. There was still the Russian Princess whom he had expected to find, or had pretended to expect to find, in the same room with the murdered man. I judged that she must now be either upstairs with the servant, or that she had, without his knowledge, already fled from the house. When I recalled his apparently genuine surprise at not finding her in the drawing-room, this latter supposition seemed the more probable. Nevertheless, I decided that it was my duty to make a search, and after a second hurried look for the weapon among the cushions of the divan and upon the floor, I cautiously crossed the hall and entered the dining-room.

The single candle was still flickering in the draught, and showed only the white cloth. The rest of the room was draped in shadows. I picked up the candle and, lifting it high above my head, moved round the corner of the table. Either my nerves were on such a stretch that no shock could strain them further, or my mind was inoculated to horrors; for I did not cry out at what I saw nor retreat from it. Immediately at my feet was the body of a beautiful woman, lying at full length upon the floor, her arms flung out on either side of her, and her white face and shoulders gleaming dully in the unsteady light of the candle. Around her throat was a great chain of diamonds, and the light played upon these and made them flash and blaze in tiny flames. But the woman who wore them was dead, and I was so certain as to how she had died that without an instant's hesitation I dropped on my knees beside her and placed my hand above her heart. My fingers again touched the thin slit of a wound. I had no doubt in my mind but that this was the Russian Princess, and when I lowered the candle to her face I was assured that this was so. Her features showed the finest lines of both the Slav and the Jewess, the eyes were black, the hair blue-black and wonderfully heavy, and her skin, even in death, was rich in colour. She was a surpassingly beautiful woman.

I rose and tried to light another candle with the one I held, but I found that my hand was so unsteady that I could not keep the wicks together. It was my intention to again search for this strange dagger which had been used to kill both the English boy and the beautiful Princess, but before I could light the second candle I heard footsteps descending the stairs, and the Russian servant appeared in the doorway.

My face was in darkness, or I am sure that at the sight of it he would have taken alarm, for at that moment I was not sure but that this man himself was the murderer. His own face was plainly visible to me in the light from the hall, and I could see that it wore an expression of dull bewilderment. I stepped quickly toward him and took a firm hold upon his wrist.

"She is not there," he said. "The Princess has gone. They have all gone."

"Who have gone?" I demanded. "Who else has been here?"

"The two Englishmen."

"What two Englishmen?" I demanded. "What are their names?"

The man now saw by my manner that some question of great moment hung upon his answer, and he began to protest that he did not know the names of the visitors, and that until the evening he had never seen them.

I guessed that it was my tone which frightened him, so I took my hand off his wrist and spoke less eagerly.

"How long have they been here?" I asked, "and when did they go?"

He pointed behind him toward the drawing-room.

"One sat there with the Princess," he said; "the other came after I had placed the coffee in the drawing-room. The two Englishmen talked together, and the Princess returned here to the table. She sat there in that chair, and I brought her cognac and cigarettes. Then I sat outside upon the bench. It was a feast day and I had been drinking. Pardon, Excellency, but I fell asleep. When I woke, your Excellency was standing by me, but the Princess and the two Englishmen had gone. That is all I know."

I believed that the man was telling me the truth. His fright had passed, and he was now apparently puzzled, but not alarmed.

"You must remember the names of the Englishmen," I urged. "Try to think. When you announced them to the Princess, what name did you give?"

At this question he exclaimed with pleasure, and, beckoning to me, ran hurriedly down the hall and into the drawing-room. In the corner furthest from the screen was the piano, and on it was a silver tray. He picked this up and, smiling with pride at his own intelligence, pointed at two cards that lay upon it. I took them up and read the names engraved upon them.

The American paused abruptly and glanced at the faces about him. "I read the names," he repeated. He spoke with great reluctance.

"Continue!" cried the Baronet sharply.

"I read the names," said the American, with evident distaste, "and the family name of each was the same. They were the names of two brothers. One is well known to you. It is that of the African explorer of whom this gentleman was just speaking. I mean the Earl of Chetney. The other was the name of his brother, Lord Arthur Chetney."

The men at the table fell back as though a trapdoor had fallen open at their feet.

"Lord Chetney!" they exclaimed in chorus. They glanced at each other and back to the American with every expression of concern and disbelief.

"It is impossible!" cried the Baronet. "Why, my dear sir, young Chetney only arrived from Africa yesterday. It was so stated in the evening papers."

The jaw of the American set in a resolute square and he pressed his lips together.

"You are perfectly right, sir," he said, "Lord Chetney did arrive in London yesterday morning, and yesterday night I found his dead body."

The youngest member present was the first to recover. He seemed much less concerned over the identity of the murdered man than at the interruption of the narrative.

"Oh! please let him go on!" he cried. "What happened then? You say

you found two visiting cards. How do you know which card was that of
the murdered man?"

The American, before he answered, waited until the chorus of excla-
mations had ceased. Then he continued as though he had not been
interrupted.

"The instant I read the names upon the cards," he said, "I ran to the
screen and, kneeling beside the dead man, began a search through his
pockets. My hand at once fell upon a card-case, and I found on all the
cards it contained the title of the Earl of Chetney. His watch and cigarette-case also bore his name. These evidences, and the fact of his
bronzed skin, and that his cheek-bones were worn with fever, convinced
me that the dead man was the African explorer, and the boy who had
fled past me in the night was Arthur, his younger brother.

"I was so intent upon my search that I had forgotten the servant, and
I was still on my knees when I heard a cry behind me. I turned and saw
the man gazing down at the body in abject and unspeakable horror.

"Before I could rise, he gave another cry of terror and, flinging himself into the hall, raced toward the door to the street. I leaped after him,
shouting to him to halt, but before I could reach the hall he had torn
open the door and I saw him spring out into the yellow fog. I cleared the
steps in a jump and ran down the garden walk, but just as the gate
clicked in front of me. I had it open on the instant, and, following the
sound of the man's footsteps, I raced after him across the open street.
He, also, could hear me, and he instantly stopped running, and there
was absolute silence. He was so near that I almost fancied I could hear
him panting, and I held my own breath to listen. But I could distinguish
nothing but the dripping of the mist about us, and from far off the
music of the Hungarian band, which I had heard when I first lost myself.

"All I could see was the square of light from the door I had left open
behind me and a lamp in the hall beyond it flickering in the draught.
But even as I watched it the flame of the lamp was blown violently to
and fro, and the door, caught in the same current of air, closed slowly. I
knew if it shut I could not again enter the house, and I rushed madly
toward it. I believe I even shouted out, as though it were something
human which I could compel to obey me, and then I caught my foot
against the kerb and smashed into the sidewalk. When I rose to my feet I
was dizzy and half stunned, and though I thought then that I was mov-

ing toward the door, I know now that I probably turned directly from it; for, as I groped about in the night, calling frantically for the police, my fingers touched nothing but the dripping fog, and the iron railings for which I sought seemed to have melted away. For many minutes I beat the mist with my arms like a man at blind man's buff, turning sharply in circles, cursing aloud at my stupidity, and crying continually for help. At last a voice answered me from the fog, and I found myself held in the circle of a policeman's lantern.

"That is the end of my adventure. What I have to tell you now is what I learned from the police.

"At the station-house to which the man guided me I related what you have just heard. I told them that the house they must at once find was one set back with others from the street within a radius of two hundred yards from the Knightsbridge Barracks, that within fifty yards of it someone was giving a dance to the music of a Hungarian band, and that the railings in front of it were about as high as a man's waist and filed to a point. With that to work upon, twenty men were at once ordered out into the fog to search for the house, and Inspector Lyle himself was despatched to the home of Lord Edam, Chetney's father, with a warrant for Lord Arthur's arrest. I was thanked and dismissed on my own recognisance.

"This morning, Inspector Lyle called on me, and from him I learned the police theory of the scene I have just described.

"Apparently I had wandered very far in the fog, for up to noon to-day the house had not been found, nor had they been able to arrest Lord Arthur. He did not return to his father's house last night, and there is no trace of him; but from what the police knew of the past lives of the people I found in that lost house they have evolved a theory, and their theory is that the murders were committed by Lord Arthur.

"The infatuation of his elder brother, Lord Chetney, for a Russian Princess, so Inspector Lyle tells me, is well known to everyone. About two years ago the Princess Zichy, as she calls herself, and he were constantly together, and Chetney informed his friends that they were about to be married. The woman was notorious in two continents, and when Lord Edam heard of his son's infatuation he appealed to the police for her record.

"It is through his having applied to them that they know so much concerning her and her relations with the Chetneys. From the police

Lord Edam learned that Madame Zichy had once been a spy in the employ of the Russian Third Section, but that lately she had been repudiated by her own Government and was living by her wits, by blackmail, and by her beauty. Lord Edam laid this record before his son, but Chetney either knew it already, or the woman persuaded him not to believe in it, and the father and son parted in great anger. Two days later the Marquis altered his will, leaving all his money to the younger brother, Arthur.

"The title and some of the landed property he could not keep from Chetney, but he swore if his son saw the woman again, that the will should stand as it was and he would be left without a penny.

"This was about eighteen months ago, when apparently Chetney tired of the Princess and suddenly went off to shoot and explore in Central Africa. No word came from him, except that twice he was reported as having died of fever in the jungle, and finally two traders reached the coast who said they had seen his body. This was accepted by all as conclusive, and young Arthur was recognised as the heir to the Edam millions. On the strength of this supposition he at once began to borrow enormous sums from the moneylenders. This is of great importance, as the police believe it was these debts which drove him to the murder of his brother. Yesterday, as you know, Lord Chetney suddenly returned from the grave, and it was the fact that for two years he had been considered as dead which lent such importance to his return, and which gave rise to those columns of detail concerning him which appeared in all the afternoon papers. But, obviously, during his absence he had not tired of the Princess Zichy, for we know that a few hours after he reached London he sought her out. His brother, who had also learned of his reappearance through the papers, probably suspected which would be the house he would first visit, and followed him there, arriving, so the Russian servant tells us, while the two were at coffee in the drawing-room. The Princess then, we also learn from the servant, withdrew to the dining-room, leaving the brothers together. What happened one can only guess.

"Lord Arthur knew now that when it was discovered he was no longer the heir the moneylenders would come down upon him. The police believe that he at once sought out his brother to beg for money to cover the *post obits,* but that, considering the sum he needed was several hundreds of thousands of pounds, Chetney refused to give it to him. No one knew that Arthur had gone to seek out his brother. They were alone. It is possible, then, that in a passion of disappointment, and crazed with the disgrace which he saw before him, young Arthur made himself the heir beyond further question. The death of his brother would have availed nothing if the woman remained alive. It is then possible that he crossed the hall and, with the same weapon which made him Lord Edam's heir, destroyed the solitary witness to the murder. The only other person who could have seen it was sleeping in a drunken stupor, to which fact undoubtedly he owed his life. And yet," concluded the Naval Attaché, leaning forward and marking each word with his finger, "Lord Arthur blundered fatally. In his haste he left the door of the house open, so giving access to the first passer-by, and he forgot that when he entered it he had handed his card to the servant. That piece of paper may yet send him to the gallows. In the meantime he has disappeared completely, and somewhere, in one of the millions of streets of this great capital, in a locked and empty house, lies the body of his brother, and of the woman his brother loved, undiscovered, unburied, and with their murder unavenged."

In the discussion which followed the conclusion of the story of the Naval Attaché the gentleman with the pearl took no part. Instead, he arose and, beckoning a servant to a far corner of the room, whispered earnestly to him until a sudden movement on the part of Sir Andrew caused him to return hurriedly to the table.

"There are several points in Mr. Sears' story I want explained," he cried. "Be seated, Sir Andrew," he begged. "Let us have the opinion of an expert. I do not care what the police think, I want to know what you think."

But Sir Andrew rose reluctantly from his chair.

"I should like nothing better than to discuss this," he said. "But it is most important that I should proceed to the House. I should have been there some time ago." He turned toward the servant and directed him to call a hansom.

The gentleman with the pearl stud looked appealingly at the Naval Attaché. "There are surely many details that you have not told us," he urged—"some you have forgotten?"

The Baronet interrupted quickly.

"I trust not," he said, "for I could not possibly stop to hear them."

"The story is finished," declared the Naval Attaché. "Until Lord Arthur is arrested or the bodies are found there is nothing more to tell of either Chetney or the Princess Zichy."

"Of Lord Chetney, perhaps not," interrupted the sporting-looking gentleman with the black tie; "but there'll always be something to tell of the Princess Zichy. I know enough stories about her to fill a book. She was a most remarkable woman." The speaker dropped the end of his cigar into his coffee-cup and, taking his case from his pocket, selected a fresh one. As he did so he laughed and held up the case that the others could see it. It was an ordinary cigar-case of well-worn pigskin, with a silver clasp.

"The only time I ever met her," he said, "she tried to rob me of this."

The Baronet regarded him closely.

"She tried to rob you?" he repeated.

"Tried to rob me of this," continued the gentleman in the black tie, "and of the Czarina's diamonds." His tone was one of mingled admiration and injury.

"The Czarina's diamonds!" exclaimed the Baronet. He glanced quickly and suspiciously at the speaker and then at the others about the table. But their faces gave evidence of no other emotion than that of ordinary interest.

"Yes, the Czarina's diamonds," repeated the man with the black tie. "It was a necklace of diamonds. I was told to take them to the Russian Ambassador in Paris, who was to deliver them at Moscow. I am a Queen's Messenger," he added.

"Oh! I see!" exclaimed Sir Andrew in a tone of relief. "And you say that this same Princess Zichy, one of the victims of this double murder, endeavoured to rob you of—of—that cigar-case?"

"And the Czarina's diamonds," answered the Queen's Messenger imperturbably. "It's not much of a story, but it gives you an idea of the woman's character. The robbery took place between Paris and Marseilles."

The Baronet interrupted him with an abrupt movement.

"No, no!" he cried, shaking his arms in protest, "don't tempt me! I really cannot listen. I must be at the House in ten minutes."

"I am sorry," said the Queen's Messenger. He turned to those seated about him. "I wonder if the other gentlemen——?" he inquired tentatively. There was a chorus of polite murmurs, and the Queen's Messenger, bowing his head in acknowledgment, took a preparatory sip from his glass. At the same moment the servant to whom the man with the black pearl had spoken slipped a piece of paper into his hand. He glanced at it, frowned, and threw it under the table.

The servant bowed to the Baronet.

"Your hansom is waiting, Sir Andrew," he said.

"The necklace was worth twenty thousand pounds," began the Queen's Messenger. "It was a present from the Queen of England to celebrate——"

The Baronet gave an exclamation of angry annoyance.

"Upon my word, this is most provoking!" he interrupted. "I really ought not to stay. But I certainly mean to hear this." He turned irritably to the servant. "Tell the hansom to wait," he commanded; and, with an air of a boy who is playing truant, slipped guiltily into his chair.

The gentleman with the black pearl smiled blandly and rapped upon the table.

"Order, gentlemen," he said. "Order for the story of the Queen's Messenger and the Czarina's diamonds."

II
The Story of the Queen's Messenger

"The necklace was a present from the Queen of England to the Czarina of Russia," began the Queen's Messenger. . . .

It was to celebrate the occasion of the Czar's coronation. Our Foreign Office knew that the Russian Ambassador in Paris was to proceed to Moscow for that ceremony, and I was directed to go to Paris and turn over the necklace to him. But when I reached Paris I found he had not expected me for a week later, and was taking a few day's vacation at Nice. His people asked me to leave the necklace with them at the Embassy, but I had been charged to get a receipt for it from the Ambassador himself, so I started at once for Nice. The fact that Monte Carlo is not two thousand miles from Nice may have had something to do with making me carry out my instructions so carefully.

Now, how the Princess Zichy came to find out about the necklace, I don't know, but I can guess. As you have just heard, she was at one time a spy in the service of the Russian Government. And after they dismissed her she kept up her acquaintance with many of the Russian agents in London. It was probably through one of them that she learned that the necklace was to be sent to Moscow, and which of the Queen's Messengers had been detailed to take it there. Still, I doubt if even that knowledge would have helped her if she had not also known something which I supposed no one else in the world knew but myself and one other man. And, curiously enough, the other man was a Queen's Messenger, too, and a friend of mine. You must know that up to the time of this robbery I had always concealed my despatches in a manner peculiarly my own. I got the idea from that play called 'A Scrap of Paper.' In it a man wants to hide a certain compromising document. He knows that all his rooms will be secretly searched for it, so he puts it in a torn envelope and sticks it up where anyone can see it on his mantelshelf. The result is that the woman who is ransacking the house to find it looks in all the unlikely places, but passes over the scrap of paper that is just under her nose. Sometimes the papers and packages they give us to carry about Europe are of very great value, and sometimes they are special makes of cigarettes and orders to Court dressmakers. Sometimes we know what we are carrying, and sometimes we do not. If it is a large sum of money or a treaty, they generally tell us. But as a rule we have no knowledge of what the package contains; so, to be on the safe side, we naturally take just as great care of it as though we knew it held the terms of an ultimatum or the Crown jewels. As a rule, my *confrères* carry the official packages in a despatch-box, which is just as obvious as a lady's jewel-bag in the hands of her maid. Everyone knows they are carrying something of value. They put a premium on dishonesty. Well, after I saw the 'Scrap of Paper' play, I determined to put the Government valuables in the most unlikely place that anyone would look for them. So I used to hide the documents they gave me inside my riding-boots, and small articles, like money or jewels, I carried in an old cigar-case. After I took to using my case for that purpose, I bought a new one, exactly like it, for my cigars. But to avoid mistakes, I had my initials placed on both sides of the new one, and the moment I touched the case, even in the dark, I could tell which it was by the raised initials.

No one knew about this except the Queen's Messenger of whom I spoke. We once left Paris together on the Orient Express. I was going to Constantinople, and he was to stop off at Vienna. On the journey I told him of my peculiar way of hiding things, and showed him my cigar-case. If I recollect rightly, on that trip it held the Grand Cross of St. Michael and St. George, which the Queen was sending to our Ambassador. The

Messenger was very much entertained at my scheme, and some months later when he met the Princess he told her about it as an amusing story. Of course, he had no idea she was a Russian spy. He didn't know anything at all about her, except that she was a very attractive woman. It was indiscreet, but he could not possibly have guessed that she could ever make any use of what he told her.

Later, after the robbery, I remembered that I had informed this young chap of my secret hiding-place, and when I saw him again I asked him about it. He was greatly distressed and said he had never seen the importance of the secret. He remembered he had told several people of it, and among others the Princess Zichy. In that way I found out that it was she who had robbed me, and I know that from the moment I left London she was following me, and that she knew then that the diamonds were concealed in my cigar-case.

My train for Nice left Paris at ten in the morning. When I travel at night I generally tell the *chef de gare* that I am a Queen's Messenger, and he gives me a compartment to myself. But in the daytime I take whatever offers. On this morning I had found an empty compartment, and I had tipped the guard to keep everyone else out, not from any fear of losing the diamonds, but because I wanted to smoke. He had locked the door, and as the last bell had rung, I supposed I was to travel alone, so I began to arrange my traps and make myself comfortable. The diamonds in the cigar-case were in the inside pocket of my waistcoat, and as they made a bulky package I took them out, intending to put them in my handbag. It is a small satchel like a bookmaker's, or those handbags that couriers carry. I wear it slung from a strap across my shoulder, and, no matter whether I am sitting or walking, it never leaves me.

I took the cigar-case which held the necklace from my inside pocket, and the case which held the cigars out of the satchel, and while I was searching through it for a box of matches I laid the two cases beside me on the seat.

At that moment the train started, but at the same instant there was a rattle at the lock of the compartment, and a couple of porters lifted and shoved a woman through the door and hurled her rugs and umbrellas in after her.

Instinctively I reached for the diamonds. I shoved them quickly into the satchel, and, pushing them far down to the bottom of the bag, snapped the spring lock. Then I put the cigars in the pocket of my coat, but with the thought that now that I had a woman as a travelling companion, I should probably not be allowed to enjoy them.

One of her pieces of luggage had fallen at my feet, and a roll of rugs had landed at my side. I thought if I hid the fact that the lady was not welcome, and at once started to be civil, she might permit me to smoke. So I picked her handbag off the floor and asked her where I might place it.

As I spoke I looked at her for the first time and saw that she was a most remarkably handsome woman.

She smiled charmingly and begged me not to disturb myself. Then she arranged her own things about her and, opening her dressing-bag, took out a gold cigarette-case.

"Do you object to smoke?" she asked.

I laughed and assured her I had been in great terror lest she might not allow me to smoke.

"If you like cigarettes," she said, "will you try some of these? They are rolled especially for my husband in Russia, and they are supposed to be very good."

I thanked her and took one from her case, and I found it so much better than my own that I continued to smoke her cigarettes throughout the rest of the journey. I must say that we got on very well. I judged from the coronet on her cigarette-case, and from her manner, which was quite as well bred as that of any woman I ever met, that she was someone of importance, and though she seemed almost too good-looking to be respectable, I determined that she was some *grande dame* who was so assured of her position that she could afford to be unconventional. At first she read her novel, and then she made some comment on the scenery, and finally we began to discuss the current politics of the Continent. She talked of all the cities in Europe and seemed to know everyone worth knowing. But she volunteered nothing about herself except that she frequently made use of the expression, "When my husband was stationed at Vienna," or, "When my husband was promoted to Rome." Once she said to me, "I have often seen you at Monte Carlo. I saw you when you won the pigeon championship." I told her that I was not a pigeon shot, and she gave a little start of surprise. "Oh! I beg your pardon," she said, "I thought you were Morton Hamilton, the English champion." As a matter of fact, I do look something like Hamilton, but I know now that her object was to make me think that she had no idea as to who I really was. She needn't have acted at all, for I certainly had no suspicions, and was only too pleased to have so charming a companion.

The one thing that should have made me suspicious was the fact that at every station she made some trivial excuse to get me out of the compartment. She pretended that her maid was travelling behind us in one of the second-class carriages, and kept saying she could not imagine why the woman did not come to look after her; and if the maid did not turn up at the next stop, would I be so very kind as to get out and bring her whatever it was she pretended she wanted?

I had taken my dressing-case from the rack to get out a novel, and had left it on the seat opposite to mine, and at the end of the compartment furthest from her. And once when I came back from buying her a cup of chocolate, or from some other fool errand, I found her standing at my end of the compartment with both hands on the dressing-bag. She looked at me without so much as winking an eye, and shoved the case carefully into a corner. "Your bag slipped off on the floor," she said. "If you've got any bottles in it, you had better look and see that they're not broken."

And I give you my word, I was such an ass that I did open the case and look all through it. She must have thought I *was* a Juggins. I get hot all over whenever I remember it. But in spite of my dullness, and her cleverness, she couldn't gain anything by sending me away, because what she wanted was in the handbag, and every time she sent me away the handbag went with me.

After the incident of the dressing-case her manner began to change. Either she had had time to look through it in my absence, or, when I was examining it for broken bottles, she had seen everything it held.

From that moment she must have been certain that the cigar-case in which she knew I carried the diamonds was in the bag that was fastened to my body, and from that time on she probably was plotting how to get it from me.

Her anxiety became most apparent. She dropped the great lady manner, and her charming condescension went with it. She ceased talking, and, when I spoke, answered me irritably or at random. No doubt her mind was entirely occupied with her plan. The end of our journey was drawing rapidly nearer, and her time for action was being cut down with the speed of the express train. Even I, unsuspicious as I was, noticed that something was very wrong with her. I really believe that before we reached Marseilles, if I had not, through my own stupidity, given her the chance she wanted, she might have stuck a knife in me and rolled me out on the rails. But as it was, I only thought that the long journey had tired her. I suggested that it was a very tedious trip, and asked her if she would allow me to offer her some of my cognac.

She thanked me and said "No," and then suddenly her eyes lighted, and she exclaimed, "Yes, thank you, if you will be so kind."

My flask was in the handbag, and I placed it on my lap, and with my thumb I slipped back the catch. As I keep my tickets and railroad guide in the bag, I am so constantly opening it that I never bother to lock it, and the fact that it is strapped to me has always been sufficient protection. But I can appreciate now what a satisfaction, and what a torment, too, it must have been to that woman when she saw that the bag opened without a key.

While we were crossing the mountains I had felt rather chilly, and had been wearing a light racing coat. But after the lamps were lighted the compartment became very hot and stuffy, and I found the coat uncomfortable. So I stood up, and, after first slipping the strap of the bag over my head, I placed the bag in the seat next to me and pulled off the racing coat. I don't blame myself for being careless; the bag was still within reach of my hand, and nothing would have happened if at that exact moment the train had not stopped at Arles. It was the combination of my removing the bag and our entering the station at the same instant which gave the Princess Zichy the chance she wanted to rob me.

I needn't say that she was clever enough to take it. The train ran in the station at full speed and came to a sudden stop. I had just thrown my coat into the rack, and had reached out my hand for the bag. In another instant I should have had the strap around my shoulder. But at that moment the Princess threw open the door of the compartment and beckoned wildly at the people on the platform. "Natalie!" she called, "Natalie! here I am. Come here! This way!" She turned upon me in the greatest excitement. "My maid!" she cried. "She is looking for me. She passed the window without seeing me. Go, please, and bring her back." She continued pointing out of the door and beckoning me with her other hand. There certainly was something about that woman's tone which made one jump. When she was giving orders, you had no chance to think of anything else. So I rushed out on my errand of mercy, and then rushed back again to ask what the maid looked like.

"In black," she answered, rising and blocking the door of the compartment. "All in black, with a bonnet!"

The train waited three minutes at Arles, and in that time I suppose I must have rushed up to over twenty women and asked, "Are you Natalie?" The only reason I wasn't punched with an umbrella or handed over to the *gendarme* must have been that they probably thought I was crazy.

When I jumped back into the compartment the Princess was seated where I had left her, but her eyes were burning with happiness. She placed her hand on my arm almost affectionately and said in a most hysterical way, "You are very kind to me. I am so sorry to have troubled you."

I protested that every woman on the platform was dressed in black.

"Indeed, I am so sorry," she said, laughing; and she continued to laugh until she began to breathe so quickly that I thought she was going to faint.

I can see now that the last part of that journey must have been a terrible half-hour for her. She had the cigar-case safe enough, but she knew that she herself was not safe. She knew if I were to open my bag, even at the last minute, and miss the case, I should know positively that she had taken it. I had placed the diamonds in the bag at the very moment she entered the compartment, and no one but our two selves had occupied it since. She knew that when we reached Marseilles she would either be twenty thousand pounds richer than when she left Paris, or that she would go to jail. That was the situation as she must have read it, and I don't envy her her state of mind during that last half-hour. It must have been hell.

I saw that something was wrong, and in my innocence I even wondered if possibly my cognac had not been a little too strong. For she suddenly developed into a most brilliant conversationalist, and applauded and laughed at everything even I said, firing off questions at me like a machine-gun, so that I had no time to think of anything else but of what she was saying. Whenever I stirred, she stopped her chattering and leaned toward me, and watched me like a cat over a mousehole. I wondered how I could have considered her an agreeable travelling companion. I thought I should have preferred to be locked in with a lunatic. I don't like to think how she would have acted if I had made a move to

examine the bag, but as I had it safely strapped around me again, I did
not open it, and I reached Marseilles alive. As we drew into the station
she shook hands with me and grinned at me like a Cheshire cat.

"I cannot tell you," she said, "how much I have to thank you for."
What do you think of that for impudence?

I offered to put her in a carriage, but she said she must find Natalie,
and that she hoped we should meet again at the hotel. So I drove off by
myself, wondering who she was, and whether Natalie was not her
keeper.

I had to wait several hours for the train to Nice, and as I wanted to
stroll around the city, I thought I had better put the diamonds in the
safe of the hotel. As soon as I reached my room I locked the door, placed
the handbag on the table and opened it. I felt among the things at the
top of it, but failed to touch the cigar-case. I shoved my hand in deeper
and stirred the things about, but still I did not reach it. A cold wave
swept down my spine, and a sort of emptiness came to the pit of my
stomach. Then I turned red-hot and the sweat sprang out all over me. I
wetted my lips with my tongue and said to myself, "Don't be an ass! Pull
yourself together, pull yourself together. Take the things out, one at a
time. It's there, of course it's there. Don't be an ass!"

So I put a brake on my nerves and began very carefully to pick out
the things one by one, but after five seconds I could not stand it another
instant, and I rushed across the room and threw out everything on the
bed; but the diamonds were not among them. I pulled the things about
and tore them open and shuffled and rearranged and sorted them, but it
was no use. The cigar-case was gone. I threw everything in the dressing-
case out on the floor, although I knew it was useless to look for it there.
I knew that I had put it in the bag. I sat down and tried to think. I
remembered I had put it in the satchel at Paris just as that woman had
entered the compartment, and I had been alone with her ever since, so it
was she who had robbed me. But how? It had never left my shoulder.
And then I remembered that it had—that I had taken it off when I had
changed my coat and for the few moments that I was searching for
Natalie. I remembered that the woman had sent me on that goose-chase,
and at every other station she had tried to get rid of me on some fool
errand.

I gave a roar like a mad bull and I jumped down the stairs six steps at
a time.

I demanded at the office if a distinguished lady traveller, possibly a Russian, had just entered the hotel.

As I expected, she had not. I sprang into a cab and inquired at two other hotels, and then I saw the folly of trying to catch her without outside help, and I ordered the fellow to gallop to the office of the Chief of Police. I told my story, and the ass in charge asked me to calm myself and wanted to take notes. I told him this was no time for taking notes, but for doing something. He got wrathy at that, and I demanded to be taken at once to his Chief. The Chief, he said, was very busy and could not see me. So I showed him my silver greyhound. In eleven years I had never used it but once before. I stated in pretty vigorous language that I was a Queen's Messenger, and that if the Chief of Police did not see me instantly he would lose his official head. The fellow jumped off his high horse at that and ran with me to his Chief—a smart young chap a colonel in the army, and a very intelligent man.

I explained that I had been robbed in a French railway carriage of a diamond necklace belonging to the Queen of England, which Her Majesty was sending as a present to the Czarina of Russia. I pointed out to him that if he succeeded in capturing the thief, he would be made for life and would receive the gratitude of three great Powers.

He wasn't the sort that thinks second thoughts are best. He saw Russian and French decorations sprouting all over his chest, and he hit a bell and pressed buttons and yelled out orders like the captain of a penny steamer in a fog. He sent her description to all the city gates, and ordered all cabmen and railway porters to search all trains leaving Marseilles. He ordered all passengers on outgoing vessels to be examined, and telegraphed the proprietors of every hotel and pension to send him a complete list of their guests within the hour. While I was standing there he must have given at least a hundred orders, and sent out enough *commissaires, sergents de ville, gendarmes,* bicycle police, and plain-clothes Johnnies to have captured the entire German army. When they had gone he assured me that the woman was as good as arrested already. Indeed, officially, she was arrested; for she had no more chance of escape from Marseilles than from the Château D'If.

He told me to return to my hotel and possess my soul in peace. Within an hour he assured me he would acquaint me with her arrest.

I thanked him, and complimented him on his energy, and left him. But I didn't share in his confidence. I felt that she was a very clever woman and a match for any and all of us. It was all very well for him to be jubilant. He had not lost the diamonds, and had everything to gain if he found them; while I, even if he did recover the necklace, should only be where I was before I lost it, and if he did not recover it I was a ruined man. It was an awful facer for me. I had always prided myself on my record. In eleven years I had never mislaid an envelope nor missed taking the first train. And now I had failed in the most important commission that had ever been entrusted to me. And it wasn't a thing that could be hushed up, either. It was too conspicuous, too spectacular. It was sure to invite the widest notoriety. I saw myself ridiculed all over the Continent, and perhaps dismissed, even suspected of having taken the thing myself.

I was walking in front of a lighted *café*, and I felt so sick and miserable that I stopped for a pick-me-up. Then I considered that if I took one drink I should probably, in my present state of mind, not want to stop under twenty, and I decided I had better leave it alone. But my nerves were jumping like those of a frightened rabbit, and I felt I must have something to quiet them or I should go crazy. I reached for my cigarette-case, but a cigarette seemed hardly adequate, so I put it back again and took out this cigar-case, in which I keep only the strongest and blackest cigars. I opened it and stuck in my fingers, but instead of a cigar they touched on a thin leather envelope. My heart stood perfectly still. I did not dare to look, but I dug my finger-nails into the letter and I felt layers of thin paper, then a layer of cotton, and then they scratched on the facets of the Czarina's diamonds!

I stumbled as though I had been hit in the face and fell back into one of the chairs on the pavement. I tore off the wrappings and spread out the diamonds on the *café* table; I could not believe they were real. I twisted the necklace between my fingers, and crushed it between my palms, and tossed it up in the air. I believe I almost kissed it. The women in the *café* stood up on the chairs to see better, and laughed and screamed, and the people crowded so close around me that the waiters had to form a bodyguard. The proprietor thought there was a fight and called for the police. I was so happy I didn't care. I laughed, too, and gave the proprietor a handful of coin and told him to stand everyone a drink. Then I tumbled into a *fiacre* and galloped off to my friend the Chief of Police. I felt very sorry for him. He had been so happy at the chance I had given him, and he would be so disappointed when he learned I had sent him off on a false alarm.

But now that I had the necklace I did not want him to find the woman. Indeed, I was most anxious that she should get clear away. For if she were caught, the truth would come out, and I was likely to get a sharp reprimand, and sure to be laughed at.

I could see now how it had happened. In my haste to hide the diamonds when the woman was hustled into the carriage I had shoved the cigars into the satchel and the diamonds into the pocket of my coat. Now that I had the diamonds safe again it seemed a very natural mistake. But I doubted if the Foreign Office would think so. I was afraid it might not appreciate the beautiful simplicity of my secret hiding-place. So, when I reached the police station and found the Princess still at large, I was more than relieved.

As I expected, the Chief was extremely chagrined when he learned of my mistake and that there was nothing for him to do. But I was feeling so happy myself that I hated to have anyone else miserable, so I suggested that this attempt to steal the Czarina's necklace might be only the first of a series of such attempts, and that I might still be in danger from an unscrupulous gang.

I winked at the Chief and the Chief smiled at me, and we went to Nice together in a saloon car with a guard of twelve carabineers and twelve plain-clothes men, and the Chief and I drank champagne all the way. We marched together up to the hotel where the Russian Ambassador was stopping, closely surrounded by our escort of carabineers, and delivered the necklace with the most profound ceremony. The old Ambassador was immensely impressed, and when we hinted that already I had been made the object of an attack by robbers, he assured us that His Imperial Majesty would not prove ungrateful.

I wrote a swinging personal letter about the invaluable services of the Chief to the French Minister of Foreign Affairs, and they gave him enough Russian and French medals to satisfy even a French soldier. So, though he never caught the woman, he received his just reward.

The Queen's Messenger paused and surveyed the faces of those about him in some embarrassment.

"But the worst of it is," he added, "that the story must have got about; for, while the Princess obtained nothing from me but a cigar-case and five excellent cigars, a few weeks after the coronation the Czar sent me a gold cigar-case with his monogram in diamonds. And I don't know yet whether that was a coincidence, or whether the Czar wanted me to know that he knew that I had been carrying the Czarina's diamonds in my pigskin cigar-case. What do you fellows think?"

III
The Solicitor's Story

Sir Andrew rose, with disapproval written in every lineament.

"I thought your story would bear upon the murder," he said. "Had I imagined it would have nothing whatsoever to do with it, I would not have remained." He pushed back his chair and bowed stiffly. "I wish you 'Good-night,' " he said.

There was a chorus of remonstrance, and under cover of this and the Baronet's answering protests a servant for the second time slipped a piece of paper into the hand of the gentleman with the pearl stud. He read the lines written upon it and tore it into tiny fragments.

The youngest member, who had remained an interested but silent listener to the tale of the Queen's Messenger, raised his hand commandingly.

"Sir Andrew," he cried, "in justice to Lord Arthur Chetney I must ask you to be seated. He has been accused in our hearing of a most serious crime, and I insist that you remain until you have heard me clear his character."

"You?" cried the Baronet.

"Yes," answered the young man briskly. "I would have spoken sooner," he explained, "but that I thought this gentleman"—he inclined his head toward the Queen's Messenger—"was about to contribute some facts of which I was ignorant. He, however, has told us nothing, and so I will take up the tale at the point where Lieutenant Sears laid it down, and give you those details of which Lieutenant Sears is ignorant. It seems strange to you that I should be able to add the sequel to this story. But the coincidence, when explained, is obvious enough. I am the junior member of the law firm of Chudleigh and Chudleigh. We have been solicitors for the Chetneys for the last two hundred years. Nothing, no matter how unimportant, which concerns Lord Edam and his two sons is unknown to us, and naturally we are acquainted with every detail of the terrible catastrophe of last night."

The Baronet, bewildered but eager, sank back into his chair.

"Will you be long, sir?" he demanded.

"I shall endeavour to be brief," said the young solicitor; "and," he added, in a tone which gave his words almost the weight of a threat, "I promise to be interesting."

"There is no need to promise that," said Sir Andrew, "I find it much too interesting as it is." He glanced ruefully at the clock and turned his eyes quickly from it.

"Tell the driver of that hansom," he called to the servant, "that I take him by the hour."

A young Mr. Chudleigh begins: For the last three days as you have probably read in the daily papers, the Marquis of Edam has been at the point of death, and his physicians have never left his house. Every hour he seemed to grow weaker; but although his bodily strength is apparently leaving him for ever, his mind has remained clear and active. Late yesterday evening word was received at our office that he wished my father to come at once to Chetney House and to bring with him certain papers. What these papers were is not essential; I mention them only to explain how it was that last night I happened to be at Lord Edam's bedside. I accompanied my father to Chetney House, but at the time we reached there Lord Edam was sleeping, and his physicians refused to have him awakened. My father urged that he should be allowed to receive Lord Edam's instructions concerning the documents, but the physicians would not disturb him, and we all gathered in the library to wait until he should awake of his own accord. It was about one o'clock in the morning, while we were still there, that Inspector Lyle and the officers from Scotland Yard came to arrest Lord Arthur on the charge of murdering his brother. You can imagine our dismay and distress. Like everyone else, I had learned from the afternoon papers that Lord Chetney was not dead, but that he had returned to England. And on arriving at Chetney House I had been told that Lord Arthur had gone to the Bath Hotel to look for his brother and to inform him that if he wished to see their father alive he must come to him at once. Although it was now past one o'clock, Arthur had not returned. None of us knew where Madame Zichy had lived, so we could not go to recover Lord Chetney's body. We spent a most miserable night, hastening to the window whenever a cab came into the square, in the hope that it was Arthur returning, and endeavouring to explain away the facts that pointed to him as the murderer. I am a friend of Arthur's, I was with him at Harrow and at Oxford, and I refused to believe for an instant that he was capable of such a crime; but as a lawyer I could not but see that the circumstantial evidence was strongly against him.

Toward early morning Lord Edam awoke, and in so much better a state of health that he refused to make the changes in the papers which he had intended, declaring that he was no nearer death than ourselves. Under other circumstances this happy change in him would have relieved us greatly, but none of us could think of anything save the death of his elder son and of the charge which hung over Arthur.

As long as Inspector Lyle remained in the house my father decided that I, as one of the legal advisers of the family, should also remain there. But there was little for either of us to do. Arthur did not return, and nothing occurred until late this morning, when Lyle received word that the Russian servant had been arrested. He at once drove to Scotland Yard to question him. He came back to us in an hour and informed me that the servant had refused to tell anything of what had happened the night before, or of himself, or of the Princess Zichy. He would not even give them the address of her house.

"He is in abject terror," Lyle said. "I assured him that he was not suspected of the crime, but he would tell me nothing."

There were no other developments until two o'clock this afternoon, when word was brought to us that Arthur had been found, and that he was lying in the Accident Ward of St. George's Hospital. Lyle and I drove there together, and found him propped up in bed with his head bound in a bandage. He had been brought to the hospital the night before by the driver of a hansom that had run over him in the fog. The cab-horse had kicked him on the head and he had been carried in unconscious. There was nothing on him to tell who he was, and it was not until he came to his senses this afternoon that the hospital authorities had been able to send word to his people. Lyle at once informed him that he was under arrest, and with what he was charged, and though the Inspector warned him to say nothing which might be used against him, I, as his solicitor, instructed him to speak freely and to tell us all he knew of the occurrences of last night. It was evident to anyone that the fact of his brother's death was of much greater concern to him than that he was accused of his murder.

"That——" Arthur said contemptuously, "that is nonsense! It is monstrous and cruel. We parted better friends than we have been for years. I will tell you all that happened—not to clear myself, but to help you to find out the truth." His story is as follows: Yesterday afternoon, owing to his constant attendance on his father, he did not look at the evening papers, and it was not until after dinner, when the butler brought him one and told him of its contents, that he learned that his brother was alive and at the Bath Hotel. He drove there at once, but was told that about eight o'clock his brother had gone out, but without giving any clue to his destination. As Chetney had not at once come to see his father, Arthur decided that he was still angry with him, and his mind, turning naturally to the cause of their quarrel, determined him to look for Chetney at the home of the Princess Zichy.

Her house had been pointed out to him, and, though he had never visited it, he had passed it many times and knew its exact location. He accordingly drove in that direction, as far as the fog would permit the hansom to go, and walked the rest of the way, reaching the house about nine o'clock. He rang, and was admitted by the Russian servant. The man took his card into the drawing-room, and at once his brother ran out and welcomed him. He was followed by the Princess Zichy, who also received Arthur most cordially.

"You brothers will have much to talk about," she said. "I am going to the dining-room. When you have finished, let me know."

As soon as she had left them, Arthur told his brother that their father was not expected to outlive the night, and that he must come to him at once.

"This is not the time to remember your quarrel," Arthur said to him; "you have come back from the dead only in time to make your peace with him before he dies."

Arthur says that Chetney was greatly moved at what he told him.

"You entirely misunderstand me, Arthur," he returned. "I did not know the governor was ill, or I would have gone to him the instant I arrived. My only reason for not doing so was because I thought he was still angry with me. I shall return with you immediately, as soon as I have said good-bye to the Princess. It is a final good-bye. After to-night I shall never see her again."

"Do you mean that?" Arthur cried.

"Yes," Chetney answered. "When I returned to London, I had no intention of seeking her again, and I am here only through a mistake."

He then told Arthur that he had separated from the Princess even before he went to Central Africa, and that, moreover, while at Cairo on his way south he had learned certain facts concerning her life there during the previous season which made it impossible for him ever to wish to see her again. Their separation was final and complete.

"She deceived me cruelly," he said; "I cannot tell you how cruelly. During the two years when I was trying to obtain the governor's consent to our marriage she was in love with a Russian diplomat. During all that time he was secretly visiting her here in London, and her trip to Cairo was only an excuse to meet him there."

"Yet you are here with her to-night," Arthur protested, "only a few hours after your return!"

"That is easily explained," Chetney answered. "I had just finished dinner to-night at the hotel when I received a note from her from this address. In it she said she had just learned of my arrival and begged me to come to her at once. She wrote that she was in great and present trouble, dying of an incurable illness, and without friends or money. She begged me, for the sake of old times, to come to her assistance. During the last two years in the jungle all my former feeling for Zichy has utterly passed away from me, but no one could have dismissed the appeal she made in that letter. So I drove here and found her, as you have seen her, quite as beautiful as ever she was, in very good health, and, from the look of the house, in no need of money.

"I asked her what she meant by writing me that she was dying in a garret, and she laughed and said she had done so because she was afraid unless I thought she needed help I would not try to see her. That was where we were when you arrived. And now," Chetney added, "I will say good-bye to her, and you had better return home. No, you can trust me. I shall follow you at once. She has no influence over me now, but I believe, in spite of the way she has used me, that she is still fond of me after her queer fashion, and when she learns that this good-bye is final there may be a scene. And it is not fair to her that you should be here. So go home at once and tell the governor that I am following you in ten minutes."

"That," said Arthur, "is the way we parted. I never left him on more friendly terms. I was happy to see him alive again, I was happy to think he had returned in time to make up his quarrel with my father, and I was happy that at last he was clear of that woman. I was never better pleased with him in my life." He turned to Inspector Lyle, who was sitting at the foot of the bed taking notes of all he told us.

"Why, in the name of common-sense," he cried, "should I have chosen that moment of all others to send my brother back to the grave again?" For a moment the Inspector did not answer him. I do not know if any of you gentlemen are acquainted with Inspector Lyle, but if you are not, I should tell you that he is a very remarkable man. Our firm often applies to him for aid, and he has never failed us yet; my father has the greatest possible respect for him. Where he has the advantage over the ordinary police official is in the fact that he possesses imagination. He imagines himself to be the criminal, imagines how he would act under the same circumstances, and he imagines to such purpose that he generally finds the man he wants. I have often told Lyle that if he had not been a detective, he would have made a great success as a poet or a playwright.

When Arthur turned on him, Lyle hesitated for a moment and then told him exactly what was the case against him.

"Ever since your brother was reported as having died in Africa," he said, "your Lordship has been collecting money on *post obits.* Lord Chetney's arrival last night turned them into waste paper. You were suddenly in debt for thousands of pounds—for much more than you could ever possibly pay. No one knew that you and your brother had met at Madame Zichy's. But you knew that your father was not expected to outlive the night, and that if your brother were dead also, you would be saved from complete ruin, and that you would become the Marquis of Edam."

"Oh! that is how you have worked it out, is it?" Arthur cried. "And for me to become Lord Edam, was it necessary that the woman should die, too?"

"They will say," Lyle answered, "that she was a witness to the murder —that she would have told."

"Then why did I not kill the servant as well?" Arthur said.

"He was asleep, and saw nothing."

"And you believe *that?*" Arthur demanded.

"It is not a question of what I believe," Lyle said gravely. "It is a question for your peers."

"The man is insolent!" Arthur cried. "The thing is monstrous! Horrible!"

Before we could stop him, he sprang out of his cot and began pulling on his clothes. When the nurses tried to hold him down, he fought with them.

"Do you think you can keep me here," he shouted, "when they are plotting to hang me? I am going with you to that house!" he cried to Lyle. "When you find those bodies, I shall be beside you. It is my right. He is my brother. He has been murdered, and I can tell you who murdered him. That woman murdered him. She first ruined his life, and now she has killed him. For the last five years she has been plotting to make herself his wife, and last night, when he told her he had discovered the truth about the Russian, and that she would never see him again, she flew into a passion and stabbed him, and then, in terror of the gallows, killed herself. She murdered him, I tell you, and I promise you that we shall find the knife she used near her—perhaps still in her hand. What will you say to that?"

Lyle turned his head away and stared down at the floor. "I might say," he answered, "that you placed it there."

Arthur gave a cry of anger and sprang at him, and then pitched forward into his arms. The blood was running from the cut under the bandage and he had fainted. Lyle carried him back to the bed again, and we left him with the police and the doctors and drove at once to the address he had given us. We found the house not three minutes' walk from St. George's Hospital. It stands in Trevor Terrace, that little row of houses set back from Knightsbridge with one end in Hill Street.

As we left the hospital, Lyle had said to me, "You must not blame me for treating him as I did. All is fair in this work, and if by angering that boy I could have made him commit himself, I was right in trying to do so; though, I assure you, no one would be better pleased than myself if I could prove his theory to be correct. But we cannot tell. Everything depends upon what we see for ourselves within the next few minutes."

When we reached the house, Lyle broke open the fastenings of one of the windows on the ground floor, and, hidden by the trees in the garden, we scrambled in. We found ourselves in the reception-room, which was the first room on the right of the hall. The gas was still burning behind the coloured glass and red silk shades, and when the daylight streamed in after us, it gave the hall a hideously dissipated look, like the foyer of a theatre at a *matinée,* or the entrance to an all-day gambling hall. The house was oppressively silent, and because we knew why it was so silent we spoke in whispers. When Lyle turned the handle of the drawing-room door, I felt as though someone had put his hand upon my throat. But I followed close at his shoulder and saw, in the subdued light of many-tinted lamps, the body of Chetney at the foot of the divan, just as Lieutenant Sears has described it. In the drawing-room we found upon the floor the body of the Princess Zichy, her arms thrown out, and the blood from her heart frozen in a tiny line across her bare shoulder. But neither of us, although we searched the floor on our hands and knees, could find the weapon which had killed her.

"For Arthur's sake," I said, "I would give a thousand pounds if we had found the knife in her hand, as he said we would."

"That we have not found it there," Lyle answered, "is to my mind the strongest proof that he is telling the truth—that he left the house before the murder took place. He is not a fool, and had he stabbed his brother and this woman he would have seen that by placing the knife near her he could help to make it appear as if she had killed Chetney and then committed suicide. Besides, Lord Arthur insisted that the evidence in his behalf would be our finding the knife here. He would not have urged that if he knew we would *not* find it, if he knew he himself had carried it away. This is no suicide. A suicide does not rise and hide the weapon with which he kills himself, and then lie down again. No, this has been a double murder, and we must look outside the house for the murderer."

While he was speaking, Lyle and I had been searching every corner, studying the details of each room. I was so afraid that, without telling me, he would make some deductions prejudicial to Arthur, that I never left his side. I was determined to see everything that he saw, and, if possible, to prevent his interpreting it in the wrong way. He finally finished his examination, and we sat down together in the drawing-room, and he took out his notebook and read aloud all Mr. Sears had told him of the murder, and what we had just learned from Arthur. We compared the two accounts, word for word, and weighed statement with statement. But I could not determine from anything Lyle said which of the two versions he had decided to believe.

"We are trying to build a house of blocks," he exclaimed, "with half of the blocks missing. We have been considering two theories," he went on: "one that Lord Arthur is responsible for both murders, and the other that the dead woman in there is responsible for one of them, and has committed suicide; but until the Russian servant is ready to talk, I shall refuse to believe in the guilt of either."

"What can you prove by him?" I asked. "He was drunk and asleep. He saw nothing."

Lyle hesitated and then, as though he had made up his mind to be quite frank with me, spoke freely.

"I do not know that he was either drunk or asleep," he answered. "Lieutenant Sears describes him as a stupid boor. I am not satisfied that he is not a clever actor. What was his position in this house? What was his real duty here? Suppose it was not to guard this woman, but to watch her. Let us imagine that it was not the woman he served, but a master, and see where that leads us. For this house has a master, a mysterious, absentee landlord, who lives in St. Petersburg, the unknown Russian who came between Chetney and Zichy, and because of whom Chetney left her. He is the man who bought this house for Madame Zichy, who sent these rugs and curtains from Petersburg to furnish it for her after his own tastes, and, I believe, it was he also who placed the Russian servant here, ostensibly to serve the Princess, but in reality to spy upon her. At Scotland Yard we do not know who this gentleman is; the Russian police confess to equal ignorance concerning him. When Lord Chetney went to Africa, Madame Zichy lived in St. Petersburg; but there her receptions and dinners were so crowded with members of the nobility and of the army and diplomats, that among so many visitors the police could not learn which was the one for whom she most greatly cared."

Lyle pointed at the modern French paintings and the heavy silk rugs which hung upon the walls.

"The unknown is a man of taste and of some fortune," he said, "not the sort of man to send a stupid peasant to guard the woman he loves. So I am not content to believe with Mr. Sears, that the man is a boor. I believe him instead to be a very clever ruffian. I believe him to be the protector of his master's honour, or, let us say, of his master's property, whether that property be silver plate or the woman his master loves. Last night, after Lord Arthur had gone away, the servant was left alone in this house with Lord Chetney and Madame Zichy. From where he sat in the hall he could hear Lord Chetney bidding her farewell; for, if my idea of him is correct, he understands English quite as well as you or I. Let us imagine that he heard her entreating Chetney not to leave her, reminding him of his former wish to marry her, and let us suppose that he hears Chetney denounce her, and tell her that at Cairo he has learned of this Russian admirer—the servant's master. He hears the woman declare that she has had no admirer but himself, that this unknown Russian was, and is, nothing to her, that there is no man she loves but him, and that she cannot live, knowing that he is alive, without his love. Suppose Chetney believed her, suppose his former infatuation for her returned, and that in a moment of weakness he forgave her and took her in his arms. That is the moment the Russian master has feared. It is to guard against it that he has placed his watch-dog over the Princess; and how do we know but that, when the moment came, the watch-dog served his master, as he saw his duty, and killed them both? What do you think?" Lyle demanded. "Would not that explain both murders?"

I was only too willing to hear any theory which pointed to anyone else as the criminal than Arthur, but Lyle's explanation was too utterly fantastic. I told him that he certainly showed imagination, but that he could not hang a man only for what he imagined he had done.

"No," Lyle answered, "but I can frighten him by telling him what I think he has done, and now when I again question the Russian servant I will make it quite clear to him that I believe he is the murderer. I think that will open his mouth. A man will at least talk to defend himself. Come," he said, "we must return at once to Scotland Yard and see him. There is nothing more to do here."

He arose, and I followed him into the hall, and in another minute we should have been on our way to Scotland Yard. But just as he opened the street-door a postman halted at the gate of the garden and began fumbling with the latch.

Lyle stopped, with an exclamation of chagrin.

"How stupid of me!" he exclaimed. He turned quickly and pointed to a narrow slit cut in the brass plate of the front door. "The house has a private letter-box," he said, "and I had not thought to look in it! If we had gone out as we came in, by the window, I should never have seen it. The moment I entered the house I should have thought of securing the letters which came this morning. I have been grossly careless." He stepped back into the hall and pulled at the lid of the letter-box, which hung on the inside of the door, but it was tightly locked. At the same moment the postman came up the steps holding a letter. Without a word Lyle took it from his hand and began to examine it. It was addressed to the Princess Zichy, and on the back of the envelope was the name of a West End dressmaker.

"That is of no use to me," Lyle said. He took out his card and showed it to the postman. "I am Inspector Lyle, from Scotland Yard," he said. "The people in this house are under arrest. Everything it contains is now in my keeping. Did you deliver any other letters here this morning?"

The man looked frightened, but answered promptly that he was now upon his third round. He had made one postal delivery at seven that morning and another at eleven.

"How many letters did you leave here?" Lyle asked.

"About six altogether," the man answered.

"Did you put them through the door into the letter-box?"

The postman said, "Yes, I always slip them into the box, and ring and go away. The servants collect them from the inside."

"Have you noticed if any of the letters you leave here bear a Russian postage-stamp?" Lyle asked.

The man answered, "Oh, yes, sir, a great many."

"From the same person, would you say?"

"The writing seems to be the same," the man answered. "They come regularly about once a week—one of those I delivered this morning had a Russian postmark."

"That will do," said Lyle eagerly. "Thank you, thank you very much."

He ran back into the hall and, pulling out his penknife, began to pick at the lock of the letter-box.

"I have been supremely careless," he said in great excitement. "Twice before when people I wanted had flown from a house I have been able to follow them by putting a guard over their mail-box. These letters, which arrive regularly every week from Russia in the same handwriting —they can come but from one person. At least we shall now know the name of the master of this house. Undoubtedly it is one of his letters that the man placed here this morning. We may make a most important discovery."

As he was talking he was picking at the lock with his knife, but he was so impatient to reach the letters that he pressed too heavily on the blade and it broke in his hand. I took a step backward and drove my heel into the lock and burst it open. The lid flew back, and we pressed forward, and each ran his hand down into the letter-box. For a moment we were both too startled to move. The box was empty!

I do not know how long we stood staring stupidly at each other, but it was Lyle who was the first to recover. He seized me by the arm and pointed excitedly into the empty box.

"Do you appreciate what that means?" he cried. "It means that some-one has been here ahead of us. Someone has entered this house not three hours before we came, since eleven o'clock this morning."

"It was the Russian servant!" I exclaimed.

"The Russian servant has been under arrest at Scotland Yard," Lyle cried. "He could not have taken the letters. Lord Arthur has been in his cot at the hospital. That is his *alibi*. There is someone else—someone we do not suspect—and that someone is the murderer. He came back here either to obtain those letters because he knew they would convict him, or to remove something he had left here at the time of the murder, something incriminating—the weapon, perhaps, or some personal arti-cle: a cigarette-case, a handkerchief with his name upon it, or a pair of gloves. Whatever it was, it must have been damning evidence against him to have made him take so desperate a chance."

"How do we know," I whispered, "that he is not hidden here now?"

"No, I'll swear he is not!" Lyle answered. "I may have bungled in some things, but I have searched this house thoroughly. Nevertheless," he added, "we must go over it again, from the cellar to the roof. We have the real clue now, and we must forget the others and work only it." As he spoke he began again to search the drawing-room, turning over even the books on the tables and the music on the piano.

"Whoever the man is," he said over his shoulder, "we know that he has a key to the front door and a key to the letter-box. That shows us he is either an inmate of the house or that he comes here when he wishes. The Russian says that he was the only servant in the house. Certainly we have found no evidence to show that any other servant slept here. There could be but one other person who would possess a key to the house and the letter-box—and he lives in St. Petersburg. At the time of the murder he was two thousand miles away." Lyle interrupted himself sud-denly with a sharp cry and turned upon me with his eyes flashing. "But was he?" he cried. "Was he? How do we know that last night he was not in London, in this very house when Zichy and Chetney met here?"

He stood staring at me without seeing me, muttering and arguing with himself.

"Don't speak to me!" he cried, as I ventured to interrupt him. "I can

see it now. It is all plain to me. It was not the servant, but his master,
the Russian himself, and it was he who came back for the letters. He
came back for them because he knew they would convict him. We must
find them. We must have those letters. If we find the one with the
Russian postmark, we shall have found the murderer." He spoke like a
madman, and as he spoke he ran around the room with one hand held
out in front of him as you have seen a mind-reader at a theatre seeking
for something hidden in the stalls. He pulled the old letters from the
writing-desk and ran them over as swiftly as a gambler deals out cards;
he dropped on his knees before the fireplace and dragged out the dead
coals with his bare fingers, and then with a low, worried cry, like a
hound on a scent, he ran back to the waste-paper basket and, lifting the
papers from it, shook them out upon the floor. Instantly he gave a shout
of triumph and, separating a number of torn pieces from the others,
held them up before me.

"Look!" he cried. "Do you see? Here are five letters, torn across in
two places. The Russian did not stop to read them, for, as you see, he
has left them still sealed. I have been wrong. He did not return for the
letters. He could not have known their value. He must have returned for
some other reason, and, as he was leaving, saw the letter-box, and taking
out the letters, held them together—so—and tore them twice across,
and then, as the fire had gone out, tossed them into this basket. Look!"
he cried, "here in the upper corner of this piece is a Russian stamp. This
is his own letter—unopened!"

We examined the Russian stamp and found it had been cancelled in
St. Petersburg four days ago. The back of the envelope bore the postmark of the branch station in Upper Sloane Street and was dated this
morning. The envelope was of official blue paper, and we had no difficulty in finding the two other parts to it. We drew the torn pieces of the
letter from them and joined them together side by side. There were but
two lines of writing, and this was the message: "I leave Petersburg on the
night train, and I shall see you at Trevor Terrace after dinner Monday
evening."

"That was last night!" Lyle cried. "He arrived twelve hours ahead of
his letter—but it came in time—it came in time to hang him!"

The Baronet struck the table with his hand.

"The name!" he demanded. "How was it signed? What was the man's
name?"

The young solicitor rose to his feet and, leaning forward, stretched out his arm. "There was no name," he cried. "The letter was signed with only two initials. But engraved at the top of the sheet was the man's address. That address was 'THE AMERICAN EMBASSY, ST. PETERSBURG, BUREAU OF THE NAVAL ATTACHÉ,' and the initials," he shouted, his voice rising into an exultant and bitter cry, "were those of the gentleman who sits opposite, who told us that he was the first to find the murdered bodies, the Naval Attaché to Russia, Lieutenant Ripley Sears!"

A strained and awful hush followed the solicitor's words, which seemed to vibrate in the air like a twanging bowstring which had just hurled its bolt. Sir Andrew, pale and staring, drew away with an exclamation of repulsion. His eyes were fastened upon the Naval Attaché with fascinated horror. But the American emitted a sigh of great content and sank comfortably into the arms of his chair. He clapped his hands softly together.

"Capital!" he murmured. "I give you my word I never guessed what you were driving at. You fooled *me*, I'll be hanged if you didn't—you certainly fooled me!"

The man with the pearl stud leaned forward with a nervous gesture. "Hush! be careful!" he whispered. But at that instant, for the third time, a servant hastening through the room handed him a piece of paper, which he scanned eagerly. The message on the paper read, "THE LIGHT OVER THE COMMONS IS OUT. THE HOUSE HAS RISEN."

The man with the black pearl gave a mighty shout and tossed the paper from him on the table.

"Hurrah!" he cried. "The House is up! We've won!" He caught up his glass and slapped the Naval Attache violently upon the shoulder. He nodded joyously at him, at the Solicitor, and at the Queen's Messenger. "Gentlemen, to you!" he cried: "my thanks and my congratulations!" He drank deep from the glass and breathed forth a long sigh of satisfaction and relief.

"But I say!" protested the Queen's Messenger, shaking his finger violently at the Solicitor, "that story won't do. You didn't play fair—and—and you talked so fast I couldn't make out what it was all about. I'll bet you that evidence wouldn't hold in a court of law—you couldn't hang a cat on such evidence. Your story is condemned tommy-rot. Now, my story might have happened, my story bore the mark——"

In the joy of creation the story-tellers had forgotten their audience, until a sudden exclamation from Sir Andrew caused them to turn guiltily toward him. His face was knit with lines of anger, doubt, and amazement.

"What does this mean?" he cried. "Is this a jest, or are you mad? If you know this man is a murderer, why is he at large? Is this a game you have been playing? Explain yourselves at once. What does it mean?"

The American, with first a glance at the others, rose and bowed courteously.

"I am not a murderer, Sir Andrew, believe me," he said; "you need not be alarmed. As a matter of fact, at this moment I am much more afraid of you than you could possibly be of me. I beg you please to be indulgent. I assure you we meant no disrespect. We have been matching stories, that is all, pretending that we are people we are not, endeavouring to entertain you with better detective tales than, for instance, the last one you read, 'The Great Rand Robbery.' "

The Baronet brushed his hand nervously across his forehead.

"Do you mean to tell me," he exclaimed, that none of this has happened? That Lord Chetney is not dead, that his solicitor did not find a letter of yours written from your post in Petersburg, and that just now, when he charged you with murder, he was in jest?"

"I am really very sorry," said the American, "but you see, sir, he could not have found a letter written by me in St. Petersburg, because I have never been in Petersburg. Until this week I have never been outside of my own country. I am not a naval officer. I am a writer of short stories. And to-night, when this gentleman told me that you were fond of detective stories, I thought it would be amusing to tell you one of mine—one I had just mapped out this afternoon."

"But Lord Chetney is a real person," interrupted the Baronet, "and he did go to Africa two years ago, and he was supposed to have died there, and his brother, Lord Arthur, has been the heir. And yesterday Chetney did return. I read it in the papers."

"So did I," assented the American soothingly. "And it struck me as being a very good plot for a story. I mean his unexpected return from the dead, and the probable disappointment of the younger brother. So I decided that the younger brother had better murder the elder one. The Princess Zichy I invented out of a clear sky. The fog I did not have to invent. Since last night I know all that there is to know about a London fog. I was lost in one for three hours."

The Baronet turned grimly upon the Queen's Messenger.

"But this gentleman," he protested, "he is not a writer of short stories; he is a member of the Foreign Office. I have seen him in Whitehall often, and, according to him, the Princess Zichy is not an invention. He says she is very well known—that she tried to rob him."

The servant of the Foreign Office looked unhappily at the Cabinet Minister and puffed nervously at his cigar.

"It's true, Sir Andrew, that I am a Queen's Messenger," he said appealingly, "and a Russian woman once did try to rob a Queen's Messenger in a railway carriage—only it did not happen to me, but to a pal of mine. The only Russian princess I ever knew called herself Zabrisky. You may have seen her. She used to do a dive from the roof of the Aquarium."

Sir Andrew, with a snort of indignation, fronted the young Solicitor.

"And I suppose yours was a cock-and-bull story, too?" he said. "Of course, it must have been, since Lord Chetney is not dead. But don't tell me," he protested, "that you are not Chudleigh's son, either."

"I'm sorry," said the youngest member, smiling in some embarrassment, "but my name is not Chudleigh. I assure you, though, that I know the family very well and that I am on very good terms with them."

"You should be!" exclaimed the Baronet; "and, judging from the liberties you take with the Chetneys, you had better be on very good terms with them, too."

The young man leaned back and glanced toward the servants at the far end of the room.

"It has been so long since I have been in the Club," he said, "that I doubt if even the waiters remember me. Perhaps Joseph may," he added. "Joseph!" he called, and at the word a servant stepped briskly forward.

The young man pointed to the stuffed head of a great lion which was suspended above the fireplace.

"Joseph," he said, "I want you to tell these gentlemen who shot that lion. Who presented it to the Grill?"

Joseph, unused to acting as master of ceremonies to members of the Club, shifted nervously from one foot to the other.

"Why, you—you did," he stammered.

"Of course I did!" exclaimed the young man. "I mean, what is the name of the man who shot it. Tell the gentlemen who I am. They wouldn't believe me."

"Who you are, my lord?" said Joseph. "You are Lord Edam's son, the Earl of Chetney."

"You must admit," said Lord Chetney, when the noise had died away, "that I couldn't remain dead while my little brother was accused of murder. I had to do something. Family pride demanded it. Now, Arthur, as the younger brother, can't afford to be squeamish, but personally I should hate to have a brother of mine hanged for murder."

"You certainly showed no scruples against hanging me," said the American, "but in the face of your evidence I admit my guilt, and I sentence myself to pay the full penalty of the law as we are made to pay it in my own country. The order of this Court is," he announced, "that Joseph shall bring me a wine-card, and that I sign it for five bottles of the Club's best champagne."

"Oh, no!" protested the man with the pearl stud, "it is not for *you* to sign it. In my opinion, it is Sir Andrew who should pay the costs. It is time you knew," he said, turning to that gentleman, "that unconsciously you have been the victim of what I may call a patriotic conspiracy. These stories have had a more serious purpose than merely to amuse. They have been told with the worthy object of detaining you from the House of Commons. I must explain to you that all through this evening I have had a servant waiting in Trafalgar Square with instructions to bring me word as soon as the light over the House of Commons had ceased to burn. The light is now out, and the object for which we plotted is attained."

The Baronet glanced keenly at the man with the black pearl and then quickly at his watch. The smile disappeared from his lips, and his face was set in stern and forbidding lines.

"And may I know," he asked icily, "what was the object of your plot?"

"A most worthy one," the other retorted. "Our object was to keep you from advocating the expenditure of many millions of the people's money upon more battleships. In a word, we have been working together to prevent you from passing the Navy Increase Bill."

Sir Andrew's face bloomed with brilliant colour. His body shook with suppressed emotion.

"My dear sir!" he cried, "you should spend more time at the House and less at your Club. The Navy Bill was brought up on its third reading at eight o'clock this evening. I spoke for three hours in its favour. My only reason for wishing to return again to the House to-night was to sup on the terrace with my old friend, Admiral Simons; for my work at the House was completed five hours ago, when the Navy Increase Bill was passed by an overwhelming majority."

The Baronet rose and bowed. "I have to thank you, sir," he said, "for a most interesting evening."

The American shoved the wine-card which Joseph had given him toward the gentleman with the black pearl.

"You sign it," he said.

❧ ❧ ❧

Big Boy, Little Boy

SIMON BRETT

Under normal circumstances he would have thrown away the letter as soon as he recognized the cramped handwriting, but Larry Renshaw was in the process of murdering his wife and needed to focus his mind on something else. So he read it.

Mario, the barman, had handed it over. Having a variety of postal addresses in pubs and bars all over London was a habit Larry had developed in less opulent days, and one that he had not attempted to break after his marriage to Lydia. The sort of letters he received had changed, though; there were fewer instructions from "business associates," fewer guilty wads of notes buying other people's extramarital secrets. Their place had been taken by confirmations of his own sexual assignations, correspondence that could, by the widest distension of the category, be classed as love letters. Marriage had not meant an end of secrets.

But it had meant an upgrading of some of the "postes restantes." Gaston's Bar in Albemarle Street was a definite advance on the Stag's Head in Kilburn. And the Saville Row suit, from which he flicked the salt shed by Mario's peanuts, was more elegant than a hotel porter's uniform. The gold identity bracelet that clinked reassuringly on his wrist was more comfortable than a handcuff—and, Larry Renshaw sincerely believed, much more his natural style.

Which was why he had to ensure that he continued to live in that style. He was nearly fifty. He resented the injustices of a world which had kept him so long from his natural milieu, and now that he had finally arrived there he had no intentions of leaving.

Nor was he going to limit his lifestyle by removing those elements—other women—of which Lydia disapproved.

Which was why, while he sipped Campari and vodka in Gaston's Bar, he was murdering his wife.

And why he read Peter Mostyn's letter to take his mind off what he was doing.

"—and those feelings for you haven't changed. I know over thirty years have passed, but those nights we spent together are still the memories I most treasure. I have never had any other *friends*. Nothing that has happened and no one I have met since has meant as much to me as the pleasure I got, not only from being with you, but also from being known as *yours*, from being made fun of at school as your Little Boy.

"I know it didn't mean as much to you, but I flatter myself that you felt *something* for me at the time. I remember how once we changed pyjamas and you let me sleep in yours in *your* bed all night. I've never felt closer to you than I did that night, as if I didn't just take on your clothes, but also a bit of you—as if I became you for a little while. I had never felt so happy. Because, though we always looked a little alike, though we were the same height and had the same colouring, I never had your strength of character. Just then, for a moment, I knew what it was like to be Larry Renshaw.

"It was wonderful for me to see you last week. I'm only sorry it was for such a short time. Remember, if there's ever *anything* I can do for you, you have only to ask. If you want to meet up again, do ring. I'm only over here sorting out some problem on my uncle's will and as I'm pretty hard up, I spend most of my time in my room at the hotel. But if I *am* out when you ring, they'll take a message. I'll be going back to France at the end of the week, but I'd really like to see you before then. I sometimes think I'll take my courage in both hands and come round to your flat, but I know you wouldn't really like it, particularly now you're *married to that woman*. It was quite a shock when you told me about your marriage. I had always had a secret hope that the reason you never *had* married was—"

Larry stopped reading. Not only had the mention of his marriage brought his mind back to the murder of Lydia, he also found the letter distasteful.

It wasn't being the object of a homosexual passion that worried or challenged him. He had no doubt where his own tastes lay. He didn't even think he had gone through a homosexual phase in adolescence, but he had always had a strong libido, and what other outlet was there in a boys' boarding school? All the other Big Boys had had Little Boys, so he had played the games tradition demanded. But as soon as he had been released from that particular prison, he had quickly discovered, and concentrated on, the instinctive pleasures of heterosexuality.

But Peter Mostyn hadn't changed. He'd make contact every few years, suggesting a lunch, and Larry, aware that a free meal was one he didn't have to pay for, would agree to meet. Their conversation would be stilted, spiralling round topics long dead, and Larry would finish up his brandy and leave as soon as the bill arrived. Then, within a week, one of the "poste restante" barmen would hand over a letter full of closely written obsequious gratitude and assurances of continuing devotion.

For Mostyn the dormitory grappling had obviously meant more and he had frozen like an insect in the amber of adolescence. That was what depressed Larry. He hated the past, he didn't like to think about it. For him there was always the hope of the big win just around the next corner, and he would rather concentrate on that than on the disasters behind him.

He could forget the past so easily, instinctively sloughing off the skin of one shady failure to slither out with a shining new identity ready for the next infallible scheme. This protean ability had enabled him to melt from stockbroker's clerk to Army recruit (after a few bounced cheques), from Army reject to mail-order manager (after a few missing boxes of ammunition), from mail-order manager to pimp (after a few prepaid but undelivered orders), and from pimp to hotel porter (after a police raid). And it had facilitated the latest metamorphosis, from hotel porter to Saville-Row-suited husband of a rich neurotic dipsomaniac (just before the inevitable theft inquiry). For Larry, change and hope went hand in hand.

So Peter Mostyn's devotion was an unpleasant intrusion. It suggested that, whatever his current identity, there remained in Larry an unchanging core that could still be loved. It threatened his independence in a way the love of women never had. His heterosexual affairs were all brisk and physical, soon ended, leaving in him no adverse emotion that couldn't be erased by another conquest and, in the women, undiluted resentment.

But Peter Mostyn's avowed love was something else—an unpleasant reminder of his continuing identity, almost a *memento mori*. And Peter Mostyn himself was even more of a *memento mori*.

They had met the previous week for the first time in six years. Once again, old habits had died hard, and Larry had instinctively taken the bait of a free meal in spite of his new opulence.

As soon as he saw Peter Mostyn, he knew it was a bad idea. He felt like Dorian Gray meeting his picture face to face. The Little Boy had aged so unattractively that his appearance was a challenge to Larry's vigour and smartness. After all, they were about the same age—no, hell, Mostyn was younger. At school he had been the Little Boy to Larry's Big Boy. A couple of forms behind, so a couple of years younger.

And yet to see him, you'd think he was on the verge of death. He had been ill, apparently; Larry seemed to remember his saying something over the lunch about having been ill. Perhaps that explained the long tubular crutches and the general air of debility. But it was no excuse for the teeth and the hair—the improvement of those was quite within his power. Okay, most of us lose some teeth, but that doesn't mean we have to go around with a mouth like a drawstring purse. Larry prided himself on his own false teeth. One of the first things he'd done after marrying Lydia had been to set up a series of private dental appointments and have his mouth filled with the best replacements money could buy.

And the hair. Larry was thinning a bit and would have been greying but for the discreet preparation he bought from his Jermyn Street hairdresser. But he liked to think that, even if he had been so unfortunate as to lose all his hair, he wouldn't have resorted to a toupé that looked like a small brown mammal that had been run over by a day's traffic on the M1.

And yet that was how Peter Mostyn had appeared, a hobbling creature with concave lips and hair that lacked any credibility. And, to match his physical state, he had demonstrated his emotional crippledom with the same adolescent infatuation and unwholesome self-pity, the same constant assertions that he would do anything for his friend, that he felt his own life to be without value and only likely to take on meaning if it could be used in the service of Larry Renshaw.

Larry didn't like any of it. Particularly he didn't like the constant use of the past tense, as if life from now on would be an increasingly crepuscular experience. He thought in the future tense, and of a future that was infinite now that he had Lydia's money.

Now that he had Lydia's money. . . . He looked at his watch. A quarter to eight. She should be a good five hours dead. Time to put thoughts of that tired old queen Mostyn behind him and get on with the main business of the day. Time for the dutiful husband to go home and discover his wife's body. Or if he was really lucky, discover that his sister-in-law had just discovered his wife's body.

He said good-bye loudly to Mario, and made some quip about the barman's new apron. He also asked if the barroom clock was right and checked his watch against it.

After a lifetime of obscuring details of timing and squeezing alibis from forgotten minutes, it was an amusing novelty to draw attention to time. And to himself.

For the same reason, he exchanged memorable banter with the driver of the taxi he picked up in a still-light Piccadilly Circus before settling back for the journey to Abbey Road.

Now he felt supremely confident. He was following his infallible instinct. The plan was the work of a mastermind. He even had a twinge of regret to think that when he had all Lydia's money that mind would be lost to crime. But no, he didn't intend to hazard his newfound fortune by doing anything mildly risky. He needed freedom to cram into his remaining rich life what he had missed out on in poorer days.

Which was why the murder plan was so good. It contained no risk at all.

In fact, although he didn't consciously realize it at the time he had got the murder plan at the same time he had got Lydia. She had come ready-packed with her own self-destruct mechanism. The complete kit.

Lydia had fallen in love with Larry when he saved her life, and had married him out of gratitude.

It had happened two years previously. Larry Renshaw had been at the lowest ebb of a career that had known many freak tides. He had been working as a porter at a Park Lane hotel, whose management was beginning to suspect him of helping himself from the wallets, handbags, and jewel cases of the guests. One afternoon he had received a tipoff that they were on to him, and determined to make one last reasonable-sized haul before another sudden exit and change of identity.

Observation and staff gossip led him to use his passkey on the door of a Mrs. Lydia Phythian, a lady whose Christmas-tree appearances in the bar left no doubts about her possession of a considerable stock of jewellery, and whose consumption of gin in the same bar suggested that she might be a little careless in locking away her decorations.

So it proved. Necklaces, brooches, bracelets, and rings lay among the pill bottles on the dressing table as casually as stranded seaweed. But there was also in the room something that promised a far richer and less risky haul than a fence's grudging prices for the gems.

There was Mrs. Lydia Phythian, in the process of committing suicide.

The scene was classic to the point of being corny. An empty gin bottle clutched in the hand of the snoring figure on the bed, on the bedside table an empty pill bottle dramatically on its side, and propped against the lamp a folded sheet of crisp blue monogrammed notepaper.

The first thing Larry did was to read the note.

This was the only way out. Nobody cares whether I live or die and I don't want to go on just being a burden. I've tried, but life's too much.

It was undated. Instinctively, Larry put it in his pocket before turning his attention to the figure on the bed. She was deeply asleep, but her pulses were still strong. Remembering some movie with this scene in it, he slapped her face.

Her eyes came woozily open. "I want to die. Why shouldn't I die?"

"Because there's so much to live for," he replied, possibly remembering dialogue from the same movie.

Her eyes rolled shut again. He rang for an ambulance. Instinct told him to get an outside line and ring the Emergency Services direct; he didn't want the manager muscling in on his act.

Then, again following the pattern of the movie, he walked her sagging body up and down, keeping her semiconscious until help arrived.

Thereafter he just followed instinct. Instinct told him to accompany her in the ambulance to the hospital; instinct told him to return (out of his hotel uniform) to be there when she came round after the ministrations of the stomach pump; instinct told him to continue his visits when she was moved to the recuperative luxury of the Avenue Clinic. And instinct provided the words which assured her that there really was a lot to live for, and that it was insane for a woman as attractive as her to feel unloved, and that he at least appreciated her true worth.

So their marriage three months after she came out of the clinic was really a triumph of instinct.

A couple of days before the registry-office ceremony, Larry Renshaw had fixed to see her doctor. "I felt, you know, that I should know her medical history now that we're going to be together for life," he said in a responsible voice. "I mean, I'm not asking you to give away any profes-sional secrets, but obviously I want to ensure that there isn't a recur-rence of the appalling incident which brought us together."

"Of course." The doctor was bald, thin, and frankly sceptical. He did not seem to be taken in by Larry's performance as the concerned hus-band-to-be. "Well, she's a very neurotic woman, she likes to draw atten-tion to herself. Nothing's going to change her basic character."

"I thought, being married . . ."

"She's been married a few times before, you must know that."

"Yes, of course, but she seems to have had pretty bad luck and been landed with a lot of bastards. I thought, given someone who really loves her for herself . . ."

"Oh yes, I'm sure she'd be a lot more stable, given *that*." The scepti-cism was now so overt as to be insulting, but Larry didn't risk righteous anger, as the doctor went on, "The trouble is, Mr. Renshaw, women as rich as Mrs. Phythian tend to meet up with rather a lot of bastards."

Larry ignored the second insult. "What I really wanted to know was—"

"What you really wanted to know," the doctor interrupted, "was whether she was likely to attempt suicide again."

Larry nodded gravely.

"Well, I can't tell you. Someone who takes as many pills and who drinks as much as she does is rarely fully rational. This wasn't her first attempt, though it was different from the others."

"How?"

"The previous ones were more obviously simply demands for atten-tion—she made pretty sure that she'd be found before anything too serious happened. In this case—well, if you hadn't walked into the room I think she'd have gone the distance. Incidentally—"

But Larry spoke before the inevitable question about why he came to be in her room. "Were there any other differences this time?"

"Small ones. The way she crushed up all the pills into the gin before she started suggested a more positive approach. And the fact that there was no note . . ."

Larry didn't respond to the quizzical look. When he left, the doctor shook him by the hand and said with undisguised irony, "I wouldn't worry. I'm sure everything will work out *for you*."

The insolent distrust was back in that final emphasis, but mixed in the doctor's voice with another feeling, one of relief. At least a new husband would keep Mrs. Phythian out of his surgery for a little while. There would just be a series of repeat prescriptions for tranquillisers and sleeping pills, and he could still charge her for those.

Subconsciously, Larry knew that the doctor had confirmed how easy it would be for him to murder his wife, but he didn't let himself think about it. After all, why should it be necessary?

At first it wasn't. Mrs. Lydia Phythian changed her name again—she was almost rivalling her husband in the number of identities she had taken on—and become Mrs. Lydia Renshaw. At first the marriage worked pretty well. She enjoyed kitting out her new husband and he enjoyed being taken round to expensive shops and being treated by her. He found her a surprisingly avid sexual partner and, although he couldn't have subsisted on that diet alone, secret snacks with other women kept him agreeably nourished and he began to think marriage suited him.

Certainly it brought him a lifestyle he had never before experienced. Having been brought up by parents whose middle-class insistence on putting him through minor public school had dragged their living standards down to working-class and below, and then having never been securely wealthy for more than a fortnight, he was well placed to appreciate the large flat in Abbey Road, the country house in Uckfield, and the choice of driving a Bentley or a little Mercedes.

In fact, there were only two things about his wife that annoyed him— her unwillingness to let him see other women and the restricted amount of pocket money she allowed him.

He had found ways around the second problem; in fact, he had reverted to his old ways to get round the second problem. He had started, very early in their marriage, stealing from his wife.

At first he had done it indirectly. She had trustingly put him in charge of her portfolio of investments, which made it very easy for him to cream off what he required for his day-to-day needs. However, a stormy meeting with Lydia's broker and accountant, who threatened to disclose all to their employer, persuaded him to relinquish these responsibilities.

So he started robbing his wife directly. The alcoholic haze in which she habitually moved made this fairly easy. Mislaying a ring or a small necklace, or even finding her wallet empty within a few hours of going

to the bank, were common occurrences and not ones to which she liked
to draw attention since they raised the question of how much her drinking affected her memory.

Larry spent a certain amount of this loot on other women, but the
bulk of it he consigned to a suitcase, which every three or four weeks
was moved discreetly to another Left Luggage office—premarital habits
again dying hard. Over some twenty months of marriage, he had accu-
mulated between twelve and thirteen thousand pounds, which was a
comforting hedge against adversity.

But he didn't expect adversity. Or at least he didn't expect adversity
until he discovered that his wife had put a private detective onto him
and had compiled a dossier of a fortnight's infidelities.

It was then that he knew he had to murder her, and had to do it
quickly, before the meeting with her solicitor she had mentioned when
confronting him with the detective's report. Larry Renshaw had no intention of being divorced from his wife's money.

As soon as he had made the decision, the murder plan that he had
shut up in the Left Luggage locker of his subconscious was revealed by a
simple turn of a key. It was so simple, he glowed from the beauty of it.

He went through it again as he sat in the cab on the way to Abbey
Road. The timing was perfect; there was no way it could fail.

Every three months Lydia spent four days at a health farm. The aim
was not primarily to dry her out but to put a temporary brake on the
runaway deterioration of her physical charms. However, the strictness of
the fashionable institution chosen to take on this hopeless task meant
that the visit did have the side-effect of keeping her off alcohol for its
duration. The natural consequence of this was that on the afternoon of
her return she would, regular as clockwork, irrigate her parched system
with at least half a bottle of gin.

And that was all the plan needed. His instinct told him it couldn't
fail.

He had made the preparations that morning, almost joyously. He had
whistled softly as he worked. There was so little to do. Crush up the pills
into the gin bottle, place the suicide note in the desk drawer, and set out
to spend his day in company. No part of that day was to be unaccounted
for. Gaston's Bar was only the last link in a long chain of alibi.

During the day he had probed at the plan, testing it for weaknesses, and found none.

Suppose Lydia thought the gin tasted funny? She wouldn't, in her haste. Anyway, in her descriptions of the previous attempt, she had said there was no taste. It had been, she said, just like drinking it neat and getting gently drowsier and drowsier. A quiet end. Not an unattractive one.

Suppose the police found out about the private detective and the appointment with the solicitor? Wouldn't they begin to suspect the dead woman's husband? No, if anything, that strengthened his case. Disillusioned by yet another man, depressed by the prospect of yet another divorce, she had taken the quickest way out. True, it didn't put her husband in a very good light, but Larry was not worried about that. So long as he inherited, he didn't care what people thought.

Suppose she had already made a will which disinherited him? He knew she hadn't. That was what she'd set up with the solicitor for the next day. And Larry had been present when she made her previous will that named him, her husband, as sole legatee.

No, his instinct told him nothing could go wrong . . .

He paid off the taxi driver and told him a joke he had heard in the course of the day.

He then went into their block of flats, told the porter the same joke, and asked if he could check the right time. Eight-seventeen. Never had there been a better-documented day.

As he went up in the lift, he wondered if the final refinement to the plan had happened. It wasn't essential, but it would have been nice. Lydia's sister had said she would drop round for the evening. If she could actually have discovered the body . . . still, she was notoriously bad about time and you can't have everything. But it would be nice . . .

Everything played into his hands. On the landing he met a neighbour just about to walk his chihuahua. Larry greeted them cheerfully and checked the time. His confidence was huge. He enjoyed being a criminal mastermind.

For the benefit of the departing neighbour and because he was going to play the part to the hilt, he called out cheerily, "Good evening, darling!" as he unlocked the front door.

"Good evening, *darling*," said Lydia.

* * *

As soon as he saw her, he knew that she knew everything. She sat poised on the sofa, and on the glass coffee table in front of her were the bottle of gin and the suicide note. If they had been labelled in a courtroom, they couldn't have been more clearly marked as evidence. On a table to the side of the sofa stood a half-empty bottle of gin. The bloody, boozy bitch—she couldn't even wait until she got home, she'd taken on new supplies on the way back from the health farm.

"Well, Larry, I dare say you're surprised to see me."

"A little," he said lightly, and smiled what he had always believed to be a charming smile.

"I think I'll have quite a lot to say to my solicitor tomorrow."

He laughed lightly.

"After I've been to the police," she continued.

His next laugh was more brittle.

"Yes, Larry, there are quite a few things to talk about. For a start, I've just done an inventory of my jewellery. And do you know, I think I've suddenly realized why you appeared in my hotel room that fateful afternoon. Once a thief, always a thief. But murder—that's going up a league for you, isn't it?"

The gin hadn't got to her; she was speaking with cold coherence. Larry slowed down his mind to match her logical deliberation. He walked over to his desk in the corner by the door. When he turned round, he was holding the gun he kept in its drawer.

Lydia laughed, loudly and unattractively, as if in derision of his manhood. "Oh, come on, Larry, that's not very subtle. No, your other little scheme was quite clever, I'll give you that. But to shoot me . . . they'd never let you inherit. You aren't allowed to profit from a crime."

"I'm not going to shoot you." He moved across and pointed the gun at her head. "I'm going to make you drink from that other gin bottle."

Again he got the harsh, challenging laugh. "Oh, come on, sweetie. What kind of threat is that? There's a basic fault in your logic. You can't make people kill themselves by threatening to kill them. If you gotta go, who cares about the method? And if you intend to kill me, I'll ensure that you do it the way that gives you most trouble. Shoot away, sweetie."

Involuntarily, he lowered the arm holding the gun.

She laughed again.

"Anyway, I'm bored with this." She rose from the sofa. "I'm going to ring the police. I've had enough of being married to a criminal mastermind."

The taunt so exactly reflected his self-image that it stung like a blow. His gun arm stiffened again and he shot her in the temple as she made her way towards the telephone.

There was a lot of blood. At first he stood there mesmerized by how much blood there was, but then, as the flow stopped, his mind started to work again.

Its deliberations were not comforting. He had blown it. The best he could hope for now was escape.

Unnaturally calm, he went to the telephone. He rang Heathrow. There was a ten o'clock flight. Yes, there was a seat. He booked it.

He took the spare cash from Lydia's handbag. Under ten pounds. She hadn't been to the bank since her return from the health farm. Still, he could use a credit card to pay for the ticket.

He went into the bedroom, where her jewellery lay in its customary disarray. He reached out for a diamond choker.

But no. Supposed the Customs searched him. That was just the sort of trouble he had to avoid. For the same reason, he couldn't take the jewellery from his case in the Left Luggage office. Where was it now, anyway? Oh, no! Liverpool Street! Fumes of panic rose to his brain. There wouldn't be time. Or would there? Maybe if he just got the money from the case and—

The doorbell rang.

Oh, my God! Lydia's sister!

He grabbed a suitcase, threw in his pyjamas and a clean shirt, then rushed into the kitchen, opened the back door, and ran down the fire escape.

Peter Mostyn's cottage was in the Department of the Lot. The nearest large town was Cahors, the nearest small town was Montaigu-de-Quercy, but neither was very near. The cottage itself was small and primitive. Mostyn was not a British trendy making a fashionable home in France; he had moved there in search of obscurity and lived very cheaply, constantly calculating how many years he could remain there on the dwindling capital he had been left by a remote uncle and hoping it would last out his lifetime. He didn't have more contact with the locals than weekly shopping demanded, and both sides seemed happy with this arrangement.

Larry Renshaw arrived there on the third night after Lydia's death. He had travelled unobtrusively by local trains, thumbed lifts, and long stretches of cross-country walking, sleeping in the fields by night. He had sold his Saville Row suit for a tenth of its value in a Paris second-hand clothes shop, where he had bought a set of stained blue overalls, which made him less conspicuous tramping along the sun-baked roads of France. His passport and gold identity bracelet were secure in an inside pocket.

If there was any chase, he reckoned he was ahead of it.

It had been dark for about four hours when he reached the cottage. It was a warm summer night. The countryside was dry and brittle, needing rain. Although the occasional car had flashed past on the narrow local roads, he had not met any pedestrians.

There was a meager slice of moon which showed him enough to dash another hope. In the back of his mind had lurked the possibility that Mostyn, in spite of his constant assertions of poverty, lived in luxury and would prove as well fleshed a body as Lydia to batten on. But the crumbling exterior of the cottage told him that the long-term solution to his problems would have to lie elsewhere. The building had hardly changed at all through many generations of peasant owners.

And when Mostyn came to the door, he could have been the latest representative of that peasant dynasty. His wig was off, he wore a shapeless sort of nightshirt and clutched a candleholder out of a Dickens television serial. The toothless lips moved uneasily and in his eye was an old peasant distrust of outsiders.

That expression vanished as soon as he recognized his visitor.

"Larry. I hoped you'd come to me. I read about it in the papers. Come inside. You'll be safe here."

Safe he certainly was. Mostyn's limited social round meant that there was no danger of the newcomer being recognized. No danger of his even being seen. For three days the only person Larry Renshaw saw was Peter Mostyn.

And Peter Mostyn still hadn't changed at all. He remained a pathetic cripple, rendered even more pathetic by his cringing devotion. For him

Renshaw's appearance was the answer to a prayer. Now at last he had the object of his affections in his own home. He was in seventh heaven.

Renshaw wasn't embarrassed by the devotion; he knew Mostyn was far too diffident to try and force unwelcome attentions on him. For a little while at least he had found sanctuary and was content for a couple of days to sit and drink his host's brandy and assess his position.

The assessment wasn't encouraging. Everything had turned sour. All the careful plans he had laid for Lydia's death now worked against him. The elaborate fixing of the time of his arrival at the flat no longer established his alibi; it now pointed the finger of murder at him. Even after he'd shot her, he might have been able to sort something out but for that bloody sister of hers ringing the bell and making him panic. Everything had turned out wrong.

On the third evening, as he sat silent at the table, savagely drinking brandy while Mostyn watched him, Renshaw shouted out against the injustice of it all. "That bloody bitch!"

"Lydia?" asked Mostyn hesitantly.

"No, you fool. Her sister. If she hadn't turned up just at that moment, I'd have got away with it. I'd have thought of something."

"At what moment?"

"Just after I'd shot Lydia. She rang the bell."

"What—about eight-thirty?"

"Yes."

Mostyn paled beneath his toupé. "That wasn't Lydia's sister."

"What? How do you know?"

"It was me." Renshaw looked at him. "It was me. I was flying back the next morning. You hadn't *rung*. I so wanted to see you before I left, so I came to the flats. I didn't *intend* to go in. But I just asked the porter if you were there and he said you'd just arrived."

"It was you! You bloody fool, why didn't you say?"

"I didn't know what had happened. I just—"

"You idiot! You bloody idiot!" The frustration of the last few days and the brandy came together in a wave of fury. Renshaw seized Mostyn by the lapels and shook him. "If I had known it was you . . . you could have saved my life! You bloody fool! You . . ."

"I didn't know, I didn't know," the Little Boy whimpered. "When there was no reply, I just went back to the hotel. Honestly, if I'd known what was happening . . . I'd do anything for you, you *know* I would. Anything . . ."

Renshaw slackened his grasp on Mostyn's lapels and returned to Mostyn's brandy.

It was the next day that he took up the offer. They sat over the debris of lunch. "Peter, you said you'd do anything for me . . ."

"Of course, and I meant it. My life hasn't been much. You're the only person that matters to me. I'd do anything for you. I'll look after you here for as long as—"

"I'm not staying here. I have to get away."

Mostyn's face betrayed his hurt. Renshaw ignored it and continued. "For that I need money."

"I've told you, you can have anything I—"

"No, I know you haven't got any money. Not real money. But I have. In the Left Luggage office at Liverpool Street Station I have over twelve thousand pounds in cash and jewellery." Renshaw looked at Mostyn with the smile he had always believed to be charming. "I want you to go to England to fetch it for me."

"What? But I'd never get it back over here."

"Yes, you would. You're the ideal smuggler. You put the stuff in your crutches. They'd never suspect someone like you."

"But I—"

Renshaw looked hurt. "You said you'd do anything for me."

"Well, I would, but—"

"You can go into Cahors tomorrow and fix the flight."

"But—but that means you'll leave me again."

"For a little while, yes. I'd come back," Renshaw lied.

"I—"

"Please do it for me." Renshaw put on an expression he knew to be vulnerable. "Please."

"All right, I will."

"Bless you, bless you. Come on, let's drink to it."

"I don't drink much. It makes me sleepy. I haven't got the head for it. I—"

"Come on, drink."

Mostyn hadn't got the head for it. As the afternoon progressed, he became more and more embarrassingly devoted. Then he fell into a comatose sleep.

The day after next, the plane ticket was on the dining-room table next to Peter Mostyn's passport. Upstairs his small case was packed ready. He was to fly from Paris in three days' time, on the Wednesday. He would be back at the cottage by the weekend with the money and jewels which would be Renshaw's lifeline.

Renshaw's confidence started to return. With money in his pocket, everything would once more become possible. Twelve thousand pounds was plenty to buy a new identity and start again. Talent like his, he knew, could not be kept down for long.

Mostyn was obviously uneasy about the task ahead of him, but he had been carefully briefed and he'd manage it all right. The Big Boy was entrusting him with a mission and the Little Boy would see that it was efficiently discharged.

A new harmony came into their relationship. Now that his escape had a date on it, Renshaw could relax and even be pleasant to his protector. Mostyn glowed with gratitude for the attention. It didn't take much to make him happy, Renshaw thought contemptuously. Once again, as he looked at the prematurely aged and crippled figure, he found it incongruous that their bodies had ever touched. Mostyn had never been other than pathetic.

Still, he was useful. And though it was making huge inroads into his carefully husbanded wealth, he kept the supply of brandy flowing. Renshaw topped up his tumbler again after lunch on the Monday afternoon. It was then that there was a knock at the door. Mostyn leapt nervously to the window to check out the visitor. When he looked back at Renshaw, his face had even less colour under its thatch. "It's a gendarme."

Moving quickly and efficiently, Larry Renshaw picked up his dirty plate, together with the brandy bottle and tumbler, and went upstairs. His bedroom window was above the sloping roof of the porch. If anyone came up, he would be able to make a quick getaway.

He heard conversation downstairs, but it was too indistinct and his knowledge of French too limited for him to understand it. Then he heard the front door shut. From his window he saw the gendarme go to his bike and cycle off towards Montaigu-de-Quercy.

He gave it five minutes and went downstairs. Peter Mostyn sat at the table, literally shaking.

"What the hell's the matter?"

"The gendarme—he asked if I'd seen you."

"So you said you hadn't."

"Yes, but . . ."

"But what? That's all there is to it, surely. There's been an Interpol alert to check out any contacts I might have abroad. They got your name from my address book back at the flat. So now the local bobby here has done his bit and will report back that you haven't seen me since last week in London. End of story. I'm glad it's happened. At least now I don't have to wait for it."

"Yes, but, Larry, look at the state I'm in."

"You'll calm down. Come on, okay, it was a shock, but you'll get over it."

"That's not what I mean. What I'm saying is, if I'm in this state now, I just won't be able to go through with what I'm supposed to be doing on Wednesday."

"Look, all you have to do is to catch a plane to London, go to the Liverpool Street Left Luggage office, get the case, go to somewhere conveniently quiet, load the stuff into your crutches, and come back here! There's no danger!"

"I can't do it, Larry. I *can't*. I'll crack up. I'll give myself away somehow. If I were like you, I could do it. You've always had a strong nerve for that sort of thing. I wish it were you who was going to do it, because I know you *could*. But I just . . ."

He petered out. Anger invaded Renshaw. "Listen, you little worm, you've got to do it! Good God, you've said enough times you'd do anything for me—and now the first time I ask for something you're bloody chicken!"

"Larry, I would do anything for you, I would. But I just don't think I *can* go through with this. I'd mess it up somehow. Honestly, Larry, if there were anything *else* I could do . . ."

"Anything else? How about getting me off the murder charge? Maybe you'd like to do that instead?" Renshaw asked with acid sarcasm.

"If I could . . . or if I had enough money to be any use . . . or if . . ."

"Oh, shut up, you useless little queen!" Larry Renshaw stomped savagely upstairs with the brandy bottle.

They did not speak to each other for over twenty-four hours.

But the next evening, as he lay on the bed drinking brandy, watching the declining sun tinge the scrubby oak trees of the hillside with gold, Renshaw's instinct started to take over again. It was a warm feeling. Once more he felt protected. His instinct was an Almighty Big Boy, looking after him, guiding him, showing him the way forward, as it always had done before.

After about an hour, he heard the front door and saw Mostyn setting off down the road that led to Montaigu-de-Quercy. Again. He'd been out more than once since their row. No doubt going to buy more brandy as a peace offering. Poor little sod. Renshaw chuckled to himself at the aptness of the description.

Alone in the cottage, he dozed. The bang of the door on Mostyn's return woke him. And he was not surprised to wake up with his plan of campaign worked out in every detail.

Peter Mostyn looked up like a mongrel fearing a kick, but Larry Renshaw smiled at him and was amused to see how gratefully the expression changed. Mostyn had all the weakness of the sort of women Renshaw had spent his life avoiding.

"Larry, look, I'm terribly sorry about yesterday afternoon. I was just a coward. Look, I really *do* want to do something for you. You know I'd give my life for you if I thought it'd be any use. It's been a pretty wasted life—I'd like it to do *something* valuable."

"But not go to London and pick up my things?" Renshaw asked lightly.

"I just don't think I *could*, Larry, I don't think I have it *in me*. But I will go to London tomorrow. There's something else I can do for you. I *can* help you. I *have* helped you already. I—"

"Never mind." Renshaw spread his hands in a magnanimous gesture of forgiveness. "Never mind. Listen, Peter," he went on intimately, "I behaved like a swine yesterday and I want to apologize. I'm sorry, this whole thing's been a dreadful strain and I just haven't been appreciating all you're doing for me. Please forgive me."

"You've been fine. I . . ." Mostyn's expression hovered between surprise and delight at his friend's change of behaviour.

"No, I've been being a swine. Peace offering." He drew his hand out of his pocket and held it towards Mostyn.

"But you don't want to give me that. It's your identity bracelet, it's got your name on. And it's gold. I mean, you'd—"

"Please . . ."

Mostyn took the bracelet and slipped it onto his thin wrist.

"Listen, Peter, I've been so confused I haven't been thinking straight. Forget the money in London. Maybe I'll get it someday, maybe I won't. The important thing is that I'm safe at the moment, with a *friend*. A very good friend. Peter, what I want to ask is—can I stay here for a bit?" He looked up humbly. "If you don't mind."

"Mind? Look, you know, Larry, I'd be delighted. *Delighted*. You don't have to ask that."

"Bless you, Peter." Renshaw spoke softly, as if choked by emotion. Then he perked up. "If that's settled then, let's drink on it."

"I won't, thank you, Larry. You know it only makes me sleepy."

"Oh, come on, Peter. If we're going to live together, we've got to learn to enjoy the same hobbies." And he filled two tumblers with brandy.

The prospect opened up by the words "live together" was too much for Mostyn. There were tears in his eyes as he drained the first drink.

It was about an hour and a half later when Renshaw judged the moment to be right. Mostyn was slurring his words and yawning, but still conscious. His eyes focused in pleasure for a moment when Renshaw murmured, "Why don't we go upstairs?"

"Whaddya mean?"

"You know what I mean." He giggled.

"Really? Really?"

Renshaw nodded.

Mostyn rose, swaying, to his feet. "Where are my crutches?"

"They won't help you stand up straight in the state you're in." Renshaw giggled again, and Mostyn joined in. Renshaw ruffled his Little Boy's hair, and the toupé came off in his hand.

"Gimme thaback."

"When I come upstairs," Renshaw murmured softly. Then, in an even lower whisper, "Go up to my room, get my pyjamas, put them on, and get into my bed. I'll be up soon."

Mostyn smiled with fuddled pleasure and started off up the stairs. Renshaw heard the uneven footsteps in his room above, then the hobbling noises of undressing, the thump of a body hitting the bed, and soon, predictably, silence.

He sat for about a quarter of an hour finishing his drink. Then, whistling softly, he started to make his preparations.

He moved slowly, but efficiently, following the infallible dictates of his instinct. First he went into the little bathroom and shaved off his remaining hair. It took a surprisingly short time. Then he removed his false teeth and put them in a glass of water.

He went cautiously up the stairs and inched open the door of his bedroom. As expected, Mostyn lay unconscious from the unaccustomed alcohol.

Unhurriedly, Renshaw placed the glass of teeth on the bedside table. Then he changed into the clothes Mostyn had just abandoned on the floor. He went into the other bedroom, picked up the overnight case that had been packed, and returned downstairs.

He picked up the air ticket and passport, which still lay accusingly on the dining table. He put on the toupé and compared his reflection with the passport photograph. The picture was ten years old and the resemblance quite sufficient. He picked up the crutches and tried them until he could reproduce the limp that appeared in the "Special Peculiarities" section.

Then he picked up the half-full brandy bottle, another unopened one, and the candle on the table, and went upstairs.

The Little Boy lay on his Big Boy's bed, in his Big Boy's pyjamas, even wearing his Big Boy's gold identity bracelet, but was in no state to appreciate this longed-for felicity. He did not stir as his Big Boy sprinkled brandy over the bedclothes, the rush matting, and the wooden floorboards. Nor did he stir when his Big Boy set the lighted candle on the floor and watched its flames spread.

Larry Renshaw felt the usual confidence that following his instinct produced as he travelled back to London in the identity of Peter Mostyn. He even found there were compensations in being a pathetic, toothless cripple on crutches. People made way for him at the airport and helped him with his bags.

On the plane he mused comfortably about his next movements. Certainly his first port of call must be the Left Luggage office at Liverpool Street. And then probably one of the fences he already knew, to turn the jewellery into cash. Then, who could say? Possibly abroad again . . . certainly a new identity . . .

But there was no hurry. That was the luxury his instinct had achieved for him. In Mostyn's identity he was safe for as long as he could stand being such a pathetic figure. There was no hurry.

He felt tense as he approached Passport Control at Heathrow. Not frightened—he was confident his instinct would see him through—but tense. After all, if there was a moment when his identity was most likely to be questioned, this was it. But if he was accepted here as Peter Mostyn, then he had nothing more to worry about.

It was slightly unnerving, because the Passport Officer seemed to be expecting him. "Ah, Mr. Mostyn," he said. "If you'd just take a seat here for a moment, I'll tell them you've arrived."

"But I—" No, better not to make a scene. Reserve righteous indignation for later. Must be some minor mix-up. He imagined how feebly Peter Mostyn would whine at the nuisances of bureaucracy.

He didn't have long to wait. Two men in raincoats arrived and asked him to go with them to a small room. They did not speak again until they were all seated.

"Now," said the man who seemed to be senior, "let's talk about the murder of Mrs. Lydia Renshaw."

"Mrs. Lydia Renshaw?" echoed Larry Renshaw, bemused. "But I'm Peter Mostyn."

"Yes," said the man, "we know that. There's no question about that. And that's why we want to talk to you about the murder of Mrs. Lydia Renshaw."

"But . . . why?" Larry Renshaw asked, quite as pathetically as Peter Mostyn would have done.

"Why?" The man seemed puzzled. "Well, because of your letter of confession that arrived this morning."

* * *

It was some time before he actually saw the document that had incriminated him, but it didn't take him long to imagine its contents:

Because of his long-standing homosexual attraction to Larry Renshaw, Peter Mostyn had gone round to see him the evening before he was due to return to his home in France. At the block of flats in Abbey Road—where he was seen by the porter—he had found, not Renshaw, but Renshaw's wife, the woman who, in his eyes, had irrevocably alienated the affections of his friend. An argument had ensued, in the course of which he had shot his rival. Larry Renshaw, returning to his flat, seeing his wife's body and guessing what had happened, had immediately set off for France in pursuit of the murderer. It was Renshaw's arrival at his home that had prompted Peter Mostyn to make a clean breast of what he had done . . .

This put Larry Renshaw in a rather difficult position. Since he was now innocent, he could in theory claim back his own identity. But he had a nasty feeling that that would raise more questions than it would answer.

His instinct, now diminished to a limping, apologetic, pathetic thing, advised him to remain as Peter Mostyn, the Little Boy who has made the supreme sacrifice to protect his Big Boy.

So it was as Peter Mostyn that he was charged with, and found guilty of, the murder of Mrs. Lydia Renshaw.

And it was as Peter Mostyn that he was later charged with, and found guilty of, the murder of Larry Renshaw.

✿ ✿ ✿

The Story of
the Lost Special

SIR ARTHUR CONAN DOYLE

The confession of Herbert de Lernac, now lying under sentence of death at Marseilles, has thrown a light upon one of the most inexplicable crimes of the century—an incident which is, I believe, absolutely unprecedented in the criminal annals of any country. Although there is a reluctance to discuss the matter in official circles, and little information has been given to the Press, there are still indications that the statement of this arch-criminal is corroborated by the facts, and that we have at last found a solution for a most astounding business. As the matter is eight years old, and as its importance was somewhat obscured by a political crisis which was engaging the public attention at the time, it may be as well to state the facts as far as we have been able to ascertain them. They are collated from the Liverpool papers of that date, from the proceedings at the inquest upon John Slater, the engine-driver, and from the records of the London and West Coast Railway Company, which have been courteously put at my disposal. Briefly, they are as follows.

On the 3rd of June, 1890, a gentleman, who gave his name as Monsieur Louis Caratal, desired an interview with Mr. James Bland, the superintendent of the Central London and West Coast Station in Liverpool. He was a small man, middle-aged and dark, with a stoop which was so marked that it suggested some deformity of the spine. He was accompanied by a friend, a man of imposing physique, whose deferential manner and constant attention suggested that his position was one of dependence. This friend or companion, whose name did not transpire, was certainly a foreigner, and probably, from his swarthy complexion, either a Spaniard or a South American. One peculiarity was

observed in him. He carried in his left hand a small black leather despatch-box, and it was noticed by a sharp-eyed clerk in the Central office
that this box was fastened to his wrist by a strap. No importance was
attached to the fact at the time, but subsequent events endowed it with
some significance. Monsieur Caratal was shown up to Mr. Bland's office,
while his companion remained outside.

Monsieur Caratal's business was quickly dispatched. He had arrived
that afternoon from Central America. Affairs of the utmost importance
demanded that he should be in Paris without the loss of an unnecessary
hour. He had missed the London express. A special must be provided.
Money was of no importance. Time was everything. If the company
would speed him on his way, they might make their own terms.

Mr. Bland struck the electric bell, summoned Mr. Potter Hood, the
traffic manager, and had the matter arranged in five minutes. The train
would start in three-quarters of an hour. It would take that time to
insure that the line should be clear. The powerful engine called Rochdale
(No. 247 on the company's register) was attached to two carriages, with
a guard's van behind. The first carriage was solely for the purpose of
decreasing the inconvenience arising from the oscillation. The second
was divided, as usual, into four compartments, a first-class, a first-class
smoking, a second-class, and a second-class smoking. The first compartment, which was the nearest to the engine, was the one allotted to the
travellers. The other three were empty. The guard of the special train
was James McPherson, who had been some years in the service of the
company. The stoker, William Smith, was a new hand.

Monsieur Caratal, upon leaving the superintendent's office, rejoined
his companion, and both of them manifested extreme impatience to be
off. Having paid the money asked, which amounted to fifty pounds five
shillings, at the usual special rate of five shillings a mile, they demanded
to be shown the carriage, and at once took their seats in it, although
they were assured that the better part of an hour must elapse before the
line could be cleared. In the meantime a singular coincidence had occurred in the office which Monsieur Caratal had just quitted.

A request for a special is not a very uncommon circumstance in a rich
commercial centre, but that two should be required upon the same afternoon was most unusual. It so happened, however, that Mr. Bland had
hardly dismissed the first traveller before a second entered with a similar

request. This was a Mr. Horace Moore, a gentlemanly man of military appearance, who alleged that the sudden serious illness of his wife in London made it absolutely imperative that he should not lose an instant in starting upon the journey. His distress and anxiety were so evident that Mr. Bland did all that was possible to meet his wishes. A second special was out of the question, as the ordinary local service was already somewhat deranged by the first. There was the alternative, however, that Mr. Moore should share the expense of Monsieur Caratal's train, and should travel in the other empty first-class compartment, if Monsieur Caratal objected to having him in the one which he occupied. It was difficult to see any objection to such an arrangement, and yet Monsieur Caratal, upon the suggestion being made to him by Mr. Potter Hood, absolutely refused to consider it for an instant. The train was his, he said, and he would insist upon the exclusive use of it. All argument failed to overcome his ungracious objections, and finally the plan had to be abandoned. Mr. Horace Moore left the station in great distress, after learning that his only course was to take the ordinary slow train which leaves Liverpool at six o'clock. At four thirty-one exactly by the station clock the special train, containing the crippled Monsieur Caratal and his gigantic companion, steamed out of the Liverpool station. The line was at that time clear, and there should have been no stoppage before Manchester.

The trains of the London and West Coast Railway run over the lines of another company as far as this town, which should have been reached by the special rather before six o'clock. At a quarter after six considerable surprise and some consternation were caused amongst the officials at Liverpool by the receipt of a telegram from Manchester to say that it had not yet arrived. An inquiry directed to St. Helens, which is a third of the way between the two cities, elicited the following reply:

"*To James Bland, Superintendent, Central L. & W. C., Liverpool — Special passed here at 4:52, well up to time.—Dowser, St. Helens.*"

This telegram was received at 6:40. At 6:50 a second message was received from Manchester:

"*No sign of special as advised by you.*"

And then ten minutes later a third, more bewildering:

"Presume some mistake as to proposed running of special. Local train from St. Helens timed to follow it has just arrived and has seen nothing of it. Kindly wire advices.—Manchester."

The matter was assuming a most amazing aspect, although in some respects the last telegram was a relief to the authorities at Liverpool. If an accident had occurred to the special, it seemed hardly possible that the local train could have passed down the same line without observing it. And yet, what was the alternative? Where could the train be? Had it possibly been side-tracked for some reason in order to allow the slower train to go past? Such an explanation was possible if some small repair had to be effected. A telegram was dispatched to each of the stations between St. Helens and Manchester, and the superintendent and traffic manager waited in the utmost suspense at the instrument for the series of replies which would enable them to say for certain what had become of the missing train. The answers came back in the order of questions, which was the order of the stations beginning at the St. Helens end:

"Special passed here five o'clock.—Collins Green."

"Special passed here six past five.—Earlestown."

"Special passed here 5:10.—Newton."

"Special passed here 5:20.—Kenyon Junction."

"No special train has passed here.—Barton Moss."

The two officials stared at each other in amazement.

"This is unique in my thirty years of experience," said Mr. Bland.

"Absolutely unprecedented and inexplicable, sir. The special has gone wrong between Kenyon Junction and Barton Moss."

"And yet there is no siding, as far as my memory serves me, between the two stations. The special must have run off the metals."

"But how could the four-fifty parliamentary pass over the same line without observing it?"

"There's no alternative, Mr. Hood. It *must* be so. Possibly the local train may have observed something which may throw some light upon the matter. We will wire to Manchester for more information, and to

Kenyon Junction with instructions that the line be examined instantly as far as Barton Moss."

The answer from Manchester came within a few minutes.

"No news of missing special. Driver and guard of slow train positive that no accident between Kenyon Junction and Barton Moss. Line quite clear, and no sign of anything unusual.—Manchester."

"That driver and guard will have to go," said Mr. Bland, grimly. "There has been a wreck and they have missed it. The special has obviously run off the metals without disturbing the line—how it could have done so passes my comprehension—but so it must be, and we shall have a wire from Kenyon or Barton Moss presently to say that they have found her at the bottom of an embankment."

But Mr. Bland's prophecy was not destined to be fulfilled. A half-hour passed, and then there arrived the following message from the station-master of Kenyon Junction:

"There are no traces of the missing special. It is quite certain that she passed here, and that she did not arrive at Barton Moss. We have detached engine from goods train, and I have myself ridden down the line, but all is clear, and there is no sign of any accident."

Mr. Bland tore his hair in his perplexity.

"This is rank lunacy, Hood!" he cried. "Does a train vanish into thin air in England in broad daylight? The thing is preposterous. An engine, a tender, two carriages, a van, five human beings—and all lost on a straight line of railway! Unless we get something positive within the next hour I'll take Inspector Collins, and go down myself."

And then at last something positive did occur. It took the shape of another telegram from Kenyon Junction.

"Regret to report that the dead body of John Slater, driver of the special train, has just been found among the gorse bushes at a point two and a quarter miles from the Junction. Had fallen from his engine, pitched down the embankment, and rolled among bushes. Injuries to his head, from the fall, appear to be cause of death. Ground has now been carefully examined, and there is no trace of the missing train."

The country was, as has already been stated, in the throes of a political crisis, and the attention of the public was further distracted by the important and sensational developments in Paris, where a huge scandal threatened to destroy the Government and to wreck the reputations of many of the leading men in France. The papers were full of these events, and the singular disappearance of the special train attracted less attention than would have been the case in more peaceful times. The grotesque nature of the event helped to detract from its importance, for the papers were disinclined to believe the facts as reported to them. More than one of the London journals treated the matter as an ingenious hoax, until the coroner's inquest upon the unfortunate driver (an inquest which elicited nothing of importance) convinced them of the tragedy of the incident.

Mr. Bland, accompanied by Inspector Collins, the senior detective officer in the service of the company, went down to Kenyon Junction the same evening, and their research lasted throughout the following day, but was attended with purely negative results. Not only was no trace found of the missing train, but no conjecture could be put forward which could possibly explain the facts. At the same time, Inspector Collins's official report (which lies before me as I write) served to show that the possibilities were more numerous than might have been expected.

"In the stretch of railway between these two points," said he, "the country is dotted with ironworks and collieries. Of these, some are being worked and some have been abandoned. There are no fewer than twelve which have small gauge lines which run trolly-cars down to the main line. These can, of course, be disregarded. Besides these, however, there are seven which have or have had proper lines running down and connecting with points to the main line, so as to convey their produce from the mouth of the mine to the great centres of distribution. In every case these lines are only a few miles in length. Out of the seven, four belong to collieries which are worked out, or at least to shafts which are no longer used. These are the Redgauntlet, Hero, Slough of Despond, and Heartsease mines, the latter having ten years ago been one of the principal mines in Lancashire. These four side lines may be eliminated from our inquiry, for, to prevent possible accidents, the rails nearest to the main line have been taken up, and there is no longer any connection. There remain three other side lines leading:

(a) to the Carnstock Iron Works;

(b) to the Big Ben Colliery;

(c) to the Perseverance Colliery.

Of these the Big Ben line is not more than a quarter of a mile long, and ends at a dead wall of coal waiting removal from the mouth of the mine. Nothing had been seen or heard there of any special. The Carnstock Iron Works line was blocked all day upon the 3rd of June by sixteen truck-loads of hematite. It is a single line, and nothing could have passed. As to the Perseverance line, it is a large double line, which does a consider-able traffic, for the output of the mine is very large. On the 3rd of June this traffic proceeded as usual; hundreds of men, including a gang of railway platelayers, were working along the two miles and a quarter which constitute the total length of the line, and it is inconceivable that an unexpected train could have come down there without attracting universal attention. It may be remarked in conclusion that this branch line is nearer to St. Helens than the point at which the engine-driver was discovered, so that we have every reason to believe that the train was past that point before misfortune overtook her.

"As to John Slater, there is no clue to be gathered from his appear-ance or injuries. We can only say that, as far as we can see, he met his end by falling off his engine, though why he fell, or what became of the engine after his fall, is a question upon which I do not feel qualified to offer an opinion." In conclusion, the inspector offered his resignation to the Board, being much nettled by an accusation of incompetence in the London papers.

A month elapsed, during which both the police and the company prosecuted their inquiries without the slightest success. A reward was offered and a pardon promised in case of crime, but they were both unclaimed. Every day the public opened their papers with the conviction that so grotesque a mystery would at last be solved, but week after week passed by, and a solution remained as far off as ever. In broad daylight, upon a June afternoon in the most thickly inhabited portion of England, a train with its occupants had disappeared as completely as if some master of subtle chemistry had volatilized it into gas. Indeed, among the various conjectures which were put forward in the public Press there were some which seriously asserted that supernatural, or, at least, preter-natural, agencies had been at work, and that the deformed Monsieur

Caratal was probably a person who was better known under a less polite name. Others fixed upon his swarthy companion as being the author of the mischief, but what it was exactly which he had done could never be clearly formulated in words.

Amongst the many suggestions put forward by various newspapers or private individuals, there were one or two which were feasible enough to attract the attention of the public. One which appeared in the *Times*, over the signature of an amateur reasoner of some celebrity at that date, attempted to deal with the matter in a critical and semi-scientific manner. An extract must suffice, although the curious can see the whole letter in the issue of the 3rd of July.

"It is one of the elementary principles of practical reasoning," he remarked, "that when the impossible has been eliminated the residuum, *however improbable,* must contain the truth. It is certain that the train left Kenyon Junction. It is certain that it did not reach Barton Moss. It is in the highest degree unlikely, but still possible, that it may have taken one of the seven available side lines. It is obviously impossible for a train to run where there are no rails, and, therefore, we may reduce our improbables to the three open lines, namely, the Carnstock Iron Works, the Big Ben, and the Perseverance. Is there a secret society of colliers, an English *camorra,* which is capable of destroying both train and passengers? It is improbable, but it is not impossible. I confess that I am unable to suggest any other solution. I should certainly advise the company to direct all their energies towards the observation of those three lines, and of the workmen at the end of them. A careful supervision of the pawnbrokers' shops of the district might possibly bring some suggestive facts to light."

The suggestion coming from a recognised authority upon such matters created considerable interest, and a fierce opposition from those who considered such a statement to be a preposterous libel upon an honest and deserving set of men. The only answer to this criticism was a challenge to the objectors to lay any more feasible explanation before the public. In reply to this two others were forthcoming (*Times*, July 7th and 9th). The first suggested that the train might have run off the metals and be lying submerged in the Lancashire and Staffordshire Canal, which runs parallel to the railway for some hundreds of yards. This suggestion was thrown out of court by the published depth of the canal, which was entirely insufficient to conceal so large an object. The second correspondent wrote calling attention to the bag which appeared to be the sole luggage which the travellers had brought with them, and suggesting that some novel explosive of immense and pulverizing power might have been concealed in it. The obvious absurdity, however, of supposing that the whole train might be blown to dust while the metals remained uninjured reduced any such explanation to a farce. The investigation had drifted into this hopeless position when a new and most unexpected incident occurred, which raised hopes never destined to be fulfilled.

This was nothing less than the receipt by Mrs. McPherson of a letter from her husband, James McPherson, who had been the guard of the missing train. The letter, which was dated July 5th, 1890, was dispatched from New York, and came to hand upon July 14th. Some doubts were expressed as to its genuine character, but Mrs. McPherson was positive as to the writing, and the fact that it contained a remittance of a hundred dollars in five-dollar notes was enough in itself to discount the idea of a hoax. No address was given in the letter, which ran in this way:

"My dear Wife,—I have been thinking a great deal, and I find it very hard to give you up. The same with Lizzie. I try to fight against it, but it will always come back to me. I send you some money which will change into twenty English pounds. This should be enough to bring both Lizzie and you across the Atlantic, and you will find the Hamburg boats which stop at Southampton very good boats, and cheaper than Liverpool. If you could come here and stop at the Johnston House I would try and send you word how to meet, but things are very difficult with me at present, and I am not very happy, finding it hard to give you both up. So no more at present, from your loving husband,

"*James McPherson.*"

For a time it was confidently anticipated that this letter would lead to the clearing up of the whole matter, the more so as it was ascertained that a passenger who bore a close resemblance to the missing guard had travelled from Southampton under the name of Summers in the Hamburg and New York liner *Vistula,* which started upon the 7th of June. Mrs. McPherson and her sister Lizzie Dolton went across to New York as directed, and stayed for three weeks at the Johnston House, without hearing anything from the missing man. It is probable that some injudicious comments in the Press may have warned him that the police were using them as a bait. However this may be, it is certain that he neither wrote nor came, and the women were eventually compelled to return to Liverpool.

And so the matter stood, and has continued to stand up to the present year of 1898. Incredible as it may seem, nothing has transpired during these eight years which has shed the least light upon the extraordinary disappearance of the special train which contained Monsieur Caratal and his companion. Careful inquiries into the antecedents of the two travellers have only established the fact that Monsieur Caratal was well known as a financier and political agent in Central America, and that during his voyage to Europe he had betrayed extraordinary anxiety to reach Paris. His companion, whose name was entered upon the passenger lists as Eduardo Gomez, was a man whose record was a violent one, and whose reputation was that of a bravo and a bully. There was evidence to show, however, that he was honestly devoted to the interests of Monsieur Caratal, and that the latter, being a man of puny physique, employed the other as a guard and protector. It may be added that no information came from Paris as to what the objects of Monsieur Caratal's hurried journey may have been. This comprises all the facts of the case up to the publication in the Marseilles papers of the recent confession of Herbert de Lernac, now under sentence of death for the murder of a merchant named Bonvalot. This statement may be literally translated as follows:

It is not out of mere pride or boasting that I give this information, for, if that were my object, I could tell a dozen actions of mine which are quite as splendid; but I do it in order that certain gentlemen in Paris may understand that I, who am able here to tell about the fate of Monsieur Caratal, can also tell in whose interest and at whose request the deed was done, unless the reprieve which I am awaiting comes to me very quickly. Take warning, messieurs, before it is too late! You know Herbert de Lernac, and you are aware that his deeds are as ready as his words. Hasten then, or you are lost!

At present I shall mention no names—if you only heard the names, what would you not think!—but I shall merely tell you how cleverly I did it. I was true to my employers then, and no doubt they will be true to me now. I hope so, and until I am convinced that they have betrayed me, these names, which would convulse Europe, shall not be divulged. But on that day . . . well, I say no more!

In a word, then, there was a famous trial in Paris, in the year 1890, in connection with a monstrous scandal in politics and finance. How monstrous that scandal was can never be known save by such confidential agents as myself. The honour and careers of many of the chief men in France were at stake. You have seen a group of nine-pins standing, all so rigid, and prim, and unbending. Then there comes the ball from far away and pop, pop, pop—there are your nine-pins on the floor. Well, imagine some of the greatest men in France as these nine-pins, and then this Monsieur Caratal was the ball which could be seen coming from far away. If he arrived, then it was pop, pop, pop for all of them. It was determined that he should not arrive.

I do not accuse them all of being conscious of what was to happen. There were, as I have said, great financial as well as political interests at stake, and a syndicate was formed to manage the business. Some subscribed to the syndicate who hardly understood what were its objects. But others understood very well, and they can rely upon it that I have not forgotten their names. They had ample warning that Monsieur Caratal was coming long before he left South America, and they knew that the evidence which he held would certainly mean ruin to all of them. The syndicate had the command of an unlimited amount of money—absolutely unlimited, you understand. They looked round for an agent who was capable of wielding this gigantic power. The man chosen must be inventive, resolute, adaptive—a man in a million. They chose Herbert de Lernac, and I admit that they were right.

My duties were to choose my subordinates, to use freely the power which money gives, and to make certain that Monsieur Caratal should never arrive in Paris. With characteristic energy I set about my commission within an hour of receiving my instructions, and the steps which I took were the very best for the purpose which could possibly be devised.

A man whom I could trust was dispatched instantly to South America to travel home with Monsieur Caratal. Had he arrived in time the ship would never have reached Liverpool; but, alas, it had already started before my agent could reach it. I fitted out a small armed brig to intercept it, but again I was unfortunate. Like all great organizers I was, however, prepared for failure, and had a series of alternatives prepared, one or the other of which must succeed. You must not underrate the difficulties of my undertaking, or imagine that a mere commonplace assassination would meet the case. We must destroy not only Monsieur Caratal, but Monsieur Caratal's documents, and Monsieur Caratal's companions also, if we had reason to believe that he had communicated his secrets to them. And you must remember that they were on the alert, and keenly suspicious of any such attempt. It was a task which was in every way worthy of me, for I am always most masterful where another would be appalled.

I was all ready for Monsieur Caratal's reception in Liverpool, and I was the more eager because I had reason to believe that he had made arrangements by which he would have a considerable guard from the moment that he arrived in London. Anything which was to be done must be done between the moment of his setting foot upon the Liverpool quay and that of his arrival at the London and West Coast terminus in London. We prepared six plans, each more elaborate than the last; which plan would be used would depend upon his own movements. Do what he would, we were ready for him. If he had stayed in Liverpool, we were ready. If he took an ordinary train, an express, or a special, all was ready. Everything had been foreseen and provided for.

You may imagine that I could not do all this myself. What could I know of the English railway lines? But money can procure willing agents all the world over, and I soon had one of the acutest brains in England to assist me. I will mention no names, but it would be unjust to claim all the credit for myself. My English ally was worthy of such an alliance. He knew the London and West Coast line thoroughly, and he had the command of a band of workers who were trustworthy and intelligent. The idea was his, and my own judgment was only required in the details. We bought over several officials, amongst whom the most important was James McPherson, whom we had ascertained to be the guard most likely to be employed upon a special train. Smith, the stoker, was also in our employ. John Slater, the engine-driver, had been approached, but had been found to be obstinate and dangerous, so we desisted. We had no certainty that Monsieur Caratal would take a special, but we thought it very probable, for it was of the utmost importance to him that he should reach Paris without delay. It was for this contingency, therefore, that we made special preparations—preparations which were complete down to the last detail long before his steamer had sighted the shores of England. You will be amused to learn that there was one of my agents in the pilot-boat which brought that steamer to its moorings.

The moment that Caratal arrived in Liverpool we knew that he suspected danger and was on his guard. He had brought with him as an escort a dangerous fellow, named Gomez, a man who carried weapons, and was prepared to use them. This fellow carried Caratal's confidential papers for him, and was ready to protect either them or his master. The probability was that Caratal had taken him into his counsels, and that to remove Caratal without removing Gomez would be a mere waste of energy. It was necessary that they should be involved in a common fate, and our plans to that end were much facilitated by their request for a special train. On that special train you will understand that two out of the three servants of the company were really in our employ, at a price which would make them independent for a lifetime. I do not go so far as to say that the English are more honest than any other nation, but I have found them more expensive to buy.

I have already spoken of my English agent—who is a man with a considerable future before him, unless some complaint of the throat carries him off before his time. He had charge of all arrangements at Liverpool, whilst I was stationed at the inn at Kenyon, where I awaited a cipher signal to act. When the special was arranged for, my agent instantly telegraphed to me and warned me how soon I should have everything ready. He himself under the name of Horace Moore applied immediately for a special also, in the hope that he would be sent down with Monsieur Caratal, which might under certain circumstances have been helpful to us. If, for example, our great *coup* had failed, it would then have become the duty of my agent to have shot them both and destroyed their papers. Caratal was on his guard, however, and refused to admit any other traveller. My agent then left the station, returned by another entrance, entered the guard's van on the side farthest from the platform, and travelled down with McPherson, the guard.

In the meantime you will be interested to know what my own movements were. Everything had been prepared for days before, and only the finishing touches were needed. The side line which we had chosen had once joined the main line, but it had been disconnected. We had only to replace a few rails to connect it once more. These rails had been laid down as far as could be done without danger of attracting attention, and now it was merely a case of completing a juncture with the line, and arranging the points as they had been before. The sleepers had never been removed, and the rails, fish-plates, and rivets were all ready, for we had taken them from a siding on the abandoned portion of the line. With my small but competent band of workers, we had everything ready long before the special arrived. When it did arrive, it ran off upon the small side line so easily that the jolting of the points appears to have been entirely unnoticed by the two travellers.

Our plan had been that Smith the stoker should chloroform John Slater the driver, and so that he should vanish with the others. In this respect, and in this respect only, our plans miscarried—I except the criminal folly of McPherson in writing home to his wife. Our stoker did his business so clumsily that Slater in his struggles fell off the engine, and though fortune was with us so far that he broke his neck in the fall, still he remained as a blot upon that which would otherwise have been one of those complete masterpieces which are only to be contemplated in silent admiration. The criminal expert will find in John Slater the one flaw in all our admirable combinations. A man who has had as many triumphs as I can afford to be frank, and I therefore lay my finger upon John Slater, and I proclaim him to be a flaw.

But now I have got our special train upon the small line two kilomètres, or rather more than one mile in length, which leads, or rather used to lead, to the abandoned Heartsease mine, once one of the largest coal mines in England. You will ask how it is that no one saw the train upon this unused line. I answer that along its entire length it runs through a deep cutting, and that, unless someone had been on the edge of that cutting, he could not have seen it. There *was* someone on the edge of that cutting. I was there. And now I will tell you what I saw.

My assistant had remained at the points in order that he might superintend the switching off of the train. He had four armed men with him, so that if the train ran off the line—we thought it probable, because the points were very rusty—we might still have resources to fall back upon. Having once seen it safely on the side line, he handed over the responsibility to me. I was waiting at a point which overlooks the mouth of the mine, and I was also armed, as were my two companions. Come what might, you see, I was always ready.

The moment that the train was fairly on the side line, Smith, the stoker, slowed-down the engine, and then, having turned it on to the fullest speed again, he and McPherson, with my English lieutenant, sprang off before it was too late. It may be that it was this slowing-down which first attracted the attention of the travellers, but the train was running at full speed again before their heads appeared at the open window. It makes me smile to think how bewildered they must have

been. Picture to yourself your own feelings if, on looking out of your
luxurious carriage, you suddenly perceived that the lines upon which
you ran were rusted and corroded, red and yellow with disuse and de-
cay! What a catch must have come in their breath as in a second it
flashed upon them that it was not Manchester but Death which was
waiting for them at the end of that sinister line. But the train was running with frantic speed, rolling and rocking over the rotten line, while
the wheels made a frightful screaming sound upon the rusted surface. I
was close to them, and could see their faces. Caratal was praying, I think
—there was something like a rosary dangling out of his hand. The other
roared like a bull who smells the blood of the slaughterhouse. He saw us
standing on the bank, and he beckoned to us like a madman. Then he
tore at his wrist and threw his despatch-box out of the window in our
direction. Of course, his meaning was obvious. Here was the evidence,
and they would promise to be silent if their lives were spared. It would
have been very agreeable if we could have done so, but business is business. Besides, the train was now as much beyond our control as theirs.

He ceased howling when the train rattled round the curve and they
saw the black mouth of the mine yawning before them. We had removed
the boards which had covered it, and we had cleared the square entrance. The rails had formerly run very close to the shaft for the convenience of loading the coal, and we had only to add two or three lengths
of rail in order to lead to the very brink of the shaft. In fact, as the
lengths would not quite fit, our line projected about three feet over the
edge. We saw the two heads at the window: Caratal below, Gomez above;
but they had both been struck silent by what they saw. And yet they
could not withdraw their heads. The sight seemed to have paralyzed
them.

I had wondered how the train running at a great speed would take the
pit into which I had guided it, and I was much interested in watching it.
One of my colleagues thought that it would actually jump it, and indeed
it was not very far from doing so. Fortunately, however, it fell short, and
the buffers of the engine struck the other lip of the shaft with a tremendous crash. The funnel flew off into the air. The tender, carriages, and
van were all mashed into one jumble, which, with the remains of the
engine, choked for a minute or so the mouth of the pit. Then something
gave way in the middle, and the whole mass of green iron, smoking

coals, brass fittings, wheels, woodwork, and cushions all crumbled to-gether and crashed down into the mine. We heard the rattle, rattle, rattle, as the *débris* struck against the walls, and then quite a long time afterwards there came a deep roar as the remains of the train struck the bottom. The boiler may have burst, for a sharp crash came after the roar, and then a dense cloud of steam and smoke swirled up out of the black depths, falling in a spray as thick as rain all round us. Then the vapour shredded off into thin wisps, which floated away in the summer sunshine, and all was quiet again in the Heartsease mine.

And now, having carried out our plans so successfully, it only re-mained to leave no trace behind us. Our little band of workers at the other end had already ripped up the rails and disconnected the side line, replacing everything as it had been before. We were equally busy at the mine. The funnel and other fragments were thrown in, the shaft was planked over as it used to be, and the lines which led to it were torn up and taken away. Then, without flurry, but without delay, we all made our way out of the country, most of us to Paris, my English colleague to Manchester, and McPherson to Southampton, whence he emigrated to America. Let the English papers of that date tell how thoroughly we had done our work, and how completely we had thrown the cleverest of their detectives off our track.

You will remember that Gomez threw his bag of papers out of the window, and I need not say that I secured that bag and brought them to my employers. It may interest my employers now, however, to learn that out of that bag I took one or two little papers as a souvenir of the occasion. I have no wish to publish these papers; but, still, it is every man for himself in this world, and what else can I do if my friends will not come to my aid when I want them? Messieurs, you may believe that Herbert de Lernac is quite as formidable when he is against you as when he is with you, and that he is not a man to go to the guillotine until he has seen that every one of you is *en route* for New Caledonia. For your own sake, if not for mine, make haste, Monsieur de ——, and General ——, and Baron —— (you can fill up the blanks for yourselves as you read this). I promise you that in the next edition there will be no blanks to fill.

P.S.—As I look over my statement there is only one omission which I can see. It concerns the unfortunate man McPherson, who was foolish enough to write to his wife and to make an appointment with her in

New York. It can be imagined that when interests like ours were at stake, we could not leave them to the chance of whether a man in that class of life would or would not give away his secrets to a woman. Having once broken his oath by writing to his wife, we could not trust him any more. We took steps therefore to insure that he should not see his wife. I have sometimes thought that it would be a kindness to write to her and to assure her that there is no impediment to her marrying again.

The Three Coffins

JOHN DICKSON CARR

I
The Problem of the Savant's Study

1
The Threat

To the murder of Professor Grimaud, and later the equally incredible crime in Cagliostro Street, many fantastic terms could be applied—with reason. Those of Dr. Fell's friends who like impossible situations will not find in his casebook any puzzle more baffling or more terrifying. Thus: two murders were committed, in such fashion that the murderer must not only have been invisible; but lighter than air. According to the evidence, this person killed his first victim and literally disappeared. Again according to the evidence, he killed his second victim in the middle of an empty street, with watchers at either end; yet not a soul saw him, and no footprint appeared in the snow.

Naturally, Superintendent Hadley never for a moment believed in goblins or wizardry. And he was quite right—unless you believe in a magic that will be explained naturally in this narrative at the proper time. But several people began to wonder whether the figure which stalked through this case might not be a hollow shell. They began to wonder whether, if you took away the cap and the black coat and the child's false-face, you might not reveal·nothing inside, like a man in a certain famous romance by Mr. H. G. Wells. The figure was grisly enough, anyhow.

The words "according to the evidence" have been used. We must be very careful about the evidence when it is not given at first-hand. And in this case the reader must be told at the outset, to avoid useless confusion, on whose evidence he can absolutely rely. That is to say, it must be assumed that *somebody* is telling the truth—else there is no legitimate mystery, and, in fact, no story at all.

Therefore it must be stated that Mr. Stuart Mills at Professor Grimaud's house was not lying, was not omitting or adding anything, but telling the whole business exactly as he saw it in every case. Also it must be stated that the three independent witnesses of Cagliostro Street (Messrs. Short and Blackwin, and Police-constable Withers) were telling the exact truth.

Under these circumstances, one of the events which led up to the crime must be outlined more fully than is possible in retrospect. It was the keynote, the whiplash, the challenge. And it is retold from Dr. Fell's notes, in essential details exactly as Stuart Mills later told it to Dr. Fell and Superintendent Hadley. It occurred on the night of Wednesday, February 6th, three days before the murder, in the back parlour of the Warwick Tavern in Museum Street.

Dr. Charles Vernet Grimaud had lived in England for nearly thirty years, and spoke English without accent. Except for a few curt mannerisms when he was excited, and his habit of wearing an old-fashioned square-topped bowler hat and black string tie, he was even more British than his friends. Nobody knew much about his earlier years. He was of independent means, but he had chosen to be "occupied" and made a good thing of it financially. Professor Grimaud had been a teacher, a popular lecturer and writer. But he had done little of late, and occupied some vague unsalaried post at the British Museum which gave him access to what he called the low-magic manuscripts. Low magic was the hobby of which he had made capital: any form of picturesque supernatural devilry from vampirism to the Black Mass, over which he nodded and chuckled with childlike amusement—and got a bullet through the lung for his pains.

A sound common-sense fellow, Grimaud, with a quizzical twinkle in his eye. He spoke in rapid, gruff bursts, from deep down in his throat; and he had a trick of chuckling behind closed teeth. He was of middle size, but he had a powerful chest and enormous physical stamina. Everybody in the neighbourhood of the Museum knew his black beard, trimmed so closely that it looked only like greying stubble, his shells of eye-glasses, his upright walk as he moved along in quick short steps, raising his hat curtly or making a semaphore gesture with his umbrella.

He lived, in fact, just round the corner of a solid old house on the west side of Russell Square. The other occupants of the house were his daughter Rosette, his housekeeper, Mme. Dumont, his secretary, Stuart Mills, and a broken-down ex-teacher named Drayman, whom he kept as a sort of hanger-on to look after his books.

But his few real cronies were to be found at a sort of club they had instituted at the Warwick Tavern in Museum Street. They met four or five nights in a week, an unofficial conclave, in the snug back room reserved for that purpose. Although it was not officially a private room, few outsiders from the bar ever blundered in there, or were made welcome if they did. The most regular attendants of the club were fussy baldheaded little Pettis, the authority on ghost stories; Mangan, the newspaperman; and Burnaby, the artist; but Professor Grimaud was its undisputed Dr. Johnson.

He ruled. Nearly every night in the year (except Saturdays and Sundays, which he reserved for work), he would set out for the Warwick accompanied by Stuart Mills. He would sit in his favourite cane armchair before a blazing fire, with a glass of hot rum and water, and hold forth autocratically in the fashion he enjoyed. The discussions, Mills says, were often brilliant, although nobody except Pettis or Burnaby ever gave Professor Grimaud serious battle. Despite his affability, he had a violent temper. As a rule they were content to listen to his storehouse of knowledge about witchcraft and sham witchcraft, wherein trickery hoaxed the credulous; his childlike love of mystification and drama, wherein he would tell a story of mediaeval sorcery, and, at the end, abruptly explain all the puzzles in the fashion of a detective story. They were amusing evenings, with something of the rural-inn flavor about them, though they were tucked away behind the gaslamps of Bloomsbury. They were amusing evenings—until the night of February 6th, when the premonition of terror entered as suddenly as the wind blowing open a door.

The wind was blowing shrewdly that night. Mills says, with a threat of snow in the air. Besides himself and Grimaud, there were present at the fireside only Pettis and Mangan and Burnaby. Professor Grimaud had been speaking, with pointed gestures of his cigar, about the legend of vampirism.

"Frankly, what puzzles me," said Pettis, "is your attitude towards the whole business. Now, I study only fiction; only ghost stories that never happen. Yet in a way I believe in ghosts. But you're an authority on attested happenings—things that we're forced to call facts unless we can refute 'em. Yet you don't believe a word of what you've made the most important thing in your life. It's as though Bradshaw wrote a treatise to prove that steam-locomotion was impossible, or the editor of the Encyclopaedia Britannica inserted a preface saying that there wasn't a reliable article in the whole edition."

"Well, and why not?" said Grimaud, with that quick, gruff bark of his wherein he hardly seemed to open his mouth. "You see the moral, don't you?"

" 'Much study hath made him mad,' perhaps?" suggested Burnaby.

Grimaud continued to stare at the fire. Mills says that he seemed more angry than the casual gibe would have warranted. He sat with the cigar exactly in the middle of his mouth, drawing at it in the manner of a child sucking a peppermint-stick.

"I am the man who knew too much," he said, after a pause. "And it is not recorded that the temple priest was ever a very devout believer. However, that is beside the point. I am interested in the causes behind these superstitions. How did the superstition start? What gave it impetus, so that the gullible could believe? For example! We are speaking of the vampire legend. Now, that is a belief which prevails in Slavonic lands. Agreed? It got its firm grip on Europe when it swept in a blast out of Hungary between 1730 and 1735. Well, how did Hungary get its proof that dead men could leave their coffins, and float in the air in the form of straw or fluff until they took human shape for an attack?"

"Was there proof?" asked Burnaby.

Grimaud lifted his shoulders in a broad gesture.

"They exhumed bodies from the churchyards. They found some corpses in twisted positions, with blood on their faces and hands and shrouds. That was their proof. . . . But why not? Those were plague years. Think of all the poor devils who were buried alive though believed to be dead. Think how they struggled to get out of the coffin before they really died. You see, gentlemen? That's what I mean by the causes behind superstitions. That's what I am interested in."

"*I also,*" said a new voice, "*am interested in it.*"

Mills says that he had not heard the man come in, although he thought he felt a current of air from the opened door. Possibly they were startled by the mere intrusion of a stranger, in a room where a stranger seldom intruded and never spoke. Or it may have been the man's voice, which was harsh, husky, and faintly foreign, with a sly triumph croaking in it. Anyhow, the suddenness of it made them all switch round.

There was nothing remarkable about him, Mills says. He stood back from the firelight, with the collar of his shabby black overcoat turned up and the brim of his shabby soft hat pulled down. And what little they could see on his face was shaded by the gloved hand with which he was stroking his chin. Beyond the fact that he was tall and shabby and of gaunt build, Mills could tell nothing. But in his voice or bearing, or maybe a trick of gesture, there was something vaguely familiar while it remained foreign.

He spoke again. And his speech had a stiff, pedantic quality, as though it were a burlesque of Grimaud.

"You must forgive me, gentlemen," he said, and the triumph grew, "for intruding into your conversation. But I should like to ask the famous Professor Grimaud a question."

Nobody thought of snubbing him, Mills says. They were all intent; there was a kind of wintry power about the man, which disturbed the snug firelit room. Even Grimaud, who sat dark and solid and ugly as an Epstein figure, with his cigar halfway to his mouth and his eyes glittering behind the thin glasses, was intent. He only barked:

"Well?"

"You do not believe, then," the other went on, turning his gloved hand round from his chin only far enough to point with one finger, "that a man can get up out of his coffin; that he can move anywhere invisibly; that four walls are nothing to him; and that he is as dangerous as anything out of hell?"

"I do not," Grimaud answered, harshly. "Do you?"

"Yes. I have done it. But more! I have a brother who can do much more than I can, and is very dangerous to you. *I* don't want your life; he does. But if *he* calls on you . . ."

The climax of this wild talk snapped like a piece of slate exploding in the fire. Young Mangan, an ex-footballer, jumped to his feet. Little Pettis peered round nervously.

"Look here, Grimaud," said Pettis, "this fellow's stark mad. Shall I—" He made an uneasy gesture in the direction of the bell, but the stranger interposed.

"Look at Professor Grimaud," he said, "before you decide."

Grimaud was regarding him with a heavy, graven contempt. "No, no, no! You hear me? Let him alone. Let him talk about his brother and his coffins—"

"Three coffins," interposed the stranger.

"Three coffins," agreed Grimaud, with bristling suavity, "if you like. As many as you like, in God's name! Now perhaps you'll tell us who you are?"

The stranger's left hand came out of his pocket and laid a grubby card on the table. Somehow the sight of that prosaic visiting-card seemed to restore sane values; to whirl the whole delusion up the chimney as a joke; and to make of this harsh-voiced visitor nothing but a scarecrow of an actor with a bee under his shabby hat. For Mills saw that the card read: PIERRE FLEY. ILLUSIONIST. In one corner was printed 2B CAGLIOSTRO STREET W.C.1., and over it was scribbled OR C/O ACADEMY THEATRE. Grimaud laughed. Pettis swore and rang the bell for the waiter.

"So," remarked Grimaud, and ticked the card against his thumb. "I thought we should come to something like that. You are a conjuror, then?"

"Does the card say so?"

"Well, well, if it's a lower professional grade, I beg your pardon," nodded Grimaud. A sort of asthmatic mirth whistled in his nostrils. "I don't suppose we might see one of your illusions?"

"With pleasure," said Fley, unexpectedly.

His movement was so quick that nobody anticipated it. It looked like an attack, and was nothing of the kind—in a physical sense. He bent across the table toward Grimaud, his gloved hands twitching down the collar of his coat, and twitching it back up again before anybody else could get a glimpse of him. But Mills had an impression that he was grinning. Grimaud remained motionless and hard. Only his jaw seemed to jut and rise, so that the mouth was like a contemptuous arc in the clipped beard. And his color was a little darker, though he continued to tick the card quietly against his thumb.

"And now, before I go," said Fley, curtly, "I have a last question for the famous professor. Some one will call on you one evening soon. I also am in danger when I associate with my brother, but I am prepared to run that risk. Some one, I repeat, will call on you. Would you rather I did—or shall I send my brother?"

"Send your brother," snarled Grimaud, getting up suddenly, "and be damned!"

The door had closed behind Fley before anybody moved or spoke. And the door also closes on the only clear view we have of the events leading up to the night of Saturday, February 9th. The rest lies in flashes and glimpses, to be interpreted in jig-saw fashion as Dr. Fell later fitted together the charred fragments between the sheets of glass. The first deadly walking of the hollow man took place on that last-named night, when the side streets of London were quiet with snow and the three coffins of the prophecy were filled at last.

2
The Door

There was roaring good-humour that night round the fire in Dr. Fell's library at Number 1 Adelphi Terrace. The doctor sat ruddy-faced and enthroned in his largest, most comfortable, and decrepit chair, which had sagged and cracked across the padding in the only way a chair can be made comfortable, but which for some reason makes wives go frantic. Dr. Fell beamed with all his vastness behind the eye-glasses on the black ribbon, and hammered his cane on the hearth rug as he chuckled. He was celebrating. Dr. Fell likes to celebrate the arrival of his friends; or, in fact, anything else. And tonight there was double cause for revelry.

For one thing, his young friends, Ted and Dorothy Rampole, had arrived from America in the most exuberant of good spirits. For another his friend Hadley—now Superintendent Hadley of the C.I.D., remember —had just concluded a brilliant piece of work on the Bayswater forgery case, and was relaxing. Ted Rampole sat at one side of the hearth, and Hadley at the other, with the doctor presiding between over a steaming bowl of punch. Upstairs the Mesdames Fell, Hadley, and Rampole were conferring about something, and down here the Messieurs Fell and Hadley were already engaged in a violent argument about something else, so Ted Rampole felt at home.

Sitting back lazily in the deep chair, he remembered old days. Across from him Superintendent Hadley, with his clipped moustache and his hair the colour of dull steel, was smiling and making satiric remarks to his pipe. Dr. Fell flourished the punch ladle in thunder.

They seemed to be arguing about scientific criminology, and photography in particular. Rampole remembered hearing echoes of this, which had roused the ribald mirth of the C.I.D. During one of his absent-minded intervals of pottering about after a hobby, Dr. Fell had been snared by his friend the Bishop of Mappleham into reading Gross, Jesserich, and Mitchell. He had been bitten. Now Dr. Fell has not, it may be thankfully stated, what is called the scientific brain. But his chemical researches left the roof on the house, since fortunately, he always managed to smash the apparatus before the experiment had begun; and, beyond setting fire to the curtains with a Bunsen burner, he did little damage. His photographic work (he said) had been very successful. He had bought a Davontel microscopic camera, with an achromatic lens, and littered the place with what resembled X-ray prints of a particularly dyspeptic stomach. Also, he claimed to have perfected Dr. Gross' method of deciphering the writing on burnt paper.

Listening to Hadley jeer at this, Rampole let his mind drift drowsily. He could see the firelight moving on crooked walls of books, and hear fine snow ticking the window panes behind drawn curtains. He grinned to himself in sheer amiability. He had nothing in the excellent world to irk him—or had he? Shifting, he stared at the fire. Little things popped up like a jack-in-the-box to jab you when you were most comfortable.

Criminal cases! Of course there was nothing to it. It had been Mangan's ghoulish eagerness to enrich a good story. All the same—

"I don't give a hoot *what* Gross says," Hadley was declaring, with a flap of his hand on the chair-arm. "You people always seem to think a man is accurate just because he's thorough. In most cases the letters against burnt paper don't show up at all. . . ."

Rampole cleared his throat pacifically. "By the way," he said, "do the words 'three coffins' mean anything to you?"

There was an abrupt silence, as he had hoped there would be. Hadley regarded him suspiciously. Dr. Fell blinked over the ladle with a puzzled air, as though he vaguely associated the words with a cigarette or a pub. Then a twinkle appeared in his eye.

"Heh," he said, and rubbed his hands. "Heh-heh-heh! Making peace, hey? Or do you by any chance mean it? What coffins?"

"Well," said Rampole, "I shouldn't exactly call it a criminal case—" Hadley whistled.

"—but it's a queer business, unless Mangan was stretching things. I know Boyd Mangan quite well; he lived on the other side for a couple of years. He's a damned good fellow who's knocked about the world a lot and has a too-Celtic imagination." He paused, remembering Mangan's

dark, slovenly, rather dissipated good looks; his slow-moving ways despite his excitable temperament; his quick generosity and homely grin.
"Anyhow, he's here in London working for the *Evening Banner* now. I
ran into him this morning in the Haymarket. He dragged me into a bar
and poured out the whole story. Then," said Rampole, laying it on with
a trowel, "when he learned I knew the great Dr. Fell—"

"Rats," said Hadley, looking at him in that sharp, watchful way of his.
"Get down to cases."

"Heh-heh-heh," said Dr. Fell, highly delighted. "Shut up, will you,
Hadley? This sounds interesting, my boy. Well?"

"Well, it seems that he's a great admirer of a lecturer or writer named
Grimaud. Also he has fallen hard for Grimaud's daughter, and that
makes him a still greater admirer of the old man. The old man and some
of his friends have a habit of visiting a pub near the British Museum,
and a few nights ago something happened which seems to have shaken
up Mangan more than the antics of a casual lunatic would warrant.
While the old man was talking about corpses getting up out of their
graves, or some such cheerful subject, in walked a tall queer-looking bird
who began babbling some nonsense about himself and his brother really
being able to leave their graves and float in the air like straw." (Here
Hadley made a disgusted noise and relaxed his attention, but Dr. Fell
continued to look curiously at Rampole.) "Actually, it seems to have
been some sort of threat against this Professor Grimaud. At the end this
stranger made a threat that his brother would call on Grimaud before
long. The odd part was that, though Grimaud didn't turn a hair, Mangan swears he was actually scared green."

Hadley grunted. "That's Bloomsbury for you. But what of it? Somebody with a scary old-womanish mind—"

"That's the point," growled Dr. Fell, scowling. "He isn't. I know
Grimaud quite well. I say, Hadley, you don't know how queer it is unless
you know Grimaud. H'mf. Ha. Go on, son. How did it end?"

"Grimaud didn't say anything. In fact, he turned it into a joke and an
anti-climax that punctured the lunacy pretty well. Just after this stranger
had gone, a street musician came up against the door of the pub and
struck up 'The Daring Young Man on the Flying Trapeze.' The whole
crowd of them burst out laughing, and sanity was restored. Grimaud
smiled and said, 'Well, gentlemen, our revived corpse will have to be

even nimbler than that if he expects to float down from *my* study window.'

"They dismissed it at that. But Mangan was curious to find out who this visitor, this 'Pierre Fley,' was. Fley had given Grimaud a card with the name of a theatre on it. So the next day Mangan followed it up in the guise of getting a newspaper story. The theatre turned out to be a rather broken-down and disreputable music-hall in the East End, staging nightly variety. Mangan didn't want to run into Fley. He got into talk with the stage-door keeper, who introduced him to an acrobat in the turn before Fley. This acrobat calls himself—Lord knows why—'Pagliacci the Great,' although he's actually an Irishman and a shrewd one. He told Mangan what he knew.

"Fley is known at the theatre as 'Loony.' They know nothing about him; he speaks to nobody and ducks out after every show. But—this is the point—he is *good*. The acrobat said he didn't understand why some West End manager hadn't tumbled to it long before, unless Fley was simply unambitious. It's a sort of super-conjuring, with a specialty in vanishing-tricks. . . ."

Hadley grunted again, derisively.

"No," insisted Rampole, "so far as I can gather it isn't just the old, old stuff. Mangan says he works without an assistant, and that all his props together can go into a box the size of a coffin. If you know anything about magicians, you'll know what a whale of an incredible thing that is. In fact, the man seems hipped on the subject of coffins. Pagliacci the Great once asked him why, and got a jump he didn't expect. Fley turned round with a broad grin and said: 'Three of us were once buried alive. Only one escaped.' Pagliacci said: 'And how did you escape?' To which Fley answered, calmly: 'I didn't, you see. I was one of the two who did not escape.'"

Hadley was tugging at the lobe of his ear. He was serious now.

"Look here," he said, rather uneasily, "this may be a little more important than I'd thought. The fellow's crazy, right enough. If he's got any imaginary grudge—You say he's an alien? I might give the Home Office a call and have him looked up. Then, if he tries to make trouble for your friend . . ."

"*Has* he tried to make trouble?" asked Dr. Fell.

Rampole shifted. "Some sort of letter has come for Professor Grimaud in every post since Wednesday. He has torn 'em up without saying anything, but somebody told his daughter about the affair at the pub, and she has begun to worry. Finally, to cap the whole business, yesterday Grimaud himself began to act queerly."

"How?" asked Dr. Fell. He took away the hand with which he had been shading his eyes. His little eyes blinked at Rampole in startling sharpness.

"He phoned Mangan yesterday, and said: 'I want you to be at the house on Saturday evening. Somebody threatens to pay me a visit.' Naturally, Mangan advised warning the police, which Grimaud wouldn't hear of. Then Mangan said: 'But hang it, sir, this fellow's stark mad and he may be dangerous. Aren't you going to take *any* precautions to defend yourself?' To which the professor answered: 'Oh yes, by all means. I am going to buy a painting.'"

"A what?" demanded Hadley, sitting up.

"A painting to hang on the wall. No, I'm not joking. It seems he did buy it: it was a landscape of some sort, weird business showing trees and gravestones, and a devil of a huge landscape that it took two workmen to carry upstairs. I say 'devil of a landscape' advisedly; I haven't seen it. It was painted by an artist named Burnaby, who's a member of the club and an amateur criminologist. . . . Anyhow, that's Grimaud's idea of defending himself."

To Hadley, who was again eyeing him suspiciously, he repeated his words with some violence. They both turned to look at Dr. Fell. The doctor sat wheezing over his double chins, his big mop of hair rumpled and his hands folded on his cane. He nodded, staring at the fire. When he spoke, the room seemed to grow less comfortable.

"Have you got the address of the place, my boy?" he asked, in a colourless voice. . . . "Good. Better warm up your car, Hadley."

"Yes, but look here—!"

"When an alleged lunatic threatens a sane man," said Dr. Fell, nodding again, "then you may or may not be disturbed. But when a sane man begins to act exactly like the lunatic, then I know *I'm* jolly well disturbed. It may be nothing at all. But I don't like it." Wheezing, he hoisted himself up. "Come on, Hadley. We'll go and have a look at the place, even if we only cruise past."

A sharp wind bit through the narrow streets of the Adelphi; the snow had stopped. It lay white and unreal on the terrace, and in the Embankment gardens below.

In the Strand, bright and deserted during the theatre hour, it was churned to dirty ruts. A clock said five minutes past ten as they turned up into Aldwych. Hadley sat quiet at the wheel, his collar turned up. At Dr. Fell's roar for more speed, Hadley looked first at Rampole and then at the doctor piled into the rear seat.

"This is a lot of nonsense, you know," he snapped. "And it's none of our business. Besides, if there has been a visitor, he's probably gone by now."

"I know," said Dr. Fell. "That's what I'm afraid of."

The car shot into Southampton Row. Hadley kept hooting the horn as though to express his own feelings—but they gathered speed. The street was a bleak canyon, opening into the bleaker canyon of Russell Square. On the west side ran few foot-tracks and even fewer wheel-marks. If you know the telephone box at the north end, just after you pass Keppel Street, you will have seen the house opposite even if you have not noticed it. Rampole saw a plain, broad, three-storied front, the ground floor of stone blocks painted dun, and red brick above. Six steps led up to a big front door with a brass-edged letter-slot and brass knob. Except for two windows glowing behind drawn blinds on the ground floor over the areaway, the whole place was dark. It seemed the most prosaic house in a prosaic neighbourhood. But it did not remain so.

A blind was torn aside. One of the lighted windows went up with a bang just as they idled past. A figure climbed on the sill, outlined against the crackling blind, hesitated, and leaped. The leap carried him far over beyond the spiked area rails. He struck the pavement on one leg, slipped in the snow, and pitched out across the kerb nearly under the wheels of the car.

Hadley jammed on his brakes. He was out of the car as it skidded against the kerb, and had the man by the arm before the latter had got to his feet. But Rampole had caught a glimpse of the man's face in the headlights.

"Mangan!" he said. "What the devil—!"

Mangan was without a hat or overcoat. His eyes glittered in the light like the glassy bits of snow streaking his arms and hands.

"Who's that?" he demanded, hoarsely. "No, no, I'm all right! Let go, damn it!" He yanked loose from Hadley and began to wipe his hands on his coat. "Who—*Ted!* Listen. Get somebody. Come along yourself.

Hurry! He locked us in—there was a shot upstairs; we just heard it. He'd locked us in, you see . . ."

Looking behind him, Rampole could see a woman's figure silhouetted against the window. Hadley cut through these incoherent words.

"Steady on. Who locked you in?"

"*He* did. Fley. He's still in there. We heard the shot, and the door's too thick to break. Well, are you coming on?"

He was already running for the front steps, with Hadley and Rampole after him. Neither of the latter had expected the front door to be un-locked, but it swung open when Mangan wrenched the knob. The high hallway inside was dark except for a lamp burning on a table far at the rear. Something seemed to be standing back there, looking at them, with a face more grotesque than any they might have imagined on Pierre Fley; and then Rampole saw it was only a suit of Japanese armour decked out in its devil mask. Mangan hurried to a door at the right, and turned the key that was in the lock. The door was opened from inside by the girl whose silhouette they had seen at the window, but Mangan held her back with his arm extended. From upstairs they could hear a heavy banging noise.

"It's all right, Boyd!" cried Rampole, feeling his heart rise in his throat. "This is Superintendent Hadley—I told you about him. Where is it? What is it?"

Mangan pointed at the staircase. "Carry on. I'll take care of Rosette. He's still upstairs. He can't get out. For God's sake be careful!"

He was reaching after a clumsy weapon on the wall as they went up thick-carpeted stairs. The floor above was dark and seemed deserted. But a light shone down from a niche in the staircase to the next floor, and the banging had changed to a series of thuds.

"Dr. Grimaud!" a voice was crying. "Dr. *Gri*maud! Answer me, will you?"

Rampole had no time to analyze what seemed the exotic, thick atmo-sphere of this place. He hurried after Hadley up the second staircase, under an open archway at its top, and into a broad hallway which ran the breadth of the house instead of the length. It was panelled to the ceiling in oak, with three curtained windows in the long side of this oblong opposite the staircase, and its thick black carpet deadened every footstep. There were two doors—facing each other from the narrow ends of the oblong. The door far down at their left was open; the door at their right, only about ten feet from the staircase, remained closed despite the man who was beating on it with his fists.

This man whirled round at their approach. Although there was no illumination in the hallway itself, a yellow light streamed through the arch from the niche on the staircase—from the stomach of a great brass Buddha in the niche—and they could see everything clearly. Full in the glow stood a breathless little man who was gesturing uncertainly. He had a big goblin-like shock of hair on his big head, and peered behind big spectacles.

"Boyd?" he cried. "Drayman? I say, is that you? Who's there?"

"Police," said Hadley, and strode past him as he jumped back.

"You can't get in there," said the little man, cracking the joints of his fingers. "But we've got to get in. The door's locked on the inside. Somebody's in there with Grimaud. A gun went off—He won't answer. Where's Madame Dumont? Get Madame Dumont! That fellow's still in there, I tell you!"

Hadley turned round snappishly.

"Stop dancing and see if you can find a pair of pliers. The key's in the lock; we'll turn it from the outside. I want a pair of *pliers*. Have you got 'em?"

"I—I really don't know where—"

Hadley looked at Rampole. "Hop down to the toolbox in my car. It's under the back seat. Get the smallest pliers you can find, and you might bring along a couple of heavy spanners. If this fellow is armed—"

Rampole turned round to see Dr. Fell emerge through the arch, wheezing heavily. The doctor did not speak, but his face was not so ruddy as before. Going downstairs three at a time, Rampole blundered for what seemed hours before he found the pliers. As he returned he could hear Mangan's voice behind the closed door in the downstairs room, and the hysterical tones of a girl. . . .

Hadley, still impassive, eased the pliers gently into the keyhole. His powerful hands clamped, and began to turn towards the left.

"There's something moving in there—" said the little man.

"Got it," said Hadley, "Stand back!"

He drew on a pair of gloves, braced himself, and threw the door inward. It flapped back against the wall with a crash that shook tinglings from the chandelier inside. Nothing came out, although something was trying to come out. Except for that, the bright room was empty. Something, on which Rampole saw a good deal of blood, was painfully trying to drag itself on hands and knees across the black carpet. It choked, rolled over on its side, and lay still.

3
The False Face

"Stay in the door, two of you," Hadley said, curtly. "And if anybody's got weak nerves, don't look."

Dr. Fell lumbered in after him, and Rampole remained in the doorway with his arm extended across it. Professor Grimaud was heavy, but Hadley did not dare wrench. In that effort to crawl to the door there had been a hemorrhage which was not altogether internal, although Grimaud kept his teeth clenched against the blood. Hadley raised him up against one knee. His face had a bluish tinge under the mask of blackish-grey stubble; his eyes were closed and sunken; and he was still trying to press a sodden handkerchief to the bullet hole in his chest. They heard his breath sink thinly. Despite a draught, there was still a sharp mist of powdersmoke.

"Dead?" muttered Dr. Fell.

"Dying," said Hadley. "See the colour? He got it through the lung." He whirled round towards the little man in the doorway. "Phone for an ambulance. Quick! There's not a chance, but he may be able to say something before—"

"Yes," said Dr. Fell, with a kind of fierce sombreness; "that's the thing we're most interested in, isn't it?"

"If it's the only thing we can do," Hadley answered, coolly, "yes. Get me some sofa pillows from over there. Make him as comfortable as we can." When Grimaud's head lolled on one pillow. Hadley bent close. "Dr. Grimaud! *Dr. Grimaud!* Can you hear me?"

The waxy eyelids fluttered. Grimaud's eyes, only half open, moved in a queer, helpless, puzzled way, like a small child's in a face that you would have described as "knowing" or "civilized." He could not seem to understand what had happened. His glasses hung down on a cord from the dressing-gown; he made a weak twitching of his fingers as though he would try to raise them. His barrel chest still rose and fell slightly.

"I am from the police, Dr. Grimaud. Who did this? Don't try to answer if you can't. Nod your head. Was it the man Pierre Fley?"

A faint look of comprehension was succeeded by an even more puzzled expression. Then, distinctly Grimaud shook his head.

"Who was it, then?"

Grimaud was eager; too eager, for it defeated him. He spoke for the first and last time. His lips stuttered in those words whose interpretation, and even the exact wording itself, was so puzzling afterwards. Then he fainted.

The window in the left-hand wall was a few inches up, and a chill draught blew through. Rampole shivered. What had been a brilliant man lay inert on a couple of pillows, spilled and torn like a sack; with something rattling like clockwork inside it to show that it lived, but no more. There was too much blood in the bright, quiet room.

"My God!" Rampole said, uncontrollably, "isn't there anything we can *do?*"

Hadley was bitter. "Nothing, except get to work. 'Still in the house?' Fine lot of dummies!—oh, myself included." He pointed to the partly open window. "Of course the fellow was out of there before we were even inside the house. He certainly isn't here now."

Rampole looked round. The sharp tang of powdersmoke was blowing away, from his vision as well as from the room. He saw the place for the first time in focus.

It was a room some fifteen feet square, with walls panelled in oak and thick black carpet on the floor. In the left-hand wall (as you stood at the door) was the window with its brown velvet draperies blowing. On either side of the window stretched high bookshelves with marble busts along the top. Just out from the window, so as to get the light from the left, stood a great flat-topped desk heavy in claw-footed carving. A padded chair was pushed back from it; at the extreme left was a lamp of mosaic glass, and a bronze ash-tray over which a dead cigar had smoldered to long ash. The blotter, on which a closed calfskin book had been put down, was clean except for a tray of pens and a pile of note-slips held down by a curious little figure—a buffalo carved in yellow jade.

Rampole looked across the room at the side directly opposite the window. In that wall was a great stone fireplace, flanked also by shelves and busts. Above the fireplace, two fencing-foils hung crossed behind a blazoned shield of arms which Rampole did not (then) examine. Only on that side of the room had furniture been disarranged. Just before the fire, a long brown-leather sofa had been knocked awry, and a leather chair rolled back in a twisted-up hearth rug. There was blood on the sofa.

And finally, towards the rear wall of the room facing the door, Rampole saw the painting. Between the bookshelves in this wall there was a vast cleared space where cases had recently been removed; removed within the last few days, for the marks of their bases were still indented in the carpet. A place on the wall had been made for the painting which Grimaud would now never hang. The painting itself lay face upwards on the floor not far from where Grimaud himself lay—and it had been slashed across twice with a knife. In its frame it was fully seven feet broad by four feet high: a thing so big that Hadley had to trundle it out and switch it round in the cleared space down the centre of the room before he could prop it up for a look.

"And that," said Hadley, propping it against the back of the sofa, "is the painting he bought to 'defend himself' with, is it? Look here, Fell, do you think Grimaud was just as mad as this fellow Fley?"

Dr. Fell, who had been owlishly contemplating the window, lumbered round. "As Pierre Fley," he rumbled, and pushed back his shovel-hat, "who *didn't* commit the crime. H'm. I say, Hadley, do you see any weapon?"

"I do not. First there isn't any gun—a high-calibre automatic is what we want—and now there isn't any knife with which this thing was cut to blazes. Look at it! It looks like an ordinary landscape to me."

It was not, Rampole thought, exactly ordinary. There was a sort of blowing power about it, as though the artist had painted in a fury and caught in oils the wind that whipped those crooked trees. You felt bleakness and terror. Its motif was sombre, with a greenish tint underlying greys and blacks, except for low white mountains rising in the background. In the foreground, through the branches of a crooked tree, you could see three headstones in rank grass. Somehow it had an atmosphere like this room, subtly foreign, but as hard to identify as a faint odour. The headstones were toppling; in one way you looked at it, there was an illusion that this was because the grave mounds had begun to heave and crack across. Even the slashes did not seem to disfigure it.

Rampole started a little as he heard a trampling of feet up the staircase in the hall. Boyd Mangan burst in, thinner and more dishevelled than Rampole remembered. Even his black hair, which clung to his head in wirelike scrolls, looked rumpled. He took a quick look at the man on the floor, the heavy brows shading his eyes, and then began to rub a parchment-like cheek. Actually he was about Rampole's age, but the slanting lines drawn under his eyes made him look ten years older.

"Mills told me," he said. "Is he—?" He nodded quickly at Grimaud. Hadley ignored this. "Did you get the ambulance?"

"Chaps with a stretcher—coming now. The whole neighbourhood's filthy with hospitals, and nobody knew where to telephone. I remembered a friend of the professor's who's got a nursing-home round the corner. They're—" He stood aside to admit two uniformed attendants, and behind them a placid little clean-shaven man with a bald head. "This is Dr. Peterson—er—the police. And that's your—patient."

Dr. Peterson sucked in his cheek and hurried over. "Stretcher, boys," he said, after a brief look. "I won't dig for it here. Take him easy." He scowled and stared curiously round as the stretcher was carried out.

"Any chance?" asked Hadley.

"He might last a couple of hours; not more, and probably less. If he hadn't had the constitution of a bull he'd be dead already. Looks as though he's made a further lesion in the lung trying to exert himself—torn it across." Dr. Peterson dived into his pocket. "You'll want to send your police surgeon round, won't you? Here's my card. I'll keep the bullet when I get it. I should guess a thirty-eight bullet, fired from about ten feet off. May I ask what happened?"

"Murder," said Hadley. "Keep a nurse with him, and if he says anything have it taken down word for word." As the doctor hurried out, Hadley scribbled on a leaf of his notebook and handed it to Mangan. "Got your head about you? Good. I wish you'd phone the Hunter Street police station with these instructions; they'll get in touch with the Yard. Tell 'em what happened if they ask. Dr. Watson is to go to the address of this nursing-home, and the rest are to come on here. . . . Who's that at the door?"

The man at the door was the small, thin, top-heavy youth who had been pounding there to begin with. In full light Rampole saw a big goblin-like shock of dark red hair. He saw dull brown eyes magnified behind thick gold-rimmed glasses, and a bony face sloping outwards to a large and loose mouth. This mouth wriggled with a sonorous precision of utterance, showing wide-spaced teeth with an upward movement of the lip like a fish. The mouth looked flexible from much speaking. Every time he spoke, in fact, he had the appearance of thinly addressing an audience, raising and lowering his head as though from notes, and speaking in a penetrating singsong towards a point over his listeners' heads. You would have diagnosed a Physics B.Sc. with Socialist platform tendencies, and you would have been right. His clothes were of a reddish-check pattern, and his fingers were laced together before him. His earlier terror had changed to inscrutable calm. He bowed a little, and replied without expression:

"I am Stuart Mills. I am, or was, Dr. Grimaud's secretary." His big eyes moved round. "May I ask what has happened to the—culprit?"

"Presumably," said Hadley, "he escaped through the window while we were all so sure he couldn't get out. Now, Mr. Mills—"

"Pardon me," the sing-song voice interposed, with a sort of aerial detachment about it. "He must have been a very extraordinary man if he did that. Have you examined the window?"

"He's right, Hadley," said Dr. Fell, wheezing heavily. "Take a look! This business is beginning to worry me. I tell you in all sincerity that, if our man didn't leave here by way of the door . . ."

"He did not. I am not," announced Mills, and smiled, "the only witness to that. I saw it all from start to finish."

". . . then he must have been lighter than air to leave by the window. Open the window and have a look. H'mf, wait! We'd better search the room first."

There was nobody hidden in the room. Afterwards, growling under his breath, Hadley eased the window up. Unbroken snow—stretching flat up to the window-frame itself—covered all the wide sill outside. Rampole bent out and looked round.

There was a bright moon in the west, and every detail stood out sharp as a wood-cut. It was a good fifty feet to the ground; the wall fell away in a drop of smooth, wet stone. Just below there was a back yard, like that of all the houses in this row, surrounded by a low wall. The snow lay unbroken in this courtyard, or any other as far as they could look, and along the tops of the walls. Below in the whole side of the house there were no windows whatever. The only windows were on this top floor; and the nearest one to this room was in the hallway to the left, a good thirty feet away. To the right, the nearest window would have been in the adjoining house, an equal distance away. Ahead there lay a vast chessboard of adjoining back yards from houses lining the square, so that the nearest house was several hundred yards away. Finally, there stretched above this window a smooth upward run of stone for some fifteen feet to the roof—whose slope afforded neither hold for the fingers nor for the attaching of a rope.

But Hadley, craning his neck out, pointed malevolently.

"All the same, that's it," he declared. "Look there! Suppose he first hitched a rope to a chimney or something, and had it dangling outside the window when he paid his visit. Then he kills Grimaud, swings out, climbs up over the edge of the roof, crawls up to untie the rope from the chimney, and gets away. There will be plenty of tracks of *that*, right enough. So—"

"Yes," said Mills voice. "That is why I must tell you that there aren't any."

Hadley looked round. Mills had been examining the fireplace, but now he regarded them with his widespaced teeth showing in an impassive smile, though his eyes looked nervous and there was sweat on his forehead.

"You see," he continued, lifting his hand with the forefinger raised, "as soon as I perceived that the man in the false face had disappeared—"

"The *what?*" said Hadley.

"The false face. Do I make myself clear?"

"No. We must see whether we can't extract some sense presently, Mr. Mills. In the meantime, what is this business about the roof?"

"There are no tracks or marks of any nature on it, you see," the other answered, with a bright expression of his eyes as he opened them wide. This was another trick of his, smiling and staring as though with inspiration, even if it sometimes seemed rather a half-witted inspiration. He raised his forefinger again. "I repeat, gentlemen: when I saw that the man in the false face had evidently disappeared, I foresaw difficulties for myself—"

"Why?"

"Because I myself had this door under observation, and I should have been compelled to asseverate that the man had not come out. Very well. It was therefore deducible that he must have left (a) by way of a rope to the roof, or (b) by means of climbing up inside the chimney to the roof. This was a simple mathematical certainty. If $PQ = pq$, it is therefore quite obvious that $PQ = pq + pB + qa + aB$."

"It is indeed?" said Hadley, with restraint. "Well?"

"At the end of this hallway which you see—that is to say, which you could see if the door were open," pursued Mills, with unshakable exactitude, "I have my workroom. From there a door leads to the attic, and thence to a trap-door opening out on the roof. By raising the trap-door I could see clearly both sides of the roof over this room. The snow was not marked in any fashion."

"You didn't go out there?" demanded Hadley.

"No. I could not have kept my footing if I had. In fact, I do not at the moment see how this could be done even in dry weather."

Dr. Fell turned a radiant face. He seemed to resist a desire to pick up this phenomenon and dangle him in the air like an ingenious toy.

"And what then, my boy?" he enquired, affably. "I mean, what did you think when your equation was shot to blazes?"

Mills remained smiling and inflexibly profound. "Ah, that remains to be seen. I am a mathematician, sir. I never permit myself to think." He folded his arms. "But I wish to call this to your attention, gentlemen, in spite of my firm statement that he did not leave by the door."

"Suppose you tell us exactly what did happen here tonight," urged Hadley, passing a hand across his forehead. He sat down at the desk and took out his notebook. "Easy, now! We'll lead up to it gradually. How long have you worked for Professor Grimaud?"

"For three years and eight months," said Mills, clicking his teeth. Rampole saw that, in the legal atmosphere of the notebook, he was compressing himself to give brief answers.

"What are your duties?"

"Partly correspondence and general secretarial duties. In greater ratio to assist him in preparing his new work, *The Origin and History of Middle-European Superstitions, Together with* . . ."

"Quite so. How many people live in this house?"

"Besides Dr. Grimaud and myself, four."

"Yes, yes, well?"

"Ah, I see! You wish their names. Rosette Grimaud, his daughter. Madame Dumont, who is housekeeper. An elderly friend of Dr. Grimaud, named Drayman. A general maid whose last name I have never yet been told, but whose first name is Annie."

"How many were here tonight when this happened?"

Mills brought the toe of his shoe forward, balanced himself, and studied it, another trick of his. "That, obviously, I cannot say with certainty. I will tell you what I know." He rocked back and forth. "At the conclusion of dinner, at seven-thirty, Dr. Grimaud came up here to work. This is his custom on Saturday evenings. He told me he did not wish to be disturbed until eleven o'clock; that is also the inviolable custom. He said, however,"—quite suddenly beads of sweat appeared on the young man's forehead again, though he remained impassive—"he said, however, that he might have a visitor about half-past nine."

"Did he say who this visitor might be?"

"He did not."

Hadley leaned forward. "Come, now, Mr. Mills! Haven't you heard of any threat to him? Didn't you hear what happened on Wednesday evening?"

"I—er—I had previous information of it, certainly. In fact, I was at the Warwick Tavern myself. I suppose Mangan told you?"

Uneasily, but with startling vividness, he sketched out the story. Meanwhile, Dr. Fell had stumped away and was going through an examination he several times made that night. He seemed most interested in the fireplace. Since Rampole had already heard an outline of the tavern incident, he did not listen to Mills; he watched Dr. Fell. The doctor inspected the blood-stains splashing the top and right arm of the disarranged sofa. There were more bloodstains on the hearth, though they were difficult to follow against the black carpet. A struggle there? Yet, Rampole saw, the fire-irons were upright in their rack, in such a position that a struggle before the hearth must have sent them clattering. A very small coal fire had been nearly smothered under a drift of charred papers.

Dr. Fell was muttering to himself. He reared up to examine the escutcheon. To Rampole, no student of heraldry, this presented itself as a divided shield in red and blue and silver: a black eagle and crescent moon in the upper part, and in the lower a wedge of what looked like rooks on a chessboard. Though its colours were darkened, it glowed with barbaric richness in a queerly barbaric room. Dr. Fell grunted.

But he did not speak until he began to examine the books in the shelves at the left of the fireplace. After the fashion of bibliophiles, he pounced. Then he began to yank out book after book, glance at the title-page, and shoot it back in again. Also, he seemed to have pounced on the most disreputable-looking volumes in the shelves. He was raising some dust, and making so much noise that it jarred across Mills' sing-song recital. Then he rose up and waved books at them in excited intent-ness.

"I say, Hadley, I don't want to interrupt, but this is very rummy and very revealing. Gabriel Dobrentei, *'Yorick 'es Eliza levelei,'* two volumes. *'Shakespere Minden Munkái,'* nine volumes in different editions. And here's a name—" He stopped. "H'mf. Ha. Do you know anything about these, Mr. Mills? They're the only books in the lot that haven't been dusted."

Mills was startled out of his recital. "I—I don't know. I believe they are from a batch that Dr. Grimaud meant for the attic. Mr. Drayman found them put away behind others when we removed some bookcases from the room last night to make room for the painting to be hung. . . . Where was I, Mr. Hadley? Ah yes! Well, when Dr. Grimaud told me that he might have a visitor tonight, I had no reason to assume it was the man of the Warwick Tavern. He did not say so."

"What exactly, did he say?"

"I—you see, after dinner I was working in the big library downstairs. He suggested that I should come upstairs to my workroom at half-past nine, sit with my door open and—and 'keep an eye on' this room, in case . . ."

"In case?"

Mills cleared his throat. "He was not specific."

"He told you all this," snapped Hadley, "and you still did not suspect who might be coming?"

"I think," interposed Dr. Fell, wheezing gently, "that I may be able to explain what our young friend means. It must have been rather a strug-gle. He means that in spite of the sternest convictions of the youngest B.Sc., in spite of the stoutest buckler emblazoned with $x^2 + 2xy + y^2$, he still had enough imagination to get the wind up over that scene at the Warwick Tavern. And he didn't want to know any more than it was his duty to know. Is that it, hey?"

"I do not admit it, sir," Mills returned, with relief, nevertheless. "My motives have nothing to do with the facts. You will observe that I carried out my orders exactly. I came up here at precisely half-past nine—"

"Where were the others then? Steady, now!" urged Hadley. "Don't say you can't reply with certainty; just tell us where you *think* they were."

"To the best of my knowledge, Miss Rosette Grimaud and Mangan were in the drawing-room, playing cards. Drayman had told me that he was going out; I did not see him."

"And Madame Dumont?"

"I met her as I came up here. She was coming out with Dr. Grimaud's after-dinner coffee; that is to say, with the remnants of it. . . . I went to my workroom, left my door open, and drew out the typewriter desk so that I could face the hallway while I worked. At exactly"—he shut his eyes, and opened them again—"at exactly fifteen minutes to ten I heard the front-door bell ring. The electric bell is on the second floor, and I heard it plainly.

"Two minutes later, Madame Dumont came up from the staircase. She was carrying one of those trays on which it is customary to place visiting-cards. She was about to knock at the door when I was startled to see the—er—the tall man come upstairs directly after her. She turned round and saw him. She then exclaimed certain words which I am unable to repeat verbatim, but whose purport was to ask why he had not waited downstairs; and she seemed agitated. The—er—tall man made no reply. He walked to the door, and without haste turned down the collar of his coat and removed his cap, which he placed in his overcoat pocket. I think that he laughed, and that Madame Dumont cried out something, shrank back against the wall, and hurried to open the door. Dr. Grimaud appeared on the threshold in some evident annoyance; his exact words were, 'What the devil is all this row about? Then he stood stockstill, looking up at the tall man; and his exact words were, 'In God's name, who are *you?*' "

Mills' sing-song voice was hurling the words faster; his smile had become rather ghastly, although he tried to make it merely bright.

"Steady, Mr. Mills. Did you get a good look at this tall man?"

"A fairly good look. As he came up under the arch from the staircase, he glanced down in my direction."

"Well?"

"The collar of his overcoat was turned up, and he wore a peaked cap. But I am endowed with what is called 'long sight,' gentlemen, and I could distinctly observe the conformation and colour of the nose and mouth. He was wearing a child's false face, a species of mask in papier-maché. I have an impression that it was long, of a pinkish colour, and had a wide-open mouth. And, so far as my observation went, he did not remove it. I think I am safe in asserting—"

"You are generally right, are you not?" asked a cold voice from the doorway. "It was a false face. And, unfortunately, he did not remove it."

4

The Impossible

She stood in the doorway, looking from one to the other of them. Rampole received the impression of an extraordinary woman without knowing why he felt it. There was nothing remarkable about her, except a certain brilliance and vividness of the black eyes, which had a sanded, reddish look as though of smart without tears. She seemed all contradiction. She was short, and of sturdy figure, with a broad face, rather high cheekbones, and a shiny skin: yet Rampole had a curious impression that she could have been beautiful if she had tried. Her dark brown hair was coiled loosely over her ears, and she wore the plainest of dark dresses slashed with white across the breast: yet she did not look dowdy.

Poise, strength, carriage, what? The word "electric" is meaningless, yet it conveys the wave that came with her; something of crackle and heat and power, like a blow. She moved towards them, her shoes creaking. The prominent dark eyes, turned a little upwards at the outer corner, sought Hadley. She was rubbing the palms of her hands together before her, up and down. Rampole was conscious of two things—that the killing of Professor Grimaud had struck her with a hurt from which she would never recover, and would have left her stunned and crying if it had not been for one other wish.

"I am Ernestine Dumont," she said, as though interpreting the thought. "I have come to help you find the man who shot Charles."

She spoke almost without accent, but with a certain slur and deadness. The palms of her hands continued to brush up and down.

"When I heard, I could not come up—at first. Then I wished to go with him in the ambulance to the nursing-home, but the doctor would not let me. He said the police would wish to speak with me. Yes, I suppose that was wise."

Hadley rose and moved out for her the chair in which he had been sitting.

"Please sit down, madame. We should like to hear your own statement in a moment. I must ask you to listen carefully to what Mr. Mills is saying, in case you should be required to corroborate. . . ."

She shivered in the cold from the open window, and Dr. Fell, who had been watching her sharply, lumbered over to close it. Then she glanced at the fireplace, where the fire had smouldered nearly out under the mass of burnt papers. Realizing Hadley's words over the gap, she nodded. She looked at Mills absent-mindedly, with a sort of vacant affection which showed almost in a smile.

"Yes, of course. He is a nice poor fool boy, and he means well. Do you not, Stuart? You must go on, by all means. I will—look."

Mills showed no anger, if he felt any. His eyelids flickered a few times, and he folded his arms.

"If it gives the Pythoness any pleasure to think so," he sang, imperturbably, "I have no objection. But perhaps I had better continue. Er— where was I?"

"Dr. Grimaud's words when he saw the visitor, you told us, were, 'In God's name, who are *you?*' Then?"

"Ah yes! He was not wearing his eye-glasses, which were hanging down by their cord; his sight is not good without them, and I am under the impression that he mistook the mask for a real face. But before he could raise the glasses, the stranger made so quick a movement that I was rather confused, and he darted in at the door. Dr. Grimaud made a movement to get in front of him, but he was too quick, and I heard him laughing. When he got inside—" Mills stopped, apparently puzzled. "This is most extraordinary. I am under the impression that Madame Dumont, although she was shrinking back against the wall, closed the door after him. I recall that she had her hand on the knob."

Ernestine Dumont blazed.

"What do you wish to be understood by that, little boy?" she asked. "You fool, be sure you know what you are saying. Do you think I would willingly have had that man alone with Charles?—He kicked the door shut behind him. Then he turned the key in the lock."

"One moment, madame. . . . Is that true, Mr. Mills?"

"I wish it clearly understood," Mills sang, "that I am merely trying to give *every* fact and even every impression. I meant nothing. I accept the correction. He did, as the Pythoness says, turn the key in the lock."

"That is what he calls his little joke, 'the Pythoness,' " Mme. Dumont said, savagely. "Ah, bah!"

Mills smiled. "To resume, gentlemen: I can well believe that the Pythoness was agitated. She began to call Dr. Grimaud's Christian name, and to shake the knob of the door. I heard voices inside, but I was some distance away, and you will perceive that the door is thick." He pointed. "I could distinguish nothing until, after an interval of about thirty seconds, during which it is deducible that the tall man removed his mask, Dr. Grimaud called out, to the Pythoness, rather angrily: 'Go away, you fool. I can handle this.' "

"I see. Did he seem—afraid, or anything of the sort?"

The secretary reflected. "On the contrary, I should have said that he sounded in a sense relieved."

"And you, madame: you obeyed and went away without further—?"

"Yes."

"Even though," said Hadley, suavely, "I presume it is not usual for practical jokers to call at the house in false faces and act in such a wild way? You knew, I suppose, of the threat to your employer?"

"I have obeyed Charles Grimaud for over twenty years," said the woman, very quietly. The word "employer" had stung her hard. Her reddish, sanded eyes were intent. "And I have never known a situation which he could *not* handle. Obey! Of course I did; I would always obey. Besides, you do not understand. You have asked me nothing." The contempt changed to a half-smile. "But this is interesting—psychologically, as Charles would say. You have not asked Stuart why *he* obeyed, and caused no fuss. That is merely because you think he would have been afraid. I thank you for the implied compliment. Please go on."

Rampole had a sensation of watching a supple wrist on a swordsman. Hadley seemed to feel this, too, although he addressed the secretary.

"Do you remember, Mr. Mills, the time at which this tall man went into the room?"

"It was at ten minutes to ten. There is a clock on my typewriter desk, you see."

"And when did you hear the shot?"

"At exactly ten minutes past ten."

"You mean to say that you watched the door all that time?"

"I did, most assuredly." He cleared his throat. "In spite of what the Pythoness describes as my timidity, I was the first to reach the door when the shot was fired. It was still locked on the inside, as you gentlemen saw—you yourselves arrived very shortly afterwards."

"During the twenty minutes while these two were together, did you hear any voices, movements, sounds of any kind?"

"At one point I was under the impression that I heard voices raised, and something which I can only describe as resembling a bumping sound. But I was some distance away. . . ." He began to rock again, and stare, as he met Hadley's cold eye. The sweat broke out again. "Now I am aware, of course, that I am under the necessity of telling what must seem an absolutely incredible story. Yet, gentlemen, I *swear* . . . !" Quite suddenly he lifted a plump fist and his voice went high.

"That is all right, Stuart," the woman said, gently. "I can confirm you."

Hadley was suavely grim. "That would be just as well, I think. One last question, Mr. Mills. Can you give an exact outward description of this caller you saw? . . . In a moment, madame!" he broke off, turning quickly. "In good time. Well, Mr. Mills?"

"I can state accurately that he wore a long black overcoat, and a peaked cap of some brownish material. His trousers were darkish. I did not observe his shoes. His hair, when he took off the cap—" Mills stopped. "This is extraordinary. I do not wish to be fanciful, but now that I recall it, his hair had a dark, painted, *shiny* look, if you understand me, almost as though his whole head were made of papier-maché."

Hadley, who had been pacing up and down past the big picture, turned on him in a way that brought a squeak from Mills.

"Gentlemen," cried the latter, "you asked me to tell you what I saw. And that is what I saw. It is true."

"Go on," said Hadley, grimly.

"I believe he was wearing gloves, although he put his hands in his pockets and I cannot be absolutely certain. He was tall, a good three or four inches taller than Dr. Grimaud, and of a medium—er—anatomical structure. That is all I can definitely assert."

"Did he look like the man Pierre Fley?"

"Well—yes. That is to say, in one way yes, and another no. I should have said this man was even taller than Fley, and not quite so thin, but I would not be prepared to swear it."

During this questioning, Rampole had been watching Dr. Fell out of the tail of his eye. The doctor, his big cloak humped and his shovel-hat under one arm, had been lumbering about the room with annoyed digs of his cane at the carpet. He bent down to blink at things until his eye-

glasses tumbled off his nose. He looked at the painting, along the rows
of books, at the jade buffalo on the desk. He went down wheezingly to
look at the fireplace, and hoisted himself up again to study the coat of
arms over it. Toward the last he seemed to become blankly amiable—
and yet always, Rampole saw, he was watching Mme. Dumont. She
seemed to fascinate him. There was something rather terrible in that
small bright eye, which would swing round the second he had finished
looking at something. And the woman knew it. Her hands were clenched
in her lap. She tried to ignore him, but her glance would come round
again. It was as though they were fighting an intangible battle.

"There are other questions, Mr. Mills," said Hadley, "particularly
about this Warwick Tavern affair and that painting. But they can wait
until we get things in order. . . . Would you mind going down and
asking Miss Grimaud and Mr. Mangan to come up here? Also Mr. Drayman, if he has returned? . . . Thanks. Stop a bit! Er—any questions,
Fell?"

Dr. Fell shook his head with broad amiability. Rampole could see the
woman's white knuckles tighten.

"*Must* your friend walk about in that way?" she cried, abruptly, and
in the shrillness of the voice she pronounced the *W* as *V.* "It is maddening. It is—"

Hadley studied her. "I understand, madame. Unfortunately, that is
his way."

"Who are you, then? You walk into my house—"

"I had better explain. I am the superintendent of the Criminal Investigation Department. This is Mr. Rampole. And the other man, of
whom you may have heard, is Dr. Gideon Fell."

"Yes. Yes, I thought so." She nodded, and then slapped the desk beside her. "Well, well, well! Even so, must you forget your manners? Must
you make the room freezing with your open windows, even? May we not
at least have a fire to warm us?"

"I don't advise it, you know," said Dr. Fell. "That is, until we see
what papers have already been burnt there. It must have been rather a
bonfire."

Ernestine Dumont said, wearily: "Oh, why must you be such fools?
Why do you sit here? You know quite well who did this. It was the fellow
Fley, and you know it. Well, well, well? Why don't you go after him?
Why do you sit here when I tell you he did it?"

There was a look about her, a trance-like and gypsyish look of hatred. She seemed to see Fley go down a trap on a gallows.

"Do you know Fley?" Hadley snapped.

"No, no, I never saw him! I mean, before this. But I know what Charles told me."

"Which was what?"

"Ah, *zut!* This Fley is a lunatic. Charles never knew him, but the man had some insane idea that he made fun of the occult, you understand. He has a brother who is"—she gestured—"the same, you understand? Well, Charles told me that he might call here tonight at half-past nine. If he did, I was to admit him. But when I took down Charles' coffee-tray at half-past nine, Charles laughed and said that if the man had not arrived by then he would not come at all. Charles said: 'People with a grudge are prompt.'" She sat back, squaring her shoulders. "Well, he was wrong. The door bell rang at a quarter to ten. I answered it. There was a man standing on the step. He held out a visiting-card, and said, 'Will you take this to Professor Grimaud and ask if he will see me?'"

Hadley leaned against the edge of the leather sofa and studied her.

"What about the false face, madame? Didn't you think that a little odd?"

"I did not *see* the false face! Have you noticed there is only one light in the downstairs hall? Well! There was a street lamp behind him, and all I could see was his shape. He spoke so courteously, you understand, and handed in the card, that for a second I did not realize . . ."

"One moment, please. Would you recognize that voice if you heard it again?"

She moved her shoulders as though she were shifting a weight on her back. "Yes! I don't know—yes, yes! But it did not sound right, you see; muffled up in that mask, I think now. Ah, why are men such—!" She leaned back in the chair, and for no apparent reason tears brimmed over her eyes. "I do not see such things! I am real, I am honest! If some one does you a hurt, good. You lie in wait for him and kill him. Then your friends go into court and swear you were somewhere else. You do not put on a painted mask, like old Drayman with the children on Guy Fawkes night; you do not hand in visiting-cards like this horror of a man, and go upstairs and kill a man and then vanish out of a window. It is like the legends they told us when I was a girl. . . ." Her cynical poise cracked across in hysteria. "Oh, my God, Charles! My poor Charles!"

Hadley waited, very quietly. She had herself in hand in a moment; she also was as still, and as foreign and inexplicable, as the big painting which faced her in tortured sombreness across the room. The gust of emotion left her relieved and watchful, though she breathed hard. They could hear the scraping noise of her finger nails on the chair-arms.

"The man said," Hadley prompted, " 'Will you take this to Professor Grimaud and ask if he will see me?' Very well. Now at this first, we understand, Miss Grimaud and Mr. Mangan were downstairs in the drawing-room near the front door?"

She looked at him curiously.

"Now that is a strange thing to ask. I wonder why you ask it? Yes—yes, I suppose they were. I did not notice."

"Do you remember whether the drawing-room door was open or shut?"

"I don't know. But I should think it was shut, or I should have seen more light in the hall."

"Go on, please."

"Well, when the man gave me the card, I was going to say, 'Step in, please, and I will see,' when I *did* see. I could not be faced with him alone—a lunatic? I wished to go up and get Charles to come down. So I said, 'Wait there and I will see.' And I very quickly slammed the door in his face, so that the spring-lock caught and he could not get in. Then I went back to the lamp and looked at the card. I still have it; I had no chance to deliver it. And it was blank."

"Blank?"

"There was no writing or printing on it at all. I went up to show it to Charles, and plead with him to come down. But the poor little Mills has told you what happened. I was going to knock at the door, when I heard somebody come upstairs behind me. I looked round, and there he was coming big and thin behind me. But I will swear, I will swear on the Cross, that I had locked that door downstairs. Well, I was not afraid of him! No! I asked him what he meant by coming upstairs.

"And still, you understand, I could not see the false face, because his back was to that bright light on the stairs, which shows up all this end of the hall and Charles's door. But he said, in French, '*Madame, you cannot keep me out like that,*' and turned down his collar and put his cap in his pocket. I opened the door because I knew he would not dare face Charles, just as Charles opened it from inside. Then I saw the mask,

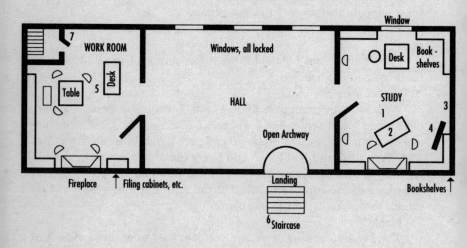

WORK ROOM

7

Desk

5

Table

Fireplace   ↑ Filing cabinets, etc.

Windows, all locked

HALL

Open Archway

Landing

6 Staircase

Window

Desk

Book-
shelves

STUDY

1

2

3

4

Bookshelves ↑

which was a pinkish colour like flesh. And before I could do anything he made a horrible jump inside, and kicked the door shut, and turned the key in the lock."

She paused, as though she had got through the worst part of the recital, and could breathe more easily now.

"And then?"

She said, dully: "I went away, as Charles ordered me to do. I made no fuss or scene. But I did not go far. I went a little way down the stairs, where I could still see the door to this room, and I did not leave my post any more than poor Stuart did. It was—horrible. I am not a young girl, you understand. I was there when the shot was fired; I was there when Stuart ran forward and began to pound the door; I was even there when you people began to come upstairs. But I could not stand it. I *knew* what had happened. When I felt myself going faint, I had just time to get to my room at the foot of that flight when I was—ill. Women sometimes are." The pale lips cracked across her oily face in a smile, shakily. "But Stuart was right; nobody left that room. God help us both, we are telling the truth. However else that horror left the room, he did not leave by the door. . . . And now please, please, will you let me go to the nursing-home to see Charles?"

5

The Jig-Saw Words

It was Dr. Fell who answered. He was standing with his back to the fireplace, a vast black-caped figure under the fencing-foils and shield of arms. He seemed to fit there, like a baron out of feudalism, with the bookshelves and white busts towering on either side of him. But he did not look like a very terrible Front de Boeuf. His eye-glasses were coming askew on his nose as he bit off the end of a cigar, turned, and expectorated it neatly into the fireplace.

"Ma'am," he said, turning back with a long challenging sound in his nose, like a battle cry, "we shall not detain you very long. And it is only fair to say that I don't in the least doubt your story, any more than I doubt Mills'. Before getting down to business, I will prove that I believe you. . . . Ma'am, do you remember what time to-night it stopped snowing?"

She was looking at him with hard, bright, defensive eyes. She had evidently heard of Dr. Fell.

"Does it matter? I think it was about half-past nine. Yes! I remember, because when I came up to collect Charles's coffee-tray I looked out of the window and I noticed that it had stopped. Does it matter?"

"Oh, very much, ma'am. Otherwise we have only half an impossible situation. . . . And you are quite right. H'mf. Remember, Hadley? Half-past nine is about the time it stopped. Right, Hadley?"

"Yes," admitted the superintendent. He also looked at Dr. Fell suspiciously. He had learned to distrust that blank stare over the several chins. "Granting that it was half-past nine, what then?"

"Not only had it stopped snowing a full forty minutes before the visitor made his escape from this room," pursued the doctor, with a meditative air, "but it had stopped fifteen minutes before the visitor even arrived at this house. That's true, ma'am? Eh? He rang the door-bell at a quarter to ten? Good. . . . Now, Hadley, do you remember when *we* arrived at this house? Did you notice that, before you and Rampole and young Mangan went charging in, *there wasn't a single footprint of the flight of steps leading up to the front door, or even the pavement leading up to the steps?* You see, I did. I remained behind to make sure."

Hadley straightened up with a kind of muffled roar. "By God! that's right! The whole pavement was clean. It—" He stopped, and swung slowly round to Mme. Dumont. "So this, you say, is your evidence of why you believe madame's story? Fell, have you gone mad, too? We hear a story of how a man rang the door-bell and walked through a locked door fifteen minutes after the snow had stopped, and yet—"

Dr. Fell opened his eyes. Then a series of chuckles ran up the ridges of his waistcoat.

"I say, son, why are you so flabbergasted? Apparently he sailed out of here without leaving a footprint. Why should it upset you to learn that he also sailed in?"

"I don't know," the other admitted, stubbornly. "But, hang it, it does! In my experience with locked-room murders, getting in and getting out are two very different things. It would throw my universe off balance if I found an impossible situation that worked sensibly both ways. Never mind! You say—"

"Please listen. I say," Mme. Dumont interposed, pale but with the bunched muscles standing out at the corners of her jaws, "that I am telling the absolute truth, so help me God!"

"And I believe you," said Dr. Fell. "You mustn't let Hadley's stern Scotch common-sense overawe you. He will believe it, too, before I'm through with him. But my point is this. I have shown you, haven't I, that I have strong faith in you—if I can credit what you have said? Very well. I only want to warn you not to upset that faith. I should not dream of doubting what you have already told me. But I fancy I shall very strongly doubt what you are going to tell me in a moment."

Hadley half-closed one eye. "I was afraid of that. I always dread the time when you begin to trot out your damned paradoxes. Seriously, now—"

"Please go on," the woman said, stolidly.

"Humph. Harrumph. Thanks. Now, ma'am, how long have you been Grimaud's housekeeper? No, I'll change that. How long have you been with him?"

"For over twenty-five years," she answered. "I was more than his housekeeper—once."

She had been looking at her interlocked fingers, which she moved in and out; but now she lifted her head. Her eyes had a fierce, steady glaze, as though she wondered how much she dared tell. It was the expression of one peering round a corner at an enemy, ready for instant flight.

"I tell you that," she went on quietly, "in the hope that you will give me your word to keep silent. You will find it in your alien records at Bow Street, and you may make unnecessary trouble that has nothing to do with this matter. It is not for myself, you understand, Rosette Grimaud is my daughter. She was born here, and there had to be a record. But she does not know it—nobody knows it. Please, please, can I trust you to keep silent?"

The glaze over her eyes was changing to a different one. She had not raised her voice, but there was a terrible urgency in it.

"Why, ma'am," said Dr. Fell, a wrinkle in his forehead, "I can't see that it's any of our business. Can you? We shall certainly say nothing about it."

"You mean that?"

"Ma'am," the doctor said, gently, "I don't know the young lady, but I'll bet you a tanner you're worrying yourself unnecessarily, and that you've both been worrying yourselves unnecessarily for years. She probably knows already. Children do. And she's trying to keep it from *you*. And the whole world goes skew-whiff because we like to pretend that people under twenty will never have any emotions, and people over forty never had. Humph, Let's forget it. Shall we?" He beamed. "What I wanted to ask you, Where did you first meet Grimaud? Before you came to England?"

She breathed hard. She answered, but vaguely, as though she were thinking of something else.

"Yes. In Paris."

"You are a Parisienne?"

"Er—what—? No, no, not by birth! I am of the provinces. But I worked there when I met him. I was a costumier."

Hadley looked up from jotting in his notebook. " 'Costumier?' " he repeated. "Do you mean a dressmaker, or what?"

"No, no, I mean what I say. I was one of the women who made costumes for the opera and the ballet. We worked in the Opéra itself. You can find record of that! And, if it will save you time, I will tell you that I was never married and my maiden name was Ernestine Dumont."

"And Grimaud?" Dr. Fell asked, sharply. "Where was he from?"

"From the south of France, I think. But he studied at Paris. His family are all dead, so that will not help you. He inherited their money."

There was an air of tension which these casual questions did not seem to warrant. Dr. Fell's next three questions were so extraordinary that Hadley stared up from his notebook, and Ernestine Dumont, who had recovered herself, shifted uneasily, with a wary brilliance in her eyes.

"What is your religious faith, ma'am?"

"I am a Unitarian. Why?"

"H'm, yes. Did Grimaud ever visit the United States, or has he any friends there?"

"Never. And he has no friends that I know of there."

"Do the words 'seven towers' mean anything to you, ma'am?"

"No!" cried Ernestine Dumont, and went oily white.

Dr. Fell, who had finished lighting his cigar, blinked at her out of the smoke. He lumbered out from the hearth and round the sofa, so that she shrank back. But he only indicated the big painting with his cane, tracing out the line of the white mountains in the background of the picture.

"I won't ask you whether you know what this represents," he continued, "but I will ask you whether Grimaud told you why he bought it. What sort of charm was it supposed to contain, anyhow? What power did it have to ward off the bullet or the evil eye? What sort of weight could its influ . . ." He stopped, as though recalling something rather startling. Then he reached out, wheezing, to lift the picture off the floor with one hand and turn it curiously from side to side. "Oh, my hat!" said Dr. Fell, with explosive absent-mindedness. "O Lord! O Bacchus! Wow!"

"What is it?" demanded Hadley, jumping forward. "Do you see anything?"

"No, I don't see anything," said Dr. Fell argumentatively. "That's just the point. Well, madame?"

"I think," said the woman, in a shaky voice, "that you are the strangest man I ever met. No. I do not know what that thing is. Charles would not tell me. He only grunted and laughed in his throat. Why don't you ask the artist? Burnaby painted it. He should know. But you people will never do anything sensible. It looks like a picture of a country that does not exist."

Dr. Fell nodded sombrely. "I am afraid you are right, ma'am. I don't think it does exist. And if three people were buried there, it might be difficult to find them—mightn't it?"

"Will you stop talking this gibberish?" shouted Hadley; and then Hadley was taken aback by the fact, that this gibberish had struck Ernestine Dumont like a blow. She got to her feet to conceal the effect of those meaningless words.

"I am going," she said. "You cannot stop me. You are all crazy. You sit here raving while—while you let Pierre Fley escape. Why don't you go after him? Why don't you *do* something?"

"Because you see, ma'am . . . Grimaud himself said that Pierre Fley did not do this thing." While she was still staring at him, he let the painting fall back with a thump against the sofa. The scene out of a country which did not exist, and yet where three gravestones stood among crooked trees, brought Rampole's mind to an edge of terror. He was still looking at the painting when they heard footsteps on the stairs.

It was a heartening thing to see the prosaic, earnest, hatchet face of Sergeant Betts, whom Rampole remembered from the Tower of London case. Behind him came two cheerful plainclothes men carrying the photographic and fingerprint apparatus. A uniformed policeman stood behind Mills, Boyd Mangan, and the girl who had been in the drawing room. She pushed through this group into the room.

"Boyd told me you wanted me," she said, in a quiet but very unsteady voice. "But I insisted on going over with the ambulance, you see. You'd better get over there as quick as you can, Aunt Ernestine. They say he's —going."

She tried to be efficient and peremptory, even in the way she drew off her gloves; but she could not manage it. She had those decided manners which come in the early twenties from lack of experience and lack of opposition. Rampole was rather startled to see that her hair was a heavy blond colour, bobbed and drawn behind the ears. Her face was squarish, with somewhat high cheek bones; not beautiful, but disturbing and vivid in the way that makes you think of old times even when you do not know what times. Her rather broad mouth was painted dark red, but in contrast to this, and to the firm shape of the whole face, the long hazel eyes were of an uneasy gentleness. She looked round quickly, and shrank back towards Mangan with her fur coat drawn tightly round. She was not far from sheer hysteria.

"Will you please hurry and tell me what you want?" she cried. "Don't you realize he's *dying?* Aunt Ernestine . . ."

"If these gentlemen are through with me," the woman said, stolidly, "I will go. I meant to go, as you know."

She was docile all of a sudden. But it was a heavy docility, with a half challenge in it—as though there were limits. Something bristled between these two women, something like the uneasiness in Rosette Grimaud's eyes. They looked at each other quickly, without a direct glance; they seemed to burlesque each other's movements, to become abruptly conscious of it, and stop. Hadley prolonged the silence, as though he were confronting two suspects with each other at Scotland Yard. Then:

"Mr. Mangan," he said, briskly, "will you take Miss Grimaud down to Mr. Mills' room at the end of the hall? Thank you. We shall be with you in a moment. Mr. Mills, just a second! Wait. . . . Betts!"

"Sir?"

"I want you to do some important work. Did Mangan tell you to bring ropes and a flashlight? . . . Good. I want you to go up on the roof of this place and search every inch of it for a footprint or a mark of any kind, especially over this room. Then go down to the yard behind this place, and both adjoining yards, and see if you can find any marks there. Mr. Mills will show you how to get to the roof. . . . Preston! Is Preston here?"

A sharp-nosed young man bustled in from the hall—the Sergeant Preston whose business it was to poke for secret places and who had discovered the evidence behind the panel in the Death Watch case.

"Go over this room for any secret entrance whatever, understand? Tear the place to bits if you like. See if anybody could get up the chimney. . . . You fellows carry on with the prints and pictures. Mark out every blood stain in chalk before you photograph. But don't disturb that burnt paper in the fireplace. . . . Constable! Where the hell's that constable?"

"Here, sir."

"Did Bow Street phone through the address of a man named Fley— Pierre Fley? . . . Right. Go to wherever he lives and pick him up. Bring him here. If he's not there, wait. Have they sent a man to the theatre where he works? . . . All right. That's all. Hop to it, everybody."

He strode out into the hall, muttering to himself. Dr. Fell, lumbering after him, was for the first time imbued with a ghoulish eagerness. He poked at the superintendent's arm with his shovel-hat.

"Look here, Hadley," he urged, "you go down and attend to the questioning, hey? I think I can be of much more service if I stay behind and assist those duffers with their photographs . . ."

"No, I'm hanged if you spoil any more plates!" said the other, with heat. "Those film packs cost money, and, besides, we need the evidence. Now, I want to talk to you privately and plainly. What's all this wild mumbo-jumbo about seven towers, and people buried in countries that never existed? I've seen you in these fits of mystification before, but never quite so bad. Let's compare notes. What did you . . . yes, yes. What is it?"

He turned irascibly as Stuart Mills plucked at his arm.

"Er—before I conduct the sergeant up to the roof," said Mills, imperturbably, "I think I had better tell you that in case you wish to see Mr. Drayman, he is here in the house."

"Drayman? Oh yes! When did he get back?"

Mills frowned. "So far as I am able to deduce, he did not get back. I should say he had never left. A short time ago I had occasion to look into his room . . ."

"Why?" enquired Dr. Fell, with sudden interest.

The secretary blinked impassively. "I was curious, sir. I discovered him asleep there, and it will be difficult to rouse him; I believe he has taken a sleeping draught. Mr. Drayman is fond of taking them. I do not mean that he is an inebriate or a drug-user, but quite literally that he is very fond of taking sleeping draughts."

"Rummiest household *I* ever heard of," declared Hadley, after a pause, to nobody in particular. "Anything else?"

"Yes, sir. There is a friend of Dr. Grimaud's downstairs. He has just arrived, and he would like to see you. I do not think it is anything of immediate importance, but he is a member of the circle at the Warwick Tavern. His name is Pettis—Mr. Anthony Pettis."

"Pettis, eh?" repeated Dr. Fell, rubbing his chin. "I wonder if that's the Pettis who collects the ghost stories and writes those excellent prefaces? H'm, yes. I dare say. Now, how would he fit into this?"

"I'm asking you how anything fits into it," insisted Hadley. "Look here. I can't see this fellow now, unless he's got something important to tell. Get his address, will you, and say I'll call on him in the morning? Thanks." He turned to Dr. Fell. "Now carry on about the seven towers and the country that never existed."

The doctor waited until Mills had led Sergeant Betts down the big hall to the door at the opposite end. A subdued mutter of voices from Grimaud's room was the only noise. The bright yellow light still streamed from the great arch of the staircase, illuminating the whole hall. Dr. Fell took a few lumbering steps round the hall, looking up and down and then across at the three brown-draped windows. He pulled back the drapes and made certain that these three windows were all firmly locked on the inside. Then he beckoned Hadley and Rampole towards the staircase.

"Scrum," he said. "A little comparing of notes, I admit, will be advisable before we tackle the next witnesses. But not for a second about the seven towers. I'll lead up to those gradually, like Childe Roland, Hadley, a few disjointed words—the only real evidence we have, because it comes from the victim—may be the most important clue of all. I mean those few mutterings from Grimaud just before he fainted. I hope to heaven we all heard 'em. Remember, you asked him whether Fley had shot him. He shook his head. Then you asked him who had done it. What did he say?—I want to ask each of you in turn what you thought you heard."

He looked at Rampole. The American's wits were muddled. He had a strong recollection of certain words, but the whole was confused by a too-vivid picture of a blood-soaked chest and a writhing neck. He hesitated.

"The first thing he said," Rampole answered, "sounded to me like *hover*—"

"Nonsense," interrupted Hadley. "I jotted it all down right away. The first thing he said was *Bath* or 'the bath,' though I'm hanged if I see—"

"Steady now. Your own gibberish," said Dr. Fell, "is a little worse than mine. Go on, Ted."

"Well, I wouldn't swear to any of it. But then I did hear the words *not suicide,* and *he couldn't use rope.* Next there was some reference to a *roof* and to *snow* and to a *fox.* The last thing I heard sounded like *too much light.* Again, I wouldn't swear it was all in consecutive order."

Hadley was indulgent. "You've got it all twisted, even if you have got one or two of the points." He seemed uneasy, nevertheless. "All the same, I'm bound to admit that my notes don't make much better sense. After the word *bath,* he said *salt and wine.* You're right about the rope, although I heard nothing about suicide. Roof and snow are correct; *too much light* came afterwards; then *got gun.* Finally, he did say something about a fox, and the last thing—I barely heard it because of that blood—was something like *Don't blame poor* . . . And that's all."

"O Lord!" groaned Dr. Fell. He stared from one to the other. "This is terrible. Gents, I was going to be very triumphant over you. I was going to explain what he said. But I am beaten by the staggering size of your respective ears. I never heard all that out of the gabble, although I dare say you're within some distance of the truth. Wow!"

"Well, what's your version?" demanded Hadley.

The doctor stumped up and down, rumbling. "I heard only the first few words. They make tolerably good sense if I'm right—*if* I'm right. But the rest is a nightmare. I have visions of foxes running across roofs in the snow, or—"

"Lycanthropy?" suggested Rampole. "Did anybody mention were-wolves?"

"No, and nobody's going to!" roared Hadley. He struck his notebook. "To put everything in order, Rampole, I'll write down what you thought you heard for comparison. . . . So. We now have:

"Your list. *Hover. Not suicide. He couldn't use rope. Roof. Snow. Fox. Too much light.*

"My list. *Bath. Salt. Wine. He couldn't use rope. Roof. Snow. Too much light. Got gun. Don't blame poor—*

"There we are. And, as usual, with your own brand of cussedness, Fell, you're most confident about the most senseless part. I might rig up an explanation that could fit together all the latter part, but how the devil does a dying man give us a clue by talking about baths and salt and wine?"

Dr. Fell stared at his cigar, which had gone out.

"H'mf, yes. We'd better clear up a little of that. There are puzzles enough as it is. Let's go gently along the road. . . . First, my lad, what happened in that room after Grimaud was shot?"

"How the hell should I know? That's what I'm asking you. If there's no secret entrance—"

"No, no, I don't mean how the vanishing-trick was worked. You're obsessed with that business, Hadley; so obsessed that you don't stop to ask yourself what *else* happened. First let's get clear the obvious things for which we can find an explanation, and go on from there. Humph. Now, then, what clearly did happen in that room after the man was shot? First, all the marks centred round the fireplace—"

"You mean the fellow climbed up the chimney?"

"I am absolutely certain he didn't," said Dr. Fell, testily. "That flue is so narrow that you can barely get your fist through. Control yourself and think. First, a heavy sofa was pushed away from in front of the fireplace; there was a good deal of blood on the top, as though Grimaud had slipped or leaned against it. The hearth rug was pulled or kicked away; there was blood on that; and a fireside chair was shoved away. Finally, I found spots of blood on the hearth and even in the fireplace. They led us to a huge mass of burnt papers that had nearly smothered the fire.

"Now, consider the behaviour of the faithful Madame Dumont. As soon as she came into that room, she was very terribly concerned about that fireplace. She kept looking at it all the time, and nearly grew hysterical when she saw I was doing so, too. She even, you recall, made the foolish blunder of asking us to light a fire—even though she must have known that the police wouldn't go fooling about with coals and kindling to make witnesses comfortable on the very scene of a crime. No, no, my boy. Somebody had tried to burn letters or documents there. She wanted to be certain they had been destroyed."

Hadley said, heavily: "So she knew about it, then? And yet you said you believed her story?"

"Yes. I did and do believe her story—about the visitor and the crime. What I don't believe is the information she gave us about herself and Grimaud. . . . Now think again what happened! The intruder shot Grimaud. Yet Grimaud, although he is still conscious, does not shout for help, try to stop the killer, make a row of any kind, or even open the door when Mills is pounding there. But he does do something. He does do something, with such a violent exertion that he tears wide open the wound in his lung: as you heard the doctor say.

"And I'll tell you what he did to. He knew he was a goner and that the police would be in. He had in his possession a mass of things that *must* be destroyed. It was more vital to destroy them than to catch the man who shot him or even save his own life. He lurched back and forth from that fireplace, burning this evidence. Hence the sofa knocked away, the hearth rug, the stains of blood. . . . You understand now?"

There was a silence in the bright bleak hall.

"And the Dumont woman?" Hadley asked, heavily.

"She knew it, of course. It was their joint secret. And she happens to love him."

"If this is true, it must have been something pretty damned important that he destroyed." said Hadley, staring. "How the devil do you know all this? What secret could they have had, anyway? And what makes you think they had any dangerous secret at all?"

Dr. Fell pressed his hands to his temples and ruffled his big mop of hair. He spoke argumentatively.

"I may be able to tell you a little of it," he said, "although there are parts that puzzle me beyond hope. You see, neither Grimaud nor Dumont is any more French than I am. A woman with those cheekbones, a woman who pronounces the silent 'h' in honest, never came from a Latin race. But that's not important. They're both Magyar. To be precise: Grimaud came originally from Hungary. His real name is Károly, or Charles, or Grimaud Horváth. He probably had a French mother. He came from the principality of Transylvania, formerly a part of the Hungarian kingdom but annexed by Rumania since the war. In the late 'nineties or early nineteen hundreds, Károly Grimaud Horváth and his two brothers were all sent to prison. Did I tell you he had two brothers? One we haven't seen, but the other now calls himself Pierre Fley.

"I don't know what crime the three brothers Horváth had committed, but they were sent to the prison of Siebenturmen, to work in the salt-mines near Tradj in the Carpathian Mountains. Charles probably escaped. Now, the rather deadly 'secret' in his life can't concern the fact that he was sent to prison or even that he escaped before finishing the sentence; the Hungarian kingdom is broken up, and its authority no longer exists. More probably he did some black devilry that concerned the other two brothers; something pretty horrible concerning those three coffins, and people buried alive, that would hang him even now if it were discovered. . . . That's all I can hazard at the moment. Has anybody got a match?"

6
The Seven Towers

In the long pause after this recital, Hadley tossed a matchbox to the doctor and eyed him malevolently.

"Are you joking?" he asked. "Or is this black magic?"

"Not about a thing like this. I wish I could. Those three coffins. . . . Dammit, Hadley!" muttered Dr. Fell, knocking his fists against his temples, "I wish I could see a glimmer—something. . . ."

"You seem to have done pretty well. Have you been holding out information, of how do you know all that? Stop a bit!" He looked at his notebook. "'Hover.' 'Bath.' 'Salt.' 'Wine.' In other words, you're trying to tell us that what Grimaud really said was, 'Horváth,' and 'salt-mine'? Take it easy, now! If that's your basis, we're going to have a lot of star-gazing on our hands to twist round the rest of those words."

"This assumption of rage," said Dr. Fell, "shows that you agree with me. Thankee. As you yourself shrewdly pointed out, dying men do not commonly mention bath salts. If your version is correct, we might as well all retire to a padded cell. He really said it, Hadley. I heard him. You asked him for a name, didn't you? Was it Fley? No. Who was it, then? And he answered. Horváth."

"Which *you* say is his own name."

"Yes. Look here," said Dr. Fell. "If it will salve your wounds, I will cheerfully admit that it wasn't fair detective work, and that I didn't show you the sources of my information from that room. I'll show you them presently, although Lord knows I tried to show them to you at the time.

"It's like this. We hear from Ted Rampole about a queer customer who threatens Grimaud, and significantly talks about people 'buried alive.' Grimaud takes this seriously; he has known that man before and knows what he is talking about, since for some reason he buys a picture depicting three graves. When you ask Grimaud who shot him, he answers with the name 'Horváth' and says something about salt-mines. Whether or not you think that's odd of a French professor, it is rather odd to find up over his mantelpiece the device of a shield graven thus: *coupé, a demi-eagle issuant sable, in chief a moon argent . . .*"

"I think we may omit the heraldry," said Hadley, with a sort of evil dignity. "What is it?"

"It's the arms of Transylvania. Dead since the war, of course, and hardly very well known in England (or France) even before that. First a Slavic name, and then Slavic arms. Next those books I showed you. Know what they were? They were English books translated into the Magyar. I couldn't pretend to read 'em—"

"Thank God."

"—but I could at least recognize the complete works of Shakespeare, and Sterne's *Letters from Yorick to Eliza,* and Pope's *Essay on Man.* That was so startling that I examined 'em all."

"Why startling?" asked Rampole. "There are all sorts of funny books in anybody's library. There are in your own."

"Certainly. But suppose a scholarly Frenchman wants to read English. Well, he reads it in English, or he gets it translated into French. But he very seldom insists on getting its full flavour by first having it translated into Hungarian. In other words, they weren't *Hungarian* books; they weren't even French books on which a Frenchman might have been practising his Magyar; they were English. It meant that whoever owned those books, his native language was Hungarian. I went through all of 'em, hoping to find a name. When I found *Károly Grimaud Horváth, 1898* faded out on one flyleaf, it seemed to put the tin hat on it.

"If Horváth was his real name, why had he kept up this pretence for so long? Think of the words 'buried alive,' and 'salt-mines,' and there is a gleam. But when you ask him who shot him, he said Horváth. A moment like that is probably the only time when a man isn't willing to talk about himself; he didn't mean himself, but somebody else named

Horváth. While I was thinking of that, our excellent Mills was telling you about the man called Fley at the public house. Mills said that there seemed something very familiar about Fley, although he had never seen him before, and that his speech sounded like a burlesque of Grimaud's. Was it Grimaud he suggested? Brother, brother, brother! You see, there were three coffins, but Fley mentioned only two brothers. It sounded like a third.

"While I was thinking about this, there entered the obviously Slavic Madame Dumont. If I could establish Grimaud as coming from Transylvania, it would narrow down our search when we tried to find out his history. But it had to be done delicately. Notice that carved figure of a buffalo on Grimaud's desk? What does that suggest to you?"

"It doesn't suggest Transylvania, I can tell you that," the superintendent growled. "It's more like the Wild West—Buffalo Bill—Indians. Hold on! Was that why you asked her whether Grimaud had ever been in the United States?"

Dr. Fell nodded guiltily. "It seemed an innocent question, and she answered. You see, if he'd got that figure in an American curio shop— H'm. Hadley, I've been in Hungary. I went in my younger and lither days, when I'd just read *Dracula*. Transylvania was the only European country where buffaloes were bred; they used 'em like oxen. Hungary was full of mixed religious beliefs; but Transylvania was Unitarian. I asked Madame Ernestine, and she qualified. Then I threw my hand grenade. If Grimaud had been innocently associated with salt-mines, it wouldn't matter. But I named the only prison in Transylvania where convicts were used to work the salt-mines. I named the Siebenturmen— or the Seven Towers—without even saying it was a prison. It almost finished her. Now perhaps you will understand my remark about the seven towers and the country that does not now exist. And for God's sake will somebody give me a match?"

"You've got 'em," said Hadley. He took a few strides round the hall, accepted a cigar from the now bland and beaming Dr. Fell, and muttered to himself: "Yes—so far as it goes, it seems reasonable enough. Your long shot about the prison worked. But the whole basis of your case, that these three people are brothers, is pure surmise. In fact, I think it's the weakest part of the case. . . ."

"Oh, admitted. But what then?"

"Only that it's the crucial joint. Suppose Grimaud didn't mean that a person named Horváth had shot him, but was only referring to himself in some way? Then the murderer might be anybody. But if there are three brothers, and he did mean that, the thing is simple. We come back to the belief that Pierre Fley *did* shoot him, after all, or Fley's brother did. We can put our hands on Fley at any time, and as for the brother—"

"Are you sure you'd recognize the brother," said Dr. Fell, reflectively, "if you met him?"

"How do you mean?"

"I was thinking of Grimaud. He spoke English perfectly, and also passed perfectly for a Frenchman. I don't doubt he did study at Paris, and that the Dumont woman did make costumes at the Opéra. Anyhow, there he went stumping round Bloomsbury for nearly thirty years, gruff, good-natured, harmless, with his clipped beard and his square bowler, keeping a check on a savage temper and placidly lecturing in public. Nobody ever saw a devil in him—though somehow I fancy it must have been a wily, brilliant devil. Nobody ever suspected. He could have shaved, cultivated tweeds and a port-wine complexion, and passed for a British squire, or anything else he liked. . . . Then what about this third brother? He's the one who intrigues me. Suppose he's right here somewhere in our midst, in some guise or other, and nobody knows him for what he really is?"

"Possibly. But we don't know anything about the brother."

Dr. Fell, struggling to light his cigar, peered up with extraordinary intentness.

"I know. That's what bothers me, Hadley." He rumbled for a moment, and then blew out the match with a vast puff. "We have two theoretical brothers who have taken French names: Charles and Pierre. Then there's a third. For the sake of clearness and argument, let's call him Henri—"

"Look here. You're not going to tell me you know something about him also?"

"On the contrary," returned Dr. Fell, with a sort of ferocity, "I'm going to emphasize just how little we know about him. We know about Charles and Pierre. But we haven't even the merest hint about Henri, *although* Pierre appears to be forever talking about him and using him as a threat. It is, 'My brother who can do much more than I can.' 'My brother who wants your life.' 'I am in danger when I associate with him.' And so on. But no shape comes out of the smoke, neither man nor goblin. Son, it worries me. I think that ugly presence is behind the whole business, controlling it, using poor half-crazy Pierre for his own ends, and probably as dangerous to Pierre as to Charles. I can't help feeling that this presence staged the whole scene at the Warwick Tavern; that he's somewhere close at hand and watchful; that—" Dr. Fell stared round, as though he expected to see something move or speak in the empty hall. Then he added: "You know, I hope your constable gets hold of Pierre and keeps hold of him. Maybe his usefulness is over."

Hadley made a vague gesture. He bit at the end of his clipped moustache. "Yes, I know," he said; "but let's stick to the facts. The facts will be difficult enough to dig out, I warn you. I'll cable the Rumanian police tonight. But if Transylvania's been annexed, in the fuss and uproar there may be few official records left. The Bolshies were storming through there just after the war, weren't they? Um. Anyhow, we want facts! Come on and let's get after Mangan and Grimaud's daughter. I'm not entirely satisfied with *their* behaviour, by the way. . . ."

"Eh? Why?"

"I mean, always provided the Dumont woman is telling the truth," Hadley amended. "You seem to think she is. But, as I've heard the thing, wasn't Mangan here tonight at Grimaud's request, in case the visitor should drop in? Yes. Then he seems to have been rather a tame watchdog. He was sitting in a room near the front door. The door-bell rings— if Dumont's not lying—and enter the mysterious visitor. All this time Mangan doesn't show any curiosity; he sits in the room with the door shut, pays no attention to the visitor, and only kicks up a row when he hears a shot and suddenly finds that the door has been locked. Is that logical?"

"Nothing is logical," said Dr. Fell. "Not even—But that can wait."

They went down the long hall, and Hadley assumed his most tactful and impassive manner when he opened the door. It was a room somewhat smaller than the other, lined with orderly books and wooden filing cabinets. It had a plain rag carpet on the floor, hard business-like chairs, and a sickly fire. Under a green-shaded hanging-lamp, Mills' typewriter desk was drawn up directly facing the door. On one side of the machine neat manuscript sheets lay clipped in a wire basket; on the other side stood a glass of milk, a dish of dried prunes, and a copy of Williamson's *Differential and Integral Calculus.*

"I'll bet he drinks mineral water, too," said Dr. Fell, in some agitation. "I'll swear by all my gods he drinks mineral water and reads that sort of thing for fun. I'll bet—" He stopped at a violent nudge from Hadley, who was speaking to Rosette Grimaud across the room. Hadley introduced the three of them.

"Naturally, Miss Grimaud, I don't wish to distress you at this time—"

"Please don't say anything," she said. She was sitting before the fire, so tense that she jumped a little. "I mean—just don't say anything about *that*. You see, I'm fond of him, but not so fond that it hurts terribly unless somebody begins to talk about it. Then I begin to think."

She pressed her hands against her temples. In the firelight, with her fur coat thrown back, there was again a contrast between eyes and face. But it was a changing contrast. She had her mother's intense personality shaped into blond, square-faced, rather barbaric Slavic beauty. Yet in one moment the face would be hard and the long hazel eyes gentle and uneasy, like the curate's daughter. And in the next moment the face would be softened and the eyes brilliantly hard, like the devil's daughter. Her thin eyebrows turned a little upwards at the outer corners, but she had a broad humorous mouth. She was restless, sleek, and puzzling. Behind her stood Mangan in gloomy helplessness.

"One thing, though," she went on, pounding her fist slowly on the arm of the chair—"one thing I've got to know, though, before you start your third degree." She nodded towards a little door across the room, and spoke breathlessly. "Stuart's—showing that detective of yours up to the roof. Is it true, *is* it true what we hear about a man getting in—and out—and killing my father—without—without—?"

"Better let me handle this, Hadley," said Dr. Fell, very quietly.

The doctor, Rampole knew, was firmly under the impression that he was a model of tact. Very often this tact resembled a load of bricks coming through a skylight. But his utter conviction that he was doing the thing handsomely, his vast good-nature and complete naïveté, had an effect that the most skilled tact could never have produced. It was as though he had slid down on the bricks himself to offer sympathy or shake hands. And people instantly began to tell him all about themselves.

"Harrumph!" he snorted. "Of course it's not true, Miss Grimaud. We know all about how the blighter worked his trick, even if it was done by somebody you never heard of." She looked up quickly. "Furthermore, there'll be no third degree, and your father has a fighting chance to pull through. Look here, Miss Grimaud, haven't I met you somewhere before?"

"Oh, I know you're trying to make me feel better," she said, with a faint smile. "Boyd has told me about you, but—"

"No, I mean it," wheezed Dr. Fell, seriously. He squinted at memory. "H'm, yes. Got it! You're at London University, aren't you? Of course. And you're in a debating circle or something? It seems to me I officiated as chairman when your team debated Woman's Rights in the World, wasn't it?"

"That's Rosette," assented Mangan, gloomily. "She's a strong feminist. She says—"

"Heh-heh-heh," said Dr. Fell. "I remember now." He was radiant, and pointed with a vast flipper. "She may be a feminist, my boy, but she has startling lapses. In fact, I remember that debate as ending in the most beautiful and appalling row I ever heard outside a Pacifist meeting. You were on the side for Woman's Rights, Miss Grimaud, and against the Tyranny of Man. Yes, yes. You entered very pale and serious and solemn, and stayed like that until your own side began to present their case. They went on something awful, but you didn't look pleased. Then one lean female carried on for twenty minutes about what women needed for an ideal state of existence, but you only seemed to get madder and madder. So when your turn came, all you did was rise to proclaim in silvery ringing tones that what women needed for an ideal existence was less talking and more copulation."

"Good God!" said Mangan, and jumped.

"Well, I felt like it—then," said Rosette, hotly. "But you don't need to think . . ."

"Or perhaps you didn't say copulation," ruminated Dr. Fell. "Anyway, the effect of that terrible word was beyond description. It was as though you had whispered, 'Asbestos!' to a gang of pyromaniacs. Unfortunately, I tried to keep a straight face by swallowing water. This, my friends, is a practice to which I am unaccustomed. The result had the general aspect, to eye and ear, of a bomb exploding in an aquarium. But I was wondering whether you and Mr. Mangan often discussed these subjects. They must be enlightening talks. What was the argument about this evening, for instance?"

Both of them began to speak at once, chaotically. Dr. Fell beamed, and they both stopped with a startled expression.

"Yes," nodded the doctor. "You understand now, don't you, that there's nothing to be afraid of in talking to the police? And that you can speak as freely as you like? It'll be better, you know. Let's face the thing and clear it up sensibly now, among ourselves, hey?"

"Right," said Rosette. "Has somebody got a cigarette?"

Hadley looked at Rampole. "The old blighter's done it," he said.

The old blighter was again lighting his cigar while Mangan fumbled in his haste to produce cigarettes. Then Dr. Fell pointed.

"Now, I want to know about a very rummy thing," he continued. "Were you two kids so engrossed in each other that you didn't notice anything tonight until the rumpus started? As I understand it, Mangan, Professor Grimaud asked you here tonight to be on the lookout for possible trouble. Why didn't you? Didn't you hear the door-bell?"

Mangan's swarthy face was clouded. He made a fierce gesture.

"Oh, I admit it's my fault. But at the time I never gave it a thought. How was I going to know? Of course I heard the door-bell. In fact, we both spoke to the fellow—"

"You *what?*" interrupted Hadley, striding past Dr. Fell.

"Certainly. Otherwise you don't think I'd have let him get past me and upstairs, do you? But he said he was old Pettis—Anthony Pettis, you know."

7

The Guy Fawkes Visitor

Of course we know now that it wasn't Pettis," Mangan pursued, lighting the girl's cigarette with an angry snap of his lighter, "Pettis must be all of five feet four inches tall. Besides, now that I think back on it, it wasn't even a very exact imitation of his voice. But he sang out and spoke in words Pettis always uses. . . ."

Dr. Fell scowled. "But didn't it strike you as queer that even a collector of ghost stories should walk about dressed up like a Fifth of November Guy? Is he addicted to pranks?"

Rosette Grimaud looked up with a startled expression. She held out her cigarette level and motionless, as though she were pointing, and then twitched to look at Mangan. When she turned back again there was a

narrow flash of those long eyes, a deepness of breathing like anger or
cruelty, or enlightenment. They had shared a thought—and Mangan
was much the more disturbed by it. He had the air of one who is trying
to be a good fellow and at peace with the world, if the world would only
let him. Rampole had a feeling that this secret thought did not concern
Pettis at all, for Mangan stumbled before he could recapture Dr. Fell's
question.

"Pranks?" he repeated, and passed a hand nervously over his wiry
black hair. "Oh! Pettis? Good Lord, no! He's as correct and fussy as they
make 'em. But, you understand, we didn't see his face. It was like this:
"We'd been sitting in that front room since just after dinner—"
"Stop a bit," interrupted Hadley. "Was the door to the hall open?"
"No. Hang it all," said Mangan in a defensive tone, and shifted, "you
don't sit in a draughty room on a snowy night with the door standing
open; not without central heating, you don't. I knew we could hear the
bell ring if it did ring. Besides—well, honestly, I didn't expect anything
to happen. The professor gave us the impression at dinner that it was a
hoax, or that it had been adjusted somehow; anyway, that he had been
inclined to get the wind up over nothing. . . ."
Hadley was looking at him with hard, bright eyes. "You got that
impression, too, Miss Grimaud?"
"Yes, in a way . . . I don't know! It's always hard to tell," she answered, with a faint anger (or rebellion?), "whether he's annoyed or
amused or just pretending both. My father has a queer sense of humour,
and he loves dramatic effects. He treats me as a child. I don't think I
ever in my life saw him frightened, so I don't know. But for the past
three days he's been acting so dashed queerly that when Boyd told me
about the man in that pub—" She lifted her shoulders.
"In what way was he acting queerly?"
"Well, muttering to himself, for instance. And suddenly roaring out
over trifles, which he seldom does. And then again he would laugh too
much. But most of all it was those letters. He began to get them in every
post. Don't ask me what was in them; he burnt all of them. They were
in plain penny envelopes. . . . I shouldn't have noticed at all if it
hadn't been for a habit of his." She hesitated. "Maybe you'll understand.
My father is one of those people who can never get a letter in your
presence without your instantly knowing what it's about or even who
it's from. He'll explode, 'Damned swindler!' or, 'Now, there's impudence

for you!' or, genially, 'Well, well, here's a letter from old So-and-so!'—in rather a surprised tone, as though he expected somebody in Liverpool or Birmingham to be at the other side of the moon. I don't know if you understand . . . ?"

"We understand. Please go on."

"But when he got these notes, or whatever they were, he didn't say anything at all. He didn't move a muscle. Yet, you see, he never openly destroyed one except yesterday morning at the breakfast table. After he'd glanced at it he crumpled it up, got up from his chair, and went over in a thoughtful sort of way and threw it in the fire. Just at that second Au —" Rosette glanced quickly at Hadley, seemed to discover her own hesitation, and blundered into confusion. "Mrs.—Madame—oh, I mean Aunt Ernestine! Just at that second she asked him if he would have some more bacon. Suddenly he whirled round from the fire and yelled, 'Go to hell!' It was so unexpected that before we had recovered our wits he'd stamped out of the room, muttering that a man couldn't have any peace. He looked devilish. That was the day he came back with that painting. He was good-humoured again; he banged about, chuckling, and helped the cabman and somebody else cart it upstairs. I—I don't want you to think—" Evidently the memories were crowding back again to this complex Rosette; she began to think, and that was bad. She added, shakily, "I don't want you to think I don't like him."

Hadley ignored the personal. "Did he ever mention this man at the public house?"

"Off-handedly, when I asked him. He said it was one of the quacks who often threatened him for jeering at—the history of magic. Of course it wasn't merely that."

"Why, Miss Grimaud?"

During a pause she looked at him unwinkingly.

"Because I felt that this was the real thing. And because I have often wondered whether there was anything in my father's past life which might bring something like that on him."

It was a direct challenge. During a long silence they could hear muffled creaking and flat, heavy footsteps shaking on the roof. Some change moved and played like firelight on her face—fear, or hatred, or pain, or doubt. That illusion of the barbaric had returned—as though the mink coat should have been a leopard-skin coat. Crossing her legs, she leaned back voluptuously, wriggling into the chair. She tilted her head against the back of the chair, so that the firelight gleamed on her throat and in her half-shut eyes. She regarded them with a faint, fixed smile; the cheek bones were outlined in shadow. All the same, Rampole saw that she was trembling. Why, incidentally, should her face seem broader than it was long?

"Well?" she prompted.

Hadley appeared mildly surprised. "Bring something on him? I don't quite understand. Had you any reason to think so?"

"Oh, no reason! I don't think so, really. Just these fancies—" The denial was quick, but the sharp rise and fall of her breast had quieted. "Probably it's living with my father's hobby. And then my mother— she's dead, you know; died when I was quite a kid—my mother was supposed to have second-sight." Rosette raised her cigarette again. "But you were asking me . . . ?"

"About tonight, first of all. If you think it would be helpful to go into your father's past, the Yard will certainly act on your suggestion."

She jerked the cigarette away from her lips.

"But," pursued Hadley in the same colourless voice, "let's get on with the story Mr. Mangan was telling. You two went to the drawing-room after dinner, and the door to the hall was shut. Now, did Professor Grimaud tell you what time he expected a dangerous visitor?"

"Er—yes," said Mangan. He had taken out a handkerchief and was mopping his forehead. Seen sideways in the firelight, there were many small wrinkles across the forehead of the thin, hollowed, sharp-angled face. "That was another reason why I didn't tumble to who it might be. He was too early. The professor said ten o'clock, and this fellow arrived at a quarter to."

"Ten o'clock. I see. You're sure he said that?"

"Well—yes! At least, I think so. About ten o'clock. Wasn't it, Rosette?"

"I don't know. He didn't say anything to me."

"I—see. Go on, Mr. Mangan."

"We had the radio on. That was bad, because the music was loud. And we were playing cards in front of the fire. All the same, I heard the door-bell, I looked up at the clock on the mantel, and it said a quarter to ten. I was getting up when I heard the door open. Then I heard Mrs. Dumont's voice saying something like, 'Wait, I'll see,' and a sound as though the door slammed. I called out, 'Ahoy there! Who is it?' But the radio was making such a row that I naturally stepped over and shut it off. And just afterwards we heard Pettis—naturally we both thought it was Pettis—call out: 'Hullo, children! It's Pettis. What's all this formality about seeing the Governor? I'm going up and break in on him.' "

"Those were his exact words?"

"Yes. He always called Dr. Grimaud the Governor; nobody else had the nerve to; except Burnaby, and he calls him Pop. . . . So we said, 'Righto,' as you do, and didn't bother any more about it. We both sat down again. But I noticed that it was getting near ten o'clock and I began to be watchful and jumpy, now that it was coming towards ten o'clock . . ."

Hadley drew a design on the margin of his notebook.

"So the man who called himself Pettis," he mused, "spoke to you through the door without seeing you? How did he know you two were there, do you think?"

Mangan frowned. "He saw us through the window, I suppose. As you come up the front steps you can see straight into the front room through the nearest window. I always notice it myself. In fact, if I see anybody in the front room I usually lean across and tap on the window instead of ringing the bell."

The superintendent was still drawing designs, meditatively. He seemed about to ask a question, but checked himself. Rosette regarded him with a sharp, unwinking gaze. Hadley merely said:

"Go on. You were waiting for ten o'clock—"

"And nothing happened," Mangan insisted. "But, a funny thing, every minute past ten o'clock I got more nervous instead of more relieved. I told you I didn't really expect the man would come, or that there would be any trouble. But I kept picturing that dark hall, and the queer suit of armour with the mask out there, and the more I thought of it the less I liked it. . . ."

"I know exactly what you mean," said Rosette. She looked at him in a strange, rather startled manner. "I was thinking the same thing. But I didn't want to talk about it in case you called me a fool."

"Oh, I have these psychic fits, too. That," Mangan said bitterly, "is why I get the sack so often, and why I shall probably get the sack for not phoning in this story tonight. News editor be damned. I'm no Judas." He shifted. "Anyway, it was nearly ten past ten when I felt I couldn't stand it any longer. I slammed down the cards and said to Rosette, 'Look here, let's get a drink and turn on all the lights in the hall—or do something.' I was going to ring for Annie, when I remembered it was Saturday and her night out. . . ."

"Annie? That's the maid? Yes. I'd forgotten her. Well?"

"So I went over to open the door, and it was locked on the outside. It was like . . . like this! You have some conspicuous object in your bedroom, like a picture or an ornament, that's so common you never fully notice it. Then one day you walk in and have a vague feeling that there's something wrong with the room. It irritates and disturbs you, because you can't imagine why. Then all of a sudden a gap jumps up, and you see with a shock that the object has been removed. Understand? I felt just like that. I *knew* something was wrong, I felt it ever since that fellow had sung out from the hall, but it never hit me with a smash until I found that door locked. Just as I began idiotically yanking at the knob, we heard the shot.

"A firearm indoors makes a devil of a noise, and we heard it even up at the top of the house. Rosette screamed—"

"I did not!"

"Then she pointed at me and said what I'd been thinking, too. She said. 'That wasn't Pettis at all. He's got in.' "

"Can you fix the time of that?"

"Yes. It was just ten minutes past ten. Well, I tried to break the door down." In spite of staring at that memory, a wry and mocking gleam of mirth twinkled in Mangan's eyes. It was as though he hated to speak, but could not help commenting. "I say, have you ever noticed how easy it is to break down doors in the stories? Those stories are a carpenter's paradise. They're an endless trail of doors smashed down on the slightest pretext, even when somebody inside won't answer a casual question. But try it on one of these doors! . . . That's about all. I banged my shoulder-bone against it for a while, and then I thought about getting out through the window and in again through the front door or the area door. I ran into you, and you know what happened."

Hadley tapped the notebook with his pencil. "Was it customary for the front door to be unlocked, Mr. Mangan?"

"O Lord! I don't know! But it was the only thing I could think of. Anyhow, it *was* unlocked."

"Yes, it was unlocked. Have you anything to add to that, Miss Grimaud?"

Her eyelids drooped. "Nothing—that is, not exactly. Boyd has told you everything that happened just as it happened. But you people always want all kinds of queer things, don't you? Even if they don't seem to bear on the matter? This probably has nothing to do with the matter at all, but I'll tell you. . . . A little while before the door-bell rang, I was going over to get some cigarettes from a table between the windows. The radio was on, as Boyd says. But I heard from somewhere out in the street, or on the pavement in front of the door, a loud sound like—like a thud, as though a heavy object had fallen from a big height. It wasn't an ordinary street noise, you see. Like a man falling."

Rampole felt himself stirring uneasily. Hadley asked:

"A thud, you say? H'm. Did you look out to see what it was?"

"Yes. But I couldn't see anything. Of course, I only pulled the blind back and peeped round the side of it, but I can swear the street was empt—" She stopped in full flight. Her lips fell open a little and her eyes were suddenly fixed. "Oh, my *God!*" she said.

"Yes, Miss Grimaud," said Hadley without inflection, "the blinds were all down, as you say. I especially noticed that, because Mr. Mangan got entangled with one when he jumped out. That was why I wondered how the visitor could have seen you through any window in that room. But possibly they weren't drawn down all the time?"

There was a silence, except for faint noises on the roof. Rampole glanced at Dr. Fell, who was propped back against one of the unbreakable doors with his chin in his hand and his shovel-hat tilted over his eyes. Then Rampole looked at the impassive Hadley, and back to the girl.

"He thinks we're lying, Boyd," said Rosette Grimaud, coolly. "I don't think we'd better say anything more."

And then Hadley smiled. "I don't think anything of the kind. Miss Grimaud. I'm going to tell you why, because you're the only person who can help us. I'm even going to tell you what did happen.—Fell!"

"Er?" boomed Dr. Fell, looking up with a start.

"I want you to listen to this," the superintendent pursued, grimly. "A while ago you were having a lot of pleasure and mystification out of saying that you believed the stories—apparently incredible—told by Mills and Mrs. Dumont; without giving any reasons why you believed them. I'll return the compliment. I'll say that I believe not only their story, but the story told by these two also. And, in explaining why, I'll also explain the impossible situation."

This time Dr. Fell did come out of his abstraction with a jerk. He puffed out his cheeks and peered at Hadley as though prepared to leap into battle.

"Not all of it, I admit," pursued Hadley, "but enough to narrow down the field of suspects to a few people, and to explain why there were no footprints in the snow."

"Oh, *that!*" said Dr. Fell, contemptuously. He relaxed with a grunt. "You know, for a second I hoped you had something. But that part is obvious."

Hadley kept his temper with a violent effort. "The man we want," he went on, "made no footprints on the pavement or up the steps because he never walked on the pavement or up the steps—after the snow had stopped. He was in the house all the time. He had been in the house for some time. He was either (a) an inmate; or (b) more probably somebody who had concealed himself there, using a key to the front door earlier in the evening. This would explain all the inconsistencies in everybody's story. At the proper time he put on his fancy rig, stepped outside the front door on the swept doorstep, and rang the door-bell. It explains how he knew Miss Grimaud and Mr. Mangan were in the front room when the blinds were drawn—he had seen them go in. It explains how, when the door was slammed in his face and he was told to wait outside, he could simply walk in—he had a key."

Dr. Fell was slowly shaking his head and rumbling to himself. He folded his arms argumentatively.

"H'mf, yes. But why should even a slightly cracked person indulge in all that elaborate hocus-pocus? If he lived in the house, the argument isn't bad: he wanted to make the visitor seem an outsider. But if he really came from outside, why take the dangerous risk of hanging about inside long before he was ready to act? Why not march straight up at the right time?"

"First," said the methodical Hadley, checking it off on his fingers, "he had to know where people were, so as to have no interference. Second, and more important, he wanted to put the finishing touches on his vanishing trick by having no footprints whatever, anywhere, in the snow. The vanishing-trick would be everything to the crazy mind of—brother

Henri, let's say. So he got in while it was snowing heavily, and waited until it had stopped."

"Who," Rosette asked in a sharp voice, "is brother Henri?"

"He's a name, my dear," Dr. Fell returned, affably. "I told you that you didn't know him. . . . Now, Hadley, here's where I enter a mild, firm objection to this whole rummy affair. We've talked glibly about snow starting and stopping, as though you could regulate it like a tap. But I want to know how in blazes a man can tell WHEN snow is going to start or stop? That is, a man seldom says to himself, 'Aha! On Saturday night I will commit a crime. On that night, I think, it will commence to snow at exactly 5:00 P.M., and leave off at exactly 9:30 P.M. This will afford me ample time to get into the house, and be prepared with my trick when the snowfall ends.' Tut, tut! Your explanation is rather more staggering then your problem. It's much easier to believe that a man walked on snow without leaving a footprint than to believe he knew precisely when he would have it to walk on."

The superintendent was irritable. "I am trying," he said, "to get to the main point of all this. But if you must fight about that—Don't you see it explains away the last problem?"

"What problem?"

"Our friend Mangan here says that the visitor threatened to pay his visit at ten o'clock. Mrs. Dumont and Mills say nine-thirty. Wait!" He checked Mangan's outburst. "Was A lying, or B? First, what sane reason could either have for lying *afterwards* about the time he *threatened* to come? Second, if A says ten o'clock and B says nine-thirty, then, innocent or guilty, one of the two should have learned beforehand the time at which the visitor really would arrive. And which was right about the time he did arrive?"

"Neither," said Mangan, staring. "It was between 'em. At 9:45."

"Yes. That's a sign that neither lied. It's a sign that the visitor's threat to Grimaud was not definite; it was 'nine-thirty or ten o'clock or thereabouts.' And, Grimaud, who was trying pretty desperately to act as though the threat hadn't scared him, nevertheless took very good care to mention both times in order to make sure everybody was there. My wife does the same thing with invitations to bridge parties. . . . Well, but *why* couldn't brother Henri be definite? Because, as Fell says, he couldn't turn off the snow like a tap. He could risk a long gamble on there being snow tonight, as there's been for several nights; but he had to wait until it stopped even if he waited until midnight. He didn't have to wait so long. It stopped at half-past nine. And then he acted exactly as such a lunatic would—he waited fifteen minutes so that there could be no argument afterwards, and rang the bell."

Dr. Fell opened his mouth to speak, looked shrewdly at the intent faces of Rosette and Mangan, and stopped.

"Now, then!" said Hadley, squaring his shoulders. "I've shown you two that I believe everything you say, because I want your help on the most important thing this tells us. . . . The man we want is no casual acquaintance. He knows this house inside out—the rooms, the routine, the habits of the occupants. He knows your phrases and nicknames. He knows how this Mr. Pettis is accustomed to address not only Dr. Grimaud, but *you*; hence he's no casual business friend of the professor whom you haven't seen. So I want to know all about everybody who's a frequent enough visitor to this house, everybody who is close enough to Dr. Grimaud, to answer the description."

She moved uneasily, startled. "You think—somebody like that. . . . Oh, it's impossible! No, no, no!" (It was a queer echo of her mother's voice.) "Not anybody like that, anyhow!"

"Why do you say that?" Hadley asked, sharply. "Do you know who shot your father?"

The sudden crack of the words made her jump. "No, of course not!"

"Or have any suspicion?"

"No. Except," her teeth gleamed, "I don't see why you should keep looking outside the house. That was a very nice little lesson in deduction you gave, and thanks awfully. But if the person had come from *inside* the house, and acted as you said, then it would really be reasonable, wouldn't it? It would apply much better."

"To whom?"

"Let's see! Well . . . that's your business, isn't it?" (He had somehow stirred a sleek tiger cat, and she was enjoying it.) "Of course, you haven't met the whole household. You haven't met Annie—or Mr. Drayman, come to think of it. But your other idea is utterly ridiculous. In the first place, my father has very few friends. Outside of the people in this house, there are only two who fit the qualifications, and neither of them could possibly be the man you want. They couldn't be in the mere matter of their physical characteristics. One is Anthony Pettis himself; he's no taller than I am, and I'm no Amazon. The other is Jerome

Burnaby, the artist who did that queer picture. He has a deformity; a slight one, but it couldn't be disguised and anybody could spot it a mile away. Aunt Ernestine or Stuart would have known him instantly."

"All the same, what do you know about them?"

She lifted her shoulders. "Both are middle-aged, well-to-do, and potter after their hobbies. Pettis is bald-headed and fastidious. . . . I don't mean he's old-womanish: he's what the men call a good fellow, and he's clever as sin. Bah! Why won't they *do* something with themselves!" She clenched her hands. Then she glanced up at Mangan, and a slow, calculating, drowsily pleasant expression came into her look. "Burnaby—yes, Jerome has done something with himself, in a way. He's fairly well known as an artist, though he'd rather be known as a criminologist. He's big and bluff; he likes to talk about crime and brag about his athletic prowess of old. Jerome is attractive in his way. He's very fond of me, and Boyd is horribly jealous." Her smile widened.

"I don't like the fellow," said Mangan, quietly. "In fact, I hate him like poison—and we both know it. But at least Rosette's right about one thing. He'd never do a thing like that."

Hadley scribbled again. "What is this deformity of his?"

"A club foot. You can see how he couldn't possibly conceal it."

"Thank you. For the moment," said Hadley, shutting up his notebook, "that will be all. I should suggest that you go along to the nursing-home. Unless . . . er—any questions, Fell?"

The doctor stumped forward. He towered over the girl, peering down at her with his head a little on one side.

"Just one last question," he said, brushing aside the black ribbon of his eye-glasses as he would a fly. "Harrumph! Ha! Now! Miss Grimaud, why are you so certain that the guilty person is this Mr. Drayman?"

8

The Bullet

He never received any answer to that question, although he received some illumination. It was all over before Rampole realized what had happened. Since the doctor had spoken with the greatest casualness, the name "Drayman" had made no impression on Rampole, and he was not even looking at Rosette. Uneasily, he had been wondering for some time what had happened to change the gusty, garrulous, beaming Mangan he used to know into this shuffling figure who backed and deprecated and talked like a fool. In the past Mangan had never talked like a fool, even when he talked like an idiot. But now—

"You *devil!*" cried Rosette Grimaud.

It was like a screech of chalk on a blackboard. Rampole whirled round to see high cheek bones gone still higher as her mouth widened, and a blaze that seemed to take the colour from her eyes: It was only a glimpse; she had flung herself past Dr. Fell, the mink coat flying, and out into the hall, with Mangan after her. The door slammed. Mangan reappeared for a moment, said to them, "Er—sorry!" and quickly closed the door once more. He looked almost grotesque in the doorway, his back bent and his head lowered, so that it seemed all wrinkled forehead and nervous dark eyes shining intensely. His hands were extended, with palms turned down, as though he were trying to quiet an audience. "Er —sorry!" he said, and closed the door.

Dr. Fell remained blinking at it.

"She's her father's daughter, Hadley," he wheezed, and shook his head slowly. "Harrumph, yes. She goes just so far under hard emotional pressure; very quiet, powder packed into a cartridge; then some little thing jars the hair trigger, and—h'm. I'm afraid she's morbid in the real sense, but maybe she thinks she has reason to be. I wonder how much she knows?"

"Oh, well, she's a foreigner. But that's not the point. It seems to me," said Hadley, with some asperity, "that you're always making a wild shot like a trick rifleman and knocking the cigarette out of somebody's mouth. What was that business about Drayman, anyhow?"

Dr. Fell seemed bothered.

"In a minute, in a minute. . . . What did you think of her, Hadley? And Mangan?" He turned to Rampole. "My ideas are a little mixed. I'd got the impression, from what you said, that Mangan was a wild Irishman of the type I know and like."

"He was," said Rampole. "Understand?"

"As to what I think of her," Hadley said, "I think she could sit here as cool as you please, analyzing her father's life (she's got a damned good head on her, by the way); and yet at this moment I'll bet she's in tears and hysterics, rushing across there, because she didn't show him enough consideration. I think she's fundamentally sound. But she's got the Old Nick in her, Fell. She wants a master in both senses. She and Mangan will never hit it off until he has sense enough to punch her head or take her own advice at the London University debate."

"Ever since you have become superintendent of the C.I.D.," declared Dr. Fell, squinting at him, "I have detected in you a certain raffish air which pains and surprises me. Listen, you old satyr. Did you honestly believe all that rubbish you talked, about the murderer sneaking into this house to wait until the snowstorm had stopped?"

Hadley permitted himself a broad grin. "It's as good an explanation as any," he said, "until I can think of a better. And it keeps their minds occupied. Always keep witnesses' minds occupied. At least I believe their story. . . . We're going to find something in the way of footprints on that roof, don't you worry. But we'll talk about that later. What about Drayman?"

"To begin with, I had stuck in my mind an odd remark made by Madame Dumont. It was so odd that it jumped out of the sentence. Not a calculated remark; she cried it out at the time she was most hysterical, when she could not understand why even murderers acted out so silly a charade. She said (if you wish to kill somebody), 'You do not put on a painter mask, like old Drayman with the children on Guy Fawkes night.' I filed away the suggestions of this Guy Fawkes spectre, wondering what it meant. Then all unintentionally, I phrased a question about Pettis— when speaking to Rosette—with the words, 'dressed up like a Fifth of November Guy?' Did you notice her expression, Hadley? Just my suggestion that the visitor was dressed like that gave her the hint, but it startled her as much as it pleased her. She didn't say anything; she was thinking. She hated the person she was thinking of. What person?"

Hadley stared across the room. "Yes, I remember. I could see she was hinting at somebody she suspected or wanted us to suspect; that was why I asked her flat out. She practically made me see it was somebody in this house. But to tell you the truth,"—he rubbed his hand across his forehead—"this is such a rum crowd that for a second I thought she was hinting at her own mother."

"Not by the way she dragged in Drayman. 'You haven't met Annie— or Mr. Drayman, come to think of it.' The important news was in the postscript. . . ." Dr. Fell stumped round the typewriter desk, peering malevolently at the glass of milk. "We must rout him out. He interests me. Who is this Drayman, this old friend and hanger-on of Grimaud, who takes sleeping draughts and wears Fifth of November masks? What's his place in the household; what's he doing here, anyway?"

"You mean—blackmail?"

"Rubbish, my boy. Did you ever hear of a schoolmaster being a black-mailer? No, no. They're much too worried about what people might find out about *them*. The academic profession has its faults, as I know for my sins; but it doesn't produce blackmailers. . . . No, it was probably only a kindly impulse of Grimaud to take him in, but—"

He paused as a rush of cold air blew his cloak. A door across the room, evidently communicating with a staircase to the attic and the roof, opened and shut. Mills popped in. His mouth was bluish and a large wool muffler was wound round his neck; but he looked warm with satisfaction. After refreshing himself with a pull at the glass of milk (impassively, with head thrown back in a way which somehow suggested a sword-swallower), he put out his hands to the fire.

He chattered: "I have been watching your detective, gentlemen, from a point of vantage at the top of the trapdoor. He has caused a few landslides, but. . . . Excuse me! Didn't you have a commission of some description for me to execute? Ah yes. I am anxious to lend assistance, but I fear I forgot—"

"Wake up Mr. Drayman," the superintendent said, "if you have to slosh him with water. And . . . Hullo! Pettis! If Mr. Pettis is still here, tell him I want to see him. What did Sergeant Betts discover up there?"

Betts answered for himself. He looked as though he had taken a header in a ski-jump; he breathed hard, stamped and slapped the snow from his clothes as he shook his way towards the fire.

"Sir," he announced, "you can take my word for it that not even a bird's lit on that roof anywhere. There's no mark of any kind in any place. I've covered every foot of it." He stripped off his sodden gloves. "I had myself tied on a rope to each of the chimneys, so I could get down and crawl straight along the gutters. Nothing round the edges, nothing round the chimneys, nothing anywhere. If anybody got up on that roof tonight, he must have been lighter than air. Now I'll go down and have a look at the back garden . . ."

"But—!" cried Hadley.

"Quite so," said Dr. Fell. "Look here, we'd better go down and see what your bloodhounds are doing in the other room. If the good Pres-ton—"

Sergeant Preston, fuming a little, pulled open the door to the hall as though he had been summoned. He looked at Betts and back to Hadley.

"It's taken me a little time, sir," he reported, "because we had to pull out all of those bookcases and shove 'em back again. The answer is nothing! No secret entrance of any kind. Chimney's solid and no funny business about it; flue's only about two or three inches wide, and goes up on an angle at that. . . . Is that all, sir? The boys have finished."

"Fingerprints?"

"Plenty of prints, except—You raised and lowered that window yourself, didn't you, sir? With your fingers on the glass up near the top of the frame? I recognized your prints."

"I am generally careful about things like that," snapped Hadley. "Well?"

"Nothing else on the glass. And all the woodwork of that window, frame and sill, is high-gloss varnish that'd take a glove-smudge as clear as a print. There's nothing, not even a smudge. If anybody went out there, he must have stood back and dived out head first without touching anything."

"That's enough, thanks," said Hadley. "Wait downstairs. Get after that back garden, Betts. . . . No, wait, Mr. Mills. Preston will fetch Mr. Pettis, if he's still there. I should like to speak to you."

"It would seem," said Mills, rather shrilly, when the other two had gone, "that we return to doubts about my own story. I assure you I am telling the truth. Here is where I sat. See for yourself."

Hadley opened the door. Ahead of them the high sombre hallway ran thirty feet to the door opposite—a door brilliantly illuminated by the glow from under the archway.

"I don't suppose there's any possibility of a mistake?" muttered the superintendent. "That he really didn't go in, or something like that? A lot of funny business might go on in a shuffle at the doorway; I've heard of its being done. I don't suppose the woman was up to any funny business, dressing up in a mask herself, or—No, you saw them together, and anyway. . . . *Hell!*"

"There was absolutely none of what you describe as funny business," said Mills. Even in his perspiring earnestness he handled the last two words with distaste. "I saw all three of them clearly and wide apart. Madame Dumont was in front of the door, yes; but towards the right. The tall man was towards the left, and Dr. Grimaud separating them.

The tall man really did go in; he closed the door behind him; and he did not come out. It is not as though the occurrence took place in half-light. There was no possibility of ever mistaking that man's gigantic stature."

"I don't see how we can doubt it, Hadley," said Dr. Fell, after a pause. "We've got to eliminate the door also." He wheeled round. "What do you know about this man Drayman?"

Mills' eyes narrowed. His sing-song voice had a guarded quality.

"It is true, sir, that he offers a subject for intelligent curiosity. Hurrum! But I know very little. He has been here some years, I am informed; in any event, before I arrived. He was forced to give up his academic work because he had gone almost blind. He is still almost blind, in spite of treatment, although you would not deduce this from the—er—aspect of his eyes. He appealed to Dr. Grimaud for help."

"Had he some sort of claim on Dr. Grimaud?"

The secretary frowned. "I cannot say. I have heard it mentioned that Dr. Grimaud knew him at Paris, where he studied. That is the only bit of information I have, except one remark which Dr. Grimaud made when he had, let us say, imbibed a convivial glass." A superior kind of smile curved round Mills' mouth without opening it; his eyes narrowed, and gleamed in drowsy satire. "Hum! He stated that Mr. Drayman had once saved his life, and described him as the best damned good fellow in the world. Of course, under the circumstances. . . ."

Mills had a jerky trick of putting one foot before the other, rocking, and tapping the toe of one shoe with the heel of the other. With his jerky movements, tiny figure, and big shock of hair, he was like a caricature of Swinburne. Dr. Fell looked at him curiously. But Dr. Fell only said:

"So? And why don't *you* like him?"

"I neither like nor dislike him. But he does nothing."

"Is that why Miss Grimaud doesn't like him, either?"

"Miss Grimaud does not like him?" said Mills, opening his eyes and then narrowing them. "Yes, I had fancied that. I watched, but I could not be certain."

"H'mf. And why is he so interested in Guy Fawkes night?"

"Guy Fa—Ah!" Mills broke off in his surprise, and uttered a flat bleat of laughter. "I see! I did not follow. You see, he is very fond of children. He had two children of his own, who were killed—by the falling of a roof, I believe, some years ago. It was one of those foolish, petty tragedies which we shall eliminate when we build the bigger, greater, more spacious world of the future." At this point in the recital Dr. Fell's face was murderous, but Mills went on: "His wife did not survive long. Then he began to lose his sight. . . . He likes to help the children in all their games, and has himself a somewhat childish mind in spite of certain mental qualities." The fish lip lifted a little. "His favourite occasion seems to be the Fifth of November, which was the birthday of one of his unfortunate progeny. He saves up throughout the year to buy illuminations and trappings, and builds a Guy for a procession to—" A sharp knocking at the door was followed by the appearance of Sergeant Preston.

"There's nobody downstairs, sir," he reported. "That gentleman you wanted to see must have left. . . . A chap from the nursing-home just brought this over for you."

He handed over an envelope and a square cardboard box like a jeweller's box. Hadley ripped open the letter, glanced down it, and swore.

"He's gone," snapped Hadley, "and not a word. . . . Here, read this!"

Rampole looked over Dr. Fell's shoulder as the latter read.

For Superintendent Hadley:

Poor Grimaud died at 11:30. I am sending you the bullet. It's a thirty-eight, as I thought. I tried to get in touch with your police surgeon, but he was out on another case, and so I am sending it to you.

He was conscious just before the end. He said certain things which can be attested by two of my nurses and myself; but he might have been wandering and I should be careful of them. I knew him pretty well, but I certainly never knew he had a brother.

First he said he wished to tell me about it; then he spoke exactly as follows:

"It was my brother who did it. I never thought he would shoot. God knows how he got out of that room. One second he was there, and the next he wasn't. Get a pencil and paper, quick! I want to tell you who my brother is, so that you won't think I'm raving."

His shouting brought in the final hemorrhage, and he died without saying anything else. I am holding the body subject to your orders. If there is any I can give, let me know.

                                        E. H. Peterson, M.D.

They all looked at each other. The puzzle stood rounded and complete; the facts stood confirmed and the witnesses vindicated; but the terror of the hollow man remained. After a pause the superintendent spoke in a heavy voice. " 'God knows,' " repeated Hadley, " 'how he got out of that room.' "

The Problem of Cagliostro Street

9

The Breaking Grave

Dr. Fell walked over aimlessly, sighed, and settled himself down in the largest chair. "Brother Henri—" he rumbled. "H'mf, yes. I was afraid we should get back to Brother Henri."

"Damn Brother Henri," said Hadley in a flat voice. "We're going after Brother Pierre first. He knows! Why haven't I had any message from that constable? Where's the man who was to pick him up at that theatre? Have the whole blasted lot of them gone to sleep and—"

"We mustn't get the wind up about this thing," interposed the other, as Hadley began to stamp and declaim rather wildly. "That's exactly what Brother Henri would want us to do. Now that we've got Grimaud's last statement, we've at least got one clue . . ."

"To what?"

"To the words he spoke to *us,* the ones we couldn't make any sense of. The unfortunate point is that they may not help us now that we can hazard a theory as to what they mean. With this new evidence, I'm afraid we were listening to Grimaud running up a blind alley. He wasn't telling us anything; he was only trying to ask us a question."

"What's all this?"

"Don't you see that's exactly what he must have been doing? Last statement: 'God knows how he got out of that room. One second he was there and the next he wasn't.' Now let's try to sort out the words from that invaluable notebook of yours. You and friend Ted have slightly different versions; but we'll begin with the words on which you both agree and which we must assume to be correct. Put aside the first puzzlers—I think we can now feel safe in saying that the words were 'Horváth' and 'salt-mine.' Put aside also the terms on which you do not agree. What words are found in both lists?"

Hadley snapped his fingers. "I begin to—Yes! The words are, 'He couldn't use rope. Roof. Snow. Fox. Too much light.' Well, then! If we try to make a composite statement; fit together the words and the sense of both statements; we have his meaning as something like this; 'God knows how he got out. He couldn't use a rope; either up on the roof or down in the snow. One second he was there, and the next he wasn't.

There was too much light for me to miss any move he made—' Stop a bit, though! What about . . ."

"And now," said Dr. Fell, with a disgusted grunt, "you can begin to fit in the differences. Ted heard, 'not suicide.' That goes into the picture as an assurance to accord with the other expressions. 'This isn't suicide; I didn't kill myself.' You heard, 'Got gun'; which isn't difficult to tie up with the sentence out of the other statement, 'I never thought he would shoot.' BAH! All the clues whirl straight round in a circle and become questions. It's the first case I ever heard of in which the murdered man was just as inquisitive as everybody else."

"But what about the word 'fox'? That doesn't fit anywhere."

Dr. Fell regarded him with a sour twinkle in his eye.

"Oh, yes, it does. It's the easiest part of all—though it may be the trickiest, and we mustn't jump to conclusions about applying it. It's a matter of how words strike the ear when they're not spelled out. If I'm using the word association test (that damned thing) on various people, and I suddenly whisper, 'Fox!' to a horseman, he will probably answer, 'Hounds!' But if I use the same word on a historian, he is likely to yell . . . quick! What?"

"Guy," said Hadley, and swore. After a lurid interval he demanded: "Do you mean that we come back to some babbling about a Guy Fawkes mask, or the resemblance to a Guy Fawkes mask?"

"Well, everybody else has been doing a tall amount of babbling about it," the doctor pointed out, scratching his forehead. "And I'm not surprised it struck the eye of somebody who saw it at somewhat closer quarters. Does that tell you anything?"

"It tells me to have a little talk with Mr. Drayman," said the superintendent, grimly. He strode towards the door, and was startled to find the bony face of Mills poked out in eager listening against the thick glasses.

"Steady, Hadley," Dr. Fell interposed as the superintendent gave indications of an explosion. "It's a queer thing about you: you can be steady as the Guards when riddles are flying, but you never seem able to keep your shirt on when we get within sight of the truth. Let our young friend stop. He should hear all this, if only to hear the end of it." He chuckled. "Does that make you suspicious of Drayman? Pfaa! On the contrary, it should be just the opposite. Remember, we haven't quite finished putting the pieces in our jig saw. There's one last bit we haven't accounted for, and it was a bit you heard yourself. That pink mask suggested Drayman to Grimaud, just as he seems to have been suggested to several others. But Grimaud knew whose face was behind the mask. Therefore we have a fairly sensible explanation of those final words you noted down, *'Don't blame poor—'* He seems to have had a great liking for Drayman, you know." After a silence, Dr. Fell turned to Mills, "Now go and fetch him up here, son."

When the door had closed, Hadley sat down wearily and took from his breast pocket the frayed cigar he had not yet lighted. Then he ran a finger round under his collar with that malevolent, broken-necked expression which people have when worry makes them think the collar is too tight.

"More trick marksmanship, eh?" he suggested. "More deductive tight-rope work, and the daring young man on the—um!" He stared at the floor, and then grunted with annoyance. "I must be losing my grip! It's no good getting fantastic notions like the one I just had. Have you got any concrete suggestions?"

"Yes. Later, if you'll permit it, I am going to apply Gross's test."

"Apply what?"

"Gross's test. Don't you remember? We were arguing about it tonight. I'm going to collect very carefully all the mass of burnt and half-burnt paper in that fireplace, to see whether Gross's test will bring out the writing. Be quiet, will you?" he roared, as Hadley made scornful noises. "I don't say all of it, or even half of it, will come out. But I should get a line here and there to give me a hint about what was more important to Grimaud than saving his own life. Purph! Hah! Yes."

"And how do you work this trick?"

"You'll see. Mind, I don't say that thoroughly burnt paper will come out satisfactorily. But there'll be something, especially in the charred parts sandwiched in and only scorched black, that *will* come out. . . . Aside from that, I haven't a suggestion, unless we ask—yes, what is it?"

Sergeant Betts, not quite so plastered with snow this time, made his report woodenly. He looked out the door behind him before he closed it.

"I've been all over that back-garden, sir. And the two adjoining ones, and the tops of all the walls. There's no footprint or any kind of mark. . . . But I believe we've caught a fish, Preston and I. As I was coming back through the house, down the stairs comes running a tallish old bloke, plunging away with his hand on the banister rail. He ran over to a clothes closet, and banged about as though he wasn't familiar with the place, until he got on his overcoat and hat, and then made for the door. He says his name's Drayman and that he lives here, but we thought—"

"I think you'll find that his sight isn't any too good," said Dr. Fell. "Send him in."

The man who entered was, in his own way, an impressive figure. His long, quiet face was hollowed at the temples; his grey hair grew far back on the skull, giving him a great height of narrow and wrinkled forehead. His bright blue eyes, which did not seem at all dimmed despite the wrinkles round them, looked gentle and puzzled. He had a hooked nose, and deep furrows running down to a kindly, uncertain mouth; and his trick of wrinkling the forehead, so that one eyebrow was slightly raised, made him look more uncertain still. Despite his stoop he was still tall; despite his bony frailty he was still powerful. He looked like a military man gone senile, a well-brushed man gone slovenly. There was nothing of humour in the face, but a great deal of muddled and apologetic good-nature. He wore a dark overcoat buttoned up to the chin. Standing in the doorway, peering hard at them from under tangled eyebrows, he held a bowler hat pressed against his chest, and hesitated.

"I am sorry, gentlemen. I am honestly very sorry," he said. His deep voice had a curious quality as though the man were unused to speech. "I know I should have come to see you before going over there. But young Mr. Mangan woke me up to tell me what had happened. I felt I had to go over and see Grimaud, to see whether there might be anything I could do—"

Rampole had a feeling that he was still dull-witted and uncertain from sleep or sleeping-drugs; that the bright stare of his eyes might have been so much glass. He moved over, and one hand found the back of a chair. But he did not sit down until Hadley asked him to do so.

"Mr. Mangan told me—" he said, "Dr. Grimaud—"

"Dr. Grimaud is dead," said Hadley.

Drayman remained sitting as bolt upright as his stoop would allow, his hands folded across his hat. There was a heavy silence in the room, while Drayman shut his eyes and opened them again. Then he seemed to stare a long way off, and to breathe with heavy, whistling sluggish-ness.

"God rest his soul," Drayman said, very quietly. "Charles Grimaud was a good friend."

"Do you know how he died?"

"Yes. Mr. Mangan told me."

Hadley studied him. "Then you will understand that to tell everything, *everything* you might happen to know, will be the only way to help us catch the murderer of your friend?"

"I—Yes, of course."

"Be very certain of that, Mr. Drayman! More certain than you are. We wish to know something of his past life. You knew him well. Where did you first know him?"

The other's long face looked muddled; an illusion as though the features had got out of line. "In Paris. He took his doctorate at the university in 1905, the same year I . . . the same year I knew him." Facts seemed to elude Drayman; he shaded his eyes with his hand, and his voice had a querulous note like a man asking where somebody has hidden his collar studs. "Grimaud was very brilliant. He obtained an associate professorship at Dijon the year afterwards. But a relative died, or something of the sort, and left him well provided for. He—he gave up his work and came to England shortly afterwards. Or so I understand. I did not see him until years afterwards. Was that what you wished to know?"

"Did you ever know him before 1905?"

"No."

Hadley leaned forward. "Where did you save his life?" he asked, sharply.

"Save his life? I don't understand."

"Ever visit Hungary, Mr. Drayman?"

"I—I have travelled on the Continent, and I may have been in Hungary. But that was years ago, when I was young. I don't remember."

And now it was Hadley's turn to pull the trigger in trick marksmanship.

"You saved his life," he stated, "near the prison of Siebenturmen, in the Carpathian Mountains, when he was escaping. *Didn't you?*"

The other sat upright, his bony hands clenched across the bowler. Rampole had a feeling that there was more dogged strength in him now than there had been for a dozen years.

"Did I?" he said.

"There's no use going on with this. We know everything—even to dates, now that you've supplied them. Károly Horváth, as a free man, wrote the date in a book in 1898. With full academic preparation behind, it would have taken him four years at least to get his doctorate at Paris. We can narrow down the time of his conviction and escape to three years. With that information," said Hadley, coolly, "I can cable to Bucharest and get the full details within twelve hours. You had better tell the truth, you see. I want to know all you know of Károly Horváth—and his two brothers. One of those two brothers killed him. Finally, I'll remind you that withholding information of this kind is a serious offence. Well?"

Drayman remained for a little time with his hand shading his eyes, his foot tapping the carpet. Then he looked up. They were startled to see that, though his puckered eyes kept their blue glassiness, the man was gently smiling.

"A serious offence," he repeated, and nodded. "Is it, indeed? Now, frankly, sir, I don't give a damn for your threats. There are very few things which can move or anger or terrify a man who can see you only in outline, as he sees a poached egg on his plate. Nearly all the fears of the world (and its ambitions, too) are caused by shapes—eyes and gestures and figures. Young people can't understand this, but I had hoped you would. You see, I am not precisely blind. I can see faces and the morning sky, and all those objects which the poets insist blind men should rave about. But I cannot *read,* and the faces I cared most to see have been for eight years blinder than mine. Wait until your whole life is built on those two things, and you will learn that not much can move you when they go." He nodded again, staring across the room. His forehead wrinkled. "Sir, I am perfectly willing to give you any information you wish, if it will help Charles Grimaud. But I don't see the sense of raking up old scandal."

"Not even to find the brother who killed him?"

Drayman made a slight gesture, frowning. "Look here, if it will help you, I can honestly tell you to forget such an idea. I don't know how you learned it. He did have two brothers. And they were imprisoned." He smiled again. "There was nothing terrible about it. They were imprisoned for a political offence. I imagine half the young fire-eaters of the time must have been concerned in it. . . . Forget the two brothers. They have both been dead a good many years."

It was so quiet in the room that Rampole heard the last collapsing rattle of the fire and the wheezing breaths of Dr. Fell. Hadley glanced at Dr. Fell, whose eyes were closed. Then Hadley regarded Drayman as impassively as though the latter's sight had been sharp.

"How do you know that?"

"Grimaud told me," said the other, accentuating the name. "Besides, all the newspapers from Budapest to Brasso were shouting about it at the time. You can easily verify all this." He spoke simply. "They died of bubonic plague."

Hadley was suave. "If, of course, you could prove this beyond any doubt . . ."

"You promise that there would be no old scandal raked up?" (That bright blue stare was difficult to meet. Drayman twisted and untwisted his bony hands.) "If I tell you exactly, and you receive the proof, will you let the dead rest?"

"It depends on your information."

"Very well. I will tell you what I saw myself." He reflected—rather uneasily, Rampole thought. "It was in its own way a horrible business. Grimaud and I never spoke of it afterwards. That was agreed. But I don't intend to lie to you and say I've forgotten it—any detail of it."

He was silent for so long a time, tapping his fingers at his temple, that even the patient Hadley was about to prompt him. Then he went on:

"Excuse me, gentlemen. I was trying to remember the exact date, so that you can verify everything. The best I can do is to say it was in August or September of nineteen hundred . . . or was it nineteen one? Anyhow, it occurs to me that I might begin, with perfect truth, exactly in the style of the contemporary French romances. I might begin, 'Towards dusk of a cool September day in the year 19— a solitary horseman might have been seen hurrying along a road,' and what a devil of a road!—'in a rugged valley below the southeastern Carpathians.' Then I should launch into a description of the wild scenery and so on. I was the horseman, it was coming on to rain, and I was trying to reach Tradj before dark."

He smiled. Hadley stirred in some impatience, though Dr. Fell opened his eyes; and Drayman was quick to take it up.

"I must insist on that sort of novelesque atmosphere, because it fitted into my mood and explains so much. I was at the romantic Byronic age, fired with ideas of political liberty. I rode horseback instead of walking because I thought I cut a good figure; I even took pleasure in carrying a pistol against (mythical) brigands, and a rosary as a charm against ghosts. But if there weren't either ghosts or brigands, there should have been. I know that I several times got the wind up about both. There was a sort of fairy-tale wildness and darkness about those cold forests and gorges. Even about the cultivated parts there was something queer. Transylvania, you see, is shadowed in on three sides by mountains. It startles an English eye to see a rye-field or a vineyard going straight up the side of a steep hill; the red-and-yellow costumes, the garlicky inns, and even, in the bleaker parts, hills made of pure salt.

"Anyhow, there I was going along a snaky road in the bleakest part, with a storm blowing up and no inn for miles. People saw the devil lurking behind every hedge in a way that gave me the creeps, but I had a worse cause for the creeps. Plague had broken out after a hot summer, and was over the whole area like a cloud of gnats, even in the chilly weather. In the last village I passed through—I've forgotten its name—they told me it was raging at the salt-mines in the mountains ahead. But I was hoping to meet an English friend of mine, also a tourist, at Tradj. Also I wanted a look at the prison, which got its name after seven white hills, like a low range of mountains, just behind. So I said I meant to go on.

"I knew I must be getting near the prison, for I could see the white hills ahead. But, just as it was getting too dark to see at all, and the wind seemed to be tearing the trees to pieces, I came down into a hollow past the three graves. They had been freshly dug, for there were still foot-marks 'round them; but no living person was 'in sight."

Hadley broke across the queer atmosphere which that dreaming voice was beginning to create.

"A place," he said, "just like the one in the painting Dr. Grimaud bought from Mr. Burnaby."

"I—I don't know," answered Drayman, evidently startled. "Is it? I didn't notice."

"Didn't notice? Didn't you see the picture?"

"Not very well. Just a general outline—trees, ordinary landscape—"

"And three headstones . . . ?"

"I don't know where Burnaby got his inspiration," the other said, dully, and rubbed his forehead. "God knows *I* never told him. It's probably a coincidence; there were no headstones over these graves. They wouldn't have bothered. There were simply three crosses made of sticks.

"But I was telling you. I sat there on my horse, looking at those graves, and with a not very pleasant feeling. They looked wild enough, with the greenish-black landscape around and the white hills beyond. But it wasn't that. If they were prison graves, I wondered why they had been dug so far away. The next thing I knew my horse reared and nearly threw me. I slewed round against a tree; and, when I looked back, I saw what was wrong with the horse. The mound of one grave was upheaving and sliding. There was a cracking noise; something began to twist and wriggle; and a dark-coloured thing came groping up out of the mound. It was only a hand moving the fingers—but I don't think I have ever seen anything more horrible."

10
The Blood on the Coat

"By that time," Drayman went on, "there was something wrong with me as well. I didn't dare dismount, for fear the horse would bolt; and I was ashamed to bolt, myself. I thought of vampires and all the legends of hell coming up out of the twilight. Frankly, the thing scared me silly. I remember battering round on that horse like a teetotum, trying to curb it with one hand while I got out my revolver. When I looked back again, the thing had climbed clear out of the grave and was coming towards me.

"That, gentlemen, was how I met one of my best friends. The man reached down and seized a spade, which somebody who dug the grave must have left there and forgotten. And still he came on. I yelled in English, 'What do you want?'—because I was so fuddled that I couldn't remember a word in any other language. The man stopped. After a second he answered in English, but with an outlandish accent. 'Help,' he said, 'help, milord; don't be afraid,' or something of the sort, and threw down the spade. The horse was quieter, but I wasn't. The man was not tall, but very powerful; his face was dark and swollen, with little scaly spots which gave it a pinkish look in the twilight. And down came the rain while he was still standing there waving his arms.

"He stood in the rain, crying out to me. I won't try to reproduce it, but he said something like, 'Look, milord, I am not dead of plague like those two poor devils,' and pointed at the graves. 'I am not infected at all. See how the rain washes it off. It is my own blood which I have pricked out of my skin.' He even stuck out his tongue to show how it was blackened with soot, and the rain made it clean. It was as mad a sight as the figure and the place. Then he went on to say that he was not a criminal, but a political offender, and was making his escape from the prison."

Drayman's forehead wrinkled. He smiled again.

"Help him? Naturally I did. I was fired by the idea. He explained things to me while we laid plans. He was one of three brothers, students at the University of Klausenburg, who had been arrested in an insurrection for an independent Transylvania under the protection of Austria; as it was before 1860. The three of them were in the same cell, and two had died of the pestilence. With the help of the prison doctor, also a convict, he had faked the same symptoms—and died. It wasn't likely that anybody would go very close to test the doctor's judgment; the whole prison was mad with fear. Even the people who buried those three would keep their heads turned away when they threw the bodies into pine coffins and nailed on the lids. They would bury the bodies at some distance from the prison. Most of all, they would do a quick job of nailing the lids. The doctor had smuggled in a pair of nail-cutters, which my resurrected friend showed me. A powerful man, if he kept his nerve and didn't use up too much air after he had been buried, could force up the lid with his head enough to wedge the nail-cutters into the loose space. Afterwards a powerful man could dig up through loose ground.

"Very well. When he found I was a student at Paris, conversation became easy. His mother had been French, and he spoke the language perfectly. We decided that he had better make for France, where he could set up a new identity without suspicion. He had a little money hidden away, and there was a girl in his native town who—"

Drayman stopped abruptly, like one who remembers that he has gone too far. Hadley merely nodded.

"I think we know who the girl was," he said. "For the moment, we can leave 'Madame Dumont' out of this. What then?"

"She could be trusted to bring the money and follow him to Paris. It wasn't likely that there would be a hue and cry—in fact, there wasn't any. He passed as dead; even if Grimaud was frightened enough to tear away from that neighbourhood before he would even shave or put on a suit of my clothes. We excited no suspicion. There were no passports in those days, and he posed on the way out of Hungary as the English friend of mine I had been expecting to meet at Tradj. Once into France . . . you know all the rest. Now, gentlemen!" Drayman drew a curiously shuddering breath, stiffened, and faced them with his hard blank eyes. "You can verify everything I have said—"

"What about that cracking sound?" interjected Dr. Fell, in an argumentative tone.

The question was so quiet, and yet so startling, that Hadley whirled round. Even Drayman's gaze groped towards him. Dr. Fell's red face was screwed up absently, and he wheezed as he poked at the carpet with his stick.

"I think it's very important," he announced to the fire, as though somebody had contradicted him. "Very important indeed. H'mf. Ha. Look here, Mr. Drayman, I've got only two questions to ask you. You heard a cracking sound—of the lid wrenching on the coffin, hey? Yes. Then that would mean it was a fairly shallow grave Grimaud climbed out of?"

"Quite shallow, yes, or he might never have got out."

"Second question. That prison, now . . . was it a well or badly managed place?"

Drayman was puzzled, but his jaw set grimly. "I do not know, sir. But I do know it was under fire at that time from a number of officials. I think they were bitter against the prison authorities for letting the disease get started—it interfered with the usefulness of the workmen at the mines. By the way, the dead men's names were published; I saw them. And I ask you again, what's the good of raking up old scandals? It can't help you. You see that it's not any particular discredit to Grimaud, but—"

"Yes, that's the point," rumbled Dr. Fell, peering at him curiously. "That's the thing I want to emphasize. It's not discreditable at all. Is it anything to make a man bury all traces of his past life?"

"—but it might become a discredit to Ernestine Dumont," said Drayman, raising his voice on a fiercer note. "Can't you see what I'm implying? What about Grimaud's daughter? And all this digging into the mess rests on some wild guess that one or both of his brothers might be alive. They're dead, and the dead don't get out of their graves. May I ask where you got such a notion as that one of Grimaud's brothers killed him?"

"From Grimaud himself," said Hadley.

For a second Rampole thought Drayman had not understood. Then the man shakily got up from his chair, as though he could not breathe. He fumbled to open his coat, felt at his throat, and sat down again. Only the glassy look of his eyes did not alter.

"Are you lying to me?" he asked—and it was with a shaky, querulous, childish tone coming through his gravity. "Why do you lie to me?"

"It happens to be the truth. Read this!"

Very quickly he thrust out the note from Dr. Peterson. Drayman made a movement to take it; then he drew back and shook his head.

"It would tell me nothing, sir. I—I—You mean he said something before he . . . ?"

"He said that the murderer was his brother."

"Did he say anything else?" asked Drayman, hesitating. Hadley let the man's imagination work, and did not reply. Presently Drayman went on: "But I tell you it's fantastic! Are you implying that this mountebank who threatened him, this fellow he had never seen before in his life, was one of his brothers? I suppose you are. I still don't understand. From the first moment I learned he had been stabbed . . ."

"*Stabbed?*"

"Yes. As I say, I—"

"He was shot," said Hadley. "What gave you the idea that he had been stabbed?"

Drayman lifted his shoulders. A wry, sardonic, rather despairing expression crept over his wrinkled face.

"I seem to be a very bad witness, gentlemen," he said in an even tone. "I persist with the best intentions, in telling you things you don't believe. Possibly I jumped to conclusions. Mr. Mangan said that Grimaud had been attacked and was dying; that the murderer had disappeared after slashing that painting to pieces. So I assumed—" He rubbed the bridge of his nose. "Was there anything else you wished to ask me?"

"How did you spend the evening?"

"I was asleep. I—You see, there are pains. Here, behind the eyeballs. I had them so badly at dinner that instead of going out (I was to go to a concert at the Albert Hall), I took a sleeping-tablet and lay down. Unfortunately, I don't remember anything from about half-past seven to the time Mr. Mangan woke me."

Hadley was studying his open overcoat, keeping himself very quiet, but with a dangerous expression like a man about to pounce.

"I see. Did you undress when you went to bed, Mr. Drayman?"

"I beg your—Undress? No. I took off my shoes, that's all. Why?"

"Did you leave your room at any time?"

"No."

"Then how did you get that blood on your jacket? . . . Yes, that's it. Get up! Don't run away, now. Stand where you are. Now take off your overcoat."

Rampole saw it when Drayman, standing uncertainly beside his chair and pulling off the overcoat, moved his hand across his own chest with the motions of a man groping on a floor. He was wearing a light grey suit, against which the stain splashed vividly. It was a darkish smear running from the side of the coat down across the right pocket. Drayman's fingers found it and stopped. The fingers rubbed it, then brushed together.

"It can't be blood," he muttered, with the same querulous noise rising in his voice. "I don't know what it is, but it can't be blood, I tell you!"

"We shall have to see about that. Take off the coat, please. I'm afraid I must ask you to leave it with us. Is there anything in the pockets you want to take out?"

"But—"

"Where did you get that stain?"

"I don't know. I swear to God I don't know, and I can't imagine. It isn't blood. What makes you think it is?"

"Give me the coat, please. Good!" He watched sharply while Drayman with unsteady fingers removed from the pockets a few coppers, a concert ticket, a handkerchief, a paper of Woodbine cigarettes, and a box of matches. Then Hadley took the coat and spread it across his knees. "Do you have any objection to your room being searched?—It's only fair to tell you I have no authority to do it, if you refuse."

"No objection at all," said the other, dully. He was rubbing his forehead. "If you'd only tell me how it happened, Inspector! I don't know. I've tried to do the right thing . . . yes. The right thing. . . . I didn't have anything to do with this business." He stopped, and smiled with such sardonic bitterness that Rampole felt more puzzled than suspicious. "Am I under arrest? I have no objection to that, either, you know."

Now, there was something wrong here: and yet not wrong in the proper way. Rampole saw that Hadley shared his own irrational doubts. Here was a man who had made several erratic misstatements. He had told a lurid tale which might or might not be true, but which had a vaguely theatrical, paste-board flimsiness about it. Finally, there was blood on his coat. And yet, for a reason he could not determine, Rampole was inclined to believe his story—or, at least, the man's own belief in his story. It might have been his complete (apparent) lack of shrewdness; his utter simplicity. There he stood, looking taller, more shrunken and bony in his shirt sleeves, the blue shirt itself faded to a dingy white, the sleeves tucked up on corded arms, his tie askew and the overcoat trailing from one hand. And he was smiling.

Hadley swore under his breath. "Betts!" he called, "Betts! Preston!" and tapped his heel impatiently on the floor until they answered. "Betts, get this coat to the pathologist for analysis of this stain. See it? Report in the morning. That's all for tonight. Preston, go down with Mr. Drayman and have a look round his room. You have a good idea what to look for; also keep an eye out for something in the mask line. I'll join you in a moment. . . . Think it over, Mr. Drayman. I'm going to ask you to come down to the Yard in the morning. That's all."

Drayman paid no attention. He blundered out in his batlike way, shaking his head and trailing the overcoat behind him. He even plucked Preston by the sleeve. "Where could I have got that blood?" he asked, eagerly. "It's a queer thing, you know, but where could I have got that blood?"

"Dunno, sir," said Preston. "Mind that doorpost!"

Presently the bleak room was quiet. Hadley shook his head slowly.

"It's got me, Fell," he admitted. "I don't know whether I'm coming or going. What do you make of the fellow? He seems gentle and pliable and easy enough; but you can keep pounding him like a punching-bag, and at the end of it he's still swinging gently in the same old place. He doesn't seem to care a rap *what* you think of him. Or what you do to him, for that matter. Maybe that's why the young people don't like him."

"H'm, yes. When I gather up those papers from the fireplace," grunted Dr. Fell, "I'm going home to think. Because what I think now . . ."

"Yes?"

"Is plain horrible."

With a gust of energy Dr. Fell surged up out of the chair, jammed his shovel-hat down over his eyes, and flourished his stick.

"I don't want to go jumping at theories. You'll have to cable for the real truth. Ha! Yes. But it's the story about the three coffins I don't believe—although Drayman may believe it, God knows! Unless our whole theory is blown to blazes, we've got to assume that the two Horváth brothers aren't dead. Hey?"

"The question being . . ."

"What happened to them. Harrumph, yes. What I think might have happened is based on the assumption that Drayman believes he's telling the truth. First point! I don't believe for a second that those brothers were sent to prison for a political offense. Grimaud, with his 'little money saved,' escapes from prison. He lies low for five years or more, and then suddenly 'inherits' a substantial fortune, under an entirely different name, from somebody we haven't heard of. But he slides out of France to enjoy it without comment. Second point, supporting! Where's the dangerous secret in Grimaud's life, if all this is true? Most people would consider that Monte Cristo escape as merely exciting and romantic; and, as for his offense, it would sound to English ears about as hideous and blasting an infamy as pinching a Belisha beacon or pasting a policeman in the eye on boat-race night. Dammit, Hadley, it won't do!"

"You mean—?"

"I mean," said Dr. Fell in a very quiet voice, "Grimaud was alive when he was nailed up to his coffin. Suppose the other two were alive, too? Suppose all three 'deaths' were faked exactly as Grimaud's was faked? Suppose there were two living people in those other coffins when Grimaud climbed out of his? But they couldn't come out . . . because he had the nail-cutters and didn't choose to use 'em. It wasn't likely that there would be more than one pair of cutters. Grimaud had 'em, because he was the strongest. Once he got out, it would have been easy for him to let the others out, as they had arranged. But he prudently decided to let them lie buried, because then there would be nobody to share the money that all three had stolen. A brilliant crime, you see. A brilliant crime."

Nobody spoke. Hadley muttered something under his breath; his face was incredulous and rather wild as he got up.

"Oh, I know it's a black business!" rumbled Dr. Fell; "a black, unholy business that would turn a man's dreams sick if he'd done it. But it's the only thing that will explain this unholy case, and why a man *would* be hounded if those brothers ever climbed up out of their graves. . . . Why was Grimaud so desperately anxious to rush Drayman away from that spot without getting rid of his convict garb as soon as he could? Why would he run the risk of being seen from the road, when a hide-away near a plague grave would be the last place any native would venture? Well, those graves were very shallow. If, as time went on, the brothers found themselves choking to death . . . and still nobody had come to let them out . . . they might begin to shriek and batter and pound in their coffins. It was just possible Drayman might have seen the loose earth trembling or heard the last scream from inside."

Hadley got out a handkerchief and mopped his face.

"Would any swine—" he said in an incredulous voice, which trailed away. "No. We're running off the rails, Fell. It's all imagination. It can't be! Besides, in that case they wouldn't have climbed up out of their graves. They'd be dead."

"Would they?" said Dr. Fell, vacantly. "You're forgetting the spade."

"What spade?"

"The spade that some poor devil in his fear or hurry left behind when he'd dug the grave. Prisons, even the worst prisons, don't permit *that* sort of negligence. They would send back after it. Man, I can see that business in every detail, even if I haven't one shred of proof to support it! Think of every word that crazy Pierre Fley said to Grimaud at the Warwick Tavern, and see if it doesn't fit. . . . Back come a couple of armed, hard-headed warders looking for that discarded spade. They see or hear what Grimaud was afraid Drayman would see or hear. They either tumble to the trick or else they act in common humanity. The coffins are smashed open; the two brothers are rolled out, fainting and bloody, but alive."

"And no hue and cry after Grimaud? Why, they'd have torn Hungary apart looking for the man who had escaped and—"

"H'mf, yes, I thought of that too, and asked about it. The prison authorities would have done just that . . . if they weren't being so bitterly attacked that their heads were in danger at the time. What do you think the attackers would have said if it became known that, through carelessness, they allowed a thing like that to happen? Much better to keep quiet about it, hey? Much better to shove those two brothers into close confinement and keep quiet about the third."

"It's all theory," said Hadley, after a pause. "But, if it's true, I could come close to believing in evil spirits. God knows Grimaud got exactly what he deserved. And we've got to go on trying to find his murderer just the same. If that's the whole story—"

"Of course it's not the whole story!" said Dr. Fell. "It's not the whole story even if it's true, and that's the worst part. You talk of evil spirits. I tell you that in some way I can't fathom there's a worse evil spirit than Grimaud; and that's X, that's the hollow man, that's brother Henri." He pointed out with his stick. "Why? Why does Pierre Fley admit he fears him? It would be reasonable for Grimaud to fear his enemy; but why does Fley even fear his brother and his ally against the common antagonist? Why is a skilled illusionist afraid of illusion, unless this gentle brother Henri is as rattlebrained as a criminal lunatic and as clever as Satan?"

Hadley put his notebook in his pocket and buttoned up his coat.

"*You* go home if you like," he said. "We've finished here. But I'm going after Fley. Whoever the other brother is, Fley knows. And he's going to tell, I can promise you that. I'll have a look round Drayman's room, but I don't anticipate much. Fley is the key to this cipher, and he's going to lead us to the murderer. Ready?"

They did not learn it until the next morning; but Fley, as a matter of fact, was already dead. He had been shot down with the same pistol that killed Grimaud. And the murderer was invisible before the eyes of witnesses, and still he had left no footprint in the snow.

11
The Murder by Magic

When Dr. Fell hammered on the door at nine o'clock next morning, both his guests were in a drowsy state. Rampole had got very little sleep the night before. When he and the doctor returned at half-past one, Dorothy had been hopping with eagerness to hear all the details, and her

husband was not at all unwilling to tell them. They equipped themselves
with cigarettes and beer, and retired to their room, where Dorothy piled
a heap of sofa pillows on the floor like Sherlock Holmes, and sat there
with a glass of beer and a sinister expression of wisdom while her husband stalked about the room, declaiming. Her views were vigorous but
hazy. She rather liked the descriptions of Mme. Dumont and Drayman,
but took a violent dislike to Rosette Grimaud. Even when Rampole
quoted Rosette's remarks to the debating society, a motto of which they
both approved, she was not mollified.

"All the same, you mark my words," said Dorothy, pointing her cigarette at him wisely, "that funny-faced blonde is mixed up in it somehow.
She's a wrong un, old boy. I mean she wants ber-lud. Bah! I'll bet she
wouldn't even make a good—um—courtesan, to use her own terms.
And if I had ever treated you the way she treats Boyd Mangan, and you
hadn't landed me a sock under the jaw, I'd never have spoken to either
of us again . . . if you see my meaning?"

"Let's omit the personal," said Rampole. "Besides, what's she done to
Mangan? Nothing that I can see. And you don't seriously think she
would kill her father, even if she hadn't been locked in the front room?"

"N-no, because I don't see how she could have put on that fancy
costume and fooled Mrs. Dumont," said Dorothy, with an expression of
great profundity in her bright dark eyes. "But I'll tell you how it is, Mrs.
Dumont and Drayman are both innocent. As for Mills—well, Mills does
sound rather a prig, but then your view is highly coloured because you
don't like science or the Vision of the Future. And you'll admit he does
sound as though he's telling the truth?"

"Yes."

She smoked reflectively. " 'M. I'm getting tremendous ideas. The people I'm most suspicious of, and the ones against whom it'd be easiest to
make out a case, are the two you haven't seen—Pettis and Burnaby."

"*What?*"

"Like this. The objection to Pettis is that he's too small, isn't it? I
should have thought Dr. Fell's erudition would have got it like a shot. I
was thinking of a story. . . . I can't remember where I've read it, but it
comes in one shape or another into several mediaeval tales. J'you remember? There's always an enormous figure in armour, with its vizor
down, who rides in a tournament and smacks everybody flat. Then
along comes ye mightiest knight to joust against it. Down he rides with

a bang, hits the tall champion's helmet squarely in the middle of the vizor, and to everybody's horror knocks the head clean off. Then up pipes a voice from inside the shell, and they discover it belongs to a handsome young lad who's not tall enough to fill up the suit of armour. . . ."

Rampole looked at her. "Beloved," said he, with dignity, "this is pure drivelling. This is beyond all question the looniest idea which. . . . Look here, are you seriously trying to tell me Pettis might walk about with a dummy head and shoulders rigged up on him?"

"You're too conservative," she said, wrinkling her nose. "*I* think it's a jolly-good idea. And do you want confirmation? Right! Didn't Mills himself comment on the shiny look about the back of the head, and say it looked as though the whole head were made of papier-maché? What have you got to say to that?"

"I say it's a nightmare. Haven't you any more practical ideas?"

"Yes!" said Dorothy, wriggling. She had obviously just been struck with the inspiration, but she passed it off as an old one. "It's about the impossible situation. *Why* didn't the murderer want to leave any footprints? You're all going after the most horribly complicated reasons. And, anyway, they generally end in your thinking that the murderer just wants to have some fun with the police. Rats, darling! What's the only real reason, the first reason anybody would think of outside a murder case, why a man mightn't want to leave any footprints? Why, because the footprints would be so distinctive that they'd lead straight to him! Because he had a deformity or something which would hang him if he left a footprint. . . ."

"And—?"

"And, you tell me," she said "this chap Burnaby has a club foot."

When towards daylight Rampole at last fell asleep he was haunted by images in which Burnaby's club foot seemed even more sinister than the man who wore a dummy head. It was all nonsense; but it was a disturbing kind of nonsense to mingle in a dream with the puzzle of the three graves.

He struggled out of bed when Dr. Fell knocked at the door towards nine o'clock on Sunday morning; he shaved and dressed hastily, and stumbled down through a silent house. It was an unearthly hour for Dr. Fell (or anybody else) to be stirring, and Rampole knew some fresh deviltry had broken overnight. The hallways were chilly; even the great library, where a roaring fire had been lighted, had that unreal look which all things assume when you get up at daybreak to catch a train. Breakfast—for three—was set out in the embrasure of the bay window overlooking the terrace. It was a leaden day, the sky already moving with snow. Dr. Fell, fully dressed, sat at the table with his head in his hands and stared at a newspaper.

"Brother Henri—" he rumbled, and struck the paper. "Oh yes. He's at it again. Hadley just phoned with more details, and he'll be here any minute. Look at this for a starter. If we thought we'd got a hard problem on our hands last night—oh, Bacchus, look at *this* one! I'm like Drayman—I can't believe it. It's crowded Grimaud's murder clean off the front page. Fortunately, they haven't spotted the connection between 'em, or else Hadley's given 'em the word to keep off. Here!"

Rampole, as coffee was poured out for him, saw the headlines. "MAGICIAN MURDERED BY MAGIC!" said one, which must have given great pleasure to the writer. "RIDDLE OF CAGLIOSTRO STREET." " 'THE SECOND BULLET IS FOR YOU!' "

"Cagliostro Street?" the American repeated. "Where in the name of sanity is Cagliostro Street? I thought I'd heard of some funny street names, but this one—"

"You'd never hear of it ordinarily," grunted Dr. Fell. "It's one of those streets hidden behind streets, that you only stumble on by accident when you're looking for a short-cut, and you're startled to find a whole community lost in the middle of London. . . . Anyway, Cagliostro Street is not more than three minutes' walk from Grimaud's house. It's a little cul-de-sac behind Guilford Street, on the other side of Russell Square. So far as I remember, it has a lot of tradesmen's shops overflowing from Lamb's Conduit Street, and the rest lodging-houses. . . . Brother Henri left Grimaud's place after the shooting, walked over there, hung about for a little time, and then completed his work."

Rampole ran his eye down the story:

The body of the man found murdered last night in Cagliostro Street, W.C. 1, has been identified as that of Pierre Fley, a French conjuror and illusionist. Although he had been performing for some months at a music-hall in Commercial Road, E.C., he took lodging two weeks ago in Cagliostro Street. About half-past ten last night, he was found shot to death under circumstances which seem to indicate that a magician was murdered by magic. Nothing was seen and no trace left—three witnesses testify—although they all distinctly heard a voice say, *"The second bullet is for you."*

Cagliostro Street is two hundred yards long, and ends in a blank brick wall. There are a few shops at the beginning of the street, closed at that time although a few night lights were burning, and the pavements were swept in front of them. But, beginning some twenty yards on, there was unbroken snow on the pavement and the street.

Mr. Jesse Short and Mr. R. G. Blackwin, Birmingham visitors to London, were on their way to visit a friend with lodgings near the end of the street. They were walking on the right-hand pavement, and had their backs to the mouth of the street. Mr. Blackwin, who was turning round to make sure of the numbers on the doors, noticed a man walking some distance behind them. This man was walking slowly and rather nervously, looking round him as though he expected to see some one near. He was walking in the middle of the street. But the light was dim, and, aside from seeing that he was tall and wore a slouch-hat, neither Mr. Short nor Mr. Blackwin noticed anything else. At the same time, P. C. Henry Withers— whose beat was along Lamb's Conduit Street—reached the entrance to Cagliostro Street. He saw the man walking in the snow, but glanced back again without noticing him. And in the space of three or four seconds the thing happened.

Mr. Short and Mr. Blackwin heard behind them a cry that was nearer a scream. They then heard some one distinctly say the words. "The second bullet is for you," and a laugh followed by a muffled pistolshot. As they whirled round, the man behind staggered, screamed again, and pitched forward on his face.

The street, they could see, was absolutely empty from end to end. Moreover, the man was walking in the middle of it, and both state that there were no footprints in the snow but his own. This is confirmed by P. C. Withers, who came running from the mouth of the street. In the light from a jeweller's window, they could see the victim lying face downward, his arms spread out, and blood jetting from a bullethole under his left shoulder blade. The weapon—a long-barrelled .38 Colt revolver, of a pattern thirty years out of date—had been thrown away some ten feet behind.

Despite the words they had all heard, and the gun lying at some distance, the witnesses thought because of the empty street that he must have shot himself. They saw that the man was still breathing, and carried him to the office of Dr. M. R. Jenkins near the end of the street, while the constable made certain there were no footprints anywhere. The victim, however, died, without speaking, not long afterwards.

Then occurred the most startling disclosures. The man's overcoat round the wound was burnt and singed black, showing that the weapon must have been pressed against his back or held only a few inches away. But Dr. Jenkins gave it as his opinion—later confirmed by the police—that suicide was not possible. No man, he stated, could have held any pistol in such a way as to shoot himself through the back at that angle, and more especially with the long-barrelled weapon which was used. It was murder, but an incredible murder. If the man had been shot from some distance away, from a window or door, the absence of a murderer and even the absence of footprints would mean nothing. But he was shot by some one who stood beside him, spoke to him, and vanished.

No papers or marks of identification could be found in the man's clothes, and nobody seemed to know him. After some delay he was sent to the mortuary—

"But what about the officer Hadley sent round to pick him up?" Rampole asked. "Couldn't he identify the man?"

"He did identify him, later," growled Dr. Fell. "But the whole hullabaloo was over by the time he got there. He ran into the policeman, Hadley says, when Withers was still making inquiries from door to door. Then he put two and two together. Meantime, the man Hadley had sent to the music-hall also in quest of Fley had phoned through that Fley wasn't there. Fley had coolly told the theatre manager he had no intention of doing his turn that night, and walked out with some sort of cryptic remark. . . . Well, to identify the body at the mortuary they got hold of Fley's landlord in Cagliostro Street. And, to make sure it was the same person, they asked for somebody from the music-hall to come along. An Irishman with an Italian name, who was also on the bill but couldn't do his turn that night because of some sort of injury, volunteered. Harrumph, yes. It was Fley, and he's dead, and we're in a hell of a mess. Bah!"

"And this story," cried Rampole, "is actually true?"

He was answered by Hadley, whose ring at the bell was belligerent. Hadley stamped in, carrying his briefcase like a tomahawk, and released some of his grievances before he would even touch bacon and eggs.

"It's true, right enough," he said, grimly, stamping his heels before the fire. "I let the papers splash it out so we could broadcast an appeal for information from anybody who knew Pierre Fley or his—— ——
——brother Henri. By God! Fell, I'm losing my mind! That damned

nickname of yours sticks in my head, and I can't get rid of it. I find myself referring to brother Henri as though I knew that was his real name. I find myself getting imaginary pictures of brother Henri. At least we soon ought to know what his real name is. I've cabled to Bucharest. Brother Henri! Brother Henri! We've picked up his trail again, and lost it again. Bro—"

"For Lord's sake go easy!" urged Dr. Fell, puffing uneasily. "Don't rave; it's bad enough now. I suppose you've been at it nearly all night? And got some more information? H'mf, yes. Now sit down and console the inner man. Then we can approach in—humph—a philosophic spirit, hey?"

Hadley said he wanted nothing to eat. But, after he had finished two helpings, drunk several cups of coffee, and lighted a cigar, he mellowed into a more normal mood.

"Now, then! Let's begin," he said, squaring himself determinedly as he took papers from the briefcase, "by checking over this newspaper account point by point—as well as what it doesn't say. Hum! First, as to these chaps Blackwin and Short. They're reliable; besides, it's certain neither of them is brother Henri. We wired Birmingham, and found they've been well known in their district all their lives. They're prosperous, sound people who wouldn't go off the handle as witnesses in a thing like this. The constable, Withers, is a thoroughly reliable man; in fact, he's painstaking to the extent of a vice. If those people say they didn't see anybody, they may have been deceived, but at least they were telling the truth as they knew it."

"Deceived . . . how?"

"*I don't know,*" growled Hadley, drawing a deep breath and shaking his head grimly, "except that they must have been. I had a brief look at the street, although I didn't go through Fley's room. It's no Piccadilly Circus for illumination, but at least it's not dark enough for any man in his five wits to be mistaken about what he saw. Shadows—I don't know! As to footprints, if Withers swears there weren't any, I'll take his word for it. And there we are."

Dr. Fell only grunted, and Hadley went on:

"Now, about the weapon. Fley was shot with a bullet from that Colt .38, and so was Grimaud. There were two exploded cartridge-cases in the magazine, only two bullets, and bro—and the murderer scored with each. The modern revolver, you see, ejects its shells like an automatic;

but this gun is so old that we haven't a ghost of a chance of being able to trace it. It's in good working order, it fires modern steel-jacket ammunition, but somebody has kept it hidden away for years."

"He didn't forget anything, Harry didn't. Well. Did you trace Fley's movements?"

"Yes. He was going to call on Henri."

Dr. Fell's eyes snapped open. *"Eh?* Look here, you mean you've got a lead about—"

"It's the only lead we have got. And," said Hadley, with bitter satisfaction, "if it doesn't produce results within a couple of hours I'll eat that briefcase. You remember, I told you over the phone that Fley had refused to perform and walked out of the theatre last night? Yes. My plainclothes officer got the story both from the theatre-manager, fellow named Isaacstein, and from an acrobat named O'Rourke, who was friendlier with Fley than anybody else and identified the body later.

"Saturday, naturally, is the big night down Limehouse way. The theatre runs continuous variety from one in the afternoon until eleven at night. Business was booming in the evening, and Fley's first night turn was to begin at eight-fifteen. About five minutes before then, O'Rourke —who had broken his wrist and couldn't go on that night—sneaked down into the cellar for a smoke. They have a coal furnace for hot-water pipes there."

Hadley unfolded a closely written sheet.

"Here is what O'Rourke said, just as Somers took it down and O'Rourke later initialled.

"The minute I got through the asbestos door and downstairs, I heard a noise like somebody smashing up kindling-wood. Then I did get a jump. The furnace door was open, and there was old Loony with a hatchet in his hand, busting hell out of the few properties he owned and shoving them all in the fire. I said, 'For cat's sake, Loony, what are you doing?' He said, in that queer way of his, 'I am destroying my equipment, Signor Pagliacci.' (I use the name of Pagliacci the Great, you understand, but then he always talked like that, so help me!) Well, he said, 'My work is finished; I shall not need them any longer'—and, zingo! in went his faked ropes and the hollow bamboo rods for his cabinet. I said, 'Loony, great goddelmighty, pull yourself together.' I said, 'You go on in a few minutes, and you're not even dressed.' He said: 'Didn't I tell you? I am going to see my brother. He will do something that will settle an old affair for both of us.'

"Well, he walked over to the stairs and then turned around sharp. Loony's got a face like a white horse, Lord pity me for saying it, and it had a queer creepy look with the fire from the furnace shining on it. He said, 'In case anything happens to me after he has done the business, you will find my brother in the same street where I myself live. That is not where he really resides, but he has taken a room there.' Just then down comes old Isaacstein, looking for him. He couldn't believe his ears when he heard Loony refuse to go on. There was a row. Isaacstein bawled, 'You know what'll happen if you don't go on?' And Loony says, as pleasant as a three-card man, 'Yes, I know what will happen.' Then he lifts his hat very courteously, and says, 'Good night, gentlemen. I am going back to my grave.' And up the stairs this lunatic walks without another word."

Hadley folded up the sheet and replaced it in his briefcase.

"Yes, he was a good showman," said Dr. Fell, struggling to light his pipe. "It seems a pity brother Henri had to . . . what then?"

"Now, it may or may not mean anything to track Henri down in Cagliostro Street, but we're sure to get his temporary hideout," Hadley went on. "The question occurred to me, where was Fley *going* when he was shot? Where was he walking to? Not to his own room. He lived at number 2B, at the beginning of the street, and he was going in the other direction. When he was shot he was a little over halfway down, between number 18 on his right and number 21 on his left—but in the middle of the street, of course. That's a good trail, and I've sent Somers out on it. He's to turn out every house past the middle, looking for *any* new or suspicious or otherwise noticeable lodger. Landladies being what they are, we shall probably get dozens, but that doesn't matter."

Dr. Fell, who was slouched as far down in the big chair as the bulk of his weight would allow, ruffled his hair.

"Yes, but I shouldn't concentrate too much on any end of the street. Rip 'em all up, say I. You see, suppose Fley was running from somebody, trying to get away from somebody, when he was shot?"

"Running away into a blind alley?"

"It's *wrong!* I tell you it's all wrong!" roared the doctor, hoisting himself up in the chair. "Not merely because I can't see anywhere a chink or glimmer of reason (which I freely admit), but because the simplicity of the thing is so maddening. It's no matter of hocus-pocus within four walls. There's a street. There's a man walking along it in the snow. Scream, whispered words, bang! Witnesses turn, and murderer gone. Where? Did the pistol come flying through the air like a thrown knife, explode against Fley's back, and spin away?"

"Rubbish!"

"I know it's rubbish. But I still ask the question," nodded Dr. Fell. He let his eye-glasses drop and pressed his hands over his eyes. "I say, how does this new development affect the Russell Square group? I mean, considering that everybody is officially under suspicion, can't we eliminate a few of those? Even if they were telling us lies at Grimaud's house, they still weren't out hurling Colt revolvers in the middle of Cagliostro Street."

The superintendent's face was ugly with sarcasm. "Now there's another bit of luck for us, kindly notice. I forgot that! We could eliminate one or two—if the Cagliostro Street business had occurred a little later, or even a little earlier. It didn't. Fley was shot at just ten-twenty-five. In other words, about fifteen minutes after Grimaud. Brother Henri took no chances. He anticipated exactly what we would do: send out a man to pick up Fley as soon as the alarm was given. Only brother Henri (or somebody) anticipated us in both ways. He was there with his little vanishing-trick."

" 'Or somebody'?" repeated Dr. Fell. "Your mental processes are interesting. Why 'or somebody'?"

"That's what I'm getting at—the unfortunate, unobserved fifteen minutes just after Grimaud's murder. I'm learning new wrinkles in crime, Fell. If you want to commit a couple of shrewd murders, don't commit one and then hang about waiting for the dramatic moment to pull off the other. Hit once—and then hit again instantly, while the watchers are still so muddled by the first that nobody, including the police, can definitely remember who was where at a given time. Can we?"

"Now, now," growled Dr. Fell, to conceal the fact that he couldn't. "It ought to be easy to work out a time-table. Let's see. We arrived at Grimaud's . . . when?"

Hadley was jotting on a slip of paper. "Just as Mangan jumped out the window, which couldn't have been more than two minutes after the shot. Say ten-twelve. We ran upstairs, found the door locked, got the pliers, and opened the door. Say three minutes more."

"Isn't that allowing a small margin of time?" Rampole interposed. "It seemed to me we were doing a good deal of tearing around."

"People often think so. In fact," said Hadley, "I thought so myself until I handled that Kynaston knifing case (remember, Fell?), where a damned clever killer depended for his alibi on the tendency of witnesses always to *over*-estimate time. That's because we think in minutes rather than seconds. Try it yourself. Put a watch on the table, shut your eyes, and look again when you think a minute is up. You'll probably look thirty seconds too soon. No, say three minutes here!" He scowled. "Mangan phoned, and the ambulance was round very quickly. Did you notice the address of that nursing-home, Fell?"

"No. I leave these sordid details to you," said Dr. Fell, with dignity. "Somebody said it was just round the corner, I remember. Humph. Ha."

"In Guilford Street, next to the Children's Hospital. In fact," said Hadley, "backed up against Cagliostro Street so closely that the back garden must be in line. . . . Well, say five minutes to get the ambulance to Russell Square. That's ten-twenty. And what about the next five minutes, the time just before the second murder, and the equally important five or ten or fifteen minutes afterwards? Rosette Grimaud, alone, rode over in the ambulance with her father, and didn't return for some time. Mangan, alone, was downstairs doing some telephoning for me, and didn't come upstairs until Rosette returned. I don't seriously consider either of 'em, but take it all for the sake of argument. Drayman? Nobody saw Drayman all this time and for a long while afterwards. As to Mills and the Dumont woman—h'm. Well, yes; I'm afraid it does clear them. Mills was talking to us all the earlier part of the time, until at least ten-thirty anyhow, and Madame Dumont joined him very shortly; they both stayed with us for a while. That tears it."

Dr. Fell chuckled.

"In fact," he said, reflectively, "we know exactly what we did before, no more or less. The only people it clears are the ones we were sure were innocent, and who had to be telling the truth if we made any sanity of the story. Hadley, it's the cussedness of things in general which makes me raise my hat. By the way, did you get anything last night out of searching Drayman's room? And what about that blood?"

"Oh, it's human blood, right enough, but there was nothing in Drayman's room that gave a clue to it—or to anything else. There were several of those pasteboard masks, yes. But they were all elaborate affairs with whiskers and goggle eyes; more the sort of thing that would appeal to a kid. Nothing, anyway, in the—the plain pink style. There was a lot of stuff for kids' amateur theatricals, some old sparklers and pinwheels and the like, and a toy theatre. . . ."

"Penny plain and twopence coloured," said Dr. Fell, with a wheeze of reminiscent pleasure. "Gone forever the glory of childhood. Wow! The grandeur of a toy theatre! In my innocent childhood days, Hadley, when I came trailing clouds of glory to the view (a thesis, by the way, which might have been open to considerable debate on the part of my parents); in my childhood days, I say, I owned a toy theatre with sixteen changes of scenery. Half of 'em, I am pleased to say, were jail scenes. Why does the young imagination run so strongly to jail scenes, I wonder? Why—"

"What the hell's the matter with you?" demanded Hadley, staring. "Why the sentimentality?"

"Because I have suddenly got an idea," said Dr. Fell, gently. "And, oh, my sacred hat, what an idea!" He remained blinking at Hadley. "What about Drayman? Are you going to arrest him?"

"No. In the first place, I don't see how he could have done it, and I couldn't even get a warrant. In the second place—"

"You don't believe he's guilty?"

"H'm," grunted Hadley, with an innate caution about doubting anybody's innocence. "I don't say that, but I think he's likely to be less culpable than anybody else. Anyhow, we've got to get a move on! Cagliostro Street first, then to interview several people. Finally—"

They heard the door-bell ring, and a sleepy maidservant tumbled down to answer it.

"There's a gentleman downstairs, sir," said Vida, poking her head into the room, "who says he wants to see either you or the superintendent. A Mr. Anthony Pettis, sir."

12
The Picture

Dr. Fell, rumbling and chuckling and spilling ashes from his pipe like the Spirit of the Volcano, surged up to greet the visitor with a cordiality which seemed to put Mr. Anthony Pettis much more at his ease. Mr. Pettis bowed slightly to each of them.

"You must excuse me, gentlemen, for intruding so early," he said. "But I had to get it off my mind, and couldn't feel easy until I did. I understand you were—um—looking for me last night. And I had an unpleasant night of it, I can tell you." He smiled. "My one criminal adventure was when I forgot to renew a dog license, and my guilty conscience was all over me. Every time I went out with that confounded dog I thought every policeman in London was eyeing me in a sinister way. I began to slink. So in this case I thought I'd better hunt you out. They gave me this address at Scotland Yard."

Dr. Fell was already stripping off his guest's overcoat, with a gesture that nearly upset Mr. Pettis, and hurling him into a chair. Mr. Pettis grinned. He was a small, neat, starched man with a shiny bald head and a startlingly booming voice. He had prominent eyes, looking more shrewd with a wrinkle of concentration between them, a humorous mouth and a square cleft chin. It was a bony face—imaginative, ascetic, rather nervous. When he spoke he had a trick of sitting forward in his chair, clasping his hands, and frowning at the floor.

"It's a bad business about Grimaud," he said, and hesitated. "Naturally I'll follow the formula of saying I wish to do everything I can to help. In this case it happens to be true." He smiled again. "Er—do you want me sitting with my face to the light, or what? Outside novels, this is my first experience with the police."

"Nonsense," said Dr. Fell, introducing everybody. "I've been wanting to meet you for some time; we've written a few things on the same lines. What'll you drink? Whisky? Brandy and soda?"

"It's rather early," said Pettis, doubtfully. "Still, if you insist—thanks! I'm very familiar with your book on the supernatural in English fiction, Doctor; you're a great deal more popular than I shall ever be. And it's sound." He frowned. "It's very sound. But I don't entirely agree with you (or Dr. James) that a ghost in a story should always be malignant . . ."

"Of course it should always be malignant. The more malignant," thundered Dr. Fell, screwing his own face up into a tolerably hideous leer, "then the better. I want no sighing of gentle airs round *my* couch. I want no sweet whispers o'er Eden. I want BLOOD!" He looked at Pettis in a way which seemed to give the latter an uncomfortable idea that it was his blood. "Harrumph. Ha. I will give you rules, sir. The ghost should be malignant. It should never speak. It should never be transparent, but solid. It should never hold the stage for long, but appear in brief vivid flashes like the poking of a face round a corner. It should never appear in too much light. It should have an old, an academic or ecclesiastical background; a flavour of cloisters or Latin manuscripts. There is an un-fortunate tendency nowadays to sneer at old libraries or ancient ruins; to say that the really horrible phantom would appear in a confectioner's shop or at a lemonade stand. This is what they call applying the 'mod-ern test.' Very well; apply the test of real life. Now, people in real life honestly *have* been frightened out of their five wits in old ruins or churchyards. Nobody would deny that. But, until somebody in actual life really does scream out and faint at the sight of something at a lemonade stand (other, of course, than that beverage itself), then there is nothing to be said for this theory except that it is rubbish."

"Some people would say," observed Pettis, cocking one eyebrow, "that the old ruins were rubbish. Don't you believe that good ghost stories can be written nowadays?"

"Of course they can be written nowadays, and there are more brilliant people to write 'em . . . if they would. The point is, they are afraid of the thing called Melodrama. So, if they can't eliminate the melodrama, they try to hide it by writing in such an oblique, upside-down way that nobody under heaven can understand what they are talking about. In-stead of saying flat out what the character saw or heard, they try to give Impressions. It's as though a butler, in announcing guests at a ball, were to throw open the drawing-room doors and cry: 'Flicker of a top-hat, vacantly seen, or is it my complex fixed on the umbrella stand faintly gleaming?' Now, his employer might not find this satisfactory. He might want to know who in blazes was calling on him. Terror ceases to be terror if it has to be worked out like an algebra problem. It may be deplorable if a man is told a joke on Saturday night and suddenly bursts out laughing in church next morning. But it is much more deplorable if a man reads a terrifying ghost story on Saturday night, and two weeks later suddenly snaps his fingers and realizes that he ought to have been scared. Sir, I say now—"

For some time an irritated superintendent of the C. I. D. had been fuming and clearing his throat in the background. Now Hadley settled matters by slamming his fist down on the table.

"Easy on, will you?" he demanded. "We don't want to hear any lec-ture now. And it's Mr. Pettis who wants to do the talking. So—" When he saw Dr. Fell's puffings subside into a grin, he went on, smoothly, "As a matter of fact, it is a Saturday night I want to talk about; last night."

"And about a ghost?" Pettis inquired, whimsically. Dr. Fell's outburst had put him entirely at his ease. "The ghost who called on poor Grimaud?"

"Yes. . . . First, just as a matter of form, I must ask you to give an account of your movements last night. Especially between, say, nine-thirty and ten-thirty?"

Pettis put down his glass. His face had grown troubled again. "Then you mean, Mr. Hadley—after all, I *am* under suspicion?"

"The ghost said he was you. Didn't you know that?"

"Said he was. . . . Good God, no!" cried Pettis, springing up like a bald-headed jack-in-the-box. "Said he was me? I mean—er—said he was —hang the grammar! I want to know what you're talking about? What do you mean?" He sat down quietly and stared as Hadley explained. But he fussed with his cuffs, fussed with his tie, and several times nearly interrupted.

"Therefore, if you'll disprove it by giving an account of your movements last night. . . ." Hadley took out his notebook.

"Nobody told me about this last night. I was at Grimaud's after he was shot, but nobody told me," said Pettis, troubled. "As for last night, I went to the theatre: to His Majesty's Theatre."

"You can establish that, of course."

Pettis frowned. "I don't know. I sincerely hope so. I can tell you about the play, although I don't suppose that's much good. Oh yes; and I think I've still got my ticket stub somewhere, or my program. But you'll want to know if I met anybody I knew. Eh? No, I'm afraid not—unless I should find somebody who remembered me. I went alone. You see, every one of the few friends I have runs in a set groove. We know exactly where he is at most times, especially Saturday evenings, and we don't try to change the orbit." There was a wry twinkle in his eye. "It's—it's a kind of respectable Bohemianism, not to say stodgy Bohemianism."

"That," said Hadley, "would interest the murderer. What are these orbits?"

"Grimaud always works . . . excuse me; I can't get used to the idea that he's dead . . . always works until eleven. Afterwards you could disturb him as much as you liked; he's a night owl; but not before. Burnaby always plays poker at his club. Mangan, who's a sort of acolyte is with Grimaud's daughter. He's with her most evenings, for that matter. I go to the theatre or the films, but not always. I'm the exception."

"I see. And after the theatre last night? What time did you get out?"

"Near enough to eleven or a little past. I was restless. I thought I might drop in on Grimaud and have a drink with him. And—well, you know what happened. Mills told me. I asked to see you, or whoever was in charge. After I had waited downstairs for a long time without anybody paying any attention to me,"—he spoke rather snappishly—"I went across to the nursing-home to see how Grimaud was getting on. I got there just as he died. Now, Mr. Hadley, I know this is a terrible business, but I will swear to you—"

"Why did you ask to see me?"

"I was at the public house when this man Fley uttered his threat, and I thought I might be of some help. Of course I supposed at the time it was Fley who had shot him; but this morning I see in the paper—"

"Just a minute! Before we go on to that, I understand that whoever imitated you used all your tricks of address, and so on, correctly? Good! Then who in your circle (or out of it) would you suspect of being able to do that?"

"Or wanting to do it," the other said, sharply.

He sat back, being careful about the knife-crease of his trousers. His nervousness was clearly giving way before the twistings of a dry, curious, insatiable brain; an abstract problem intrigued him. Putting his fingertips together, he stared out of the long windows.

"Don't think I'm trying to evade your question, Mr. Hadley," he said, with an abrupt little cough. "Frankly, I can't think of anybody. But this puzzle bothers me apart from the danger, in a way, to myself. If you think my ideas suffer from too much subtlety, or from too much plain damned nonsense, I'll put it up to Dr. Fell. Let's suppose, for the sake of argument, that I am the murderer."

He looked mockingly at Hadley, who had straightened up.

"Hold on! I am not the murderer, but let's suppose it. I go to kill Grimaud in some outlandish disguise (which, by the way, I *would* rather commit a murder than be seen wearing). Hum! I indulge in all the rest of the tomfoolery. Is it likely that, after all these things, I would blatantly sing out my real name to those young people?"

He paused, tapping his fingers.

"That's the first view, the short-sighted view. But the very shrewd investigator would answer: 'Yes, a clever murderer might do just that. It would be the most effective way of bamboozling all the people who had jumped to the first conclusion. He changed his voice a very little, just enough so that people would remember it afterwards. He spoke as Pettis because he wanted people to think it *wasn't* Pettis.' Had you thought of that?"

"Oh yes," said Dr. Fell, beaming broadly. "It was the first thing I did think of."

Pettis nodded. "Then you will have thought of the answer to that, which clears me either way. If I were to do a thing like that, it isn't my voice I should have altered slightly. If the hearers accepted it to begin with, they might not later have the doubts I wanted them to have. *But,*" he said, pointing, "what I should have done was to make one slip in my speech. I should have said something unusual, something wrong and obviously not like myself, which later they would have remembered. And this the visitor didn't do. His imitation was too thorough, which seems to excuse me. Whether you take the forthright view or the subtle one, I can plead not guilty either because I'm not a fool or because I am."

Hadley laughed. His amused gaze travelled from Pettis to Dr. Fell, and he could keep his worried expression no longer.

"You two are birds of a feather," he said. "I like these gyrations. But I'll tell you from practical experience, Mr. Pettis, that a criminal who tried anything like that would find himself in the soup. The police wouldn't stop to consider whether he was a fool or whether he wasn't. The police would take the forthright view—and hang him."

"As you would hang me," said Pettis, "if you could find contributory evidence?"

"Exactly."

"Well—er—that's frank, anyhow," said Pettis, though he seemed acutely uneasy and startled at the reply. "Er—shall I go on? You've rather taken the wind out of my sails."

"Go on, certainly," urged the superintendent, with an affable gesture. "We can get ideas even from a clever man. What else have you to suggest?"

Whether or not that was a deliberate sting, it had a result nobody had expected. Pettis smiled, but his eyes had a fixed quality and his face seemed to become more bony.

"Yes, I think you can," he agreed. "Even ideas you should have had yourselves. Let me take one instance. You—or somebody—got himself quoted at some length in all the papers this morning, about Grimaud's murder. You showed how the murderer was careful to ensure unbroken snow for his vanishing-trick, whatever it was. He could be sure that it would snow last night, lay all his plans accordingly, and gamble on waiting until the snow stopped for the working of his scheme. In any event, he could reasonably depend on there being some snow. Is that correct?"

"I said something of the sort, yes. What of it?"

"Then I think you should have remembered," Pettis answered, evenly, "that the weather forecast said he could do nothing of the kind. Yesterday's weather forecast announced that there would be no snow at all."

"Oh, Bacchus!" boomed Dr. Fell, and brought his fist down on the table after a pause in which he blinked at Pettis. "Well done! I never thought of it. Hadley, this changes things altogether! This—"

Pettis relaxed. He took out a cigarette-case and opened it. "Of course, there is an objection. I mean, you can make the obvious retort that the murderer knew it was bound to snow because the weather forecast said it wouldn't. But in that case *you'd* be the one who took subtlety to the edge of comedy. I can't follow it so far. Fact is, I think the weather forecast comes in for as many untrue jeers as the telephone service. It dropped a brick in this instance, yes . . . but that doesn't matter. Don't you believe me? Look up last night's papers and see."

Hadley swore, and then grinned.

"Sorry," he said. "I didn't mean to touch you on the raw, but I'm glad I did. Yes, it does seem to alter matters. Blast it, if a man intended to commit a crime that depended on snow, he'd certainly treat the forecast with some sort of consideration." Hadley drummed on the table. "Never mind; we'll come back to that. I seriously ask for ideas now."

"That's all, I'm afraid. Criminology is more in Burnaby's line than in mine. I only happened to notice," Pettis admitted, with a jeering look at his own clothes, "so as to decide whether I ought to wear overshoes. Habit! . . . As to the person who imitated my voice, why try to implicate *me?* I'm a harmless enough old codger, I assure you. I don't fit into the rôle of gigantic nemesis. The only reason I can think of is that I'm the only one of the group who has no definite orbit on Saturday night and might not be able to prove an alibi. But as to who could have done it. . . . Any good mimic could have pulled it off; still, who knew just how I addressed those people?"

"What about the circle at the Warwick Tavern? There were others besides the ones we've heard about, weren't there?"

"Oh yes. There were two other irregulars. But I can't see either as a candidate. There's old Mornington, who has had a post at the Museum for over fifty years; he's got a cracked tenor that would never pass for me. There's Swayle, but I believe he was speaking on the wireless last night, about ant life or something, and should have an alibi . . ."

"Speaking at what time?"

"Nine forty-five or thereabouts, I believe, although I wouldn't swear to it. Besides, neither of them ever visited Grimaud's house.—And casual drifters at the pub? Well, some may have listened or sat down at the back of the room, though nobody ever joined the conversation. I suppose that's your best lead, even if it's a very thin one." Pettis took out a cigarette and closed the case with a snap. "Yes. We'd better *decide* it was an unknown quantity, or we shall be in all kinds of quicksand, eh? Burnaby and I were Grimaud's only close friends. But I didn't do it, and Burnaby was playing cards."

Hadley looked at him. "I suppose Mr. Burnaby really was playing cards?"

"I don't know," the other admitted, with flat candour. "But I'll give you odds he was, all the same. Burnaby's no fool. And a man would have to be rather an outstanding fathead to commit a murder on the one night when his absence from a certain group would be certain to be noticed."

Clearly this impressed the superintendent more than anything Pettis had yet said. He continued to drum on the table, scowling. Dr. Fell was occupied with some obscure, cross-eyed meditation of his own. Pettis looked curiously from one to the other of them.

"If I have given you food for thought, gentlemen—?" he suggested, and Hadley became brisk.

"Yes, yes! No end! Now, about Burnaby: you know he painted the picture which Dr. Grimaud bought to defend himself?"

"To defend himself? How? From what?"

"We don't know. I was hoping you might be able to explain it." Hadley studied him. "The taste for making cryptic remarks seems to run in his family. Do you know anything about his family, by the way?"

Pettis was evidently puzzled. "Well, Rosette is a very charming girl. Er —though I shouldn't say she had a taste for making cryptic remarks. Quite the contrary. She's a little too modern for my taste." His forehead wrinkled. "I never knew Grimaud's wife; she's been dead some years. But I still don't see—"

"Never mind. What do you think of Drayman?"

Pettis chuckled. "Old Hubert Drayman is the most unsuspicious man I ever met. So unsuspicious that some people think it hides a deep and devilish cunning. Excuse me, but have you got him on the carpet? If you have, I should forget it."

"We'll go back to Burnaby, then. Do you know how he came to paint that picture, or when he did it, or anything about it?"

"I think he did it a year or two ago. I remember it particularly, because it was the biggest canvas at his studio; he used it as a screen or a partition, turned up endways, whenever he needed one. I asked him once what it was intended to represent. He said, 'An imaginative conception of something I never saw.' It had some French name, *Dans l'Ombre des Montagnes du Sel,* or something of the sort." He stopped tapping the still unlighted cigarette on the case. His curious, restless brain was probing again. "Hullo! Now that I remember it, Burnaby said, 'Don't you like it? It gave Grimaud a hell of a turn when he saw it.'"

"Why?"

"I paid no attention. I naturally supposed it was some joke or piece of bragging; he laughed when he said it, and Burnaby's like that. But the thing had been lying about the studio, collecting dust, for such a long time that I was surprised when Grimaud came charging in on Friday morning and asked for it."

Hadley leaned forward sharply. "You were there then?"

"At the studio? Yes. I'd dropped in early for some reason or other—I forget what. Grimaud came stumping in . . ."

"Upset?"

"Yes. N-no. Say excited." Pettis reflected, studying Hadley covertly. "Grimaud said, with that machine-gun snap of his, 'Burnaby, where's your salt-mountain picture? I want it. What's your price?' Burnaby looked at him in a queer way. He came hobbling over and pointed to the picture and said, 'The thing's yours, man, if you want it; take it.' Grimaud said, 'No, I have a use for it and I insist on buying it.' Well, when Burnaby named some fool price like ten shillings, Grimaud quite solemnly got out a cheque-book and wrote a cheque for ten shillings. He would say nothing except that he had a place on the wall where it ought to go, in his study. That's all. He took the picture downstairs, and I got him a cab to take it away in. . . ."

"Was it wrapped up?" asked Dr. Fell, sharply; so sharply that Pettis jumped a little.

Dr. Fell had been showing more interest, not to say fierce concentration, in this recital than in anything Pettis had yet said. The doctor was bending forward with his hands clasped over his stick, and Pettis regarded him curiously.

"I wonder why you ask that?" he said. "It's what I was just going to mention—the fuss Grimaud made about wrapping it. He asked for paper, and Burnaby said, 'Where do you think I'd get a sheet of paper big enough to go round that? Why be ashamed of it? Take it as it is.' But Grimaud insisted on going downstairs and getting yards of brown paper off one of those rolls in somebody's shop. It seemed to annoy Burnaby a good deal."

"You don't know whether Grimaud went straight home with it?"

"No . . . I think he was going to have it framed, but I'm not sure."

Dr. Fell sat back with a grunt and let the subject go without more questions, in spite of Pettis's hints. Although Hadley kept on questioning for some time, nothing of importance was elicited so far as Rampole could see. On the personal side Pettis spoke guardedly; but there was, he said, little to conceal. There had been no friction in Grimaud's household, and none in the immediate circle except an antagonism between Mangan and Burnaby. Burnaby, although nearly thirty years older, had a strong interest in Rosette Grimaud, at once lazy and jealous. Dr. Grimaud had said nothing about this; if anything, he encouraged it, although so far as Pettis could observe he made no objection to Mangan.

"But I think you'll find, gentlemen," concluded Pettis, as he rose to go when Big Ben was striking ten, "that all these are side issues. It would be difficult to associate the *crime passionel* with any of our group. As to the financial side of affairs, I can't tell you much, either. Grimaud was fairly well-to-do, I should think. His solicitors, I happen to know, are Tennant and Williams of Gray's Inn. . . . By the way, I wonder if you'd all have lunch with me on a dreary Sunday? I'm just at the other side of Russell Square, you know; I've had a suite of rooms at the Imperial for fifteen years. You're investigating in that neighbourhood, and it might be handy; besides, if Dr. Fell feels inclined to discuss ghost stories—?"

He smiled. The doctor cut in to accept before Hadley could refuse, and Pettis left with a much more jaunty air than he had worn at his entrance. Afterwards they all looked at each other.

"Well?" growled Hadley. "Straightforward enough, it seemed to me. Of course we'll check it up. The point, the impressive point is: why should *any* of them commit a crime on the one night when absence would be bound to be noticed? We'll go after this chap Burnaby, but he sounds out of it, too, if only for that reason. . . ."

"And the weather forecast said it wouldn't snow," said Dr. Fell, with a kind of obstinacy. "Hadley, that shoots everything to blazes! It turns the whole case upside down somehow, how, but I don't see . . . Cagliostro Street! Let's go on to Cagliostro Street. Anywhere is better than this darkness."

Fuming, he stumped over after his cloak and shovel-hat.

13
The Secret Flat

London, on the morning of a grey winter Sunday, was deserted to the point of ghostliness along miles of streets. And Cagliostro Street, into which Hadley's car presently turned, looked as though it would never wake up.

Cagliostro Street, as Dr. Fell had said, contained a thin dingy overflow of both shops and rooming-houses. It was a backwater of Lamb's Conduit Street—which itself is a long and narrow thoroughfare, a shopping centre of its own, stretching north to the barrack-windowed quiet of Guilford Street, and south to the main artery of traffic along Theobald's Road. Towards the Guilford Street end on the west side, the entrance to Cagliostro Street is tucked between a stationer's and a butcher's. It looks so much like an alley that you would miss it altogether if you were not watching for the sign. Past these two buildings, it suddenly widens to an unexpected breadth, and runs straight for two hundred yards to a blank brick wall at the end.

This eerie feeling of streets in hiding, or whole rows of houses created by illusory magic to trick you, had never deserted Rampole in his prowlings through London. It was like wondering whether, if you walked out your own front door, you might not find the whole street mysteriously changed overnight, and strange faces grinning out of houses you had never seen before. He stood with Hadley and Dr. Fell at the entrance, staring down. The overflow of shops stretched only a little way on either side. They were all shuttered, or had their windows covered with a folding steel fretwork, with an air of defying customers as a fort would defy attackers. Even the gilt signs had an air of defiance. The windows were at all stages of cleanliness, from the bright gloss of a jeweller's farthest down on the right, to the grey murkiness of a tobacconist's nearest on the right: a tobacconist's that seemed to have dried up worse than ancient tobacco, shrunk together, and hidden itself behind news placards headlining news you never remembered having heard of. Beyond there were two rows of flat three-story houses in dark red brick, with window-frames in white or yellow, and drawn curtains of which a few (on the ground floor) showed a sportive bit of lace. They had darkened to the same hue with soot; they looked like one house except where iron railings went to the front doors from the lone line of area rails; they sprouted with hopeful signs announcing furnished rooms. Over them the chimney-pots stood up dark against a heavy grey sky. The snow had melted to patches of grey slush, despite a sharp wind that was swooping through the entrance and chasing a discarded newspaper with flaps and rustlings round a lamp-post.

"Cheerful," grunted Dr. Fell. He lumbered forward, and there were echoes of his footsteps. "Now, let's get this all straight before we attract attention. Show me where Fley was when he was hit. Stop a bit! Where did he live, by the way?"

Hadley pointed at the tobacconist's near which they were standing.

"Up over that place; just at the beginning of the street, as I told you. We'll go up presently—although Somers has been there, and says there's nothing at all. Now, come along and get roughly the middle point of the street. . . ." He went ahead, pacing off a yard at a stride. "The swept pavements and the marked street ended somewhere about here; say, more or less, a hundred and fifty feet. Then unmarked snow. A good distance beyond that, nearer to another hundred and fifty . . . *here.*"

He stopped and turned round slowly.

"Halfway up, centre of the roadway. You can see how broad the road is; walking there, he was a good thirty feet from any house on *either* side. If he'd been walking on the pavement, we might have constructed some wild theory of a person leaning out of a window or an areaway, with the gun fastened to the end of a pole or something, and—"

"Nonsense!"

"All right, nonsense; but what else can we think?" demanded Hadley, with some violence, and made a broad gesture with his briefcase. "As you said, yourself, here's the street; it's plain, simple, and impossible! I know there was no hanky-panky like that, but what *was* there? Also, the witnesses didn't see anything; and, if there had been anything, they must have seen it. Look here! Stay where you are, now, and keep facing the same direction." He paced again to a point some distance farther on, and turned after inspecting the numbers. Then he moved over to the right-hand pavement. "Here's where Blackwin and Short were when they heard the scream. You're walking along there in the middle of the street. I'm ahead of you. I whirl around—so. How far am I from you now?"

Rampole, who had drawn off from both of them, saw Dr. Fell standing big and alone in the middle of an empty rectangle.

"Shorter distance this time. Those two chaps," said the doctor, pushing back his shovel-hat, "were not much more than thirty feet ahead! Hadley, this is even rummier than I thought. He was in the middle of a snow desert. Yet they whirl round when they hear the shot . . . h'm . . . h'mf. . . ."

"Exactly. Next, as to lights. You're taking the part of Fley. On your right—a little distance ahead, and just beyond the door of number 18— you see a street lamp. A little distance behind, also on the right, you see that jeweller's window? Right. There was a light burning in that; not a bright one, but still it was there. Now, can you explain to me how two people, standing where I'm standing now, could possibly be mistaken about whether they saw anybody near Fley?"

His voice rose, and the street gave it a satiric echo. The discarded newspaper, caught again by an eddy of the wind, scuttled along with a sudden rush; and the wind tore with a hollow roar among chimney-pots as though it blew through a tunnel. Dr. Fell's black cloak flapped about him, and the ribbon on his eye-glasses danced wildly.

"Jeweller's—" he repeated, and stared. "Jeweller's! And a light in it. . . . Was there anybody there?"

"No. Withers thought of that and went to see. It was a show-light. The wire fretwork was stretched across both the window and the door; just as it is now. Nobody could have got in or out of there. Besides, it's much too far away from Fley."

Dr. Fell craned his neck round, and then went over to look owlishly into the protected window. Inside were displayed velvet trays of cheap rings and watches, an array of candlesticks, and in the middle a big round-hooded German clock with moving eyes in its sun of a face, which began to tinkle eleven. Dr. Fell stared at the moving eyes, which had an unpleasant effect of seeming to watch with idiot amusement the place where a man had been killed. It lent a touch of the horrible to Cagliostro Street. Then Dr. Fell stumped back to the middle of the street.

"But that," he said—obstinately, as though he were continuing an argument—"that is on the right-hand side of the street. And Fley was shot through the back from the *left* side. If we assume, as apparently we must assume, that the attacker approached from the left . . . or at least the flying pistol travelled over from the left . . . I don't know! Even granting that the murderer could walk on snow without leaving a foot-print, can we at least decide where he came from?"

"*He came from here,*" said a voice.

The rising of the wind seemed to whirl the words about them, as though they came from empty air. For one second in that gusty half-light Rampole experienced a worse shock than he had known even in the days of the Chatterham Prison case. He had a mad vision of flying things, and of hearing words from an invisible man exactly as the two witnesses had heard the hollow murderer whisper the night before. For one second, then, something took him by the throat—before he turned and, with a drop of anti-climax, saw the explanation. A thick-set young man with a reddish face and a bowler pulled down on his forehead (which gave him a somewhat sinister air) was coming down the steps from the open door of number 18. The young man grinned broadly as he saluted Hadley.

"He came from here, sir. I'm Somers, sir. You remember, you asked me to find out where the dead one, the Frenchie, was going when he was killed? And to find out what landlady had any sort of rum lodger that might be the man we're looking for? . . . Well, I've found out about the rum lodger, and it oughtn't to be difficult to find him. He came from *here*. Excuse my interrupting you."

Hadley, trying not to show that the interruption had been unpleasantly startling, growled a pleased word. His eyes travelled up to the doorway, where another figure stood hesitating. Somers followed the glance.

"Oh no, sir. That's not the lodger," he said, and grinned again. "That's Mr. O'Rourke; chap from the music-hall, you know, who identified the Frenchie last night. He's been giving me a bit of help this morning."

The figure detached itself from the gloom and came down the steps. He looked thin despite his heavy overcoat; thin and powerful, with the quick smooth steps carried on the ball of the foot which mark the trapeze or high-wire man. He was affable, easy, and bent slightly backwards as he spoke, like a man who wants room for his gestures. In looks he was rather swarthily reminiscent of the Italian: an effect that was heightened by a luxuriant black moustache with waxed ends, which curled under his hooked nose. Beneath this a large curved pipe hung from one corner of his mouth, and he was puffing with evident enjoyment. His wrinkled eyes had a humorous blue gleam; and he pushed back an elaborate fawn-coloured hat as he introduced himself. This was the Irishman with the Italian pseudonym; he spoke like an American, and in point of fact was, he explained, a Canadian.

"O'Rourke's the name, yes," he said. "John L. Sullivan O'Rourke. Does anybody know what my middle name is? You know, the name of the—" He squared back and took a hard right-hander at the empty air —"the greatest of 'em all? I don't. My old man didn't, when he named me. L. is all I know. I hope you don't mind my butting in. You see, I knew old Loony—" He paused, grinned, and twisted his moustache. "I see, gents! You're all looking at this soup-strainer of mine. Everybody does. It's on account of that goddam song. You know. The management thought it'd be a good idea if I got myself up like the fellow in the song. Oh, it's real! Look"—he pulled—"nothing phony about it, see? But I was telling you, excuse my butting in. I'm damn sorry for old Loony. . . ." His face clouded.

"That's all right," said Hadley. "Thanks for all the help as it is. It saves me seeing you at the theatre—"

"I'm not working, anyway," said O'Rourke, gloomily. He thrust his left hand out of a long overcoat sleeve. The wrist was wound into a cast and bandaged. "If I'd had any sense I'd have followed Loony last night. But here! Don't let me interrupt. . . ."

"Yes. If you'll come along, sir," Somers interposed, grimly, "I've got something pretty important to show you. As well as tell you. The landlady's downstairs getting dressed up, and she'll tell you about the lodger.

There's no doubt he's the man you want. But first I'd like you to see his rooms."

"What's in his rooms?"

"Well, sir, there's blood, for one thing," replied Somers. "And also a very queer sort of rope. . . ." He assumed an expression of satisfaction as he saw Hadley's face. "You'll be interested in that rope, and in other things. The fellow's a burglar—at least a crook of some sort, by the look of his outfit. He's put a special lock on the door, so that Miss Hake (that's the landlady) couldn't get in. But I used one of my keys—there's nothing illegal about that, sir; the fellow's evidently cleared out. Miss Hake says he's had the rooms for some time, but he's only used them one or two times since . . ."

"Come *on*," said Hadley.

Somers, closing the door behind, led them into a gloomy hallway and up three flights of stairs. The house was narrow, and had on each floor one furnished flat which ran the whole depth from back to front. The door of the top floor—close up near a ladder which led to the roof—stood open, its extra lock gleaming above the ordinary keyhole. Somers took them into a darkish passage with three doors.

"In here first, sir," he said, indicating the first on the left. "It's the bathroom. I had to put a shilling in the electric meter to get any light—now!"

He pressed a switch. The bathroom was a dingy converted box-room, with glazed paper on the wall in imitation of tile, worn oilcloth on the floor, a top-heavy geyser-bath whose tank had gone to rust, and a wavy mirror hung over a washstand with bowl and pitcher on the floor.

"Effort made to clean the place up, you see, sir," Somers went on. "But you'll still see reddish traces in the bath where the water was poured out. That was where he washed his hands. And over behind this clothes-hamper, now—"

With dramatic satisfaction he swung the hamper to one side, reached into the dust behind, and produced a still damp face cloth with sodden patches that had turned to dull pink.

"—he sponged his clothes with that," said Somers, nodding.

"Well done," said Hadley, softly. He juggled the face-cloth, glanced at Dr. Fell, smiled, and put down the find. "The other rooms, now. I'm curious about that rope."

Somebody's personality permeated those rooms like the sickly yellow of the electric lights; like the chilly chemical smell which was not quite obliterated by the strong tobacco O'Rourke smoked. It was a den in more senses than one. Heavy curtains were drawn across the windows in a fairly large front room. Under a powerful light on a broad table lay an assortment of little steel or wire tools with rounded heads and curved ends, (Hadley said, "Lockpicks, eh?" and whistled), an assortment of detached locks, and a sheaf of notes. There was a powerful microscope, a box fitted with glass slides, a bench of chemicals on which six labelled test-tubes were arranged in a rack, a wall of books, and in one corner a small iron safe at the sight of which Hadley uttered an exclamation.

"If he's a burglar," said the superintendent, "he's the most modern and scientific burglar I've seen in a long time. I didn't know this trick was known in England. You've been dipping into this, Fell. Recognize it?"

"There's a big hole cut right out of the iron in the top, sir," put in Somers. "If he used a blow-pipe, it's the neatest acetylene-cutting job I ever saw. He—"

"He didn't use a blow-pipe," said Hadley. "It's neater and easier than that. This is the Krupp preparation. I'm not strong on chemistry, but I think this is powdered aluminum and ferrous oxide. You mix the powder on top of the safe, you add—what is it?—powdered magnesium, and set a match to it. It doesn't explode. It simply generates a heat of several thousand degrees and melts a hole straight through the metal. . . . See that metal tube on the table? We have one at the Black Museum. It's a detectascope, or what they call a fish-eye lens, with a refraction over half a sphere like the eye of a fish. You can put it to a hole in the wall and see everything that's going on in the next room. What do you think of this, Fell?"

"Yes, yes," said the doctor, with a vacant stare as though all this were of no importance; "I hope you see what it suggests. The mystery, the— But where's that rope? I'm very much interested in that rope."

"Other room, sir. Back room," said Somers. "It's got up in rather grand style, like an Eastern . . . you know."

Presumably he meant divan; or even harem. There was a spurious Turkish floridity and mysteriousness about the rich-coloured couches and hangings; the tassels, gimcracks, and weapon-groups; yet your eye was almost startled into belief by finding such things in such a place. Hadley flung back the curtains. Bloomsbury intruded with winter daylight, making sickly the illusion. They looked out on the backs of the houses along Guilford Street, on paved yards below, and an alley winding up towards the back of the Children's Hospital. But Hadley did not consider that for long. He pounced on the coil of rope that lay across a divan.

It was thin but very strong, knotted at intervals of two feet apart; an ordinary rope except for the curious device hooked to one end. This looked like a black rubber cup, something larger than a coffee-cup, of great toughness and with a grip edge like a car tire.

"Wow!" said Dr. Fell. "Look here, is that—?"

Hadley nodded. "I've heard of them, but I never saw one before and I didn't believe they existed. See here! It's an air-suction cup. You've probably seen the same sort of thing in a child's toy. A spring toy-pistol fires at a smooth card a little rod with a miniature suction-cup in soft rubber on the end. It strikes the card, and the suction of the air holds it."

"You mean," said Rampole, "that a burglar could force that thing against the side of a wall, and its pressure would hold him on the rope?"

Hadley hesitated. "That's how they *say* it works. Of course, I don't—"

"But how would he get it loose again? That is, would he just walk away and leave it hanging there?"

"He'd need a confederate, naturally. If you pressed the edges of this thing at the bottom, they would let the air in and destroy the grip. Even so, I don't see how the devil it could have been used for—"

O'Rourke, who had been eyeing the rope in a bothered way, cleared his throat. He took the pipe out of his mouth and cleared his throat again for attention.

"Look, gents," he said in his hoarse, confidential voice. "I don't want to butt in, but I think that's all bunk."

Hadley swung round. "How so? Do you know anything about it?"

"I'll make you a little bet," nodded the other, and poked at the air with his pipe-stem for emphasis, "that this thing belonged to Loony Fley. Give it to me for a second and I'll see. Mind, I don't *swear* it belonged to Loony. There are plenty of queer things in this joint. But—"

He took the rope, and ran his fingers gently along it until he reached the middle. Then he winked and nodded with satisfaction. He twirled his fingers, and then suddenly held his hands apart with the air of a conjuror. The rope came in two pieces.

"Uh-huh. Yes. I thought it was one of Loony's trick ropes. See this?

The rope's tapped. It's fitted with a screw in one side and a thread in the other, and you can twist it together just like a screw in wood. You can't see the joint; you can examine the rope all you like, and yet it won't come apart under any pressure. Get the idea? Members of the audience tie the illusionist, or whatdyecallum—tie him up tight in his cabinet. This joint of the rope goes across his hands. The watchers outside can hold the ends of the rope tight to make sure he don't try to get out of it. See? But he unscrews the thing with his teeth, holds the rope taut with his knees, and all kinds of hell start to pop inside the cabinet. Wonder! Mystification! Greatest show on earth!" said O'Rourke, hoarsely. He regarded them amiably, put the pipe back in his mouth, and inhaled deeply. "Yes. That was one of Loony's ropes, I'll bet anything."

"I don't doubt that," said Hadley. "But what about the suction-cup?"

Again O'Rourke bent slightly backwards to give room for his gestures.

"We-el, Loony was as secretive as they make 'em, of course. But I haven't been around with magic acts and the rest of that stuff without keeping my eyes peeled. . . . Wait a minute; don't get me wrong! Loony had tricks that were GOOD, and I mean good. This was just routine stuff that everybody knew about. Well. He was working on one. . . . You've heard of the Indian rope trick, haven't you? Fakir throws a rope up in the air; it stands upright; boy climbs up it—whoosh! he disappears. Eh?"

A cloud of smoke whirled up and vanished before his broad gesture.

"I've also heard," said Dr. Fell, blinking at him, "that nobody has ever yet seen it performed."

"Sure! Exactly! That's just it," O'Rourke returned, with a sort of pounce. "That's why Loony was trying to dope out a means of doing it. God knows whether he did. I think that suction-cup was to catch the rope somewhere when it was thrown up. But don't ask me how."

"And somebody was to climb up," said Hadley, in a heavy voice; "climb up, and disappear?"

"We-el, a kid—!" O'Rourke brushed the idea away. "But I'll tell you this much: that thing you've got won't support a full-grown man's weight. Look, gents! I'd try it for you, and swing out the window, only I don't want to break my goddam neck; and besides, my wrist is out of kilter."

"I think we've got enough evidence just the same," said Hadley. "You say this fellow's bolted, Somers? Any description of him?"

Somers nodded with great satisfaction.

"We shouldn't have any difficulty in pulling him in, sir. He goes under the name of 'Jerome Burnaby,' which is probably a fake; but he's got a pretty distinctive appearance—and he has a club foot."

14
The Clue of
The Church Bells

The next sound was the vast, dust-shaking noise of Dr. Fell's mirth. The doctor did not only chuckle; he roared. Sitting down on a red-and-yellow divan, which sagged and creaked alarmingly, he chortled away and pounded his stick on the floor.

"Stung!" said Dr. Fell. "Stung, me bonny boys! Heh-heh-heh. Bang goes the ghost. Bang goes the evidence. Oh, my eye!"

"What do you mean, stung?" demanded Hadley. "I don't see anything funny in getting our man dead to rights. Doesn't this pretty well convince you that Burnaby's guilty?"

"It convinces me absolutely that he's innocent," said Dr. Fell. He got out a red bandana and wiped his eyes as the amusement subsided. "I was afraid we should find just this sort of thing when we saw the other room. It was a little too good to be true. Burnaby is the Sphinx without a secret; the criminal without a crime—or at least this particular sort of crime."

"If you would mind explaining . . . ?"

"Not at all," said the doctor, affably. "Hadley, take a look around and tell me what this whole place reminds you of. Did you ever know of any burglar, any criminal at all, who ever had his secret hideaway arranged with such atmospheric effect, with such romantic setting? With the lockpicks arranged on the table, the brooding microscope, the sinister chemicals and so on? The real burglar, the real criminal of any kind, takes care to have his haunt looking a little more respectable than a churchwarden's. This display doesn't even remind me of somebody playing at being a burglar. But if you'll think for a second you'll see what it does remind you of, out of a hundred stories and films. I know that," the doctor explained, "because I'm so fond of the atmosphere, even the theatrical atmosphere, myself. . . . It sounds like somebody playing detective."

Hadley stopped, rubbing his chin thoughtfully. He peered round.

"When you were a kid," pursued Dr. Fell, with relish, "didn't you ever wish for a secret passage in your house?—and pretend that some hole in the attic *was* a secret passage, and go crawling through it with a candle, and nearly burn the place down? Didn't you ever play the Great Detective, and wish for a secret lair in some secret street, where you could pursue your deadly studies under an assumed name? Didn't somebody say Burnaby was a fierce amateur criminologist? Maybe he's writing a book. Anyhow, he has the time and the money to do, in rather a sophisticated way, just what a lot of other grown-up children have wished to do. He's created an *alter ego*. He's done it on the quiet, because his circle would have roared with laughter if they had known. Relentlessly the bloodhounds of Scotland Yard have tracked down his deadly secret; and his deadly secret is a joke."

"But, sir—!" protested Somers, in a kind of yelp.

"Stop a bit," said Hadley, meditatively, and gestured him to silence. The superintendent again examined the place with a half-angry doubt. "I admit there's an unconvincing look about the place, yes. I admit it has a movieish appearance. But what about that blood and this rope? This rope is Fley's, remember. And the blood . . ."

Dr. Fell nodded.

"H'mf, yes. Don't misunderstand. I don't say these rooms mightn't play a part in the business; I'm only warning you not to believe too much in Burnaby's evil double life."

"We'll soon find out about that. And," growled Hadley, "if the fellow's a murderer I don't care how innocent his double life as a burglar may be. Somers!"

"Sir?"

"Go over to Mr. Jerome Burnaby's flat—yes, I know you don't understand, but I mean his other flat. I've got the address. H'm. 13A Bloomsbury Square, second floor. Got it? Bring him here; use any pretext you like, but see that he comes. Don't answer any questions about this place, or ask any. Got that? And when you go downstairs, see if you can hurry up that landlady."

He stalked about the room, kicking at the edges of the furniture, as a bewildered and crestfallen Somers hurried out. O'Rourke, who had sat down and was regarding them with amiable interest, waved his pipe.

"Well, gents," he said, "I like to see the bloodhounds on the trail, at that. I don't know who this Burnaby is, but he seems to be somebody you already know. Is there anything you'd like to ask *me*? I told what I knew about Loony to Sergeant, or whatever he is, Somers. But if there's anything else . . . ?"

Hadley drew a deep breath and set his shoulder back to work again. He went through the papers in his briefcase.

"This is your statement—right?" The superintendent read it briefly. "Have you anything to add to that? I mean, are you positive he said his brother had taken lodgings in this street?"

"That's what he said, yes, sir. He said he'd seen him hanging around here."

Hadley glanced up sharply. "That's not the same thing, is it? Which did he say?"

O'Rourke seemed to think this a quibble. He shifted. "Oh, well, he said that just afterwards. He said, 'He's got a room there; I've seen him hanging around.' Or something. That's the honest truth, now!"

"But not very definite, is it?" demanded Hadley. "Think again!"

"Well, hell's bells, I *am* thinking!" protested O'Rourke in an aggrieved tone. "Take it easy. Somebody reels off a lot of stuff like that; and then afterwards they ask you questions about it and seem to think you're lying if you can't repeat every word. Sorry, partner, but that's the best I can do."

"What do you know about this brother of his? Since you've known Fley, what has he told you?"

"Not a thing! Not one word! I don't want you to get the wrong idea. When I say I knew Loony better than most people, that don't mean I know anything about him. Nobody did. If you ever saw him, you'd know he was the last person you could get confidential with over a few drinks, and tell about yourself. It would be like treating Dracula to a couple of beers. Wait a minute!—I mean somebody who looked like Dracula, that's all. Loony was a pretty good sport in his own way."

Hadley reflected, and then decided on a course.

"The biggest problem we have now—you'll have guessed that—is an impossible situation. I suppose you've seen the newspapers?"

"Yes." O'Rourke's eyes narrowed. "Why ask me about that?"

"Some sort of illusion, or stage trick, must have been used to kill both those men. You say you've known magicians and escape artists. Can you think of any trick that would explain how it was done?"

O'Rourke laughed, showing gleaming teeth under the elaborate moustache. The wrinkles of amusement deepened round his eyes.

"Oh, well! That's different! That's a lot different. Look, I'll tell you straight. When I offered to swing out the window on that rope, I noticed you. I was afraid you were getting ideas. Get me? I mean about me." He chuckled. "Forget it! It'd take a miracle man to work any stunt like that with a rope, even if he had a rope and could walk without leaving any tracks. But as for the other business. . . ." Frowningly O'Rourke brushed up his moustache with the stem of his pipe. He stared across the room. "It's this way. I'm no authority. I don't know very much about it, and what I do know I generally keep mum about. Kind of"— he gestured—"kind of professional etiquette, if you get me. Also, for things like escapes from locked boxes, and disappearances and the rest of it . . . well, I've given up even talking about 'em."

"Why?"

"Because," said O'Rourke, with great emphasis, "most people are so damned disappointed when they know the secret. Either, in the first place, the thing is so smart and simple—so simple it's funny—that they won't believe they could have been fooled by it. They'll say, 'Oh, hell! don't tell us that stuff! I'd have seen it in a second.' Or, in the second place, it's a trick worked with a confederate. That disappoints 'em even more. They say, 'Oh, well, if you're going to have somebody to help—!' as though anything was possible then."

He smoked reflectively.

"It's a funny thing about people. They go to see an illusion; you tell 'em it's an illusion; they pay their money to see an illusion. And yet for some funny reason they get sore because it isn't *real* magic. When they hear an explanation of how somebody got out of a locked box or a roped sack that they've examined, they get sore because it *was* a trick. They say it's farfetched when they know how they were deceived. Now, it takes BRAINS, I'm telling you, to work out one of those simple tricks. And, to be a good escape-artist, a man's got to be cool, strong, experienced and quick as greased lightning. But they never think of the cleverness it takes just to fool 'em under their noses. I think they'd like the secret of an escape to be some unholy business like real magic; something that nobody on God's earth could ever do. Now, no man who ever lived can make himself as thin as a post-card and slide out through a crack. No man ever crawled out through a keyhole, or pushed himself through a piece of wood. Want me to give you an example?"

"Go on," said Hadley, who was looking at him curiously.

"All right. Take the second sort first! Take the roped and sealed sack trick: one way of doing it." O'Rourke was enjoying himself. "Out comes the performer—in the middle of a group of people, if you want him to —with a light sack made out of black muslin or sateen, and big enough for him to stand up in. He gets inside. His assistant draws it up, holds the sack about six inches below the mouth, and ties it round tightly with a long handkerchief. Then the people watching can add more knots if they want to, and seal his knots and theirs with wax, and stamp 'em with signets . . . anything at all. Bang! Up goes a screen round the performer. Thirty seconds later out he walks, with the knots still tied and sealed and stamped, and the sack over his arm. Heigh-ho!"

"Well?"

O'Rourke grinned, made the usual play with his moustache (he could not seem to leave off twisting it), and rolled on the divan.

"Now, gents, here's where you take a poke at me. There's duplicate sacks, exactly alike. One of 'em the performer's got all folded up and stuck inside his vest. When he gets into the sack, and he's moving and jerking it around, and the assistant is pulling it up over his head—why, out comes the duplicate. The mouth of the other black sack is pushed up through the mouth of the first; six inches or so; it *looks* like the mouth of the first. The assistant grabs it round, and what he honest-to-God ties is the mouth of the duplicate sack, with such a thin edge of the real one included so that you can't see the joining. Bang! On go the knots and seals. When the performer gets behind his screen, all he does is shove loose the tied sack, drop the one he's standing in, stick the loose sack under his vest, and walk out holding the duplicate sack roped and sealed. Get it? See? It's simple, it's easy, and yet people go nuts trying to figure out how it was done. But when they hear how it *was* done, they say, 'Oh, well, with a confederate—!' " He gestured.

Hadley was interested in spite of his professional manner, and Dr. Fell was listening with a childlike gaping.

"Yes, I know," said the superintendent, as though urging an argument, "but the man we're after, the man who committed these two murders, couldn't have had a confederate! Besides, that's not a vanishing-trick. . . ."

"All right," said O'Rourke, and pushed his hat to one side of his head. "I'll give you an example of a whopping-big vanishing-trick. This is a stage illusion, mind. All very fancy. But you can work it in an outdoor theatre, if you want to, where there's no trapdoors, no wires from the flies, no props or funny business at all. Just a stretch of ground. Out rides the illusionist, in a grand blue uniform, on a grand white horse. Out come his gang of attendants, in white uniforms, with the usual hoop-la like a circus. They go round in a circle once, and then two attendants whisk up a great big fan which—just for a moment, see?—hides the man on the horse. Down comes the fan, which is tossed out in the audience to show it's O.K.; but the man on the horse has vanished. He's vanished straight from the middle of a ten-acre field. Heigh-ho!"

"And how do you get out of that one?" demanded Dr. Fell.

"Easy! The man's never left the field. But you don't see him. You don't see him because that grand blue uniform is made of paper—*over* a real white one. As soon as the fan goes up, he tears off the blue one and stuffs it under the white. He jumps down off the horse, and just joins in the gang of white-uniformed attendants. Point is, nobody ever takes the trouble to *count* them attendants beforehand, and they all exit without anybody ever seeing. That's the basis of most tricks. You're looking at something you don't see, or you'll swear you've seen something that's not there. Hey presto! Bang! Greatest show on earth!"

The stuffy, gaudily coloured room was quiet. Wind rattled at the windows. Distantly there was a noise of church bells, and the honking of a taxi that passed and died. Hadley shook his notebook.

"We're getting off the track," he said. "It's clever enough, yes; but how does it apply to this problem?"

"It don't," admitted O'Rourke, who seemed convulsed by a noiseless mirth. "I'm telling you—well, because you asked. And to show you what you're up against. I'm giving you the straight dope, Mr. Superintendent: I don't want to discourage you, but if you're up against a smart illusionist, you haven't got the chance of a snowball in hell; you haven't got the chance of *that*." He snapped his fingers. "They're trained to it. It's their business. And there ain't a prison on earth that can hold 'em."

Hadley's jaw tightened. "We'll see about that when the time comes. What bothers me, and what's been bothering me for some time, is why Fley sent his brother to do the killing. Fley was the illusionist. Fley would have been the man to do it. But he didn't. Was his brother in the same line?"

"Dunno. At least, I never saw his name billed anywhere. But—"

Dr. Fell interrupted. With a heavy wheeze, he lumbered up from the couch and spoke sharply.

"Clear the decks for action, Hadley. We're going to have visitors in about two minutes. Look out there!—but keep back from the window."

He was pointing with his stick. Below them, where the alley curved out between the blank windows of houses, two figures shouldered against the wind. They had turned in from Guilford Street; and, fortunately had their heads down. One Rampole recognized as that of Rosette Grimaud. The other was a tall man whose shoulder lunged and swung as he walked with the aid of a cane; a man whose leg had a crooked twist and whose right boot was of abnormal thickness.

"Get the lights out in those other rooms," said Hadley, swiftly. He turned to O'Rourke. "I'll ask you a big favour. Get downstairs as quickly as you can; stop that landlady from coming up and saying anything; keep her there until you hear from me. Pull the door shut after you!"

He was already out into the narrow passage, snapping off the lights. Dr. Fell looked mildly harassed.

"Look here, you don't mean we're going to hide and overhear terrible secrets, do you?" he demanded. "I've not got what Mills would call the anatomical structure for such tomfoolery. Besides, they'll spot us in a second. This place is full of smoke—O'Rourke's shag."

Hadley muttered profanities. He drew the curtains so that only a pencil of light slanted into the room.

"Can't be helped; we've got to chance it. We'll sit here quietly. If they've got anything on their minds, they may blurt it out as soon as they get inside the flat and the door is shut. People do. What do you think of O'Rourke, by the way?"

"I think," stated Dr. Fell, with energy, "that O'Rourke is the most stimulating, enlightening, and suggestive witness we have heard so far in this nightmare. He has saved my intellectual self-respect. He is, in fact, almost as enlightening as the church bells."

Hadley, who was peering through the crack between the curtains, turned his head round. The line of light across his eyes showed a certain wildness.

"Church bells? What church bells?"

"Any church bells," said Dr. Fell's voice out of the gloom. "I tell you that to me in my heathen blindness the thought of those bells has brought light and balm. It may save me from making an awful mistake. . . . Yes, I'm quite sane." The ferrule of a stick rapped the floor and his voice became tense. "Light, Hadley! Light at last, and glorious messages in the belfry."

"Are you sure it's not something else in the belfry? Yes? Then for God's sake will you stop this mystification and tell me what you mean? I suppose the church bells tell you how the vanishing-trick was worked?"

"Oh no," said Dr. Fell. "Unfortunately not. They only tell me the name of the murderer."

There was a palpable stillness in the room, a physical heaviness, as of breath restrained to bursting. Dr. Fell spoke in a blank, almost an incredulous voice which carried conviction in its mere incredulity. Downstairs a back door closed. Faintly through the quiet house they heard footsteps on the staircase. One set of footsteps was sharp, light, and impatient. The other had a drag and then a heavy stamp; there was the noise of a cane knocking the banisters. The noises grew louder, but no word was spoken. A key scraped into the lock of the outer door, which opened and closed again with a click of the spring-lock. There was another click as the light in the hallway was snapped on. Then—evidently when they could see each other—the two burst out as though they had been the ones who held in breath to suffocation.

"So you've lost the key I gave you," a man's thin, harsh, quiet voice spoke. It was mocking and yet repressed. "And you say you didn't come here last night, after all?"

"Not last night," said Rosette Grimaud's voice, which had a flat and yet furious tone; "not last night or any other night." She laughed. "I never had any intention of coming at all. You frightened me a little. Well, what of it? And now that I *am* here, I don't think so much of your hideout. Did you have a pleasant time waiting last night?"

There was a movement as though she had stepped forward, and been restrained. The man's voice rose.

"Now, you little devil," said the man, with equal quietness, "I'm going to tell you something for the good of your soul. I wasn't here. I had no intention of coming. If you think all you have to do is crack the whip to send people through hoops—well, I wasn't here, do you see? You can go through the hoops yourself. I wasn't here."

"That's a lie, Jerome," said Rosette, calmly.

"You think so, eh? Why?"

Two figures appeared against the light of the partly opened door. Hadley reached out and drew back the curtains with a rattle of rings.

"We also would like to know the answer to that, Mr. Burnaby," he said.

The flood of murky daylight in their faces caught them off-guard; so much off-guard that expressions were hollowed out as though snapped by a camera. Rosette Grimaud cried out, making a movement of her raised arm as though she would dodge under it, but the flash of the previous look had been bitter, watchful, dangerously triumphant. Jerome Burnaby stood motionless, his chest rising and falling. Silhouetted against the sickly electric light behind, and wearing an old-fashioned broad-brimmed black hat, he bore a curious resemblance to the lean Sandeman figure in the advertisement. But he was more than a silhouette. He had a strong, furrowed face, that ordinarily might have been bluff and amiable like his gestures; an underhung jaw, and eyes which seemed to have lost their colour with anger. Taking off his hat, he tossed it on a divan with a swash-buckling air that struck Rampole as rather theatrical. His wiry brown hair, patched with grey round the temples, stood up as though released from pressure like a jack-in-the-box.

"Well?" he said with a sort of thin, bluff jocularity, and took a lurching step forward, on the club foot. "Is this a hold-up, or what? Three to one, I see. I happen to have a sword-stick, though—"

"It won't be needed, Jerome," said the girl. "They're the police."

Burnaby stopped; stopped and rubbed his mouth with a big hand. He seemed nervous, though he went on with ironical jocularity. "Oh! The police, eh? I'm honoured. Breaking and entering, I see."

"You are the tenant of this flat," said Hadley, returning an equal suavity, "not the owner or landlord of the house. If suspicious behaviour is seen . . . I don't know about suspicious, Mr. Burnaby, but I think your friends would be amused at these—Oriental surroundings. Wouldn't they?"

That smile, that tone of voice, struck through to a raw place. Burnaby's face became a muddy colour.

"Damn you," he said, and half raised the cane, "what do you want here?"

"First of all, before we forget it, about what you were saying when you came in here. . . ."

"You overheard it, eh?"

"Yes. It's unfortunate," said Hadley, composedly, "that we couldn't have overheard more. Miss Grimaud said that you were in this flat last night. Were you?"

"I was not."

"You were not. . . . Was he, Miss Grimaud?"

Her colour had come back; come back strongly, for she was angry with a quiet, smiling poise. She spoke in a breathless way, and her long hazel eyes had that fixity, that luminous strained expression, of one who determines to show no emotion. She was pressing her gloves between the fingers, and in the jerkiness of her breathing there was less anger than fear.

"Since you overheard it," she answered, after a speculative pause while she glanced from one to the other, "it's no good my denying it, is there? I don't see why you're interested. It can't have anything to do with —my father's death. That's certain. Whatever else Jerome is," she showed her teeth in an unsteady smile, "he's not a murderer. But since for some reason you *are* interested, I've a good mind to have the whole thing thrashed out now. Some version of this, I can see, is going to get back to Boyd. It might as well be the true one. . . . I'll begin by saying, yes, Jerome was in this flat last night."

"How do you know that, Miss Grimaud? Were you here?"

"No. But I saw a light in this room at half-past ten."

15

The Lighted Window

Burnaby, still rubbing his chin, looked down at her in dull blankness. Rampole could have sworn that the man was genuinely startled; so startled that he could not quite understand her words, and peered at her as though he had never seen her before. Then he spoke in a quiet, common-sense tone which contrasted with his earlier one.

"I say, Rosette," he observed, "be careful now. Are you sure you know what you're talking about?"

"Yes. Quite sure."

Hadley cut in briskly. "At half-past ten? How did you happen to see this light, Miss Grimaud, when you were at your own home with us?"

"Oh, no, I wasn't—if you remember. Not at that time. I was at the nursing-home, with the doctor in the room where my father was dying. I don't know whether you know it, but the back of the nursing-home faces the back of this house. I happened to be near a window, and I noticed. There was a light in this room; and, I think, the bathroom, too, though I'm not positive of that. . . ."

"How do you know the rooms," said Hadley, sharply, "if you've never been here before?"

"I took jolly good care to observe when we came in just now," she answered, with a serene and imperturbable smile which somehow reminded Rampole of Mills. "I *didn't* know the rooms last night; I only knew he had this flat, and where the windows were. The curtains weren't quite drawn. That's how I came to notice the light."

Burnaby was still contemplating her with the same heavy curiosity.

"Just a moment, Mr.—Inspector—er—!" He humped his shoulder. "Are you sure you couldn't have been mistaken about the rooms, Rosette?"

"Positive, my dear. This is the house on the left hand side at the corner of the alley, and you have the top floor."

"And you say you saw *me?*"

"No, I say I saw a light. But you and I are the only ones who know about this flat. And, since you'd invited me here, and said you would be here . . ."

"By God!" said Burnaby. "I'm curious to see how far you'll go." He hobbled over, with a trick of pulling down the corner of his mouth each time he lunged on the cane; he sat down heavily in a chair, and continued to study her out of his pale eyes. That upstanding hair gave him somehow a queerly alert look. "Please go on! You interest me. Yes. I'm curious to see how far you have the nerve to go."

"Are you really," said Rosette, in a flat voice. She whirled round; but her resolution seemed to crack and she succeeded in looking only miserable to the point of tears. "I wish I knew myself! I—I wish I knew about *you!* . . . I said we'd have this out," she appealed to Hadley, "but now I don't know whether I want to have it out. If I could decide about him, whether he's really sympathetic, and just a nice bluff old—old—"

"Don't say friend of the family," snapped Burnaby. "For Lord's sake don't say friend of the family. Personally, I wish I could decide about you. I wish I could decide whether you think you're telling the truth, or whether you're (excuse me for forgetting my chivalry for a moment!) a lying little vixen."

She went on steadily: "—or whether he's a sort of polite blackmailer. Oh, not for money!" she blazed again. "Vixen? Yes. Bitch if you like. I admit it. I've been both—but why? Because you've poisoned everything with all the hints you've dropped . . . if I could be sure they were hints and not just my imagination; if I could even be sure you were an honest blackmailer! . . ."

Hadley intervened. "Hints about what?"

"Oh, about my father's past life, if you must know." She clenched her hands. "About my birth, for one thing, and whether we mightn't add another nice term to bitch. But that's not important. That doesn't bother me at all. It's this business about some horrible thing—about my father—I don't know! Maybe they're not even hints. But . . . I've got it in my head somehow that old Drayman is a blackmailer. . . . Then, last night, Jerome asked me to come over here—why, why? I thought: well, is it because that's the night Boyd always sees me, and it will tickle Jerome's vanity no end to choose just that night? But I don't and I didn't—please understand me!—want to think Jerome was trying a little blackmail himself. I do like him; I can't help it; and that's what makes it so awful. . . ."

"We might clear it up, then," said Hadley. "Were you 'hinting,' Mr. Burnaby?"

There was a long silence while Burnaby examined his hands. Something in the posture of his bent head, in his slow heavy breathing, as though he were bewilderedly trying to make up his mind, kept Hadley from prompting him until he raised his head.

"I never thought—" he said. "Hinting. Yes. Yes, in strict accuracy, I suppose I was. But never intentionally, I'll swear. I never thought—" He stared at Rosette. "Those things slip out. Maybe you mean only what you think is a subtle question. . . ." He puffed out his breath in a sort of despairing hiss, and shrugged his shoulders. "To me it was an interesting deductive game, that's all. I didn't even think of it as prying. I swear I never thought anybody noticed, let alone taking it to heart. Rosette, if that's the only reason for your interest in me—thinking I was a blackmailer, and afraid of me—then I'm sorry I learned. Or am I?" He looked down at his hands again, opened and shut them, and then looked slowly round the room. "Take a look at this place, gentlemen. The front room especially . . . but you'll have seen that. Then you know the answer. The Great Detective. The poor ass with the deformed foot, dreaming."

For a second Hadley hesitated.

"And did the Great Detective find out anything about Dr. Grimaud's past?"

"No. . . . If I had, do you think I'd be apt to tell you?"

"We'll see if we can't persuade you. Do you know that there are bloodstains in that bathroom of yours, where Miss Grimaud says she saw a light last night? Do you know that Pierre Fley was murdered outside your door not long before half-past ten?"

Rosette Grimaud cried out, and Burnaby jerked up his head.

"Fley mur . . . Blood-stains! No! Where? Man, what do you mean?"

"Fley had a room in this street. We think he was coming here when he died. Anyhow, he was shot in the street outside here by the same man who killed Dr. Grimaud. Can you prove who you are, Mr. Burnaby? Can you prove, for instance, that you are not actually Dr. Grimaud's and Fley's brother?"

The other stared at him. He hoisted himself up shakily from the chair.

"Good God! man, are you mad?" he asked, in a quiet voice. "Brother! Now I see! . . . No, I'm not his brother. Do you think if I were his brother I should be interested in . . ." He checked himself, glanced at Rosette, and his expression became rather wild. "Certainly I can prove it. I ought to have a birth certificate somewhere. I—I can produce people who've known me all my life. Brother!"

Hadley reached round to the divan and held up the coil of rope.

"What about this rope? Is it a part of your Great Detective scheme, too?"

"That thing? No. What is it? I never saw it before. Brother!"

Rampole glanced at Rosette Grimaud, and saw that she was crying. She stood motionless, her hands at her sides and her face set; but the tears brimmed over her eyes.

"And can you prove," Hadley continued, "that you were not in this flat last night?"

Burnaby drew a deep breath. Relief lightened his heavy face.

"Yes, fortunately I can. I was at my club last night from eight o'clock

—or thereabouts; maybe a little earlier—until past eleven. Dozens of people will tell you that. If you want me to be specific, ask the three I played poker with the whole of that time. Do you want an alibi? Right! There's as strong an alibi as you're ever likely to get. I wasn't here. I didn't leave any blood-stains, wherever the devil you say you found some. I didn't kill Fley, or Grimaud, or anybody else." His heavy jaw came out. "Now, then, what do you think of *that?*"

The superintendent swung his batteries so quickly that Burnaby had hardly finished speaking before Hadley had turned to Rosette.

"You still insist that you saw a light here at half-past ten?"

"Yes! . . . But, Jerome, truly, I never meant—!"

"Even though, when my man arrived here this morning, the electric meter was cut off and the lights would not work?"

"I . . . yes, it's still true! But what I wanted to say—"

"Let's suppose Mr. Burnaby is telling the truth about last night. You say he invited you here. Is it likely that he invited you here when he intended to be at his club?"

Burnaby lurched forward and put a hand on Hadley's arm. "Steady! Let's get this straightened out, Inspector. That's what I did. It was a swine's trick, but—I did it. Look here, have I *got* to explain?"

"Now, now, now!" struck in the quiet, rumbling, deprecating tones of Dr. Fell. He took out the red bandana and blew his nose with a loud honking noise, to attract attention. Then he blinked at them, mildly disturbed. "Hadley, we're confused enough as it is. Let me put in a soothing word. Mr. Burnaby did that, as he expressed it himself, to make her jump through a hoop. Hurrum! Excuse my bluntness, ma'am, but then it's all right because that particular leopard wouldn't jump, eh?— About the question of the light not working, that's not nearly so ominous as it sounds. It's a shilling meter, d'ye see. Somebody was here. Somebody left the lights burning, possibly all night. Well, the meter used up a bob's worth of electricity, and then the lights went out. We don't know which way the switches were turned, because Somers got here first. Blast it, Hadley, we've got ample proof that there *was* somebody here last night. The question is, who?" He looked at the others. "H'm. You two say that nobody else knew of this place. But—assuming your story to be straight, Mr. Burnaby; and you'd be a first-class fathead to lie about a thing so easily checked up as that story—then somebody else must have known of it."

"I can only tell you I wasn't likely to speak of it," insisted Burnaby, rubbing his chin. "Unless somebody noticed me coming here . . . unless . . ."

"Unless, in other words, I told somebody about it?" Rosette flared again. Her sharp teeth bit at her under lip. "But I didn't. I—I don't know why I didn't"—she seemed fiercely puzzled—"but I never mentioned it to anybody. There!"

"But you have a key to the place?" asked Dr. Fell.

"I had a key to this place. I lost it."

"When?"

"Oh, how should I know? I never noticed." She had folded her arms and was walking round the room with excited little movements of her head. "I kept it in my bag, and I only noticed this morning, when we were coming over here, that it was gone. But one thing I insist on knowing." She stopped, facing Burnaby. "I—I don't know whether I'm fond of you or whether I hate you. If it was only a nasty little fondness for detective work, if that's all it really was and you didn't mean anything, then speak up. What do you know about my father? Tell me! I don't mind. They're the police, and they'll find out anyway. Now, now, don't act! I hate your acting. Tell me. What's this about brothers?"

"That's good advice, Mr. Burnaby. You painted a picture," said Hadley, "that I was going to ask about next. What did you know about Dr. Grimaud?"

Burnaby, leaning back against the window with an unconsciously swaggering gesture, shrugged his shoulders. His pale grey eyes, with their pin-point black pupils, shifted and gleamed sardonically.

He said: "Rosette, if I had ever known, if I had ever suspected, that my detective efforts were being interpreted as. . . . Very well! I'll tell you in a few words, what I'd have told you long ago, if I had known it worried you at all. Your father was once imprisoned at the salt-mines in Hungary, and he escaped. Not very terrible, is it?"

"In prison! What for?"

"For trying to start a revolution, I was told. . . . My own guess is for theft. You see, I'm being frank."

Hadley cut in quickly. "Where did you learn that? From Drayman?"

"So Drayman knows, does he?" Burnaby stiffened, and his eyes narrowed. "Yes, I rather thought he did. Ah! Yes. That was another thing I tried to find out, and it seems to have been construed into. . . . And, come to think of it, what do *you* fellows know about it, anyhow?" Then he burst out, "Look here, I'm no busybody! I'd better tell you if only to prove it. I was dragged into the thing; Grimaud wouldn't let me alone. You talk about that picture. The picture was the cause rather than the effect. It was all accident—though I had a bad time persuading Grimaud of that. It was all on account of a damned magic-lantern lecture."

"A what?"

"Fact! A magic-lantern lecture. I ducked into the thing to get out of the rain one night; it was out in North London somewhere, a parish hall, about eighteen months ago." Wryly Burnaby twiddled his thumbs. For the first time there was an honest and homely expression on his face. "I'd like to make a romantic story out of this. But you asked for the truth. Right! Chap was lecturing on Hungary: lantern-slides and plenty of ghostly atmosphere to thrill the church-goers. But it caught my imagination; by George, it did!" His eyes gleamed. "There was one slide—something like what I painted. Nothing effective about it; but the story that went with it, about the three lonely graves in an unhallowed place, gave me a good idea for a nightmare. The lecturer inferred that they were vampires' graves, you see? I came home and worked like fury on the idea. Well, I frankly told everybody it was an imaginative conception of something I never saw. But for some reason nobody believed me. Then Grimaud saw it . . ."

"Mr. Pettis told us," Hadley remarked, woodenly, "that it gave him a turn. Or that you said it did."

"Gave him a turn? I should say it did! He hunched his head down into his shoulders and stood as quiet as a mummy, looking at it. I took it as a tribute. And then, in my sinister innocence," said Burnaby, with a kind of leer, "out I came with the remark, 'You'll notice how the earth is cracking on one grave. He's just getting out.' My mind was still running on vampires, of course. But he didn't know that. For a second I thought he was coming at me with a palette knife."

It was a straightforward story Burnaby told. Grimaud, he said, had questioned him about that picture; questioned, watched, questioned again, until even a less imaginative man would have been suspicious. The uneasy tension of being always under surveillance had set him to solve the puzzle in ordinary self-defence. A few pieces of handwriting in books in Grimaud's library; the shield of arms over the mantelpiece; a casual word dropped. . . . Burnaby looked at Rosette with a grim smile. Then, he continued, about three months before the murder Grimaud had collared him and, under an oath of secrecy, told him the truth. The "truth" was exactly the story Drayman had told Hadley and Dr. Fell last night: the plague, the two dead brothers, the escape.

During this time Rosette had been staring out of the window with an incredulous, half-witted blankness which ended in something like a tearfulness of relief.

"And that's *all?*" she cried, breathing hard. "That's all there is to it? That's what I've been worrying about all this time?"

"That's all, my dear," Burnaby answered, folding his arms. "I told you it wasn't very terrible. But I didn't want to tell it to the police. Now, however, that you've insisted . . ."

"Be careful, Hadley," grunted Dr. Fell in a low voice, and knocked against the superintendent's arm. He cleared his throat. "Harrumph! Yes. We have some reason to believe the story, too, Miss Grimaud."

Hadley took a new line. "Supposing all this to be true, Mr. Burnaby: you were at the Warwick Tavern the night Fley came in first?"

"Yes."

"Well, then? Knowing what you did, didn't you connect him with that business in the past? Especially after his remarks about the three coffins?"

Burnaby hesitated, and then gestured. "Frankly, yes. I walked home with Grimaud on that night—the Wednesday night. I didn't say anything, but I thought he was going to tell me something. We sat down on either side of the fire in his study, and he took an extra large whisky, a thing he seldom does. I noticed he seemed to be looking very hard at the fireplace. . . ."

"By the way," Dr. Fell put in, with such casualness that Rampole jumped, "where did he keep his private and personal papers? Do you know?"

The other darted a sharp glance at him.

"Mills would be better able to tell you that than I," he returned. (Something veiled, something guarded, some cloud of dust here?) "He may have had a safe. So far as I know, he kept them in a locked drawer at the side of that big desk."

"Go on."

"For a long time neither of us said anything. There was one of those uncomfortable strains when each person wants to introduce a subject, but wonders whether the other is thinking about it, too. Well, I took the plunge, and said, 'Who was it?' He made one of those noises of his like a dog just before it barks, and shifted round in the chair. Finally he said: 'I don't know. It's been a long time. It may have been the doctor; it looked like the doctor.' "

"Doctor? You mean the one who certified him as dead of plague at the prison?" asked Hadley. Rosette Grimaud shivered, and suddenly sat down with her face in her hands. Burnaby grew uncomfortable.

"Yes. Look here, must I go on with this? . . . All right, all right! 'Back for a little blackmail,' he said. You know the look of the stoutish opera stars, who sing Mephistopheles in 'Faust'? He looked just like that when he turned round towards me, with his hands on the arms of the chair, and his elbows hooked as though he were going to get up. Face reddish with the firelight, clipped beard, raised eyebrows—everything. I said 'Yes, but actually what can he do?' You see, I was trying to draw him out. I thought it must be more serious than a political offence or it wouldn't carry any weight after so long. He said 'Oh, *he* won't do anything. He never had the nerve. *He* won't do anything.'

"Now," snapped Burnaby, looking round, "you asked for everything, and here it is. I don't mind. Everybody knows it. Grimaud said, with that barking directness of his, 'You want to marry Rosette, don't you?' I admitted it. He said, 'Very well; you shall,' and began nodding and drumming on the arm of the chair. I laughed and said . . . well! I said something about Rosette's having preference in another direction. He said: 'Bah! the young one! I'll fix that.' "

Rosette was looking at him with a hard, luminous, inscrutable stare, her eyes nearly closed. She spoke in a tone too puzzling to identify. She said:

"So you had it all arranged, did you?"

"O Lord, don't fly off the handle! You know better than that. I was asked what happened, and here it is. The last thing he said was that, whatever happened to him, I was to keep my mouth shut about what I knew—"

"Which you didn't . . ."

"At your express orders, no." He turned back to the others. "Well, gentlemen, that's all I can tell you. When he came hurrying in on Friday morning to get that picture, I was a good deal puzzled. But I had been told to keep out of it entirely, and I did."

Hadley, who had been writing in his notebook, went on without speaking until he came to the end of the page. Then he looked at Rosette, who was sitting back on the divan with a pillow under her elbow. Under the fur coat she wore a dark dress, but her head was bare as usual; so that the heavy blonde hair and square face seemed to fit with the gaudy red-and-yellow divan. She turned her hand outward from the wrist, shakily.

"I know. You're going to ask me what *I* think of all this. About my father . . . and all." She stared at the ceiling. "I don't know. It takes such a load off my mind, it's so much too good to be true, that I'm afraid somebody's not telling the truth. Why, I'd have admired the old boy for a thing like that! It's—it's awful and terrible, and I'm glad he had so much of the devil in him! Of course if it was because he was a thief"—she smiled in some pleasure at the idea—"you can't blame him for keeping it quiet, can you?"

"That was not what I was going to ask," said Hadley, who seemed a good deal taken aback by this frankly broad-minded attitude. "I do want to know why, if you always refused to come over here with Mr. Burnaby, you suddenly decided on coming this morning?"

"To have it out with him, of course. And I—I wanted to get drunk or something. Then things were so unpleasant, you see, when we found that coat with the blood on it hanging in the closet . . ."

She stopped as she saw faces change, and jerked back a little.

"When you found *what?*" said Hadley, in the midst of a heavy silence.

"The coat with blood inside it, all stained down the inside of the front," she answered, with something of a gulp. "I—er—I didn't mention it, did I? Well, you didn't give me any chance! The minute we walked in here, you leaped out at us like . . . like . . . yes, that's it! The coat was hanging up in the coat-closet in the hall. Jerome found it when he was hanging up his own."

"Whose coat?"

"Nobody's! That's the odd part! I never saw it before. It wouldn't have fitted anybody at our house. It was too big for father—and it's a flashy tweed overcoat of the kind he'd have shuddered at, anyway; it would have swallowed Stuart Mills, and yet it isn't quite big enough for old Drayman. It's a new coat. It looks as though it had never been worn before. . . ."

"*I see*," said Dr. Fell, and puffed out his cheeks.

"You see what?" snapped Hadley. "This is a fine state of affairs now! You told Pettis you wanted blood. Well, you're getting blood—too infernally much blood!—and all in the wrong places. What's on your mind now?"

"I see," replied Dr. Fell, pointing with his stick, "where Drayman got the blood on him last night."

"You mean he wore the coat?"

"No, no! Think back. Remember what your sergeant said. He said that Drayman, half-blind, came blundering and rushing downstairs; blundered round in the clothes-closet getting his hat and coat. Hadley, he brushed close up against that coat when the blood was fresh. And it's no wonder he couldn't understand afterwards how it got there. Doesn't that clear up a good deal?"

"No. I'm damned if it does! It clears up one point by substituting another twice as bad. An extra coat! Come along. We're going over there at once. If you will go with us, Miss Grimaud, and you, Mr. . . ."

Dr. Fell shook his head. "You go along, Hadley. There's something I must see now. Something that changes the whole twist of the case; something that has become the most vitally important thing in it."

"What?"

"Pierre Fley's lodgings," said Dr. Fell, and shouldered out with his cape whirling behind him.

III

The Problem of Seven Towers

16
The Chameleon Overcoat

Between that discovery and the time they were to meet Pettis for lunch, Dr. Fell's spirits sank to a depth of gloom Rampole would not have believed possible, and which he certainly could not understand.

To begin with, the doctor refused to go straight back to Russell Square with Hadley, although he insisted Hadley should go. He said the essential clue must be at Fley's room. He said he would keep Rampole behind for some "dirty work of a strenuous pattern." Finally, he swore at himself with such heart-felt violence that even Hadley, sometimes sharing the views he expressed, was moved to remonstrate.

"But what do you expect to find there?" insisted Hadley. "Somers has already been through the place!"

"I don't expect anything. I can only say I hope," grumbled the doctor, "to find certain traces of brother Henri. His trademark, so to speak. His whiskers. His . . . oh, my hat, brother Henri, damn you!"

Hadley said that they could forego the Soliloquy in a Spanish Cloister, and could not understand why his friend's rage at the elusive Henri seemed to have grown to the status of a mania. There appeared nothing fresh to inspire it. Besides, the doctor, before leaving Burnaby's lodging-house, held up everybody for some time with a searching examination of Miss Hake, the landlady. O'Rourke had been gallantly keeping her downstairs with reminiscences of his trouping days; but both of them were tall talkers, and it is to be doubted whether he reminisced any more than Miss Hake did.

The questioning of Miss Hake, Dr. Fell admitted, was not productive. Miss Hake was a faded, agreeable spinster with good intentions but somewhat wandering wits, and a tendency to confuse erratic lodgers with burglars or murderers. When she was at last persuaded out of her belief that Burnaby was a burglar, she could give little information. She had not been at home last night. She had been at the moving pictures from eight o'clock until eleven, and at a friend's house in Gray's Inn Road until nearly midnight. She could not tell who might have used Burnaby's room; she had not even known of the murder until that morning. As to her other lodgers, there were three: an American student and his wife on the ground floor, and a veterinary surgeon on the floor above. All three had been out on the night before.

Somers, who had returned from his futile errand to Bloomsbury Square, was put to work on this lead; Hadley set out for Grimaud's house with Rosette and Burnaby, and Dr. Fell, who was doggedly intent on tackling another communicative landlady, found instead an uncommunicative landlord.

The premises over and under the tobacconist's shop at number 2 looked as flimsy as one of those half-houses which stand out from the side of the stage in a musical comedy. But they were bleak, dark-painted, and filled with the mustiness of the shop itself. Energy at a clanking bell at last brought James Dolberman, tobacconist and news agent, materializing slowly from the shadows at the back of his shop. He was a small, tight-lipped old man with large knuckles and a black muslin coat that shone like armour in a cave of fly-blown novelettes and mummified peppermints. His view of the whole matter was that it was no business of his.

Staring past them at the shop window, as though he were waiting for some one to come and give him an excuse to leave off talking, he bit off a few grudging answers. Yes, he had a lodger; yes, it was a man named Fley—a foreigner. Fley occupied a bed-sitting-room on the top floor. He had been there two weeks, paying in advance. No, the landlord didn't know anything about him, and didn't want to, except that he gave no trouble. He had a habit of talking to himself in a foreign language, that was all. The landlord didn't know anything about him, because he hardly ever saw him. There were no other lodgers; he (James Dolberman) wasn't carrying hot water upstairs for anybody. Why did Fley choose the top floor? How should he know? They had better ask Fley.

Didn't he know Fley was dead? Yes, he did; there had been a policeman here asking fool questions already, and taking him to identify the body. But it wasn't any business of his. What about the shooting at twenty-five minutes past ten last night? James Dolberman looked as though he might say something, but snapped his jaws shut and stared even harder at the window. He had been belowstairs in his kitchen with the radio on; he knew nothing about it, and wouldn't have come out to see if he had.

Had Fley ever had any visitors? No. Were there ever any suspicious-looking strangers, any people associated with Fley, hereabouts?

This had an unexpected result: the landlord's jaws still moved in a somnambulistic way, but he grew almost voluble. Yes, there was something the police ought to see to, instead of wasting taxpayer's money! He had seen somebody dodging round this place, watching it, once even speaking to Fley and then darting up the street. Nasty-looking customer. Criminal most likely! He didn't like people who dodged. No, he couldn't give any description of him—that was the police's business. Besides, it was always at night.

"But isn't there anything," said Dr. Fell, who was nearly at the limit of his affability and was wiping his face with the bandana, "you can give as description? Any clothes, anything of that sort? Hey?"

"He might," Dolberman conceded, after a tight-lipped struggle with the window, "he *might* have been wearing a kind of fancy overcoat, or the like. Of a light yellow tweed; with red spots in it, maybe. That's your business. You wish to go upstairs? Here is the key. The door is outside."

As they were stamping up a dark and narrow stairway, through a house surprisingly solid despite its flimsy appearance, Rampole fumed.

"You're right, sir," he said, "in saying that the whole case has been turned upside down. It has been—on a matter of overcoats—and it makes less sense than anything else. We've been looking for the sinister figure in the long black overcoat. And now along comes another figure in a bloodstained tweed coat that you can at least call gay in colour. Which is which, and does the whole business turn on a matter of overcoats?"

Dr. Fell puffed as he hauled himself up. "Well, I wasn't thinking of that," he said, doubtfully, "when I said that the case had been turned upside down—or perhaps I should say wrong way round. But in a way it may depend on overcoats. H'm. The Man with Two Overcoats. Yes, I think it's the same murderer, even if he doesn't happen to be sartorially consistent."

"You said you had an idea as to who the murderer might be?"

"I know who he is!" roared Dr. Fell. "And do you know why I feel an urge to kick myself? Not only because he's been right under my nose all the time, but *because he's been practically telling me the truth the whole time,* and yet I've never had the sense to see it. He's been so truthful that

it hurts me to think of how I disbelieved him and thought he was innocent!"

"But the vanishing-trick?"

"No, I don't know how it was done. Here we are."

There was only one room on the top floor, to which a grimy skylight
admitted a faint glow on the landing. The room had a door of plain
boards painted green; it stood ajar, and opened on a low cave of a room
whose window had evidently not been opened in some time. After fumbling round in the gloom, Dr. Fell found a gas-mantle in a tipsy globe.
The ragged light showed a neat, but very grimy, room with blue cab-
bages on the wall-paper and a white iron bed. On the bureau lay a
folded note under a bottle of ink. Only one touch remained of Pierre
Fley's weird and twisted brain: it was as though they saw Fley himself, in
his rusty evening clothes and top-hat, standing by the bureau for a performance. Over the mirror hung framed an old-fashioned motto in
curly script of gilt and black and red. The spidery scrollwork read, *Vengeance is Mine, Saith the Lord; I Will Repay.* But it was hung upside
down.

Wheezing in the quiet, Dr. Fell lumbered over to the bureau and
picked up the folded note. The handwriting was flowery, Rampole saw,
and the short message had almost the air of a proclamation.

James Dolberman, Esq.
  I am leaving you my few belongings, such as they are, in lieu of a
week's notice. I shall not need them again. I am going back to my grave.
                                                        Pierre Fley.

"Why," said Rampole, "this insistent harping on 'I am going back to
my grave'? It sounds as though it ought to have a meaning, even if it
doesn't. . . . I suppose there really was such a person as Fley? He existed: he wasn't somebody else pretending to be Fley, or the like?"

Dr. Fell did not answer that. He was at the beginning of a mood of
gloom which sank lower and lower as he inspected the tattered grey
carpet on the floor.

"Not a trace," he groaned. "Not a trace or a bus ticket or anything.
Serene and unswept and traceless. His possessions? No, I don't want to
see his possessions. I suppose Somers had a look through those. Come
on; we'll go back and join Hadley."

They walked to Russell Square through a gloom of mind as well as overcast sky. As they went up the steps, Hadley saw them through the drawing-room window and came to open the front door. Making sure the drawing-room door was closed—there was a mutter of voices beyond—Hadley faced them in the dimness of the ornate hallway. Behind him the devil mask on the suit of Japanese armour gave a fair caricature of his face.

"More trouble, I perceive," said Dr. Fell, almost genially. "Well, out with it. I have nothing to report. I was afraid my expedition would be a failure, but I have no consolation merely from being a good prophet. What's up?"

"That overcoat—" Hadley stopped. He was in such a state that wrath could go no farther; he touched the other side, and ended with a sour grin. "Come in and listen to it, Fell. Maybe it'll make sense to you. If Mangan is lying, I don't see any good reason why he could be lying. But that overcoat . . . we've got it right enough. A new coat, brand new. Nothing in the pockets, not even the usual grit and fluff and tobacco ash that you get when you've worn a coat a little while. But first we were faced with the problem of two overcoats. Now we have what you would probably call the Mystery of the Chameleon Overcoat. . . ."

"What's the matter with the overcoat?"

"It's changed colour," said Hadley.

Dr. Fell blinked. He examined the superintendent with an air of refreshed interest. "I don't imagine by any chance," he said, "that this business has turned your brain, has it? Changed colour, hey? Are you about to tell me that the overcoat is now a bright emerald green?"

"I mean it's changed colour since . . . Come on!"

Tension was thick in the air when he threw open the door on a drawing-room furnished in heavy old-fashioned luxury, with bronze groups holding lights, gilt cornices, and curtains stiff with such an overdose of lace that they looked like frozen waterfalls. All the lights were on. Burnaby lounged on a sofa. Rosette was walking about with quick, angry steps. In the corner by the radio stood Ernestine Dumont, her hands on her hips and her lower lip folded across the upper, amused, or satiric, or both. Finally, Boyd Mangan stood with his back to the fire hopping a little and moving from one side to the other as though it burnt him. But it was excitement, or something else, that burnt him.

". . . I know the damn thing fits me!" he was saying, with an air of fierce repetition. "I know it. I admit it. The overcoat fits me, but it's not my coat. In the first place, I always wear a waterproof; it's hanging up in the hall now. In the second place, I could never afford a coat like that; the thing must have cost twenty guineas if it cost a penny. In the third place—"

Hadley figuratively rapped for attention. The entrance of Dr. Fell and Rampole seemed to soothe Mangan.

"Would you mind repeating," said Hadley, "what you've just been telling us?"

Mangan lit a cigarette. The match-flame gleamed in dark eyes that were a little bloodshot. He twitched out the match, inhaled, and expelled smoke with the air of one who is determined to be convicted in a good cause.

"Personally, I don't see why everybody should want to jump all over me," he said. "It may have been another overcoat, although I don't see why anybody should want to strew his wardrobe all over the place. . . . Look here, Ted, I'll put it up to you." He seized Rampole's arm and dragged him over in front of the fire as though he were setting up an exhibit. "When I got here for dinner last night, I went to hang up my coat—my waterproof, mind you—in the clothes-closet in the hall. Generally you don't bother to turn on the light in there. You just grope round and stick your coat on the first convenient hook. I wouldn't have bothered then, but I was carrying a parcel of books I wanted to put on the shelf. So I switched on the light. And I saw an overcoat, an extra coat, hanging by itself over in the far corner. It was about the same size as the yellow tweed one you've got; just the same, I should have said, only it was black."

"An extra coat," repeated Dr. Fell. He drew in his chins and looked curiously at Mangan. "Why do you say an extra coat, my boy? If you see a line of coats in somebody's house, does the idea of an extra one ever enter your head? My experience is that the least noticed things in a house are coats hanging on a peg; you have a vague idea that one of 'em must be your own, but you're not even sure which it is. Eh?"

"I knew the coats people have here, all the same. *And,*" replied Mangan, "I particularly noticed this one, because I thought it must be Burnaby's. They hadn't told me he was here, and I wondered if he was. . . ."

Burnaby had adopted a very bluff, indulgent air towards Mangan. He was not now the thin-skinned figure they had seen sitting on the divan in Cagliostro Street; he was an elder chiding youth with a theatrical wave of his hand.

"Mangan," he said, "is very observant, Dr. Fell. A very observant young man. Ha-ha-ha! Especially where I am concerned."

"Got any objections?" asked Mangan, lowering his voice to a calm note.

". . . But let him tell you the story. Rosette, my dear, may I offer you a cigarette? By the way, I may say that it wasn't my coat."

Mangan's anger grew without his seeming to know exactly why. But he turned back to Dr. Fell. "Anyway, I noticed it. Then, when Burnaby came here this morning and found that coat with the blood inside it . . . well, the light one was hanging in the same place. Of course, the only explanation is that there were two overcoats. But what kind of crazy business is it? I'll swear that coat last night didn't belong to anybody here. You can see for yourself that the tweed one doesn't. Did the murderer wear one coat, or both, or neither? Besides, that black coat had a queer look about it—"

"Queer?" interrupted Dr. Fell, so sharply that Mangan turned round. "How do you mean, queer?"

Ernestine Dumont came forward from beside the radio, her flat-heeled shoes creaking a little. She looked more withered this morning; the high cheek bones more accentuated, the nose more flat, the eyes so puffed round the lids that they gave her a hooded, furtive appearance. Yet, despite the gritty look, her black eyes still had their glitter.

"Ah, bah!" she said, and made a sharp, somehow wooden gesture. "What is the reason to go on with all this foolishness? Why do you not ask me? I would know more about such things than he. Would I not?" She looked at Mangan and her forehead wrinkled. "No, no, I think you are trying to tell the truth, you understand. But I think you have mixed it up a little. That is easy, as the Dr. Fell says. . . . The yellow coat was there last night, yes. Early in the evening, before dinner. It was hanging on the hook where he says he saw the black one. I saw it myself."

"But—" cried Mangan.

"Now, now," boomed Dr. Fell, soothingly. "Let's see if we can't straighten this out. If you saw the coat, there, ma'am, didn't it strike you as unusual? A little queer, hey, if you knew it didn't belong to anybody here?"

"No, not at all." She nodded towards Mangan. "I did not see him arrive. I supposed it was his."

"Who did let you in, by the way?" Dr. Fell asked Mangan, sleepily.

"Annie. But I hung up my things myself. I'll swear—"

"Better ring the bell and have Annie up, if she's here, Hadley," said Dr. Fell. "This problem of the chameleon overcoat intrigues me. Oh, Bacchus, it intrigues me! Now, ma'am, I'm not saying you're not telling the truth any more than you say it of our friend Mangan. I was telling Ted Rampole a while ago how unfortunately truthful a certain person has been. Hah! Incidentally have you spoken to Annie?"

"Oh yes," Hadley answered, as Rosette Grimaud strode past him and rang a bell. "She tells a straight story. She was out last night, and didn't get back until past twelve. But I haven't asked her about this."

"I don't see what all the fuss is about!" cried Rosette. "What difference does it make? Haven't you better things to do than go fooling about trying to decide whether an overcoat was yellow or black?"

Mangan turned on her. "It makes a lot of difference, and you know it. I wasn't seeing things. No, and I don't think she was, either! But somebody's got to be right. Though I admit Annie probably won't know. God! I don't know anything!"

"Quite right," said Burnaby.

"Go to hell," said Mangan. "Do you mind?"

Hadley strode over between them and spoke quietly but to the point. Burnaby, who looked rather white, sat down on the couch again. The fray and strain of nerves showed raw in that room; everybody seemed eager to be quiet when Annie answered the bell. Annie was a quiet, long-nosed serious-minded girl who showed none of that quality which is called nonsense. She looked capable; she also looked hard-worked. Standing rather bent at the doorway, her cap so precise on her head that it seemed to have been stamped there, she regarded Hadley with level brown eyes. She was a little upset, but not in the least nervous.

"One thing I neglected to ask you about last night—er," said the superintendent, not too easy himself. "Hum! You let Mr. Mangan in, did you?"

"Yes, sir."

"About what time was that?"

"Couldn't say, sir." She seemed puzzled. "Might have been half an hour before dinner. Couldn't say exactly."

"Did you see him hang up hat and coat?"

"*Yes*, sir! He never gives them to me, or of course I'd have—"

"But did you look into the clothes-closet?"

"Oh, I see. . . . Yes, sir, I did! You see, when I'd let him in, I went straight back to the dining-room, but then I discovered I had to go downstairs to the kitchen. So I went back through the front hall. And I noticed he'd gone away and left the light on in the clothes-closet so I went down and turned it out. . . ."

Hadley leaned forward. "Now be careful! You know the light tweed overcoat that was found in that closet this morning? You knew about that, did you? Good! Do you remember the hook it was hanging from?"

"Yes, sir, I do." Her lips closed tightly. "I was in the front hall this morning when Mr. Burnaby found it, and the rest came round. Mr. Mills said we must leave it where it was, with the blood on it and all, because the police . . ."

"Exactly. The question, Annie, is about the colour of that coat. When you looked into that closet last night, was the coat a light brown or a black? Can you remember?"

She stared at him. "Yes, sir, I can re— light brown or black, sir? Do you mean it? Well, sir, strictly speaking, it wasn't either. *Because there was no coat hanging from that hook at all.*"

A babble of voices crossed and clashed: Mangan furious, Rosette almost hysterically mocking, Burnaby amused. Only Ernestine Dumont remained wearily and contemptuously silent. For a full minute Hadley studied the set, now fighting-earnest face of the witness: Annie had her hands clenched and her neck thrust out. Hadley moved over towards the window, saying nothing in a markedly violent fashion.

Then Dr. Fell chuckled.

"Well, cheer up," he urged. "At least it hasn't turned another colour on us. And I must insist it's a very revealing fact, although I shall be in some danger of having that chair chucked at my head. H'mf. Hah! Yes. Come along, Hadley. Lunch is what we want. Lunch!"

17

The Locked-Room
Lecture

The coffee was on the table, the wine-bottles were empty, cigars lighted. Hadley, Pettis, Rampole, and Dr. Fell sat round the glow of a red-shaded table lamp in the vast, dusky dining-room at Pettis's hotel. They had stayed on beyond most, and only a few people remained at other tables in that lazy, replete hour of a winter afternoon when the fire is most comfortable and snowflakes begin to sift past the windows. Under the dark gleam of armour and armorial bearings, Dr. Fell looked more than ever like a feudal baron. He glanced with contempt at the demitasse, which he seemed in danger of swallowing cup and all. He made an expansive, settling gesture with his cigar. He cleared his throat.

"I will now lecture," announced the doctor, with amiable firmness, "on the general mechanics and development of that situation which is known in detective fiction as the 'hermetically sealed chamber.' "

Hadley groaned. "Some other time," he suggested. "We don't want to hear any lecture after this excellent lunch, and especially when there's work to be done. Now, as I was saying a moment ago—"

"I will now lecture," said Dr. Fell, inexorably, "on the general mechanics and development of the situation which is known in detective fiction as the 'hermetically sealed chamber.' Harrumph. All those opposing can skip this chapter. Harrumph. To begin with, gentlemen! Having been improving my mind with sensational fiction for the last forty years, I can say—"

"But, if you're going to analyze impossible situations," interrupted Pettis, "why discuss detective fiction?"

"Because," said the doctor, frankly, "we're in a detective story, and we don't fool the reader by pretending we're not. Let's not invent elaborate excuses to drag in a discussion of detective stories. Let's candidly glory in the noblest pursuits possible to characters in a book.

"But to continue: In discussing 'em, gentlemen, I am not going to start an argument by attempting to lay down rules. I mean to speak solely of personal tastes and preferences. We can tamper with Kipling thus: 'There are nine and sixty ways to construct a murder maze, and every single one of them is right.' Now, if I said that to me every single one of them was equally interesting, then I should be—to put the matter as civilly as possible—a cock-eyed liar. But that is not the point. When I say that a story about a hermetically sealed chamber is more interesting than anything else in detective fiction, that's merely a prejudice. I like my murders to be frequent, gory, and grotesque. I like some vividness of colour and imagination flashing out of my plot, since I cannot find a story enthralling solely on the grounds that it sounds as though it might really have happened. All these things, I admit, are happy, cheerful, rational prejudices, and entail no criticism of more tepid (or more able) work.

"But this point must be made, because a few people who do not like the slightly lurid insist on treating their preferences as rules. They use, as a stamp of condemnation, the word 'improbable.' And thereby they gull the unwary into their own belief that 'improbable' simply means 'bad.'

"Now, it seems reasonable to point out that the word improbable is the very last which should ever be used to curse detective fiction in any case. A great part of our liking for detective fiction is *based* on a liking for improbability. When A is murdered, and B and C are under strong suspicion, it is improbable that the innocent-looking D can be guilty. But he is. If G has a perfect alibi, sworn to at every point by every other letter in the alphabet, it is improbable that G can have committed the crime. But he has. When the detective picks up a fleck of coal dust at the seashore, it is improbable that such an insignificant thing can have any importance. But it will. In short, you come to a point where the word improbable grows meaningless as a jeer. There can be no such thing as any probability until the end of the story. And then, if you wish the murder to be fastened on an unlikely person (as some of us old fogies do), you can hardly complain because he acted from motives less likely or necessarily less apparent than those of the person first suspected.

"When the cry of 'This-sort-of-thing-wouldn't happen!' goes up, when you complain about half-faced fiends and hooded phantoms and blond hypnotic sirens, you are merely saying, 'I don't like this sort of story.' That's fair enough. If you do not like it, you are howlingly right to say so. But when you twist this matter of taste into a rule for judging the merit or even the probability of the story, you are merely saying, 'This series of events couldn't happen, because I shouldn't enjoy it if it did.'

"What would seem to be the truth of the matter? We might test it out by taking the hermetically-sealed-chamber as an example, because this situation has been under a hotter fire than any other on the grounds of being unconvincing.

"Most people, I am delighted to say, are fond of the locked room. But —here's the damned rub—even its friends are often dubious. I cheerfully admit that *I* frequently am. So, for the moment, we'll all side together on the score and see what we can discover. Why are we dubious when we hear the explanation of the locked room? Not in the least because we are incredulous, but simply because in some vague way we are *disappointed*. And from that feeling it is only natural to take an unfair step farther, and call the whole business incredible or impossible or flatly ridiculous.

"Precisely, in short," boomed Dr. Fell, pointing his cigar, "what O'Rourke was telling us today about illusions that are performed *in real life*. Lord! gents, what chance has a story got when we even jeer at real occurrences? The very fact that they do happen, and that the illusionist gets away with it, seems to make the deception worse. When it occurs in a detective story, we call it incredible. When it happens in real life, and we are forced to credit it, we merely call the explanation disappointing. And the secret of both disappointments is the same—we expect too much.

"You see, the effect is so magical that we somehow expect the cause to be magical also. When we see that it isn't wizardry, we call it tomfoolery. Which is hardly fair play. The last thing we should complain about with regard to the murderer is his erratic conduct. The whole test is, *can* the thing be done? If so, the question of whether it *would* be done does not enter into it. A man escapes from a locked room—well? Since apparently he has violated the laws of nature for our entertainment, then heaven knows he is entitled to violate the laws of Probable Behaviour! If a man offers to stand on his head, we can hardly make the stipulation that he must keep his feet on the ground while he does it. Bear that in mind, gents, when you judge. Call the result uninteresting, if you like, or anything else that is a matter of personal taste. But be very careful about making the nonsensical statement that it is improbable or far fetched."

"All right, all right," said Hadley, shifting in his chair. "I don't feel very strongly on the matter myself. But if you insist on lecturing—apparently with some application to this case—?"

"Yes."

"Then why take the hermetically sealed room? You yourself said that Grimaud's murder wasn't our biggest problem. The main puzzle is the business of a man shot in the middle of an empty street. . . ."

"Oh, that?" said Dr. Fell, with such a contemptuous wave of his hand that Hadley stared at him. "That part of it? I knew the explanation of that as soon as I heard the church bells. —Tut, tut, such language! I'm quite serious. It's the escape from the room that bothers me. And, to see if we can't get a lead, I am going to outline roughly some of the various means of committing murders in locked rooms, under separate classifi-cations. This crime belongs under one of them. It's got to! No matter how wide the variation may be, it's *only* a variation of a few central methods.

"H'mf! Ha! Now, here is your box with one door, one window, and solid walls. In discussing ways of escaping when both door and window are sealed, I shall not mention the low (and nowadays very rare) trick of having a secret passage to a locked room. This so puts a story beyond the pale that a self-respecting author scarcely needs even to mention that there is no such thing. We don't need to discuss minor variations of this outrage: the panel which is only large enough to admit a hand; or the plugged hole in the ceiling through which a knife is dropped, the plug replaced undetectably, and the floor of the attic above sprayed with dust so that no one seems to have walked there. This is only the same foul in miniature. The principal remains the same whether the secret opening is as small as a thimble or as big as a barn door. . . . As to legitimate classification, you might jot some of these down, Mr. Pettis. . . ."

"Right," said Pettis, who was grinning. "Go on."

"First! There is the crime committed in a hermetically sealed room which really is hermetically sealed, and from which no murderer has escaped because no murderer was actually in the room. Explanations:

"1. It is not murder, but a series of coincidences ending in an accident which looks like murder. At an earlier time, before the room was locked, there has been a robbery, an attack, a wound, or a breaking of furniture which suggests a murder struggle. Later the victim is either accidentally killed or stunned in a locked room, and all these incidents are assumed to have taken place at the same time. In this case the means of death is usually a crack on the head—presumably by a bludgeon, but really from some piece of furniture. It may be from the corner of a table or the sharp edge of a chair, but the most popular object is an iron fender. The murderous fender, by the way, has been killing people in a way that looks like murder ever since Sherlock Holmes' adventure with the Crooked Man. The most thoroughly satisfying solution of this type of plot, which includes a murderer, is in Gaston Leroux's *The Mystery of the Yellow Room* —the best detective tale ever written.

"2. It is murder, but the victim is impelled to kill himself or crash into an accidental death. This may be by the effect of a haunted room, by suggestion, or more usually by a gas introduced from outside the room. This gas or poison makes the victim go beserk, smash up the room as though there had been a struggle, and die of a knife-slash inflicted on himself. In other variations he drives the spike of the chandelier through his head, is hanged on a loop of wire, or even strangles himself with his own hands.

"3. It is murder, by a mechanical device already planted in the room, and hidden undetectably in some innocent-looking piece of furniture. It may be a trap set by somebody long dead, and work either automatically or be set anew by the modern killer. It may be some fresh quirk of devilry from present-day science. We have, for instance, the gun-mechanism concealed in the telephone receiver, which fires a bullet into the victim's head as he lifts the receiver. We have the pistol with a string to the trigger, which is pulled by the expansion of water as it freezes. We have the clock that fires a bullet when you wind it; and (clocks being popular) we have the ingenious grandfather clock which sets ringing a hideously clanging bell on its top, so that when you reach up to shut off the din your own touch releases a blade that slashes open your stomach. We have the weight that swings down from the ceiling, and the weight that crashes out on your skull from the high back of a chair. There is the bed that exhales a deadly gas when your body warms it, the poisoned needle that leaves no trace, the—

"You see," said Dr. Fell, stabbing out with his cigar at each point, "when we become involved with these mechanical devices we are rather in the sphere of the general 'impossible situation' than the narrower one of the locked room. It would be possible to go on forever, even on mechanical devices for electrocuting people. A cord in front of a row of pictures is electrified. A chessboard is electrified. Even a glove is electrified. There is death in every article of furniture, including a tea-urn. But these things seem to have no present application, so we go on to:

"4. It is suicide, which is intended to look like murder. A man stabs himself with an icicle; the icicle melts! and, no weapon being found in the locked room, murder is presumed. A man shoots himself with a gun fastened on the end of an elastic—the gun, as he releases it, being carried up out of sight into the chimney. Variations of this trick (not locked-room affairs) have been the pistol with a string attached to a weight, which is whisked over the parapet of a bridge into the water after the shot; and, in the same style, the pistol jerked out of a window into a snowdrift.

"5. It is a murder which derives its problem from illusion and impersonation. Thus: the victim, still thought to be alive, is already lying murdered inside a room, of which the door is under observation. The murderer, either dressed as his victim or mistaken from behind for the victim, hurries in at the door. He whirls round, gets rid of his disguise, and instantly comes out of the room *as himself*. The illusion is that he has merely passed the other man in coming out. In any event, he has an alibi; since, when the body is discovered later, the murder is presumed to have taken place some time after the impersonated 'victim' entered the room.

"6. It is a murder which, although committed by somebody outside the room at the time, nevertheless seems to have been committed by somebody who must have been inside.

"In explaining this," said Dr. Fell, breaking off, "I will classify this type of murder under the general name of the Long-Distance or Icicle Crime, since it is usually a variation of that principle. I've spoken of icicles; you understand what I mean. The door is locked, the window too small to admit a murderer; yet the victim has apparently been stabbed from inside the room and the weapon is missing. Well, the icicle has been fired as a bullet from outside—we will not discuss whether this is practical, any more than we have discussed the mysterious gases previously mentioned—and it melts without a trace. I believe Anna Katherine Green was the first to use this trick in detective fiction, in a novel called *Initials Only*.

"(By the way, she was responsible for starting a number of traditions. In her first detective novel, over fifty years ago, she founded the legend of the murderous secretary killing his employer, and I think present-day statistics would prove that the secretary is still the commonest murderer in fiction. Butlers have long gone out of fashion; the invalid in the wheel-chair is too suspect; and the placid middle-aged spinster has long ago given up homicidal mania in order to become a detective. Doctors, too, are better behaved nowadays, unless, of course, they grow eminent and turn into Mad Scientists. Lawyers, while they remain persistently crooked, are only in some cases actively dangerous. But cycles return! Edgar Allan Poe, eighty years ago, blew the gaff by calling his murderer Goodfellow; and the most popular modern mystery-writer does precisely the same thing by calling his arch-villain Goodman. Meanwhile, those secretaries are still the most dangerous people to have about the house.)

"To continue with regard to the icicle: Its actual use has been attributed to the Medici, and in one of the admirable Fleming Stone stories an epigram of Martial is quoted to show that it had its deadly origin in Rome in the first century A.D. Well, it has been fired, thrown, or shot from a crossbow as in one adventure of Hamilton Cleek (that magnificent character of the *Forty Faces*). Variants of the same theme, a soluble missile, have been rock-salt bullets and even bullets made of frozen blood.

"But it illustrates what I mean in crimes committed inside a room by somebody who was outside. There are other methods. The victim may be stabbed by a thin swordstick blade, passed between the twinings of a summerhouse and withdrawn; or he may be stabbed with a blade so thin that he does not know he is hurt at all, and walks into another room before he suddenly collapses in death. Or he is lured into looking out of a window inaccessible from below; yet from above our old friend ice smashes down on his head, leaving him with a smashed skull but no weapon because the weapon has melted.

"Under this heading (although it might equally well go under head number 3) we might list murders committed by means of poisonous snakes or insects. Snakes can be concealed not only in chests and safes, but also deftly hidden in flowerpots, books, chandeliers, and walking-sticks. I even remember one cheerful item in which the amber stem of a pipe, grotesquely carven as a scorpion, comes to life a real scorpion as the victim is about to put it into his mouth. But for the greatest long-range murder ever committed in a locked room, gents, I commend you to one of the most brilliant short detective stories in the history of detective fiction. (In fact, it shares the honours for supreme untouchable top-notch excellence with Thomas Burke's, *The Hands of Mr. Ottermole*, Chesterton's, *The Man in the Passage*, and Jacques Futrelle's, *The Prob-*

lem of Cell 13.) This is Melville Davisson Post's, *The Doomdorf Mystery* —and the long-range assassin is the sun. The sun strikes through the window of the locked room, makes a burning-glass of a bottle of Doomdorf's own raw white wood-alcohol liquor on the table, and ignites through it the percussion cap of a gun hanging on the wall: so that the breast of the hated one is blown open as he lies in his bed. Then, again, we have. . . .

"Steady! Harrumph. Ha. I'd better not meander; I'll round off this classification with the final heading:

"7. This is a murder depending on an effect exactly the reverse of number 5. That is, the victim is presumed to be dead long before he actually is. The victim lies asleep (drugged but unharmed) in a locked room. Knockings on the door fail to rouse him. The murderer starts a foul-play scare; forces the door; gets in ahead and kills by stabbing or throat-cutting, while suggesting to other watchers that they have seen something they have not seen. The honour of inventing this device belongs to Israel Zangwill, and it has since been used in many forms. It has been done (usually by stabbing) on a ship, in a ruined house, in a conservatory, in an attic, and even in the open air—where the victim has first stumbled and stunned himself before the assassin bends over him. So—"

"Steady! Wait a minute!" interposed Hadley, pounding on the table for attention. Dr. Fell, the muscles of whose eloquence were oiling up in a satisfactory way, turned agreeably and beamed on him. Hadley went on: "This may be all very well. You've dealt with all the locked-room situations—"

"All of them?" snorted Dr. Fell, opening his eyes wide. "Of course I haven't. That doesn't even deal comprehensively with the methods under that particular classification: it's only a rough offhand outline; but I'll let it stand. I was going to speak of the other classification: the various means of hocussing doors and windows so that they can be locked on the inside. H'mf! Hah! So, gentlemen. I continue—"

"Not yet you don't," said the superintendent, doggedly. "I'll argue the thing on your own grounds. You say we can get a lead from stating the various ways in which the stunt has been worked. You've stated seven points; but, applied to *this* case, each one must be ruled out according to your own classification-head. You head the whole list, 'No murderer escaped from the room because no murderer was ever actually in it at the time of the crime.' Out goes everything! The one thing we definitely do know, unless we presume Mills and Dumont to be liars, is that the murderer really was in the room! What about that?"

Pettis was sitting forward, his bald head gleaming by the glow of the red-shaded lamp as he bent over an envelope. He was making neat notes with a neat gold pencil. Now he raised his prominent eyes, which seemed more prominent and rather froglike as he studied Dr. Fell.

"Er—yes," he said, with a short cough. "But that point number 5 is suggestive, I should think! Illusion! What if Mills and Mrs. Dumont really didn't see somebody go in that door; that they were hoaxed somehow or that the whole thing was an illusion like a magic-lantern?"

"Illusion my foot," said Hadley. "Sorry! I thought of that, too. I hammered Mills about it last night, and I had another word or two with him this morning. Whatever else the murderer was, he wasn't an illusion and he did go in that door. He was solid enough to cast a shadow and make the hall vibrate when he walked. He was solid enough to talk and slam a door. You agree with that, Fell?"

The doctor nodded disconsolately. He drew in absent puffs on his dead cigar.

"Oh yes, I agree to that. He was solid enough, and he did go in."

"And even," Hadley pursued, while Pettis summoned the waiter to get more coffee, "granting what we know is untrue. Even granting a magic-lantern shadow did all that, a magic-lantern shadow didn't kill Grimaud. It was a solid pistol in a solid hand. And for the rest of the points, Lord knows Grimaud didn't get shot by a mechanical device. What's more, he didn't shoot himself—and have the gun whisk up the chimney like the one in your example. In the first place, a man can't shoot himself from some feet away. And in the second place, the gun can't whisk up the chimney and sail across the roofs to Cagliostro Street, shoot Fley, and tumble down with its work finished. Blast it, Fell, my conversation is getting like yours! It's too much exposure to your habits of thought. I'm expecting a call from the office any minute, and I want to get back to sanity. What's the matter with you?"

Dr. Fell, his little eyes opened wide, was staring at the lamp, and his fist came down slowly on the table.

"Chimney!" he said. "Chimney! Wow! I wonder if—? Lord! Hadley, what an ass I've been!"

"What about the chimney?" asked the superintendent. "We've proved the murderer couldn't have got out like that: getting up the chimney."

"Yes, of course; but I didn't mean that. I begin to get a glimmer, even if it may be a glimmer of moonshine. I must have another look at that chimney."

Pettis chuckled, tapping the gold pencil on his notes. "Anyhow," he suggested, "you may as well round out this discussion. I agree with the superintendent about one thing. You might do better to outline ways of tampering with doors, windows, or chimneys."

"Chimneys, I regret to say," Dr. Fell pursued, his gusto returning as his abstraction left him, "chimneys, I regret to say, are not favoured as a means of escape in detective fiction—except, of course, for secret passages. There they are supreme. There is the hollow chimney with the secret room behind; the back of the fireplace opening like a curtain; the fireplace that swings out; even the room under the hearthstone. Moreover, all kinds of things can be dropped *down* chimneys, chiefly poisonous things. But the murderer who makes his escape by climbing up is very rare. Besides being next to impossible, it is a much grimier business than monkeying with doors or windows. Of the two chief classifications, doors and windows, the door is by far the more popular, and we may list thus a few means of tampering with it so that it seems to be locked on the inside:

"1. Tampering with the key which is still in the lock. This was the favourite old-fashioned method, but its variations are too well-known nowadays for anybody to use it seriously. The stem of the key can be gripped and turned with pliers from outside; we did this ourselves to *open* the door of Grimaud's study. One practical little mechanism consists of a thin metal bar about two inches long, to which is attached a length of stout string. Before leaving the room, this bar is thrust into the hole at the head of the key, one end under and one end over, so that it acts as a lever; the string is dropped down and run under the door to the outside. The door is closed from outside. You have only to pull on the string, and the lever turns the lock; you then shake or pull out the loose bar by means of the string, and when it drops, draw it under the door to you. There are various applications of this same principle, all entailing the use of string.

"2. Simply removing the hinges of the door without disturbing lock or bolt. This is a neat trick, known to most schoolboys when they want to burgle a locked cupboard; but of course the hinges must be on the outside of the door.

"3. Tampering with the bolt. String again: this time with a mechanism of pins and darning-needles, by which the bolt is shot from the outside by leverage of a pin stuck on the inside of the door, and the string is worked through the keyhole. Philo Vance, to whom my hat is lifted, has shown us this best application of the stunt. There are simpler, but not so effective, variations using one piece of string. A 'tomfool' knot, which a sharp jerk will straighten out, is looped in one end of a long piece of cord. This loop is passed round the knob of the bolt, down, and under the door. The door is then closed, and, by drawing the string along to the left or right, the bolt is shot. A jerk releases the knot from the knob, and the string drawn out. Ellery Queen has shown us still another method, entailing the use of the dead man himself—but a bald statement of this, taken out of its context, would sound so wild as to be unfair to that brilliant gentleman.

"4. Tampering with a falling bar or latch. This usually consists in propping something under the latch, which can be pulled away after the door is closed from the outside, and let the bar drop. The best method by far is by the use of the ever-helpful ice, a cube of which is propped under the latch; and, when it melts, the latch falls. There is one case in which the mere slam of the door suffices to drop the bar inside.

"5. An illusion, simple but effective. The murderer, after committing his crime, has locked the door from the outside and kept the key. It is assumed, however, that the key is still in the lock on the inside. The murderer, who is first to raise a scare and find the body smashes the upper glass panel of the door, puts his hand through with the key concealed in it, and 'finds' the key in the lock inside, by which he opens the door. This device has also been used with the breaking of a panel out of an ordinary wooden door.

"There are miscellaneous methods, such as locking a door from the outside and returning the key to the room by means of string again, but you can see for yourselves that in this case none of them can have any application. We found the door locked on the inside. Well, there are many ways by which it could have been done—but it was *not* done, because Mills was watching the door the whole time. This room was only locked in a technical sense. It was watched, and that shoots us all to blazes."

"I don't like to drag in famous platitudes," said Pettis, his forehead wrinkled, "but it would seem plenty sound to say exclude the impossible and whatever remains, however improbable, must be the truth. You've excluded the door; I presume you also exclude the chimney?"

"I do," grunted Dr. Fell.

"Then we come back in a circle to the window, don't we?" demanded Hadley. "You've gone on and on about ways that obviously couldn't have been used. But in this catalogue of sensationalism you've omitted all mention of the only means of exit the murderer *could* have used. . . ."

"Because it wasn't a locked window, don't you see?" cried Dr. Fell. "I can tell you several brands of funny business with windows if they're only locked. It can be traced down from the earliest dummy nail-heads to the latest hocus-pocus with steel shutters. You can smash a window, carefully turn its catch to lock it, and then, when you leave, simply replace the whole pane with a new pane of glass and putty it round; so that the new pane looks like the original and the window is locked inside. But this window wasn't locked or even closed—it was only inaccessible."

"I seem to have read somewhere of human flies . . ." Pettis suggested.

Dr. Fell shook his head. "We won't debate whether a human fly can walk on a sheer smooth wall. Since I've cheerfully accepted so much, I might believe that if the fly had any place to light. That is, he would have to start from somewhere and end somewhere. But he didn't; not on the roof, not on the ground below. . . ." Dr. Fell hammered his fists against his temples. "However, if you want a suggestion or two in that respect, I will tell you—"

He stopped, raising his head. At the end of the quiet, now deserted dining-room a line of windows showed pale light now flickering with snow. A figure had darted in silhouette against them, hesitating, peering from side to side, and then hurrying down towards them. Hadley uttered a muffled exclamation as they saw it was Mangan. Mangan was pale.

"Not something else?" asked Hadley, as coolly as he could. He pushed back his chair. "Not something else about coats changing colour or—"

"No," said Mangan. He stood by the table, drawing his breath in gasps. "But you'd better get over there. Something's happened to Drayman; apoplectic stroke or something like that. No, he's not dead or anything. But he's in a bad way. He was trying to get in touch with you when he had the stroke. . . . He keeps talking wildly about somebody in his room, and fireworks, and chimneys."

18
The Chimney

Again there were three people—three people strained and with frayed nerves—waiting in the drawing-room. Even Stuart Mills, who stood with his back to the fireplace, kept clearing his throat in a way that seemed to drive Rosette half frantic. Ernestine Dumont sat quietly by the fire when Mangan led in Dr. Fell, Hadley, Pettis, and Rampole. The lights had been turned off; only the bleakness of the snow-shadowed afternoon penetrated through heavy lace curtains, and Mills' shadow blocked the tired gleam of the fire. Burnaby had gone.

"You cannot see him," said the woman, with her eyes fixed on that shadow. "The doctor is with him now. Things all come at once. Probably he is mad."

Rosette, her arms folded, had been pacing about with her own feline grace. She faced the newcomers and spoke with harsh suddenness.

"I can't stand this, you know. It can go on just so long, and then— *Have* you any idea of what happened? Do you know how my father was killed, or who killed him? For God's sake say something, even if you only accuse me!"

"Suppose you tell us exactly what happened to Mr. Drayman," Hadley said, quietly, "and when it happened. Is he in any grave danger?"

Mme. Dumont shrugged. "That is possible. His heart . . . I do not know. He collapsed. He is unconscious now. As to whether he will ever come alive again, that I do not know, either. About what happened to him, we have no idea what caused it. . . ."

Again Mills cleared his throat. His head was in the air, and his fixed smile looked rather ghastly. He said:

"If, sir, you have any idea of—um—foul play, or any suspicion that he was murderously set upon, you may dismiss it. And, strangely enough, you will receive confirmation of it from us in—what shall I say

—pairs? I mean that the same people were together this afternoon who were together last night. The Pythoness and I," he bowed gravely towards Ernestine Dumont, "were together upstairs in my little workroom. I am given to understand that Miss Grimaud and our friend Mangan were down here. . . ."

Rosette jerked her head. "You had better hear it from the beginning. Did Boyd tell you about Drayman coming down here first?"

"No. I didn't tell 'em anything," Mangan answered, with some bitterness. "After that business of the overcoat, I wanted somebody to give me a little confirmation." He swung round, the muscles tightening at his temples. "It was about half an hour ago, you see. Rosette and I were here alone. I'd had a row with Burnaby—well, the usual thing. Everybody was yelling and fighting about that overcoat affair, and we'd all separated. Burnaby had gone. I hadn't seen Drayman at all; he'd kept to his room this morning. Anyhow, Drayman walked in here and asked me how he could get in touch with you."

"You mean he had discovered something?"

Rosette sniffed. "Or wanted us to think he had. Very mysterious! He came in with that doddering way of his, and as Boyd says, asked where he could find you. Boyd asked him what was up . . ."

"Did he act as though he might have—well, found something important?"

"Yes, he did. We both nearly jumped out of our shoes. . . ."

"Why?"

"So would you," said Rosette, coolly, "if you were innocent." She twitched her shoulders, her arms still folded, as though she were cold. "So we said, 'What is it, anyhow?' He doddered a little, and said, 'I've found something missing from my room, and it makes me remember something I'd forgotten about last night.' It was all a lot of nonsense about some subconscious memory, though he wasn't very clear on the point. It came down to some hallucination that, while he was lying down last night after he'd taken the sleeping-powder, somebody had come into his room."

"Before the—crime?"

"Yes."

"Who came into his room?"

"That's it! He either didn't know, or wouldn't say, or else the whole thing was a plain dream. Of course that's probably what it was. I won't suggest," said Rosette, still coolly, "the other alternative. When we asked him, he simply tapped his head, and hedged, and said, 'I really can't say,' in that infuriating way of his. . . . Lord! how I hate these people who won't come out and say what they mean! We both got rather annoyed—"

"Oh, he's all right," said Mangan, whose discomfort appeared to be growing. "Only, damn it all, if I hadn't said what I did. . . ."

"Said what?" asked Hadley, quickly.

Mangan hunched his shoulders and looked moodily at the fire. "I said, 'Well, if you've discovered so much, why don't you go up to the scene of the 'orrid murder and see if you can't discover some more?' Yes, I was sore. He took me seriously. He looked at me for a minute and said: 'Yes, I believe I will. I had better make sure.' And with that out he went! It was maybe twenty minutes later that we heard a noise like somebody banging downstairs. . . . You see, we hadn't left the room, although—" He checked himself suddenly.

"You might as well go on and say it," Rosette told him, with an air of surprised indifference. "I don't mind who knows it. I wanted to sneak up after him and watch him. But we didn't. After that twenty minutes, we heard him blundering downstairs. Then, apparently when he'd just got to the last step, we heard a choking sound and a thud—*flap*, like that. Boyd opened the door, and there he was lying doubled up. His face was all congested, and the veins up round the forehead were standing out in a blue colour; horrible business! Of course we sent for the doctor. He hasn't said anything except to rave about 'chimneys' and 'fireworks.' "

Ernestine Dumont still remained stolid, her eyes not moving from the fire. Mills took a little hopping step forward.

"If you will allow me to take up the story," he said, inclining his head, "I think it probable that I can fill the gap. That is, of course, with the Pythoness' permission. . . ."

"Ah, bah!" the woman cried. Her face was in shadow as she looked up, there was about her a rigidity as of whale-bone, but Rampole was startled to see that her eyes blazed. "You must always act the fool, must you not? The Pythoness this, the Pythoness that. Very well, I must tell you. I am Pythoness enough to know that you did not like poor Drayman, and that my little Rosette does not like him, either. God! what do you know of human men or sympathy or . . . Drayman is a good man, even if he may be a little mad. He may be mistaken. He may be full of drugs. But he is a good man at the heart, and if he dies I shall pray for his soul."

"Shall I—er—go on?" observed Mills, imperturbably.

"Yes, you shall go on," the woman mimicked, and was silent.

"The Pythoness and I were in my workroom on the top floor; opposite the study, as you know. And again the door was open. I was shifting some papers, and I noticed Mr. Drayman come up and go into the study . . ."

"Do you know what he did there?" asked Hadley.

"Unfortunately, no. He closed the door. I could not even venture a deduction as to what he might be doing, since I could hear nothing. After some time he came out, in what I can only describe as a panting and unsteady condition—"

"What do you mean by that?"

Mills frowned. "I regret, sir, that it is impossible to be more precise. I can only say that I received an impression as though he had been indulging in violent exercise. This, I have no doubt, caused or hastened the collapse, since there were clear evidences of an apoplectic stroke. If I may correct the Pythoness, it had nothing to do with his heart. Er—I might add something which has not yet been mentioned. When he was picked up after the stroke, I observed that his hands and sleeves were covered with soot."

"The chimney again," Pettis murmured, very softly, and Hadley turned round towards Dr. Fell. It gave Rampole a shock to see that the doctor was no longer in the room. A person of his weight and girth can, as a rule, make small success of an effort to fade mysteriously away; but he was gone, and Rampole thought he knew where.

"Follow him up there," Hadley said quickly to the American. "And see that he doesn't work any of his blasted mystification. Now, Mr. Mills—"

Rampole heard Hadley's questions probing and crackling as he went out into the sombre hall. The house was very quiet; so quiet that, as he mounted the stairs, the sudden shrilling of the telephone bell in the lower hall made him jump a little. Passing Drayman's door upstairs, he heard hoarse breathing inside, and quiet footfalls tiptoeing about the room: through the door he could see the doctor's medicine-case and hat on a chair. No lights burned on the top floor; again such a stillness that he could distinctly hear Annie's voice answering the telephone far below.

The study was dusky. Despite the few snowflakes, some faint lurid light, dull red-and-orange with sunset, glimmered through the window. It made a stormy glow across the room; it kindled the colours of the shield of arms, glittered on the crossed fencing-foils above the fireplace, and made vast and shadowy the white busts on the bookshelves. The shape of Charles Grimaud, half-studious, half-barbaric like the room, seemed to move and chuckle here after Charles Grimaud was dead. That vast blank space in the panelled wall, where the picture was to have hung, faced Rampole in mockery. And, standing motionless in his black cloak before the window, Dr. Fell leaned on his cane and stared out into the sunset.

The creaking of the door did not rouse him. Rampole, his voice seeming to make echoes, said:

"Did you—?"

Dr. Fell blinked round. His breath, when he puffed it out with a sort of weary explosiveness, turned to smoke in the sharp air.

"Eh? Oh! Did I what?"

"Find anything."

"Well, I think I know the truth. I think I know the truth," he answered, with a sort of reflective stubbornness, "and tonight I shall probably be able to prove it. H'mf. Hah. Yes. D'ye see, I've been standing here wondering what to do about it. It's the old problem, son, and it becomes more difficult each year I live: when the sky grows nobler, and the old chair more comfortable, and maybe the human heart—" He brushed his hand across his forehead. "What is justice? I've asked it at the end of nearly every case I ever handled. I see faces rise, and sick souls and bad dreams. . . . No matter. Shall we go downstairs?"

"But what about the fireplace?" insisted Rampole. He went over, peered at it, hammered it, and still he could see nothing out of the way. A little soot had been scattered on the hearth, and there was a crooked streak in the coating of soot on the back of the fireplace. "What's wrong with it? Is there a secret passage, after all?"

"Oh no. There's nothing wrong with it in the way you mean. Nobody got up there. No," he added, as Rampole put his hand into the long opening of the flue and groped round. "I'm afraid you're wasting your time; there's nothing up there to find."

"But," said Rampole, desperately, "if this brother Henri—"

"Yes," said a heavy voice from the doorway, "brother Henri."

The voice was so unlike Hadley's that at the moment they did not recognize it. Hadley stood in the doorway, a sheet of paper crumpled in his hand; his face was in shadow, but there was such a dull quietness in his tones that Rampole recognized something like despair. Closing the door softly behind him, Hadley stood in the darkening room and went on calmly:

"It was our own fault, I know, for being hypnotized by a theory. It ran away with us—and now we've got to start the whole case afresh. Fell, when you said this morning that the case had been turned upside down, I don't believe you knew just how true it was. It's not only upside down; it's non-existent. Our chief prop is knocked to blazes. Damn the rotten, impossible . . . !" He stared at the sheet of paper as though he meant to crush it into a ball. "A phone-call just came through from the Yard. They've heard from Bucharest."

"I'm afraid I know what you're going to say," Dr. Fell nodded. "You're going to say that brother Henri—"

"There is no brother Henri," said Hadley. *"The third of the three Horváth brothers died over thirty years ago."*

The faint reddish light had grown muddy; in the cold, quiet study they could hear from far away the mutter of London awaking towards nightfall. Walking over to the broad desk, Hadley spread out the crumpled sheet on the desk so that the others could read. The shadow of the yellow jade buffalo lay across it sardonically. Across the room they could see the slashes gaping in the picture of the three graves.

"There's no possibility of a mistake," Hadley went on. "The case is a very well-known one, it seems. The whole cablegram they sent was very long, but I've copied the important parts verbatim from what they read over the phone. Take a look."

No difficulty about information desired [it ran]. Two men now in my personal service were at Siebenturmen as warders in 1900, and confirm record. Facts: Károly Grimaud Horváth, Pierre Fley Horváth, and Nicholas Revéi Horváth were sons of Professor Károly Horváth (of Klausenburg University) and Cécile Fley Horváth (French) his wife. For robbery of Kunar Bank at Brasso, November, 1898, the three brothers were sentenced, January, 1899, to twenty years' penal servitude. Bank watchman died of injuries inflicted, and loot never recovered; believed to have been hidden. All three, with aid of prison doctor during plague scare of August, 1900, made daring attempt at escape by being certified as dead, and buried in plague-ground. J. Lahner and R. Görgei, warders, returning to graves an hour later with wooden crosses for marking, noticed disturbance had taken place on earth at grave of Károly Horváth. Investigation showed coffin open and empty. Digging into other two graves, warders found Pierre Horváth bloody and insensible, but still alive. Nicholas Horváth had already suffocated to death. Nicholas reburied after absolute certainty made the man was dead; Pierre returned to prison. Scandal hushed up, no chase of fugitive, and story never discovered until end of war. Pierre Fley Horváth never mentally responsible afterwards. Released January, 1919, having served full term. Assure you no doubt whatever third brother dead.

—*Alexander Cuza, Policedirector, Bucharest*

"Oh yes," said Hadley, when they had finished reading. "It confirms the reconstruction right enough, except for the little point that we've been chasing a ghost as the murderer. Brother Henri (or brother Nicholas, to be exact) never did leave his grave. He's there yet. And the whole case . . ."

Dr. Fell rapped his knuckles slowly on the paper.

"It's my fault, Hadley," he admitted. "I told you this morning that I'd come close to making the biggest mistake of my life. I was hypnotized by brother Henri! I couldn't think of anything else. You see now why we knew so remarkably little about that third brother, so little that with my cursed cocksuredness I put all kinds of fantastic interpretations on it?"

"Well, it won't do us any good just to admit the mistake. How the devil are we going to explain all those crazy remarks of Fley's now? Private vendetta! Vengeance? Now that that's swept away, we haven't a lead to work on. Not one lead! And, if you exclude the motive of vengeance on Grimaud and Fley, what is there left?"

Dr. Fell pointed rather malevolently with his stick.

"Don't you see what's left?" he roared. "Don't you see the explanation of those two murders that we've got to accept now or retire to the madhouse?"

"You mean that somebody cooked up the whole thing to make it look like the work of an avenger?—I'm at the state now," explained the superintendent, "where I could believe nearly anything. But that strikes me as being a good bit too subtle. How would the real murderer ever know we could dig so far into the past? We'd never have done it if it hadn't been, saving your presence, for a few lucky shots. How would the real murderer know we should ever connect Professor Grimaud with a Hungarian criminal, or connect him with Fley or any of the rest of it? It strikes me as a false trail far *too* well concealed." He paced up and down, driving his fist into his palm. "Besides, the more I think of it the more confusing it gets! We had damned good reason to think it was the third brother who killed those two . . . and, the more I think of that possibility, the more I'm inclined to doubt that Nicholas is dead. Grimaud *said* his third brother shot him!—and when a man's dying, and knows he's dying, what earthly reason would he have for lying? Or . . . stop a bit! Do you suppose he might have meant *Fley*? Do you suppose Fley came here, shot Grimaud, and then afterwards somebody else shot Fley? It would explain a lot of the puzzles—"

"But," said Rampole, "excuse the interruption, I mean, but it wouldn't explain why Fley kept talking about a third brother as well! Either brother Henri is dead or he isn't. Still, if he is dead, what reason have both victims got to lie about him all the time? If he's really dead, he must be one hell of a live ghost."

Hadley shook the briefcase. "I know. That's exactly what I'm kicking about! We've got to take somebody's word for it, and it seems more reasonable to take the word of two people who were shot by him, rather than this cablegram which might be influenced or mistaken for several reasons. Or—h'm! Suppose he really is dead, but the murderer is pretending to be that dead brother come to life?" He stopped, nodded, and stared out of the window. "Now I think we're getting warm. That would explain all the inconsistencies, wouldn't it? The real murderer assumes the rôle of a man neither of the other brothers has seen for nearly thirty years; well? When the murders are committed, and we get on his track— if we do get on his track—we put it all down to vengeance. How's that, Fell?"

Dr. Fell, scowling heavily, stumped round the table.

"Not bad . . . no, not bad, as a disguise. But what about the motive for which Grimaud and Fley were really killed?"

"How do you mean?"

"There has to be a connecting thread, hasn't there? There might be any number of motives, plain or obscure, why a person would kill

Grimaud. Mills or Dumont or Burnaby or—yes, anybody *might* have killed Grimaud. Also, anybody might have killed Fley: but not, I must point out, anybody in the same circle or group of people. Why should Fley be killed by a member of Grimaud's group, none of whom had presumably ever seen him before? If these murders are the work of one person, where is the connecting link? A respected professor in Bloomsbury and a tramp actor with a prison record. Where's the human motive that ties those two together in the murderer's mind, unless it is a link that goes back into the past?"

"I can think of one person who is associated with both from the past," Hadley pointed out.

"Who? You mean the Dumont woman?"

"Yes."

"Then what becomes of somebody impersonating brother Henri? Whatever else you decide on, you must decide that she's not doing that. No, my lad. Dumont is not only a bad suspect; she's an impossible suspect."

"I don't see that. Look here, you're basing your whole belief that Dumont didn't kill Grimaud on the grounds that you think she loved Grimaud. No defence, Fell—no defence at all! Remember that she told the whole fantastic story to begin with . . ."

"In coöperation with—Mills," boomed Dr. Fell, with a sardonic leer. He was puffing again. "Can you think of any two less likely conspirators to band together at the dark of the moon and hoodwink the police with their imaginative fairy-tales? She might wear a mask; I mean a figurative mask in life. Mills might wear a mask. But the combination of these two masks, and their activities, is too much. I prefer the one literal false face. Besides, bear in mind that as the double killer Ernestine D. is absolutely O-U-T. Why? Because, at the time of Fley's death sworn to by three good men and true, she was here in this room, talking to us." He pondered, and a twinkle began to appear in his eye. "Or will you drag in the second generation? Rosette is Grimaud's daughter; suppose the mysterious Stuart Mills is really the son of the dead brother Henri?"

About to reply, Hadley checked himself and studied Dr. Fell. He sat down on the edge of the desk.

"I know this mood. I know it very well," he asserted, with the air of one who confirms a sinister suspicion. "It's the beginning of some more blasted mystification, and there's no use arguing with you now. Why are you so anxious for me to believe the story?"

"First," said Dr. Fell, "because I wish to force it into your head that Mills told the truth. . . ."

"You mean, as a point in the mystification, in order to prove later that he didn't? The sort of low trick you played me in that Death Watch case?"

The doctor ignored this with a testy grunt. "And, second, because I know the real murderer."

"Who is somebody we've seen and talked to?"

"Oh yes; very much so."

"And have we got a chance of—?"

Dr. Fell, an absent, fierce, almost pitying expression on his red face, stared for some time at the desk.

"Yes, Lord help us all," he said, in a curious tone, "I suppose you've got to. In the meantime, I'm going home. . . ."

"Home?"

"To apply Gross's test," said Dr. Fell.

He turned away, but he did not immediately go. As the muddy light deepened to purple, and dust-coloured shadows swallowed up the room, he remained for a long time staring at the slashed picture which caught the last glow with its turbulent power, and the three coffins that were filled at last.

19

The Hollow Man

That night Dr. Fell shut himself up in the small cubbyhole off the library which was reserved for what he called his scientific experiments and what Mrs. Fell called "that horrible messing about." Now, a liking for messing about is one of the best of human traits, and Rampole and Dorothy both offered to assist. But the doctor was so serious, and so unwontedly troubled, that they left off with an uncomfortable feeling that to make a joke would be bad taste. The tireless Hadley had already gone off to check alibis. Rampole left the matter with only one question.

"I know you're going to try to read those burnt letters," he said, "and I know you think they're important. But what do you expect to find?"

"The worst possible thing," replied Dr. Fell. "The thing that last night could have made a fool of me."

And with a sleepy shake of his head he closed the door.

Rampole and Dorothy sat on opposite sides of the fireplace, looking at each other. The snow was whirling outside, and it was not a night to venture far. Rampole at first had an idea that he ought to invite Mangan out to dinner, to renew old times; but Mangan, when he telephoned, said that obviously Rosette could not go, and he had better remain with her. So the other two, Mrs. Fell being at church, had the library to themselves for argument.

"Ever since last night," commented her husband, "I've been hearing about Gross's method for reading burnt letters. But nobody seems to know what it is. I suppose you mix chemicals or something?"

"I know what it is," she told him, with an air of triumph. "I looked it up while you people were dashing about this afternoon. And what's more, I bet you it won't work even if it is simple. I bet you *anything* it won't work!"

"You read Gross?"

"Well, I read it in English. It's simple enough. It says something like this. It says that anybody who has thrown letters on the fire will have noticed that the writing on the charred fragments stands out quite clearly, usually white or grey against a black background, but sometimes with the colours reversed. Did you ever notice that?"

"Can't say I have. But then I've seen very few open fires before I came to England. Is it true?"

She frowned. "It works with cardboard boxes that have printing on them, boxes of soap flakes or things like that. But regular writing. . . . Anyway, here's what you're supposed to do. You get a lot of transparent tracing-paper and pin it to a board with drawing-pins. As you pick up each of the charred pieces of paper you cover a place on the tracing-paper with gum, press the charred paper down on it . . ."

"When it's crumpled up like that? It'll break, won't it?"

"Aha! That's the trick, Gross says. You have to soften the fragments. You arrange over and around the tracing-paper a frame two or three inches high, with all the bits under it. Then you stretch across a damp cloth folded several times. That puts the papers in a damp atmosphere, and they straighten out. When they're all flattened out and fixed, you cut out the tracing-paper round each separate fragment. Then you reconstruct them on a sheet of glass. Like a jig-saw puzzle. Afterwards you press a second sheet of glass over the first, and bind the edges, and look through both against the light. But I'll bet you anything you like—"

"We'll try it," said Rampole, impressed and afire with the idea.

The experiments at burning paper were not a complete success. First he got an old letter out of his pocket and touched a match to it. Despite his frantic manoeuvring, it soared up into flame, twitched round, sailed out of his hand, and shrank to rest on the hearth as not more than two inches of shrivelled blackness rolled up like an umbrella. Though they got down on their knees and scrutinized it from every angle, no writing was visible. Rampole burnt several more pieces, which sailed apart like gentle skyrockets and powdered the hearth. Then he began to get mad and burn everything within reach. And, the madder he got, the more convinced he grew that the trick could be worked somehow if he did it properly. Typewriting was tried; he tapped out "Now is the time for all good men to come to the aid of the party" a number of times on Dr. Fell's machine and presently the carpet was littered with floating fragments.

"Besides," he argued, with his cheek against the floor and one eye closed as he studied them, "these aren't charred—they're burnt to hell. They're too far gone to fulfill the conditions. Aha! Got it! I can see 'party' as plain as day. It's much smaller than the actual typing; it seems to be indented on the black; but here it is. Have you got anything out of that handwritten letter?"

Her own excitement was growing as she made a discovery. The words "East 11th Street" stood out in dirty grey letters. With some care, but much powdering of the brittle pieces, they at last deciphered plainly the words, "Saturday night," "ginch," "hangover," and "gin." Rampole got up with satisfaction.

"If those pieces can be straightened out by dampness, then it works!" he declared. "The only thing is whether you could get enough words out of any letter to make sense of it. Besides, we're only amateurs; Gross could get the whole thing. But what does Dr. Fell expect to find?"

This was the subject of an argument which was carried on far into the night.

"And with the case turned upside down," Rampole pointed out, "where do we go now for a motive? That's the crux of the whole busi-

ness. There's no motive that could connect both Grimaud and Fley with
the murderer! By the way, what's become of your wild theories last
night, that the guilty person must be either Pettis or Burnaby?"

"Or the funny-faced blonde," she corrected, with a certain emphasis
on the term. "I say, you know, what bothers me most is that overcoat
changing colour and disappearing and all the rest of it. It seems to lead
straight back to that house, or does it?" She brooded. "No, I've changed
my mind altogether. I don't think Pettis or Burnaby can be implicated. I
don't even think the blonde is. The possible murderer, I'm certain now,
can be narrowed down to two other people."

"Well?"

"It's either Drayman or O'Rourke," she said, firmly, and nodded.
"You mark my words."

Rampole stifled a strong protest. "Yes, I'd thought of O'Rourke," he
admitted. "But you're picking him for just two reasons. First because
he's a trapeze man, and you associate a flying escape of some sort with
the way this thing was done. But, so far as I can see, it's impossible.
Second and more important, you're picking him for the reason that he
doesn't seem to have any connection with this case at all; that he's
standing around for no good reason, and that's always a suspicious sign.
Isn't that so?"

"Maybe."

"Then Drayman . . . yes, Drayman might have been the only one
who could now be associated with both Grimaud and Fley in the past.
That's a point! H'm. Also, nobody saw him during the whole evening
from dinner time until a much later hour—eleven o'clock, anyhow. But
I don't believe he's guilty. Tell you what: let's make a rough time-table of
last night's events to get this thing straightened out. We'll put in everything, from before dinner on. It'll have to be a very rough time-table,
with a lot of guessing on smaller points. We don't know much definitely
except the time of the actual murders and a few statements leading up to
them, but we can make a stab at it. Our times before dinner are vague
too. But let's say . . ."

He took out an envelope and wrote rapidly.

(About) 6:45 Mangan arrives, hangs his coat in the hall closet, and
sees a black overcoat hanging there.

(About) 6:48 (give her three minutes) Annie comes from the dining-room, switches off the light in the hall closet left burning by Mangan, and sees no overcoat at all.

(About) 6:55 (this is not specified, but we know it was before dinner), Mme. Dumont looks into the hall closet and sees a yellow overcoat.

"I arrange it like that," said Rampole, "because presumably in the very brief time between Mangan's hanging up his own coat and going away with the light left on, Dumont didn't rush out to look in there before Annie came to turn the light off."

The girl's eyes narrowed. "Oo, wait! How do you know that? I mean, if the light wasn't on, how did she see a yellow coat at all?"

There was a pause while they looked at each other. Rampole said:

"This is getting interesting. And, if it comes to that, why did she look in there, anyhow? The point is this: If the sequence of times can be established at what I've written, that's reasonable. First, there's a black coat, which Mangan sees. Well, then somebody swipes the black coat just after Mangan goes—for what reason we don't know—and Annie sees nothing. Later the coat is replaced with a light tweed one. That sounds all right. *But,*" he cried, stabbing out with his pencil, "if it worked the other way around, then either somebody is lying or the whole thing is impossible. In that case it doesn't matter what time Mangan arrived, because the whole business must have taken place in a matter of minutes or even seconds. See it? Boyd gets there, hangs his coat up, and walks away. Out comes Dumont, looks in, and walks away. Along comes Annie immediately afterwards, turns out the light, and *she* goes. In that short flash a black overcoat has first turned yellow and then disappeared. Which is impossible."

"Well done!" said the other, beaming. "Then which one was lying? I suppose you'll insist it wasn't your friend—"

"I certainly will. It's the Dumont woman, I'll bet you anything you like!"

"But she's not guilty. That's been proved. Besides, I like her."

"Don't mix me up, now," Rampole urged. "Let's go on with this time-table and see if we can discover anything else. Haa! Where were we?

Yes. Dinner we'll put at seven o'clock, because we know it was over at seven-thirty. Hence—

"7:30 Rosette G. and Mangan go to drawing-room.

7:30 Drayman goes upstairs to his room.

7:30 E. Dumont—where she goes is not known, except that she remains in the house.

7:30 Mills goes to downstairs library.

7:30 Grimaud joins Mills in downstairs library, tells him to come upstairs about 9:30, since he expects a visitor then.

"Whoa! Here's a snag. I was just going to write that then Grimaud goes on to the drawing-room, and tells Mangan the visitor is expected at ten o'clock. But that won't do, because Rosette knew nothing about it, and yet she was with Mangan! The trouble is, Boyd didn't say exactly when he was told that. But it isn't important—Grimaud might have taken him aside or something like that. Similarly, we don't know when Madame Dumont was told to expect the visitor at nine-thirty; probably earlier. It amounts to the same thing."

"Are you sure it does?" enquired Dorothy, searching after cigarettes. "H'm! Well, carry on."

"(About) 7:35 Grimaud goes up to his study.

7:35 to 9:30 no developments. Nobody moves. Heavy snow.

(About) 9:30 snow stops.

(About) 9:30 E. Dumont collects coffee-tray from Grimaud's study. Grimaud remarks that visitor will probably not come that night. E. Dumont leaves study just as—

9:30 Mills comes upstairs.

"I don't think anything noticeable happened in the next interval. Mills was upstairs, Drayman in his room, and Rosette and Boyd in the front room with the radio on. . . . Wait! I'm forgetting something. A little while before the door-bell rang, Rosette heard a thud from somewhere out in the street, as though somebody had fallen off a high place. . . ."

"How did she hear that if they had the radio on?"

"Apparently it wasn't playing loudly enough to— Yes, it was, though. It made such a racket they could hardly hear the fake 'Pettis's' voice. But put that in order:

"9:45 Door-bell rings.

9:45 to 9:50 E. Dumont goes to answer door; speaks to visitor (failing to recognize voice). She receives card, shuts the door on him, examines card and finds it blank, hesitates, and starts upstairs. . . .

9:45 to 9:50. Visitor, after E. D. has started upstairs, gets inside somehow, locks Rosette G. and Boyd M. in front room, answers their hail by imitating the voice of Pettis—"

"I don't like to keep on interrupting you," cut in Dorothy. "But doesn't it seem to have taken them a terribly long time to sing out and ask who the caller was? I mean, would anybody wait so long? If I were expecting a visitor like that, I know I should have piped up, 'Hullo! who is it?' as soon as I heard the door open."

"What are you trying to prove? Nothing? Sure of that? Don't be so hard on the blonde! It was some time before they expected anybody, remember—and that sniff of yours indicates prejudice. Let's continue, with the still inclusive times of nine forty-five to nine-fifty, the interval between the moment X entered the house and the moment he entered Grimaud's study:

"9:45 to 9:50. Visitor follows E. Dumont upstairs, overtakes her in upper hall. He takes off cap and pulls down coat collar, but does not remove mask. Grimaud comes to the door, but does not recognize visitor. Visitor leaps inside and door is slammed. (This is attested by both E. Dumont and S. Mills.)

9:50 to 10:10. Mills watches door from end of hall; Dumont watches same door from staircase landing.

10:10 Shot is fired.

10:10 to 10:12. Mangan in front room finds door to hall locked, on the inside.

10:10 to 10:12. E. Dumont faints or is sick, and gets to her room. (N. B. Drayman, asleep in his room, does not hear shot.)

10:10 to 10:12. Mangan in front room finds door to hall locked, attempts to break it and fails. He then jumps out window, just as—

10:12 We arrive outside; front door unlocked; we go up to study.

10:12 to 10:15. Door is opened with pliers, Grimaud found shot.

10:15 to 10:20. Investigation, ambulance sent for.

10:20 Ambulance arrives. Grimaud removed. Rosette goes with him in ambulance. Boyd M. at orders from Hadley, goes down stairs to telephone police.

"Which," Rampole pointed out with some satisfaction, "absolutely clears both Rosette and Boyd. I don't even need to set down minute times there. The ambulance-men coming upstairs, the doctor's examination, the body taken down to the ambulance—all that in itself would have taken at least five minutes if they'd moved fast enough to slide down the banisters with that stretcher. By God! it's as plain as print when you write it out! It would have taken a good deal longer before they could get to the nursing-home . . . and yet Fley was shot in Cagliostro Street at just ten twenty-five! Now, Rosette did ride over with the ambulance. Boyd was in the house when the ambulance-men arrived, because he came upstairs with them and went down after them. There's a fairly perfect alibi."

"Oh, you don't need to think I'm so anxious to convict them!—especially Boyd, who's rather nice what little I've seen of him." She frowned. "That's always granting your guess that the ambulance didn't arrive at Grimaud's before ten-twenty."

Rampole shrugged. "If it did," he pointed out, "then it flew over from Guilford Street. It wasn't sent for before ten-fifteen, and even so it's something like a miracle that they had it at Grimaud's in five minutes. No, Boyd and Rosette are out of it. Besides, now that I remember, she was at the nursing-home—in the presence of witnesses—when she saw the light in the window of Burnaby's flat at ten-thirty. Let's put the rest into the record and exonerate anyone else we can.

"10:20 to 10:25. Arrival and departure of ambulance with Grimaud.

10:25 Fley shot in Cagliostro Street.

10:20 to (at least) 10:30. Stuart Mills remains with us in study, answering questions.

10:25 Madame Dumont comes into study.

10:30 Rosette, at nursing-home, sees a light in the window of Burnaby's flat.

10:25 to 10:40. Madame Dumont remains with us in the study.

10:40 Rosette returns from nursing-home.

10:40 Arrival of police at Hadley's call."

Rampole, sitting back to run his eye down the scrawl, drew a long flouish under the last item.

"That not only completes our time-table as far as we need to go," he said, "but it unquestionably adds two more to our list of innocents. Mills and Dumont are out. Rosette and Boyd are out. Which accounts for everybody in the house except Drayman."

"But," protested Dorothy, after a pause, "it's getting even worse tangled up. What happens to your brilliant inspiration about the overcoat? You suggested somebody was lying. It could only have been either Boyd Mangan or Ernestine Dumont; and both are exonerated. Unless that girl Annie—But that won't do, will it? Or it shouldn't."

Again they looked at each other. Wryly he folded up his list and put it into his pocket. Outside, the night wind whirled by in a long blast, and they could hear Dr. Fell blundering round his cubbyhole behind the closed door.

Rampole overslept the next morning, partly from exhaustion and partly because the following day was so overcast that he did not open his eyes until past ten o'clock. It was not only so dark that the lights were on, but a day of numbing cold. He had not seen Dr. Fell again last night, and, when he went downstairs to breakfast in the little back dining-room, the maid was indignant as she set out bacon and eggs.

"The doctor's just gone up to have a wash, sir," Vida informed him. "He was up all night on them scientific things, and I found him asleep in the chair in there at eight o'clock this morning. I don't know what Mrs. Fell will say, indeed I don't. Superintendent Hadley's just got here, too. He's in the library."

Hadley, who was impatiently knocking his heels against the fender as though he were pawing the floor, asked for news with some eagerness.

"Have you seen Fell?" he demanded. "Did he go after those letters? And if so—?"

Rampole explained. "Any news from you?"

"Yes, and important news. Both Pettis and Burnaby are out. They've got cast-iron alibis."

Wind whooped past along Adelphi Terrace, and the long window-frames rattled. Hadley continued to paw the hearth rug. He went on: "I saw Burnaby's three card-playing friends last night. One, by the way, is an Old Bailey judge; it'd be pretty difficult to drag a man into court when the judge on the bench can testify to his innocence. Burnaby was playing poker on Saturday night from eight o'clock to nearly half-past eleven.—And this morning Betts has been round to the theatre where Pettis said he saw the play that night. Well, he did. One of the bar-attendants at the theatre knows him quite well by sight. It seems that the second act of the show ends at five minutes past ten. A few minutes afterwards, during the interval, this attendant is willing to swear he served Pettis with a whisky-and-soda in the bar. In other words, he was having a drink at just about the exact moment Grimaud was shot nearly a mile away."

"I expected something like that," said Rampole, after a silence. "And yet, to hear it confirmed. . . . I wish you'd look at this."

IIc handed over the time-table he had made last night. Hadley glanced over it.

"Oh yes. I sketched out one of my own. This is fairly sound; especially the point about the girl and Mangan, although we can't swear too closely to time in that respect. But I think it would hold." He tapped the envelope against his palm. "Narrows it down, I admit. We'll have another go at Drayman. I phoned the house this morning. Everybody was a bit hysterical because they've brought the old man's body back to the house, and I couldn't get much out of Rosette except that Drayman was still only half-conscious and under morphia. We—"

He stopped as they heard the familiar, lumbering step with the tap of the cane, which seemed to have hesitated just outside the door as though at Hadley's words. Then Dr. Fell pushed open the door. There was no twinkle in his eye when he wheezed in. He seemed a part of the heavy morning, and a sense of doom pervaded that leaden air.

"Well?" prompted Hadley. "Did you find out what you wanted to know from those papers?"

Dr. Fell fumbled after, found, and lit his black pipe. Before he answered he waddled over to toss the match into the fire. Then he chuckled at last but very wryly.

"Yes, I found out what I wanted to know.— Hadley, twice in my theories on Saturday night I unintentionally led you wrong. *So* wrong, with such a monstrous and dizzying stupidity, that if I hadn't saved my self-respect by seeing the truth of this thing yesterday, I should have deserved the last punishment reserved for fools. Still, mine wasn't the only blunder. Chance and circumstance made an even worse blunder, and they've combined to make a terrifying, inexplicable puzzle out of what is really only a commonplace and ugly and petty murder-case. Oh, there was shrewdness to the murderer; I admit that. But—yes, I've found out what I wanted to know."

"Well? What about the writing on those papers? What was on those papers?"

"Nothing," said Dr. Fell.

There was something eerie in the slow, heavy way he spoke the word. "You mean," cried Hadley, "that the experiment didn't work?"

"No, I mean that the experiment did work. I mean that there was *nothing* on those papers," boomed Dr. Fell. "Not so much as a single line or scrap or shred of handwriting, not so much as a whisper or pothook of the deadly secrets I told you on Saturday night we might find. That's what I mean. Except—well, yes. There were a few bits of heavier paper, rather like thick cardboard, with one or two letters printed there."

"But why burn letters unless—?"

"Because they weren't letters. That's just it; that's where we went wrong. Don't you see even yet what they were? . . . Well, Hadley, we'd better finish this up and get the whole mess off our minds. You want to meet the Invisible Murderer, do you? You want to meet the damned ghoul and hollow man who's been walking through our dreams? Very well; I'll introduce you. Got your car? Then come along. *I'm going to see if I can't extract a confession.*"

"From—?"

"From somebody at Grimaud's house. Come on."

Rampole saw the end looming, and was afraid of it, without an idea in his whirling head as to what it might be. Hadley had to spin a half-frozen engine before the car would start. They were caught in several traffic blocks on the way up, but Hadley did not even curse. And the quietest of all was Dr. Fell.

All the blinds were drawn on the house in Russell Square. It looked even more dead than yesterday, because death had come inside. And it was so quiet that even from outside they could hear the ringing of the bell when Dr. Fell pressed it. After a long interval Annie, without her cap or apron, answered it. She looked pale and strained, but still calm.

"We should like to see Madame Dumont," said Dr. Fell.

Hadley jerked his head round to look, even though he remained impassive. Annie seemed to speak out of the darkness in the hall as she moved back.

"She is in with the—she's in there," the girl answered, and pointed towards the drawing-room door. "I'll call—" She swallowed.

Dr. Fell took his head. He moved over with surprising quietness and the drawing-room door.

own blinds were drawn, and the thick lace curtains muffled what little light filtered through. Although the room looked vaster, its furniture was lost in shadow; except for one piece of furniture, of gleaming black metal lined with white satin. It was an open coffin. Thin candles were burning around it. Of the dead face Rampole afterwards remembered that from where he stood he could see only the tip of a nose. But those candles alone, or the faint thickness of flowers and incense in the air, moved the scene weirdly from dun London to some place of crags and blasts among the Hungarian mountains: where the gold cross loomed guard against devils, and garlic wreaths kept off the prowling vampire.

Yet this was not the thing they first noticed. Ernestine Dumont stood beside the coffin, one hand gripping its edge. The high, thin candle-light above turned her greying hair to gold; it softened and subdued even the crumpled posture of her bent shoulders. When she turned her head slowly round, they saw that her eyes were sunken and smeared—though she still could not weep. Her breast heaved jerkily. Yet round her shoulders she had wound a gay, heavy, long-fringed yellow shawl, with red brocade and bead embroidery that burnt with a shifting glitter under the light. It was the last touch of the barbaric.

And then she saw them. Both hands suddenly gripped the edge of the coffin, as though she would shield the dead. She remained a silhouette, one hand outspread on either side, under the unsteady candles.

"It will do you good, madame, to confess," said Dr. Fell, very gently. "Believe me, it will do you good."

For a second Rampole thought she had stopped breathing, so easy was every motion to follow in the unearthliness of that light. Then she made a sound as though she were half-coughing, which is only grief before it becomes hysterical mirth.

"Confess?" she said. "So that is what you think, all you fools? Well, I do not care. Confess! Confess to murder?"

"No," said Dr. Fell.

His voice, in that one quiet monosyllable, had a heavy note across the room. And now she stared at him, and now for the first time she began to stare with fright as he moved across towards her.

"No," said Dr. Fell. "You are not the murderer. Let me tell you what you are."

Now he towered over her, black against the candlelight, but he still spoke gently.

"Yesterday, you see, a man named O'Rourke told us several things. Among them was the fact that most illusions either on or off the stage are worked with the aid of a confederate. This was no exception. You were the confederate of the illusionist and murderer."

"The hollow man," said Ernestine Dumont, and suddenly began to laugh hysterically.

"The hollow man," said Dr. Fell, and turned quietly to Hadley, "in a real sense. The hollow man whose naming was a terrible and an ironic jest, even if we did not know it, because it was the exact truth. That is the horror and in a way the shame. Do you want to see the murderer you have been hunting all through this case?—The murderer lies *there*," said Dr. Fell, "but God forbid that we should judge him now."

And with a slow gesture he pointed to the white, dead, tight-lipped face of Dr. Charles Grimaud.

20
The Two Bullets

Dr. Fell continued to look steadily at the woman, who had again shrunk against the side of the coffin as though to defend it.

"Ma'am," he went on "the man you loved is dead. He is beyond the reach of the law now, and, whatever he has done, he has paid for it. Our immediate problem, yours and mine, is to hush this thing up so that the living may not be hurt. But, you see, you are implicated, even though you took no actual hand in the murder. Believe me, ma'am, if I could have explained the whole thing without bringing you into it at all, I should have done so. I know you have suffered. But you will see for yourself that such a course was impossible if I were to explain the entire problem. So we must persuade Superintendent Hadley that this affair must be hushed up."

Something in his voice, something of the unweary, unchanging, limitless compassion that was Gideon Fell, seemed to touch her as gently as sleep after tears. Her hysteria had gone.

"Do you know?" she asked him, after a pause, and almost eagerly. "Do not fool me! Do you really know?"

"Yes, I really know."

"Go upstairs. Go to *his* room," she said in a dull voice, "and I will join you presently. I—I cannot face you just now. I must think, and—

But please do not speak to anybody until I come. Please! No, I will not run away."

Dr. Fell's fierce gesture silenced Hadley as they went out. Still in silence they tramped up the gloomy stairs to the top floor. They passed no one, they saw no one. Once more they came into the study, where it was so dark that Hadley switched on the mosaic lamp at the desk. After he had made sure the door was closed, Hadley turned round rather wildly.

"Are you trying to tell me that Grimaud killed Fley?" he demanded.

"Yes."

"While he was lying unconscious and dying under the eyes of witnesses in a nursing-home, he went to Cagliostro Street and—!"

"Not then," said Dr. Fell quietly. "You see, that's what you don't understand. That's what led you wrong. That's what I meant by saying that the case had been turned not upside down, but *the wrong way round*. Fley was killed before Grimaud. And, worst of all, Grimaud was trying to tell us the exact, literal truth. He did tell us the exact truth, when he knew he was dying beyond hope—it's one of the good gleams in him—but we chose to misinterpret it. Sit down, and I'll see if I can explain it. Once you have grasped the three essential points, you will need no deduction and very little elucidation from me. The thing will explain itself."

He lowered himself, wheezing, into the chair behind the desk. For a little time he remained staring vacantly at the lamp. Then he went on:

"The three essential points, then, are these. (1) There is no brother Henri; there are only two brothers. (2) Both these brothers were speaking the truth. (3) A question of time has turned the case wrong way round.

"Many things in this case have turned on a matter of brief spaces of time, and how brief they are. It's a part of the same irony which described our murderer as the hollow man that the crux of the case should be a matter of mistaken time. You can easily spot it if you think back.

"Now remember yesterday morning! I already had some occasion to believe there was something queer about that business in Cagliostro Street. The shooting there, we were told by three (truthful) witnesses who agreed precisely and to a second, took place at just ten twenty-five. I wondered, in an idle sort of way, why they corroborated each other with such startling exactitude. In the case of the usual street accident, even the most cool witnesses don't usually take such notice, or are care-

ful to consult their watches, or (even if they do) agree about the time
with such uncanny precision. But they were truthful people, and there
must have been some reason for their exactitude. The time must
have been thrust on them.

"Of course there was a reason. Just across from where the murdered
man fell there was a lighted show-window—the only lighted window
thereabouts—of a jeweller's shop. It was the most noticeable thing in the
foreground. It illuminated the murdered man; it was the first place to
which the constable rushed in search of the murderer; it quite naturally
focussed their attention. And, facing them from that window, there was
an enormous clock of such unusual design that it immediately took the
eye. It was inevitable that the constable should look for the time, and
natural that the others should also. Hence their agreement.

"But one thing, not apparently important at that time, bothered me a
little. After Grimaud was shot, Hadley summoned his men to this house,
and instantly dispatched one of them to pick up Fley as a suspect. Now,
then, those men arrived here . . . about what time?"

"About ten-forty," said Rampole, "according to a rough calculation.
I've got it in my time-table."

"And," said Dr. Fell, "a man was sent immediately to get Fley. This
man must have arrived in Cagliostro Street—when? Between fifteen and
twenty minutes after Fley was presumed to have been killed. But in the
space of that brief time what has happened? An incredible number of
things! Fley has been carried down to the doctor's house, he has died, an
examination has been made, a fruitless effort undertaken to identify
Fley; and then, 'after some delay' in the words of the newspaper account,
the van is sent for and Fley removed to the mortuary. All this! For, when
Hadley's detective arrived in Cagliostro Street to pick up Fley, he found
the whole business finished—and the constable back making inquiries
from door to door. The entire excitement had died down. Which seemed
incredible.

"Unfortunately, I was so dense that I didn't see the significance of this
even yesterday morning when I saw the clock in the jeweller's window.

"Think back once more. Yesterday morning we had breakfast at my
house; Pettis dropped in, and we talked to him—until what time?"

There was a pause.

"Until exactly ten o'clock," Hadley answered, suddenly, and snapped his fingers. "Yes! I remember, because Big Ben was striking just as he got up to go."

"Quite right. He left us, and afterwards we put on our hats and coats and drove *straight* to Cagliostro Street. Now, allow any reasonable margin of time you like for our putting on our hats, going downstairs, driving a short distance on deserted roads Sunday morning—a drive that took us only ten minutes when there was Saturday-night traffic. I think you'll say the whole process can hardly have taken twenty minutes in all. . . . But in Cagliostro Street you showed me the jeweller's shop, and that fancy clock was just striking *eleven*.

"Even then in my musing density it never occurred to me to look at that clock and wonder, just as in their excitement it never occurred to the three witnesses last night. Just afterwards, you recall, Somers and O'Rourke summoned us up to Burnaby's flat. We made quite a long investigation, and then had a talk with O'Rourke. And while O'Rourke was speaking, I noticed that the earlier dead quiet of the day—the quiet when in the street we heard only the wind—had a new sound. I heard church bells.

"Well, what time *do* church bells begin to ring? Not after eleven o'clock; the service has begun. Usually before eleven, for a preparatory bell. But, if I accepted the evidence of that German clock, it must then be a very long time past eleven o'clock. Then my dull mind woke up. I remembered Big Ben and our drive to Cagliostro Street. The combination of those bells and Big Ben—against (hem!) a trumpery foreign clock. Church and State, so to speak, couldn't both be wrong. . . . In other words, *the clock in that jeweller's window was more than forty minutes fast. Hence the shooting in Cagliostro Street the night before could not have taken place at twenty-five minutes past ten. Actually it must have taken place a short time previous to a quarter to ten. Say, roughly, at nine-forty.*

"Now, sooner or later somebody would have noticed this; maybe somebody has noticed it already. A thing like that would be bound to come out in a coroner's court. Somebody would come forward to dispute the right time. Whether you'd have instantly seen the truth then (as I hope), or whether it would have confused you even more, I don't know. . . . But the solid fact remains that the affair in Cagliostro Street took place some minutes before the man in the false face rang the bell of this house at nine forty-five."

"But I still don't see—!" protested Hadley.

"The impossible situation? No; but I have a clear course now to tell you the whole story from the beginning."

"Yes, but let me get this straightened out. If Grimaud, as you say, shot Fley in Cagliostro Street just before nine forty-five—"

"I didn't say that," said Dr. Fell.

"What?"

"You'll understand if you follow my patient elucidation from the beginning. On Wednesday night of last week—when Fley first appeared out of the past, apparently out of his grave, to confront his brother with rather a terrible threat at the Warwick Tavern—Grimaud resolved to kill him. In the whole case, you see, Grimaud was the only person with a motive for killing Fley. And, my God! Hadley, but he did have a motive! He was safe, he was rich, he was respected; the past was buried. And then, all of a sudden, a door blows open to admit this thin grinning stranger who is his brother Pierre. Grimaud, in escaping from prison, had murdered one of his brothers by leaving him buried alive; he would have murdered the other except for an accident. He could still be extradited and hanged—and Pierre Fley had traced him.

"Now, bear in mind exactly what Fley said when he suddenly flew in to confront Grimaud that night at the tavern. Study *why* he said and did certain things, and you will see that even shaky-minded Fley was very far from being as mad as he liked to pretend. Why, if he were intent merely on private vengeance, did he choose to confront Grimaud in the presence of a circle of friends and speak in just the innuendoes he used? He used his *dead* brother as a threat; and it was the only time he did speak of that *dead* brother. Why did he say, 'He can be much more dangerous to you than I can? Because the dead brother could hang Grimaud! Why did he say, 'I don't want your life; he does'? Why did he say, 'Shall I have him call on you'? And then why, just afterwards, did he hand Grimaud his card on which his own address was carefully written? The giving of that card, combined with his words and later actions, is significant. What Fley really meant, veiled so that he could throw a scare into Grimaud before witnesses, was just this: 'You, my brother, are fat and rich on the proceeds of a robbery we both committed when we were young. I am poor—and I hate my work. Now will you come and call on me at my address, so that we can arrange this matter, or shall I set the police on you?"

"Blackmail," said Hadley, softly.

"Yes. Fley had a bee in his bonnet, but Fley was far from being a fool. Now mark how he twisted round his meaning in his last threatening words to Grimaud. 'I also am in danger when I associate with my brother, but I am prepared to run that risk.' And in that case, as always afterwards, he was referring in strict truth to *Grimaud*. 'You, my brother, might also kill me as you killed the other, but I will risk it. So shall I call on you amiably, or will my other dead brother come to hang you?'

"For think of his behaviour afterwards, on the night of his murder. Remember the glee he had of smashing up and getting rid of his illusion-properties? And what words did he use to O'Rourke? Words which, if you look at them squarely in the light of what we know, can have only one explanation. He said:

> " 'I shall not need them again. My work is finished. Didn't I tell you? I am going to see my brother. He will do something that will settle an old affair for both of us.'

"Meaning, of course, that Grimaud had agreed to come to terms. Fley meant that he was leaving his old life for good; going back to his grave as a dead man with plenty of money; but he couldn't be more specific without blowing the gaff. Still, he knew that his brother was tricky; he'd had good reason in the past to know it. He couldn't leave behind him a big warning when he spoke with O'Rourke, in case Grimaud really meant to pay; but he threw out a hint:

> " 'In case anything happens to me, you will find my brother in the same street where I myself live. That is not where he really resides, but he has a room there.'

"I'll explain that last statement in just a moment. But go back to Grimaud. Now, Grimaud never had any intention of coming to terms with Fley. Fley was going to die. That wily, shrewd, theatrical mind of Grimaud's (who, as you know, was more interested in magical illusions than anybody else we have met) was determined not to suffer any nonsense from this inconvenient brother of his. Fley must die—but this was more difficult than it looked.

"If Fley had come to him in private, without anybody in the world ever being able to associate Fley's name with his, it would have been simple. But Fley had been too shrewd for that. He had blazoned forth his own name and address, and hinted at mysterious secrets concerning Grimaud, before a group of Grimaud's friends. Awkward! Now if Fley is found obviously murdered, somebody is likely to say, 'Hullo! Isn't that the same chap who—?' And then presently there may be dangerous enquiries; because Lord knows what Fley may have told *other* people about Grimaud. The only thing he isn't likely to have confided to somebody else is his last deadly hold over Grimaud; and that is the thing about which he must be silenced. Whatever happens to Fley, however he dies, there are likely to be enquiries concerning Grimaud. The only thing to do is frankly to pretend that Fley is after his life; to send himself threatening letters (not too obviously); to stir up the household in an ingenious way; finally, to inform everybody that Fley has threatened to call on him on the night he himself intends to call on Fley. You will see very shortly just how he planned to work out a very brilliant murder.

"The effect he intended to produce was this: The murderous Fley should be seen calling on him on Saturday night. There should be witnesses to this. The two should be together alone when Fley goes into his study. A row is heard, the sound of a fight, a shot, and a fall. The door being opened, Grimaud should be found alone—a nasty-looking but superficial wound from a bullet scratched along his side. No weapon is there. Out of the window hangs a rope belonging to Fley, by which Fley is assumed to have escaped. (Remember, it had been predicted that there would be *no* snow that night, so it would have been impossible to trace footprints.) Grimaud says: 'He thought he killed me; I pretended to be dead; and he escaped. No, don't set the police on him, poor devil. I'm not hurt.'— And the next morning Fley would have been found dead in his own room. He would have been found, a suicide, having pressed his own gun against his chest and pulled the trigger. The gun is beside him. A suicide note lies on the table. In despair at thinking he has killed Grimaud, he has shot himself. . . . That, gentlemen, was the illusion Grimaud intended to produce."

"But how did he do it?" demanded Hadley. "And, anyway, it didn't turn out like that!"

"No. You see, the plan miscarried badly. The latter part of the illusion of Fley calling on him in his study when actually Fley would already have been dead in the Cagliostro Street house—I'll deal with in its proper place. Grimaud, with the aid of Madame Dumont, had already made certain preparations.

"He had told Fley to meet him at Fley's room on the top floor over the tobacconist's. He had told Fley to meet him there at nine o'clock on the Saturday night, for a cash settlement. (You recall that Fley, gleefully throwing up his job and burning his properties, left the theatre in Lime-house at about eight-fifteen.)

"Grimaud had chosen Saturday night because that night, by inviolable custom, he remained alone all evening in his study without anyone being allowed to disturb him for any reason whatsoever. He chose that night because he needed to use the areaway door, and go and come by way of the basement; and Saturday night was the night out for Annie, who had her quarters there. You'll remember that, after he went up to his study at seven-thirty, nobody *did* see him until, according to the evidence, he opened the study door to admit the visitor at nine-thirty. Madame Dumont claimed to have spoken to him in the study at nine-thirty, when she gathered up the coffee things. I'll tell you shortly why I disbelieved that statement—the fact is, he was not in the study at all: he was in Cagliostro Street. Madame Dumont had been told to lurk round the study door at nine-thirty, and to come out for some excuse. Why? Because Grimaud had ordered Mills to come upstairs at nine-thirty, you see, and watch the study door from the room down the hall. Mills was to be the dupe of the illusion Grimaud meant to work. But if—as he came upstairs near the study door—Mills had for any reason taken it into his head to try to speak with Grimaud, or see him, Dumont was there to head him off. Dumont was to wait in the archway, and keep Mills away from that door if he showed any curiosity.

"Mills was chosen as the dupe of the illusion: why? Because, although he was so meticulously conscientious that he would carry out his instructions to the tick, he was so afraid of 'Fley' that he would not interfere when the hollow man came stalking up those stairs. It was not only that he must not attack the man in the false face in those dangerous few moments before the man got into the study (as, for instance, Mangan or even Drayman might have done), but also that he must not even venture out of his room. He had been told to stay in that room, and he would. Finally, he had been chosen because he was a very short man, a fact which will presently become clear.

"Now, he was told to go upstairs and watch at nine-thirty. This was because the hollow man was timed to make his appearance only a little afterwards; although, in fact, the hollow man was late. Mark one discrepancy. Mills was told nine-thirty—but Mangan was told ten o'clock! The reason is obvious. There was to be somebody downstairs to testify that a visitor had really arrived by the front door, confirming Dumont. But Mangan might be inclined towards curiosity about this visitor; he might be inclined to challenge the hollow man . . . unless he had first been jokingly told by Grimaud that the visitor would probably not arrive at all, or, if he did arrive, it could not possibly be before ten o'clock. All that was necessary was to throw his mind off, and make him hesitate long enough, for the hollow man to get upstairs past that dangerous door. And, if the worst came to the worst, Mangan and Rosette could always be locked in.

"For everybody else: Annie was out, Drayman had been supplied with a ticket to a concert, Burnaby was unquestionably playing cards, and Pettis at the theatre. The field was clear.

"At some time before nine o'clock (probably about ten minutes) Grimaud slipped out of the house, using the area door up to the street. Trouble had already started. It had been snowing heavily for some time, contrary to rules. But Grimaud did not regard it as serious trouble. He believed he could do the business and return by half-past nine, and that it would still be snowing heavily enough to gloss over any footprints that he would make, and cause no comment on the absence of any footprints the visitor later *should* have made when the visitor would be supposed to have swung down from his window. In any case, his plans had been carried too far for him to back out.

"When he left the house he was carrying an old and untraceable Colt revolver, loaded with just two bullets. The sort of hat he wore I don't know, but his overcoat was a light yellow, glaring tweed with chicken-pox spots. He bought this coat several sizes too large. He bought it because it was the sort of coat he had never been known to wear and because nobody would recognize him in it if he were to be seen. He—"

Hadley intervened.

"Stop a bit! What about that business of the overcoats changing colour? That would come earlier in the evening. What had happened there?"

"Again, I've got to ask you to wait until we get to the last illusion he worked; that's a part of it.

"Well, Grimaud's purpose was to call on Fley. There he would speak with Fley amiably for a time. He would say something like: 'You must leave this hovel, brother! You will be comfortably off now; I will see to that. Why not leave these useless possessions behind and come to my house? Let your landlord have the damned things in place of notice!"— Any sort of speech, you see, the purpose being to make Fley write one of his ambiguous notes for the landlord. 'I am leaving for good.' 'I am going back to my grave.' Anything *that could be understood as a suicide note when Fley was found dead with a gun in his hand."*

Dr. Fell leaned forward. "And then Grimaud would take out his Colt, jam it against Fley's chest, and smilingly pull the trigger.

"It was the top floor of an empty house. As you have seen, the walls are astonishingly thick and solid. The landlord lived far down in the basement, and was the most incurious man in Cagliostro Street. No shot, especially a muffled shot with the gun held against Fley, could have been heard. It might be some time before the body was discovered; it would certainly not be before morning. And in the meantime, what will Grimaud do? After killing Fley he will turn the same gun on himself to give himself a slight wound, even if he has to imbed the bullet—he had, as we know from that little episode of the three coffins years before, the constitution of an ox and the nerve of hell. Then he would leave the gun lying beside Fley. He would quite coolly clap a handkerchief or cotton wool across this wound, which must be *inside* the coat and across the shirt; bind it with adhesive tape until the time came to rip it open—and go back home to work his illusion, which should prove that Fley came to see him. That Fley shot him, and then returned to Cagliostro Street and used the same gun for suicide, no coroner's jury would afterwards doubt. Do I make it clear so far? It was crime turned the wrong way round.

"That, as I say, was what Grimaud *intended* to do. Had he performed it as he intended, it would have been an ingenious murder; and I doubt whether we should ever have questioned Fley's suicide.

"Now, there was only one difficulty about accomplishing this plan. If anybody—not anybody recognizable as himself, but anybody at all— were seen visiting Fley's house, the fat would be in the fire. It might not appear so easily as suicide. There was only one entrance from the street —the door beside the tobacconist's. And he was wearing a conspicuous coat, in which he had reconnoitred the ground before. (By the way, Dolberman, the tobacconist, had seen him hanging about previously.) He found the solution of his difficulty in Burnaby's secret flat.

"You see, of course, that Grimaud was the likeliest person of all to have known of Burnaby's flat in Cagliostro Street? Burnaby himself told us that, some months before when Grimaud suspected him of having an ulterior motive in painting that picture, Grimaud had not only questioned him—he had *watched* him. From a man who was in such fancied danger, it would have been real watching. He knew of the flat. He knew from spying that Rosette had a key. And so, when the time came and the idea occurred to him, he stole Rosette's key.

"The house in which Burnaby had his flat was on the same side of the street as the house where Fley lived. All those houses are built side by side, with flat roofs; so that you have only to step over a low dividing wall to walk on the roofs from one end of the street to the other. Both men, remember, lived on the top floor. You recall what we saw when we went up to look at Burnaby's flat—just beside the door to the flat?"

Hadley nodded. "Yes, of course. A short ladder going to a trap-door in the roof."

"Exactly. And, on the landing just outside Fley's room, there is a low skylight also communicating with the roof. Grimaud had only to go to Cagliostro Street by the back way, never appearing in the street itself, but going up the alley which we saw from Burnaby's window. He came in the back door (as we saw Burnaby and Rosette do later), he went up to the top floor and thence to the roof. Then he followed the roofs to Fley's lodgings, descended from the skylight to the landing, and could both enter and leave the place without a soul seeing him. Moreover, he knew absolutely that that night Burnaby would be playing cards elsewhere.

"And then everything went wrong.

"He must have got to Fley's lodgings before Fley arrived there himself; it wouldn't do to make Fley suspicious by being seen coming from the roof. But we know that Fley had some suspicions already. This may have been caused by Grimaud's request for Fley to bring along one of his long conjuring-ropes. . . . Grimaud wanted that rope as a piece of evidence to use later against Fley. Or it may have been caused by Fley's knowledge that Grimaud had been hanging about in Cagliostro Street for the past couple of days; possibly seeing him duck across the roofs towards Burnaby's after one reconnoitering, and thereby making Fley believe he had taken a room in the street.

"The two brothers met in that gaslit room at nine. What they talked about we don't know. We may never know. But evidently Grimaud lulled Fley's suspicions; they became pleasant and amiable and forgot old scores; Grimaud jocularly persuaded him to write that note for the landlord. Then—"

"I'm not disputing all this," said Hadley, quietly, "but how do you happen to know it?"

"Grimaud told us," said Dr. Fell. Hadley stared.

"Oh yes. Once I had tumbled to that terrible mistake in times, I could understand. You'll see. But to continue:

"Fley had written his note. He had got into his hat and coat for departure—because Grimaud wished it to be assumed that he had killed himself just after having returned from a journey *outdoors:* his return from the phantom visit to Grimaud, in other words. They were all ready to go. And then Grimaud leaped.

"Whether Fley was subconsciously on his guard; whether he twitched round to run for the door, since he was no match for the powerful Grimaud; whether it happened in the twisting and scuffle—this we do not know. But Grimaud, with the gun against Fley's coat as Fley wrenched round from him, made a hellish mistake. He fired. And he put the bullet in the wrong place. Instead of getting his victim through the heart, he got him under the left shoulder blade: a wound of almost the same sort, although at the back, as the one from which Grimaud later died himself. It was a fatal wound, but far from instantly fatal. The poetic ironies were working to kill these brothers, with interchangeable methods, in precisely the same way.

"Of course Fley went down. He could do nothing else; and it was the wisest course, or Grimaud might have finished him. But Grimaud, for a second, must have lost his nerve in sheer terror. This might have wrecked his whole plan. *Could* a man shoot himself in that spot? If not, God help the murderer. And worse—Fley, not caught quickly enough, had screamed out before the bullet went home, and Grimaud thought he heard pursuers.

"He had sense enough, and guts enough, even in that hellish moment, to keep his head. He jammed the pistol into the hand of the motionless Fley, lying on his face. He picked up the coil of rope. Somehow, in spite of crash and fuddlement, the plan must go on. But he had more sense than to risk the noise of another shot to be heard by people possibly listening, or to waste more time. He darted out of the room.

"The roof, do you see! The roof was his only chance. He heard imaginary pursuers everywhere; maybe some grisly recollection came back to him of three graves in a storm below the Hungarian mountains. He imagined that they would hear him and track him across those roofs. So he dashed for the trap door at Burnaby's, and down into the dark of Burnaby's flat.

"It was only then that his wits began to recover themselves. . . .

"And, meantime, what has happened? Pierre Fley is fatally hurt. But he still has the ribs of that iron frame which once enabled him to survive being buried alive. The murderer has gone. And Fley will *not* give in. He must get help. He must get to—

"*To a doctor*, Hadley. You asked yesterday why Fley was walking towards the other end of the street, towards the end of a blind alley. Because (as you saw in the newspaper) a doctor lived there: the doctor to whose office he later was carried. He is mortally hurt and he knows it; but he will not be beaten! He gets up, still in his hat and overcoat. The gun has been put into his hand; he rams it in his pocket, for it may be useful. Down he goes, downstairs as steadily as he can, to a silent street where no alarm has been raised. He walks on. . . .

"Have you asked yourself why he was walking in the middle of the street and kept looking so sharply round? The most reasonable explanation is not that he was going to visit anybody; but that he knew the murderer to be lurking somewhere, and he expected another attack. He thinks he is safe. Ahead of him, two men are walking rapidly. He passes a lighted jeweller's, he sees a street lamp ahead on the right. . . .

"But what has happened to Grimaud? Grimaud has heard no pursuit, but he is half-insane with wondering. He does not dare go back to the roof and risk investigation. But stop a moment! If there has been any discovery, he will be able to know by looking for a second out into the street. He can go down to the front door, look out, and peer up the street, can't he? No danger in that, since the house where Burnaby lives is deserted.

"He goes softly downstairs. He opens the door softly, having unbuttoned his coat to wind the coil of rope round him inside that overcoat. He opens the door—full in the glow of a street lamp just beyond that door—and facing him, walking slowly in the middle of the street, is the man he left for dead in the other house less than ten minutes ago. And for the last time those brothers come face to face.

"Grimaud's shirt is a target under that street lamp. And Fley, driven mad with pain and hysteria, does not hesitate. He screams. *He* cries the words, 'The second bullet is for *you!'*—just before he whips up the same pistol and fires.

"That last effort is too much. The hemorrhage has got him, and he knows it. He screams again, lets go of the gun as he tries to throw it (now empty) at Grimaud; and then he pitches forward on his face. That, my lads, is the shot which the three witnesses heard in Cagliostro Street. It was the shot which struck Grimaud in the chest just before he had time to close the door."

21
The Unravelling

And then?" prompted Hadley, as Dr. Fell paused and lowered his head.

"The three witnesses did not see Grimaud, of course," said Dr. Fell, wheezing, after a long pause, "because he was never outside the door; never on the steps at all; never within twenty feet of the man who seemed to have been murdered in the middle of a snow desert. Of course Fley already had the wound, which jetted blood from the last convulsion. Of course any deduction from the direction of the wound was useless. Of course there were no fingerprints on the gun, since it landed in snow and in a literal sense had been washed clean."

"By God!" said Hadley, so quietly that he seemed to be making a statement. "It fulfills every condition of the facts, and yet I never thought of it. . . . But go on. Grimaud?"

"Grimaud is inside the door. He knows he's got it in his chest; but he doesn't think it's very serious. He's survived worse things than bullets, and other things (he thinks) *are* more serious.

"After all, he's only got what he was going to give himself—a wound. He could bark out that chuckle of his at such a thing. But his plan has crashed to hell! (How is he to know, by the way, that the clock at the jeweller's will be fast? He doesn't even know that Fley is dead, for there is Fley walking in the street with fire and sting still in him. Luck—by reason of the jeweller's clock—is with him when he thought it had deserted him, but how is he to know it?) All he is sure of is that Fley will never now be found, a suicide, up in that little room. Fley—probably dangerously wounded, yes, but still able to talk—is out in that street with a policeman running towards him. Grimaud is undone. Unless he can use his wits, he's on his way to the hangman, for Fley will not keep silent now.

"All this comes an instant after the shot, the rush of fancies crowding in. He can't stay here in this dark hall. He'd better have a look at that wound, though, and make sure he doesn't leave a trail of blood. Where? Burnaby's flat upstairs, of course. Up he goes, gets the door open, and switches on the lights. Here's the rope wound round him . . . no use for *that* thing now; he can't pretend Fley came to call on him when Fley may now be talking with the police. He flings the rope off and leaves it.

"A look at the wound next. There's blood all over the inside of that light tweed overcoat, and blood on his inner clothes. But the wound is of small consequence. He's got his handkerchief and his adhesive tape, and he can plug himself up like a horse gored in the bull-ring. Károly Horváth, whom nothing can kill, can afford to chuckle at this. He feels as steady and fresh as ever. But he patches himself up—hence the blood in the bathroom of Burnaby's flat—and tries to collect his wits. What time is it? Good God! He's late; it's just on a quarter to ten. Got to get out of here and hurry home before they catch him. . . .

"And he leaves the lights on. When they burnt up a shilling's worth and went out in the later course of the night, we don't know. They were on three-quarters of an hour afterwards, anyhow, when Rosette saw them.

"But I think that his sanity returns as he hurries home. *Is* he caught? It seems inevitable. Yet is there any loophole, any ghost of a fighting chance, however thin? You see, whatever else Grimaud is, he's a fighter. He's a shrewd, theatrical, imaginative, sneering, common-sense black-guard: but don't forget that he's also a fighter. He wasn't all of a black colour, you know. He would murder a brother, but I question whether he would murder a friend or a woman who loved him. In any case, *is* there some way out? There's one chance, so thin that it's almost useless; but the only one. That's to carry through his original scheme and pre-tend that Fley has called on him and given him that wound *in his own house*. Fley still has the gun. It will be Grimaud's word, and his wit-nesses' word, that he never left the house all evening! Whereas they can swear that Fley did come to see him—and then let the damned police try to prove anything! Why not? The snow? It's stopped snowing, and Fley won't have left a track. Grimaud has thrown away the rope Fley was supposed to have used. But it's a toss-up, a last daring of the devil, the only course in an extremity. . . .

"Fley shot him at about twenty minutes to ten. He gets back here at a quarter to ten or a little after. Getting into the house without leaving a footprint? Easy! for a man with a constitution like an ox, and only slightly wounded. (By the way, I believe he was really wounded only slightly, and that he'd live now to hang, if he hadn't done certain things; you'll see.) He'll return by way of the steps down to the areaway, and the area door, as arranged. —How? Well, there is a coating of snow on the areaway steps, of course. But the entrance to the areaway steps is beside the next house, isn't it? Yes. And, at the foot of the area steps, the basement door is protected from snow by a projection: the projection of the main front steps overhanging. So that there is no snow exactly in front of the area door. If he can get down there without leaving a mark—

"He can. He can approach from the other direction, as though he were going to the house next door, and then simply jump down the area steps to the cleared patch below. . . . Don't I seem to remember a *thud,* as of some one falling, which some one heard just before the front-door bell rang?"

"But he didn't ring the front-door bell!"

"Oh yes, he did—but from inside. After he'd gone into the house by way of the area door, and up to where Ernestine Dumont was waiting for him. Then they were ready to perform their illusion."

"Yes," said Hadley. "Now we come to the illusion. How was it done, and how do you know how it was done?"

Dr. Fell sat back and tapped his finger tips together as though he were marshalling facts.

"How do I know? Well, I think my first suggestion was the weight of that picture." He pointed sleepily at the big slashed canvas leaning against the wall. "Yes, it was the weight of the picture. That wasn't very helpful, until I remembered something else. . . ."

"Weight of the picture? Yes, the picture," growled Hadley. "I'd forgotten that. How does *it* figure in the blasted business, anyhow? What did Grimaud mean to do with that?"

"H'mf, ha, yes. That's what I wondered, you see."

"But the weight of the picture, man! It doesn't weigh very much. You yourself picked it up with one hand and turned it round in the air."

Dr. Fell sat up with an air of some excitement. "Exactly. You've hit it. I picked it up with one hand and swung it round. . . . Then why should it take two husky men, the cabman and one extra, to carry it upstairs?"

"What?"

"It did, you know. That was twice pointed out to us. Grimaud, when he took it from Burnaby's studio, easily carried it downstairs. Yet, when he returned here with that same painting late in the afternoon, two people had a job carting it up. Where had it picked up so much weight all of a sudden? He didn't have glass put in it—you can see that for yourself. Where was Grimaud all that time, the morning when he bought the picture and the afternoon when he returned with it? It's much too big a thing to carry about with you for pleasure. Why was Grimaud so insistent on having the picture all wrapped up?

"It wasn't a very far-fetched deduction to think that he used that picture as a blind to hide something that the men were carrying up, unintentionally, along with it. Something in the same parcel. Something very big . . . seven feet by four . . . h'm. . . ."

"But there couldn't have been anything," objected Hadley, "or we'd have found it in this room, wouldn't we? Besides, in any case the thing must have been almost absolutely flat, or it would have been noticed in the wrappings of the picture. What sort of object is it that's as big as seven feet by four, and yet thin enough not to be noticed inside the wrappings of a picture; what's as huge a business as that picture, which can nevertheless be spirited out of sight whenever you wish?"

"A mirror," said Dr. Fell.

After a sort of thunderous silence, while Hadley rose from his chair, Dr. Fell went on sleepily: "And it can be spirited out of sight, as you put it, merely by being pushed up the flue of that very broad chimney—where we've all tried to get our fists, by the way—and propped up on the ledge inside where the chimney turns. You don't need magic. You only need to be damnably strong in the arms and shoulders."

"You mean," cried Hadley "that damned stage trick . . ."

"A new version of the stage trick," said Dr. Fell, "and a very good one which is practical if you care to try it. Now, look round this room. You see the door? What do you see in the wall directly opposite the door?"

"Nothing," said Hadley. "I mean, he's had the bookcases cleared away in a big space on either side. There's blank panelled wall, that's all."

"Exactly. And do you see any furniture in a line between the door and that wall?"

"No. It's cleared."

"So if you were out in that hall looking in, you would see only black carpet, no furniture, and to the rear an expanse of blank oak-panelled wall?"

"Yes."

"Now, Ted, open the door and look out into the hall," said Dr. Fell. "What about the walls and carpet out there?"

Rampole made a feint of looking, although he knew. "They're just the same," he said. "The floor is one solid carpet running to the baseboards, like this one, and the panelling is the same."

"Right! By the way, Hadley," pursued Dr. Fell, still drowsily, "you might drag out that mirror from behind the bookcase over there. It's been behind the bookcase since yesterday afternoon, when Drayman found it in the chimney. It was lifting it down that brought on his stroke. We'll try a little experiment. I don't think any of the household will interrupt us up here, but we can head off anybody who does. I want you to take that mirror, Hadley, and set it up just inside the door—so that when you open the door (it opens inwards and to the right, you see, as you come in from the hall) the edge of the door at its outermost swing is a few inches away from the mirror."

The superintendent with some difficulty trundled out the object he found behind the bookcase. It was bigger than a tailor's swinging mirror; several inches, in fact, higher and wider than the door. Its base rested flat on the carpet, and it was supported upright by a heavy swing-base on the right-hand side as you faced it. Hadley regarded it curiously.

"Set it up inside the door?"

"Yes. The door will only swing open a short distance; you'll see an aperture only a couple of feet wide at the most. . . . Try it!"

"I know, but if you do that . . . well, somebody sitting in the room down at the end of the hall, where Mills was, would see his own reflection smack in the middle of the mirror."

"Not at all. Not at the angle—a slight angle, but enough; a poor thing, but mine own—not at the angle to which I'm going to tilt it. You'll see. The two of you go down there where Mills was while I adjust it. Keep your eyes off until I sing out."

Hadley, muttering that it was damned foolishness, but highly interested in spite of that, tramped down after Rampole. They kept their eyes off until they heard the doctor's hail, and then turned round.

The hallway was gloomy and high enough. Its black-carpeted length ran down to a closed door. Dr. Fell stood outside that door, like an overfat master of ceremonies about to unveil a statue. He stood a little to the right of the door, well back from it against the wall, and had his hand stretched out across to the knob. "Here she goes!" he grunted, and quickly opened the door—hesitated—and closed it. "Well? What did you see?"

"I saw the room inside," returned Hadley. "Or at least I thought I did. I saw the carpet, and the rear wall. It seemed a very big room." "You didn't see that," said Dr. Fell. "As a matter of fact, you saw the reflection of the panelled wall immediately to the right of the door where you're standing, and the carpet going up to it. That's why it seemed so big a room: you were looking at a double length of reflection. This mirror is bigger than the door, you know. And you didn't see a reflection of the door itself because it opens inwards to the right. If you looked carefully, you might have seen a line of what looks like a shadow just along the top edge of the door. That's where the top edge of the mirror inevitably reflects, being taller, an inch or so of the *inner* top edge of the door. But your attention would be concentrated on any figures you saw. . . . Did you see me, by the way?"

"No; you were too far over. You had your arm across the door to the knob, and kept back."

"Yes. As Dumont was standing. Now try a last experiment before I explain how the whole mechanism worked. Ted, you sit down in the chair behind that desk—where Mills was sitting. You're very much taller than he is, but it will illustrate the idea. I'm going to stand outside, with this door open, and look at myself in the mirror. Now, you can't mistake ME, either from the front or the rear; but then I'm more distinguishable than some people. Just tell me what you see."

In the ghostly light, with the door partly open, the effect was rather eerie. A figure of Dr. Fell stood inside the door, peering out at another figure of Dr. Fell standing on the threshold and confronting himself—fixed and motionless, with a startled look.

"I don't touch the door, you see," a voice boomed at them. By the illusion of the moving lips Rampole would have sworn that the Dr. Fell inside the door was speaking. The mirror threw the voice back like a

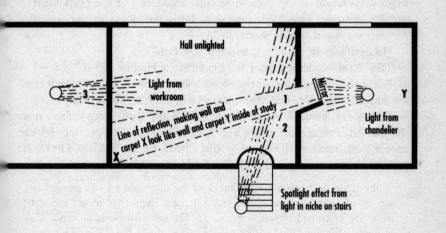

Hall unlighted

Light from workroom

3

Mirror

1

Line of reflection, making wall and carpet X look like wall and carpet Y inside of study

2

X

Y

Light from chandelier

Spotlight effect from light in niche on stairs

sounding-board. "Somebody obligingly opens and closes the door for me—somebody standing at my right. I don't touch the door, or my reflection would have to do likewise. Quick, what do you notice?"

"Why—one of you is very much taller," said Rampole, studying the images.

"Which one?"

"You yourself; the figure in the hall."

"Exactly. First because you're seeing it at a distance, but the most important thing is that you're sitting down. To a man the size of Mills I should look like a giant. Hey? H'mf. Hah. Yes. Now if I make a quick move to dodge in at that door (supposing me to be capable of such a manoeuvre), and at the same time my confederate at the right makes a quick confusing move with me and slams the door, in the muddled illusion the figure inside seems to be—?"

"Jumping in front of you to keep you out."

"Yes. Now come and read the evidence, if Hadley has it."

When they were again in the room, past the tilted mirror which Hadley moved back, Dr. Fell sank into a chair, sighing wheezingly.

"I'm sorry, gents. I should have realized the truth long before, from the careful, methodical, exact Mr. Mills' evidence. Let me see if I can repeat from memory his exact words. Check me up, Hadley. H'm." He rapped his knuckles against his head and scowled. "Like this:

" 'She [Dumont] was about to knock at the door when I was startled to see the tall man come upstairs directly after us. She turned round and saw him. She exclaimed certain words. . . . The tall man made no reply. He walked to the door, and without haste turned down the collar of his coat and removed his cap, which he placed in his overcoat pocket. . . .'

"You see, gents? He had to do that, because the reflection couldn't show a cap and couldn't show a collar turned up when the figure inside must appear to be wearing a dressing-gown. But I wondered *why* he was so methodical about that, since apparently he didn't remove the mask—"

"Yes, what about that mask? Mills says he didn't—"

"Mills didn't see him take it off; I'll show you why as soon as we go on with Mills:

" 'Madame Dumont cried out something, shrank back against the wall, and hurried to open the door. Dr. Grimaud appeared on the threshold—'

"Appeared! That's precisely what he did do. Our methodical witness is uncomfortably exact. But Dumont? There was the first flaw. A frightened woman, looking up at a terrifying figure while she's standing before the door of a room in which there's a man who will protect her, doesn't *shrink back*. She rushes towards the door to get protection. Anyhow, follow Mills' testimony. He says Grimaud was not wearing his eyeglasses (they wouldn't have fitted behind that mask). But the natural movement of a man inside, I thought, would have been to raise his glasses. Grimaud—according to Mills—stands *stockstill* the whole time; like the stranger, with his hands in his pockets. Now for the damning part. Mills says: 'I am under the impression that Madame Dumont, although she was shrinking back against the wall, closed the door after him. I recall that she had her hand on the knob.' Not a natural action for her, either! She contradicted him—but Mills was right." Dr. Fell gestured.

"No use going on with all this. But here was my difficulty: if Grimaud was alone in that room, if he simply walked in on his own reflection, what became of his clothes? What about that long black overcoat, the brown peaked cap, even the false face? They weren't in the room. Then I remembered that Ernestine's profession had been the making of costumes for the opera and ballet; I remembered a story O'Rourke had told us; and I knew—"

"Well?"

"That Grimaud had burnt them," said Dr. Fell. "He had burnt them because they were made of paper, like the uniform of the Vanishing Horseman described by O'Rourke. He couldn't risk the long and dangerous business of burning real clothes in that fire; he had to work too fast. They had to be torn up and burnt. And bundles of loose, blank sheets of writing paper—perfectly blank!—had to be burned on top of them to hide the fact that some of it was coloured paper. Dangerous letters! Oh, Bacchus, I could murder myself for thinking such a thing!" He shook his fist. "When there was no blood-trail, no blood-stain at all, going to the drawer in his desk where he did keep his important papers! And there was another reason for burning papers . . . they had to conceal the fragments of the 'shot.' "

"Shot?"

"Don't forget that a pistol was supposed to have been fired in that room. Of course, what the witnesses really heard was the noise of a heavy firecracker—pinched from the hoard Drayman always keeps, as you know, for Guy Fawkes night. Drayman discovered the missing thunderbolt; I think that's how he tumbled to the scheme, and why he kept muttering about 'fireworks.' Well, the fragments of an exploding firecracker fly wide. They're heavy reënforced cardboard, hard to burn, and they had to be destroyed in the fire or hidden in that drift of papers. I found some of them. Of course, we should have realized no bullet had really been fired. Modern cartridges—such as you informed me were used in that Colt revolver—have smokeless powder. You can smell it, but you can't see it. And yet there was a *haze* in this room (left by the firecracker) even after the window was up.

"Ah, well, let's recapitulate! Grimaud's heavy crêpe-paper uniform consisted of a black coat—black like a dressing-gown, long like a dressing-gown, and having at the front shiny lapels which would show like a dressing-gown when you turned down the collar to face your own image. It consisted of a paper cap, to which the false face was attached—so that in sweeping off the cap you simply folded both together and shoved 'em into your pocket. (The real dressing-gown, by the way, was already in this room while Grimaud was out.) And the black 'uniform,' early last evening, had been incautiously hung up in the closet downstairs.

"Mangan, unfortunately, spotted it. The watchful Dumont knew that he spotted it, and whisked it out of that cupboard to a safer place as soon as he went away. She, naturally, never saw a yellow tweed coat hanging there at all. Grimaud had it upstairs here with him, ready for his expedition. But it was found in the closet yesterday afternoon, and she had to pretend it had been there all the time. Hence the chameleon overcoat.

"You can now make a reconstruction of just what happened when Grimaud, after killing Fley and getting a bullet himself, returned to the house on Saturday night. Right at the start of the illusion he and his confederate were in dangerous trouble. You see, Grimaud was late. He'd expected to be back by nine-thirty—and he didn't get there until a quarter to ten. The longer he delayed, the nearer it got to the time he had told *Mangan* to expect a visitor, and now Mangan would be expecting the visitor he had been told to watch. It was touch-and-go, and I rather imagine the cool Grimaud was fairly close to insane. He got up through the basement entrance, where his confederate was waiting. The tweed coat, with the blood inside it, went into the hall closet to be disposed of presently—and it never was, because he died. Dumont eased open the door, rang the bell by putting her hand out, and then went to 'answer' it while Grimaud was getting ready with his uniform.

"But they delayed too long. Mangan called out. Grimaud, with his wits still not functioning well, grew a little panicky and made a blunder to ward off immediate detection. He'd got so far; he didn't want to fail then from the nosiness of a damned penniless kid. So he said that he was Pettis, and locked them in. (You notice that Pettis is the only one with a voice of the same bass quality as Grimaud's?) Yes, it was a spur-of-the-moment error, but his only wish was to writhe like a footballer down a field and *somehow* escape those hands for the moment.

"The illusion was performed; he was alone in his room. His jacket, probably with blood on that, had been taken in charge by Dumont; he wore the uniform over his shirtsleeves, open shirt, and bandaged wound. He had only to lock the door behind him, put on his real dressing-gown, destroy the paper uniform, and get that mirror up into the chimney. . . .

"That, I say again, was the finish. The blood had begun to flow again, you see. No ordinary man, wounded, could have stood the strain under which he had already been. He wasn't killed by Fley's bullet. He ripped his own lung like a rotted piece of rubber when he tried to—and super-humanly did—lift that mirror into its hiding-place. That was when he knew. Then was when he began to bleed from the mouth like a slashed artery; when he staggered against the couch, knocked away the chair, and reeled forward in his last successful effort to ignite the firecracker. After all the hates and dodgings and plans, the world was not spinning in front of him: it was only slowly going black. He tried to scream out, and he could not, for the blood was welling in his throat. And at that moment Charles Grimaud suddenly knew what he would never have believed possible, the breaking of the last and most shattering mirror-illusion in his bitter life. . . ."

"Well?"

"He knew that he was dying," said Dr. Fell. "And, stranger than any of his dreams, he was glad."

The heavy leaden light had begun to darken again with snow. Dr. Fell's voice sounded weirdly in the chill room. Then they saw that the door was opening and that in it stood the figure of a woman with a damned face. A damned face and a black dress, but round her shoulders was still drawn a red-and-yellow shawl for the love of the dead.

"You see, he confessed," Dr. Fell said in the same low, monotonous tone, "he tried to tell us the truth about his killing of Fley, and Fley's killing of him. Only we did not choose to understand, and I didn't understand until I knew from the clock what must have happened in Cagliostro Street. Man, man, don't you see? Take first his final statement, the statement made just before he died:

" 'It was my brother who did it. I never thought he would shoot. God knows how he got out of that room—' "

"You mean Fley's room in Cagliostro Street, after Fley had been left for dead?" demanded Hadley.

"Yes. And the horrible shock of coming on him suddenly, as Grimaud opened the door under the street light. You see:

" 'One second he was there, and the next he wasn't . . . I want to tell you who my brother is, so you won't think I'm raving. . . .'

"For, of course, he did not think anybody knew about Fley. Now, in the light of that, examine the tangled, muddled, half-choked words with which—when he heard the statement that he was sinking—he tried to explain the whole puzzle to us.

"First he tried to tell us about the Horváths and the salt-mine. But he went on to the killing of Fley, and what Fley had done to him. *'Not suicide.'* When he'd seen Fley in the street, he couldn't make Fley's death the suicide he pretended. *'He couldn't use the rope.'* Fley couldn't, after that, be supposed to use the rope that Grimaud had discarded as useless. *'Roof.'* Grimaud did not mean this roof; but the other roof which he crossed when he left Fley's room. *'Snow.'* The snow had stopped and wrecked his plans. *'Too much light.'* There's the crux, Hadley! When he looked out into the street, there was too much light from the street lamp; Fley recognized him, and fired. *'Got gun.'* Naturally, Fley had got the gun then. *'Fox.'* The mask, the Guy Fawkes charade he tried to work. But finally, *'Don't blame poor—'* Not Drayman; he didn't mean Drayman. But it was a last apology for the one thing, I think, of which he was ashamed; the one piece of imposture he would never have done. 'Don't blame poor Pettis; I didn't mean to implicate him.' "

For a long time nobody spoke.

"Yes," Hadley agreed, dully. "Yes. All except one thing. What about the slashing of that picture, and where did the knife go?"

"The slashing of the picture, I think, was an extra touch of the picturesque to help the illusion; Grimaud did it—or so I imagine. As for the knife, I frankly don't know. Grimaud probably had it here, and put it up the chimney beside the mirror so that the invisible man should seem to be doubly armed. But it isn't on the chimney ledge now. I should suppose that Drayman found it yesterday, and took it away—"

"That is the one point," said a voice, "on which you are wrong."

Ernestine Dumont remained in the doorway, her hands folded across the shawl at her breast. But she was smiling.

"I have heard everything you said," she went on. "Perhaps you can hang me, or perhaps not. That is not important. I do know that after so many years it is not quite worthwhile going on without Charles. . . . I took the knife, my friend. I had another use for it."

She was still smiling, and there was a blaze of pride in her eyes. Rampole saw what her hands were hiding. He saw her totter suddenly, but he was too late to catch her when she pitched forward on her face. Dr. Fell lumbered out of his chair and remained staring at her with a face as white as her own.

"I have committed another crime, Hadley," he said. "I have guessed the truth again."

The End
❧